FATAL INHERITANCE

By Catherine Shaw

FATAL INHERITANCE

CATHERINE SHAW

Allison & Busby Limited
12 Fitzroy Mews
London W1T 6DW
www.allisonandbusby.com

First published in Great Britain by Allison & Busby in 2013.

A CIP catalogue record for this book is available from
the British Library.

First Edition

ISBN 978-0-7490-1322-6

Typeset in 11/16 pt Sabon by
Allison & Busby Ltd.

The paper used for this Allison & Busby publication
has been produced from trees that have been legally sourced
from well-managed and credibly certified forests.

Printed and bound by
CPI Group (UK) Ltd, Croydon, CR0 4YY

To the daughter whose cello fills my soul with music

VANESSA WEATHERBURN'S CASE DIARY

Winter 1900

CHAPTER ONE

*In which Vanessa listens to a concert of chamber music
and learns of a suicide*

The music spilt forth, welled up, flooded over, and ran down and away in twinkling rivulets that thinned as they disappeared into unfathomable distance.

The piano rose up in a roar, then subsided as the deep voice of the cello became audible, and swelled to ride the crest of the piano's wave. The violin entered then, its pure and steady tones bringing to mind a small but sturdy boat, handled by competent sailors, forging a path through wild seas under a mad Northern sky filled with streaks of swaying light and gleaming stars.

I listened to the trio for more than a quarter of an hour, allowing free rein to the images which the music evoked naturally in my mind, before beginning, imperceptibly at first, then more clearly, to wonder if they were really the images that the composer would have intended. The cockle boat, tossed up and down by the violent waves, always at risk but never quite succumbing, had provoked my admiration; now it began to cause a certain irritation. Listen to this theme, now – why so tame? I thought. Should the violin not be soaring ever higher and more powerful, dominating the underlying clamour of the other instruments, representing the very power of nature, like a gigantic ocean bird, wings outstretched, gliding unaffected over the turmoil below? Or a powerful ship, the captain stern at the helm, cleaving the water in spite of the troubled waves and crashes beneath?

The prick of irritation jerked me back to conscious thought, and I turned my eyes to the offending violinist, then glanced down at the programme to see his name.

John Milrose sat on the edge of his chair, his dark hair parted at the side and combed smoothly over his broad, clear forehead. His fingers flew over the ebony fingerboard, and his bow swept the strings with large and generous gestures; his tone was pure and melodic, he paid careful attention to his partners, there was no cheap showmanship in his playing, his love of the music was patent and sincere. In fact, he played altogether beautifully, and really, I exhorted myself, there was nothing one could reproach him with.

Except . . . that little cockle boat!

The piano took the theme again. The young woman playing had white hands which lifted high into the air like flying birds after each sweeping chord; her face was lowered, her cheeks flushed, and sometimes I thought she closed her eyes. Rose, my little pupil Rose – a blooming young woman now – sat near her, playing her cello with total abandon; she almost never glanced at the music on the stand low in front of her, but watched now the pianist, now the violinist, and melted her entrances into theirs, or paused with a waiting as alive as breathing, till they had reached the very point of diminishment to allow a new voice to rise up in all its ripeness. The sound of her instrument, thick as honey, strong as mead, overshadowed the violin in intensity, though never fully covering its fluting higher notes.

The trio came to an end, and the three players stood up and bowed. They were dressed in deep mourning, and the small stage had been decorously draped in crêpe. I fingered my programme. It was black-edged and folded over; the front held only a box enclosed in a small wreath of black leaves, containing the words:

IN MEMORIAM

The remainder of the information about the concert lay within the flap.

A concert by the Cavendish Trio
dedicated to the memory of Sebastian Cavendish

John Milrose, violin
Claire Merrivale, piano
Rose Evergreene, violoncello

Piano Trio in D major ('Ghost')   Ludwig van Beethoven, 1770–1827
Piano Trio No. 2 in E-flat major   Franz Schubert, 1797–1828

Inside my programme lay the small note that I had received along with it in my mail earlier in the week, the note which had brought me to London without a moment's

11

hesitation, and for which I was seated presently in this small theatre, with its dim lights and lugubrious atmosphere of mourning.

Dear Vanessa,

It has been at least three years since we last saw each other. I know the fault is entirely mine. I have been so busy, and I am really very remiss! I hope you forgive me enough to attend the concert shown in the enclosed programme. It would give me immense pleasure to see you again, and also – I wish to speak to you about a very strange matter.

Very sincerely,
Your former pupil,
Rose Evergreene

I slipped the note back into the programme and closed it as applause began and grew all around me. I joined in, but my gloved hands made almost no noise; I wondered for a moment whether it was worth removing the gloves, and then decided not to, for the sound of the applause in general was muted and respectful as befitted a mourning ceremony. The clapping went on for exactly the seemly amount of time; the three musicians, having left the stage, returned, bowed once again politely, and left again in single file. They were deadly serious; the face of the young pianist was ravaged.

The audience began to rise and gather up fans, programmes, handkerchiefs, reticules and other personal items. The large double doors at the back of the hall opened up, leading into the foyer. I joined the line forming in front of this door and, after some minutes of advancing very slowly up the aisle between the seats, reached it and emerged into the large space, dazzling with lights, gilt mouldings and a shining copper counter on which glasses and bottles had been placed, surrounded with piles of snowy but black-edged napkins.

A hall led away from this foyer, curving around the concert hall itself from the outside. I followed it, and passing through a baize door at the end, found myself in the rooms behind the stage set aside for the use of the artists. A murmur of voices led me to the area where the three musicians were still engaged in packing away their instruments and their scores. A man's voice was speaking; the youthful violinist.

'You're kind to say that, but I know it isn't true. I can't be part of the Cavendish trio. It was just for this evening; for this one time. I can't replace Sebastian and you know it.'

'Oh, John, can we not always play together?' asked the pianist, who was holding his arm, looking straight up into his face. 'It isn't a question of replacing Sebastian. Of course no one can replace him, ever. But you *understand* about him – you were his friend! That's why I couldn't bear the idea of anyone but you playing with us tonight.'

Rose said nothing; her back was turned to the other two, and she was kneeling down in front of the large, open cello case, fitting her instrument carefully into its velveteen bed. This done, she took a silken square and dusted the traces of rosin carefully from the burnished wooden surface, passing under all the strings. She then used the square to tuck in the instrument as tenderly as a child, after which she closed and latched the lid. The round shape of her shoulders as she concentrated made me suspect that she wished to stay out of the discussion. I thought that perhaps she did not wish for John Milrose to continue as part of the trio.

'Well, we'll see, Claire,' Mr Milrose was saying. The baize door behind me swung again, and two or three more people entered to greet the artists; an elderly couple, a dark-haired young lady, then a moment after, two young men. One of them wore the red, rubbed mark of a violinist under the left side of his chin. Mr Milrose and Miss Merrivale separated immediately and turned to greet the newcomers. Rose stood up and came forward also. Her face lit up with a wonderful smile as she saw me.

'Vanessa!' she cried eagerly. 'I am so glad that you came. It has been much too long! Let me introduce you to Claire and John.' She kissed me warmly, and taking me by the hand, drew me over to where John was now talking to the people who had entered behind me. Claire was standing near him, listening, but her attention had wandered to Rose, and she took a quick step towards us as we approached.

'This is Vanessa Weatherburn,' Rose told her, in a tone which clearly indicated that she had already spoken of me to Claire, and that Claire was expecting, for some reason, to meet me. I shook her hand and spoke admiringly of her playing. But still holding my right hand in hers, she brushed off my praise with a quick sweep of her left, and said,

'Rose tells me I can talk to you – I *must* talk to someone, I don't know what to do – I can't bear it any longer!'

'Just ten more minutes,' said Rose quickly, 'we must be polite. Let's just wait until everyone's gone.'

A few more people had entered. Claire saw them, and drew herself together sharply.

'There's his mother,' she said, and crossed over, as though pulled by a string, reluctant but compelled, to a somewhat elderly lady who was speaking to John Milrose. I drew nearer to observe, and noticed how the woman's banal words seemed charged with meaning, because of the quiet intensity and poise with which she spoke them. Her hair, a greying ash-blonde, was dressed with the kind of simplicity that bespeaks taste in ample quantities, compensating, perhaps, a certain lack of wealth. Like the three members of the trio, she was wearing deep mourning; the cut of her gown was just fashionable enough to hint at an awareness of fashion without the slightest ostentation. The shoulders puffed too gently to be qualified as leg-of-mutton sleeves, underlining the slender waist without unduly attracting the eye. The skirt was close fitting, deeply gored at the back but devoid of ruffles and ribbons, and the collar rose high on the neck. A row of jet buttons gleamed down the front of the bodice. The woman who wore this dress was a woman of quality.

Her voice was quite extraordinary; it was of an exceptionally rich timbre, as though it came more directly from the chest cavity than from the throat, and her speech was very slow, each syllable enunciated carefully and yet without any sign of particular effort. She radiated a strong personality in which Claire Merrivale seemed caught like a little silver fish in a net. She looked up at the older woman, her voice trembled, she seemed unable to find words.

'That's Mrs Cavendish,' Rose explained in my ear, 'Sebastian's mother.' She tapped the *In Memoriam* on

15

the front of the programme that still dangled from my fingers. 'We'll tell you everything in a minute.' She went to join Claire, and half-consciously laying a comforting hand on the other girl's arm, she undertook to answer the lady's remarks herself, with more aplomb than her friend. I watched intently, guessing that this little scene and everything concerning the defunct Sebastian Cavendish would soon become the focal point of my attention.

Claire and Rose were much of a size, and Mrs Cavendish dominated them by a good five inches; however Claire appeared slight and weightless in front of her, whereas Rose stood firm and strong. I found it odd how, although the lady spoke with only the kindest words, her remarkable tallness and the sheer force of her character produced a desire to oppose some resistance to it, even though there was not the slightest conflict in her speech or attitude. But perhaps this impression did not emanate from the lady only, but also from Claire's display of weakness; she seemed on the point of breaking down. Perceiving this, Mrs Cavendish bent down a little towards her, taking her hand, and I heard her say,

'Try not to yield to despair, my dear. You must take courage from your art.'

She then kissed her affectionately, turned away, and departed upon the arm of an extremely elegant gentleman with side-whiskers and a gold-topped cane, who had been waiting silently at some little distance. The room having emptied considerably, Rose addressed a vigorous goodbye, tantamount to a dismissal, to John Milrose who was still standing amongst a few remaining friends. He smiled at the girls, took up his violin case and left with his group, and we found ourselves entirely alone in the green room.

'There,' said Rose. 'Now, Claire, you can tell Vanessa everything.'

There was a short silence, during which Claire struggled with tears.

'Well, I had better begin,' said Rose, although even she seemed to have some difficulty finding the words to tell me what had happened. 'You see, Vanessa,' she explained finally, 'the violinist of our trio, Sebastian Cavendish – Claire was engaged to him – he – well, he died a month ago. Tonight's concert was already planned; we turned it into a memorial concert for him . . . we had to find another violinist . . . John Milrose was one of Sebastian's closest friends . . . No, why am I talking about him? The problem is . . .'

Her voice tailed off, and I perceived that although more stable and less emotional than her friend, she was also deeply troubled. A cold fear seized me. What dreadful thing could have so disturbed her?

'How did he die?' I asked gently, leaning forward to look in her face.

'He committed suicide,' said Rose with what was clearly a conscious effort to steady her voice. 'He left a note for Claire. That is what she wants to ask you about. Claire – Claire? Come, you must explain things to Vanessa. And show her the note.'

Claire was already fumbling with the clasp of a little black brocade bag she held in her hands. The note she took out was written on a sheet of small, thick letter-paper of admirable quality. The ink had penetrated deeply into the soft fibres. The gentleman's handwriting was large and dashing. The short note filled the entire page, which had been rendered soft and grey by Claire's incessant handling of it.

Darling Claire,

How can I say this to you? I've found out something about myself – I can't go on with it any more. I'm sorry. I'm so sorry. Cursed inheritance – it's too dangerous to take such risks. Please try to understand.

Comforting words usually fall easily from my lips in the face of distress, but this event seemed so utterly dreadful, so totally beyond comfort of any kind, that I remained silent, staring at the letter. I admired Mrs Cavendish for having been able to find kind words for this young girl, when her own bereavement was so sudden and so awful. Rose echoed my thoughts.

'You saw Sebastian's mother, who was here earlier. Did you notice what she's like? So upright, so tall, so strong somehow; well, Sebastian was like her in some ways. He had that strength, that vitality – except that he was almost too emotional. And the way he played . . .'

'Like a god,' finished Claire. 'I never heard a violinist like him. Even though he was still young, he had everything – technique beyond most violinists' wildest dreams, infinite imagination and the power to express it. When he played, people in the audience were always in tears. *I* used to cry. It was almost beyond human.' Her words came out in a rush, as though once she had overcome the initial difficulty of talking about him, she couldn't stop. 'He used to play the Paganini Caprices as though they were a sort of joke. I've never heard anyone play so fast . . . Did you know that people used to say that the devil stood behind Paganini when he performed, helping him? Sebastian was like that. You couldn't believe he was just an ordinary person; when you saw him play, sometimes it was as though he was possessed.'

'Sometimes,' interjected Rose hastily. 'When he played madly difficult pieces. But he wasn't like that for chamber music. There was nothing diabolical about him then. He played as though the trio was a single instrument. We worked so hard; we were reaching for something very rare, and I think . . . we were approaching it.' She stopped. I said nothing, feeling humble in the face of a disaster, wondering why they had asked to talk to me.

'But what can I possibly do?' I asked.

'I want to understand why he killed himself,' said Claire, in a small, stern voice. 'Nothing foreshadowed it – nothing! The week before, he was exactly as always – and he was *happy*. Happy and vital and intense and full of projects. Oh, Mrs Weatherburn, I've lost my sleep from wondering and wondering and wondering, why, why, why? What do his words mean? What did he find out? What was that *something* that made him not want to live any more? What dreadful thing can it have been? Why did he kill himself? Why? Why? Why?'

Her words startled me. I had read his message differently, as though he had written 'I've found out something about myself: that I can't go on.' As though he had discovered that he had not the strength to live up to what was required

19

of him. But Claire was understanding something else – that he had found out some particular mysterious *thing*, some actual thing that had driven him to despair. I saw at once that she might, indeed, be right, if it were true that a few days before his suicide, he had not a care in the world. If a man is not depressive or miserable; if he has no visible cause to be deeply despairing or disappointed, and is perceived by those closest to him as happy, vital, intense; then there must indeed be some essential outside *something* to drive him to sudden suicide.

'You believe that he found out something specific? Some dreadful thing that he could not endure?' I asked.

'He must have! What else could it mean?' she exclaimed, clutching her little bag convulsively with her fingers.

'I agree with Claire,' said Rose. 'I have thought about it also, again and again. We have talked it over and discussed everything we can remember about Sebastian, especially about the days and weeks before he died. If you are willing to investigate this for Claire, we will tell you everything we know. The only trouble is that we don't see how what we know could help you, because Sebastian was absolutely fine until the last time we saw him. And he wasn't the type of person who could easily have hidden something that was disturbing him deeply. He was very extroverted, very emotional. And it would have been especially difficult for him to hide anything from Claire, I think.'

'I could easily tell if something was amiss with him,' she agreed, rubbing her eyes although they contained no tears; she had reached a stage of grief beyond such expression. 'The last time I saw him was five days before . . . it happened. It was the day after Christmas. We hadn't spent

Christmas Day together, because he had to be with his mother. But we met the next day, the 26th. We rehearsed the *Geistertrio* together—' she glanced at Rose, who nodded in confirmation, 'and then when we stopped, Rose left, but I stayed and Sebastian and I played Brahms. It was utterly beautiful. And he kissed me goodbye . . .'

'It isn't easy to recall everything exactly,' said Rose, 'and yet it is. Because there isn't anything special to say about that day. We've been through it again and again, and it was just as usual. That doesn't mean dull or routine. Sebastian was like a wire when you see the electricity go crackling down it, with sparks.' (I noted with pleasure that some of the scientific lessons I had provided during Rose's tender childhood appeared to have left some trace.) 'I wish we could describe him to you better. Imagine his mother – a bit larger than life, you know – but young, handsome, and happy. Yes, he was happy, not contented or cheerful, but with a happiness that was like – like bated breath, for life was so unexpected, and the things it brings so fearfully wonderful. Oh, Vanessa, you don't have to believe just us! If you're willing to do this, you should talk to his friends, his teachers. Then you'll see what he was like. No one, but *no one* could believe that he had killed himself.'

I steeled myself to ask a terrible question.

'How did he . . . ?'

'He drank a cup of poison. The police told me; they say he took something that he found in the house, and put it in a cup of coffee that he left next to his bed. Something must have happened on his trip – something dreadful, unspeakable, to provoke such a gesture!'

'He went on a trip?' I asked.

'Yes – he left in the evening, after the last time we saw him, that we just told you about,' she replied. 'He took a night train to Zürich, where he had been invited to play the E minor Mendelssohn Concerto with the Tonhalle Orchester. It was a great honour – they've built a new concert hall and it's said to be the best in the world. He was going to talk to them about the three of us coming, to play the Beethoven Triple Concerto . . .' She stopped speaking, and swallowed.

'Have you tried to find out anything about what he did in Zürich, and whom he saw there?' I asked.

'No,' replied Rose in a small voice. 'We're not detectives. We didn't actually *do* anything. We didn't know what to do. We just tried to think.'

'And you are sure there was nothing strange about his behaviour before he left? He didn't seem to have any special plans?'

'No-o,' Claire put in. 'But there was something strange afterwards. His concert was on December 28th, and I'm sure he meant to come home the day after. At least, I had understood that, although I can't remember that he specifically said so, but I'm sure he would have told me if he actually meant to spend time away. But he didn't. Then when I didn't hear from him, I did wonder what he was doing, but of course I wasn't in the least bit worried. I just thought that he must have met some interesting people, and stayed on.'

'Because he did not return home, in fact?'

'It seems that he didn't, until he was found dead.'

'And when was that?'

'In the morning of January 1st, by the charwoman who

comes in by the day. Mrs Cavendish was at home in bed, but she had come in late from a New Year's celebration and had seen nothing of him.'

'We had an idea,' intervened Rose. 'We thought that maybe he discovered that he was ill with some horrible illness which would kill him. We thought he might have felt ill and gone to see a doctor. Not that he ever seemed at all ill, but we couldn't think of anything else. So after the inquest, we asked the doctor who . . . who . . .' She glanced awkwardly at her friend.

'. . . performed the post-mortem?' I helped her.

'But he said there was nothing,' she replied quickly, 'no illness of any kind. Nothing was wrong with him.'

'Still, some doctor somewhere could have made a terrible mistake, couldn't he?' said Claire. 'And told him he was dying? Or something like that. I just want to understand . . . I *must* understand what happened, and whose fault it was. I must . . . I can't sleep . . .'

She stood up and wandered half-blindly across the room and out of the door which led directly onto the stage. After a moment, a turbulent storm of music flowed into the room.

'Chopin's twenty-fourth prelude,' murmured Rose. 'It was the piece he most loved to hear her play.'

'If I understand rightly,' I said, 'the police are not actually undertaking any investigation.'

'No, they're not. For them, it's just an ordinary suicide, nobody's fault, and there is nothing to investigate. As long as they can make sure he did it, they're not interested in his private reasons. But we are! Oh, please say you'll try to find out what happened. Please! It's – I can't tell you what it's done – it was so sudden, it shattered our lives.

Claire's worse than mine, but it isn't just that they loved each other; it was the music, too. We were all together in that; we were doing something like – like one person. We put our whole lives into it; we were discovering new ways to interpret, new ways to express the music, something really, truly different. How could he have smashed it all and abandoned us? What could have been more important to him than music, that was his very soul?'

The sound of the piano continued to flow in from the stage, its voice so gripping that it absorbed and held all my attention. I found it hard to continue to speak, hard to organise my thoughts.

'I will do it,' I said. 'I can only try, you understand that. I have no idea what I may or may not find out. Whatever I find, I will tell you about it frankly, Rose – but only you. What you do with what I tell you is up to you.'

I glanced towards the stage, from which the last notes of Chopin's prelude resonated despairingly.

'I understand,' she whispered, clasping my hand in hers. 'Thank you, Vanessa.'

CHAPTER TWO

In which Vanessa visits the charming town of Basel
and meets an orchestra conductor

Old, crooked houses leant together along the Rheinsprung as though for support, like a group of elegant dowagers. Crowned with ancient tiles dusted with chill powdery snow, painted in unexpected pinks, blues and greens, frozen flowerpots ready at the windows, awaiting the advent of spring, the houses spoke of centuries devoted to order, duty and gentility. I moved along the row admiringly, my eyes hesitating between the delightfulness of the pretty row of house-fronts and the glorious beauty of the Rhine shimmering in front of me. On I went past Münsterplatz and down the Rittergasse, then right on the broad St Alban-Graben to the Steinenberg, where the Stadtcasino concert hall rose impressively in front of my eyes.

This was my first experience of Switzerland, and it had lasted all in all barely an hour until this point. Arriving from Paris and then Mulhouse, the train never really left France, but deposited one upon the very boundary between the two countries; only upon crossing some corridors on foot and displaying suitable papers to uniformed guards was one permitted to actually enter the country. And from the Basel train station to the centre of the old town was but a short ride, although one so remarkably charming, as the cab wound its way among narrow cobbled streets, as to fill the mind with enduring impressions. I sat happily, thinking how many of the most extraordinary experiences of my life had come to me through my detecting efforts, and how very lucky I was to have stumbled into the profession, almost by sheer accident.

The cab deposited me at a small pension, the name of which had been given to me by my dear friend Mrs Burke-Jones as being highly reputable and filled with travelling English ladies. I was not completely sure that this was the kind of company I most desired, but on the other hand, my German was so very rudimentary – and the language that I heard spoken all about me, in any case, so very unlike even my elementary notions of German! – that I thought it must surely be useful to be able to communicate in English. So I booked a room, spent the entire night crossing the Continent, and arrived at midday, ready to offer myself the gift of an afternoon and evening devoted to exploration, before presenting myself at the rendezvous so kindly granted me by Maestro Friedrich Hegar in Basel, where he was conducting a special concert.

I had written to him immediately after the conversation with Rose and Claire, for it seemed as clear to me as to them that whatever had driven Sebastian Cavendish to sudden suicide, it was something that he had learnt within the course of his five days' absence, and I could think of nothing more urgent or more useful than to retrace every step that he took during that short period of time. It was so recent that the project struck me as eminently possible, and I determined to begin in Zürich, whither he had travelled to give his concert with the Tonhalle Orchester.

I hesitated over leaving at once, but my husband advised me that it would be more prudent to write to the conductor, explaining the situation and requesting an interview at his convenience. Arthur said that orchestra conductors are busy and often widely-travelled men, and he turned out to be quite right, for the Maestro informed me that he would be out of the country for a few days, and then he would be spending a short time in Basel for a series of concerts with the Chorale there, before returning to Zürich. If I could not wait until his return home, he offered to receive me in Basel for a short meeting, and gave me a most precise day and hour during which I might come to the concert hall; it was very nearly the only free time that he would have. I accepted immediately by telegraph, made my preparations, deposited my things at the pension and went for a roundabout walk: and thus I found myself wandering along the banks of the Rhine in the wintry sunshine, somewhat early, somewhat timid, but very much charmed by my surroundings.

Upon the stroke of four o'clock I entered the building, and soon found the main concert hall. The orchestra members were putting away their instruments and leaving; the conductor, who must be none other than Herr Hegar, was gathering up his music. I approached him with a little

27

trepidation, hoping that he had not entirely forgotten about our meeting.

He turned as he heard me coming up to the stage from the seats, and I saw a head of white hair brushed artistically back, giving a peculiar effect of being rigidly windblown, a pair of sharp, commanding blue eyes, and a general air of being used to authority and to public observation. Then he came forward, his hand outstretched, and shook mine. His score under his arm, he invited me to join him in the room set aside for his use before and after concerts, and I followed him there under the curious glances of the musicians. It was a simple, pleasant little room furnished with a wardrobe and a mirror – important accessories for the conductor, certainly – a desk and lamp, and two or three armchairs. He settled down in one of them – it seemed almost too small in character, although not in size, for such a personality – and ushering me into another, leant forward to speak.

'So you have come about Sebastian Cavendish,' he said. 'Terrible, terrible, that he should be dead. I can hardly believe it. He was so young, so vigorous, so extraordinarily talented – a true artist, such as one meets but few over a lifetime of music. Only weeks ago he was playing here in Switzerland – only weeks ago. And now he is dead. I am horrified. I would wish to express my greatest sympathy and condolences to his family. If I may be so blunt, how did he die?'

His English was elegant, carefully pronounced yet strongly accented with the rhythmic singsong and peculiar vowels that characterised the incomprehensible Swiss German I heard spoken all about me in the streets. It made me want to smile, but the very thought of the dreadful nature of the response I must give to his question effaced that desire at once.

'He committed suicide by drinking poison,' I replied, unwilling or unable to be flowery on the matter.

His expression changed; he looked stern.

'Really,' he said. 'I had thought it must be some accident. I am sorry to hear what you tell me. Some tragedy of love, perhaps. But it is not clear to me why you wished to meet with me upon the subject. I was hardly acquainted with young Mr Cavendish, though I would gladly have hoped to become more so in the coming years.'

'We, his friends and family,' I began, smoothly adopting a polite fiction that I often used to avoid presenting myself as a detective, 'believe that he had no reason to wish to do away with himself before he left on his trip to Zürich. All are of one mind that he was happy, excited, hopeful and full of plans and projects, as well as being engaged to a charming young lady who was also a brilliant pianist and a member of his trio, the Cavendish Trio. In fact, it seems that he meant to broach the subject of a possible return to Zürich with the trio, in view of a performance of the Beethoven Triple Concerto.'

'Ah yes. He did speak of that,' replied the conductor with a wave of his hand. 'We had a discussion at the party that followed the concert, about his possible return. I expressed my preference that he should return as a soloist, to play something in contrast with the splendidly romantic Mendelssohn; something that would electrify rather than move. Paganini, perhaps. The Beethoven Triple Concerto is extremely difficult to organise; three soloists, three payments, and then generally more than the usual three rehearsals to put everything together. As an established trio, of course, they would have been able to prepare it in detail beforehand. On the other hand, the names of the other two members were unknown to me, although I cannot imagine that Cavendish would have participated in a mediocre trio. Still, I would have wished for further guarantees, and in addition, both the pianist and the cellist are women, which seemed to me to be a poor arrangement.'

'Oh,' I said. 'And why would that be?'

'We Swiss are lovers of tradition!' he responded firmly. 'Our women are not expected to attack the professions, as so many do in your advanced English society. We do not wish for such forwardness here. Women are content to stay at home in their kitchens, and they do not rush about getting up on stages to show themselves in public, or clamour loudly for the vote. Not even to mention the peculiar appearance of a young man travelling with *two* young women. It would not have done here, not at all, I assure you.'

I wondered inwardly whether to laugh or cry over the description of England as an advanced place for women, then decided that it is always best to count one's blessings. I could not guess whether Swiss women were truly as he described them, or whether this was a man's description, offered under the optimistic assumption that women were as he wished them to be. It is not that I am not acquainted with a certain number of Englishmen who would be likely enough to hold the same discourse (except, of course, that they would be obliged, additionally, to fulminate against the modest progress we women have achieved in attaining to the professions, and against the multiple demonstrations women have unsuccessfully staged in order to obtain university degrees, the right to vote, and other carefully protected male prerogatives). The question is both infinite and close to my heart, so I considered it wisest to nod my head sagely and appear as kitchen-oriented and profession-free as possible.

'I see,' I said humbly but encouragingly.

'However, I did assure young Cavendish that he would be invited again for next year's opening season,' continued Herr Hegar, 'without yet specifying what concerto would be played. He had a very bright future in front of him and seemed very enterprising, full of energy, and happiness also. I assure you that I cannot have the slightest notion of why he should have committed suicide.'

'Neither do we,' I answered slowly. 'It seems to all the members of his family that when he left, he was as you describe him. Therefore, we have determined to follow his traces and attempt to discover everything he did while he was away, to see if we can recapture what led to the tragedy. I ought to explain to you that he left a note to his fiancée, telling her that he had "found out something" and "could not go on". We are all quite certain that whatever it was, he must have found it out during the course of his trip to Switzerland, for he left in good spirits and died immediately upon his return. That is why I am trying to go to the places where he went, do the things that he did and speak to the people that he met: in order to discover the cause of his sudden despair. Perhaps the most I can ask of you is to tell me how much you saw of him while he was in this country, and if you know where he stayed, or of any other people he was in contact with while he was here?'

He hesitated, then shook his head.

'I cannot be of much help to you, I am afraid,' he began. 'I do not know exactly when he arrived, but he was certainly here on December 27th, the day before the concert, for we had a three-hour rehearsal in the evening of that day. Cavendish did not stay for the three hours, of course. He waited while we went through the overture to Fidelio, then we rehearsed Mendelssohn, and he left while we worked through the second half of the program, Schubert's unfinished symphony. The first rehearsal was only moderately successful in that his playing was so free that it was not easy to comprehend his style and predict his rubato. For the next morning's rehearsal, I summoned him an hour early to discuss the score in detail, and he explained his interpretation to me with a high level of technical mastery and also poetic expression. The rehearsal went much better. The concert was on the evening of that day. After the concert, there was a soirée during which Mr Cavendish appeared at the top of his form; that was when we had the conversation about his possible return for next year's season. This is all that I saw of him. I cannot tell you anything further.'

'But that is already a great deal,' I said. 'He played on the 28th of December. The . . . the death occurred during the night of December 31st; he was supposed to join some friends celebrating the arrival of the New Year. What did he do in between? Did he stay on in Zürich?'

'I have no idea what he did or where he may have gone after the evening of the 28th,' said Herr Maestro Hegar, beginning to look slightly impatient.

'I quite understand, and you have already given me some most important information,' I said hastily. 'Perhaps I may ask you if he received many people backstage after the concert, and who organised the soirée?'

'The soirée was organised and hosted by one of our most faithful sponsors,' he replied, a faint smile hovering over his lips. 'Her name is Frau Adelina Bochsler, and she is a great lover and supporter of music and musicians. She would certainly have gone to greet the evening's soloist after his concert and can tell you more than I about what occurred there. As it happens, she is also the person to ask about who was invited to the soirée. As always in her home, it was a formal and carefully organised affair, so I should not be surprised if she could provide you with a list of guests. I will write you a letter of recommendation to her, so that you may present yourself at her home in Zürich.' He seemed relieved at the idea of handing me over to the care of someone else, and, moving over to a small writing table, he wrote, folded and sealed a letter which he gave me, together with a note containing the lady's name and address.

'You may present yourself directly at her home and leave a card,' he said, 'upon which you should write that you are sent by me. If she is in, she will receive you, and otherwise she will certainly send for you at her earliest convenience. I am certain that she will be willing to render this service to the cause of Music. I would be happy to accompany you to visit dear Frau Bochsler, if I could, but I will not be returning to Zürich for several days. Basel is a lovely place,' he added, looking around him, then out of the window, with a smile. 'I lived here as a child and still

33

have excellent friends here, who sometimes even come to visit me in Zürich for the concerts. This city is filled with old associations that, by some mysterious contrast, serve to refresh and renew me. It is good for the soul. But I expect that when I return to Zürich, you will probably no longer be there.'

It was clearly a dismissal, but I estimated myself successful with all that I had obtained, and bid the Maestro goodbye with the greatest respect. I felt optimistic about my next step, hoping for much rich conversation from a music-loving and party-arranging lady.

CHAPTER THREE

*In which Vanessa visits Zürich
and hears all about a charming party which took place there*

Frau Adelina Bochsler was very friendly, very helpful, and very, very voluble. She was horrified by the so gifted young virtuoso's dreadful death. She had seen in him a great future. She was always, but always, looking out for young geniuses such as he. She had hoped for a long and fruitful collaboration. She had heard him in London, and it was her idea that he should come to Zürich. She had persuaded Herr Maestro Hegar, who had hesitated to take risks on yet unknown youth, but the young man's gold medal at a famous competition had helped convince him. Sebastian was so young, so strong, so handsome, so appealing. Those who had never met him could not even understand, was it not, dear Frau Vetherburn? She had been lucky to meet him even once. As for myself, how lucky I had been, and how sad my bereavement! I nodded until I felt like a Chinese mandarin.

I asked if dear Sebastian had stayed on in Zürich after his concert. No, Frau Bochsler did not believe that he had. In fact, she had asked him, for if he had been staying longer, she would have gladly taken him on an outing in her carriage to see the sights. But he was leaving the very next morning. Where was he going? Why, she didn't know. She supposed he was returning home. But had he said so? She didn't remember, but she did remember that he was quite – how could she say? He seemed eager to go. It was as though something important was awaiting him next. But she hadn't seen anything out of the ordinary in this. Surely the life of such a handsome young man must be filled with exciting events.

So he had seemed nervous? No, nervous would be the wrong word. Not nervous, but tense, excited, wound up. He was to leave quite early in the morning. The trip to London was a very long one. Such musicians were in great demand; they must resolve themselves to a great deal of travel.

Had poor Sebastian spoken to her of his trio, or his fiancée? Why yes, he had. He had told her of his hopes to come with his trio to play the Beethoven Triple Concerto with the Tonhalle Orchester. But Frau Bochsler had felt a twinge of dismay, as she did not know whether it would be right to encourage him in this idea. She was not at all certain that Herr Hegar would agree, and of course it was Herr Hegar who took all such decisions. She did not say so, but she seemed very much to prefer the idea of Sebastian coming all by himself, to be petted and taken under her wing. The idea of his arriving flanked by two radiant young ladies did not seem to appeal to her much. She sighed, and

36

agreed that of course his fiancée must be utterly devastated.

Could she tell me anything she had noticed about Sebastian's mood over the course of the evening? You see, I told her, we were convinced that at some point between his leaving for Zürich and his death, he had learnt something which had a profound and terrible effect on him. We were trying to trace his every movement and gesture during that lapse of time in order to pinpoint the moment at which this had happened. She understood perfectly. But she could not see how anything of the kind could have happened at her soirée. Well, obviously, there had been many people there. Thirty-five or forty people. Dear Sebastian was not previously acquainted with any of them, as far as she knew. She had kept him near her for the whole first part of the evening, introducing him to the cream of music-loving Zürich society; magistrates, doctors, men of law, men of government, and their elegant, artistic wives. He had not encountered any familiar faces that she knew of, except for Herr Hegar's, of course. At least there had been no sign that he had done so. His mood was excellent, and he was such a lovely young man, so full of charm, such easy manners. Of course he spoke mainly English, but he had some German, and these two languages sufficed for him to enter into many a more or less broken conversation. No, he was not in the least bit shy; quite the contrary. And he seemed to enjoy making friends. What a personality; he was truly the star of the evening, truly, truly. To think he was dead, it was dreadful. Frau Bochsler took out a handkerchief and wiped her eyes.

Yet he seemed somehow tense when he spoke of hurrying home. Why would that be? She didn't know, hadn't thought about it. Probably he simply missed his fiancée. Perhaps, indeed. But, I asked, could it possibly be that he had had a particular conversation at the soirée which had disturbed him? She could hardly imagine it, yet – her eyes sparkled with excitement – it was not impossible; no, she supposed that it was not impossible. Did she think that Sebastian had spoken with more or less everyone at the soirée? Yes, he had probably exchanged at least a few words with nearly everyone. Had she noticed him in particular conversation with anyone? Well, on and off she saw him talking and laughing with several people. What did they talk about in general? Well, music was the subject of the evening. Sebastian's talent, his superb interpretation of Mendelssohn, his gold medal, his budding career, his future. He spoke of it all with such grace; he was modest and at the same time eager and hopeful and so gifted it was quite impossible to believe that he was gone. Frau Bochsler wiped her eyes again.

How could we possibly find out if he had had any particularly striking conversation that evening? Well, she was eager to help. What could she do? She herself had participated in the most fascinating moment when Mr Cavendish had actually taken out his violin to show it to some of the assembled guests. It was a most extraordinary violin, but I would know all about it, of course. (More nodding.) A lion's head was carved at the end of the fingerboard, at the place where there is usually a scroll; a lion's head with a strangely long, extended tongue. The young soloist had explained that the violin was made by a certain Jacob Stainer of Austria. I perked up my ears at the mention of an actual name, only to learn further that Jacob

Stainer had lived and died in the 17th century. Frau Bochsler believed that the name meant no more to her guests than it did to herself – namely, nothing whatsoever – although some of them had appeared to pretend to know all about him. Mr Cavendish had smilingly explained that the sound of the violin was not as powerful as certain others that had been made in Italy, but that it was so extraordinary an instrument in tone and quality that he would not wish to change it; he felt it belonged to him by destiny. She remembered that he had said that the violin had been inherited from his grandfather. Was it not remarkable that grandfather and grandson should both be violinists? But perhaps it was quite a normal thing. Frau Bochsler herself loved embroidery, and she had shared this taste with her grandmother. Her mother had not seemed to enjoy it so much, she recalled. Frau Bochsler's mother had been given to making lace, and she had taught her daughter to make lace, but little Adelina had preferred to embroider poppies and cornflowers and violets, like her grandmother. She had made these napkins herself, she recalled, extracting some from a drawer to show me. I admired the ability of a child to form such perfect stitches, and wondered fleetingly if my own little Cecily would be able to hold still long enough to master such an art. But this was a digression. I drew Frau Bochsler firmly back to the matter at hand. Yes, yes, she said, her eyes still on the napkins, but Sebastian had not wanted anyone to say that he inherited his gift from his grandfather just as he had inherited the violin. The joke had been made, but he had said it was impossible, out of the question. Frau Bochsler did not see why it should be out of the question. Such things could be inherited, certainly.

She continued to finger the napkins. But Sebastian had said it was impossible. Then he had laughed. He was a young man of infinite vitality; the guests had been won over by his charm.

All this was relevant enough, but although it appeared that the guests were learning many an interesting fact from Sebastian, I could hardly imagine what he might have learnt from any of them during the course of such banal conversations. Yet it was tantalising. The violin must have been of tremendous importance to him – I could well imagine a flamboyant personality on the cusp of a grand career appreciating the effect produced on his public by the unusual sight of a lion's head at the tip of his instrument. The fact that he associated the violin with his 'destiny' was also intriguing, indicative of something fundamental in his life. Yet, what on earth could he have possibly learnt that night about his own violin? And what fact about a violin could possibly provoke a suicide? Even discovering that it was a fake or a fraud would surely not produce so dramatic an effect. My imagination was failing me.

I drew Frau Bochsler back to the subject of Sebastian's suicide. She could not imagine any relation whatsoever between this terrible event and anything that had transpired during the soirée. It seemed to her, alas, much more probable that poor Sebastian had made some dreadful discovery in London. Could it not be – she leant towards me, dropping her voice to a whisper – that he had found out something *about his fiancée*? Such things had been known to shatter the happiness of young men.

I told her that the fiancée was more distraught by the mystery of it all than anyone else, and described the

40

note that Sebastian had left for her. Frau Bochsler sighed deeply upon hearing about it, and the distaste for having doubts shed upon the absolute success of her party was slightly overshadowed by the glowing account I gave of the mystery of it all, and the realisation that she might possibly yet play a role in its elucidation. I asked again if she could be sure that there had been no other significant moments for Sebastian during the evening, and if she had noticed his mood when he finally left. Well, it was as she had told me; he left somewhat early as he had an early train to Paris on the following morning, and he was definitely tense when he told her this, as he shook her hand. Perhaps there had been something to cause that. It was possible, after all, although she had certainly thought nothing of it at the time.

Could I, perhaps, arrange to meet some of the other guests and ask them the question?

It would be a little socially awkward. Yet, she thought it could be done. Without saying so directly, she intimated that certain people might be quite interested to hear details about the terrible tragedy that had passed so close to them. She could arrange something. She had the list of guests, of course. Her soirées were highly prestigious, highly desirable. Everyone who was anyone in Zürich wished to be invited. She must keep lists and be careful to exclude undesirables. Anything might happen if one were not strict; people who were not received because of a social scandal could attach themselves to other people and, on the grounds of visiting them, could worm their way in. Frau Bochsler had had to yield on such matters many a time when she was younger and less experienced, and more than once she'd had a soirée ruined by the presence of an obnoxious or unwanted guest. She knew better now. She had precise lists and they were given to the servants. Yes, we could consult her list. It would be awkward but not impossible to visit her guests and explain the situation. There were not as many visits to make as it might seem, since many of the guests had come as couples or families. She found it very hard to believe that I would discover anything of significance, however. As the hostess, she had spent the larger part of the evening near Sebastian and heard whatever people had to say to him. Music was much discussed; the young man's studies, his professor, his musical preferences, his concert experiences, his future plans, and his instrument. She could not remember any other topics; she had heard nothing that struck her as the slightest bit unusual. Of course, there were necessarily many things that she had not heard. And I, who knew Sebastian personally, might perhaps pick up some allusion, some reference that others had not noticed, although she could not even imagine what it might be. She really could not believe it possible that the fatal knowledge acquired by the poor young man before his death could have been learnt at her soirée. No, truly she could not. For if it had been, why would he not have committed suicide that very night, at the Pension Limmat, where she herself had organised his lodging. What a horror that would have been; a horror and a scandal! All the more so because she knew the lady who ran the Pension Limmat quite well. It was a very proper place, and Frau Dossenbach would not have liked a suicide there. She, Frau Bochsler, would never have lived it down. It was indeed fortunate that it had not occurred thus. The mere idea made her feel faint. Well, in any case, she quite saw how important it was for the family to try to understand why he had felt that he had to die. A true tragedy. Although Frau Bochsler had many engagements, she was free the next morning, and, if I wished, we might begin our round of calls then.

In the meantime, she recommended me to the Pension Limmat. It was right on the Limmatquai, a short and pleasant walk over the bridge from the Tonhalle. If I did not yet have a room somewhere, I should certainly go there. It was short notice, but she would write a letter of recommendation to Frau Dossenbach, which I could show her directly I presented myself there. It was not extremely far, and very easy to find; I need only walk straight down the Kirchgasse to the river and then turn along the quay. I could go there by foot if my bag was not too heavy.

I thanked her, took the missive which she sealed with a large ring, and left, feeling a slight relief, in spite of all her kindness, at leaving the plush and pillowy surroundings of her parlour behind and emerging into the crisp, sunny air.

I was in a hurry to reach the pension, but my eyes and my feet had other desires, for the daintiness of the streets, the fresh colours of the houses, the old beams and the bright flowers at every window constantly distracted my attention so that I found myself pausing on my way, staring about me in delight. When I reached the river, instead of turning left along it, I walked onto the Quaibrücke and spent an enchanted moment hanging over the edge. A solid mass of black ducks, many dozens of them, was wedged into the corner formed by the river and the old bridge, reposing or simply socialising, and amongst them, two enormous white swans were etched out against the black background. I forgot momentarily where I was in the contemplation of this astonishing spectacle of Nature, then suddenly remembered Sebastian. Had he also paused on this bridge, on his way to the Tonhalle which lay just a short distance from the other end? He must have, surely. It was so beautiful, and he had loved beauty.

Sebastian was still a mystery to me. His feet had probably trod the very same bridge; his smile had lit up the very same parlour in which I had just now been offered some overly sugary tea, his music had blended with that of my darling Rose whom I had known since her childhood. But human beings are mysterious enough to one another even face-to-face. And those who had known Sebastian best had not understood why he had done what he had done. How could I hope to penetrate his secret?

What was most important to Sebastian? His violin and his music, on the one hand, and on the other hand the people he loved: his mother, presumably, and Claire. Was there anything else? For the time being, I should proceed on the assumption that there was not; otherwise, surely Claire would have known. So, the terrible thing that he had found out must have concerned these things, or been triggered by one of them. The violin – the music – the mother – Claire. In asking Frau Bochsler's guests to recall their conversations with Sebastian, I would concentrate on these four points. Something, somewhere, had triggered a terrible realisation in him. Surely it could not be impossible to find out what it was.

If only I had met him. It was so hard, feeling my way blindly, trying to understand the innermost thoughts of a young man I had never met. If only I had seen him but once. But I shook my head briskly, and scolded myself. I must stop thinking this way: as though I had missed my chance. Frau Bochsler had met him and Herr Hegar had met him, and they understood as little as I. Having met him was not the point. Trying to understand the secrets of his mind was not the point. The point was simply factual, I reassured myself. Sebastian had been to Frau Bochsler's; I had been to Frau Bochsler's. He had walked to the Pension Limmat; I was walking the same way. He had met some people whom I would meet tomorrow. *Somewhere* along that path that he had trod, and that I would tread after him: *somewhere*, his secret must be hidden. If, after having followed it, it still seemed to me that everyone I spoke to said nothing more than platitudes and banalities – my greatest fear at that very moment – why then, somewhere, I would have missed the single pebble that was actually a pearl. I might do so. Yet that did not mean that the pearl was not there. Its existence was a matter of plain fact: of that much I was certain.

I left the bridge and wandered on up the street in the direction of the pension. Doubt was not an option.

CHAPTER FOUR

In which Vanessa meets a retired violinist
and asks him a number of questions

I sat in a comfortable armchair in front of a small table decorously laid with small pastries. It was already the fifth of my morning calls in the company of Frau Bochsler, and each host had offered us something to eat. I was beginning to feel foolish, frustrated and exhausted. It had been obvious to me in the first five minutes of each call that no information was to be had, and yet we had been obliged to spend another ten minutes each time in polite conversation, most of which took place between Frau Bochsler and the host or hostess, and escaped me entirely, held as it was in singsong Swiss German.

My enquiries had begun on the previous evening when I interviewed Frau Dossenbach, the proprietress of the low-ceilinged, medieval Pension Limmat, but from her I had learnt nothing but the barest of facts. Frau Dossenbach's English was rudimentary: she appeared to possess an exactly equal and minimal knowledge of English, French, Italian and high German; precisely those words and phrases necessary to attend to the immediate wants of her numerous foreign guests, such as 'Do you wish for hot water now?' and 'The evening meal is at seven o'clock precisely'. My attempt to pose a few modest questions about Sebastian Cavendish had met with blank incomprehension until I was rescued by a gentleman passing through the hall. He took the trouble to interpret my questions and Frau Dossenbach's answers, but as might be expected from one so entirely devoted to the necessities of her daily work, she had only facts of this nature to tell (and some reluctance, due no doubt to the natural discretion of one in her profession, to mention even those). I could learn absolutely nothing about Sebastian's state of mind, and gleaned only the simple confirmation of the fact that he had departed early on the morning of the 29th of December, whether to Paris, London or elsewhere she could not say.

Giving up on this source of information, I turned to thank the gentleman who had helped me, but he had already disappeared up the narrow, crooked staircase that led to the chambers above. I was left to my imaginings as I went up to my room and proceeded to freshen myself with a pitcher of hot water carried in by an obliging maid not two minutes later. In entirely incomprehensible words proffered in the local dialect, but using the most unmistakeable gestures, she was able to communicate to me the fact that dinner would be served when I should hear the sound of a bell or gong belowstairs, and leaving me with this welcome piece of information, she removed herself and I removed my shoes and reclined upon the bed.

I felt anxious and troubled, and was worried that I would have difficulty finding sleep in such unfamiliar surroundings. However, after consuming the extremely heavy meal of a bowl of cabbage-and-rice soup followed by breaded veal, together with potatoes cut to tiny ribbons and fried to a crisp golden brown, I felt overcome by exhaustion, and dragged myself up the stairs to my room again, feeling as laden as though I were carrying a weighty suitcase. I went to bed at once, in order to be at Frau Bochsler's at as early an hour as was reasonable to begin our round of visits.

Some two hours after we had started forth, bored to tears by endless repetition of banalities, I began to wonder if Frau Bochsler was not becoming as impatient and sceptical of the whole procedure as myself, and was on the very point of calling it all off from sheer enervation, when her carriage stopped in front of an elegant town house, and she rang at the doorbell, saying,

'Now you shall meet a very dear friend.'

The door was opened by a sempiternal aproned maid, who ushered us into a sempiternal velvet-upholstered parlour. After a young lady, an elderly lady, a middle-aged couple and an elderly couple, it was now a single gentleman who entered the room: a gentleman of a certain age, small, wiry and friendly.

'I am so pleased to meet you,' he said in excellent English, once Frau Bochsler had explained something of the nature of our call. 'My name is Leopold Ratner. Please, do sit down and by all means let us discuss this strange story.' For the fifth time that morning, we sat down and the maid was sent for something to offer the unexpected guests.

'I was greatly interested in Sebastian Cavendish, and terribly shocked to hear of his sudden death,' Herr Ratner told me with sincere feeling. 'You see, I follow the careers of as many of the rising young violinists of Europe as I reasonably can. Luckily for me, my dear Tonhalle is one of the very best of all the European orchestras, so that some of the most extraordinary players come to perform right here where I live. I attended Cavendish's phenomenal concert in December, and afterwards, of course, the charming evening party at Frau Bochsler's home.'

I noticed then that half-hidden underneath his grey beard, Herr Ratner had an old, well-rubbed mark on the left side of his neck.

'You are a violinist also?' I asked.

'I was one, not so long ago,' he replied with a smile. 'I was an orchestral musician for several decades. When I was young, I had some talent and I thought I might go far, but such a career is not given to many. Ah, then, when I was still young and energetic and filled with dreams of ambition, I travelled far and wide to hear the greatest violinists of my day, and that is how I came to hear Josef Krieger – or Joseph Krieger, as he called himself after moving to England – and to be inspired to become his pupil. You wish to know what I discussed with young Cavendish during the evening: we talked about my teacher, Joseph Krieger. Alas, what I learnt above all from Krieger was that I would never be a great violinist. He used to shout at me during the lessons, which I believe he gave only because he was in need of money at certain times; his career knew some dramatic ups and downs because of the terrible disputes he had with some of his patrons and protectors. He was, to be straightforward about it, a cruel and violent man. I remember one time when an eminent professor from the Royal Academy of Music had come to visit. He arrived early and I was still having a lesson, on the Saint-Saëns concerto. Start from the beginning, my teacher told me. Eagerly I lifted my violin to my chin, fired up to give my best on this splendid work in front of the stranger. After the first two notes of the superb initial theme, Herr Krieger stopped me with a cry of "Too high!" Undaunted, I began again, only to be stopped after the same two notes by "Too low!" He continued in this manner for a full quarter of an hour. I never played more than those first two notes, after which he declared my lesson over and turned to talk with his colleague as though I no longer existed. I cannot even remember my thoughts as I packed my instrument and left his house, so black were they. He destroyed my ambitions, and if he had lived longer, he would probably have succeeded in destroying my love of playing and even my love of music.'

'How horrid he sounds,' said Frau Bochsler consolingly. 'Why ever did you stay on?'

'You don't know how things were then,' he said. 'They have perhaps changed a little nowadays, although I am not so certain about it. For the young and aspiring musician, his teacher was like a god. One did not shop for a teacher as for a pair of shoes. One selected a teacher, and humbly requested that he deign give lessons, and accepted that his rebukes were merely the thorns along the path to greatness. I did not realise the harm that Joseph Krieger was doing me until long after his death. I was too used to habits of respect.'

I thought of Rose's tone, on divers occasions when I had

heard her speak of her cello teacher, and recognised the same phenomenon of infinite and unquestioning respect. Yet in Rose's experience, that respect and admiration went hand in hand with an attachment as deep as love, that contained no trace of pain or humiliation. Perhaps she was one of the lucky ones, and there were still students who suffered as poor Herr Ratner had done at a time when young whippersnappers were not expected to protest ill-treatment at the hands of their masters, but to profit from it, and improve.

'However,' the elderly violinist was continuing, 'he died when I had been with him for less than two years, and I found myself suddenly obliged to make my own way as best I could. In that same year, Sir Charles Hallé formed a new symphony orchestra in Manchester, and to my great good fortune, I was able to become a member. Thus I had the infinite joy of making the splendid music in a group that I did not feel able to make by myself. Then, ten years later, when the Tonhalle Orchester was formed here in Zürich, I chose to join it, and thus to return to my native country. I retired only a few years ago, and since then, it continues to be my greatest pleasure to attend the concerts.'

Something in his tone and manner indicated that he was not merely indulging in a flow of memory, but that all this had some connection with Sebastian Cavendish. I encouraged him to continue with a nod and a murmur.

'Now, Joseph Krieger possessed a very remarkable violin,' he went on. 'I had occasion to see and even to hold and play his violin very frequently, over the two years I spent attempting to learn something from him, while he fulminated against my playing and told me that my accent in music compared to the composer's intentions was no better than my Swiss compared to his own pure and elegant High German. However, all of that is past and finished, and Joseph Krieger has been dead for nearly half a century. I meant to speak of his violin, because when young Cavendish showed us his instrument that evening at Frau Bochsler's, I felt absolutely certain that I recognised it. It was not just the astonishing lion's head, although this caused me to identify the violin at once as a Jacob Stainer. Stainer made more than one violin of that type, although they are rare, but here there was something more: I felt quite certain, seeing and running my hands over the violin, that it was none other than the very instrument that had belonged to my former teacher. A certain stain and discoloration on the back, certain worn marks, and then, the very sound of the instrument itself, as I had heard it during Cavendish's concert – fiery and infinitely subtle – I was quite certain that this was the same instrument!'

'Did you tell Sebastian about it?'

'Not at once. I have always felt a nearly insurmountable repugnance at mentioning the name of Joseph Krieger, such was the burden of resentment that remained within me even after his death. I cannot speak of it without bitterness even today; even now that the ice has been broken, you cannot but sense something of my feelings. Cavendish was far too young to have ever known Krieger, of course, and I thought it quite possible that he had bought the violin from a dealer, or that it had been lent to him by an anonymous foundation, and that I might be able to indulge my curiosity about the instrument without mentioning the name of Krieger at all. But before I had time to put the question, I heard him telling others that Joseph Krieger was his own grandfather, and that the violin was a family heirloom.'

'Quite,' I assented. 'Sebastian certainly knew that his grandfather was a famous virtuoso, although I do not know whether he knew much about his character. But the violin was certainly a treasured inheritance.'

'I should say not just the violin, but the extraordinary, flamboyant talent as well! As soon as I heard it, I realised how much his playing resembled his grandfather's in style. Yet the boy must have been born a good quarter of a century after his grandfather's death, and cannot have had any more idea of his playing than what reputation and family tradition may have communicated to him. Is it not strange that something as intangible as the manner of playing the violin can be inherited in just the same way as a material object like the violin? Yet the evidence of it was there before me!'

'It is extraordinary,' I agreed. 'And so, once you knew that he was Joseph Krieger's grandson, did you tell him anything about his grandfather?'

'What do you think?' he smiled sadly. 'Politeness dictated that I tell him only the facts; that his grandfather was my teacher, and that he was one of the greatest of violinists. Nothing more.'

'Did you tell him what you just told us about his playing being in the same style as his grandfather's?'

'Yes, that I certainly did.'

'And what did he answer?'

'He laughed it off and denied the possibility; said he did not believe such a thing could be inherited, and at any rate in his case he knew it to be impossible.'

'What could he have meant by that?'

'I have no idea. I suppose he was merely enjoying feeling original.'

'Did you tell him anything else about his grandfather?'

'Nothing; certainly not a word of all I have just told you. Indeed, I have never spoken of those feelings to a living soul until this very moment. It is strange, but when I realised that this blithe young man with the ready smile was Krieger's grandson, I felt a wave of pleasure; it seemed to me as though a chance had been offered me, to undo the twisted knot that Krieger had left in my heart. I intended to continue to see the young man, to be his friend, and to follow the development of his career, without ever telling him why. It would have been a kind of redemption! And then – I heard about his sudden death. I cannot tell you the effect the news had on me. I had just begun to feel that my hidden shame was finally to be dissolved in friendship, that my anger against the grandfather could finally dissolve in the form of kindness to the grandson. And then the process was suddenly cut short! I will not deny that at first I was literally in despair. But after some days, I came to realise that something had changed within me after all. It was as though the brief contact with the young man's vibrant personality had somehow broken the hold that Krieger has exercised over me through all these years. His playing and his personality provoked in me the old feelings of passion for the violin that I had lost long ago, without the despair and frustration caused by my teacher's attitude. In that short evening, he gave back to me what his grandfather took from me. And although I spoke of this to no one, I realise now, with you, that I am able to speak of it after all, and that this signifies that indeed, everything has changed.'

He sighed and paused for a moment, then continued.

'It is indiscreet of me, but may I ask you how Cavendish died?'

The sadness in his eyes communicated itself directly to my soul as Claire's mourning had not. Love is essentially intimate, and although I could sympathise, I could not really share her sorrow at her loss. But music is for everyone, and although I am no more than a mildly appreciative member of the audience at the best of times, Herr Ratner had suddenly made me feel that a musician like Sebastian could bring people a sense of the power, the marvel, the sap of new life. I acutely regretted never having seen him, and never having heard him play. For the first time, I felt more than merely handicapped in my research by my ignorance of what he was: I felt a sharp pang of regret at not having known him. I wanted to comfort this old man, or at least explain to him simply and exactly how and why Sebastian had died, but I didn't know! And the little I could say was anything but comforting. Sadly I was obliged to explain to him that Sebastian, his newly discovered fountain of life, had committed suicide for a reason that no one understood. I told him frankly that my quest in Zürich was to find out if that reason had anything to do with Sebastian's visit. I told him about the words 'I've found out something about myself'. I asked him if he, who had been acquainted with the grandfather that Sebastian himself had never known, believed that the connection with Joseph Krieger could have anything whatsoever to do with Sebastian's suicide.

'I cannot imagine how it could,' replied the old gentleman

in a subdued tone. 'He knew of his grandfather already. What could he possibly have "found out" from our brief discussion?'

'Perhaps he knew very little of his grandfather. Are you sure you told him nothing at all that might have been new to him?'

'I told him that I had known his grandfather long ago and heard him play often, in the years just before his death. I mentioned being his student, frequenting his home over that space of two years. I cannot remember mentioning anything else in particular. Not one word, I repeat, of the things I have just told you. I spoke of Joseph Krieger only with admiration and respect.'

'Since Sebastian's name is not Krieger,' I observed, 'I presume that his mother must have been Mr Krieger's daughter. Did you know her? She must have been quite a child when you were still taking lessons.'

'Ah yes. I remember knowing that Professor Krieger had a wife and children, though I never met them that I can recall. I may have glimpsed his wife once or twice, but I have no clear memories. She must have been very self-effacing. I cannot imagine being able to live with a man like Joseph Krieger otherwise. I do not recall his children learning to play music, for example, as many musicians oblige their children to do. In fact, now that you mention it, I believe he had only daughters, because I recall his once telling me that it was a pity he had no son, as I would have been just good enough to serve as his practising tutor. That was the way he spoke in general. And mind you, many girls did learn to play musical instruments or sing even in those days. But that would not have been the way of a man like

Professor Krieger. Women learnt music for the betterment of their lives and the lives of those around them, not as a profession, and Joseph Krieger was only interested in music as a life-dominating profession, and, even then, only in those who might have the capacity to reach the heights of genius. I do not believe his children were trained at all. It is all the more striking a miracle that the gift should survive intact into the next generation, is it not?'

Herr Ratner did not seem to recall anything further about his conversation with Sebastian Cavendish; it really seemed unlikely that he had said anything that could have produced such a tremendous shock as to drive a man to suicide. We were both somewhat disappointed by the paucity of the information we were able to provide to each other. But try as I might, I simply could not imagine why hearing any mention of the grandfather who had died so long before his birth should suddenly appear important to Sebastian now. Nevertheless, I noted down Herr Ratner's address, ostensibly in order to write to him if any deeper understanding of Sebastian's sad fate should be obtained, but also simply as a source of information about the past if such should be needed. And upon that we said goodbye, and I left to continue the round of calls with Frau Bochsler; without, however, discovering anything further of interest.

'Whatever poor Mr Cavendish learnt, it was not said at my soirée,' she pronounced finally, with a mixture of relief and disappointed curiosity, at the close of the wearisome and monotonous day. Wearisome and monotonous for me, at least. She, to be sure, had many more reasons to enjoy it than I; the people we had visited were her friends, and she had the benefit of a common language to communicate with them; and, being quite generously built, she had presumably suffered less from the ceaseless intake of pastries than had I.

'It is a pity that dear Dr Bernstein is not in Zürich at the moment,' she said later, as we sat in her parlour, taking stock of the day. 'He has been a dear friend of mine for decades, and of Herr Ratner's as well. You would like him. He is so highly educated, so cosmopolitan, our dear doctor, and I did notice him speaking for some time with that poor young man. He seemed quite excited, but that is not surprising, such a lover of music as our Dr Bernstein is. You would have appreciated his intellect and knowledge. As a matter of fact, he wrote a book . . . I have it here somewhere. Ah yes, I remember, here it is. I have never read it, but I am sure that it is most interesting.' She took from the mantelpiece a bound volume whose dustless state was obviously due to careful work on the part of the housemaids rather than to any effort at reading the contents by anyone whatsoever, given that the pages were still uncut. I read the title: *Automatische Schreibung: Diagnose und Bedeutung.*

'Diagnosis and meaning of automatic writing. What is that?'

'Yes, our dear doctor is greatly fascinated by the phenomenon, and has been for as long as I have known him. Don't you know about it? The patient writes down all kinds of nonsense in a state of unawareness, like a medium in a trance. Such things used to be all the rage and people were convinced that spirits were speaking through the writers, but Dr Bernstein insists that true understanding of the phenomenon is still lacking, though it has nothing at all to do with spirits from the other world. I know that he speaks of a patient of his own somewhere in the book. Take it, if you like. Perhaps you will enjoy it. You speak some German, as I heard. Do you also read?'

'Haltingly, but with a dictionary I can manage,' I said, thanking her and taking the book. Automatic writing! Either the doctor was a charlatan or – or he was not, and there was something interesting behind a phenomenon that my husband Arthur had taught me to consider essentially as a swindle. I felt intrigued, and determined to spell my way through at least part of the book before coming to a conclusion of my own.

'Well, if the subject interests you, you may have a chance to meet Dr Bernstein in person, and then you can ask him the questions you wished. He moved from Zürich to Basel some years ago, but he travels quite regularly to London, to attend the meetings of the Society for Psychical Research there.'

'Really!' I exclaimed. During a previous case, I had already had some dealings with members of the SLR, in a manner that had deeply affected my natural scepticism. 'Thank you so much for telling me about this. I shall certainly look for him at their next meeting.'

CHAPTER FIVE

In which Vanessa returns home to Cambridge
and discovers the existence of a theory of heredity

Sitting in the winter sunshine in my little Cambridge garden, I took Cecily's small face between my hands and stared at it closely. Heredity! What was it? What secret lay behind Sebastian's 'cursed inheritance'? Was it material, or did he refer to the incorporeal conveyance of traits and features between the generations? Cecily wriggled and gave me a kiss, and all the mystery of motherhood, of the miraculous transmission of flesh to flesh and blood to blood lay revealed before me: her brown eyes, her soft hair, her little upturned nose, my features inexplicably reflected in the enigma of her face, radiant with love and the joy of being reunited.

The magical moment passed and the mystery sank into opaqueness once again; the children grasped my hands and pulled me into a dance of wild Indians about an improvised totem pole, and the capacity for rational thought melted away from my mind, leaving behind a mass of confused images and associations. The scales, which had fallen momentarily from my eyes and showed me the reflection of my own face in my child's, returned and I perceived it no longer; Cedric's resemblance to Arthur was pronounced (and he even looked a little like me – another mystery, as Arthur and I do not resemble each other in the least), but Cecily was once again nothing other than a little elf who had strayed into our garden by mistake.

As a matter of fact, as I watched her dancing about, I was reminded, not for the first time, of my own dearest sister, Dora. I used to think this was nothing but pure foolishness, since Dora and I are identical twins, and therefore I could hardly imagine a likeness to her and none to myself. But over time the impression persisted, and I came to understand that as Cecily's character was closer to Dora's (far sweeter, gentler and more thoughtful than I seemed to recall myself as ever having been!), I came to believe that the ephemeral similarities I sometimes fleetingly perceived arose as much from expressions and from movements as from the plastic features.

How often it is said that children have inherited their looks from Papa, their character from Grandmamma, and even their very troubles, which are imputed to Uncle James or Auntie Joan! But what can such a thing mean? How can a character, how can even a face be inherited in the same way that a material object, such as a violin, is inherited? How is it that we humans so freely confuse these two types of inheritance, even using the same word, although one is simple and the other complex and beyond all comprehension? That the face of a child can reflect both mother and father, and even back to the previous generations, is a phenomenon so familiar that we no longer question it. Although we do not understand it, we accept it and it seems natural to us; yet surely there must be some physical mechanism by which our physical attributes pass through our bodies to the child we create together.

I could not help mulling over the question, to the point of making theories whose expression would have been a perfect example of scandalous impropriety. It was a delicate subject to broach at dinner (for Arthur hates unseemliness), but I did so with tact, and encountered unexpected enthusiasm!

'Why,' he answered with the characteristic pleasure that exposure to new scientific ideas invariably gives him, 'there is more known about the mystery of inheritance than you might think! In fact, I heard a very fascinating lecture on the subject some time ago, by a visiting German professor engaged in some research that I'm sure you would find very interesting. He told a story you would like, although I cannot quite remember the details, about someone having reached an extraordinary level of understanding of the subject and then having died and all his work having disappeared. Now, why would that have been? I'm sorry, I can't recall; it's the kind of thing you would remember better than me. What struck me in the lecture, the reason why I went, was the role of mathematics in the whole theory; probability, to be exact. For example, if a certain physical feature appears in the parents, then certain physical features may appear in the children with greater or lesser probabilities, which can be mathematically calculated, and certain other physical characteristics may be totally precluded in the children of

a given couple. Theoretically, at least. Professor Correns'
studies concerned plants, which have a simpler constitution
than human beings. But he strongly expressed the belief
that humans, animals and plants function analogously.

'But plants do not have children,' I said. 'What is the
means of transmission?'

'Ah, but they do! When you take a pea (I believe he
spoke of peas) from a pea plant and plant it to obtain a new
pea plant, that is considered to be a child, and, according to
Professor Correns, it is not so different from . . .'

He paused and blushed, but I finished his sentence with
a smile.

'Than the planting done by us humans. So, the pea-plant
plays the role of the father and the earth that of the mother?'

'No, I believe there is a matter of two pea plants . . . Now
you are getting me all interested! I can't think how I
managed not to seize the physical aspects of the theory, so
interested was I by the mathematical.'

'That doesn't surprise me in the least. It is too bad,
however,' I remarked.

'Well, it should be an easy affair to manage to encounter
Professor Correns at some social event around Cambridge,
if you would enjoy that. If it would compensate for my
foolish distraction, I will be happy to speak to my friends in
the department of biology and see if such an event cannot
be arranged, or, if it is already arranged, if we cannot be
allowed to join.'

'I should love that!' I exclaimed, with sudden impatience.
Could it be that a light would suddenly be shone directly,
and for me personally, upon one of the greatest mysteries
of life? Could it be that scientists understood the secrets of

heredity, if only for peas? It was, to be sure, a mystery that had never occupied my spirit particularly until that very day. But now that it appeared as one of the most important elements in a puzzle that concerned me, it suddenly seemed to me to be one of the essential secrets of nature, and I could not resist the desire to learn as soon as possible whatever there was to be known on the subject. I felt as impatient to meet fusty old Professor Correns as a young girl waiting for a midnight tryst with her first lover.

Professor Correns was being much celebrated in Cambridge, and as it happened, I was destined to meet him quite by chance on that very same afternoon, for as I was returning home along Silver Street carrying a few purchases of haberdashery, a carriage drew up in front of the Darwin house and a woman emerged with a very small girl, followed by two top-hatted gentlemen. One of them was familiar to me as one of Mr George Darwin's brothers; I knew he was also a professor at the university, but could not remember of what subject. The other was a tall, dashing fellow, obviously a foreigner, with striking blonde hair and beard worn in a longer style than is usual hereabouts.

As these gentlemen approached the gate, the Darwin children appeared *en masse* from the stable where they often play, and greeted the newcomers effusively. The youngest one, William, spotted me as he was displaying his prowess to impress the visitors by climbing atop the high wall that separates the Darwin property from the road, and running eagerly back and forth along the top. Though I no longer live next door to them, the children still treat me cordially as a neighbour.

'Mrs Weatherburn!' Willliam cried out with great

enthusiasm, as an additional means of drawing attention to himself. 'Here's Uncle Francis and Aunt Ellen with a German for tea! Do come!'

I glanced through the gate, not certain whether an invitation proffered by a six-year-old was to be taken at face value, and encountered the welcoming smile of Mr Darwin's lovely American wife, who had emerged from the house in her relaxed fashion, without a wrap, to take charge of her unruly brood, two more of whom had now joined their brother atop the wall.

'Please, do join us if you can,' she said. 'Professor Correns must not be kept isolated amongst dons! He ought to meet as many as possible of the ladies of Cambridge as well, don't you think? Such a different style of conversation!'

My heart leapt at the mention of his name; this was really a stroke of luck, for the satisfaction of my impatience, at least! Arthur being out for tea and the twins with their nanny, I accepted the invitation with pleasure. As I entered, another carriage drew up, and a couple of a certain age stepped out and entered the house behind me. Mrs Darwin's maid took all the shawls and wraps, and we settled down in front of a roaring fire. Children ran in and out, tea was brought in and poured, various cakes were served, and introductions were made all around.

Professor Francis Darwin, I learnt with some excitement, was a naturalist, and Professor Carl Correns from Tübingen his guest in Cambridge!

'I am very honoured to meet you,' the eminent professor said to me in that respectful and somewhat weighty tone that a German accent always appears to lend to the English language.

'And I to meet you,' I said with an enthusiasm that

he probably found surprising. 'My husband was at your lecture on heredity, and what he told me has made me very eager to meet you and learn more about it.'

'So, you have a scientific mind?' he answered pleasantly. 'It is something of a rarity to meet a woman with true scientific curiosity in the tradition of old, such as the legendary Marquise du Châtelet.'

'I am honoured by the comparison!' I laughed. 'I have heard about the marquise, who brought the discoveries of Newton to the scientists of the French court. It is said that she studied day and night. I only wish I possessed such capacities!'

'Yet you are interested by the sciences, and perhaps often like to meet and discuss with the scientists who work or visit the university?'

'Yes, well,' I said. 'I do get very curious about some of the discoveries I learn of through my husband. I admit to a certain interest, even if my understanding must necessarily remain superficial. But I was particularly intrigued by what my husband described to me of your lecture. I must say that heredity is a topic that fascinates me deeply. However, he was only able to tell me just enough to whet my appetite for more, without giving satisfactory answers to any of my questions.'

'Perhaps I can do better,' responded Professor Correns with delighted gallantry. 'At any rate, I am quite ready to try, and where I fail, my colleagues will certainly help me.'

Mrs Darwin was chatting quietly with her sister-in-law during this conversation and Professor Bates was standing at the sideboard together with the two Professors Darwin. Mrs Bates, seated on the same sofa as myself, was following our conversation without participating.

Professor Correns settled into an armchair that he drew up nearer the sofa. I took advantage of his proximity to examine him more closely.

He looked no older than Arthur, and his eyes were of a bright Teutonic blue with a merry twinkle. He seemed to be playing at a very entertaining game, yet there was an air of melancholy behind his laughter. I found him an intriguing and attractive personality, but my desire to know about his science was stronger than my desire to draw him out.

'Well then,' I said, 'let us see if you can possibly explain the secrets of heredity to an ignorant being such as myself.'

He sat back and smiled.

'Part of the secret of heredity is beyond my own knowledge,' he said, 'and another part must always remain mysterious to us humans because it is dependent on no other laws than the laws of chance, which as you know are unpredictable. I don't know if you are aware that the laws of chance give precise predictions only over very large numbers, but never over a single occurrence of some event. For example, if I flip a die, I cannot make any prediction about which number will come up, but if I flip it six thousand times, I can predict that the number of times that a one will appear will be quite close to one thousand. Do you see?'

'Yes, I do see,' I said. 'I see it for a die, because there are only six possibilities and we know them all and we know that there is an equal chance for any of them to occur. But it doesn't seem possible that those simple rules could apply to a situation as complex as that of heredity in living beings, where it would seem that the number of possibilities are absolutely endless and impossible to enumerate.'

'Very true, for complex living beings like humans. But there are much simpler living beings whose study has allowed us to understand the grand discovery, namely that the rules of chance governing the dice are the same identical rules which govern heredity; it is simply the number of possible combinations which is infinitely greater.'

I paused to think for a moment.

'Well,' I said, 'I can conceive somehow that such a thing might be true. It seems to us that the possibilities for two human beings to create another one are endless, but perhaps, as you say, they are really only in the many millions and that seems like an infinite number to us because we cannot tell the difference. Theoretically, I can see that what you are saying might be the case. But I must admit that I have not the faintest idea of how, even having conceived of this theory, it could possibly ever be proven.'

'It takes a genius, madam,' said the German professor with a sudden ponderousness, and I glanced at him in surprise, wondering if he could possibly be using this term in reference to himself. But no. This sudden earnestness was of that which is inspired by the contemplation of an extraordinary phenomenon.

'I will tell you how it was done,' he explained, 'but I must first tell you by *whom* it was done. It is a surprising story, and a sad one. The story is about a monk in a monastery in Brünn who, some thirty-five years ago, published a paper which was misunderstood and utterly ignored and forgotten, until I myself discovered it barely one year ago – and it has changed my life, so that I now consider my scientific mission to be the bringing of this seminal work to the light of day!

'The story is about a monk who asked himself the same question that you are asking about the secret of heredity, and who actually devised a way to make a scientific investigation of the answer, by studying plants in the monastery garden! It is the story of a monk who spent years making the most extraordinary, intelligent controlled experiments and painstaking notes of the results, then analysing their mathematical meaning with the brilliance of genius, to come to a final result. A result which is, to my mind, one of the most astounding scientific discoveries of our century, in no way inferior to Charles Darwin's theory of natural selection.' Here he broke off and glanced at the men at the sideboard, hoping, no doubt, that he had said nothing to offend the sons of the eminent naturalist. But they were paying no attention to him, so he went on.

'And finally, it is the story of a monk who, on becoming the abbot of his monastery, ceased to pursue his research, and whose notes were burnt at his death by his successor, who had no understanding of the genius contained therein. His name was Gregor Mendel, and it has been the crowning glory of my professional life to be the one to rediscover that old, forgotten published paper, the only remaining trace of all his careful work, and to recognise its potential importance. I gave myself the task of reproducing his experiments in order to confirm his astounding theory, and have met with total success. And therefore, I can now trumpet the work of Gregor Mendel to the entire world: *heredity is governed by the laws of chance*! A sentence which must be properly understood, of course, since to the layman it may sound like heredity is a matter of chance. But that is not what is meant at all; the laws of chance, which are mathematically known as the laws of probability, are strict, and they govern heredity according to fully understood rules. This, by my reproduction of Mendel's work, has now been definitively proven!'

'The descent from theory to experiment is always liable to render a theoretical idea more accessible to the layman's mind,' I said. 'Would it be possible to describe your experiments?'

'Nothing could be easier,' he said. 'The experiments themselves were so simple that you could do them yourself, if you were interested. They are based on the careful study of pea plants. Do you cultivate vegetables?'

'I do, in fact,' I said, glancing automatically out the window at the Darwins' garden, whose wintry aspect left all visions of peas and the usual tomatoes and beans entirely to the imagination. 'At least, I do in the springtime, but nothing is happening there now, unfortunately.'

'But still, I will tell you how the experiments are done, and you can try them for yourself. But please do not forget to pay careful attention to the fact that the beauty of the theory is not in the experiments themselves, but in the fact that Mendel was able to see that he might be able to deduce the secret laws of heredity from making sufficiently many of these experiments, and carefully observing the results. He never claimed to understand *how* the traits are passed from one generation to the next – that delicate mechanism still remains beyond our knowledge. But he created an experiment to test the laws governing the frequency at which certain given features will be inherited by the offspring, and this is a shining example of genius.'

I agreed to bear this in mind. Professor Francis Darwin,

catching the mention of plants even from some distance away, now came towards us and sat down to listen.

Professor Correns continued, 'Mendel began by making a careful examination of the common pea plant, *pisum sativum*, that grew abundantly in the monastery kitchen garden, and he noticed that, unlike the human being, in which each physical trait (for instance, the colour of the eyes) can take a myriad of different shades and hues, many distinguishing traits of the pea plant took just two possible forms. For instance, the flowers of the pea plant always grow either at the top of the plant, or on the side, never both. The plants are either noticeably tall or noticeably short; there does not seem to be the possibility of every kind of height, as with humans. The colour of the pods on a given plant are either all green or all yellow, never some of each or some strange greenish-yellow combination, and the pods themselves are either smooth or pinched in between each pea. Finally, the peas themselves are either green or yellow, either round or wrinkled. Mendel studied these properties, and the first observation he made was this: if you take a single pea plant and write down all of its properties (for instance, tall with flowers at the top, smooth green pods and round green peas), and you take a pea from this plant, plant it and observe the plant that then grows, it will have all the same properties exactly, and so on down the generations.'

'So in fact, a pea plant is a creature that has but a single parent,' I observed. 'I was wondering about that. Does Mother Earth really play no role in the genesis of the new plant?'

'None at all. The pea is naturally a monoparental plant practising self-fertilisation, but it can be made to have two parents by the method of cross-fertilisation. This is the experiment that Mendel made.'

'He was not alone to make such experiments,' interjected Francis Darwin suddenly. 'My father did many such, over a period of years, and even published a book called *The Effects of Cross and Self-Fertilisation in the Vegetable Kingdom.*'

'But of course,' rejoined Professor Correns placatingly, then added, 'your father's book is a classic of the subject, and his methods are certainly similar to those of Mendel. Cross-fertilisation and breeding of plants has been practised by gardeners for hundreds of years. Mendel's research took place several years earlier than Darwin's, of course, since he published his article in 1865 and that already followed years of research, whereas your father's book, if I am not mistaken, appeared in 1876. But that is not the point. Mendel's particularity was the mathematical study of the results, and the mathematical theory he devised to explain them. It is in this that he differed from all who preceded and followed him in the study of cross-fertilisation of plants.'

His father's honour saved, Francis Darwin subsided, and, with the true interest of the scientist, prepared to listen as attentively as I to the German professor's explanations.

'To return to your point,' he began, 'Mother Earth certainly plays a role in the genesis of plants, since a plant could not be born and grow without nutrients. But she plays no role in their hereditary properties. Father Plant, Mother Earth – it is a beautiful analogy, but it is not correct here. There is a proper analogy within the pea plant itself to the role of both mother and father, and it takes place within the flower. You see, within the petals of the flower of the pea plant, like most common flowers such as crocuses and tulips, there are two organs, the pistil which is the centre part, and the stamens which are the tiny stems containing a little yellow spot on the top of each. It is the stamens which play the role of the male organ, as their pollen ferti—?'

The professor's voice ground to a halt as his attention was drawn to the strange behaviour of my neighbour upon the sofa, Mrs Bates. For some moments already she had been fanning herself vigorously with a Chinese fan decorated with pagodas and flying herons, from which depended a green tassel decorated with a bead, and now she leant back, closed her eyes and slipped into a near faint. Her pale lips murmured something that I didn't catch, since I was paying attention to the maid, who was already hastening forward holding out smelling salts. I took them and agitated them under Mrs Bates' nose, and she revived somewhat and remonstrated in a voice of deep dismay.

'I cannot stand it – such language! I have never heard such a conversation. The stamens – the male – indeed! I cannot bear it – I am sorry – I am not accustomed . . .'

Her voice trailed away in a show of weakness, but her husband, rushing forward to her aid, added his protests to hers.

'Whatever have you been saying to shock my wife so deeply?'

'Oh, the conversation took a turn – dear Thomas, I know that it is science, but I really could not hear it!'

'Well, it shan't go on, my dear. Would you like me to take you home?'

'No, no,' said Mrs Darwin soothingly. 'Here, dear Mrs Bates, do have your tea, it will revive you in a moment. We shan't have any more scientific conversation, shall we? Let us all speak of ordinary things!'

Calm returned to the company, and everyone present was relieved that the moment of tension had passed. Everyone, that is, except for myself. I was overcome by a great wave of anger and frustration, so powerful that it risked entirely ruining the atmosphere of a pleasant social occasion, and leaving an unpleasant trace and strained relations behind. My delight at being asked to tea had been uniquely due to the possibility of having my questions answered, and now the tea party had transformed itself into an obstacle blocking my way to the knowledge I so dearly wanted. Even though Mrs Bates' fainting spell was genuine enough, I could not help feeling that there was something hateful about it – something artificial and untruthful; not that she herself was counterfeiting her emotion – I did not think that of her – but yet how in Heaven's name could the words 'male organ', pronounced in the most abstract scientific manner, on the subject of the stamens of a flower, cause such an effect upon a woman who was a wife and very probably a mother? Whence exactly came the shock to her nervous system upon hearing those words? Certainly not in the actual fact of the existence of the corresponding object! What hypocrisy, that the pronunciation of a word should cause a shock where the thing itself presumably caused none! I was truly suffused with rage and unable to pronounce a single word, for I saw that not only was Professor Correns' fascinating discourse destined to be interrupted, but there should be no chance of its being resumed at any time during the course of the party, which at once became a dreary duty that I must perform, puppet-like, while hiding my feelings to the best of my ability.

By a miracle of the same kind of intuition that had allowed him to sense the importance of Gregor Mendel's published but utterly unrecognised work, Professor Correns detected my thoughts and drew me aside.

'I perceive your deep interest in these questions,' he said, 'and that you do not suffer from the sensitivity of certain English ladies with regard to certain somewhat delicate questions. Or perhaps it is that you, like myself, belong to a new and younger generation. So, I would propose, if you wish, that we meet again, perhaps to take a quiet walk through one of Cambridge's lovely parks, and discuss these things in privacy and at leisure. It would afford me great pleasure to do so.'

The world returned to rights, and I felt a great smile of gratefulness spread over my face as I accepted joyfully and fixed a date that unfortunately could not, due to other obligations, be nearer than two days hence. But the professor's understanding compensated for the delay, and, thanks to his words, I was able to resume the tea-drinking and the now relentlessly proper and correct conversation that ensued, with everyone gathered round the tea table together, and nothing left to chance, the husbands apparently not ready to abandon their wives once again to the unknown dangers of science.

CHAPTER SIX

*In which Vanessa reads a book in German
and one chapter in particular*

The art of automatic writing, I wrote, painstakingly translating the foreword to Dr Bernstein's book in the hopes of developing an honest interest in the material, and thus providing myself with a perfect reason to ask for an introduction to the good doctor at the very next SPR meeting in London – *is one of the most mysterious and ill-understood phenomena of our time. This is partly due to the many aspects of the phenomenon and the deep divergences of opinion of observers as to its origin and meaning. The major trends of popular beliefs could be listed as follows:*

1. Swindle, pure and simple, for the gain of attention or even financial advantage.
2. Communication from otherworldly spirits whether dead, distant or planetary.

In this case, two currents of thought are to be noted:

2.a. The communication is made in order to carry messages from the spirit to our world, through the medium;

2.b. The communication is made in order for the all-wise spirit (possibly identified with the Lord or one of his angels) to teach the medium, if she is willing to listen, hidden but important aspects of herself.

3. Fragmented impressions produced from the unconscious brain, not unlike the images produced in dreams.

In this case again, two possibilities present themselves, as for dreams:

3.a. Haphazard and fragmentary reproductions, in arbitrary arrangements, of sights, physical experiences, or mental experiences (such as anxiety over a particular coming event or over a type of event in general) from the daily life of the subject;

3.b. Mental constructions which are totally meaningful according to a logic which is different from that of the conscious mind, but which merely requires possessing the key to unlock its mysteries entirely.

The purpose of the present volume is, by the study of various cases, to indicate that true automatic writing does exist, independently of the many cases of imitation for purposes of gain, and to provide some case histories that may provide evidence for the last of these interpretations. In spite of intensive personal study of one of the cases presented in this book, the author has not yet discovered the key to unlock the meaning of her writings, yet so strong is the impression of hidden meaning that the author is convinced that all who read the writings selected here must share it, and he writes this book in order to present it to the world, in the hopes that some more experienced or more enlightened colleague may use it as a springboard to reach the ultimate truth.

Each chapter of the book was devoted to a different case history, but from the first few lines of each, it was clear that the doctor had not personally analysed most of the cases, if he had even actually met them. Thus, his ability to link their writings (often quite coherent in themselves) to a deeper meaning connected to the unconscious personal life of the writer was in the majority of chapters limited by his lack of knowledge of even the quite basic facts of that life. For this reason, it made sense that the final and longest chapter should be devoted to the one case that was actually a patient of his own: a British subject named Lydia K. I skipped over the other chapters and went straight to Lydia K.

I treated Lydia K. for a period of nearly four years, of which she spent the first part residing in my clinic for mental patients, and then the final years in my home, for I came to the conclusion that she did not belong in the clinic, being in no way insane, but a very lovely young woman.

Over this period of time, I grew to know her

extremely well, in spite of the fact that my study of her case was somewhat handicapped by the fact that she had been forbidden to speak of her family or to give her true name. I communicated with the family through her legal guardian, who checked regularly on her well-being through the visits of a deputy who was sent to the clinic on a monthly basis, and also came regularly in June to bring Lydia home for the annual summer holidays. The family was clearly desirous of keeping her identity entirely secret. She had been instructed to refuse to answer any questions whatsoever about the subject, whether it be on her name, her parents, her siblings, or her more distant relatives. Aided by a natural tendency to discretion, she kept these promises faithfully, no doubt as convinced as the rest of the family of the shame that her 'illness' or 'abnormality' might afford to what I imagined must be a noble or prominent family. Throughout the time she spent in Basel, she was known to me as Lydia K., the K. standing for the name of her guardian, a name very widespread in England. I was quite certain that this name was not her real name, for she sometimes did not react to it very naturally, yet I never knew her by any other.

Lydia's greatest desire in life was to please others, and possessing a naturally sweet and compliant disposition, she was able to follow her family's directives and the requirements of my own treatment perfectly insofar as they did not enter into conflict with each other. When they did, she invariably chose to keep faith with the promises made to her family.

Since she was a ward, I supposed her to be an orphan, and she eventually confirmed that this was the case, telling me that her father had died when she was four and her mother when she was fourteen. Apart from these bare facts, I was left in the most complete ignorance of many facts of her childhood that, I am certain, would have aided me to come to a deeper understanding of the ailment that afflicted her.

Yet even without such information, I believe that as the years passed I was coming closer and closer to some kind of comprehension, and, at the same time, her own writings were evolving in interesting ways, although to a superficial eye they may not have appeared significantly different from those she produced from the very beginning of her stay at my clinic.

Although the guardian, Mr C. K., steadfastly refused to give me the information that I felt I needed to know on the subject of Lydia's family, he was desirous that she should be cured, and willingly answered various other questions that I asked him during the course of an exchange of correspondence that lasted throughout the four years of her treatment (I never met him personally). He told me, for example, that according to the family she had no noticeable peculiarity of writing before reaching the age of fourteen, apart from a tendency to occasionally mar the margins of her copybooks with stray words, phrases or lines of poetry, but nothing which could in any way cause alarm, although to a trained mind these might have served as the first indications of the direction that the subsequent abnormality was to follow. Lydia herself told me that as a child she had no consciousness of writing the stray words and was usually quite surprised to see them there when her governess had corrected her work. However, there was no cause for concern, and Lydia was able to complete her education altogether normally; indeed she was a cultivated and well-read young person.

At the age of fourteen, coinciding in her case with the onset of puberty and (as I eventually learnt) following the death of her mother, Lydia's tendency to absent-mindedness while writing began to increase noticeably, until it became necessary to stand over her and call her attention repeatedly to the matter at hand whenever she had to perform an ordinary writing task such as a letter or invitation. A moment's inattention on the part of the governess would result in sentences turning, seemingly of their own accord, into something quite different from what was intended: snatches of poetry, confused images and the like. This tendency continued and intensified in spite of (perhaps partly because of) repeated scoldings and punishments, until Lydia could no longer take pen in hand without slipping into a state in which her hand alone functioned and her will could inject no sense at all into the process. By the age of nineteen or twenty she had reached a state of complete inability to write anything on purpose.

From our discussions I became convinced that, in spite of appearances, Lydia's slow slide into automatic writing after her mother's death represented a *progressive relief from repression rather than a descent into confusion. This reasoning was the first step towards my conviction that by her writing she was expressing inner thoughts that were totally inaccessible and incomprehensible to her conscious mind, and from that point on, my efforts were all bent on understanding the message itself. I believed that if I could understand it, I would hold the key to understanding the reason for which the message had been mentally suppressed, and something of the mechanism by which the human brain is able to accomplish such a feat. Everyone has the experience of forgetting something just when it is needed, only to have it spring into the mind at some entirely irrelevant moment, proving conclusively that the fact in question has not really been forgotten by the brain at all, but was only made temporarily unavailable. This phenomenon in itself is not mysterious, or, at least, it is familiar to everyone, but the mechanism which puts into direct opposition the brain's intention of hiding something with the soul's urgent desire to express that same thing, and the manifestation of this struggle by such rare and extraordinary phenomena as automatic writing, are mysteries, the unlocking of which would lead us deep into the secrets of human psychology.*

The patient came to me in the autumn of the year 1870, at the age of twenty-four. She had previously been living at home. I was not sure what particular event had motivated her suddenly being sent for treatment after six years of a stable although strange condition. It occurred to me that the family probably saw her condition as an obstacle to marriage, for which she was in every other way entirely suitable, being a sweet-natured and very presentable young woman with polished manners. In the absence of any contact with pen and paper, it would have been nearly impossible to notice anything at all peculiar about her, were it not for a tendency to dreaminess and a certain lack of ability to reason efficiently, but these are of course traits shared by many young women and in no way prejudicial to her marrying happily and raising a family. Later, when I learnt that Lydia was an orphan, it occurred to me that she may have become a burden on her siblings for some reason, perhaps due to their own marriages into other families.

I began Lydia's treatment simply by a series of examinatory sessions, during which I gave her pen and paper and observed her writing with no interference.

The sight of pen and paper produced an immediate although scarcely visible effect on her; her eyes developed a dreamy look, almost as though they were covered by a film, and she appeared to look inwards inside herself. She confirmed to me that she saw and heard nothing while writing, nor could she recall any thoughts that went through her head. She spontaneously wrote for periods of time that would typically last from one to several minutes, after which she would appear to awaken. When she read what she had written, she used to shake her head with a laugh, exclaiming 'What nonsense!' in a casual tone I felt certain that she had been taught, probably by family usage. Her writings were all very similar to each other in tone and in vocabulary, with a very small number of continuously recurring themes. Here is one example from the earliest days of her treatment.

Sky arches overhead, clouds over trees, world is large, world is vast, sky covers all, world and sky contain all. Nothing is more secret than any other thing to the eye of God, which knows and sees all equally like the sky covers all equally. God the Father made that which is Natural and that which is Unnatural thus the Unnatural is as natural as the Natural and pain is as natural as joy and all comes from the Father. Joy and abomination are both expressions of the love of the Father. Not one thing is right and one wrong but all are equal being sent by God as they are equal under the sky.

Attempting to analyse writings such as this one together led us far along the path of religious investigation, as we explored the writings of Calvin and the roots of Protestantism. However, Lydia repeatedly told me that these writings did not express her own consciously-held religious and moral views, and that she was herself shocked by reading 'Not one thing is right and one wrong but all are equal' which in no way corresponded to the manner in which she had been brought up. She was occasionally tempted to believe that a spirit from outside herself was dictating such words to her, but her belief in this theory was and had always been tempered by the complete absence of any kind of self-identification of the said spirit (unlike in many of the other cases cited in this book). Of herself, Lydia made no attempt to comprehend her own writings, dismissing them as nonsense as observed above.

Having obtained a grasp of her habitual procedure when writing, I began to make a series of very gentle experiments with her. My goal early on in the treatment was exclusively one of curing a peculiar and rare disease for which no kind of treatment had yet been developed; I was not, at that stage, as profoundly fascinated by the disease itself as I later became. In the desire to restore to her, little by little, control over her own writing, I began by suggesting that she include certain specific words in her texts. Before handing her the pen and paper or even showing them to her, I would impress upon her that she should attempt to write down a certain word, for example 'house', as many times as possible within her text. However, these efforts bore no fruit whatsoever. The moment the pen was in her hand, she lost contact with the conscious world and all memory of my request to her was effaced.

The next strategy I adopted, after some weeks of trial and reflection, had more success, although of an unpredictable and confusing nature. By its very nature, this technique could only be used rarely, as it could be easily recognised and I did not wish her to know my intentions. It occurred to me that if *her writings were reflecting a repressed reality, then perhaps if I gave her some knowledge purposely destined to be somehow repressed, echoes of it might emerge in her writing. I decided to make her the confidante of a secret – not an important one, of course; indeed one that I invented for the occasion – yet I told it to her with no reference whatsoever to its relevance to her treatment, but rather as though I wished to ask her advice, and I repeated to her many times the necessity for complete secrecy and discretion, which she of course whole-heartedly promised. The story I told her was one of a slightly embarrassing skin ailment, asking for her opinion as to whether I should inform my wife of it, or visit a doctor. In order to perceive the traces of my effort, I chose a topic – 'skin' – which had not yet made an appearance in any of her writings.*

I was immediately rewarded by the emergence in the following treatment sessions of the new word in her automatic writing, yet so disguised as to keep the secret perfectly. The word 'skin' now appeared occasionally, but in contexts not even remotely associated to the secret I had confided to her, and so disguised that, had I not been especially on the lookout for it, I would have missed its presence entirely.

Truth is what comes from God and not what we ourselves believe is the truth for we are subject to error. Whatever comes to us from God is the truth and our difficulty is to distinguish truth from error, truth from Him and error from ourselves. This is the only task and not distinguishing the wrong from the right, the pain from the joy, the outer from the inner for these are one so long as they come to us from the Source. We have a body and there is the world and we perceive it as the inner and the outer, our skin is the frontier between our sense of Inner and our sense of Outer yet this is an illusion for within us there are elements of the outer and outside of us of the inner. All Truth is outer, all Lies inner. On the Day of Judgement, the Truth will emerge. When man rips the fabric of God's Truth then only then is he Evil. Before condemning a man for Evil be certain that his thoughts and deeds were not sent to him for a purpose beyond our understanding.

In style and essential content her writings were as before. Only I could be aware of the introduction of an entirely new word into the mental processes that produced them. In order to verify my findings, I repeated this experiment a few times, but at quite long intervals so as not to make the patient aware of my proceedings. Each time, some fundamental word or words from the secret emerged in a different context in her writing.

By this time, Lydia had been with me for more than one year with no noticeable change in her condition. Standard exercises geared towards a practical outcome of allowing her to write something in a conscious manner systematically failed as soon as she took the writing instrument in her hand, be it pen, pencil, or any other implement. I tried to fabricate such peculiar writing instruments for her as should continue to attract her attention and keep her in a conscious state during the writing, but had no success in this venture. Using chalk in front of a blackboard, she fell into her usual trance and covered the blackboard repeatedly at a tremendous speed, writing again and again over what was already written without any erasures. I once believed I was on the brink of success when I suddenly asked her to trace the letter A with her toe in the sand. I saw her listen to my request and attempt to obey; her foot made some disjointed movements, something vaguely triangular emerged, but she was so acutely troubled as to fall in a kind of faint directly afterwards, somewhat discouraging me from trying the experiment again. I did so, nonetheless, one further time, after having obtained her agreement; in her normal state, she even spoke humorously about the possibility of her learning to write with her foot, but the exercise once again turned awry as she underwent a kind of seizure, her limbs becoming rigid and her eyes rolling upwards, before falling into an unconscious trance during which time she sank to the floor and her hand made rapid although illegible gestures of writing in the sand until she awoke a few minutes later.

By the time Lydia had been in my clinic for two years, I had come to the conclusion that there could be no possible cure for her without coming to a complete understanding of what was causing her writings; in other words, their hidden meanings. At the same time, I began to feel that it was entirely useless for her to live in the clinic together with the patients suffering from serious mental problems when she was quite normal in her everyday behaviour. It began to seem to me, although this was perhaps in my imagination and a consequence of a certain worry, that the clinic was having a negative effect on her mental state, and that she was becoming stranger and more dreamy and absent-minded there, and even more distant from ordinary reality, so I determined to restore her to a normal daily life by taking her into my home, which I did with the consent of my wife. She lodged in a room at our house, embroidering, reading, and singing. She sang extremely well; astonishingly, in fact for a young woman who had never had music lessons, as she told us. For the rest, she accompanied us on our walks and outings and took her meals with us, while I continued to hold regular writing sessions with her, now more in order to probe the secrets I felt convinced her writings were revealing than to effect any kind of pragmatic cure in which I no longer believed.

In the summer of 1874, her family sent for her to pass the holidays with them. She had returned home for the summer each year since she first came. All seemed entirely normal – yet I was never to see her again.

I never received any further explanation. A man was sent to fetch her things, bearing a short note to the effect that the treatment was to be terminated, and that was the last I ever saw or heard of one of the most fascinating cases it has been given to me to encounter in the whole of my career.

CHAPTER SEVEN

In which Vanessa is treated to a fascinating discourse
on Mendel's theory of genetics

Having told Professor Correns to come and pay us a visit on Wednesday afternoon, I had left the garden gate invitingly open, and upon hearing his step upon the path at three o'clock precisely, I hurried out to greet him. He was looking all about him with an air of great pleasure.

'The poetry of your garden, Mrs Weatherburn!' he said admiringly.

I dearly love my garden, which is quite ample compared to others along Malting Lane, stretching up the side of the house to the street as well as behind the house. In spring and summer it is a riot of flowers and sunshine. January, however, is not usually the season at which I most appreciate it. Thanks to the clemency of Cambridge weather it is very green, but the taller plants tend to wilt sadly and have an air of awaiting the spring with the same glum patience I sometimes feel myself when the wintry weeks stretch on for too long. But Professor Correns had already spotted the nearly-empty vegetable patch at the back, in which nothing remained but a few blackened and broken stems.

'Ah,' he said, hurrying over eagerly to have a closer look. 'Yes. I see that you do know peas.'

'Just the ordinary type,' I said.

'*Pisum sativum*,' he said. 'That is exactly what my own research was concerned with. Having cultivated them, you probably noticed that the peas produced are sometimes green and sometimes a yellow colour; also that they are sometimes round and sometimes wrinkly.'

I had never paid much attention to these details, and dared not mention that the peas that I harvested for the enjoyment of a summer day's gardening were generally shelled by Mrs Widge. But my conscience was relieved by calling up the image of the dishes of roast mutton that she fondly served us, accompanied by our own garden peas and tiny carrots. Yes, a few were wrinkled and the colour of the peas was not entirely even. Although if any peas looked too yellowish, I suspected that Mrs Widge might actually throw them away. However, I nodded vigorously, and seeing that the professor was on the point of launching into a discourse, I asked him whether he would like to come indoors.

He looked up at the sky, then at the house through the open door of which the wild shouts of the children could be heard, and then suggested that as it was a particularly lovely day for January, we could perhaps take a turn. The idea did not displease me, and hurrying indoors to put on hat and wraps, I called out to the children's nurse that I was going for a walk and hastened quickly out again before they had time to cling to me with a show of wild protestations performed uniquely for the histrionic fun of it, which tended to redouble in intensity in the presence of outsiders.

'Let us walk about the Lammas Land,' I said as we started down the lane. The professor accompanied my steps, looking around him with unmitigated delight.

'It is like a country village here,' he said. 'It is almost difficult to imagine that we are but ten minutes' walk from the busy colleges.'

'Less than that, if you count Newnham,' I said, pointing towards Sidgwick Avenue. 'It's just a two-minute walk that way.' But Professor Correns was not interested in Newnham College. Reaching the end of the lane, we entered Laundress Green, and I began to do the honours of the place, pointing to the public house on the bridge and to the back of the Darwins' granary with its little white balcony, but he seemed to have something else on his mind. As we crossed over a small bridge under which the river runs sluggishly through the fen grasses, he turned to me with an air of secrecy, and I thought that he was going to pick up the interrupted conversation about the mating habits of pea plants, when instead he said in a hushed tone,

'Rumour has it that last year you discovered a body floating in this place.'

'Oh!' I said. For many months I had been unable to cross the Lammas Land without recalling the events surrounding that murder, but of late that association had begun to fade away under the influence of other more recent events. 'No, no, rumour exaggerates. I did not find the body, I merely helped in understanding the facts that had led to its being there.'

'But it was here?'

'Not quite. It was more over there, I believe. Caught in the reeds and grasses.'

'I have heard that you are regularly involved in detective activities,' he went on, and I noted in his tone respect mingled with a curiosity of which he was slightly ashamed but unable to completely repress. The enquiry in his blue eyes was intense and alive with intelligence. Normally I loathe talking about these things, or perceiving the prurient interest they occasionally arouse. But I did not feel that now, and I became aware with a blush that it was because his interest was not directed at the grisly tales of murder, but at myself. This sensation was unusual and, to be quite honest, not unpleasant. In any case, it provoked in me an uncharacteristic expansiveness, and I found myself telling him not only about the girl who had been killed, but, to my own surprise, all about Sebastian and the source of my sudden interest in heredity. And by this circuitous route, having crossed and circled the Lammas Land and Laundress Green from top to bottom, edge to edge and bridge to bridge, we found ourselves naturally back at the subject which had first brought us together, and caused such emotion to Mrs Bates.

'You were telling me about heredity in peas,' I said.

'Of course! Exactly. I was telling you that the stamens of the flower function as the male,' he responded at once, launching into a lecture with the natural flow of an experienced professor, 'and the pistil functions as the female organ, which is fertilised by the stamens in the following manner: they shed the yellow powder that you can see upon their tips, the pollen, onto the pistil, and that fertilises it and allows it to produce a pea pod containing peas.

'Now, if you allow the flower to self-fertilise and obtain a pea pod, from which you extract a pea which you then use as a seed for another pea plant, you will, as I said earlier, obtain a pea plant having characteristics identical to the parent plant; green or yellow, round or wrinkly and so forth. That is because, in this case, the mother and father are from the same plant, so of the same type. Such plants are called purebred, and they carry the strains of their characteristics from generation to generation, exactly as one might see certain characteristics carried down in strains of purebred horses or dogs, for example.

'What Gregor Mendel wished to do was to see if it was possible to comprehend whether the transmission of visible features in peas and the role of the pollen and the pistil is governed by a discernible theory. To separate the role of pollen and pistil, he cross-fertilised plants of different strains. This is a technique which has been practised by farmers for many, perhaps hundreds, of years: it consists in opening the immature flowers of the pea plant and cutting off the stamens, and then using a small brush or even the fingers to remove pollen from a different plant and brush it onto the immature pistil. One then carefully closes the flower petals and leaves the whole situation alone until the pea pod emerges, after which one can study the properties of the individual peas in the pod, and then plant them and observe the properties of the plants they produce. He was a monk, if you recall, in Brünn, and had all the necessary time and leisure to do as he pleased in the monastery garden, and the approval of his superior as well.

'In order to carry out numerical observations, Mendel repeated his experiments on many hundreds of plants, crossing the same type with the same type, for each of the many possibilities, again and again, observing and counting the results. What had been believed at first – that crossing a plant with green peas and a plant with yellow peas could produce a plant with either green or yellow peas (regardless of which parent was green and which yellow), and that it was merely a matter of chance – turned out to be false. In fact, crossing purebred strains yielded very clear and observable results. Considering just the property of the peas being green or yellow, he saw over a great number of experiments that crossing two purebred green plants could only produce green plants, and crossing two purebred yellow plants could only produce yellow, whereas crossing a green and a yellow invariably produced a green.

'He then proceeded to mate purebred plants with those of the second generation of mixings, and now he observed something new. Mating a purebred green with a green that was actually of green and yellow parentage produced only green offspring, but mating a purebred yellow with a green of mixed parentage produced green exactly half the time, and yellow exactly half the time. As for the mating of two mixed plants, the result was a green offspring three-quarters of the time, and a yellow offspring one quarter. Can you guess the rule? It is a purely mathematical question by now!'

I stopped and leant my elbows on the railing of a bridge, ruminating over the pattern he was describing. He stopped next to me, and extracting a crumpled envelope from his pocket together with a stub of pencil, he drew the following diagram.

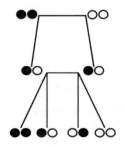

'Look!' he exclaimed. 'This is Mendel's stroke of genius, and the picture explains it all! Each organ, whether stamen or pistil, must contain two *markers* of some kind, which can be either green or yellow. From the stamens only one of the two can pass to the offspring, and from the pistils again only one, and these are selected by random chance! In a purebred green plant, both markers will be green for the stamens and the pistils, so, if they are crossed, they can only pass green markers to the offspring, and for purebred yellow it will be the same. But when you cross the plants – then what happens to a plant with one green and one yellow marker?'

'Well,' I said, 'you claimed that crossing a green and a yellow purebred always creates a green, so I am obliged to conclude that a plant with one green and one yellow marker must be green.'

'Logically spoken!' he cried and again looked at me with an undue measure of admiration. 'Mendel called these markers *alleles*, and the fact that green and yellow together make green, he described by saying that the green allele is dominant and the yellow recessive. Thus, of the four possible father-mother combinations green-green, green-yellow, yellow-green and yellow-yellow, only the last one will actually show yellow peas – so only one quarter of the offspring, on average, will be yellow! But the mixed plants will contain alleles that are totally invisible when observing the plants themselves, but that will affect a certain number of the offspring, according to the laws of probability. Generalise this theory to all possible physical traits, and you have the entire theory of their heredity and the manner in which they are passed down through the generations.'

'Is that mystery not contained in the nature of the alleles?' I said. 'They seem to hold the secret of it, whatever they are.'

'We do not yet know their precise nature,' he said confidently, 'but we will. They are some kind of purely physical entity, microscopically small and carried within each living creature. When we have sufficiently powerful microscopes, we will perhaps be able to observe them physically. As to the mechanism that ensures that each creature carries a pair of alleles and passes exactly one of them to the offspring, that is also a physical reality. The power of Mendel's theory is that it proves that the choice of which allele passes down proceeds according to the laws of probability. For the rest, the only mystery that remains is how God could fabricate machines as utterly complex and fascinating as living creatures surely are. And the question of God's power will no doubt remain forever beyond our grasp.'

'You mean that human beings must be content to be satisfied with the physical explanation, as long as it is complete.'

'For myself,' he said, 'between the physical description of the alleles, and the mathematical description of their behaviour, it is the theory that I find the most interesting. Can you imagine that Mendel understood why, when a yellow pea plant is crossed with a purebred green, they will have only green offspring, but exactly one quarter of the grandchildren provided by mating those offspring will be yellow? And how many typical human characteristics of heredity are explained by that same observation?'

'You're right – that is striking,' I said, my thoughts reverting suddenly to Sebastian. 'I have often heard that many traits are seen to "skip a generation", and to pass directly from grandparent to grandchild without being visible in the parents. Do you think that Mendel's theory could really explain it?'

'But it is certain!' he said. 'For one particular example of such a thing, one might say that it could be due to many complex combinations of heredity, but when such a thing is perceived very generally, there is no doubt that it must be interpreted as a consequence of the theory.'

'This is one of the most fascinating things I have ever heard,' I declared. I was bemused and seduced by it all: it seemed so very revealing, so daring, so deep and yet so fundamentally simple – and so patently true! 'But still,' I went on, 'there is something I don't understand. If your theory explains the hereditary transmission of physical features – and I quite understand that human features are subject to a great many more variations than pea plants, and therefore the number of possibilities is gigantic, yet the mathematical laws governing them would be the same – what about the transmission of non-physical attributes?'

'You mean such as character?' he asked.

'Yes. Such as often-noted family tendencies such as a quick temper, or a high intelligence. Or – or musical gifts.'

'The question is both deep and subtle,' he said, 'and I have pondered it myself a great deal. I have finally arrived at the conclusion that, in spite of appearances, there is no way to be certain that these traits are not just as much consequences of a physical disposition as visible features are. Could not a musical talent be a consequence of a physical superiority of the ears, causing more acute appreciation of sounds that already seem beautiful to everyone?'

'But surely the love of music, the feelings of emotion connected to art and the ability to communicate them are more than just a fine ear,' I said.

'Can we be certain? Could not an emotional, artistic temperament be a consequence of a more fragile heart, thus more easily and more strongly moved, again, by visions that are considered lovely by all? Could not a tendency to rage be due to some physical quality of the brain or the body?'

'We do speak of "hot blood",' I replied thoughtfully. 'Someone, somewhere, must have had an intuition of your claim that character traits are purely physical, to invent such a phrase. Yet it shocks my feelings!'

'It shocked mine also, at the beginning,' he said. 'And, of course, it is true that education can be another powerful vehicle for transmission of certain things between the generations, but not this kind of thing. Certainly, Mendel's ideas go beyond and even against many received notions about character. Yet I have come to believe in them absolutely. If I see any remarkable resemblances between any two members of a family, I now attribute them automatically to heredity, and begin to reflect upon what physical peculiarity they might reflect.'

'I suspect that if I think about it enough, I will soon begin to do the same,' I admitted. 'It is too convincing. It opens up new vistas of possibilities – albeit slightly frightening ones. But now that I understand it, I cannot help believing in it. Even before I have had time to get used to it.'

'That is because you are a very unusual young woman,' he said, taking my arm.

CHAPTER EIGHT

In which Vanessa attempts to understand
what the suicide note might have meant

'Vanessa! It's me! I'm visiting at home for a few days – I simply had to see how you were getting on!' Rose's delightful face beamed at me from the doorway. The afternoon sun shone on her thick, wavy hair, once gold, now burnished to the colour of ripe honey. Her whole being radiated joie de vivre; the kind of happiness that simply comes from inside, with no cause and no explanation; some people are born happy and the happiness wells up inside them no matter what the circumstances. I felt how lucky it was for Rose, and for those around her, that she could express her feelings in music.

'I was going to write to you,' I told her. 'Do come in. It's nearly teatime.' As I spoke, a tornado stormed through the front room in the form of the twins, who flung themselves bodily upon Rose, one clinging to her legs and the other attempting to scale the vertical surface of her back with the aid of her hair, which immediately came down.

'Rose! Rose! Rose!' they screamed in a cacophonous medley. I had already noticed with pleased astonishment how deeply they were attached to her, even though they rarely had occasion to see her; still, she had known them from the earliest moments of their existence, and in their little minds she was as familiar as their own nursery. It was a charming feature of their love for her, that they were able to sit silent and attentive through an entire concert of cello music, if only it was Rose who was playing.

'Dear me,' I remonstrated, trying to pull them off her as they shouted for her to come up to the nursery to see their newest toys. 'It seems we will not get any calm if we have tea at home. They won't stay upstairs if they know you're here. I propose a bargain,' I added, grasping each twin firmly by the arm in order to get its complete attention. 'Rose will play with you in the nursery for half an hour, and then Rose and Mamma will go out to tea and you will have yours in the nursery with Nurse.'

'I should love to,' said Rose warmly. 'It is amazing how they grow each time I look away for a few moments!' And she sailed off up the stairs, towed like a little ship by two eager tugs. An unseemly racket was immediately heard to proceed from the nursery, but I forbore to interfere.

Half an hour later I collected my things and went to fetch Rose, causing something of an uproar, which was fortunately soon quelled by the sight of three severe adult faces combined with the sudden production of a sponge cake for nursery tea. Rose and I took ourselves outside, and walked across the Green to a tea shop I was fond of, tucked away in Little St Mary's Lane.

It was not until tiny sandwiches, scones, jam, cream and a steaming teapot had been set before us that I undertook to tell Rose something of what I had learnt, and to ask her the questions that were troubling me. I recounted to her the entire tale of my Swiss adventure, and she listened intently, but at the end of my tale she sighed.

'I only wish he had really heard something on that evening!' she exclaimed. 'But I simply can't pick out anything special from what you describe. If only the doctor you haven't seen yet told him something special. But probably that would be too much to hope. For the rest, it sounds so banal that I'd have died if I had been there. Sebastian loved that kind of attention, though. He basked in it, he really did. He always wanted to be the centre of attention; always centre stage.'

I looked up quickly.

'You almost sound as though you didn't like him,' I remarked.

'No, no – I didn't mean it that way! I loved him, really. How could I not? Everyone did. He was so magnetic. He had such energy, and when he looked at you the effect was tremendously strong. He was ardent like flame. He made you feel drawn up in the whirlwind of his life when he paid attention to you, and everything seemed possible. Sebastian really reached for the stars, Vanessa. He wanted the fame and the wealth and the success, but only to laugh over. What he really wanted was to play music the way no one ever had before. I know what I'm trying to say even if it isn't coming out right. I should love to be able to make you see what he was like. He was inhabited by a kind of devil. I don't mean something evil, but something wild and strange, uncontrolled, that drove him, that made him too beautiful, too attractive, too irresistible from the outside, but that was burning him up inside. You know, there were times when he really seemed a little out of control. He could actually be a bit frightening, because he reacted to things so strongly and violently sometimes. He really needed to play the violin, to play out that thing that was inside him. The violin is really the devil's instrument, isn't it? Because it's also wild. Can you imagine the devil playing the harpsichord?'

'No, I suppose not,' I said, 'but perhaps I should have thought of him playing the drums.'

'Drums express the savage within us, not the devil,' she said, smiling. 'Anyway, this is all a digression. I wanted to tell you something about Sebastian. You know, I'm glad he was engaged to Claire, because that made it impossible for me to fall in love with him. I mean, it helped me keep my distance and protect myself. Otherwise, I might very well have fallen in love with him, and that wouldn't have been good at all.'

'Why not?'

'Because of the centre stage thing.' She blushed. 'Claire was content to be his shadow and to pour all her love for him into her music, which she offered to him as the supreme gift. She is enormously talented, but her interpretations were largely adapted to his. For the trio, of course, we all adapted to each other to some extent, and I found his approach exciting and experimental, and also very beautiful. But when I play sonatas for piano and cello,

I don't want to be upstaged by the pianist. I want to play them *my* way. I want someone who will share my ideas and help them bloom, without sacrificing either my ideas or his. Playing with Sebastian helped me discover many things about music, but not much about myself. And that's what I will really need from the person I fall in love with. I don't think I could do what Claire did.'

'If one is lucky, one's husband can be remarkably good about letting one be what one truly needs to be,' I said philosophically, spooning up some cream. I had a fleeting feeling of guilt which, upon closer examination, turned out to be a mixture of a suspicion that Arthur, while indeed being remarkably good, was making something of a sacrifice in letting me do quite so very much as I pleased with regards to detective work, and a feeling that I oughtn't to be enjoying such a delightful tea without the twins. But I ignored it firmly.

'Enough about me,' said Rose eagerly, pouring herself another cup of tea and smiling at the waitress who hovered near her elbow with a pot of hot water. 'Now that you've told me what you found out, tell me what you think! Do you have any ideas? Have you put two and two together?'

'Not yet,' I admitted. 'I don't know enough. It doesn't make sense to me yet in the least. I have been thinking over the possibilities, but none of them seem to be particularly supported by the facts.'

'Well,' she said, 'let's hear them.'

'I asked myself what kind of thing Sebastian could have found out about himself, and I decided we could divide the possibilities into two types: on the one hand, he found out something about his own character – for example, by a spontaneous reaction to some event of which his higher self disapproved; on the other, he could have found out something purely factual about himself – for example, that he was suffering from some illness.'

'That makes sense,' she said. 'Well said. It's an important distinction. Pity he didn't say more in his note. *Please try to understand* – what a thing to say, as if one could!'

'Perhaps he tried to say more, but found himself unable to explain,' I suggested. 'His note does sound a bit like a beginning, as though he had meant to say more, and then gave it up as a bad job. Well, that is our task, isn't it? To find out what it may have been. So, returning to my classification, I want first to try to imagine what kind of thing might have provoked Sebastian to feel negatively about himself. Does anything I've said give you any ideas?'

'No. Really not, I'm afraid. You know, I simply can't imagine Sebastian feeling really badly about himself. Even if he discovered some feeling inside him that he didn't know about, he would be more likely to observe it with fascination, even with delight. He really loved living, Vanessa. Much more than with morality, he was concerned with life itself.'

'But surely, if it were something really bad, he could hardly feel delight.'

'Well, but what could possibly be so very bad? He discovered that he liked to smoke opium? He fell madly in love with somebody else? He committed a crime? And liked it, perhaps?'

'Such levity! No, nothing I've learnt indicates that anything of that sort happened. But I was wondering about the fact that Herr Hegar was reluctant to schedule a concert of your trio playing the Beethoven Triple Concerto.'

'That was a pity, to be sure. But if Sebastian were to kill himself over not being able to play such a concert, then the concert would be even more impossible than it already was. That makes no sense at all, Vanessa!'

'Oh, I wasn't suggesting that he felt disappointment. I was wondering if he thought of himself as betraying the trio, by accepting to return and play other concerts without you. Perhaps he realised that he would actually be able to sacrifice the trio for the sake of ambition, and disliked observing such a trait in himself.'

'But Vanessa, surely you don't think it would have been a problem if Herr Hegar had preferred to invite him back alone to play some virtuoso violin concerto instead of the Beethoven? Of course we'd have understood. It was just an idea, that Beethoven concert. The musical world is like that. You play the concerts that you can; it's no use crying over those you can't.'

'I suppose so. But you don't think that Sebastian might have been troubled inside by the knowledge that he risked always keeping his wife in what she might perceive as a subordinate position, professionally?'

'Vanessa – have you looked around you? Do you know any couples in which the wife is not in a subordinate position? I know we've just entered the twentieth century, Vanessa dear, and that we both expect great strides in the advancement of women from it! But I think you need to give it a little time. We've had it for less than a month!' She laughed, and so did I.

'You mean that Claire would not have expected anything different?'

'Of course not. Claire would probably have stopped playing concerts once she had children, and stayed at home, teaching them their scales.'

'Does that really go without saying? Will you do that?'

'Well . . . no, I don't think I will. A woman doesn't absolutely *have* to, you know. There are some exceptions. You've heard of Clara Schumann, the wife of the composer? She went on playing concerts while having eight children and then losing her husband first to madness, then to death. She never stopped playing publicly until she was seventy! She died just a few years ago. And yet, you know, it can't have been easy for the children. And Clara too considered herself subordinate to her husband, musically speaking. He composed, she interpreted. She longed to compose, but she didn't have the time because she needed to play to support the family. Crowds adored her, and she adored her husband. Well, why not? She was famous, she was celebrated, she enjoyed the limelight as much as anybody, and yet her husband came first. That corresponds to the idea of the perfect couple, doesn't it? I do wonder if the twentieth century will eventually change that ideal, or not.'

'So you think that Claire would have accepted that Sebastian pursue a grand career in music, at some point leaving her behind, without any resentment?'

'Without resentment towards him, in any case. Surely women sometimes feel a little resentment against their destiny in general. But Claire is not much of a fighter. Believe me, Vanessa, Sebastian did not kill himself over such a thing.'

'I do believe you.'

'But then, what other possibilities exist?'

'Perhaps he fell in love, and committed some mad act on the way home from Switzerland?'

'You think he might have done that? But then, I think he would simply have broken off his engagement to Claire. He'd have written to her – why, now that I think of it, he'd have written just what he did write. *Darling Claire, how can I say this to you? I've found out something about myself – I can't go on with it any more. I'm sorry. I'm so sorry. Please try to understand.* He might have written exactly that!'

'But you've forgotten the most important part, the bit about cursed inheritance and the danger of taking risks. If this idea is right, what would he have meant by that? Could Sebastian's father have been a known philanderer?'

Rose burst out laughing.

'Oh dear. No, I'm afraid not. From what I've heard, poor Mr Cavendish was a very upright old gentleman afflicted with gout. He was ill and in pain for many months before he died. Sebastian says he was always correct and just, and he does remember him with respect, even though he was a rather cold and distant kind of father. He never played with Sebastian as a boy or anything like that, and always talked about improvement. Still, though, he encouraged him to excel and allowed him to follow his bent and study music when so many other fathers would have wanted him to study law as he did himself. He said that if that was Sebastian's choice, he would have to make his own way in the world, but Sebastian says he didn't mean this disapprovingly; he thought it was good for a young man to make his own way in the world. He left nothing to Sebastian when he died, by the way. His will left all of his worldly goods to his wife. I don't think it was an awful lot, though. Sebastian says they were wealthier when he was a child, but the family fortunes declined badly, and they live very simply now. But Mrs Cavendish is to be married next summer, to Lord Warburton, the gentleman who accompanied her to the memorial concert.'

'Really,' I said. 'That will improve her circumstances. Still, though, what if her first husband was a rake in his youth, and then settled down?'

'If that was the case, Sebastian knew nothing about it. I can promise you that, because Mrs Cavendish is awfully keen on keeping up appearances. She would never have told him such a thing, even if she knew about it herself. No, I can't believe that Sebastian suddenly discovered that he had inherited libertine tendencies by meeting some lovely maiden on the way home in the sleeping car. You know, if he had had a tendency to fall in love easily, we would have known about it already. It's not as though he wasn't surrounded by female admirers. He wasn't like that, and even if it happened once, that would prove nothing.'

'I suppose so. Oh dear. Anyway, I hardly believe that such a trait can even be inherited. I suspect it's more of a caprice of nature, or else an act of rebellion against a strict upbringing.'

'So, we have to exclude this possibility as being as unlikely as the previous one.'

'Well, then. Who else might Sebastian have inherited anything from? Who else was in his family?'

'No one that he knew,' she said. 'Mr Cavendish's parents

died long before Sebastian was born. Mr Cavendish's father was a merchant, and I recall Sebastian saying that he felt he had nothing in common with his father's side of the family. And he had no aunts or uncles, no sisters or brothers. It was just his mother and him.'

I set down my teacup and leant back. 'We seem to have run out of ideas as to what he might actually have learnt about himself and considered as inherited,' I said. 'Let's think about the other idea: he realised something quite different – not a feeling, but a fact. A dreadful fact of some kind; something he simply couldn't live with.'

Rose giggled nervously.

'I'm sorry, Vanessa. Sebastian is dead, and he was so much a part of my life, in a way much deeper than just friendship. He brought me a passionate intensity of music making that was a miracle each time. I miss him more than you can imagine, musically. Whenever I play with John instead of Sebastian, it simply hurts inside. Yet this whole conversation is making me realise that I'm just not able to take his suicide seriously. I simply can't face that it really happened, or make myself understand that there must have been a reason. Everything you're suggesting seems outrageous, ridiculous, out of the question! What could he possibly have discovered that could have such an effect? The more you make me think about it, the more it seems absurd!'

'Could it have been something to do with his violin? I heard that he inherited that from his grandfather.'

'Oh yes. He loved his violin. It was an extraordinary instrument, just right for his playing, although sometimes he would have wished for more power. But he could produce strains of madness on this one. It went so well with him. It had a lion's head instead of the scroll. Have you heard about that? That was just the kind of thing that appealed to him; something peculiar, mad, different, full of energy. A roaring lion instead of a dainty scroll. That was Sebastian all over.'

'Perhaps he discovered that the violin was stolen?' I suggested. 'That it didn't really belong to him?'

This time she laughed outright.

'He died because he couldn't face life without his violin? Or because he was going to be flung into prison for the rest of his life on account of his grandfather's theft? No, I'm afraid not. The violin was offered to Sebastian's grandfather by a patron, because he was an incredible violinist. It was quite common in those days; it still is, for that matter. It went to Sebastian's mother, and she gave it to him. It really was his.'

'Well,' I said, 'you say he inherited nothing from his father, but at least here we have an inheritance from the grandfather. What else did he inherit?'

'Don't say that he inherited his gift – he used to hate it when people said that and he would deny it outright. That's rather odd, now that I think of it. I wonder why he cared?'

'I have heard about that. Yes, it is striking; the refusal to accept what everyone noticed. Perhaps that might be the key. It's a pity I know so little about the nature of musical talent.'

'I have an idea,' exclaimed Rose eagerly. 'You should come with me to the Royal Academy once, and talk to my professor. He often talks about musical inheritance! I think he has heaps of ideas. Oh, Vanessa, he is a marvellous, luminous man; a darling, but also a genius. You would love him. He is certainly the best person to talk to about this. And now that I think of it, we can try to arrange for you to meet Sebastian's professor as well. Who knows what you might learn from him?'

'I should love to meet them,' I said. 'But the problem seems very difficult. I hardly know what to ask them. I must admit, I am sorely puzzled.'

'Please don't give up!' she exclaimed. 'Please, Vanessa, do go on trying to understand! He deserves it. He loved Claire; he loved children – he wanted lots. He was so vibrant. It must have been something enormous to take his life away so suddenly. We do have something to go on – after all, he *did* kill himself, so there *was* a reason – it really does exist! Please, do go on trying to understand. I think I'll never really rest until I know. And for Claire it's a matter of life or death. She's like a ghost with not knowing. Please don't give up!'

'I'm not going to,' I said firmly. 'Absolutely not. I shall be in London next week for a meeting of the Society for Psychical Research. Yes, I know it's strange, but I'll explain it later. Anyway, when I come I shall visit you as well, and you shall take me to meet your teacher. I promise, I'm far from giving up. As you say, the reason most definitely exists, and we have only to find it!'

CHAPTER NINE

In which Vanessa attends a meeting of
the Society for Psychical Research,
sees some very strange things, and hears their explanation

I hastened into the large lecture hall, removed my wrap, which was unpleasantly damp from the disagreeable sleet falling steadily outside, and slipped into one of the last remaining empty seats, situated modestly near the back of the hall. The president of the Society for Psychical Research stepped onto the stage, introduced himself as Mr Frederic Myers, and began to say a few words on the subject of the presentation about to take place.

'What is the purpose of our Society?' he began, very pertinently, as I thought. 'Why, faced with the scepticism and derision of the public, do we pursue against all odds a direction of knowledge guided by observations which suffer from their irregularity, their doubtfulness and their frequent infestation with the forces of vanity and dishonesty? What, ultimately, is our goal?'

He paused and glanced around challengingly, then continued.

'Starting from various standpoints, we are endeavouring to carry the newer, the intellectual virtues into regions where dispassionate tranquillity has seldom yet been known. First, we adopt the ancient belief, implied in all monotheistic religion, and conspicuously confirmed by the progress of modern science, that the world as a whole – spiritual and material together – has in some way a systematic unity: and on this we base the novel presumption that there should be a unity of method in the investigation of all fact. We hold therefore that the attitudes, the habits of mind, the methods by which physical science has grown deep and wide should be applied also to the spiritual world. We endeavour to approach the problems of that world by careful collection, scrutiny, testing of particular facts; and we account no unexplained fact too trivial for our attention.[1]

'We are exceptionally lucky today, ladies and gentlemen,' he went on, 'to have the opportunity of welcoming to our premises one of the world's most fascinating and impressive mediums: Mademoiselle Hélène Smith of France! Mademoiselle Smith discovered her amazing talents eight years ago, and since that time she has provided us, the students of the spiritist world, with an incredible wealth of information from abroad, from the past, from the dead, and most recently and extraordinarily – a phenomenon truly unheard-of hitherto – from the planet Mars! As Mademoiselle Smith is presently in contact with spirits

---

[1] Actual words of Frederic Myers, president of the SPR in 1900, cited from the preface to the book *From India to the Planet Mars* (1899) by Th. Flournoy.

from Mars, you will very likely hear, when she appears on this stage and allows herself to be led into a trance, actual words of the Martian language, together with their translation into French by a Martian spirit. I myself will stand here to the side, out of the way, and write upon this large board, as silently as possible, the English translation of the French for your benefit.

'Following the session, we will hear two analyses of Mademoiselle Smith's visions, one by famed spiritualist Mrs Ellen Jackson from the United States of America, and the second by Professor Theodore Flournoy, expert in psychology and psychophysiology, from the University of Geneva. I beg you, ladies and gentleman, to welcome Mademoiselle Hélène Smith!'

I felt an expression of total mystification painting itself upon my face as Mr Myers described the medium's accomplishments, and I noticed the same expression reflected in many of the faces around me. Yet equally many were upturned towards the stage with every sign of delight and rapt attention. I firmly put aside the voice of reason that screeched with dismay within me. I do believe that Arthur and his scientific friends have had too much influence over me of late. I *know* there is much in life than can startle even the most rational of scientists.

But – Mars?

The audience applauded politely as the curtain at the back of the stage parted, letting through a tall and striking woman with black hair piled high in a manner befitting an earlier century. This woman greeted us with reserve, then took her place in an easy chair that Mr Myers pushed forward for her, and closed her eyes. The electric lights on

117

the stage and in the hall were dimmed until her outline was blurred in the shadows. Only a tiny light remained, brightening the board upon which Mr Myers was to write his translations. This gentleman then approached the medium and laid his hand upon her forehead, reciting the following words in French with a strong British accent:

Pose bien doucement ta main sur son front pâle
Et prononce bien bas le doux nom d'Esenale!

He spoke the name of Esenale with the strong emphasis of one who calls for a person, then removed his hand from the lady's forehead and walked quickly and silently to the edge of the stage.

A great sigh proceeded from Mademoiselle Smith's lips, and in a ringing voice, she proclaimed:

'*Cé évé pléva ti di benez essat riz tes midée durée!*'

There was a short silence, then Mr Myers called out:

'Esenale! Please translate into French!'

'*Je-suis-chagrin-de-te-retrouver-vivant-sur-cette-laide-terre!*' emerged, in a foreign-sounding staccato, from the mouth of the medium. Mr Myers hastily wrote: *I am sad to find you still living upon this ugly Earth.*

'*Mitchma mitchmon mimini tchouainem mimatchineg masichi-nof mézavi patelki abrésinad navette naven navette mitchichénid naken chinoutoufich,*' she burst forth suddenly, and then, spinning out of control, she continued so rapidly that one could only catch syllabic snatches such as '*ték . . . katéchivist.. méguetch . . . kété . . . chimék*'. At length her voice slowed to nearly a stop, and in a sepulchral tone she clearly enunciated:

'*Dodé né ci haudan té méss métiche Astané!*'

'Translate, Esenale!' shouted Mr Myers quickly, into the moment of silence that followed these words.

'*Ceci-est-la-maison-du-grand-homme-Astané!*' stuttered the medium. *This is the house of the great man Astané!* wrote Mr Myers. And then she fell completely silent. Her eyes stared up at the ceiling with a weirdly empty expression, and occasionally her body was shaken by strange shudders, or she made peculiar motions with her hands. The audience waited in transfixed silence as the minutes passed. After perhaps a quarter of an hour, during which the attempts of the more impatient spectators to while away the time by whispering together were sharply quelled by Mr Myers holding up his hand like a severe schoolteacher, she stirred, and slowly awoke. Mr Myers hurried forward with a glass of water, from which she weakly sipped, then she sat up and looked out at us as though astonished to find herself in such a place.

'Will you recount to us what you saw?' he asked her respectfully. She answered in a lovely, musical voice totally unlike that which had pronounced the words we heard before.

'I stood before an astonishing house of a shape and colour I had never seen before. A man of dark complexion emerged and took me by the hand and led me away. I knew that this was Astané. I saw before me a landscape and some peculiar people. I was on the border of a beautiful blue-pink lake. A bridge with transparent sides formed of yellow tubes like the pipes of an organ seemed to have one end plunged into the water. The earth was peach-colour; some of the trees had trunks widening as they ascended, while

119

those of others were twisted. Later a crowd approached the bridge, in which one woman was especially prominent. The women wore hats that were flat, like plates. I do not know exactly who these people were, but I had the feeling of having conversed with them before. Astané went onto the bridge. He carried in his hands an instrument somewhat resembling a carriage-lantern in appearance, but which, when pressed, emitted flames, and which seemed to be a flying-machine. By means of this instrument the man left the bridge, touched the surface of the water, and returned again to the bridge. He took me by the hand and led me back through the emptiness of space.'

Upon this, the lady arose from her seat, crossed the stage, and arriving in front of the board where Mr Myers had noted down the two brief Martian sentences that had been translated into French, she proceeded to make a drawing of a square house of unusual shape, with decorations like battlements at the top and strange trees on either side.

'This is the house I saw; the house of Astané,' she told us in quite a normal tone. She smiled with pleasure and modestly inclined her head as the audience burst into spontaneous applause and Mr Myers led her off the stage to some quiet place, no doubt, where she could recover her strength over a cup of strong tea.

A moment later, another woman appeared upon the stage, and was introduced to us as Mrs Ellen Jackson from Connecticut. She took her place confidently behind a lectern that was quickly pulled forward in place of the easy chair. Dressed to the height of fashion in a tailor-made suit with a sailor collar which firmly structured her rather generous forms, she began to speak with an American accent, a loud voice, and a degree of enthusiasm typical of our visitors from the other side of the Atlantic but which is rarely or never visible here in England, where its original freshness has been blunted, perhaps, by the passage of too many centuries. Mrs Jackson assured us that Hélène Smith was the most astonishing medium she had ever encountered, and this in a long tradition of association with the most reputed mediums of America, including herself.

'When I found,' she told us emphatically, 'that poor Hélène was having to work in a department store for her living, standing behind the counter for up to eleven hours each day till her health was worn to a thread, I said to myself, "Something must be done about this!" I was travelling across Europe to hear all the most famous mediums from over here, and what I heard from Hélène left me just utterly spellbound, as you probably are right this minute. I simply couldn't let such a treasure go to waste selling gloves and scarves, I thought, with all her knowledge of secrets withheld from the rest of us! We need to hear everything that Hélène has to tell us! And I want to tell you today that I have decided to free dear Hélène from the need to earn her living, thanks to my own good fortune which has enabled me to support people in need wherever and whenever I find them. I want to say that I've helped many a fascinating medium reach the apex of her talent, and none of them has ever seemed to me as worthy as Hélène Smith! People such as she are contributing to the advancement of knowledge beyond anything that science can achieve! Worthy as our astronomers are, they have not been able to reach as far as the planet Mars, and I never thought I would know what goes on in that mysterious place during my lifetime. I'm not going to talk about any kind of analysis of what Hélène says, because it doesn't need any. I am certain that it is all quite literally true. I have had enough experience of spirit communication to know about the invisible reality it reveals, and that it can tell us about places beyond the reach of science. Hélène's visions represent the only chance we have to learn about the planet Mars! And that's why I have offered Hélène the means to pursue her mediumistic activities without constraint, for the rest of her life! *Vive Mademoiselle Hélène Smith!*' And upon this, she burst into a spontaneous applause into which the audience joined with a general feeling of laughter and astonishment.

As we clapped, Mr Myers returned to the stage from the side, accompanied by a short professorial gentleman with a pointy beard. This was Professor Flournoy, specialist in psychology and psychophysiology from the University of Geneva: the very man who had discovered the amazing talents of Hélène Smith, or at least, revealed them to the world. Having been close to her for six years now, and having thus had the opportunity to observe every detail of the development and evolution of her visions, he had recently completed a book upon the subject, containing a full analysis of her visions and of the Martian language that spoke through her mouth. This book was to appear very shortly in print, and as Mr Myers informed us with some pride, we were now to be the first to hear some of the most significant parts of its contents.

Professor Flournoy greeted Mrs Jackson with a slight bow and, turning to the audience, pronounced a few words of grateful recognition for her grand and generous gesture.

She thanked him, and proceeded to sail off the stage in a stately manner with Mr Myers, upon which the professor began his speech.

'The first task which investigators of obscure mental phenomena set themselves is, naturally, that of separating and sifting the real, actually existent facts from the mass of fraud and deception created by mercenary charlatans. These, aided by the easy credulity of the simple-minded, have contrived so completely to bury from sight the true phenomena, that for a long time now the intelligent public has utterly refused to believe in the existence of any real phenomena of the kind, but insisted that everything when fully probed would be found to be mere delusion, the result of trickery and fraud.

'Probably no scientific fact since the dawn of modern science has required so great a weight of cumulative evidence in its favour to establish the reality of its existence in the popular mind than have the phenomena in question. I am glad to be able to say, however, that this task has finally been accomplished!

'Mademoiselle Smith is a high-minded, honourable woman, regarded by all her neighbours and friends as wholly incapable of conscious fraud. Moreover, she has been subjected to the closest surveillance on the part of a number of eminent physicians and scientists of Geneva for more than five years past, while Mrs Jackson, the famous medium from Connecticut whom we have just had the honour to hear, has been subjected to an even closer scrutiny by the Society for Psychical Research for the past fifteen years.

'Yet in spite of the fact that this society has announced

its willingness to become responsible for the entire absence of fraud in both cases, there still remain a considerable number of ultra-sceptical persons who persist in asserting that fraud and deceit are at the bottom of, and account for, all this species of phenomena.

'The endeavour to explain these mysterious phenomena by scientific investigators has resulted in their adoption of one or other of two hypotheses, namely:

'1. That the phenomena are really of supernormal origin and emanate from the disincarnate spirits of the other beings, who return to earth and take temporary possession of the organism of the medium, talking through her mouth and writing with her hand while she is in a somnambulistic state.

'2. That the phenomena are the product of and originate in the subliminal consciousness of the medium.

'The first theory, exemplified by Mrs Jackson's earlier address, adduces as the essential argument in its support the frequently observed occurrence of mediums in trances speaking languages or expressing information that they do not know and cannot possibly know in their ordinary lives.

'The second theory, instead, credits the subliminal consciousness of the true medium with quite extraordinary powers of knowledge, memory, invention and understanding. When I first began regularly attending the séances of Hélène Smith, I hesitated for some time before coming to a final conclusion about which theory best describes the phenomena I then saw, and of which you have all been a witness today. In my present lecture, I will defend the hypothesis of the second theory.

'Let me attempt to explain why, by first saying that

of all the traits that I discover in her tale of Martian romance – which consists in several dozen sessions similar to that which you witnessed today, but greatly varied and containing very little repetition of information – the most salient feature is undoubtedly this: *its profoundly infantile character.*'

The audience gasped collectively. Surely this was unheard-of insolence, stated so bluntly in the hallowed circles of the SPR!

'The candour and imperturbable naivety of childhood,' continued the professor, ignoring the noise, 'which doubts nothing because it is ignorant of everything, is necessary in order for one to launch himself seriously upon an enterprise such as the pretended exact and authentic depictions of an unknown world. An adult who is at all cultivated and has any experience of life would never waste time in elaborating similar nonsense; Mademoiselle Smith less than anyone, intelligent and cultivated as she is in her normal state.

'In general, it is the sitters who gather as much as they can of the strange words pronounced by Mademoiselle Smith in her states of trance, but, as you have just seen, that is very little, since Hélène, in her Martian state, often speaks with a tremendous volubility. Moreover, a distinction must be made between the relatively clear and brief phrases that are later translated by Esenale, and the rapid and confused gibberish the signification of which can never be obtained, probably because it really has none, being only a pseudo-language.

'Although as you saw, Hélène can preserve a certain memory of her visions in the waking state, and make reproductions of some of the things she saw, her verbo-motor hallucinations of articulation and of writing seem to be totally incompatible with her preservation of the waking state, and are invariably followed by amnesia. Hélène is always totally absent or entranced while her hand writes mechanically, and she is not aware of speaking Martian automatically, and does not recollect it. This incapacity of the normal personality of Mademoiselle Smith to observe at the time or remember afterwards any of her verbo-motor automatisms denotes a more profound perturbation than that which she experiences during her reception of visual hallucinations. For this reason, it is not surprising to me that her visual experiences bear an obvious resemblance to those which surround her in her ordinary life: the Martians closely resemble the human beings of our own planet in their appearance, and their houses and trees are mere fanciful variations upon ours.

'The Martian language, produced in a state of deeper trance leaving no memory behind, appears far less similar to anything familiar to us. Yet proceeding by analogy, I determined to inspect it more closely to see whether, in fact, it was not actually much more similar to Mademoiselle Smith's native French than it appeared on the surface. I began by a complete examination of the strange alphabet in which she wrote down the Martian sentences during her experiences of automatic writing.

'Now, it is not always easy to represent a language and its pronunciation by means of the typographical characters of another. Happily, the Martian, upon detailed examination and in spite of its strange appearance and the fifty millions of leagues which separate us from the red planet, turned out to be in reality so near a neighbour to French in both alphabet and syntax, that one can only conclude that either French-speakers are astoundingly lucky in having a language that is so close a neighbour to Martian, or that Mademoiselle Smith has invented the Martian language entirely, based on her intimate subliminal knowledge of her mother tongue. Let me give two simple examples supporting my claim that the pretended Martian language is nothing but an infantile travesty of French: it will suffice for you to contemplate for one moment the two sentences spoken in Martian here in this hall, whose translations are written upon the board before you:

'*Cé évé pléva ti di benez essat riz tes midée durée!*'

'*Dodé né ci haudan té méss métiche Astané!*'

'If you compare these sentences to their English translations, you may already be struck by a general similarity in sentence structure, compared for example with that of the Chinese. However, a moment's examination will show you that their relationship to French is yet one degree closer, in that the French translation admits of a word-by-word correspondence! Take for example the first sentence, rendered in English as "I am sad to find you still living upon this ugly Earth", which is as good a translation from the French as can be expected. But consider now the actual French as it proceeded from Hélène's very mouth: "*Je suis chagrin de te retrouver vivant sur cette laide terre!*" Here, each word in Martian has its exact equivalent in French, and, as a further indication, we note that the short words "*de*", "*te*", "*sur*" in French correspond to equally short monosyllables in the Martian. Comparing the French and the English of the second sentence reveals the same peculiarity: whereas "This is the house of the great man

Astané" will not allow for a word-for-word correspondence, the French "*Ceci est la maison du grand homme Astané*" does, thanks to the contraction of the two words "of the" into the single French "*du*" which, remarkably, also exists in the Martian "*té*".

'If I add that the consonants which appear in the Martian language correspond very exactly to equivalent consonants in French, and that I have verified these claims on a great number of other Martian sentences pronounced over the course of dozens of séances, this will explain why I have been led to the inescapable conclusion that the Martian language is nothing but French, metamorphosed and carried to a higher diapason.

'Now, my argument would not be complete if I did not have a theory justifying, at the same time, the complete dissimilarity of the individual Martian words with those of the French, for it must be acknowledged that there is no trace of parentage, of filiation, of any resemblance whatever between the Martian and French vocabularies.

'But in fact, this apparent contradiction carries its explanation in itself, and gives us the key to Martian. This fantastic idiom is quite evidently the naive and somewhat puerile work of an infantile imagination, which had the idea of creating a new language, but which even while creating strange and unknown words, caused them to run in the accustomed moulds of the only real language that it knew. The Martian of Mademoiselle Smith, in other words, is the product of a brain or a personality which certainly has taste and aptitude for linguistic exercises, but which never knew that French takes little heed of the logical connection of ideas, and did not take the trouble to make innovations in the matter of phonetics, of grammar, or of syntax.

'The process of creation of Martian seems to have consisted in simply taking certain French phrases as such and replacing each word by some other chosen at random. That is why not only the order but even the structure and number of syllables of French words can be recognised in many Martian words.

'Yet the search for originality inherent in the creation of new language represents an effort of imagination with which Mademoiselle Smith must certainly be credited. Homage must also be rendered to the labour of memorisation necessitated by the making of a mental dictionary. She has sometimes, indeed, fallen into errors; the stability of her vocabulary has not always been perfect. But, finally, after the first hesitation and independently of some later confusions, it gives evidence of a praiseworthy terminological consistency, and which, no doubt, in time, and with some suggestive encouragement, would result in the elaboration of a very complete language.

'The preceding analysis of the Martian language furnishes its support to the considerations which the content of the romance has already suggested to us in regard to its author. To imagine that by twisting the sounds of French words a new language capable of standing examination could actually be created, and to wish to make it pass for that of the planet Mars, would be the climax of silly fatuity or of imbecility were it not simply a trait of naive candour well worthy of the happy age of childhood.

'If, however, one takes into account the great facility for

languages known to have been possessed by Mademoiselle Smith's father, the question naturally arises whether in the Martian we are not in the presence of an awakening and momentary display of a hereditary faculty, dormant under the normal personality of Hélène, and from which she has never profited in an effective or conscious manner. It is a fact of common observation that gifts and aptitudes often skip a generation and seem to pass directly from the grandparents to the grandchildren, forgetting the intermediate link. Who knows whether Mademoiselle Smith, someday, may not cause the polyglot aptitudes of her father to bloom again with greater brilliancy, for the glory of science, through a brilliant line of philologists and linguists of genius?

'Let me insist once again upon my total conviction that while everything learnt from Hélène's visual and auditive hallucinations is a pure production of her subliminal consciousness, thus revealing the infantile elements which all of us carry deep within and which rarely or never emerge in our conscious state, I do not for one moment suggest the slightest effort at fraud or conscious manipulation on her part. Knowing Hélène as I do, I would lay down my honour as a guarantee that she is totally unaware of the tricks her subconscious is playing upon her, and hears and sees the messages exactly as though they proceed from the exterior. And above and beyond this statement, I would also beg to observe that while clearly containing, as I have shown, all the hallmarks of the infantile subconscious, her inventions reveal tremendous and impressive powers of creation and imagination which can only lead me to have the greatest admiration for a brain able to produce such a wealth of visionary material and, furthermore, unlike most, able to find its own startling and unusual manner of bringing this material to its conscious attention when it usually remains unrecognised, or expressed only through the confusion of dreams.

'It is hardly necessary to add, in conclusion, that the whole spiritistic or occult hypothesis seems to me to be absolutely superfluous and unjustified in the case of the Martian of Hélène Smith. Autosuggestibility set in motion by certain stimulating influences of the environment amply suffices to account for the entire Martian romance.'

He stopped speaking and laid his papers down upon the lectern. But poor Professor Flournoy – his carefully thought-out efforts had fallen largely on deaf ears! None of the enthusiasm which had greeted Mrs Jackson's address was expressed now, and it was only due to an extreme of courtesy that scattered and unenthusiastic applause was heard at all, while a couple of voices even cried out observations such as 'Shocking!' and 'Boo!' He gave a resigned smile, bowed slightly, and left the stage.

I remained in my seat as people stood up all around me, collecting their scarves and wraps. My head was spinning with the ideas set in motion by the professor's speech, which so remarkably pulled together the ideas that had been knocking about loosely in my head. Subliminal consciousness, unconscious infantile impulses emerging in states of trance, their expression by automatic writing, the role of heredity – even the mention of heredity from the grandfather that I had so lately discussed with Carl – or Professor Correns, rather. I sat turning these notions over in my mind, trying to find out what notion within them was tickling my brain, until I suddenly realised that the room was nearly empty, and only a few grey-bearded men remained clustered together near the door! I recognised Professor Flournoy and Mr Myers amongst them, as well as the famous Sir Oliver Lodge. But what about Dr Bernstein, the man I had come here to see! I jumped out of my seat at once. Had I in my stupidity let him disappear?

CHAPTER TEN

In which Vanessa meets a Swiss doctor of psychology
who recalls something that might or might not be important

Approaching the group, I addressed myself to Sir Oliver, reminding him of the circumstances in which we had last met. He hesitated for a moment, then laughed as the recollection struck him.

'Mrs Weatherburn – of course! Delighted to see you here. So, you have become a believer!' he exclaimed with enthusiasm. 'As I remember, you used to be something of a sceptic. Am I not right?'

'I was,' I said diplomatically. 'But now I realise that we are surrounded by mysteries that science is not yet able to explain. Today's demonstration was particularly fascinating. I had read about automatic writing, but never witnessed it. In fact, ever since reading this book I have greatly wished to meet its author,' I added, extracting Dr Bernstein's volume from my muff and showing it around.

'Why, then you are in luck,' he said, 'for the very man is standing in front of you,' and he indicated the gentleman next to him, short of stature, wearing the pointed beard that all doctors of psychology seemed to feel the need to sport as a badge of their identification with the ideas of Dr Freud, and smiling in surprised amusement at being so suddenly and so anxiously sought. Sir Oliver kindly performed the necessary introductions.

'To tell the truth, I wished to speak to you on a very particular matter,' I confided to the doctor in a low tone as soon as the general conversation about the day's events had died down somewhat, and the other gentlemen had taken up their canes and umbrellas in preparation for departure. 'If you are willing, perhaps we could talk in private for some moments?'

'But certainly,' he replied, casting me a glance bright with interest, and he led me out of the lecture room into the front hall of the building. After a glance outside, where freezing sleet continued to pour down as it had been doing relentlessly since the morning, he led me across the hall into a smaller, empty room equipped with desks and a blackboard.

'We shall be quite quiet here,' he said kindly. 'Now, do tell me how I can be of service to you.'

'Do you remember a concert in Zürich at the end of December, in which you heard a violinist named Sebastian Cavendish?'

He started visibly and looked at me with an entirely new expression. Clearly he had not expected this: Frau Bochsler must not have had the opportunity to tell him about my visit to her. Although he controlled it carefully, his reaction struck me as quite strong; there was a tension, a sudden attention that intrigued me greatly, and something fleeting in his eyes. What was it? A stab of pain?

I also took care to show nothing particular, but I felt very alert. The more so since the man, a trained psychologist, must probably know more about my thoughts and feelings than an ordinary person would. It was not, of course, that I had anything to hide; only that I preferred to remain in the shadows, as it were, observing while providing no food for observation. A difficult task before a man who looked at one like a mind-reader.

'Of course, of course,' he said in quite a natural voice, belying the palpable strain I noticed in his jaw and shoulders. 'A beautiful concert, quite unforgettable. I read about the sad death of the young artist in the newspaper a short time afterwards. A terrible loss.'

Ordinary words, and yet how significant they sounded in his mouth. Was this simply the way of all psychologists, to bring out the deeper meaning behind the everyday?

'The reason I am here,' I explained, 'is that his family has asked me to make some attempt to understand why he killed himself. You know that it was a suicide?'

'I read it,' replied the doctor, 'but I know nothing more.'

'Neither do they,' I told him. 'You see, all appeared to be going wonderfully well in his life. He was engaged to a lovely young woman, his career was brilliant, he was a beloved and successful artist. He left a note, however, which seems to indicate that he learnt something deeply troubling about himself in those final days before his death. His mother and his fiancée seem to have no idea what that thing could possibly be. Yet it was something terrible enough for him to take his own life, without even choosing to share it with them. They have remained stunned by it all.'

'That seems hard,' he said softly. 'He really gave no explanation?'

'All he said in his note was that he had found out this terrible thing, and could not go on. The only clue is that he used the words 'cursed inheritance' and said it was too dangerous to take risks with it. His fiancée is quite desperate. She has asked me to find out, if I can, exactly what it was that he discovered in those last days. I am trying to follow his traces step by step during the last days of his life, and to speak to everyone he spoke to then, in the effort to discover something, anything at all, out of the ordinary. I have already been in Zürich, and with the help of Frau Bochsler I have talked with nearly everyone who attended the party at her home that followed Sebastian's concert. You, however, were away, and as Frau Bochsler remembers seeing you having an animated conversation with Sebastian, she encouraged me to try to meet you here.'

'I see,' he said slowly. 'I see. Yet you have also read my book.' He came to a complete stop.

'Frau Bochsler gave it to me,' I told him, 'and I did read some of it, particularly the chapter about your own patient, Lydia K. It was fascinating. But I admit that that is not the reason why I wished to see you. I am sorry,' I added, taking his silence as a sign of disappointment.

'No, no,' he said. 'That is not why I ask you whether you read it. It is because of something that did happen, on that evening at Frau Bochsler's.'

An electric tingle traversed me.

'I cannot possibly see how what I said could have any connection to the young man's suicide,' he went on. 'And yet, it was strange. Perhaps it was wrong of me to mention it to him, but, you see, I was violently excited and moved by his physical appearance. I really do not think I am dreaming when I tell you that he bore a remarkable resemblance to a person I once knew well. To Lydia K., in fact.'

'He resembled Lydia K.!' I exclaimed, truly surprised.

'Astonishingly, to my eyes,' he replied, 'although there is no one else who could verify my feelings on the matter. But I will tell you that I could hardly take my eyes off him for the entire evening. He was a lively young man, full of laughter. It was only when he remained calm and stationary that the resemblance sprang to view; when he was talking and laughing, it ceased to be visible to me. Thus, I felt the need to stare at him continually, in an attempt to catch him at those moments when he should be listening attentively, in order to question and confirm what I was seeing again and again, a hundred times.'

'Did you think there was a chance that it was a family resemblance?' I asked.

'Naturally I did! If you have read my book, you know how much I searched for Lydia after she disappeared from my life. No, what am I saying? Of course you cannot know that – obviously I did not write about it in the book. But I can tell you now that I wrote many letters to Mr Charles King, her guardian, and called at his house in London more than once in the years after she was taken away from me. But he neither answered my letters nor received me, and I was unable to find out the true identity of the ward who had been using his name. He died five or six years later, and with him my last hope of finding her. But the dream of seeing her again someday has never left my heart. She was a most interesting person; a most extraordinary case.'

'And you talked to Sebastian about this?' I said, much excited. Surely, after the violin, here was yet another tale of inheritance arising out of the mists of time.

'I did, and I mentioned the name of Lydia King, but he had no knowledge of any such person, not even of the Christian name Lydia. Everyone in the room was referring to the fact that Sebastian was the grandson of a famous violinist named Joseph Krieger, so I even suggested to him that Lydia Krieger might have been her true name, but he told me that his mother's name was Tanis, not Lydia; he knew of no Lydia. My gently probing questions revealed that his mother had not the slightest peculiarity in writing, nor any strong physical resemblance to her son other than a general effect of height and bearing, and also that she married in 1869, before I ever met Lydia.'

'How did he seem when he reacted to your remarks?' I asked. 'Shocked or surprised?'

'Not at all. Slightly amused and not particularly interested,' he said. 'I believe he actually remarked that it was rather a pity that there was no Lydia in his family, for he had always regretted being the only child of a widowed mother, and would have much appreciated the sort of extended family filled with grandparents, uncles, aunts and cousins that some of his friends enjoyed. But he certainly did not say this in a tragic manner. He was not a tragically minded person, but one more inclined, I should say, to laugh off adversity.'

'And that is all you told him? Only that you noticed a

138

physical resemblance to a Lydia King you once knew, who would be in her fifties at the present time? And you asked if he was acquainted with any such person?'

'Well, I told him a few words about how I had known Lydia and what kind of patient she was, and that I had lost sight of her long ago and often wondered what had become of her.'

'And he did not appear especially moved.'

'No. Perhaps he would have been more interested if his attention had not been solicited by so many other admirers that evening, but it is certain that what I was telling him did not strike any particular chord.'

'You are a psychologist,' I said thoughtfully, 'you are used to reading human reactions. You do not think it possible that what you told him actually had a stronger effect than what he showed? That it really did provoke a deep inner disturbance? That it meant something to him which he was able to successfully hide?'

'Unless he was one of the greatest actors in the world, and able to control himself so completely in a situation of which he had no previous warning, I should have to say that that is completely impossible. His reaction corresponded in every way to that of a person who had never heard of any Lydia, K., King, Krieger or otherwise. I think I can state with certainty that the name simply meant nothing to him, and neither did the mention of automatic writing. He seemed perfectly unfamiliar with the phenomenon, probably viewing it as no more than a fad which fascinates the kind of person who attends meetings such as today's in this building.'

'But that "cursed inheritance",' I persisted. 'If, stimulated by your remarks, he did make enquiries, and discovered that he was related in some distant way to your Lydia, might not the cursed inheritance then refer to madness?'

'But Lydia was not mad! She was as sane as you or I – or as Sebastian himself – outside of her trances. And he was not likely to consider himself mad, either. Gifted with a wild and creative imagination he certainly was, but without a trace of hysteria or any other mental disease. Unless, perhaps, he too was subject to trances?'

'I have heard absolutely nothing of the kind,' I admitted.

'Then I cannot see what it could have meant to him. No, however we turn it around, it seems quite impossible to me that our conversation could possibly have led to his suicide. I would be most surprised to learn that he had even gone so far as to make enquiries. He did not seem to take the idea of a connection between Lydia and himself at all seriously.'

'And what about you? You must have been very disappointed by his reaction,' I said.

'Not by his reaction, but by the plain fact that he knew nothing,' he admitted. 'For me, on that evening when I saw his face and the traits that reminded me so strongly of her, I knew a moment of ecstatic hope that was then dashed. I did not say this to anyone, of course. But Lydia was like a shooting star that once traversed my life, illuminating everything, and then lost forever. Nothing has ever been the same for me since then. Nothing.'

I squeezed the old man's hand as I shook it goodbye, for the sadness in his eyes was deeper than tears. To my surprise, he squeezed mine gently back.

'I have never spoken of all this to a living soul,' he said. 'Not a single person has known of my feelings for Lydia. For years after she went, I hoped for some message from her. Of course, she could not write, but I thought that perhaps she might manage to have a message conveyed to me someday, through another person. But nothing came, nothing but the years of silence. And then suddenly, from out of the chaos and turmoil of existence, an echo of her face was flung up at me from an unexpected source – and now it is lost again.' He sighed deeply, and added philosophically, 'Surprising physical resemblances can occasionally occur as the result of pure chance. I have been told more than once that I myself greatly resemble Sigmund Freud.'

'That is just because of the beard,' I said.

'The beard and more,' he replied with the ghost of a smile. 'Inheritance is not merely something passed from parents to children, you know. Its consequences spread through entire countries, entire races. You must not give it too much importance.'

But Sebastian did, I thought, as I forced my way out of the front door into the blast of icy wind that hurled itself inside the building, as though for shelter. Something about inheritance was important enough for him to die for.

CHAPTER ELEVEN

In which it is stated that suicide is selfish
and that the cello is an instrument for women

'Professor Wilcox?' Rose said timidly, opening the door a crack, once her preliminary knock had produced a rather sharp 'Come in!' in response.

'Come in.' The professor was sitting at a desk laden with papers, mostly musical scores, in the process of making annotations on one of them with a pencil. He wrote with his right hand; his left, turned palm upwards, was agitated by a continuous wiggling of the fingers which I momentarily took for a disease before suddenly comprehending that he was playing an imaginary violin, visualising fingerings that he was then transporting onto the score by means of tiny numbers. He looked as though our arrival was something of an unwelcome interruption, I thought, but then surely the worry lines etched into his forehead indicated a state of more general strain than that caused by our momentary apparition.

'We're very sorry to bother you,' said Rose politely, 'but my friend is trying to help Sebastian's family – Sebastian Cavendish – and we thought . . .' Her voice trailed off suddenly at the sight of the hostile storm gathering upon the professor's face.

'I have no interest in discussing Sebastian Cavendish,' he said shortly.

Abashed, I was on the point of melting meekly away, and I am sure that Rose did not mean to be insolent. The sudden 'But why not?' that sprang from her lips echoed nothing but a most sincere reaction of bewilderment.

Professor Wilcox stood up and, bracing himself on his desk with his two fists, leant forward to add emphasis to his chopped-off words.

'Why not?' he repeated coldly. 'Why not? Has it ever occurred to you that there is no act more indicative of utter egotism, selfishness and cruelty than suicide?'

There was a brief pause, during which Rose and I glanced at each other and each perceived that such a thought had never crossed either of our minds. A shocking, iconoclastic notion, this, cutting across the accepted – and surely not entirely mistaken – view of the suicide as having been harassed to his death by the unbearable weight of inner or outer circumstances.

'I spent years of my life nurturing Sebastian,' Professor Wilcox was continuing, the muscles of his face strained. 'I invested countless hours, limitless effort, unspoken depths of feeling in that boy. And if I, a teacher, can say this, think for one moment of his mother! So much devotion, so much love, so much care went into him. What right had he, on the edge of manhood, on the very cusp of the fruition of all our dreams, to throw it all away? I don't want to speak of it. I don't even wish to think about it. Did he have a single thought for anyone else before rushing into that mad act? Probably not. What Sebastian did has thrown me into a mental state of disgust with teaching that I will take months or years to overcome, if I ever succeed.' He glared at us for a long moment, and finally spat, 'I wish never to hear his name again,' leaving the clear impression that the name was ceaselessly before his troubled mind.

There was no possible rejoinder to this argument, so bitter and yet so undeniably justified. All of my eager questions faded upon my lips, and we could think of nothing better to do than murmur confused apologies as we hurried simultaneously out of the room in a swish of mingling skirts, and closed the door carefully behind us. Only when we had put an entire corridor and staircase between ourselves and the intensity and resentment of the wounded teacher did we stop to breathe.

'Oh dear,' said Rose, not knowing whether to laugh or cry.

'Oh dear, indeed,' I said. 'Oh dear, oh dear. I do hope the others won't be like that.'

'But they might, for he really is right in a way. From his point of view, I mean. I do see that now, although I would never have thought of it before.'

'I believe it takes an egotist to see into the heart of an egotist,' I observed sagely. 'Performing musicians, star soloists like Sebastian or his grandfather, must necessarily have a strong ego, otherwise they would not be able to lead the life they do, or even to desire it.'

'I suppose so,' she assented glumly. 'At any rate, that

was absolutely useless, and very disagreeable to boot. I wonder who else would know? Oh, I have an idea, if you feel courageous. We'll go straight to the Director. He's a very formal person, but really he's a dear at heart, and surely he can't feel quite as personally involved in it all as Professor Wilcox does.'

She led me to the Director's office, where we were told by a forbidding secretary that the Director was out and that in any case he could only be seen by appointment, and asked what the object of our visit was to be.

'It's about Sebastian Cavendish,' Rose began. The woman looked up sharply, and repeated the name in a questioning tone. It struck me that everyone in the school knew Sebastian or at least knew of him, and that much might be learnt from speaking to them.

By a stroke of pleasing good fortune, the outer door opened at that precise moment, and the Director entered just in time to hear the secretary repeat the name.

'What about Sebastian?' he asked, without any formality at all.

'Oh, Professor Mackenzie,' she said, her stiffness melting slightly in a flutter at having been observed unexpectedly. 'I was just about to make an appointment for you with these two young women. I recognise you,' she added in Rose's direction. 'You are a student here, are you not? Rose Evergreene, I believe.' She ran her pen down the pages of the appointment book that lay open upon the desk before her, searching for an empty spot.

'You wished to speak to me about Sebastian?' the Director said, coming nearer and ignoring the secretary and her book.

'Yes, Professor Mackenzie,' said Rose quickly, 'you see, we . . .'

'Come into my office, why don't you,' he interrupted, and, passing behind the secretary, he unlocked and opened the door to his inner sanctum, ushered us through, and closed it behind us. I remained for a moment staring at the beauty and luxury of his office, which contained as many artworks as a museum. Exquisite vases stood upon tables and paintings lined the walls: portraits, Flemish still-lives, and a pastoral scene by Watteau. The professor caught my eye.

'The paintings honour the role of Director of the Royal Academy of Music,' he said with a smile. 'They belong to the Academy and to this office, whoever occupies it. Directors come and go: the paintings remain.'

There was a kindly modesty in his remark that made me smile as I took the seat he offered me. Rose took a deep breath and began to explain to Professor Mackenzie that she I and were making an effort to understand the reason behind Sebastian's suicide.

'But my dear,' said the professor, 'attempting to discover the cause of a suicide is a difficult and thankless task. It may so easily be that there is no precise cause, but a general state of depression and despair. Or,' he added, no doubt noting the contrast between his description and the impression that Sebastian had left on people, 'it can be a consequence of hidden, inner doubts. I do admit that although I knew Sebastian but little as an individual, having encountered him only in the contexts of my classes, I would never have guessed that his life would end this way. It is a tragedy for him and for the Academy, and I would not be averse to understanding better what occurred. But I do not see exactly what you are trying to do, and even less how I can be of help to you.'

'I am particularly concerned by the fact that he spoke of inheritance in his last note,' I told him. 'Since it seems there can be no question of money involved, I believe that he must have been speaking of something more personal, more intimate; something about himself, and I particularly wanted to find out more about his grandfather, the violinist Joseph Krieger.'

'Ah yes,' he said, 'I recall now hearing that he was Joseph Krieger's grandson. Quite right. An interesting point. Krieger was the greatest soloist in England in his time. I never heard him, of course. He must have died just about the time when I was born. But his performances were still spoken of twenty years later. Indeed, even today they are remembered as legendary, although there must be relatively few people alive now who actually heard him.'

'It is possible that Sebastian was referring to something personal about his grandfather and not merely his reputation as a violinist, with which he must have been familiar all his life,' I said. 'That is why I was hoping to discover someone who had personal memories of the man and his family.'

'The professors here are all too young for that,' he said. 'But someone here may know someone . . . wait – you give me an idea. When I first came here as a student in 1862, I studied with Prosper Sainton, a Frenchman who came here from Bordeaux. He had been my father's teacher also, and I recall that he had known Joseph Krieger quite well at one time. In fact, he had cultivated his acquaintance assiduously at the time when he was involved in the establishment of the popular concerts. They were friends for a time, and then I believe that they quarrelled. Now, what was it that he told me about Krieger? Wait, it is coming back to me. Something about adoption. Did Krieger adopt a child? Was that what it was?' He blinked, lost in the effort of memory. 'A little girl, perhaps? Do you know anything about this?'

'Well,' I said, 'Sebastian's mother was Joseph Krieger's daughter.'

'Quite right, of course she was. Possibly my vague memories on the subject of adoption may concern that lady.'

'Perhaps we could ask Professor Sainton?' I said hopefully.

'Oh, he died ten years ago,' said the professor. 'But do you know, he left all of his musical papers and writings to one of the professors here, Hans Wessely. We hired Wessely in 1889; Sainton was already an old man then who no longer gave lessons, but he came here often and followed the musicians of the Academy with great interest. They became very close during the last months of Sainton's life. Wessely tells me that there are some interesting things amongst the papers that Sainton left behind; many years' worth of reflections on the teaching of orchestral musicians, and other recollections. Why don't you ask him? If it can be of help, I will write him a personal note requesting him to show you whatever he has. If there really was an adopted child, the circumstance may be mentioned in private papers or letters. I don't see how you can do any better, for anyone alive now who knew Krieger would have had to have been very young at the time, and would probably not have been a familiar of his household. I remember Sainton's telling me that Krieger was quite standoffish and could be downright unpleasant.'

He wrote the note, sealed it and gave it to us, and we set out into the corridors once again, now in the direction of Professor Wessely's office. But he was not in, and his door was closed and locked.

'Bother,' said Rose, 'but fortunately I know that he will be here the day after tomorrow. He teaches on Thursdays.'

'Urgh,' I said. 'I am so impatient to see the old papers that might talk about Joseph Krieger. Well, I will just have to wait. You know, it makes sense that Mrs Cavendish might have been an adopted child.'

'Does it?' she said, surprised. 'I shouldn't have said so! Everyone connects Sebastian's talent with his grandfather – and he wouldn't even really have been his grandfather after all!'

'That's true,' I rejoined thoughtfully. 'But there was one person who always refused to make that connection. Do you see?'

'Oh? Why, yes, I do see – you mean Sebastian himself! I know he always denied that his gift could have anything to do with inheritance. After we talked about this in the tea shop, I decided that he must have been resentful of its being attributed in some way to family, like a person who would prefer to earn his own fortune rather than merely inherit one.'

'Well, that might have been what it was,' I said, 'but I'm not sure. I mean, I've never met anyone who had inherited a family fortune and denied it when it was mentioned. Family heritage is usually a source of pride. Think back,

Rose. Do you think there's any possibility that Sebastian might have been aware all along that his mother was an adopted child?'

'I see now that that's possible; it does seem as though he was hinting at it, though he never said it outright,' she admitted. 'But if his mother didn't want it known, he would have respected that. Pity it's such an embarrassing question to put to Mrs Cavendish directly. That's annoying; she must know the answer, but we can't ask. He might have told Claire – but no, he can't have. If she had known that, she would have known that the cursed inheritance couldn't come from the grandfather.'

'But this raises a whole new set of possibilities!' I said suddenly. 'Perhaps he unexpectedly found out something about his *mother's* real parents!'

Rose gave her head a little shake.

'I can't get that idea into my head,' she said. 'Everyone always associated him with Joseph Krieger. Oh dear, I don't know what to think. I have an idea, Vanessa – do let's go now and see if *my* professor is in. He's a cello teacher, of course, but he's old, he's been here for ever so long, and I think there isn't much that goes on here that he doesn't know. And he's so lovely! Come – let's go and find him. He's a marvellous old gentleman. I adore him. It's true what Professor Wilcox was saying about gratefulness, you know. I hadn't thought of it for Sebastian, but for myself, when I think about all that Professor Pezze has done for me – and more than that, all has given to me of himself – I can't even think about how he would feel if I died. He's like a darling grandparent, only even better because he transmitted all that music to me out of choice, out of a love that didn't come into being because of any bond of blood. The love of the teacher for the student is something different, perhaps even deeper in some ways. Oh, I don't know how to explain it. But it's something strong that builds you up and stays with you for your whole life. Here we are. Listen – he's in! That's his cello sound. He may be almost seventy, but he still has such energy in his playing. Oh, I do love him!'

She knocked, and flung open the door at once without waiting for an invitation. The white-haired professor holding the cello turned his face to the door, and it lit up immediately with an expression of delighted pleasure.

'Rose, Rose! You do not come to see me so often any more!' he exclaimed with a warm voice and a strong Italian accent.

'I'm sorry,' she said contritely, while the blooming womanliness of her seemed to melt away, leaving the place to a loving little girl.

'What have you been doing lately? I have not seen you since your recital with the sonata of Grieg, but I heard wonderful zings about your Beethoven,' he said. 'Ah, and your trio.' His face grew suddenly sad, but not with a tragic look; rather, with the sadness of an old man who has seen a great deal already, and is prepared to endure more as the years go on.

'You were doing a beautiful work wiz the trio, Rose,' he went on, the music taking the major place in his mind, above the sordid realities of life and death. 'The last time I heard you there was much, much progress since one year ago when you began! Eet was all much more harmonious in style. You worked hard to tame the wild one, the lion, did you not? You must teach him that his voice ees not ze only one, yes? And to bring forth the storm hidden inside the timid miss at ze piano, and to find her hidden passion. I felt it, zat if Sebastian was ze energy driving the trio, you were ze glue which bound it togezer. It was wonderful work, Rose. *Brava!* Eet ees terrible zat it has finished so. What will you do now? Find anozer violinist?'

'Oh, I don't know!' A point of impatience crept into her tone. 'Claire wants us to play with John Milrose. He says he shouldn't, and can't replace Sebastian, but it's obvious that he wants to, and Claire wants him too. It's all wrong, Professor Pezze. John's style goes well enough with the old Claire, the way she used to play, but she's come so far since then! I don't think we can make a go of it with John, but I don't know how to tell them what I really feel. Oh dear. I do wish I didn't have to be in this situation!'

'No, you must not do eet eef eet ees so, Rose. Better to cut eet short sooner zan later.'

'But that would hurt Claire, and I can't hurt her right now, Professor. She is already devastated! Oh dear, oh dear. But don't let's talk about me. See, I've brought you a friend, Mrs Weatherburn from Cambridge, on purpose to meet you.'

'Yes, I see. How do you do, Mrs Wezzerburn? Eet ees a pleasure. To what do I owe such a rare honour as a visit from Rose, in company even? You are a musician?'

'No, no,' I said blushing, 'although I love music.'

'No, she isn't a musician, but she's trying to understand about Sebastian, Professor Pezze.'

'Understand what?'

'Understand why he died. I mean, why he killed himself. You see, we don't understand.'

'But one cannot hope to understand such zings,' said the old man, giving the same argument that we had already heard more than once that day, but with a air of gentle philosophy. 'Ze boy was perhaps disappointed wiz something. It happens so often, sadly. Ze young people, zey do not always zink.'

'But he wasn't really, Professor. It's very strange. But Mrs Weatherburn really wanted to ask you some other questions. Questions about music, and about musicians. For example, about Sebastian's grandfather. Did you know him?'

'Joseph Krieger, you mean? I encountered him once or twice, yes, when I was young.'

'What was he like?'

'What was he like? He was . . . vain, domineering, proud, hard, and brilliant. One who must always be at ze forefront of everyzing. You could not approach him wiz friendship. He zought he was always right, knew everyzing best. He was a very difficult man. His students at ze time, I recall, suffered sadly at his hands. When zey could not stand it any more, zey would sometimes come here, to ze Academy, to get a decent education.'

'Did you ever play with him?'

'I? No, no. No one played wiz him. He played no chamber music. Only grand concertos wiz ze orchestra, or else solo upon ze stage.'

'But he played well?'

'Oh yes, he played marvellously, if you like zis way of playing. A little bit wizout a heart. Passion, yes, but no warmth of ze heart. For virtuoso playing, he was of ze very best of his generation. Zey say he had some gypsy blood in him, alzough he came from Germany. I don't know if zat is true, or if it is just a story he liked to spread to mark his difference wiz all ozers. Ze violin is a dangerous instrument, you know. It is a devilish instrument as we have known since Tartini, ze greatest violinist of his time, actually saw ze devil playing incredible music upon ze violin and wrote it down. Ze violin sometimes sheds somezing of its dangerous character on ze violinist. When ze capacity is too great, zere is some danger.'

'You think the cello is fundamentally different, then?'

'Oh, yeeeees. Ze cello ees completely different! Fundamentally, you know what?' The old man leant forward with a gleam in his eye, as though to confide to us a most humorous secret. 'The cello ees a woman's instrument,' he whispered, and sat back squatly in his chair, his pudgy hands resting on his short thighs, which hardly jutted out farther than the round stomach which rested comfortably upon them. His eyes twinkled merrily. 'Zat is what ze people do not yet realise – no! Zey zink because eet ees big, because eet has a deep voice, eet ees an instrument for men! Zey forget zat ze cello sings wiz ze voice of thrilling tenderness – ze woman's voice! Zey forget zat ze low, sweet tones are feminine; ze loud, brash tones are masculine. And ze women are practically forbidden to play it, are zey not? In ze Academy, one hundred cello students, how many women are zere? Two – only two! And why is zis? I will tell you why. It is because you must hold ze cello between ze knees. *Knees?* But in zis country, ze women may not have knees; zey are not allowed to admit having knees!'

He sat back in his chair again, and a mellow laugh rippled forth.

'Not to mention ze word *between*,' he added. 'Zis word, I zink, evokes ze worst of sin to ze English. But you will see, or perhaps you will not see . . . but zings will change wiz time, zings will change. One hundred years from now, I will bet zat all ze cellists will be ze women, and ze men will be playing ze drums and ze trombone.'

'That would be lovely,' said Rose decidedly. 'Vanessa, do ask him our question.'

'How can I put it?' I said thoughtfully. 'Professor Pezze, can incredible musical talent arise in a person whose family is not at all musical?'

'Certainly,' he said. 'Zere are many examples. Rose, eet ees so wiz you, no?'

'And what about the opposite,' I went on. 'If the parents are musical, how likely is it that the children will be?'

'It happens,' he replied, 'but eet ees not certain. Zere are examples of entire families gifted wiz unbelievable gifts. You know Manuel García? He was our professor of singing here at ze Academy until he retired just a few years ago. He lives nearby still. You have seen him?'

'I have,' volunteered Rose. 'He's awfully old, isn't he?'

'He is 95 zis year, he taught here until he was 90! Can you imagine? But did you know zat his sister is ze famous soprano, Pauline Viardot? And zat his ozer sister is the legendary Malibran?'

'Really! Why, how can that be? La Malibran – she was famous sixty or seventy years ago, wasn't she?'

'Yes, but she was a young zing when she died, no older zan our Sebastian, I zink. Her sister Pauline is still alive, but very old. Zeir parents were both singers, you know. And ze children of Pauline Viardot, zey are all fine musicians also.

Zere is a talent which is inherited wizin an entire family. You see? Yet on ze ozer hand, musical parents can have children wiz no talent at all. I have seen some here, sadly. The parents force zem so zat zey can play, but zere is no real talent. And zen, many times I have seen ze gift pass directly from grandfather to grandson. Just as in ze case of Joseph Krieger and Sebastian Cavendish. Or perhaps, who knows, it may be zat the children of Joseph Krieger were also filled wiz talent. I have some memory of hearing zat he would not have zem learning any music. It does not surprise me. He wanted always to be ze focus of attention himself. I cannot imagine his taking ze time to teach his children, or taking ze risk zat zey might become so brilliant as la Malibran, more famous zan himself. Who knows?'

'What if you found out that Sebastian was not really Joseph Krieger's grandson after all?' Rose said. 'We think he might not have been – we heard a rumour that his mother was adopted. Would that surprise you?'

'Ha? *Davvero?* You heard such a zing? No, impossible! Zat would be really astonishing.'

'Why astonishing? You told us that talent can spring up anywhere,' she said.

'But not een this case, surely! I heard zem both, you know. Fifty years apart, I heard zem both. Perhaps not many people have. Ze same bearing, ze same attack, ze same flair, ze same technical prowess. Krieger not Sebastian's grandfather?' He shook his head doubtfully. 'If he was not, zen ze whole zing is truly a miracle.'

CHAPTER TWELVE

In which Vanessa suddenly puts two and two together
and finds that it might make five (or even six)

Two days later, I crossed Hanover Square, turned into Tenterden Street and entered the imposing square door of the Royal Academy of Music quite by myself for the first time. I almost felt something of a fraud as I walked through the hall and up the stairs, following the directions that Rose had given me to locate her at the end of her trio rehearsal. All around me, students passed carrying all kinds of instrument cases, some of shapes so lumpy and irregular that I could hardly guess at the identity of the instrument inside. A tall young man carrying a tiny box that probably contained a flute accompanied a diminutive girl lugging a contrabass taller than her companion. Feeling oddly naked with nothing but my handbag, I walked along briskly, trying to look quite as though I belonged there, and soon reached the padded door where Rose had told me I should find her.

I stood outside the door and cocked my ear. Faint strains of music filtered through, muted and lovely, facilitating the necessary wait, for I did not want to interrupt the musicians at their work. Crossing notes and fragments wafted through the corridors from all of the different doors along it. I found the place pervaded by a stimulating atmosphere of hard work and deep concentration. My own thoughts were in something of a whirl, for Rose was to accompany me to visit Professor Wessely, and armed with the kind note scribbled by the Academy's director, I thought to be allowed to have access to the private diaries and letters of a musician who had known Joseph Krieger closely and well.

The idea that Tanis Cavendish might have been an adopted and not a natural child of her father intrigued me to the highest degree, and I longed for some kind of confirmation. I stood there in the hall thinking it over, and trying to remember what the old Swiss violinist Herr Ratner had said about the Krieger family. He had spent about two years visiting the house regularly for lessons, I recalled, but he could hardly remember Krieger's wife; he had called her a self-effacing person, a remark which might have been a deduction as much as a memory. He had also said that Joseph Krieger had no sons, for if he had, Herr Ratner might have found employment as their musical tutor. But there had been only daughters, Herr Ratner had recalled.

Until now, I had not taken any particular notice of these words, taking them to mean nothing more the expression of Joseph Krieger's not being childless, yet having no sons. But now, I wondered suddenly. *Daughters?* Might it not be possible that Herr Ratner remembered daughters, because there really were daughters, and not just one daughter? And had Professor Mackenzie not quoted Sainton as saying that Krieger had not had his *children* trained in music? It could be just confusion or poor memory, of course – but could it not also mean that Sebastian's mother Tanis might have had a sister? And if she had, what were the chances that that sister's name was nothing other than *Lydia*?

I made a rapid calculation of ages in my mind. According to Dr Bernstein's book, Lydia had been twenty-four in 1870: she would be fifty-four today. Mrs Cavendish must be of much the same age.

My heart began to beat as a mental scene began to unroll itself before me. There was the party in Zürich, in Frau Bochsler's padded, plushy parlour, filled with pillows and little porcelain objects. There was Dr Bernstein, telling Sebastian with eyes full of memory about a woman called Lydia, of nearly the same age as Sebastian's mother, whom he resembled astonishingly. I saw Sebastian smiling indulgently, having never heard a word about the existence of any such person, and paying scant attention, probably putting it down to coincidence or to the faulty memory of a romantic old man. And later on, at that very same party, there was Herr Ratner, chatting away with the young star of the evening, telling him this and that about how he had once known his grandfather – and mentioning *daughters*.

Why should he not have mentioned them that evening, as naturally as he had mentioned them to me? And if he had, then might not the very same idea have sprung into Sebastian's mind as now sprang into mine?

I knew nothing of Sebastian's family, but he had lived

near his mother for his entire life, and must have been sensitive to her every mood, reserved and cool though she was. If my idea was right, if Tanis Cavendish had had a sister whose existence had been concealed from her son, then how would she have reacted when he asked her, in all the innocence of childhood, why he had no aunts, uncles or cousins as his friends all did? She would have kept her secret if she wished, of course, but as for the underlying minuscule tensions that invariably accompany a lie – who is better equipped to detect them than a mother in her child, or a child in his mother? I smiled to myself, remembering a time not days ago when, upon being asked, little Cedric had asserted with a broad smile of angelic beatitude that *of course* he had already cleaned his teeth. How was it that I was able to laugh at him without the slightest feeling of doubt, and tell him to stop telling untruths and to go and clean them at once? I could hardly even define to myself what made me so certain; it was not that he had looked sly or shifty, it was far more subtle than that: some elusive, inexpressible difference between that cheery smile and his usual one. Might not Sebastian have felt a similar minuscule pinprick when his mother told him that she had no family at all? Without ever having the slightest indication of the contrary, he had probably dismissed it from his mind. But perhaps the two facts he had learnt almost simultaneously that night had suddenly made that pinprick blossom into a full-fledged doubt, accompanied by an urgent desire to *know*!

The door before me opened and Rose looked out into the corridor.

'Oh, Vanessa, you found the room!' she exclaimed. 'You

didn't need to wait out here. You'd have been welcome to enter. Do come in.' The dark-haired, solidly built young violinist that I had already seen, John Milrose, was standing with Claire, his hands on her shoulders, and was talking to her softly and seriously, his eyes locked into hers. Rose's glance followed mine and she shrugged, with a faint air of annoyance.

But Claire wrenched away from him when she saw me, and hurried over, her hand outstretched.

'Mrs Weatherburn,' she said. 'Rose says you have found out some things, but she wouldn't tell us anything till you came! Oh, I did so want to see you. Do you think you understand what might have happened? I'm sorry,' she added, recovering her manners, yet with a nervous stammer still causing her voice to shake, 'I have barely even asked you how you are. And about – about your expenses. Rose says you have been travelling. Of course I will—'

'Please, do not even think about that now,' I said firmly. 'We can discuss it at the end. I do have some things to tell you, although nothing is yet certain. But I am continuing to discover new information.' In a few words, I told her about Lydia K., then about the mention of daughters in the plural, and the possibility that Sebastian had made a connection between the two things. She looked doubtful.

'But you say that he didn't pay much attention to what the doctor told him,' she said, biting her lip. 'You really think—'

'There is one more thing,' I interrupted. 'We learnt yesterday that there seems to be some rumour, some possibility, that Sebastian's mother may not have been the true daughter of Joseph Krieger, but an adopted child. Rose and I were wondering if it is true, and if Sebastian knew it, and if that fact could perhaps explain the way he always used to deny that he had inherited his musical abilities from his grandfather. I wondered if you knew anything about that. I thought perhaps he might have told you, if he told anyone at all.'

Her startled glance reminded me of a wren.

'I—no,' she began. 'No, I didn't know that. He never told me. But you know, I wonder – it's strange, because he did hint at something of the kind, now that you mention it. He made some remarks once or twice, but I never paid any attention, because I thought it was just his way of declaring his independence. You know, from the all-dominating grandfather thing.'

'Quite. However, it has occurred to us that, if true, this piece of information might completely change the meaning we have been giving to the words "cursed inheritance",' I said. 'We were thinking that he might have found out something about his mother's real parents, perhaps.'

'Yes, I see. Yet I still don't understand why he should have cared so dreadfully, whatever it could have been.'

'I only wish we could confirm that his mother really was adopted,' I said, 'and that Sebastian knew about it.'

'He did,' said John Milrose unexpectedly, coming nearer to us. He had been standing aside, out of politeness, but he could hear everything we were saying, and as Rose and Claire seemed to consider this perfectly acceptable, I did as well.

It was far too early for Claire to even think of falling in love again; it was obvious that Sebastian still reigned over her heart, but it was also clear that John had an interest in helping her in any way he could to recover her peace of mind. It had not occurred to me, though, that he might know anything intimate about Sebastian that had not been confided even to Claire.

I was, however, mistaken. John explained to us how Sebastian had told him the truth some months earlier, when they had entered into a serious argument on the subject of hereditary artistry.

'He was actually angry with me for insisting,' he admitted, 'and that's why he told me. His mother had told him the truth because of what happened at his debut concert, his very first solo concert with orchestra. He was just thirteen, and after the concert dozens of people came and told him that he was the worthy heir of his grandfather and that it was easy to see where his gift came from. He said that after they were all gone he actually cried with rage; no one was talking about him – it was just Joseph Krieger, Joseph Krieger, Joseph Krieger, like he didn't even exist, like he was nothing but a reincarnation. That's when his mother told him that it wasn't even true, that Krieger was not his real grandfather because she was an adopted child. She said he must never tell anyone, but should always keep that knowledge inside himself to give him strength.'

'So that's it,' I exclaimed, astonished to have so suddenly obtained an answer from this unexpected source to one of the many questions that assailed me. 'Did he say whether he knew anything about his mother's real parents?'

'He said she didn't know and didn't wish to,' he replied. 'Actually, I believe he regretted telling me about it, afterwards. Not that he cared much himself whether people knew, but it isn't a thing one spreads about really;

and then, his mother did not want it to known. It was not that she drew any special pride or glory from being the great violinist's daughter – she never behaved in that way at all – but still, with her engagement to Lord Warburton, questions of family were taking on a certain importance, what with Warburton being a proponent of Galton's eugenics and all. Sebastian asked me to keep the secret for his mother's sake, so I never mentioned it again.'

'But Sebastian's note didn't make you think about it at once?' cried Rose in amazement. 'I mean, the words "cursed inheritance" – I'd have thought of that right away, if I'd known what you knew!'

'He wrote those words in his note?' he said in surprise. 'I had no idea. Claire never showed it to me. I thought I had understood that he hadn't given any explanation at all.' He put his arm around Claire's shoulders, as though to defend her from the cruelty of such an empty message. Rose hoisted her cello case over her shoulder.

'Oh dear,' she said, 'it was probably silly of us not to think of asking you before. I do hope we haven't missed too many opportunities like that. Of course, there's Mrs Cavendish herself, but we simply *can't* ask her about this – and anyway, it's probably true that she doesn't know much about it. We think the best place to find out would be from older musicians who knew Joseph Krieger. We're going to chase up a source right now. Come, Vanessa, let's go see if Professor Wessely is free.'

She led me through the halls in the direction of his office.

'Urgh,' she said, 'John Milrose annoys me. It's not nice of me, and I don't even know exactly why it is, but the way he's pressing Claire with his feelings – can't he see that it's much too soon? It's in poor taste. Sebastian died barely a month ago!' With the energy of irritation, she knocked vigorously upon the door. No response, however, was forthcoming.

'I know he's here today,' she said, and she hailed a young man passing by with a violin case slung over his shoulder.

'Professor Wessely is teaching in the grand studio right now,' he told us, consulting his pocket watch. 'It's on the ground floor to left. But he won't like being interrupted. He hates that, you know.'

'We'll just wait until he's free,' said Rose, and down we went, to a very grand door that seemed to indicate passage into an unusually elegant room. Through this door we heard a few notes, which were quickly interrupted by a long string of remarks in heavily accented English. Rose knocked gently and opened the door a crack.

The studio was indeed large, with a burnished parquet floor covered with remarkable carpets, portraits upon the walls, and an immense shining grand piano before which sat a woman, her fingers on the keys, waiting for instructions. To my surprise, the student was just a little boy no more than ten years old, with a bony, sensitive face, a large nose, deep eyes sparkling with intelligence and a violin that looked too large for him. I was alarmed at Rose's boldness and half-expected a sharp reproach at our interruption, but the professor, a dynamic man in the prime of his life, smiled cordially.

'Ah yes,' he said, 'that is quite perfect. Please, do come in and sit down. Wolfe, you will play the Tartini for these visitors. Enter, enter,' he added, beckoning us forward and ushering us to two of the brocaded chairs that surrounded the walls. 'This is my youngest student: Wolfe Wolfinsohn, from South Africa. An extraordinary youngster. He will play for you the Devil's Trill.'

Rose poked my arm. It was the very piece that her professor had mentioned! The small boy slid into the performance with a theme so wistful that it brought to mind images of infinite sadness and nostalgia, interrupted once or twice by strident chords indicative of a sudden spurt of rage. Just as I was allowing myself to be lulled by the spirit of this part, he launched into something quite different; a kind of dance of Puckish sprites which leapt and laughed without a stop as though they were rushing all over the room. After a few minutes of this, the air was suddenly filled with wrenching chords, like sobs torn from the very entrails, ending with a tragic weeping. Then began the real madness, accompanied by the gentle touch of the woman at the piano, whose role, essentially a series of soft chords, served to accentuate the wild peculiarity of the violin music, which now soared and dived, slowed and rushed forth again, leapt and above all trilled – lengthening the whole notion of trill from the usual pretty ornament to a terrifying, unending cackle of diabolical laughter, twisting agilely in and out of the realm which links beauty and madness. It ended with a single note repeated manically again and again to distraction – and then the burst of a grand farewell.

Rose and I began spontaneously to clap, and heaped praise upon the young artist. Rising, we then thanked the professor for having given us the opportunity to hear this extraordinary student, and asked if there might be a moment when he could see us privately. He seemed quite pleased and gave us an appointment in his office upstairs for six o'clock. Closing the door behind us, we emerged into the grey, chilly day and bent our steps towards a nearby tea room. My excitement had been stimulated to fever pitch by the wait, but even more so by the music itself, which was obsessional, possessing. I hurried Rose inside and ordered tea, and we set to discussing the events of the day.

'Do you think Mrs Cavendish was really adopted, or did she just tell Sebastian that in order to console him?' Rose asked.

'Oh, I think it must be true. I can't imagine that anyone would invent a thing like that. There would be plenty of other ways of learning to deal with Sebastian's feelings, and this one might become rather a burden in the end, what with his hinting it but not feeling right about saying it openly.'

'That's true. It would be a very odd thing to invent. But you do see why I still think it might be possible?'

'No. Tell me.'

'Why, it's because of what Professor Pezze said about Sebastian's resemblance to Joseph Krieger. I wouldn't believe it from anyone else, perhaps, but with him – it would be the first time I ever put even one syllable he pronounced in doubt. He knows and feels music right through every fibre of his body. It would be astonishing if he were wrong about this.'

'Well,' I said thoughtfully, 'but he did know beforehand that Krieger was the grandfather – it's not as though he deduced it just from seeing Sebastian play. So perhaps he had a prejudice in his mind.'

'You don't know Professor Pezze. It's simply inconceivable

that he could imagine some musical relationship that doesn't really exist!'

'Sebastian – the grandson and yet not the grandson,' I said, and suddenly a great flash of light burst blindingly into my mind! 'I have an idea, Rose! Perhaps Sebastian was not actually his mother's son, after all! Perhaps he, too, was adopted! Maybe his real mother was Lydia K – and maybe she really was Krieger's own daughter!'

So excited was I by this seemingly incredible discovery that I could hardly breathe. I tried to remember exactly what Dr Bernstein had written about Lydia K. She had left Basel when she was 24 years old, and it was in the summer of 1874.

'Exactly how old was Sebastian?' I asked Rose.

'He was twenty-four.'

'So he would have been twenty-five this year; he must have been born in 1875. That would be the reason why she never returned to Basel! It's possible, it's very possible. It would explain so much!'

'You mean that you think that the Kriegers might have adopted Mrs Cavendish even if they had a daughter of their own? Why would they do that?'

'There could be any number of reasons. Perhaps close friends of theirs died and left an orphan child behind. Rose, I believe we are getting closer to the truth. Just think! Here's Sebastian, denying outright that he can have inherited anything from his grandfather, and certain that he's right, because he knows that his mother is an adopted child. Yet people keep mentioning it, perhaps people like Professor Pezze, people he trusts, so he can't help but be puzzled somewhere deep inside. On that evening in Zürich, he unexpectedly receives indications that his mother might have had a sister whom he resembles remarkably and whose existence was completely hidden from him. Do you not think he might jump to the conclusion that the mysterious Lydia could be his real mother – and also the real daughter of his grandparents? I can imagine that such an idea would send him rushing to try to discover the truth!'

'Oh, Vanessa, it all hangs together – it's very possible!' she cried. 'If only we could find out more.'

'Well, perhaps we will. Hopefully, we will be leafing through Prosper Sainton's papers in less than an hour.'

'Hum. We'd probably better be prepared for disappointment,' she warned wisely. Who knows what Professor Wessely might have done with his old papers – who knows if he even actually really kept them, or whether they might not be somewhere unavailable, like in his far-off home in Hungary. And even if we find them, who knows whether they contain anything more than remarks about music – or boring information like "Saw J.K. today" – or even worse, no information about Joseph Krieger at all!'

'Stop, stop! We must be optimistic!' I answered firmly, calling the waitress over to pay for our tea.

'All right, we shall be.' She stood up and gave her head a little shake. 'But Vanessa, there's still something I don't understand. If this new idea is right, then Sebastian couldn't have discovered anything dreadful about his mother's true parents. I mean about Mrs Cavendish's true parents. What I mean is, if he realised she wasn't his real mother, then no matter who they were, it wouldn't matter to him. Not in terms of the "cursed inheritance", at any rate.'

'No, that's true,' I agreed. 'This would change all of

that. If we're right, it was Lydia K he was concerned with.'

'Still, though. Even if our theory is true, no matter how angry he might have been to discover that his mother had hidden it all from him, I simply can't see why he should kill himself over it!'

'The "cursed inheritance",' I said. 'I wonder if somehow, he found out something terrible about Lydia herself. I wonder what happened to Lydia? If her sister adopted her baby, it could be that she died—'

'—or went raving mad! Could that be it?'

'It could. And yet, even if she did—'

'—no matter how dreadfully, it still doesn't seem like a reason for Sebastian to take his own life! It doesn't, Vanessa. No matter what happened to her, it doesn't. Does it?'

'No,' I admitted. 'No, it doesn't. There's still a lot we don't know.'

Unspoken words remained in the air as we gathered up our things and left.

CHAPTER THIRTEEN

In which the logical progression of ideas encounters an obstacle

When we arrived at the eminent music teacher's office at six o'clock precisely, we found his door standing welcomingly open. He was inside, bent over a musical score in the company of the small boy we had heard earlier, and they were studying it together with animation. Professor Wessely looked up as we entered, waved us to some leather chairs, and packed the boy off, carrying the music and his violin, to go and practise it by himself.

'I am so glad that you have come,' he said. 'Young Wolfe is an exceptional child. I believe that he may be the greatest talent I have ever seen among my students; perhaps the greatest that the Royal Academy has ever seen. You heard his playing. It is astounding for a boy of ten. With proper teaching and nurturing, I believe there is no limit that he may not surpass.'

Rose and I glanced at each other, slightly surprised.

'He is quite wonderful,' she agreed. 'We are really delighted to have had the opportunity to hear him play. Now, what we—'

'The search for some kind of financial support is not easy,' the professor went on firmly. 'People are not used to such cases nowadays. But this is something really special. When I was a child in Hungary, there, at that time, there were children who were able to work and learn like this child. I do not say they necessarily possessed the same gift. I myself, for instance, realised as I grew up that my vocation was to be a teacher; that passing on to students the wonderful secrets of technical accomplishments and the splendid approach to musical interpretation that I had learnt from the best of the Hungarian teachers, laden with all of their traditions, was my true destiny in life, and not to play solo upon the grand stages of Europe. But the devotion, the inspiration, the effort I devoted to the violin as a child – these have all but disappeared in our modern time. Young Wolfe is the first child I have seen of the young generation to possess this kind of depth. It would be impossible to choose a more worthy object of aid and support.'

He paused expectantly, but we did not know what to say in the face of what was turning out to be quite an embarrassing misunderstanding. Apparently the professor had been expecting possible sponsors to come and hear his prodigy, and had taken us for them. This was unfortunate, as neither Rose nor I commanded the kind of finances that could cover the support of a young child over a period of years, however deserving.

'Wolfe comes from South Africa,' Professor Wessely

said, deciding to pursue his effort in the face of our silence, 'and he arrived in this country on the recommendation of his teacher there, who wrote a letter to me explaining that no teacher in the country could do justice to a talent of this magnitude. He has come with his mother, leaving father and siblings behind. But the mother is not sure that she should stay; helping this gifted youngster deprives the others of a mother, but returning to them would leave this one nearly in the situation of an orphan, although of course I would look after him as much as time would allow me to do so. In the meantime, however, they have barely enough money to survive. That is why it is so important to find some person who will accept to offer the gift of a scholarship. I believe that that person will be gratified, in just a few years, by seeing young Wolfe Wolfinsohn become the name of one of the legendary violinists of the new century.'

I sat calculating a number of possible but unsatisfactory remarks in my mind and discarding them all. But Rose began to speak, and I realised as I listened that she had had a stroke of genius which might just turn out to be of benefit to everyone, as well as satisfying our immediate purposes.

'Unfortunately, we ourselves are not in a situation to be able to provide the amount of financial help that Wolfe would need,' she said kindly, 'but the reason we are here is because we are acquainted with someone who is in such a situation, and who, we believe, seeks an opportunity to do some good in the musical world, having recently undergone a terrible loss. I am speaking of Mrs Cavendish, the mother of Sebastian Cavendish. You know about him, I presume?'

'Mrs Cavendish! Of course I know of the terrible tragedy,' he replied. 'The poor woman. Is it possible that she can be thinking of helping others at a time like this? That would be very courageous of her, indeed.'

'It is something of a consolation, or perhaps, I should better say, a manner of actively expressing her grief,' said Rose smoothly. 'It is not something she is determined upon yet, merely a vague idea, and, as you can imagine, she is not in a state to search out the possibilities for herself. You are acquainted with her?'

'I am not, although I have seen her more than once, at the recitals and auditions here,' he replied. 'Naturally, I knew her son and even coached him in the occasional chamber music group when he was a student. A phenomenal talent, although not so astonishing an early-bloomer as Wolfe, and perhaps more brash than deep in a certain manner. But that is merely according to my taste and my tradition. Sebastian is a great loss to the future of British violin playing, there is no doubt about that. I will write to Mrs Cavendish.'

I paused at this, wondering whether our inventions might not end up by getting us into trouble, but it was impossible to back off now. And even if she disliked the idea, I could not imagine Mrs Cavendish answer the professor's request otherwise but courteously. 'There is another thing,' I gabbled, in a hasty desire to steer the conversation away from scholarships. 'You probably know that Mrs Cavendish's father was the late Joseph Krieger.'

'Yes, I have heard that,' he assented, his interest aroused.

'Well, having lost her father as a very young child, she has always been interested in learning anything she could about him, and now, at this dreadful time, it seems she has vaguely had the idea of beginning to write his biography.'

Rose glanced at me quickly, then added,

'It would be a way of remembering family ties, and those who have passed away.'

'I quite understand,' he said, looking as though he didn't, which was perfectly natural, given the hasty and haphazard nature of our inventions. I quickly handed him Professor Mackenzie's note.

'The Director told us that you may have quite a lot of interesting information about Joseph Krieger in your possession,' I explained, 'amongst the private papers of Prosper Sainton. He remembers that they used to be friends, and then quarrelled.'

'I have heard that Joseph Krieger quarrelled with everyone,' he murmured. 'It would not make much of a topic for biographical writing.'

'But he had a family, many important acquaintances in the musical world, and innumerable concerts and interesting encounters and experiences,' I improvised. 'Professor Mackenzie thinks that Prosper Sainton may have written about these things during the period of their friendship.'

'It is possible,' he said. 'I have not read much of his private papers, I must tell you honestly, because they are mostly written in French. From the little I have seen, they may be historically quite interesting. It has been one of my long-standing projects to find a French student to properly read and classify them for the Archives of the Academy. Do you read French?' Upon our both nodding breathlessly, he pulled out his watch, glanced at it, and said,

'I must go and teach for one hour now. An extra lesson for a student who has not been working well lately. I would not wish the documents to leave my office. May I entrust you with them here until my return?'

We assented with alacrity, almost unable to believe our luck, as he opened the cupboard directly behind him and extracted two large piles of disordered notebooks and papers. Much of the heap consisted of annotated musical scores and exercises. He swiftly separated those out and put them back, leaving us with a large quantity of yellowed envelopes addressed in the scratchy copper-plate of fifty years ago, and more than a dozen notebooks covered with writing in a crabbed but legible hand.

The moment the door had closed behind him, Rose took up a handful of papers and said,

'Well – our first worry has melted into thin air. Now we just have to hope that Monsieur Sainton was a terrific gossip at heart!' And she set to examining the letters in the envelopes with a great speed that was no doubt due more to the three or four summers she had spent at chamber music festivals in the mountains of France than to the rudiments of French grammar that I had dutifully inculcated into her as a child. Not to mention the helpful fact that, unlike the diaries, at least half of the letters were actually written in a language we both spoke fluently.

I took up the notebooks, and soon found that as I became used to the old Frenchman's handwriting, the speed of my ability to spell out his words increased. I put aside everything concerned with the years following Joseph Krieger's death, and concentrated on the earlier ones, going through them from the year 1844, in which Prosper Sainton had first arrived in England. I saw immediately that the diaries were a wonderful place to look for information. He wrote in their pages no more than once or twice each month, but when he did, he described concerts, encounters and anecdotes in a breezy and amusing tone which made me suspect that he was perhaps doing it with a view to writing his memoirs one day. And a fascinating book they would have made. The names of musicians and composers, familiar and unfamiliar, filled the pages as he followed their careers: he had known Berlioz, Alkan, Chopin, Mazas, Liszt while at the Paris Conservatoire, and followed their careers all through the years, attending their concerts in London and playing their orchestral music. He described leading his orchestra in the position of concertmaster through innumerable concerts, of which the most unforgettable, he wrote with an eager hand, was an extraordinary performance of Beethoven's violin concerto conducted by none other than the great Mendelssohn himself, and performed by a boy of twelve whose name, Joseph Joachim, returned repeatedly in the pages of the diary. I searched in vain, however, for a mention of Joseph Krieger.

Rose was the first to make a find.

'Vanessa, Vanessa, quick, look!'

I jumped out of my seat and read over her shoulder a short note written in English, in a bold handwriting whose pointed letters denoted a German origin. The note mentioned that the author had been invited to a luncheon and had heard that Mr Sainton was also to be there. 'It will be a good opportunity for us to discuss the questions you raised the other day,' it read. I turned over the sheet to read the back, and my eye fell upon the signature.

'Joseph Krieger!'

'Yes – isn't it eerie? We've heard so much about him, and now we have something concrete: a letter from his very own hand! Look at the date; August 1848. So we know they knew each other then. Perhaps you could skip directly to there in the diaries.'

The notebooks for 1844, 1845 and 1846 having proved disappointing, I followed the hint, took up the one from 1848, and was rewarded almost at once. In that year, Joseph Krieger had played a large part in the life of Prosper Sainton. Sainton had left the Royal Italian Opera to lead an orchestra known as the Queen's Band, and he desired to consolidate the reputation of the Queen's Band by organising a series of concerts presenting the most prestigious soloists of Europe. The invitations closest to his heart, the ones he took care of personally, concerned the violinists, and detailed descriptions of his correspondence and negotiations with them filled a generous portion of the diary's pages. While they mainly sought the great soloists from the continent – Henri Vieuxtemps from Belgium, Joseph Joachim from Germany – London did provide Joseph Krieger, who was persuaded, once, twice and then a third time to perform with the orchestra, playing some of the most splendid concertos in the world, and invariably astounding the audience by following them up with encore pieces played with a virtuosity that had not been seen since the days of Paganini! Sainton spoke of the lion's head violin and of Krieger's hands and his long and exceptionally flexible fingers. I showed the passage to Rose.

'They sound exactly like Sebastian's hands,' she said, looking up at me.

Soon after the beginning of 1848, it became obvious that Sainton was courting Krieger, professionally speaking, and their contacts were increasingly frequent. Sainton managed to be at many a social event where Krieger was invited as well, and even became acquainted with the ephemeral figure of Mrs Krieger, a thin, sad, pale woman (*'maigre, triste et pâle'*), as he wrote, who seemed 'lost when not standing at her husband's side, and nervous when she was'.

A few weeks farther on in the diary, I read something which made me sit up.

'As we played for a moment with our host's delightful three-year-old daughter,' I read, 'Mrs Krieger's eyes filled with tears, which began to run down her cheeks. I felt quite embarrassed (*'gêné'*) and yet very sympathetic, and she explained to me that she, also, had once had a daughter, named Xanthe, who had been very ill and died in the countryside where she had been sent to get well. Controlling her weeping with difficulty, she told me that she longed for children to love and care for. But she cannot be much under fifty, and will surely never have another. It is very sad.'

I went on and on, with Rose now reading over my shoulder, and it was in the entries for the month of September that we suddenly struck gold.

'All musical London is buzzing with the rumour that Joseph Krieger and his wife have adopted two small orphans. In my opinion, it is his wife's desire alone, but it was good of him to comply with her wishes.'

And in December, giving an account of one of the carefully organised concerts with the Queen's Band, complete with a description of Joseph Krieger's flabbergasting rendition of Mozart's fifth violin concerto (*'he played the so-called Turkish chromatic passages in the final movement with a lascivious daring that could leave no doubt as to his interpretation, if the question may still be asked about*

Mozart's intentions'), he recounted seeing Mrs Krieger after the concert and asking after the children. '*She seems a different woman,*' he wrote, '*still nervous, tense and shy, certainly, but stronger. The little girls have given her a new purpose in life. I am glad for her, because she is a good woman, and deserves this happiness.*'

'Rose,' I said. 'Oh, Rose, I don't know what to think!'

'We've found Lydia,' she said. 'We simply must have. The two little girls were Lydia and Tanis. They must have been!'

'Yes,' I replied, 'but don't you see the problem? Both girls were adopted – so our idea that Lydia was the true daughter of the Kriegers must have been wrong. So even if Sebastian was her son and not Tanis' – why, it still does nothing to explain the "cursed inheritance"!'

'Oh, blow,' she said, 'you're right. We had it differently in our heads, didn't we?'

'We had thought that Tanis might be the daughter of friends of the Kriegers who had died,' I recalled. 'Maybe both girls were. Any friends of the Kriegers were probably musicians, and perhaps that would explain where Sebastian's talent came from.'

She laughed. 'If one admits that it needs any explanation at all,' she said. 'You know that Sebastian wouldn't agree. Anyway, it isn't the talent that needs explaining, it's what Professor Pezze said. He saw a *real* resemblance to Joseph Krieger, Vanessa. I can't not believe him – but neither can I see how it could be true! Oh, this is annoying – just when we were getting everything to be so plausible!'

'We simply must find out who the children really were, and where they came from,' I said, and at that moment, well before we had had time to finish reading the diaries, let alone digest the new information, the door opened and Professor Wessely came back in.

'You seem very busy,' he remarked. 'Have you found interesting things?'

'Extraordinarily interesting,' I blurted out. 'Did you know that Mrs Cavendish was adopted by Joseph Krieger and his wife?'

'Really?' He looked surprised. 'No, I didn't know that. I always assumed that Sebastian's talent came from his grandfather through his mother. It seemed something that ran in the family. I am not aware that Sebastian's mother played any instrument, but I noticed more than once that she has a profound feeling for and understanding of music. From seeing her over the course of several years at the concerts and recitals that take place here at the Academy, it was clear to me that she had a remarkable ear. In fact, I have more than once noticed her actually wincing at a wrong note, and when I say a wrong note, I am speaking of something very subtle, just the smallest bit off-colour, not something that would disturb an ordinary amateur.' He smiled. 'In any case, what importance does it have? None at all. As I told you, talent can flower anywhere, and the important thing is to nurture it once it is discovered. I am very grateful for the idea you have given me. I will certainly write to Mrs Cavendish about Wolfe.'

'Please, do not mention our visit!' said Rose quickly. 'We are acting on what we felt to be an unspoken wish of hers. She does not know of our search on her behalf, and might perhaps be annoyed by it.'

'Of course, of course,' he replied understandingly.

'Rest assured, I shall be most delicate.' He hesitated for a moment, glancing at his watch. 'I am sorry, I must lock the office and leave now. But you have been very helpful. Is there something that you would like to borrow from all this?' He indicated the papers scattered over his desk.

I gratefully took the notebooks for the years 1849 and 1850, and stowed them in my bag.

'I will take the best possible care of them,' I promised him, 'and bring them back to you tomorrow.'

He smiled again, warmly.

'They have lain untouched for a long time,' he said. 'Monsieur Sainton would be pleased, I think, to know that someone was reading them. It is important not to forget those who are dead.'

'They have much to say to us,' I agreed, but I was thinking of Sebastian, not Prosper Sainton.

'And many ways of saying it,' added Rose, and I knew her thoughts were running in the same channels as mine.

CHAPTER FOURTEEN

Vanessa takes a trip to a graveyard
that also leads into the past

I stood with Rose in the wind and cold damp which rendered even the luxurious gardens and splendid monuments of the Highgate Cemetery drab and gloomy, and stared down at the smooth earthen plot where Sebastian Cavendish reposed, his vibrant voice forever silent. The grass had been replanted, but the chill had not encouraged it to flourish, and only a couple of patches showed some straggling blades. Faded bouquets with brownish petals, tied with discoloured ribbons, still lay at the foot of the large stone cross, together with a few fresher ones. Clutching her own bunch of white lilies, Rose stood and contemplated them motionlessly.

The base of the cross was a solid four-sided block in grey stone, and in the frontal panel were carved the words:

IN MEMORY OF
JOSEPH KRIEGER
WHO DIED APRIL 10, 1850
AGED 60 YEARS

Joseph Krieger had prepared a tomb for his family, but they were not there. The other three sides of the block were bare and smooth. In front of one of them, a small wooden cross had been planted, upon which was mounted a tiny brass plate containing the words:

Sebastian Cavendish
1875–1900
Rest in Peace

'They haven't had time to carve it into the stone yet,' said Rose. 'It's such a little epitaph.'

'It's more beautiful so,' I said. 'Adding words wouldn't make it any better.'

'No one knows exactly what time he died, before or after midnight,' she went on with a catch in her voice. 'The carvers offered him 1900 as a kind of gift; that he should have seen the new century before he died.'

'That is a touching thought,' I said, and she burst into tears.

'No, it isn't,' she sobbed. 'He could have been spared those last hours. They must have been horrible.'

I had never asked about the precise circumstances of Sebastian's death, contenting myself with the brief mention of taking poison that Rose had let fall on that first day at the memorial concert. Even now, when Rose spoke of it spontaneously, I felt inhibited about asking for details. Whatever Sebastian had taken, it would not make any difference, and I had no need to know.

If he had really taken it. Of his own will.

The thought entered my head unbidden, but not for the first time. In the last few days, it had presented itself there with a persistence that increased in proportion to the tenacity with which I pushed it away. I did not want to behave like a seeker after sensation – and yet – it did seem that the unfolding pattern was leading to discoveries which, exciting though they were and liable to cause a tumult of emotions, could not comprehensibly have led to a state of suicidal despair.

Consciously, at least, I tried to reject the idea. I told myself repeatedly that there might be, there must be, a missing link of some kind, and that I was not to jump to conclusions before knowing the full detail of Sebastian's actions on the day he died. But it lingered stubbornly in the recesses of my mind.

Someone could have been jealous of Sebastian.

Someone could have been angry with him.

Or someone could have been afraid of him, or of something he might do, or discover.

It wasn't difficult to construct mad theories. It was perhaps useless, and in any case certainly premature. But Rose's tearful words gave me an opening to find out something I had not known how to ask.

'Was it very dreadful?' I asked, taking her hand in both of mine.

'It was arsenic,' she wept. 'It was right there in the house; it had always been there. It's a terrible death, Vanessa, they say. Hours of terrible illness before you die.'

'Why on earth did he have arsenic in the house?' I asked, instantly alert. Chemists do not sell pure arsenic. Anyone in possession of arsenic may be justly suspected of planning a suicide.

'He took it from a porcelain pot on his mother's dressing table,' she said, wiping her eyes. 'She bought it in America. We went there three years ago on tour with the Academy orchestra. Sebastian was concertmaster, and we also played solo – we played the Brahms Double Concerto together. It was so exalting – I'll never forget it. The way we played that night. Oh, Sebastian!' Leaning forward, she suddenly set her bouquet of lilies in the middle of the patch of earth over the grave. She laid it down with both hands, almost pressing it, as though she could push the message of loving memory through the earth to the body below. She remained there for a moment, bent over, her hands on the flowers, communing silently. Then she stood up, her face calmer. Drawing my arm through hers, I led her towards the large entrance gate as she went on speaking.

'Mrs Cavendish came with us on the tour; she took care of some of the organisation. I suppose she enjoyed the opportunity to hear Sebastian, and also to see something of the United States. It really was great fun, and fascinatingly different, too. One of the things we found out was that American women believe that tiny doses of arsenic are splendid for the complexion. You can buy pots of it over there, and Mrs Cavendish got one. I found out later that some ladies actually do use it over here as well, but they've got to soak it off fly-papers. Personally, I should hate the idea of poisoning myself every day, but Mrs Cavendish does have a marvellous complexion for her age; she quite glows. Sebastian took the powder from her pot and put nearly all of it into a cup of coffee. He was all alone; alone and too ill to go for help.'

'He didn't want help,' I said. Again that little voice inside me argued. And Rose argued, too.

'I know why you say that, Vanessa. But he did want help – I know he did! He wasn't made to lie down and give up. Maybe his brain didn't want to be helped, but the life-force running through his veins – it must have!'

She was upset again, but she pulled herself together as a man in a black coat came towards us, holding up an umbrella against the rain that had now begun to fall, and a second one in his hand.

'It's coming down, ladies,' he said kindly, 'and it'll be worse in a minute. Would you like to take shelter in the lodge till it's over?' He looked at Rose's face and added, 'We'll make a nice cup of tea over my spirit lamp.'

The caretaker's room was stuffy, but it was not too cold and there was a bench covered with a ragged blanket upon which we sat while he bustled about with kettle and mugs.

'You been visiting a new grave?' he asked conversationally.

'Yes, Sebastian Cavendish's,' I told him. 'The epitaph hasn't been carved yet.'

'Oh right. 'E 'asn't started yet on that one, our carver. 'E's finishing another one; a posh one it is, in the Circle of Lebanon. Someone new in a family vault. 'E'll do the Cavendish stone next.'

He glanced out of a tiny window divided into even tinier panes, dimmed with raindrops on the outside and grime and spiderwebs within.

''E was out there working this morning. I expect 'e'll

come in 'ere in a minute. 'E doesn't much like the rain. Oh, 'ere 'e comes now.'

The man who entered the lodge, the collar of his rain-streaked workman's jacket pulled up over his head, was grizzled and so old that I was surprised he could still manage such a demanding task. But his knotted hands were strong. He set down a few tools and sat next to me on the bench. I squeezed over a little to make room for him, and we greeted each other.

'Sheltering from the rain, eh?' he said. 'Visiting tombs, were you?'

'Yes. And you have been working?'

'Oh yes, I have. Gold leaf inside the letters on that one,' and he smiled largely, showing a missing front tooth. 'Which is yours? Or were you just seeing the sights?'

'No, we were visiting a new one. Sebastian Cavendish.'

'Oh right, yes. I'll be doing that one next. Poor old Joseph's finally got some company.' He smiled again gappily, and took the mug of very sugary tea that the caretaker offered him, remarking sympathetically,

'Been lonely for a long time, 'e 'as.'

'The dead people here are your friends,' I said, seeing suddenly how simple and obvious this was, and how much sense it made.

'Why, of course they are,' said the caretaker. 'We know 'em all, every one in-di-vi-dually, don't we, Jack?'

'Carved dozens o' their stones with me own 'ands,' answered the carver with quiet pride. 'And no worse than the ones that came before, if I do say so myself.'

'Did you carve Joseph Krieger's?'

'No, I didn't do that one, but I saw it done. I was

serving my apprenticeship then. I 'ad a good master; good technique and plenty of style. Those words will be legible for a long, long time yet. I'm going to use the same lettering for young Sebastian's.'

'What about Joseph Krieger's wife?' I asked, suddenly curious. 'Why isn't anything carved for her?'

'She's not buried 'ere,' he said, and then added unexpectedly, 'I remember 'er well. She came to the grave with 'er daughters twice a year to garden it a bit, clean it up, set in some flowers. Every year twice, she came. In the autumn, and she'd plant bulbs around the edge, and then in the spring, when they bloomed, to clear off the winter's debris. Only one kind of flower: yellow tulips. Never anything else. The *Black Tulip* novel came out that year, and 'alf the graves 'ere 'ad them on it the next spring, only it was the purple ones that everyone was planting – there weren't no black ones for real. But Mrs Krieger, she went on year after year, always the same thing: a ring of yellow tulips right around the edge and a grass plot in the middle. That's why I remember it so well. As soon as I'd see those tulip buds in February, I'd start expecting 'er next visit.'

Mesmerised by this discourse, I waited until he had stopped speaking and even several seconds after, afraid to disrupt the natural flow of his memory by insistent questions. When I finally spoke, it was just to gently repeat his words.

'She used to come with her daughters?'

'That's right. Just little things they were in the beginning, all dressed in black like their mother. Energetic little creatures, quite a 'andful they must have been and she a

191

widow. I saw them grow from little girls into big ones and then one year they stopped coming.'

'Do you know why?'

'I didn't then,' he said, 'but I do now, for I asked young Sebastian's mother about it last month when I met with 'er about the epitaph. One of the little girls, she was. The littler one. Anyway, it seems that the Kriegers 'ad 'ad a child who died out in the country somewhere, and was buried there, and Joseph Krieger's wife wanted to be buried with 'er child.'

'I would want the same thing, in that situation,' I said.

'She might easily 'ave asked for the child's coffin to be exhumed and brought 'ere,' he said with a note of huffiness in his voice. 'The Krieger plot is for four; all paid for and everything, it is. I wonder she didn't do that. No one told 'er, perhaps. A pity. They could 'ave all been together. It isn't too late now, either,' he added. 'I told Mrs Cavendish, I did. "Why don't you 'ave your mother brought 'ome," I said to 'er, "so you can all be together?" '

'And what did she say?'

'She said they were well where they were. But I'm thinking that she wants to keep one of the places for 'erself. Save 'er 'aving to buy one, and they're getting more expensive than they were. And it stands to reason that she'll want to be with 'er son. Poor woman,' he added in a slightly perfunctory tone, a token of respect for the unofficial aspects of mourning, so much less familiar to him than the formal ones, amongst which he felt easy and comfortable.

The rain stopped and a feeble ray of sunshine gleamed palely through the grey clouds. Rose and I got up to leave, handing our mugs back to the caretaker.

'Vanessa, everywhere we go, we find out something,' she said as we made our way out of the gate. 'Now we *know* it's all true, what we read in the notebooks about the adopted children! It's not that I didn't believe it, of course, but meeting someone who actually saw them does make a difference, doesn't it? The younger one was Tanis, and the bigger girl simply must have been Lydia!'

'Illegitimate children of Joseph Krieger,' I blurted out. This thought had been vaguely in my head since we had read about the adoption of both girls in Prosper Sainton's notebooks. But I had not liked to mention it to Rose; it seemed to open doors upon such a world of impropriety and sin and evil.

Rose looked at me in surprise.

'You really think that?' she said. 'But surely Mrs Krieger would not have wanted to adopt her husband's children by some mistress, and love them, and bring them up as her own.'

'You've heard of Edith Nesbit?' I asked thoughtfully. 'You know, the woman socialist – one of the founders of the Fabian Society. My friend Sir Oliver Lodge belongs, and so does Bertrand Russell, the mathematician – I met him once. She's published some absolutely wonderful children's books; I've read them to the twins. Anyway, they are all very advanced, these people, and everyone knows that Edith Nesbit lives with her husband and his mistress all together in one house, and they're bringing up the children of both women as one big family.'

'You call that advanced?' said Rose. 'It sounds to me like the behaviour of people from a primitive tribe somewhere, or from Biblical times.'

'No,' I said, 'the difference is that these women bring up their children together from their own choice. They feel that they are in the vanguard of a movement to break out of the bonds of conventional morality.'

She looked at me askance.

'You think Mrs Krieger was like that?'

'Well, not really,' I admitted. 'But she wouldn't have had to live with the mistress or even know her. Perhaps the mistress died. And she did long for little children to care for.'

'You're sure there was nothing at all in the rest of Sainton's diary?' she said hopefully. 'If Krieger had a mistress, there might have been rumours.'

'Oh, believe me, I looked,' I exclaimed. 'When I went to give back the ones I borrowed, I stayed in Professor Wessely's office for a long time and re-read all the earlier ones. There's no mention of such a thing at all. In fact, to be honest, Sainton actually says that Krieger did not much like women. But I wouldn't pay much attention to that. A man can dislike or despise women and have a mistress all the same. Anyway, soon after the bit we read, where they were friends, they quarrelled. Sainton would have accepted that Krieger didn't wish to play again with the Queen's Band, but Krieger went overboard being offensive about it. So they stopped seeing each other, and then in 1850 Krieger died. Sainton just mentions it in passing, and says it was a tragedy for the musical scene of London, and totally unexpected. I remember reading in Dr Bernstein's book that Lydia's father died when she was four, so it hangs together perfectly with her having been adopted in 1848 when she would have been two and her sister just a baby.'

'And then, when Mrs Krieger finally died, she wanted to go away and be buried with her dead child,' said Rose. 'She must have left specific instructions to avoid being buried here instead. If she'd said nothing, she certainly would have been.'

'Yes. It was funny how lightly that man spoke of exhumation, wasn't it? He doesn't realise that it makes us ordinary mortals shudder.'

'I don't think that was the problem,' said Rose moodily. 'I think Mrs Krieger wanted to get away from her husband. Nobody liked him. He must have been quite horrid. Why should she lie next to him for eternity instead of being in a peaceful, quiet little corner of countryside with the child that she loved? And this way she could leave the empty spaces for the two adopted children, who had barely known Krieger and needn't feel the same way about him.'

I smiled. 'I have to say in his favour that it's nice he let her adopt them,' I said. 'He probably didn't want them at all. So you have to give him some credit, as Monsieur Sainton did.'

We left the cemetery and took a cab for the long ride back to town. I sat still, letting the conversations I had just been having run through my mind. There had been a little question in my head as Rose and I were walking away from the tombstone together, but it had disappeared underneath all the information from the epitaph carver. Now it came back to me.

'Rose,' I said, 'I wonder why Sebastian was alone at home on the evening of December 31st, when everyone in the entire country was going to a party?' *Who knew he was going to be alone at home?* whispered a little voice somewhere inside me. But no – I repressed it. I was simply supposed to be finding out exactly what Sebastian had been doing all through that final day. *Yes*, came back the stubborn little voice, *and whom he was doing it with? And who might have wished that Sebastian would die?*

'He wasn't supposed to be alone at home,' she said. 'He was supposed to go to a party – Lord Warburton's grand Centennial Ball. I know it, because he and Claire and I had all three been invited to another party for the new century, but Sebastian couldn't come with us, because Mrs Cavendish wanted him to go to Lord Warburton's ball with her. Only he didn't go there, either, because he wasn't home. He hadn't been home since he had left for Zürich; he hadn't slept at home the night before, so she simply didn't know where he was. On the 31st, she expected that he would arrive or at least send a message, but he didn't, so she left by herself, thinking that he could always join them if he did get home later on.'

'She wasn't worried about his unexpected disappearance?'

'Not when he didn't arrive on the 30th as he should have. She simply thought that he had had an opportunity to stay in Zürich for another day. That wouldn't have been unusual. He was twenty-four, after all. You'd think he might have sent a telegram, but he wasn't always a particularly thoughtful person, you know. He liked to be free, and she respected that and never made him give an account of himself. On the 31st she probably felt annoyed as well as worried, as she was expecting him to accompany her to Lord Warburton's ball, and it would have been unthinkable for her not to be there, since they are engaged to be married and she was to act as hostess.

Till the last minute, she thought he would turn up, but he never did.'

'So she went to the ball by herself?'

'Yes, she really had no choice, and once she was there she had to stay nearly all night. There were fireworks and dancing and a midnight supper. The guests didn't leave the party till dawn, and then she came home exhausted to a perfectly silent house and saw Sebastian's coat and hat on the hall stand, so she assumed that he had arrived too late for the ball and had simply gone straight to bed. I know all this because the police went through it with her and then they explained everything to Claire. Mrs Cavendish went directly to bed herself, and the next morning she rose fairly early and went out. Sebastian kept irregular hours and often slept late, so she did not disturb him. It was the charwoman who found him when she came in to do the daily cleaning.'

'I wonder why Mrs Cavendish employs a charwoman,' I said. 'I would have thought she would have servants.'

'The Cavendishes didn't have enough money for live-in servants,' said Rose. 'I told you about that; Mr Cavendish left too many debts when he died. Mrs Cavendish was able to pay Sebastian's school fees, and she gave him a small allowance. He was already starting to make a living from his concerts, and they got by. They had no servants at all except for this charwoman who came in by the day, to clean the house and prepare the afternoon and the evening meal.'

'Well,' I said, 'Mrs Cavendish puts a good face upon it. She looks for all the world like an elegant lady with a personal maid to take care of her hair and her dresses.'

'She is very elegant, that's true. She must have a sewing

girl in from time to time. I don't imagine she actually does her own sewing.'

'Or her washing,' I added.

'That probably gets sent out as well,' said Rose. 'It all costs less than having servants living in the house. And when she marries Lord Warburton, she'll be very wealthy and have all the service she wants. I suppose the prospect of beginning a new and much easier life cannot but help her a little at this awful time. Lord Warburton is a widower himself; from the little I've seen of them together, they seem very well suited. Of a similar temperament, somehow. Very traditional, very upright, very proper.'

'I hope all will be well for them,' I said thoughtfully. 'I suppose that the charwoman will no longer be employed by Mrs Cavendish once the marriage takes place.'

'Surely not. They'll have plenty of servants then. But I'm sure the poor woman will find another place of work. Only too many people need charwomen nowadays, don't they? And probably Mrs Cavendish will give her a recommendation.'

'I would like to talk to that charwoman,' I said. 'I really would. I wonder if you could find out, or ask Claire to find out who she is.'

'I suppose that wouldn't be difficult,' said Rose. 'But what on earth do you expect to learn from her?'

'I don't know,' I said. 'But it occurs to me that it's quite incredible what servants can know about the secrets hidden within families, and I suppose that the same must apply to charwomen.'

'Charwomen, gravediggers and who knows who else,' she said. 'You're right, of course. I'll find out about her for you.'

CHAPTER FIFTEEN

*In which Vanessa meets a charwoman who knows no secrets
but a little fact which suddenly changes everything*

I stood waiting patiently outside the imposing building
where Mrs Cavendish had her flat, occasionally glancing at
my watch. Rose had obtained from Claire the information
that the charwoman, Mrs Munn, generally arrived at the
Cavendish home at eleven in the morning and left at nine
o'clock, after dinner had been served and cleared away.
The woman had spent ten hours of every day but Sunday,
for years, probably, in Sebastian's home. There could be
little, I thought, that she did not know about the family.

Rose, who had seen Mrs Munn briefly once or twice at
the house while visiting, had described her to me as a small,
thin woman in black. This description perfectly fit the
woman who stepped out of the front door at some minutes
before nine o'clock, carrying a handbag and an umbrella.

'Mrs Munn?' I said in a quiet and reassuring voice,

stepping out of the shadows. In spite of these precautions, she jumped, and threw me a look of suspicion and deep annoyance.

'Certainly not!' she snapped. 'My name is Mrs Davenport-Brown, and I would be very grateful if you would take yourself away from these premises at once, and cease importuning the residents!' She stalked away in a huff, her nose in the air, and, watching her, I berated myself for having failed, in the dusk, to notice her haughty bearing and the refined cut of her coat.

Five minutes later another small, thin woman in black emerged, this one carrying a generous holdall. I took a closer look before speaking again.

'Mrs Munn?'

Startled, she looked at me with an expression not dissimilar to Mrs Davenport-Brown's. I was, however, fingering one of those notes that are, sadly, so useful and necessary to working people as to quite modify their behaviour on occasion, and I now slipped this into her hand.

'I should very much like to speak with you for a short time,' I said gently. 'I do not mean to disturb you, but perhaps you could spare me a few moments?'

'I need to get home,' she said, looking me up and down. But perhaps home was not such a very alluring prospect for her, for her reluctance to accompany me appeared quite ready to be overcome.

'We could perhaps sit down somewhere for half an hour,' I proposed, and her face brightened.

'And get a bite to eat, maybe?' she said hopefully.

'Of course, if you wish! Have you not dined yet? You don't eat dinner at your work?'

'You've no idea how difficult the times are, madam,' she said, peering at me closely in the gloaming, as though to gauge whether I was of a class that could possibly comprehend her problems. 'What with my husband sick at home, it's been years now he can't walk, after his accident falling off the building at work.' She fingered her bag almost unconsciously while speaking.

'You bring your food home to him?' I guessed, observing her gesture.

'And it isn't a great deal, either,' she said defensively. 'Mrs Cavendish don't eat like a queen, she don't. A cutlet and some beans and pudding, that will be her dinner. It's next to nothing since the young man died. I don't know how we'll manage. There used to be leftovers, there did. Before.'

'Oh my goodness,' I said. 'I should like to take you to dinner. I know a perfect place, truly I do. It's very near here; just behind King's Cross. A ten-minute walk. Would you come there with me?'

'I'd like to, madam, only my husband won't know where I am.'

As we drew under a gaslight, I saw that the poor woman looked altogether torn and distressed by my proposal. She was indeed very thin, and the prospect of a good meal must have been an attractive one indeed. I had a glimpse of a life lived on the very boundary of misery. If an extra penny ever came the way of this poor woman, she was probably obliged to spend it on having her shoes repaired or other details required in order to look at least decent enough to enter the handsome building on Russell Square.

'It should be all right if I don't take too long,' she said.

'It happens that I stay extra some evenings, when Mrs Cavendish needs it. It brings in a few more pennies, so even if supper is late on those days, sometimes it runs to a sausage. He don't mind waiting if it's for a good reason.'

We walked together to Jenny's Corner, a little restaurant that I would never have discovered, let alone dined at, had it not been for extraordinary circumstances linked to another mystery, of many years ago now. Jenny had been warm and comforting in those difficult days, and now, distinctly older and distinctly rounder, she was still warm and comforting, and her little restaurant still served the weekly round of customer favourites that had kept her making a modest but tidy profit year after year. Arthur and I went there at least once each year as a matter of friendship and of memory, and even though we were perhaps a slightly strange sight in the busy little place crowded with working bachelors, we were always made welcome in a corner and treated with a warm-hearted and spontaneous kindness that was worth more than any ceremonious courtesy in the world.

I was eager to take Mrs Munn there; it seemed to me of all possible places in London the one I knew most suited to making her feel at home and drawing her out. As we walked, talking of nothing more than the wintry chill and the difficulties of sore feet and aching backs, I saw that she was agitated by a certain anxiety, as well she might be, having no idea where we were going. However, as we drew within sight of the bustling little restaurant, from whose slightly open door emerged a cloud of steam, smoke and conversation, she heaved a pleased sigh. We entered, and a sallow girl in a checked dress and apron came to show us to a table.

'Please, bring us two of the daily specials,' I told her, 'and do tell Jenny that Mrs Weatherburn is here. I should love to greet her when she has a moment.'

Jenny arrived moments later, carrying a plate in each hand, piping hot and laden with a generous quantity of beef, gravy, mashed potatoes and green beans. Having set them down in front of us, she enveloped me in a quick hug – a tradition of many years' standing – and asked after Arthur and the twins. Then she turned to examine my guest, summed her up in a moment, and extended a plump, red hand in friendship.

'Glad to meet you, love,' she said, grasping Mrs Munn's bony one. 'Any friend of Mrs Weatherburn's is a friend of mine. Please do enjoy your suppers. There'll be pudding when you want it, and a cup o' tea if you need it.' And she bustled back to her kitchen.

Mrs Munn looked at the food with an expression of ineffable sadness. I thought of the poor remains she had packed away in her bag, which were to constitute her husband's meagre dinner. It seemed unfair, but I could not think of any way to mend it right now; one could hardly put mashed potatoes and gravy into a holdall. But here was Mrs Munn, who worked hard all day, sitting in front of a succulent and well-deserved meal looking sad, and it seemed to me that the most urgent thing right now was that she should enjoy it as much as she could. So I picked up my silverware and encouragingly scooped up a generous forkful, and was sincerely delighted to see her follow suit.

I did not attempt to enter into any explanations until the meal was finished, and Mrs Munn must have been a bit overwhelmed by it all, for she did not ask a single question.

But over steaming teacups, while I was searching for the right words to begin, she spoke suddenly.

'There must be a reason, madam, for you doing all this,' she said. 'But I can't guess what it might be, not even now that I've eaten a square meal and my head is straight. You want something of me, madam, I'm certain, but I'm afraid I shan't be able to give it to you, for I can't imagine what such as I might be able to do or say could be useful to someone like you. At any rate, though, as long as you don't tell me, it's certain I won't know.' She smiled for the first time that evening, and I suddenly perceived a little glimpse of a past Mrs Munn, probably gay and laughing and hopeful that life would hold many pleasant surprises in store.

London is filled with women such as Mrs Munn; women who work so hard they are practically enslaved, who eat so little they nearly faint, and who have the sole care of helpless dependents. Surely something is very wrong with our society, which allows such a thing to be so common that no one even takes any notice.

'All I want,' I told her, 'is to know a little bit about Sebastian Cavendish. You see, his friends are very upset about the way he died. They have asked me to see if I can try to understand why he did it.'

'There, I'm not surprised,' she said. 'You've gone and asked me a question that I've no idea about. I can't tell you why he did it, madam. It's a terrible sad thing, and he died in a terrible way, too. Very sick, horrible sick all night he was. To think of anyone wanting to do that to themselves.'

'You were the one who found the body? That must have been a terrible experience for you.'

'I knew something was wrong the moment I came in

the house that morning,' she said. 'It was so weirdly quiet. I saw right away that Mrs Cavendish was out, her things being gone from the coat rack, but Master Sebastian was still in, yet everything was silent. It seems to me now that it was too silent, and I knew something was wrong as I came in the door. But perhaps I didn't know it quite so clearly. I did think he might simply be sleeping, as a lot of people had come home from their parties in the wee hours that night. I didn't do anything at first, but, around midday, I wondered if I should be preparing something for him to eat or not, and I just knocked on the door and opened it a crack, to check. Oh, madam, there was a terrible smell of sickness! I just made out that he was lying on his bed, but dressed in his clothes, and that something was horribly wrong! I couldn't bear it – I didn't take one step inside the room. I ran out of the flat screaming and calling for help, and the neighbours came out and they helped me; one lady gave me some smelling salts and a gentleman went in to see what it was, and then he ran for the police. I couldn't bear to take another look, not at anything, madam; not even when they carried out the body. Then I had to clean up the room, though. It was a bad way to die; a bad, horrible business. Poor Master Sebastian. Whatever made him do such a thing!'

'Had you known him for many years?'

'Going on for ten years now,' she said. 'He was a big lad already when I first came, but such a nice one. A bit wild, perhaps, about getting his own way and such, but with a good heart. Always a smile and a nice word for me, he had, and when Christmas time came and Mrs Cavendish would give me an envelope, he'd always add something from his own pocket, and a bunch of flowers, every single Christmas for ten years although I told him it was too much for a poor old woman like me, flowers in December. Every year a bunch of flowers. They were the only flowers anyone's ever given me since the day I was married. They did look nice in a jug on the table at home. Brightened up the room, they did.'

'You must have known Sebastian well after all those years. Do you really not have any idea at all why he wanted to die? Any reason at all?'

'No, madam. I have asked myself. But really, it can't have been anything that I could know about. He must have kept it very close, whatever it was.'

'Or,' I said, 'it happened because of something he found out in the last few days before he died. Some secret about the family, perhaps.'

'I wouldn't know about anything like that.'

'Really not? You never overheard any talk with his mother about anything particular having to do with the family? I do have a reason for asking. I really think that Sebastian did discover something about his family before he died.'

'I don't remember any such discussion, madam; not any kind of talk between them about anything you might call secret, or intimate. They didn't have that kind of relation together. I'd say that if they had any secrets at all, they'd most likely have kept them from one another. They weren't close like some mothers are with their sons. Mrs Cavendish is a very private person.'

'Quite. Well, did you ever happen to hear any talk about Mrs Cavendish's father? There wouldn't have been anything secret about him, I suppose.'

'Him, the old violinist? Yes, I heard him mentioned. Guests spoke of him pretty often. When Master Sebastian was still at school, he'd often get out his violin to play for guests. I'd be serving dinner and clearing up, so I heard him many a time. What a noise he could make on that violin of his! Sometimes the upstairs neighbours even banged on the ceiling, if they thought it was going on too long.'

'And what did you hear about Sebastian's grandfather?'

'Not much. Now that I think of it, Mrs Cavendish and Master Sebastian didn't seem to like to talk of him much. Guests would ask sometimes if Mrs Cavendish had any memories of her dad, or souvenirs or pictures, and she'd say that he'd died when she was a baby and she knew nothing of him at all. She'd get a bit short sometimes when he was spoken of, though she was always polite, of course, but I don't think she much liked to talk about him.'

'Did you ever hear anything about Mrs Cavendish having been an adopted child? That the old violinist was not really her father at all?'

She looked at me in surprise.

'No, I never heard a breath about such an idea as that. Is it true?'

'Apparently it is, and it seems that both Mrs Cavendish and Sebastian knew about it. Can you not remember ever hearing anything of the sort at all?'

She thought for a while.

'Not that. But there was a feeling that the memory of the old man wasn't much appreciated. I recall as Mrs Cavendish used to not like when visitors would say that Master Sebastian played like his grandfather. "His way of playing comes from inside himself," she'd say. I don't think she actually even liked him playing music very much at all. She hoped he wouldn't become a musician. You asked about discussions; there were some when he left school and had to choose a profession. Then he said there was no question he'd go anywhere but to that music school, and she was very much against it and tried to persuade him to study law like his father.'

'Was Sebastian's father alive then? Did you know him?'

'Why, of course he was. He only died – let me see, when was it? It was five or six years ago. Yes, he was alive when I first came, though in poor health. He suffered badly from the gout, poor man. Such twinges he used to have in his toe. I helped him bathe his feet with special salts sometimes. Terrible, the shape they had.'

'Poor man,' I sympathised. 'And tell me, what did he say about Sebastian becoming a musician?'

'He said what will be, will be, and Sebastian should do what he wanted if he could make a success of it. Mrs Cavendish didn't like it. She would have rather her husband support her point of view, I guess, but she was never one to make any kind of quarrel, so she put the best possible face on it and let him go to the music school and didn't say anything about it any more. I guess she became proud of him later, when he started to play concerts in front of people and all. At least she would keep the concert programmes on her dressing table.'

'I should think so,' I said, quite intrigued by all that I was hearing. 'I would be proud, too, to have a son who played the violin as well as that. But if the old violinist was really not her father, I suppose I can imagine that it might annoy her if people kept saying that Sebastian's talent came from him, since she knew it wasn't true yet didn't like to publicly explain why. A person can hardly go around shouting that she is adopted.'

'I don't know anything about her being adopted or not,' Mrs Munn repeated.

'I have also heard that Mrs Cavendish had a sister,' I said.

'A sister? That's news to me as well. I never saw anyone from the mistress's family. I thought it was clear there wasn't a soul left.'

'Well, I know there was a sister, but I don't know if she's alive or dead now. But I have a rather strong suspicion that Sebastian didn't know about that sister, and that he found out that she existed just before he died.'

'You mean, when he looked in the papers in the desk?' said Mrs Munn with a gleam of understanding. I looked up sharply.

'What do you mean? When did he look at papers?'

'I noticed him looking through some of his mother's papers before he went away again,' she said with an air of backing down quickly. 'It doesn't mean anything, though. He was just looking at papers.'

'Why do you say that he went away again? Why "again"?'

'Well, he had already been and gone to Switzerland with his violin, for some grand concert over there.'

'Yes, of course. But that's only one trip.'

'Yes. And he came back, and left again.'

I was so excited that I forced myself to remain perfectly still for several moments, not wanting her to be startled and clam up, realising she had said something very important.

Her words constituted the very first clue I had yet obtained about the gap – the missing hours between his arrival in London on December 30th (assuming that he had really left Zürich on December 29th as it seemed that he had) and his death on December 31st. From December 30th to December 31st, I still had no idea what he had been doing with himself. And now it seemed that a clue had suddenly fallen into my lap. And such a simple one!

'When did you see him looking at papers?' I asked very quietly.

'On the afternoon of the day before the day he died. On the 30th, it would have been.'

'At home, at the flat?'

'Of course, that's where I work. Naturally he came home after his trip. I did think that after having travelled in the train all day and all night, he'd be happy to get home and just stay there, but no. He was a restless one, he was. Off again right away, the same evening, and didn't sleep in his bed.'

'And you don't know where he went?'

'No, I've not the least idea. How should I?'

'Did he talk to you at all?'

'No, only just to say "Hello, Mrs Munn, how are you today?" He didn't even call out to me when he left. And when he saw that I saw him at the desk, he closed the study door.'

'Tell me exactly what you remember. What time did he come in and what did he do?'

'I can't be so exact. He came in in the afternoon and put his hat and overcoat and his violin and his suitcase all down in the hall. I heard him come in, then I don't know, he poured himself a drink, I think, and went about the house. I heard nothing at first, being in the kitchen in the back. But after a while, I came looking for him to ask him if he'd like a bite to eat after all the travelling. He was sitting on the floor in the study with the desk drawers all open. Mrs Cavendish keeps her desk locked, but I never thought there was anything special in there, only that she kept her money inside sometimes. Not even that she'd have private letters or anything like that. It's always been locked; no one ever paid attention, that was just her way. Master Sebastian grew up in that house, but I don't think he ever bothered to wonder what was in his mother's desk, for what should be there but ordinary papers and bills and such? Still, I'll wager he knew where the key was, for she'd open the desk sometimes to take out some money, and she used to open it up to put in his school reports when he was younger. Kids are like monkeys – they know everything about their home.'

'You must know quite everything there is to know about that flat, too, don't you?' I asked innocently. 'After so many years, I mean.'

'I never knew where she kept the key before and never asked myself,' she replied. 'I never came upon it in any of my work. But I know where it is now, for Master Sebastian put it away after he put the papers back. He came out of the study and I saw him go into his mother's room, and I went in after he had gone to check nothing was out of place and I saw that the grey hatbox wasn't stacked straight on top of the striped one as always, so I looked in. It was right inside the ribbons of the black bonnet she wore for mourning. It was a clever place to keep the key; no one would ever have any reason to look inside one of Mrs Cavendish's hatboxes and come upon the key by accident. I certainly never did.'

'What did you do with the key when you found it?'

'Why nothing, I left it there, of course.'

'And you never told Mrs Cavendish that Sebastian had looked through the desk?'

'Certainly not. What business was it of mine? I never even thought of it. I mean, when I saw him looking in there, all I thought was that he was needing a bit of money quickly. It didn't seem important.'

'And then he left?'

'Yes. Well, first asked me to draw him a bath, and he bathed and changed his clothing. And then he left.'

'Did he take the suitcase with him?'

'Yes, madam, he did. And the violin, too.'

I stared at her, digesting all of this information.

'And you didn't tell anyone about this?'

'No one asked me about it,' she said. 'I don't even know why you're asking me now, madam. I can't see that it has any importance. After all, he's dead, poor young man.'

CHAPTER SIXTEEN

In which Vanessa persuades a youngster
to allow himself to be led into doubtful ways

The day after Mrs Munn's extraordinary revelations, I came to a decision: there was something that absolutely had to be done, but I could not do it by myself. I needed help, and I thought I knew just where I might find it. At least, I thought I knew, but now I began to feel slightly lost. I went past Petticoat Lane and on down the Whitechapel Road, hesitating slightly. Where was the place exactly?

Around me bustled the life of the East End, as familiar as my own past and as foreign as an exotic, distant country. Yes, this was it. I turned onto Fieldgate Street and walked along, studying the miserable surroundings, until I came to the dingy little opening to Settles Street and stopped in front of the familiar tenement house where I had once visited David and Rivka Mendel for help in solving a case, only to discover that they were more deeply involved that I could have imagined. Rivka's cousin Jonathan had been courting my dearest friend Emily at the time, and although her subsequent engagement to the brilliant young mathematician Roland Hudson had put a stop to that, they had remained friends, and she mentioned him and his cousins to me now and again. Emily was always busy, however, trying to accomplish the feat of writing a doctoral thesis in mathematics at the University of London – the only one that would admit women to such a course of work – and I didn't see her often any more. Four years had gone by since those days, and I was not even sure whether Rivka and David still lived in the same flat.

A strange woman, her head wrapped up in a turban-like shawl, answered my knock at once. She was both unfriendly and suspicious at first, and did not appear to have a particularly advanced grasp of the English language, but my querying repetitions of David and Rivka's names eventually brought forth a response. She called forth a somewhat dirty small girl wearing an oversized dress and braids, and spoke to her in her own tongue. The girl grabbed me by the hand without ceremony and towed me unresistingly out of the house, down the street and around the corner to Greenfield Street. Unable to express the full wealth of her ideas, she grinned up at me, revealing an amusing mixture of large, small and half-grown teeth, and contented herself by repeating 'Rivka, Rivka Mendel' and nodding vigorously. She seemed to know exactly where she was going, so I followed along, emitting a concurring 'Rivka Mendel' with a satisfying feeling that our communication was by no means as impossible as might have been thought.

At a distance of between five and ten minutes from the

old place, she stopped at another house, somewhat less peeling and rickety than her own. The front door stood open and a number of small children ran in and out, their faces, hands and knees of divers shades of lighter and darker grey.

'Sammy!' shouted the spunky child holding my hand, and one boy detached himself from the group and came over to her. I stared at him, admiring the wonders of time. A long-legged and knobbly-kneed child with bright brown eyes looked up at me, and I recalled the little Samuel tumbling about his mother's knees four years ago, now a great lad of six. A smaller boy drew up next to him, and then a third, successively decreasing in size. These three listened to the girl's explanations for a moment, then the oldest one turned to me and confirmed the situation by enquiring in perfect English: 'You want to see Rivka Mendel? She is my mother. Come upstairs.'

I followed him, and the two smaller lads followed me; like a small train chugging up a mountain, we mounted higher and higher until we arrived at the very top floor, where Samuel flung open the door and shouted out,

'Someone to see you, Ima!'

'Oh!' She turned around from where she had been bending over a baby, and straightened up, her hand to her head, pushing stray locks underneath the scarf that covered it, tied up in a knot at her nape.

'Vanessa!' she cried with real emotion as soon as she saw me, and ran into my arms with such pleasure that I felt that I had almost let slip a cherished friendship by keeping away for so long.

'Are all these your children?' I asked, amazed as the

little group milled about the room, too curious to disappear back down the stairs.

'Yes, four of them now,' she said proudly. 'This is our baby Esther; a precious little girl, finally, after three great boys!' She picked up the little creature, enveloped in a cloud of pink and frills as though to celebrate the tiny femininity of her, and gestured me to an armchair, while she set about with one hand preparing a pot of tea, chattering all the while about the family's improved circumstances, her husband's promotion at his bank, the new flat with its three rooms and its own water closet and bath.

'And you, Vanessa?' she asked with interest, setting the teapot on the table and adding teacups, spoons, milk and sugar.

I was mentally searching for some explanation as to the stubborn invariability in the number of my children, when she clarified the real import of her question by adding,

'Are you still solving mysterious cases?'

'Sometimes,' I admitted. 'In fact, to be honest, that is why I came. I need help, and I thought that your husband's brother, young Ephraim, might be able to do something for me.' I blushed as I spoke, for I suspected that the plan I had in mind for the said Ephraim would not please his family, were they to know about it in any detail, although it would surely appeal to the adventurous temperament I remembered him to possess from my acquaintance with him four years earlier as an 11-year-old imp of exceptional capabilities.

A look of surprise crossed Rivka's face, and she reflected for a moment, then said,

'Well, I must say that I cannot imagine anything that

would please him more.' But she didn't look absolutely delighted, and went on, 'I must tell you that Ephraim has never forgotten you and your work and the help he gave you, and ever since that time he has nourished the desire to become a detective. David does not really approve of such intentions on the part of his young brother. He would much prefer him to start work as an errand boy in his own bank, and rise through the ranks. But he says that Ephraim's fantasy will probably pass before he is an adult, and, at worst, he says it is surely better than the professions of most of the people in this part of town, who run about the streets of London with boxes, hawking everything from oranges to spectacles, and never knowing if they will sell enough to feed their family on any given day. Still, though, I'm afraid David won't much like your idea.' She stopped and sipped tea, then added, 'And yet, finding out the truth as you do is a *mitzvah*. An act of pure goodness.'

Another moment of reflection, during which I remained prudently silent, and she finally said, 'I think the fairest thing would be for you to talk to Ephraim yourself. He will be home from school at any moment. In fact, he may be home already if he has not dallied too much with his friends on the road. Shall I send Samuel to fetch him? Or perhaps we could simply walk there together? It is not far, and it will provide little Esther with an outing.'

She wrapped the baby up well – clearly there was no such item as a perambulator anywhere about, nor would it have been possible to negotiate one up and down four flights of stairs – and carried her in her arms, leaving her three tiny ones under the supervision of the oldest boy of the group at play about the doorway. She bounced the child gently up and down as we walked along the lane and around the corner, and turned right and left amongst ever more of the gloomy, dirty and rickety tenement houses that lined the road. Even the flowerpots in front of the occasional window, that must have cheered the miserable aspect of it all with a few bright-coloured geraniums in the spring, now held nothing but frostbitten, blackened stalks, and the roadway itself was covered with traces of slush, grit and unidentifiable filth. Yet the streets were very lively, filled with people, young and old, bustling about their activities; some stood at the doorways of their grimy shops and others wheeled carts, all calling out their wares; adults were making purchases and arguing about the prices, children were running about, playing, getting in the way and occasionally snatching a fruit that had rolled upon the ground with a gesture as quick as a monkey's, to the tune of shouting and scolding from the annoyed vendor.

Eventually we reached the house where Ephraim still lived with his older brother and their mother, Rivka's mother-in-law, and knocked at their door, from behind which enough sounds could be heard to tell us that more than one person was certainly at home.

The door was flung welcomingly wide, and Ephraim's freckled face looked out. It burst into a spontaneous grin of pleasure at the sight of me, which unmistakably corroborated Rivka's assertions. The impish child had grown up into a red-haired young man of fifteen, taller than me now in his stockinged feet, and with something of the relaxed pleasantness of his brother David, but more of a twinkle in his laughing eyes.

'Mrs Weatherburn!' he shouted, half at me, half back over his shoulder at the other occupants of the flat.

'Mrs Weatherburn wishes to speak to you particularly,' said Rivka in a low voice, glancing at me. 'I think it might be better if she could speak to you alone, rather than go inside now. I will visit with your mother for a while, if that is all right; not for too long, however, since I've left the boys at home.' Ephraim caught on instantly, pulled on his boots, leaving the laces dragging, and ushered Rivka inside with her baby – then he hurried onto the landing, pulling the door closed behind him.

'Better not say anything to my mother,' he said, 'she'll ask where I'm going and all. Oh, I'm pleased to see you again! I have so many things to ask you! But do tell me – how are you? What have you come for? You look very well indeed. Do tell me why you have come? Is it another mystery? Is it?'

He led me down the stairs and out of the building as we spoke, and we walked along the road. In spite of the crowd and the cold, it was certainly the best possible place for a discreet conversation, as no one had a spare moment to notice or overhear a thing, not even to mention that few of the people surrounding us had the good fortune to speak English as well as Ephraim. Like his brothers, he had been awarded a scholarship to a regular British day-school, to which his mother had wisely elected to send him instead of keeping him at the local institutions where the children studied nothing but the Bible and the laws of the Jewish religion, entirely in their own language. In my opinion this rendered them unfit to ever emerge from their own miserable corner of London, which resembled nothing

219

more than an Eastern European village transported bodily across the continent and set down unexpectedly on the edge of the metropolis.

'I do need help,' I said, 'and I cannot think of anyone who could possibly do what I need, except for you.' I stopped and purposely heaved a melancholy sigh. 'But I am afraid you will not want to do it. It is a problem.'

'Oh, but I will!' he said eagerly. 'Of course I will! Why wouldn't I?'

'Because,' I said, 'it is unfortunately something that might appear to be both bad and somewhat dangerous. But it's in a good cause.'

'Oh,' he said, very slightly crestfallen. He appeared to reflect for a moment, and I could hardly blame him. Surely if one is going to launch oneself into bad and dangerous activities at someone else's behest, one wishes to be certain that the instigator is trustworthy. Our previous experiences together had left me with a great stock of moral credit within the Mendel family, but still, that was four long years ago and they knew very little about me. Ephraim had doubtless been brought up with strict moral values. I awaited his final decision with interest.

'But you will tell me exactly what it is all about?' he finally said, a little meekly.

I laughed.

'It's a bargain. I will, and, moreover, you are only to do what I ask if you are as convinced as I am that it is necessary, possible, and ultimately not harmful,' I said. 'What do you want to know first: the what, or the why?'

'The what,' he responded at once. 'And probably I'd better know the when, as well!'

I hesitated. In spite of my innermost conviction of the justice, the necessity and the importance of what I was about to propose doing, some fundamental inhibition still prevented me from feeling quite open and above board about going so far as to rope a young and perfectly innocent boy into my plans. Yet I felt it really could not go wrong – at least, hardly – and the danger was only slight. A vision of Ephraim tearing down the streets of London pursued by bobbies shouting and waving their sticks streamed through my head.

'If I were to ask you to commit a small crime in a just cause,' I said, 'which would very soon be made good, and in which no one is hurt, would you be able to consider it?'

'Why not, if no one is the worse for it?' he said cheerily. 'What kind of crime?'

'I need you to snatch an elderly lady's bag and run away with it as fast as you can,' I told him, 'to a secret place which I will tell you, where I will be waiting for you. In her bag is a key to a flat. If you are willing to help me, we will go there together and you will stand guard at the door while I search inside as fast as I can.'

A frank mixture of astonishment, shock, dismay and admiration gleamed into his eyes.

'Oh my,' he remarked. 'But you will you tell me what you've found, won't you? But no, before I ask that, I should ask whether you mean the poor old lady to get her things back?'

'Certainly. As soon as I am finished, you will take the bag to the lady's house and give a penny to a small boy to carry it in to her, keeping an eye on him to see that he does it at once. And I will put something inside the bag to compensate her for the disagreeable experience. But we must make the search directly we get the key, for although I don't think she would go to the police, she might just do so if an officer happened to be passing by on his beat. And if she tells him that she is frightened because she has a key to this flat in her bag and it was just stolen, he might rush there post-haste to check for thieves. I'm a little worried about that, and so we'll have to work incredibly fast.'

'Oh my,' he said again. 'Do you know what we are looking for? Are you actually going to take anything?'

'I don't know exactly what I am looking for, but I do know exactly where to look. It won't take long, and, with luck, I don't think I will need to take anything or to leave any trace at all of my presence in the house. Hopefully no one will ever know.'

'How exciting,' he said. 'When is this all to happen?'

'Very soon,' I said. 'I have simply been waiting for an opportunity to be absolutely certain that the lady who lives in the flat will be out when I need to go there, and, as a matter of fact, that opportunity has just arisen. Next Thursday there is to be a private concert and ceremony at the town house of a certain Lord, who is engaged to be married to this lady, and she is certain to attend.'

Indeed, contrary to all my expectations, Professor Wessely's letter to Mrs Cavendish, which must have been redacted with an unusual level of tact, had met with astonishing success. She had apparently consulted her betrothed, for the result was that Lord Warburton had accepted to become the patron of young Wolfe Wolfinsohn until his majority, and an event had been organised at which the guests were to combine such friends of Lord

Warburton as might also be interested by the possibility of transforming themselves into patrons of the arts, and musicians, both eminent professionals and friends of Sebastian. Not only was little Wolfe to be publicly presented with the gift of a monthly pension, modest indeed in view of Lord Warburton's fortune but quite sufficient to cover the child's expenses, but he was to play a short concert, and there was also to be a grand surprise, revealed to no one before the ceremony itself.

Rose and Claire were of course invited, and Rose passed me her card.

'This will get you inside,' she said, 'and no one will notice a thing. Lord Warburton and Mrs Cavendish will each think you were on the other's list of guests, and there will be quite enough people present for you to remain perfectly unnoticed. Do go – you never know whom you might meet, or what you might observe.'

'So it is to be Thursday?' said Ephraim, counting off the days on his fingers.

'Yes. Thursday, at nine o'clock in the evening. We will be at our posts from eight-thirty. I mustn't miss this opportunity.'

'We shall do it all right,' he said confidently. 'But when are you going to tell me what it's all about?'

'This minute, if you like,' I said, spotting the gold and white front of a Lyons a short distance up the Whitechapel Road, along which I was trying to keep up with Ephraim's step, whose rapidity was probably representative of a half-conscious effort to distance himself from his mother, the hub of his world and the human embodiment of his conscience. I drew him inside and ordered tea and cakes, as always blessing Mr Lyons for the recent creation of these unpoetic but clean and orderly places, which offered to an incalculable number of chilled, lonely women and shy, impoverished working girls a cup of tea or a sausage roll when no other place would be safe or suitable.

Since the first Lyons had opened six years ago, they had multiplied like mushrooms all over London, thus proving the existence of a widespread, long-repressed and frustrated demand. If only there were more Mr Lyons about, I thought, to answer the multitude of other ignored needs of women; all the infinity of little needs that combined into one great, giant need to be allowed to emerge from the shadows of a uniquely private life into the sunshine of the grand world of ideas and actions. I should not grudge them their profit, and should wish all of their pockets filled with gold, if only they would be so noble as to come to our aid and free us from our prison, the bars of which are made of unsuitability, modesty and masculine decree. Poor dear Queen Victoria, as long as she continues to champion by word, act and example, the familiar concept that woman's sphere is the home and that public appearance is to be shunned, her reign will not have the honour of being the cradle of revolutionary change. But she is eighty and a new century is beginning, and we shall see what we shall see. In the meantime, thank goodness for Lyons, and for all the individual efforts of women – with particular attention to mathematicians, cellists and detectives – to thrust vibrant green shoots out from the rich soil of the private home, and let them grow and thrive in the open air.

In front of the steaming cups, I told Ephraim the story from the beginning. His life kept him at such a distance from the people concerned in my story that I felt as discreet in talking to him about them as though I had been talking to myself, or simply telling him the story of a novel. He drank it all in with passionate interest. It was much more than a mere story to him. It was an initiation.

'How dreadful to have wanted to die without explaining why. You *must* find out,' he cried, and his words and his tone reflected the sympathy, the innate curiosity, and the profound desire to understand and penetrate to the heart of things that characterises the heart of a detective. I spoke to him as to a younger colleague, he responded in kind, and my heart was pleasantly warmed with the prospect of having a willing and able travelling companion to accompany me over some of the worst humps in my lonely and disturbing journeys.

CHAPTER SEVENTEEN

*In which Vanessa causes an infraction to be committed
and commits one herself*

I stood by the long, cloth-covered table laden with sumptuous refreshments, holding the champagne flute with which a white-gloved footman had kindly provided me from a circulating tray, and trying to keep out of the way of bumping by the people who crowded all about. Everyone was eating, drinking and uttering pleasant remarks on the subject of the delightful concert to which we had just been treated, the remarkable talent on the part of one so young, the admirable generosity of Lord Warburton who was undertaking the support of the boy for the duration of his studies, and the extraordinary, unexpected and touching gesture of Mrs Cavendish. Indeed, at the conclusion of the formal words pronounced by Lord Warburton on the subject of his pleasure at being able to contribute something useful to so worthy a cause, she had stepped forward, dressed in the deepest mourning, and, with no more than an inaudible mumble, thrust a violin case into the boy's hands and then sat down again abruptly. Lord Warburton helped the child open the case and extract from it a violin so beautiful that those in the audience not familiar with it gasped as it was held up to view: the rich tones of red-gold varnish, the burnished appearance that only age could provide, and above all the extraordinary lion's head with its roaring open mouth that replaced the traditional scroll.

This, then, was the announced surprise: Mrs Cavendish had given Wolfe Sebastian's violin. The splendid beauty and generosity of this gift, from a woman so grievously bereaved, was much admired by the assembled guests. Even with all the admirable self-control at her command, I noticed that Mrs Cavendish closed her eyes momentarily as the dark rectangular case left her hands, and averted her gaze from the violin when it was shown. I thought of the recently dug grave at Highgate, and of my twins, and of the unspeakable pain of losing a child to grinning death. Mrs Cavendish's mother had also known that pain, I recalled, and a sudden urge rose up inside me to know more about what had happened to that other girl, so long ago.

The concert that followed lasted no longer than a half-hour, as Lord Warburton was no doubt wary of unduly taxing the concentration abilities of his aristocratic guests, but it displayed young Wolfe to his best advantage as he played turn by turn religious music, lilting melodies and pieces of astonishing virtuosity. His teacher sat in the front row, the new violin on his lap, fingering its wood and strings gently, listening, and nodding his head. When it was over there was polite applause, and a pair of wide double doors was opened, leading into the dining room in which the long and well-laden tables had been exquisitely prepared.

I stood by the table, trying to be unnoticeable, and kept my eyes on Mrs Cavendish. My one fear was that the emotion of the evening would prove too much for her, and that she would request to be taken home – which would have seriously interfered with my plans! I was relieved to see, however, that between the compliments of the guests, a glass of champagne, and above all the considerate and protective behaviour of Lord Warburton, who stood near her, his hand on her elbow, she appeared to be reasonably master of the situation, and to have no intention of retiring. As I waited and watched, I followed Lord Warburton with my eyes, and admired his kind air and his upright bearing.

And I wondered suddenly.

How would such a man react if told that the sister of his bride-to-be was a madwoman? A man of noble birth, who bore an ancient tradition in his blood, and a man who, according to John Milrose, was a believer in Galton's plan of eugenics, according to which the English race must be improved and strengthened by enforced sterilisation of anyone who was suspected of any kind of hereditary mental disease.

If the truth were known, he might no longer wish to marry Mrs Cavendish. Even though she was beyond the age of bearing children, such a marriage would fly in the face of his beliefs and render him a laughing-stock amongst his peers and colleagues. Might not Sebastian have been forcibly stopped from bringing the knowledge of Lydia's existence to the attention of the eugenicist Lord? My eyes, which were resting on Mrs Cavendish, moved slowly over to her betrothed.

What if, in fact, Lord Warburton had been told the truth – what if Sebastian had discovered that Lydia was still alive, hidden away somewhere, and had gone to Lord Warburton to tell him about her and demand help. What if, shocked by the discovery, Lord Warburton realised that it would render his marriage impossible, and yet simultaneously that his love for Mrs Cavendish was too strong to be denied? What if, locked in a dreadful bind, he could neither renounce nor accept his coming marriage? Reserved and aristocratic as he was, it was obvious that he was deeply enamoured, and, indeed, Mrs Cavendish was a very beautiful woman, even if some of her glow was due to arsenical treatment. This evening, she was the very picture of noble and touching grief, allied with the infinite benevolence of a goddess. Was it out of the question that he might wish to solve the problem by suppressing all possibility of the unpleasant knowledge ever being revealed, by silencing the interfering youth?

Ah, the insistent idea of murder, sneaking yet again into my mind of its own accord, taking me unawares. Sebastian was considered to have killed himself. He *may* have killed himself. Why was I so suspicious, so doubting?

I simply could not picture Sebastian being driven to despair and self-immolation by the discoveries that were emerging, little by little. Lydia K. – Lydia Krieger, I was now convinced – had been no madder than Hélène Smith; Dr Bernstein had said so clearly. And even if she had become so – even if beautiful, gentle Lydia had somehow, in the twenty-five years since he had lost sight of her, become so uncontrollably and so incurably mad that she was now lost amongst the very dregs of humanity; those that are locked away in the deepest and most miserable dungeons of the insane asylums – even then, I still did not believe that Sebastian would go home and kill himself over it.

But!

Now, at this very instant, while standing next to the tables, my dazed eyes following Lord Warburton as he circulated amongst his guests, holding in his hand a porcelain dish edged with a ring of gold and containing a tiny silver fork and a dainty and diminutive mince pie, I suddenly had enough of mere ruminations. There was information waiting for me in Mrs Cavendish's desk drawers, and now was the very time to go and find it! Setting down my teacup, I passed back towards the double doors opening into the drawing room in which the concert had been held. On each side of these, a pair of enormously thick curtains had been gathered, leaving the opening free. As I went through the doorway, I became aware of movements within the green velvet folds. I paused for the slightest moment.

There were two people. I heard very muffled whispers.

'No! You mustn't! John, stop!'

'I love you, Claire. I adore you. Please – let me speak!'

'No! I can't – I mustn't hear it!'

I went through, but turned my head and glanced back as I left. Claire hurried out from the curtains alone, her face flushed with confusion and distress, and walked unsteadily towards the tea table. I waited until John Milrose followed her, a long moment later. His face was grim, but also determined.

John Milrose was so in love with Claire that he couldn't

even bring himself to respect her grief, let alone the memory of his friend.

He, too, had a reason to wish Sebastian out of the way.

My mind was out of control, it seemed, in a turmoil of wild suspicion; terrible, generic suspicion that seemed ready to be directed upon anyone who happened to pass in front of me. This was quite unacceptable! I hurried outside, and immediately took a cab and directed it to Russell Square. An unbearable pressure seemed to work upon me from within, and Mrs Cavendish's desk drawers took on, in my mind, the features of the Oracle of Delphi. I did not know what I should find there, and perhaps when I found it, I would not understand it. Yet it hardly mattered, as long as there was *something*.

I stood in the garden in the centre of Russell Square, sheltered from the drizzle underneath a large umbrella which further served to hide my features from the occasional passer-by (who in any case was too occupied with dogs on leashes or squalling children to care), and looked over at Mrs Cavendish's building, to see if I could spot young Ephraim lurking in the shadows, ready and waiting according to our plan. It was not easy to see in the darkness and rain, but I could just make out the occasional movements of a dim figure in a nearby doorway. The appointed hour was drawing near.

At nine o'clock the door opened, letting out a shaft of light that reflected in a thousand twinkles on the rain-shimmering pavement. Out came Mrs Munn – I made sure it was really she – and paused to reach into her large holdall and extract an umbrella, which she opened before setting off along the side of the square.

Yes! A swift and silent shadow was following her, at a short distance.

The two figures disappeared around the corner, and there was nothing for me to do but wait, whilst imaginary pictures of the events that were to take place thrust themselves into my mind in richly coloured contradictions. Here, Ephraim attacked the poor old lady, accidentally throwing her to the ground in his haste, and then stopped to raise her to her feet, drowning in humble apologies, his natural politeness smothering all the nefarious intentions I had so carefully introduced into his innocently boyish mind. There, the poor woman unexpectedly hailed a passing omnibus and hopped nimbly inside, taking Ephraim by surprise and leaving him standing empty-handed under the pouring rain. Finally, I imagined him succeeding in snatching away the bag and hotfooting it back towards Russell Square, pursued by Mrs Munn's shrieks of 'Stop thief!', several angry passers-by and a bobby, all of whom would stop directly in front of me and stare squarely into my face while Ephraim handed me his booty with a sheepish expression.

Lost in these visions of distress, I never even heard a sound as Ephraim actually approached me in reality. His step suddenly sounding in my very ear caused me to jump out of my skin, and I turned around with a gasp. The boy handed me Mrs Munn's capacious bag in silence, his expression a mixture of relief, guilt and sadness.

'Ah, thank you,' I said, somewhat absurdly.

'It was much harder than I thought it would be,' he said, following my hurried steps out of the garden and onto the street. 'I mean, it was very easy, in fact. I simply snatched the bag from her hand and ran. She cried out something,

233

but there was no one around. I didn't even have to run fast. But I thought I wasn't going to be able to bring myself to do it. It's awful, awful. I can't believe I just did this to that poor old lady. I thought I wasn't going to be able to. I didn't realise that there was such a big, strong thing inside me trying to stop me. I thought I wasn't going to be able to make myself do it. It was so mean. I feel so bad.'

Water streamed down his face, but as he was absolutely dripping with rain, I made no assumptions, but laid my hand gently upon his arm.

'We will get it back to her and make it up to her,' I promised. 'Just as soon as I'm finished here. Come quickly, now.'

'But she has to take a 'bus and she'll not have the fare,' he sniffled.

'I know. I'm sorry. But Mrs Munn has lived through much greater difficulties in her life than this. It's not such a catastrophe. She will manage. Come now, we may have only a few minutes. Quick!'

We crossed the road together and Ephraim stationed himself in front of the door of the building as a lookout, ready to rush up and call me to come running out the very moment he should spy anyone approaching. I climbed the stairs, quickly removed my wet wrap and boots, and laid them with my umbrella outside the flat so as to leave no traces at all inside. Then I located the key with my fingers inside Mrs Munn's bag, unlocked the door without difficulty, and entered Sebastian's flat for the first time.

The flat was eerily quiet. I knew it would be empty, yet the silence was disturbing – though a sudden or mysterious noise would certainly have been worse! In my stockings,

I stepped down the corridor, passing the open doors to the parlour on my left and the dining room on my right. Farther down, the doors were closed. I tentatively opened the first one, then closed it again quickly, then opened it again. So this was Sebastian's room.

It perfectly neat and perfectly clean, but probably no more so than it had been on a daily basis even during his life. I raised a corner of the quilted cover laid upon the bed, and saw that it was laid over the bare mattress; the bed had been stripped. But a music stand in the corner, books and music on the shelves, and clothes in the closet, spoke for the heart that had beat in this room.

I had no time to contemplate it further, although I would have liked to absorb something of the personality that had left its traces there. I went out and peered into the next room: it was the study. Leaving the door ajar, I finally found my way into Mrs Cavendish's bedroom.

Like the rest of the flat, the room was a compromise between the style in which it had originally been furnished, some decades earlier, and a nature more attuned to a sort of stark simplicity in which two words would never do when one was enough. The heavy furniture spoke of another time, but their smooth surfaces were bare of the vases and pictures that must have once been crowded upon them. The heavy bed curtains were drawn back and held by thick braided ropes, opening to view what had been conceived as a secretive, cosy nook. Upon the dressing table, which was covered with a piece of plain white damask, were laid ivory brushes, combs and mirrors and a modest selection of pots and flasks. I lifted the lid of a porcelain pot with a shock, but it contained only the most ordinary powder, surmounted by a tiny puff. Of arsenic, there was none to be seen. I supposed that Mrs Cavendish would hardly have kept the pot, even if the police had returned it to her, which was most unlikely. Upon the washstand next to the dressing table stood a large porcelain bowl and jug, perfectly white, the latter filled with fresh water. The whole room denoted a struggle between the clutches of the dim, heavy styles of the past – an echo of collector's objects all crowded together could still faintly be felt in the dense but faded garlands of the wallpaper and the intricate fruits and leaves carved on the wardrobe doors – and a striving for absolute simplicity and purity. Something about it was tremendously revealing. I felt as though I had had an unexpected glimpse into Mrs Cavendish's very soul.

But there was no time to waste, and I dragged a chair to the wardrobe and climbed upon it to reach the hatboxes perfectly stacked upon the top. The grey one was, as Mrs Munn had told me, on top of the striped one, and during the few seconds it took me to lift it down, I worried myself into a panic over whether she might have moved the key. I knew something was wrong the second I touched the box, for it was too light. My fears were confirmed as soon as I opened it. The box contained no hat at all, only a crumple of protective tissue paper.

Stupid me – why had I expected to find the hat here? Had not Mrs Munn specifically said that the key was tucked into the loops of ribbon on the black hat that Mrs Cavendish wore for mourning? Obviously, she hadn't been wearing it on the day that Sebastian came home, but, just as obviously, she was wearing it today. In fact, I had seen it not more than an hour ago atop her beautifully arranged silvery blonde hair.

I fingered the tissue paper, and the tiny key dropped into my hand.

In a wink, I was out of the room and in the study, where I unlocked the drawers and began to go through them with feverish haste, listening all the while for Ephraim's warning cry.

With an efficiency partly born, I admit it, from a certain amount of practice, I rifled through the contents of one drawer after another. Unsurprisingly, Mrs Cavendish's papers were perfectly organised, everything classified in carefully arranged folders of bills, household affairs and correspondence, through all of which I anxiously flipped, until in the very bottom drawer I finally came upon a single slim folder containing an exchange of no more than a dozen or so letters. No sooner had my eye caught sight of the letterhead on the top of each than I grew cold and shivered, while the letters themselves burnt my fingers.

Holloway Sanatorium, Virginia Water, Surrey was printed in beautifully calligraphed letters across the top of each page. The name of Lydia Krieger jumped out at me at once, a blinding confirmation of everything I had guessed.

It did not take long to read them all.

In 1875, Mr Edward Cavendish, brother-in-law to Miss Lydia Krieger, became her legal guardian in the place of Mr Charles King, who had played that role since the death of her mother. The reason given was that Lydia's mental deficiency necessitated a continued guardianship, and that, given certain events that had transpired while she was his ward, Mr Charles King found that he could not provide the necessary surveillance and desired to relinquish his responsibility.

Mr Cavendish took the decision to consign Lydia Krieger to the Holloway Sanatorium, an institution specialised in the care and treatment of mentally deranged patients. The fees charged and paid by Mr Cavendish proved that the sanatorium was not intended for members of the poorer classes. These monthly fees had been paid by Mr Cavendish for nearly twenty years, until his death in 1894. The individual bills had not been kept, but only a complete yearly financial statement whose figure gave me a clearer understanding of what had happened to at least a significant part of Mr Cavendish's money, both before and after his death. Indeed, I discovered that his widow received a not unreasonable pension, which should have been quite sufficient to allow her to afford servants and the usual luxuries of a ladies' life; if she could not, it was essentially on account of the expense of keeping her sister at Holloway.

The last letter in the folder was dated March 1899 and contained a fact that gave me a painful shock. In that month, another person assumed full responsibility for the payments of Lydia's fees, indefinitely or until further notice – and that person was no other than Lord George Warburton! This information consigned more than one of my different theories about why Sebastian might possibly have been murdered to the rubbish bin. Whatever had been the reason for Sebastian's death, it was not to prevent Lord Warburton finding out about Lydia's existence – nor did that existence appear to have provided any incentive for breaking off his coming marriage. It was sorely disappointing. Yet inexplicably, even as the motives I had sketched out in my mind thus melted away, my intimate conviction that Sebastian's death was not suicide but murder grew stronger.

I put the papers back, locked the desk, hurried to the bedroom, dropped the key back into the hatbox, piled it perfectly symmetrically atop the wardrobe, put back the chair, closed the bedroom door, rushed out of the flat, locked it, hastily scooped up boots, wrap and umbrella and rushed down the stairs to the main entrance with them all bundled in my arms, to find a trembling Ephraim standing in the cold, pale with anxiety. His interest in the crimes of others appeared to have evaporated; he thought only of rushing off to erase his own as soon as possible, and he literally pawed the ground with impatience as I buttoned my boots, and heaved an immense sigh of relief as I handed him the key and some money to put inside Mrs Munn's bag and gave him careful instructions on how to reach her home, located in the poorest section of Bermondsey. Off he went at a run, and I walked away by myself, deep in thought.

Lydia Krieger had existed; she still existed, and now I knew exactly where she was.

Lord Warburton knew it as well.

But what of Sebastian?

He had seen the same papers that I had, and he must have understood that the person named there was his aunt, if not actually his real mother. He had rushed away from the flat after reading them – where else but directly to Holloway? He must have seen her there. And what had happened? Had he somehow received an unbearable shock to his nervous system? Had he, rather, blundered unforgivably into the middle of a secret that was not really his? Or was his death due to reasons quite apart from his discovery of Lydia's existence and her refuge? To a hidden jealousy, for example, burgeoning within the heart of a friend?

If he had not killed himself, then what was I to make of the suicide note? I recalled its words.

Darling Claire,

How can I say this to you? I've found out something about myself – I can't go on with it any more. I'm sorry. I'm so sorry. Cursed inheritance – it's too dangerous to take such risks. Please try to understand.

Not for the first time, I was struck by the lack of signature. But now I suddenly understood it differently.

Was this not merely the beginning of a letter? A letter breaking off an engagement, not a life?

CHAPTER EIGHTEEN

In which Vanessa does not accomplish the object of her visit but something quite different instead

Holloway Sanatorium was pointed out to me by the porter as soon as I emerged from the Virginia Water railway station. Vast and impressive with its multiple wings and gables, surmounted by a great square tower, it was as grand and imposing as any castle, and a monument to the founders' intentions of bringing the treatment of mental illness to the middle classes and applying the most progressive methods to the patients, with the firm intention of effecting actual cures and sending them back to the bosom of their families. In principle, it was not intended as a place to permanently harbour mad patients, but the case of Lydia Krieger was obviously an exception of some kind.

The sanatorium was visible at a short distance from the station, and I set forth to walk to it in a great state of suppressed excitement. The grounds stretched, rolling,

241

pleasant and richly wooded, all about the enormous building, bestowing upon the entire property the agreeable pastoral atmosphere that people generally expect from their country estates. A large and forbidding iron railing, however, surrounded the entire property, leaving the visitor no possible ingress – and the patients no exit – except for the tried and true method of the well-guarded main gate.

I followed the road leading to this very place and, as I approached, a surly-faced porter emerged from a small shed placed just within, and proceeded to unlock and swing open the gates to let me in. He did not allow me to go towards the building, however, but detained me while he rang for a person to come. I had to wait idly for several long minutes before a white-capped figure appeared at a distance, approaching with hasty steps. Only when she had nearly reached us did the porter consent to allow me to advance a few steps on my own and join her on the path, never removing his suspicious eyes from me until she had, by means of enquiring as to my name and purpose there, taken over from him the role of officially designated escort and guardian to the intruder.

When I explained that I had come as a visitor to one of the patients, she immediately extracted a large watch from her pocket and made a show of examining the time, but said nothing, as I had taken the precaution of informing myself that proper visiting hours were from two to four – unlike Sebastian, who must have come rushing straight here from London directly he had discovered the letters concerning Lydia, but who would certainly have arrived too late in the afternoon to be admitted before the following day. He must have been beside himself with impatience, and I could well imagine that he did not feel like returning home to face his mother before he had plumbed the depths of the situation. He had probably found himself a room at an inn in Virginia Water on the night of December 30th.

The nurse did not me ask any further questions, but led me into an impressive entrance hall with a vaulted ceiling supported by arched wooden beams worthy of some of the loveliest of our Cambridge colleges, and from there into a spacious office at the side. Here, another nurse, significantly older, severer and invested with greater authority than the one at my side, received me from behind an immense oaken desk.

After mulling over a hundred possibilities, I had decided to ask in the simplest manner to be allowed to visit one of the patients, a Miss Lydia Krieger.

The woman's face took on a look of surprise and momentary doubt, then cleared to resume her previous rather impassive expression.

'Miss Krieger; you wish to visit Miss Krieger,' she repeated, raising her eyebrows slightly. 'Let me see. I am not sure that will be possible. Please excuse me for a moment. I must check in her file.' She rose, went into a room behind, and came back bearing a thin file in her hand, into whose contents I should have dearly liked to have a glimpse. However, as she turned over the pages, I perceived from upside down that they were letters, no doubt exactly those whose answers I had already read at Mrs Cavendish's flat. The patient's medical history could not possibly fit into such a small file; it must be kept in a different place. The nurse extracted the very last document and read it over carefully. Then she said,

'No, it is as I thought. Miss Krieger is not allowed to receive visits. I am very sorry that you have come all this way for nothing.'

Her voice held a tone of simple finality that aroused a sense of immediate furious frustration inside me. I turned my tongue around seven times in my mouth while collecting my spirits.

'Surely it is not so,' I replied as soon as I felt able to speak in a level tone. 'A friend of mine visited her less than one month ago, and encouraged me to do so.'

She looked up a little sharply.

'What friend would that have been?'

'A Mr Cavendish. Mr Sebastian Cavendish,' I replied, risking my all.

'Quite. I see. Let me explain. The fact is that precisely following the visit of that gentleman, we received a letter from Miss Krieger's guardians explicitly forbidding her to be disturbed by any further visits. It appears that Mr Cavendish's visit caused a serious problem which is not to be allowed to recur.'

'A problem for Miss Krieger herself?' I said, playing innocent and hoping to extract some information.

'I do not know. I know nothing about it except that we received this letter.'

'But I am certain that the visit caused no harm to Miss Krieger, quite the contrary,' I persisted, 'and I do not see why she should be the one to suffer for the problems of another, of which she may not even be aware.'

'It is not in my hands,' she replied coldly, beginning (as well she might) to be annoyed. 'I am very sorry I cannot help you,' she added, and rang a bell, probably to summon someone to escort me out. I quickly staved off the moment of absolute failure by insisting upon speaking to Miss Krieger's physician.

'Dr Richards is excessively busy, as are all the physicians here, with over six hundred patients,' she replied. 'He cannot be disturbed for a mere question of visits. Besides, there is no more to be said. The letter is quite explicit.'

'Surely,' I said, 'even from guardians as severe as these, there cannot be any letter explicitly forbidding the physician to receive a visit.'

She pressed her lips together, and when the young nurse who had met me earlier near the gate knocked gently and opened the door, she said,

'Run to Dr Richards' room, Sister Theresa, and tell him that there is a visitor for Miss Krieger here, who wishes if possible to speak to him.'

She gestured with her hand to a pretty brocade chair against the wall, and I sat down and waited. At length Sister Theresa returned and said that Dr Richards was with a patient, that he could spare a few moments in a quarter of an hour, and would I please save time by waiting in his ante-room? I followed her up many stairs and down many halls, and we passed a vast number of people bustling in every direction; patients, some in white robes and others normally dressed, doctors, nurses, young girls pushing carts laden with cups and dishes or medical equipment, and groups of well-dressed people who were possibly visitors like myself. As we went, I tried to pump the young nurse discreetly, but I met with no success at all, not least because, in her anxiety not to waste a single second of the doctor's precious time, she was hurrying me along at a pace nearly worthy of a footrace. This species of nurse is clearly trained to a high degree of functionality and discretion.

She finally stopped, opened a door without knocking, and inserted me, like a letter in the postbox, into a beautifully decorated room that had little or no relation to how I would have imagined a mental doctor's waiting room to appear. Here she left me alone, to hurry on to other duties.

An inner door of this room was closed, but certainly led to the room or office where the doctor received his patients; indeed I could make out the muffled sound of his voice, alternating with a woman's tones. I tried to make out some of his words, but could not, yet their tone evoked a spirit of reasoning. After many minutes, the door opened, and the white-clad doctor ushered a plain woman with a sickly, indifferent expression on her face quickly out of the waiting room and into the hall, where a nurse – yet another one – was waiting to accompany her to some other place. I could not help noticing a long red scratch on the woman's cheek as she passed. Dr Richards then closed the door to the hall, came towards me and said in a quick, businesslike manner,

'You are the visitor who came to see Miss Krieger? How may I help you? I do not have much time, I'm afraid.'

Alas, before he even spoke these words, I perceived in him the very type of doctor (and, let me add, of man) that I most dislike. Too refined to look openly self-important, he nonetheless had the air of a man who is in command and knows it. Here was a person imbued with a sense of his power; not a constructive sense, I felt, but an unfortunate, unhealthy sense, fed and nourished daily by the knowledge of his actual, perfectly real power over all those around him – helpless patients and respectful, obedient and scuttling nurses. Here was a man whose professional word was law, whose personal decisions bore the weight of law in the truest sense, for were he called to a court of law for any reason, either to aid in a judge's decision or to defend his own medical doings, his expert words would no doubt be held to be unassailable and his expert opinion trusted implicitly. Such people raise my hackles; I feel an instinctive abhorrence for them, and am sometimes driven, I confess it, to flout their power for the pure pleasure of being able to do so.

But this did not seem to be a moment when such a course of action was advisable. Speaking respectfully, I explained my great wish to visit Miss Krieger, adding a totally untruthful tale about having been begged to do so by a dear friend of mine, now deceased, who had seen her quite lately and was aware that the visit had done her the greatest good.

The nurse downstairs may or may not have been ignorant of the entire story surrounding Sebastian's visit; her discretion made it impossible for me to guess. But the quick glance in Dr Richards' sharp blue eyes told me that he knew exactly what had occurred, and certainly much more about it than I did.

'Surely you were told downstairs that Miss Krieger is to receive no visits?' he said coldly, and snapped his lips shut. If possible, my dislike of the man increased by a notch.

'I was,' I said, 'but I wished to enquire further, to learn why this was suddenly the case, and to make sure that it was truly for Miss Krieger's benefit. For it appears to me possible that the family's request to bar her from visits was made for a very different reason, and that it is equally essential, if not more so, to consider her own well-being. As her doctor, you must surely agree.'

It was a losing battle.

'As her doctor, I am quite able to judge for myself of the best manner of ensuring my patients' well-being,' he said. 'Visits are not useful to Miss Krieger. She is a patient whose peace of mind is fragile and must be preserved at all costs.'

'I quite understand,' I replied smoothly. 'Holloway Sanatorium is reputed, of course, for curing its patients and releasing them into their normal lives. I presume your care for her well-being is oriented towards such a cure?'

'Naturally,' he replied, his tone yielding nothing to mine. 'Miss Krieger's case is, however, particularly complex, and it will take an amount of time which cannot be determined at present.'

'Twenty-five years seems quite long already, does it not?' I murmured.

'It is long, too long. However, the methods of psychological treatment of one or two decades ago were not what they are now, and I may hope to succeed where my predecessors failed.'

I felt convinced that he was lying; that he had been tacitly or openly charged with the task of keeping Miss Krieger a prisoner for the rest of her life – for no really adequate reason, I was sure – and that he knew it, just as his predecessors had known it.

'I am delighted to think that you believe you have a chance of bringing Miss Krieger to make a normal use of writing,' I chanced, having no idea whether some earnest doctor along the way – or simply the passage of time –

had actually improved Lydia's condition years ago. 'In that case, she could certainly leave the premises at once, could she not? For I am informed that she has no other psychological problems.'

The doctor's face stiffened.

'That is the assessment of an amateur,' he stated. 'A psychological problem is never confined to one narrow domain, although it may appear so to a layman. In any case, I am not at liberty to discuss my patients' medical conditions. I beg that you will not trouble yourself about Miss Krieger's well-being. You have seen our building, met our nurses. Look out of this window and you will see our gardens. You can judge for yourself whether the patients here are adequately cared for.'

He pointed out of the window as he spoke, and I followed his glance eagerly, for the window was not set in the ante-room where we were, but on the wall of his inner office, facing the door. The doctor had left this communicating door wide open when he ushered the patient out, and I had been dying to have a glance inside, but it was out of the question to let my eyes pry about indiscreetly, when his own were fixed so sharply upon my very face. Pretending to admire the grounds (which were indeed lovely), I took one or two steps forward and scanned what I could of his office. I immediately spotted the fact that behind his desk stood a set of large oaken filing cabinets with drawers, each of which was labelled with a card bearing a letter of the alphabet. A delightful idea suddenly entered my head, having the immediate effect of causing all of my spirit of rebellion to creep modestly back into the place in which it lives when it is invisible. Bowing my head submissively,

I said that I would leave now. I added hopefully that I could find my own way out, but the doctor was not to be manipulated. 'That is against our rules here,' he said shortly, and rang a bell. I had perforce to wait until Sister Theresa appeared with a firm step to guide me directly to the exit, down the path, and inexorably out of the grounds.

It was an emergency!

If she were to once put me out of the gate and see it locked behind me, my last chance of learning anything about Lydia Krieger would be definitively lost. I simply could not allow that to happen! Could I dash away suddenly? No, that was impossible. What about fainting? As convincingly as possible, I made a sudden show of terrible weakness, and clutching the nurse's arm, begged to be allowed to sit down somewhere and have a cup of tea before I should have to shoulder the burden of my disappointment and return home.

Sister Theresa looked annoyed, but she must have been used to women with vapours and did not appear suspicious. Leading me to a small empty sitting room, she rang a bell which brought a little housemaid running in. I smiled inwardly at the sight of her. This was the kind of girl I knew and liked; a rosy country girl with a smile lurking behind her dimpled cheeks. If only I could arrange to spend a few moments with her alone!

'Bring tea for this lady, Polly, and be quick, please,' said Sister Theresa. The girl disappeared and I waited silently, fanning myself gently with a handkerchief and wishing that Sister Theresa would leave, but suspecting I would have no such luck. Various plans revolved in my mind, and then, to my delight, the girl returned with the tea and said,

'There's a visitor just come, Sister Theresa, and you're wanted to show him in.'

Sister Theresa rose. 'I must return to my duties,' she said to me, then drew young Polly aside and delivered to her a murmured lecture, which I easily guessed to be a strict injunction not to leave my side, and to escort me to the main gate just as soon as I should be pleased to shake off my indisposition.

Sister Theresa left and Polly stayed. Conversation flowed at once with ease and cheer, and within two minutes I had led the conversation around to the topic of Lydia Krieger. I was excited to learn that Polly knew who she was, although with six hundred patients and she nothing but a housemaid, she didn't have much actual contact with most of them. At first her comments were but simple, essentially summarised by the repetition of the words 'poor dear lady'. She told me that Miss Krieger was known to most of the staff because she had been at Holloway forever, longer than almost any other patient except the famous Mr Turner who sometimes thought he was Napoleon and sometimes Disraeli, and had already been pronounced cured and released twelve times.

But Miss Krieger had never been released, I persisted, bringing the conversation back in the direction that interested me.

'No, poor dear lady. She never gets any better, nor any worse.'

'Is she actually ill?'

'Not as you can see. A sweet quiet lady and beautiful, too. Tall. She likes to read, to sew, to walk in the garden. She likes animals, too; the patients cannot have animals here, but some of the visitors come with a little dog or such.

I've seen her holding and petting them. She never has those crises like what the others do, some of them, or believe they're something else than what they really are. We get all kinds here. But Miss Krieger seems no different from you and me. Just dreamy, like, but then, there's not much for her to do here.'

A new image of Lydia Krieger arose in my mind, far more vivid than the previous ghostly shadows: the medieval Lady of the Unicorn. Seated in her garden of tapestry flowers, surrounded by dogs and rabbits and an earnest-looking lion, her gentle hand resting on a tame unicorn who smiles at her adoringly. That otherworldly beauty, quiet elegance, infinite gentleness. And with that vision, the very last shred of possibility that Sebastian had discovered something so dreadful he had wanted to end his life faded away. He had come here to see the woman who was his aunt – perhaps, very possibly, his mother – and he had found the Lady of the Unicorn.

'Do you know why they've forbidden me to visit her?' I asked.

'Have they really?' she said with great sympathy. 'That's not kind.'

'It seems that her family sent a letter forbidding visitors after a visit that she had last month, where something bad happened. A young man came to visit her, and then he died.'

'Oh, of course! I remember that! We were all talking about it last month. That was the young man who killed himself, wasn't it? Sister Matilda who sits at the front desk saw his name in the paper and realised that she'd written that very name down in the visitor's book herself; it was still open to the same page, even. He killed himself on the very day that he was here, didn't he? We all heard about how the young man came here for a visit and then went and killed himself in London. But I didn't know he had come to see Miss Krieger. Sister Matilda didn't tell us that. She's very close; I think she wouldn't have even told anyone about what she saw in the paper if it hadn't been such a coincidence. But as she wasn't alone when she saw the name, she naturally cried out something right then when she recognised it, and it got around. Poor young man, I do wonder why he did it. Some people are madder outside than the ones in here, don't you think?'

'Did you see him when he came?'

'Not I, ma'am, but the ones who did said he was lovely.'

I leant forward, enjoying myself, but worried lest Sister Theresa should find a spare moment to come back and check upon our whereabouts, and lowered my voice to a conspiratorial whisper.

'Polly, can you tell me anything about Miss Krieger's writing?'

Her eyes grew round.

'We're not allowed to talk about the patients, ma'am,' she said.

I smiled kindly.

'There's no harm in talking with me,' I said. 'In fact, you could help me. You see, I'm trying to find out why the poor young man who came here went and killed himself. I'm trying to understand the reason.'

'Surely it had nothing to do with his visit here, did it?' she said.

'Well, I think that it did. Because if not, why would her

family suddenly write to the sanatorium forbidding her to receive any more visitors?'

'Why, I don't know. It's strange. Miss Krieger never had any other visitors anyway. That was the only one. That's why it caused such a to-do. She never had any other. That's what they all say, at least.'

'Do you know if Miss Krieger spoke about the visit after it happened?'

'No, I wouldn't know that, I don't talk to the patients myself,' she replied. 'She might have done, to her doctor, but then again she might not. She doesn't say much as a rule. There's not much to say, really, in here, it's so shut away. If I didn't get out to see my family on my half-days, I sometimes think I'd go all strange myself.'

'What do the doctors do here, to cure the patients?' I asked. 'Do you know anything about that?'

'They've all kinds of machines,' she said. 'They have the patients spinning round or taking cold baths; ever so many things. A French doctor came here once and he put some of the patients into funny trances, so they'd do anything he said. But with Miss Krieger, they say the doctor only gets her to write. She's not allowed to write any other time, you see. We've been told to keep papers and pens away from her, and she mayn't go into the writing room. She may only write for Dr Richards. But she doesn't need the cold baths and other things, because she's always calm.'

The idea that had sprung up in my mind in the doctor's waiting-room was fast becoming an absolute determination. Time was short and no elaborate planning would be possible. But simplicity is often the best way, in any case. The vastness of the building and its long empty corridors could be turned to my advantage.

'Polly,' I said, rising and gathering my things, 'I need to find out why Miss Krieger's visitor killed himself, and I know it has something to do with what she writes. I want you to help me.'

'Oh, ma'am, I can't,' she said, turning pale. 'It's as much as my place is worth. Why, if I don't take you straight down to the gatehouse in a minute, I'll be in trouble already.'

'I won't ask you to anything forbidden,' I promised. 'In fact, I'm asking you almost nothing at all. Do take me to the gatehouse. Let's go there now.' I rose, and something passed from my purse to my hand, and from my hand to Polly's. She uttered a little cry and it disappeared into her apron pocket.

'When the porter opens the gate to let me out, you turn back to go up the path,' I said. 'Then you trip and fall down and cry out. He'll come to you and help you get up. Cry out that it hurts and get him to look at your knee, so he doesn't look at me for a few moments. That's all I want you to do. Don't even think about me after that. Don't pay attention to anything. Just go back to the house, and go about your duties.'

She looked at me with great curiosity.

'Oh – I think I can do that!' she said. 'But are you not going to go out at all?'

'You don't need to know anything about that,' I replied firmly.

'It'll be the porter's fault, not mine, if they do find you back inside,' she said, and burst into a merry laugh. Out we went, along the corridors into the grand main foyer, out the front door, and straight down the path to the gatehouse, Polly wearing a great air of doing her duty. The porter stood up and unlocked the gate, pulling it inwards to let me out. I took a step to the side, and Polly turned away. I held my breath. A shriek from behind me made the porter whirl around, and in the flash of a second, I was hiding in the thick shrubbery next to the gate, peering through the prickly leaves to see how he raised Polly from the ground as she bent over, and clutching her knee and howling, 'Oh, it's broken, it's broken; oh please look at it, do; oh, is it bleeding?' like a five-year-old child. If he was a little surprised by my total disappearance during the short time it took him to pull her upright and utter something between a consolation and a remonstrance, he did not show it, but contented himself with locking the gate as she followed him, limping, whimpering realistically and demanding attention.

At length he sent her off, and she went back up the path, still hobbling, and disappeared into the building. I had in the meantime taken advantage of the racket to slip through the shrubbery as far away from the gate as possible, and had by now reached a place where I thought the rustling caused by my movements would not be noticeable. It seemed that I could continue to creep behind the shrubbery around the entire perimeter of the sanatorium's enormous grounds, which, apart from the bushes along the railings, were green and quite empty even of trees. I continued my thorny trajectory for what seemed an immense distance, until finally the porter's cabin was out of sight. Then I came out, brushed leaves and twigs from my clothing, and crossed the lawn with what I hoped was a confident step.

I was naturally worried about detection, but not excessively so, for several other people were dotted about the grounds; doctors and nurses, and even a number of normally dressed people quite like myself, going back and forth from the outlying buildings for reasons of their own. They did not appear to be patients, and I soon realised that the patients were not free to wander about the full extent of the grounds, but were confined to a particular, rather large and quite lovely garden of their own, set behind the building and to one side, and surrounded with its own set of iron railings. Here was a much thicker concentration of nurses, together with a number of people, some of whom appeared normal enough, but others who disported themselves strangely, uttered peculiar noises, or were covered in rugs and pushed about in wheeled chairs. There were even a few visitors who actually stood outside the railings, conversing with patients on the inside; an excellent arrangement allowing patients to receive visits while taking the air, and while protecting the more sensitive visitors from sights or sounds that might alarm them when experienced at close quarters.

I joined these people and stood looking in. The weather was unusually bright, but extremely cold, and it was not surprising that of the six hundred patients in the sanatorium, there were no more than forty or fifty in the garden at that particular moment, most of them walking about quite briskly. My heart beat; Polly had said that Lydia Krieger enjoyed walking in the garden. In the strictly regulated life of the sanatorium, this particular moment must correspond to the hour for visits and garden walks and it was perhaps the only chance during the day at which patients were allowed outside. She might well be there.

After some moments, my eyes located a figure that I thought might be Lydia. There was no way to be certain, but the gentle demeanour, the dreamy expression, the greying hair of the rather lovely woman I saw, wearing an elegant fur stole and hat, denoted the right age and style, and it seemed to me that I could detect a faint family resemblance to Tanis Cavendish. Resemblances are infinitely subtle, but my instinct told me that this could well be Lydia Krieger, and my heart beat faster as I tried to imagine a way to attract her attention. Sebastian had come here just a month ago, and he had seen Lydia, just as I believed I was seeing her now. And he had spoken to her – and perhaps she had written for him, as I would wish her to write for me, and some secret had been thence revealed. And Sebastian had died, and Lydia remained a prisoner, and no one but she now knew exactly what had taken place here on that day.

My determination to understand grew and intensified, and plans rushed through my head. But she was at too much of a distance for me to call out to her, and I was afraid of drawing attention to myself; there was nothing to do but wait and hope that she would draw nearer in her circulation. I observed her carefully, I tried to catch her eye, I readied myself – and then suddenly, I saw a young nurse hurry from the building into the garden, straight up to the very woman I was watching so closely, and speak to her urgently, taking her arm to lead her inside. The woman replied, making a gesture indicating the garden and the sky, as though she would wish to remain there, but the young nurse was adamant and drew her indoors as fast as she could, casting a hasty glance about the garden as she did so.

My disappointment was keen, but not as strong as the sudden piercing sensation of fear. What could be the meaning of the little scene I had just witnessed, other than that the alarm had somehow been raised, and the staff informed that I was still within their gates and probably determined to force a meeting with Lydia Krieger? The porter must have been surprised not to see me walking away down the road after the little scene with Polly, suspected that I hadn't left at all, and decided to alert someone. And not knowing where I might be hiding, the hospital had been very quick to spirit Lydia out of the way of a possible encounter. It might seem like a rather grand reaction to such a little thing, but Lydia's previous visit had ended with a suicide, and I could imagine how desirous they might be of avoiding any repetition of such a tragedy.

I left the garden at once, and circled the building back towards the front entrance with as tranquil and confident an air as I could muster. From what I had seen, the giant foyer with its towering arched ceiling contained no official person in the role of watchdog; this was not necessary, as visitors were accompanied up to the house from the gate, and led immediately to their proper destination. My best hope, then, was to behave as normally as possible and thus remain unnoticed. With a firm, unhesitant gesture, I pushed open the great entrance door, went in, crossed the foyer and tried to take the same path along which I had been led so speedily less than an hour before.

On I went, through a veritable maze of corridors, trying to recognise this or that landmark, occasionally returning the way I had come to search for a more familiar scene. I crossed a few busy employees, carrying domestic items or leading patients, but they ignored me and I ignored them, and kept moving along rather quickly as though I had a specific task to accomplish – which, indeed, I did.

Thanks to my observation of the route we had taken previously, I did eventually manage to arrive at a door I recognised as being the suite attributed to Dr Richards. There was no one in the hall, and, as slowly and silently as possible, I turned the knob and gave the gentlest possible push at the door, not to open it even by the smallest crack, but simply to test whether or not it was locked. Finding that it yielded, I released the knob, moved a little way down the hall to the top of a staircase, and concealed myself behind the heavy drapes that hung in front of all the corridor windows.

Ideally, what I wanted was a moment in which I could be certain that Dr Richards was alone inside. If he should be out of the office, I feared he would probably lock the door, and if a patient or someone else were inside with him, my plan would certainly fail. I waited and observed and watched until my legs were full of pins-and-needles.

Now and then, someone passed down the corridor in one direction or the other. Through a crack in the curtains I saw people being escorted away, and knew that visiting hours had come to an end. A little later, a nurse arrived with a patient who continually dragged her fingers through her hair, pulling and deforming the neat bun which the nurse pinned back for her repeatedly with perfunctory remonstrances of 'Now, dear'. These two stopped at the door of the doctor's ante-room, and the nurse opened it, went in, and knocked gently on the inner door. A murmured word, a moment's wait, and the doctor ushered a gentleman patient out into the nurse's capable hands and led the woman with her hair now half-falling down one side of her face into his inner room. He closed the door and the nurse went away with the gentleman, who was mumbling in a ceaseless monotone. I waited for twenty minutes or half an hour.

At the end of this time, my hopes were raised by the sight of a tea-trolley being wheeled along the corridor: the long rows of white cups with little dishes next to each containing scones were probably for the patients, but surely the doctors were also soon to be served. And indeed, the nurse returned, the lady with her hair now completely down around her face and shoulders came out and went away with her, and a minute later a little maid – not Polly, unfortunately, but some other similar little village Molly or Sally – arrived carrying a beautifully decked tea tray laden with much nicer things than what the patients were having. Having delivered this, she departed, and I knew that the doctor was alone, and that my moment was at hand.

I gave myself three minutes just to let the good doctor get properly relaxed, then set up a sudden and tremendous cry of 'Dr Richards! Oh, please! Oh, Dr Richards, come quickly! Please!' I was gratified to see him come rushing out of his office, hasten down the hall in the direction of my voice, and hurry down the steps near the top of which I was concealed.

I almost flew down the hall in the direction of his rooms; within a mere three or four seconds I was standing inside his private office, which was filled with the pleasant aroma of buttered toast. Another second and I was pulling open the drawer marked 'K' that my eyes had already accurately located at my earlier visit. Five seconds later my trembling fingers found and snatched out the file marked 'Krieger', and I clapped the drawer shut. I could not hurry away now without risking crossing the doctor's path as he returned, but the risk of discovery would be too great if I remained in the room; the ante-room was the least dangerous place, and I was there in the flash of an instant, clutching my prize, lying at full length behind the settee, and trying not to breathe.

There were calls and voices from outside, and the doctor returned, flushed and displeased to judge by his breathing, and stalked into his room to finish his tea. Alas, he did not quite close the door of his private office, thereby foiling my plans for immediate escape. I remained perfectly still, and occupied myself in hoping that this obstacle might lead to some interesting event, such as a visit from Lydia Krieger. But nothing so exciting occurred, and the next person to enter was no other than little Molly-Sally, on her way to collect the tea tray. With great good manners, she balanced it on one arm while pulling the doctor's door shut behind her, and then left, also closing the door to the hall. Instantly I was on my feet and following her, hoping that the doctor would attribute the double sound of the door, if he could hear it at all, to the struggle of the young girl with a heavy tray. I had no choice but to follow her straight out – there was no time to check whether anyone else was standing in the hall right then, but as a matter of fact the coast was clear – and off I went down the stairs, along the corridors and right out the front door, happily carrying my heavy prize concealed beneath my shawl.

Now came the difficulty of getting out of the grounds. I

was afraid that the porter might recognise me from earlier, especially if he had noticed my disappearance (or rather, my failure to have properly disappeared) and raised the alarm. It was awkward, and I could not think of anything better to do than to insert myself into a group of four or five working women, probably daily assistants from the village hired to aid with the cooking, cleaning or caring for patients, by the simple expedient of asking them if they could be so kind as to show me the way to the train station. I made sure to engage them in conversation so as to look as much as possible like part of their group, and in return they were very friendly. We all exited together as easily as possible; indeed, it was quite dark outside by this time, being after five o'clock, and the porter didn't notice a thing. I allowed myself the luxury of a tremendous sigh of relief accompanied by some nervous giggles, hurried to the train station, purchased a ticket, and leapt upon the first train to London with a feeling of unspeakable triumph. I may not have been able to talk to Lydia, but I believed I had seen her – and I had obtained a tremendously important set of documents, and played a trick on the obnoxious doctor to boot!

I settled back into my seat, extracted the thick folder of documents from the folds of my shawl, and began to examine the contents. I read, and I read, and I read.

But if I had expected a revelation – and I realised now that clearly I had – I was destined to be sorely disappointed.

According to her medical records, Lydia had been pilled and syruped, hypnotised and lectured, subjected to innumerable constraints, told to speak while writing and write while speaking, to write with her left hand, to write copying what the doctor wrote, to write with her hand guided by the doctor and a multitude of even more peculiar, irrelevant and unfortunate experiments, all of which had met with total failure and left her condition quite unchanged. As time passed, the doctor's notes became briefer, his experiments rarer, and, above all, the expression of his inability to comprehend her meaning moved over the years from the description 'indicative of internal logic incommunicable to outside world' in the early stages to 'incomprehensible' and even 'ranting' towards the end.

By an unfortunate psychological mechanism which I could not rationally explain to myself, my contempt for Dr Richards' failure was not in the least diminished by the fact that, had I been shown the many dozens of pages covered in Lydia Krieger's characteristic flowing handwriting under any ordinary circumstances, I might well have been capable of using the very same words to describe their contents myself. I read them through, and read them through again, then shook my head.

Their contents were utterly beyond me. Dr Bernstein had believed that a repressed secret was forcing its way forth between the lines, but I could not perceive any trace of such a thing. Her writings strongly resembled the samples I had read in Dr Bernstein's book: they expressed a kind of religious obsession with neurotic repetitiveness, and I could see nothing more. No strange incoherencies marred their natural flow. I shuffled them all back into the stolen file, and sat back, thinking.

If there was any sense at all to be made of this nonsense, any clue to the mystery of Lydia's secret and Sebastian's death, there was only one person in the world who could help me find it. And by asking for his help, I would also be granting him his heart's desire.

When the train pulled into London, I immediately went and sent an urgent telegram to Dr Bernstein at his Basel home. I had really had enough of trains, and would have been delighted to hear that I was never to see another one, but it was not to be. Twenty-four hours later I was spending yet another night trundled and jumbled in yet another sleeping-car, on my way to yet another destination, in the search for the elusive truth.

CHAPTER NINETEEN

In which a discovery takes place
at a most astonishing moment

The doctor rose, struck a match, and lit another candle, then pushed the brass candlestick closer to the papers that lay scattered over his desk. I sat near him in his study, my eyes heavy, but any idea of sleep was out of the question, for the doctor was buzzing about like a frantic bee. Shock, anger, joy, indignation, fury, and a feverish desire to understand crowded together to occupy all of his possibilities of expression, so that the poor man felt the need to slap his head, utter sighs and groans, take dancing steps about the room, pronounce imprecations and evolve yet another new theory, all at the same time. We had been there for hours, and the manservant who had brought us tea and then prepared a light dinner had long since gone to bed, but Dr Bernstein's state would not admit of his stopping for a moment. It was a Sunday, and he had had no patients, and our work and discussion had been going on for hours, interrupted only by meals over which he asked me ever more questions, and reminisced with increasing openness about the past.

Alerted by my telegram – in which, in order to be certain of his immediate reaction, I had included the words 'Lydia Krieger found' – the doctor had come to fetch me at the Basel railway station, and the sight of the emotion painted upon his bearded face as he recognised me erased any impulse I might normally have had to respect the social conventions by preceding the moment of revelation with lengthy formal greetings. Instead, I lifted up the heavy file that I had been clutching almost without stopping for the last forty-eight hours, and plunked it straight into his arms with a feeling of relief at thus transferring an insoluble problem to one more competent than myself. He opened it, glanced at the first pages, and then looked at me. We had not yet exchanged a single word, and for several moments, he seemed unable to pronounce one. When he finally did, it was simply: 'Come.'

Luncheon, to say the least, was a tense affair. His eyes burning, the doctor questioned me in detail, breaking off abruptly every time his manservant entered to bring or remove the dishes. I told him all I knew and all I had done, and had the pleasure of seeing him smile for the first time as I somewhat blushingly explained about the unusual use I had made of Dr Richards' settee. I hid nothing from him, at least not a single fact or incident. I kept to myself only certain suspicions. It was his turn to question me for the present. My own time for questioning would come, and I should know to seize the opportunity when it was ripe.

The meal over, we settled into the doctor's study, coffee was brought in, and we remained undisturbed. The doctor took out the file and spread the papers over the desk.

Being a physician, Dr Bernstein began his examination of the contents with the document I had considered last; the medical report. Of this, there was only one entry of significant interest, which was the very first one, established by a certain Dr Enderson on the day of Lydia's arrival at Holloway. The moment I had read it, I had felt a tingling down my spine, for it confirmed at least one of my suspicions.

April 18, 1875

Lydia Krieger, 29 years of age, born August 1, 1846, in good physical health, primiparous.

Mr and Mrs Edward Cavendish have brought Miss Lydia Krieger, sister of the second-named, for examination in view of confinement and treatment for mental illness.

I first spoke with Mr and Mrs Cavendish in the absence of the patient. Mrs Cavendish recounts that her sister has displayed increasingly abnormal psychological behaviour, in particular for anything concerned with the act of writing, since the age of 13 or 14 years. Miss Krieger was sent for treatment to a private clinic in Switzerland at the age of 24. Miss Krieger is now aged 29. Miss Krieger left the clinic one year ago for her annual summer holiday in England, and did not return. Mr Cavendish told me that the reason for her remaining in England was that she was found to be with child. Miss Krieger either would not say or was unaware of how this situation had come about. Mrs Cavendish moved with her to the countryside for six months, remaining with her until the birth of the child. When her sister was entirely recovered, she returned with her to London, leaving the child in the care of a local woman. Mrs Cavendish states that her sister's mental condition has become even more fragile than it was previous to the birth, and, given what has happened, she believes it would be unwise to allow her to continue to roam freely within society, when any unscrupulous person might take advantage of her mental disability.

I then saw Miss Lydia Krieger. The initial cursory examination of the patient confirmed Mrs Cavendish's observations of pronounced mental abnormality and fragility. Mr and Mrs Cavendish refuse to communicate any information concerning the Swiss clinic where Miss Krieger received treatment. They claim that the reason is that 'they wish Miss Krieger's whereabouts to remain entirely unknown to the circle of friends she had formed there, for reasons that should be obvious', even at the price of excluding all possibility of obtaining her previous medical records. In any case, Mrs Cavendish claims that contrarily to her original expectations, the Swiss treatment had no positive effect on her sister, that if anything she worsened under its influence, and that the records of it would be of no use to us. She categorically refused to give any further details on this matter. In fact, the couple had never had any direct communication with the Swiss clinic at all, the whole affair having been handled by a third person, who had been named as the sisters' legal guardian upon their mother's death.

Holloway Sanatorium agrees to accept Miss Lydia Krieger as a patient for a trial period of one month, during which time she will be examined and diagnosed for further treatment. At the end of the one-month period, a final decision will be made as to whether she may be profitably kept.

One sentence had leapt out at me in letters of flame: *the birth of the child*! So I was right, I had to be right: the age was the same, the resemblance was there: the child could not be anyone but Sebastian. He was, as I had guessed, and somehow in the depths of my soul even hoped, Lydia's son.

I waited for Dr Bernstein to say something about it, any remark at all, any hypothesis about what might have happened when Lydia left Basel, but he did not mention it, and his face was inscrutable. I bided my time, and he continued to read through the documents one by one, handing each one to me as he finished. I had glanced through the file on the train to London, of course, and read it all in greater detail during the long, long trip across the continent, but it was interesting to read it again together with him, for he kept up a running commentary on the purely medical aspects of the case that were outlined on each page; every minor illness, every drug and medicine that Lydia had ever received merited his scathing commentary, and on the whole the experience was an enlightening one even if he did avoid precisely the points that most interested me. The doctor was in no hurry. He did not rush through the pages as I had done; he read them one by one in detail, frowned often, stopped occasionally to look things up in certain large medical books he kept upon his shelves, and finally concluded his examination of the medical report with a fiery diatribe against institutional treatment in general, during which he actually took notes of his own words, probably in view of some future written complaint! Then, perhaps in deference to my nationality, he peered at the clock which was ticking loudly upon the mantelpiece and rang for the manservant to bring us tea and biscuits on a tray, draw the curtains, and light the lamps, for it was already growing dusky outside. Setting aside the large sheaf of Lydia's own writings for later, he now pulled towards him the thick notebook in which Dr Richards had recorded the efforts of five years of psychiatric treatment. The file did not contain the records of the efforts of the doctors who had held the position before his arrival at Holloway in the month of September of 1895. They must have been archived in some separate place; presumably they were too bulky to fit inside. After all, most patients did not spend twenty-five years receiving treatment, and the square files had been constructed of a limited thickness. Thus, Lydia's file contained nothing but the records of the four and half years during which Dr Richards attended her.

During the first few weeks, Dr Richards' comments upon the writing samples that emerged from Lydia's pen expressed strenuous efforts at comprehension, accompanied by somewhat forced analyses. As Dr Bernstein read them, he grunted, shook his head, slapped his forehead in deep irritation and occasionally uttered smothered imprecations.

I had experienced some of the same reactions upon reading them, although I did not have the professional qualifications that he did. But Dr Richards' approach struck me as unconvincing, unlikely, and, in fact, altogether unbelievable. This feeling was strengthened, I admit, by my secret rationalistic suspicion that Lydia's madness was simply too mad to be meaningful, and no analysis could possibly make sense of it. With all my heart I desired Dr Bernstein to prove me wrong, to discover something, to convince me, yet I was conscious of a pinch of fear that the evening might end in disappointment, either because he might find nothing, or worse, because he might enter into some slippery psychological terrain upon which I could not follow him, interpreting weird occult meanings into Lydia's words that I could not perceive myself at all.

Dr Richards' overbearing personality shone through his writings, exasperating me even though I knew that he was simply and conscientiously doing his professional job. '*The previous doctors have made a mess of the case*' was the very first phrase he had consigned to the notebook devoted to the study of his recalcitrant patient.

No modern methods have been applied, only clumsy efforts at persuasion and moderate coercion, which, as might be expected, have had no effect whatsoever. It was necessary for me to proceed to a new and complete interview with the family, which is at present reduced only to the sister, now a widow. Modern psychoanalytical theory indicates repressed trauma from early childhood, which may or may not be linked to the act of writing. The patient's history of childhood communicated by the sister does not indicate the latter, but although she shared the patient's childhood, the difference in age indicates that she may not have been conscious or even born at the time of the original trauma. This is a clear possibility in view of the fact that the children were adopted together, indicating that if the second child was a baby at that time, the older one had already reached the age of two, an age at which the great impressionability and consciousness of the child does not match its ability to express itself, leading, as recent theories reveal, to frequent cases of traumatic repression. Neither the patient nor her sister has any memories of or knowledge of anything concerning the time previous to their adoption.

On the other hand, they were not told that they were adopted until the mother revealed it to them on her deathbed, when the sisters were aged fourteen and twelve respectively. She told them that they should be aware of the fact, so that they would not be surprised if they learnt it later from some unexpected source, such as an old family acquaintance who had witnessed the adoption. Both the patient and her sister claim that they were far more shocked by the death of their adoptive mother, which left them orphans for a second time (their adoptive father having died ten years earlier when the children were aged four and two), than by this revelation. Certainly the patient's irregular behaviour dates from this time. It is possible in the case of the patient that the combination of the two events, losing her single remaining parent and *learning of her adoption, produced the impulse to compulsive behaviour.*

In order to determine the truth, a cure of this patient must be effected, which can only be done by causing the memory of the trauma to emerge. Previous doctors have been incapable of perceiving the original cause and thus of providing adapted treatment.

'He does seem to have some idea of why Lydia began to write so strangely,' I said, after reading this page together with the doctor. We were both leaning over his broad oak desk covered with a layer of dark green leather, and the page laid open upon it was bathed in the mellow circle of light from the lamp. A very faint but not disagreeable odour of cigar smoke clung to the doctor's jacket. Together, we read through Dr Richards' efforts with Lydia over the following weeks and months, which consisted largely in applications of recently developed methods of dream-analysis and free association.

'He is missing the main point,' exclaimed the doctor. 'All these suppositions are well and good, but he cannot hope to find the answer through attempts at direct analysis such as these!' He turned another page, then half-covered it with his hand. Then he glanced at me, and took his hand away.

'Hum,' he mumbled, 'please recall that a doctor's job involves a certain necessary intimacy.' I smiled and nodded gently. I had already read the entire text and seen everything embarrassing that there might be to see, as, in fact, he might have known had he taken a moment to think about it. But there seemed no point in saying so; his delicacy was kindly meant.

By two months after the beginning of his treatment, Dr Richards was displaying frustration with the case, leading him to explore the domains that Dr Bernstein feared might embarrass me. But he needn't have worried; if anything, I found all the commentaries disappointingly tame.

The patient resists all attempts to unearth the original source of trauma, opposing a consistent attitude of dreamy absent-mindedness to my questions. Her responses are indicative of a deeper resistance than the respect for appearance and manners that has certainly been inculcated into her. No matter how I phrase them, she deflects my questions about sexuality with vague and general remarks. She will not react to any hints and shows no will whatsoever to investigate her deeper self, or, in fact, to be cured of her affliction at all. She will not rise to the bait even if asked whether she does not wish to leave this place and to live outside like other people. She has been here for twenty years now, and any desire to return to the real world has been lost, perhaps replaced by the nameless and unspoken fear of freedom well known in long-term patients and prisoners. She opposes all insistence, even provocation, with a fatalistic sigh.

On we read together, through the months and years of efforts on the part of the doctor to understand the origin of Lydia's problem, and to influence or modify the static condition of the problem itself.

December 4, 1895

I asked Miss Krieger if she remembered the very beginnings of her condition. She replied that she did remember more or less, but that it had been gradual, not sudden. I asked her to describe these gradual beginnings, and she told me that it had begun at the age of fourteen, after the death of her mother. Until that time, she had been schooled by governesses, and had not experienced any difficulties. She recalls that after her mother died, she occasionally felt a strong desire to write down certain words. Encouraged by friends who were involved in spiritualism, she associated these with the desire of her mother to send her messages from beyond. She had no precise memory of exactly what those first words might have been. At that time, the inner pressure to write down words became increasingly strong, but it took a year before it actually began to interfere severely with her attempts to write other texts. At that point it became necessary for her to keep a second paper near her when writing anything, which she used to note down the irrelevant words that pressed into her mind. Over the course of a second year, she gradually lost the ability to write words of her own choice. She did not recall this development as being particularly unpleasant, and had no sense of being mentally ill. She described it as a person who slowly begins to limp while walking, due to some developing defect of the leg. At first it seems like nothing, and then little by little one accepts the situation without making a fuss about it. For many months, she continued to believe that she was receiving messages from her defunct mother, but her sister shed doubt upon this idea. This situation continued until the two sisters reached the ages of twenty-two and twenty-four. At that time, the patient's sister married, and the couple came to the decision, to which the patient did not object, to send her to a clinic in Switzerland specialising in psychiatric treatment of trance and automatic writing. The patient spent four years in Switzerland, returning home only during the summer holidays. Details and records from this clinic have not been provided for use in the present treatment; neither the patient nor her sister consent to speak of it or even to identify it. It is very possible that the treatments she received there provoked a new trauma. I reserve the possibility of discovering more about this at a later stage, if investigation of the original source of trauma does not yield results.

I peeked at Dr Bernstein out of the corner of my eye as we read this passage. After all, it was his clinic and his treatment that were being referred to here in such cavalier terms! He twitched nervously; indeed, I noticed that his forehead was glistening and he was clearly in the grip of a strong emotion. But once again he said nothing about what interested me so particularly.

December 18, 1895

I asked the patient if she understood that other people were able to write down anything that they were able to think in their heads. She replied that she understood this. I asked her if she understood that a person might, at will, take a piece of paper and write a note, for example thanking someone for a gift. We discussed at some length the words 'Thank you for your kind gift' and the awkwardness and difficulty caused by the fact of being unable to make such communications by writing. The patient stated that in her youth she had overcome such difficulties by the expedient of dictation, then by the use of the telegraph, and later occasionally even the telephone. She denied that her disability had ever placed her in a position of being unable to behave normally in social situations, or compelled her to be rude. Indeed, she seemed shocked at the suggestion. I asked if it had not made her uncomfortable to be always dependent on her friends and family. She replied that such was the lot of women in our society, and that perhaps, were they granted a general freedom from the yoke of such forced dependence, the psychological effect induced by this freedom would have had some effect upon her own condition. We then entered into a discussion of social mores which convinced me that she is no fool and has a penetrating understanding of the forces and necessities that govern the order of society. Whilst she may deplore, she does not protest, being of a character more attuned to resignation than to rebellion.

December 31, 1895
    Today, I decided to perform a thought experiment with the patient's collaboration. First, she was

to watch me writing a short thank-you note, simultaneously concentrating on the movements of my arm and hand, and on the words appearing on the page, which she was to read out as they appeared. I concentrated upon the notion of thanks, feeling that expressions of simple courtesy and polite gratefulness were very natural to her, a condition reinforced by careful upbringing and a sense of duty.

Having ascertained that she was able to perform this action with the utmost normality, I set her to a more difficult task, asking her to imagine someone she knew well, her sister, for example, in the process of writing a similar note. Now she was to visualise the situation in detail, imagining each gesture, seeing the pen dipping into the ink and tracing the words. She was then to read out the words just as her imagination caused them to be traced one by one upon the imaginary paper. She was to follow all gestures of arm, hand and pen, just as she had done with me, but entirely in her imagination. This exercise was exactly as successful as the previous one. There could be no distinction between the patient's performance and that of a perfectly ordinary person. Finally, I asked her to apply the same concentration to envisioning a picture of herself writing the same now-familiar note. I asked her to envision the scene in detail and to describe to me everything that she saw. She appeared to undertake the exercise willingly enough, and described herself moving towards the writing-table, sitting down, drawing the paper in front of her and taking the pen in her hand. She then stopped her description. I encouraged her to continue.

She told me that no sooner was the pen in her hand in her imagination, than the thoughts in her brain began to be taken over by the words which seemingly poured into it from an outside source, and she felt the stirrings of the irresistible compulsion to write them down in an automatic manner, even though there was no actual pen in her hand. As she pronounced the word 'outside', she unconsciously pointed her finger towards heaven. She explained that because she felt slightly distanced from the situation of writing due to its being in her imagination and not real, she felt able to slide in and out of the state of trance at will, exactly as though she were opening and shutting her ears to the flow of words. Letting her imagination show her the picture of herself putting pen to paper immediately activated the flow of words, whereas focusing her eyes upon real objects in the room, in particular her own empty hands, brought her back to reality. I asked if she could envision herself writing and pronounce, rather than write, the words that flowed into her mind. She said that this would be possible and indeed she had been aware of the possibility for many years, but that she avoided engaging in the exercise, from a fear of thereby opening a door to the entrance of the trance-words into other aspects of her life than that associated purely with writing. I explained to her that I thought it possible that if the trance-words could be made to intrude into other aspects of ordinary life, then ordinary life could also be induced to arise in moments of trance, and perhaps mingling them would be a positive catalyst for change. She resisted my suggestion, asserting that she was convinced that trance-words would enter her ordinary life but not the contrary, as the one had always seemed to be within her power and the other not. I very much wished to make the experiment, for I believe that if there is to be any hope of a treatment, some change must be provoked in a situation which has remained static for thirty years, even by somewhat violent means. But the patient refused absolutely, claiming that she has always been aware of the risk of a complete slide into madness, and held it at bay by maintaining a certain mental discipline.

I recalled as we read this passage that the following one was of particular significance, and kept an eye firmly trained upon the good doctor as he read.

January 7, 1896
  Today I decided to make an attempt to break through the patient's resistance by confronting her directly on one sensitive point that I have chosen to avoid completely until this point: the birth of her child. While obviously unconnected with the original trauma, the source of her troubles, I have reached a stage where I believe that any means must be used to break down the wall she opposes to any penetration into her inner mental life. I reflected at length before coming to this decision and choosing a strategy, and finally decided to ask her point-blank what she could remember of the birth itself.
  As I had expected, she was sincerely shocked by

the question, and refused to discuss it in the most absolute terms. Alternating between attitudes of brutality and gentleness, a system that often produces excellent results, I admitted that her attitude was quite understandable, and amended my question to asking whether she actually possessed specific memories of the event itself, without requiring any description. She replied that she did not, as she had been plied with chloroform by the attending physician, and repeated that in any case she would not speak about this. Reverting to the direct approach, I asked her whether she did not wish to know what her child had become. She replied that she did, but that destiny had decided otherwise. I asked if she was even aware now of the child's age, phrasing the question in a slightly provocative tone, as though to question whether the fact of her own motherhood held any importance for her. She replied quietly that he had just passed his twenty-first birthday, but that it was quite useless my asking her any further information upon the subject, for none had been vouchsafed her and therefore she had none to provide.

I took this moment to explain to the patient that by the very nature of repression, unconnected pieces of repressed knowledge become associated with each other in the unconscious mind, and that by digging forth one such piece of which she had at least some conscious knowledge, I hoped to unearth the other, which was the initial cause of her malady. I said that it might be a painful procedure, analogous in some ways to the extraction of bad teeth, but was

283

unavoidable if a cure was to be effected. She replied that the project seemed reasonable, but that she had no knowledge on the subject of her child to share with me, repressed or otherwise. I responded that this was certainly untrue, for if nothing else, she must be aware of the identity of the father.

She would not discuss this subject. I developed a thesis upon the notions of social conceptions of morals and honour, and the necessity of rejecting such a system of values in the context of a psychological analysis. She replied that she disagreed, considering that dignity was more important than health. I objected very strongly to this, claiming that a medical operation deprived no one of dignity, and using the example of a purely physical operation to remove something like a tumour located in an intimate place. Would she say that the patient undergoing such an operation had lost his dignity? Was he not, on the contrary, being helped to regain that dignity which illness had partially removed from him? She replied that the doctor's calling was a noble one, but that the loss of dignity was something which must be felt differently by each individual and that it could be that there were some who would rather die than undergo the operation, and she could not fault them if such were their feelings. As for herself, she would not continue with any discussion on the subject of her past. It was impossible for her to imagine discussing these things with a stranger or with anyone at all apart from God, who alone was and would ever be witness to her memories.

From this time on, it became clear that the doctor lost interest in his patient – if it would not be better said that the patient lost interest in her doctor. The doctor's conclusion after the failure of his efforts was expressed as follows:

This patient is unfortunately handicapped, in view of any possible treatment, by a sexual repression entirely supported by her social and moral conditioning, which prevents any access to her inner world. The prognosis under these conditions is not hopeful. The patient's experience with motherhood has not served to increase her conscious self-awareness, but rather, having been so abruptly and perhaps ill-advisedly interrupted, has sealed her even more tightly from any possibility of normal self-expression.

It was the end of any attempt on the doctor's part to perform anything like an analysis. Lydia's treatments now evolved into regular sessions of rather rudimentary physical and medical experiments, training activities, guided movements, sedatives, even a session of hypnosis performed, as little Polly had told me, by a visiting French doctor who specialised in that area of treatment. All these methods and more were applied in the attempt to modify her writing activity directly, without any further examination into its deeper cause, nor for that matter any success whatsoever. The sessions became increasingly rare – no more than one a month in the last year or two – and the doctor's entries increasingly perfunctory. We were able to read through the later ones far more quickly than the first. The very last consultation marked in the book, as I pointed out to Dr Bernstein, had taken place on the day following Sebastian's visit to Holloway, and followed the previous one by a mere ten days. Clearly the unusual event had caused a spark of interest in the doctor, but he had fallen too far into Lydia's disfavour to be able to obtain anything important from her now, no matter how striking the stimulus.

January 1, 1900

I called the patient in for an unscheduled visit today, after learning that yesterday she received an unexpected visit, her first in the twenty-five years that she has spent within the walls of this institution. Although I was not informed of this visit until after it had occurred, and therefore had no chance to see the visitor with my own eyes, the description of the visitor provided me by the accompanying nurse, as a young man of about twenty-five bearing a strong physical resemblance to the patient, convinces me that this person can have been no other than the child she is known to have borne in 1875, about whom she has had no knowledge or information from the time of his birth. If I had been aware that there was any possibility whatsoever of such a visit, I would have left instructions for the visitor to see me before leaving, for much information on the patient's state of mind might have been had in this way. Furthermore, I was informed by the nurse that at the termination of visiting hours, the young man left carrying a sheaf of papers in his hand which she did not recall him holding upon his arrival, and I conclude from this that the patient wished to demonstrate to her visitor the reason for which she has spent half her life under psychological treatment, and provided him with several pages of her automatic writing. In general the patient is forbidden access to paper and pencil, but it is to be presumed that if she told him of her abnormality, the visitor procured them for her in order to witness it for himself.

I could not possibly have foreseen this event, especially as the patient's sister had made quite clear that she herself had no intention of visiting at any time, and had mentioned no other possible visitors at all. As for the patient herself, she refused to respond to my probing queries, giving only her usual bland remark that she did not wish to speak of these things. In spite of her stubborn silence, however, it was quite clear that she was very much moved by the unexpected troubling of the peaceful course of her life. She appeared unusually disturbed, and her hand trembled as she allowed herself to be placed at the table for her customary writing. For this session, I allowed her to write in complete freedom without any form of interference, for I wished to see if the emotions produced by yesterday's visit would have any tangible effect on her writing. In this, though, I was disappointed, for the sample appears identical in spirit to those that I have obtained from her over the past five years.

'It is a pity that the doctor managed to so completely lose Lydia's confidence,' I observed mournfully when Dr

Bernstein had finished reading this final entry. 'If only she had told him all about Sebastian's visit, and he had written it all down here, we would finally know what it was that Sebastian learnt that day.'

'No, I do not think that we would,' replied the doctor. 'You see, even if we may safely assume that Sebastian learnt for sure on that day that Lydia Krieger was his true mother, you who are seeking the cause of his death must seek deeper than this. What matters here, what Sebastian must have discovered, is the hidden secret, the one that Lydia herself could not express in any other way than through her writing. And this Dr Richards was not capable of understanding that even after studying Lydia for so long.'

'So you really believe there is such a secret,' I said, and in spite of my doubts, I prayed that he was right, for otherwise my investigation was at a dead end. 'You really believe that her writings actually mean something.'

'Of course,' he said. 'Even that fool of a doctor realised that, with all his talk of repression and trauma, but he did not understand *where* to look for it! Lydia is not mad – her writings are not the products of an insane mind. There is no nonsense in automatic writing; it is like another language, invented by the writer to simultaneously hide things and yet speak them. You know this – you have read my book, and you saw Hélène Smith at work! That imbecile doctor never looked in the right place for what he sought. He should have been examining the writings themselves, not her thoughts and actions while producing them. *These* writings!' And he slapped his hand down upon the thick sheaf of papers that we had not yet begun to look over together. Lydia's own productions.

By now the evening was already well advanced, and the doctor, seeming unusually agitated, ran his fingers through his short grey beard several times, took up the pile and put it down again, rose nervously, strode about the room, and finally suggested that we have supper before starting work upon them, as it was likely to take a considerable amount of time. I was more than willing, so we left them on the desk and went into the small dining room, to partake of a light meal consisting of mushroom soup, followed by a cheese omelette, all prepared by the admirable manservant. During this repast, we avoided the subject of Lydia Krieger by common consent; instead, the doctor entertained me with a sketch of the development in methods of psychoanalytical treatment since the ideas of Sigmund Freud had begun to be adopted all over Europe. It was fascinating, but I could not bring myself to believe in it all. My own dreams being often quite nonsensical, I found it difficult to convince myself that they represented anything more than a great collection of visions, observations, hopes and fears, all ephemerally tied together in a random hodgepodge of kaleidoscopic images. Freud's theory of the interpretation of dreams, published in a book which had appeared but last November and which the doctor could not resist fetching and thrusting under my nose in the middle of the omelette, struck me as most inapplicable to myself. Goodness me, if some of the nocturnal messes in my head really represent desires, whatever am I to think?

After dinner, we returned to the study, the manservant brought coffee and was given his well-deserved dismissal for the night, and the doctor, who did not seem to know weariness, eagerly snatched up the first page of Lydia's writings, radiating a tense and silent expectation which I observed with mixed feelings. Fascination at seeing the man at work, flushed with the conviction of his beliefs and irrepressible hope that complete understanding was finally at hand were tempered by doubts and fears. Quelling all expression of these conflicting emotions, I joined the doctor at his desk and we began to read.

The writings in the file began from the time of Dr Richards' arrival at Holloway; her earlier work must have been archived somewhere along with the medical observations of the preceding psychiatrists. Dr Richards had taken up his post at Holloway in September of 1895, and the first sample dated from that month. There were at least a hundred of them collected through the years, the last one dating from the day following Sebastian's visit to Holloway. They were piled in inverse order, with the latest one on top, and quite naturally, just as I had, Dr Bernstein began to read them as they appeared, from the last one to the first. In a style reminiscent of Sebastian's suicide note, Lydia's large, flowing handwriting dominated the space on the paper, covering an entire page with just a few sentences.

In the final sample, from the day after she saw Sebastian, Lydia had written:

The Father, the Son and the Holy Ghost. The Father, the Son and the Holy Ghost, redeem our sins and our transgressions. The transgressors of long ago give birth to the sinners of today, the transgressions of long ago give birth to the sins of today. The Son will redeem the transgressors, the Son will redeem the sinners. On the Day of Judgement the truth will emerge and the sinner and the Son will be reunited. Unnatural no longer, sinful but natural, pure love, sin redeemed, abomination redeemed by lesser sin and lesser sin redeemed by the Son, all truth will emerge and shine on the Day of Judgement.

On December 20th, she had written:

Child of the Father, look to the Father, look to Heaven for salvation, there is no evil but abomination, there is no abomination but denial of the Father, there is no denial but the unnatural. Unnatural is the ripping of the veil, when the child of God rips the veil of God then is Evil done, all natural sin is not evil for man does not decide, all comes from God, yet Evil exists, but then how could he do this? How could he do this?

Back we travelled through the months and years of Lydia's incarceration, and though I could make out nothing more than a prophetic ring to her outpourings, I could not but be impressed by the power of the inner, unconscious force that had compelled her to continue producing them so unchangingly for so long, resisting all efforts and all pressures.

April 18, 1899:
  Birth from sin, birth from abomination, pain of the abomination, joy of the birth, right and wrong, good and evil, mingled in a birth of joy and abomination. On the day of judgement will emerge the truth. Suffer

the little children to come unto me. Children of God born of sin and abomination, children of the Father, it is his will though the fabric of the universe was rent as the veil of the Temple was rent, from top to bottom.

January 7, 1899:

The meaning is hidden it is God's will, it is God's will for all is God's will, but the unnatural is Evil and how can Evil be God's will? All that exists is God's will and Abomination exists and so it is God's will but it is God's will that abomination should exist, then how could he do this? The world is full of sinners, sin is natural and God will forgive. There is no sin, there is no right and wrong for all can be forgiven. Sin is not evil, evil is not sin, all comes from God and the heavens above and the earth below glow with beauty and God's gift to us is this beauty and so he cannot be angry with our sin. But abomination is not sin: is abomination evil sent by the Father to his Child? Should not the Father love his Child and does he not, for we are surrounded by beauty. But then how?

July 15, 1898:

God sees below with the eye that sees all and the acts of his children are all visible to Him. All are equal, the acts of the children of God, all are equal in the eye of God because they are sent by Him. Sin is not evil in the eye of God because sin is natural and natural is the harmony of the universe sent by God to his child. What looks like sin may be Good and what *looks like Good may be evil for we have not the eye of God. The truth will emerge on the day of Judgement and then and only then may we know that all is right in the eye of God for all comes from Him. The truth cannot now be known because the sinners are aware of their sin and not aware that in Heaven sin is no sin and all sin is forgiven and right and wrong are not. Only Abomination is not forgiven.*

Dr Bernstein read each passage slowly several times, sometimes murmuring the words aloud, and examining them with a detailed thoughtfulness that seemed to take forever. By the time we reached the bottom of the pile, I was possessed by alternating feelings of dreadful boredom and acute despair, with little room left for optimism. I felt more than ever as though I could easily write such stuff myself, given a quiet hour and a sufficient heap of paper, and were Dr Bernstein to seek a deeper meaning within it, he should be wasting his time. It was with a sense of relief that I saw that we had reached the very last page, which was really the earliest one, from the day of Lydia's first encounter with Dr Richards.

September 11, 1895:
Madness in the red sky, mad red storm in the swirling sky, madness of abomination and evil in the mad spinning red clouds, clouds of our confusion and our sin. The eye of the storm is the eye of God, centre of all things, seer of all things, the mad confusion of the wild red churning sky, tumult of sin we are blind here below. All that comes from God is given

by the Father to his child, but the mad storms hide
the Truth from us, that will emerge only on the day
of Judgement.

I pushed the papers aside, and leant back for a moment's repose, but Dr Bernstein was far from finished. He looked through them all again, concentrating with fevered intensity, driven by a will to understand which could only be explained by a more powerful passion than the purely intellectual desire to know. He bent his eyes close to the pages, he read and re-read the same sentences again and again as though they did not occur in a hundred other places, he murmured words aloud – he even wrote things down. Some of the passages he read out to me, and doing my best to encourage him, I sought inside myself some observations of my own, so as to stimulate at least some kind of a discussion.

Dr Bernstein had only one clear intention in his mind: the search for a coherent, deeper meaning. He rambled on, speaking half to me and half to himself, suddenly holding forth in spurts as an idea struck him, then falling silent. He spoke of historical references, he tried anagrams of certain words and phrases, he tried substituting certain words in a systematic way for others. He took thick books from his shelves and read out to me strange and astonishing accounts of long-past cases of automatic writing and prophetic seizures. I watched him at work, sometimes joyfully influenced by his certainty, at others feeling merely dull and increasingly tired. Sometimes I tried to gently oppose a little simple logic to some of his wilder ideas. Hours passed; it was the middle of the night now, and I was quite exhausted, but I dared not interrupt the flow of his inspired research. Once, I pronounced the name of Dr Richards, only to find myself violently interrupted, in a tone whose indignation seemed proportional to the doctor's own feelings of frustration.

'Do not mention his name to me any more! The doctor was a fool – he utterly missed the point! He did not *read* what she wrote! He asked stupid questions, he probed vulgarly and stupidly – but he did not *read*!'

He strode about the room, clutching a paper in his hands, his eyes like glowing coals, reading out snatches, repeating them aloud and under his breath, changing the order of the words as Lydia herself frequently did.

'The truth will emerge on the day of Judgement!'

'All truth will emerge and shine on the day of Judgement!'

'The Truth, that will emerge only on the day of Judgement!'

Periodically he relit the lamp and also one or two candles, whose flicker added an element of peculiar mystery to the whole venture. Midnight passed, one o'clock, two o'clock, then three. Eventually the doctor fell silent, staring moodily at the papers and books piled and scattered over his desk, and I found myself drifting into sleep. To prevent myself from nodding, I rose and wandered over to the window, pushed aside the heavy curtain and leant my forehead against the icy cold glass, peering out into the night, across which light snowflakes were spreading their soft curtain of fairy dust through the glowing light of . . .

Dozens of lanterns, held in a hundred utterly immobile white-gloved hands!

A voiceless Inquisition? A silent troop of ghosts come

to fetch me to the land of mystery into whose secrets I was trying so hard to penetrate?

I jumped backwards, pale with shock and disbelief, closed my eyes for a moment, then carefully advanced and peered once again out of the foggy pane. No, it was not a vision. The unearthly sight was there as before, soundless under the falling snow, hoods, hats and wigs grouped in a frozen pantomime.

'Dr Bernstein!' I managed to articulate. 'What on earth is happening in the street?'

He came to the window, glanced out and smiled. Now I saw that under shocks of yellow and red woolly hair were the most grotesque masks I had ever seen; mad weird distorted faces, some with giant noses, others with fixed wide open mouths or gigantic teeth spilling over the painted lips. All were poised in positions of activity as though caught in a moment of petrified time: some held drumsticks aloft, others fifes and flutes, but of music, motion or sound there was none. On the pavements on either side, a few people in ordinary dress, also clutching lanterns and bundled to the nose in woollen wraps and scarves, stood watching them. The utter silence and immobility of so many people, the monstrous masks illuminated from below by the shafts of eerie light emanating from the many lanterns, came together to form a terrifying and magical vision.

'Why, tonight is Fasnacht – the beginning of the carnival,' said the doctor. 'I had forgotten. Take your coat, and let us go down into the street.'

I wrapped myself up solidly against the cold, imbued with a strong feeling of unreality. The doctor led me down the stairs and outside. Standing with other spectators on the pavement, we now became not just observers, but a very part of the uncanny scene. I stood still, staring about me, having no idea what to expect. I had never seen or heard of any carnival consisting of freakish masks standing utterly still in the pitch darkness in the deepest part of the night.

Then the cathedral bells began to toll, and struck four.

As though on an instantaneous cue, the masked figures came alive together and began to play music, strange, ancient, gay little marching tunes, while stepping forward at a regular pace. We followed them up the street and around the corner; at each crossroads we saw other groups in ever more outlandish and wild dress, proceeding up and down the cobbled streets, some, like ours, with fife and drum, others with blaring of trumpets, still others with violins. The masks were enormous, twice the size of a normal head; a group of twenty shocking Mozart-faces with mouths open in fixed toothy grins, bird-heads with bodies covered in multi-coloured feathers, stiff golden-faced Napoleons in clown suits with giant buttons and tri-cornered hats, and the weirdest figures of all, with grins stretching from one eye to the other, mops of blue or yellow hair, noses reaching up to their foreheads, teeth nearly down to their chins, and a general air of insane glee.

I asked no questions, for the whole appearance of the carnival was itself a conundrum of cosmic dimensions, and I did not want to spoil my profound intuition that it was all somehow closely connected with the object of our research by the acquisition of any dry factual information. I continued to look about me, trying to absorb impressions, to observe only, and not to think. A shower of tiny paper confetti rained over our heads and shoulders, drenching us both in bits of red, whilst crazy laughter echoed behind and around us.

'What do I want? What am I seeking here?' I asked myself, as we wandered on through the icy cold amongst the crazy masks and falling snowflakes. 'Something here is trying to speak to me. There is a message for me somewhere in all this. There is something that I have to realise, or to do.' And all at once, I knew what it was; something very simple, something that I should have sought already, inside myself, but that I had not sought because I was inhibited. In such surroundings, inhibition seemed to belong to another world, a world of normality that was shut into the tight walls of the warm, protected houses, shut away from the wild streets that were the scene of wild freedom from normal behaviour.

I myself was free now, and the fact that had slipped through my mind without leaving a trace strong enough to rise to the surface came easily to my tongue. A group of harlequins in white satin with giant black buttons, playing a wistful and yearning tune on tiny flutes, passed us and disappeared around a corner, and I found myself with the doctor, momentarily isolated in a little island of quiet. I could hear another group approaching from a distance.

'I think Lydia conceived her child whilst she was living in Basel,' I said, wondering incongruously why I had not seen this before, why I had allowed my mind to assume that it was while under her sister's uncaring protection that Lydia had been led astray. 'She first came to Holloway in April 1875, and the child was already born. In early January, she said that he had just passed his birthday.'

The doctor did not reply, and I went on.

'The child was Sebastian. I am certain of it, and so was Dr Richards. Lydia's sister had been married for five years already when Lydia's baby was born, and she must have feared, or perhaps even known for certain, that she herself would never bear a child, so she adopted her sister's. He must have been a beautiful baby.'

Still no response.

'Lydia must have been already expecting her child when she left Basel in June for her holiday that summer.'

Nothing. But in my new, wild state, I did not feel inclined to let the matter rest. If Lydia had fallen pregnant while living in the doctor's house, then chances were that he knew or could guess who the father was. A vague vision of Herr Ratner floated through my mind. He had been a younger man then, and a friend of the doctor's.

'Did you know anything about it?' I asked relentlessly.

'I must have been blind,' he replied finally, with an effort. 'No, I did not know. I am a doctor, yet I did not see.'

'It was very early days, of course,' I said.

'But I should have guessed! I should never have let her go! I should have told the family that she was unwell and could not travel. I should have kept her near me forever!' He was not looking at me, but into space, into the darkness, or perhaps simply into the past.

'If you think back now,' I said, 'can you guess who fathered the child? I have been wondering – is it not possible that while he was in Zürich Sebastian guessed the identity of his true father as well as that of his mother?'

'No. That is impossible,' he replied, and now his eyes came to rest on mine with defiant certainty.

'How can you be sure? The father could have been there, at the concert, and at the party that evening. He could have noticed Sebastian's resemblance to Lydia just as you did. He could have realised the truth, and told Sebastian about it.'

'You are not guessing right,' said the doctor into the feathery snowflakes that floated between our faces. 'Yes, the father of Lydia's child was there that evening, and he saw what you say that he saw. But he was not certain of what it meant. He could not be certain, for he had never known of the existence of a child, and could not quite convince himself of something so momentous, not when it might be nothing but an error, and when the young man himself seemed so perfectly convinced of having his own quite different parents. His mind was in a turmoil, and in the end he did not utter a single word on the subject of paternity.'

'But now he knows?' I asked carefully, feeling my way into the intricacies of this discourse.

'Yes. Now he knows for certain. Sebastian was his child.'

'He told you?' Like the flame of the candles in the lanterns, the truth flickered in my mind.

'Have you not understood?' he responded, and turning, he moved out of the square, away from the direction from which the newest group of masked revellers was now nearly upon us.

'It was you?'

'It was I.'

Without quite knowing this, somehow I must have known it, for I was not really surprised. The doctor began to speak, rebelliously, quickly, loudly into the darkness, flinging the weight of his guilt at me as though I should be able to catch it and take some of its burden from him.

'Yes, it was I. Yes, I betrayed the marriage bond and I betrayed the doctor's oath: a double infidelity. That is exactly what I did. In moral terms, there could hardly be a more heinous sin. But it was a sin of love such as is beyond expression and beyond morality. Her family took her away from me. They spirited her away and I could not find her although I searched for months and years. My letters remained unanswered, her guardian died, I could not find her trace! I lost her suddenly and without knowing why. And the passion I felt for her has continued petrified, unchanged and undiminished in my heart since that day. It was that passion that made me speak, the evening I saw Sebastian. I did not speak of my love, of course – I did not say much, yet I said too much, for what I told him drove him to the search for Lydia that ended with his death! I did not understand then that it was the death of my own son. That knowledge only came to me from you.' He had been shouting almost convulsively, but the last words came out in a whisper, and I understood with a kind of shock why he had remained silent, pressing his lips together, about precisely the points on which I most wanted his opinion, those concerning Lydia's motherhood, and what it was that he had come to understand over the course of the evening that had driven him into such a frenzy.

I did not know what to say to one who has discovered the existence of his child only after that child is dead. But the doctor clutched my arm, and I realised that there was someone even more important to him than the son whom, after all, he had never known.

'Thanks to you, though, I have found the treasure that I lost. Our son died because he found her, but I shall not die, because I am stronger than my enemies, who are *her* enemies. Twenty-five years too late, I will find her and free her, and, if she will, I will marry her.'

'What enemies? Who are they?' I said in confusion, staring in surprise at his transformed face.

'Her words tell the story of what happened,' he said. 'Now I see it plainly! It is all in the words themselves, just as I told you! Do you not remember what she wrote on the day after Sebastian came? *The Father, the Son and the Holy Ghost*?'

'Yes, I remember that,' I said.

'The Son! Do you not see?'

'Yes.' I paused. 'The Son', indeed; she had written that word directly after Sebastian's visit. But her writings were all full of religious phrases. What was the doctor so certain that he saw? Was there really a meaning to it all?

'I described that,' he exclaimed, and now he was walking quickly, almost running towards his home, dragging me along by the sleeve. 'In my book, I told how the words of a secret shared with Lydia would emerge in an unrecognisable context the next time she wrote!'

'Yes, I remember,' I said, hurrying and slipping on the slushy cobbles. 'But was that really the first time that she ever used the word "Son"?'

'You tell me. Do you remember any other instances through all the pages that we read?'

I tried to recall another, but failed.

'There are none!' he exclaimed in confirmation. 'Look again, and you will see that she never used the word "Son" before that day. It is the words, the words we must consider! We must find out which are the true ones. Come, hurry, hurry! We have work to do!'

302

CHAPTER TWENTY

The dawn was leaking palely through the window by the time we had finished the task upon which Dr Bernstein insisted: counting the number of times each word and phrase appeared in the hundred samples of Lydia's writing, and setting them down one by one in order of frequency. But all desire to sleep had fled. So clear, so unexpected and so diabolical were the conclusions necessarily provoked by the list finally tabulated and thrust under my nose by the trembling hand of the overexcited doctor, that I pushed it away with a spontaneous cry.

'Impossible!'

Yet I took it back and stared at it, horrified and mesmerised. It read:

Unnatural
Love
Birth
Abomination
Father
Child
How could he do this?
Evil
Sin
On the day of judgement the truth will emerge.

CHAPTER TWENTY-ONE

'But what does it mean?' I said at length, sitting down weakly. I felt the perspiration break out on my brow and my legs weaken beneath me. I did not understand, but the feeling of the presence of evil was so strong and so convincing that there was no need to know the identities of transgressor and victim to sense the truth at the heart of the list of words.

'Such words never came from Lydia herself,' the doctor was saying. 'These are undoubtedly words and fragments of sentences that were told to her in secret.'

'You think so? They were words that she heard? You do not think these reflect some experience of her own?'

'Incest? For that is what is being described here; there is no doubt about it. No, this was not Lydia's own story. The birth of a child was involved in the story echoed here, and when Lydia came to me she was innocent and without sexual experience. That is certain.'

'But she did have a child before writing these,' I said, blushing in the darkness at the awkwardness of thus referring to the doctor's transgression.

'Yes, but during the years she spent with me, she wrote the same things, repeatedly. I recognise them all. If only I had understood it then!'

Tears of emotion stood in his eyes. Between the shame of the horror revealed by Lydia's words and that associated with the doctor's illicit relationship with his patient, the conversation was fraught with awkwardness and difficulty, but as I have often noted, there is nothing better in such circumstances than to keep as calm as possible, to breathe deeply, and to say what needs to be said. I did so, and felt the wrestling match taking place in my mind between doubt and certainty diminish in intensity and disappear, the former yielding definitively to the latter. In my heart, I knew now that contrarily to what I had believed, the list of words in front of me did carry a meaningful message. My eyes were opened, and I could see it clearly, even if I did not fully understand. I had been blind, stupid and stubborn, that was all. A rather large all.

'Think,' the doctor was continuing. 'Lydia's father died when she was four. The psychological scars left by incest are strong even when repressed, but she was entirely free of them. Lydia did not suffer an incestuous relationship, but all the signs point to her having heard talk about someone who did.'

'But why would the talk she overheard not simply have brought the fact to her consciousness?'

'Either because she was sworn to secrecy, or because she did not understand what she heard. I suspect the latter reason is the right one, for surely she would have chosen to reveal the secret in confidence to a doctor, rather than suffer endless years of incarceration in order to keep it. And then, she did not have the knowledge to understand such things; she had been brought up very protected. I think it far more probable that she did not understand the words she heard, yet she sensed that something was deeply wrong. Remember that I knew Lydia very well. I am certain that she had no conscious memory of these words at any time, and no awareness that the words emerging in her writing had either the meaning or the origin that I see in them now.'

'But how could she have heard and remembered words unconsciously but not consciously?'

'It would be possible if, for instance, she was extremely young. A very small child, unable to understand anything other than the seriousness of what she was hearing. Small children often have strong memories of which they are unaware, which can emerge unexpectedly many years later.'

'But she only began the spontaneous writing at fourteen,' I said. 'Why would she have carried the words inside her silently for all those years, and then suddenly begun expressing them?'

'Do you remember what event triggered the beginning of her writing?'

'It started when her mother died. Is that it?'

'Yes. It seems rather as if, at that point, Lydia lost the only person with whom she could share her trouble, even if she was conscious of neither the trouble nor of sharing it.'

'So you believe the words were spoken by her mother?'

'I believe so. I think it is possible that the mother held the child close to her for comfort in her pain, and expressed her feelings of horror and despair, perhaps simply murmuring broken words, feeling secure in the knowledge that the child was much too small to understand. The words survived in the unconscious memory of the child, together with the child's sense that the words corresponded to a dreadful secret that must be repressed at all costs. As long as the mother lived, the unconscious mind of the child would not have to bear the full burden of the secret. But after her death, the weight of bearing it alone must have produced a strong urge to discover another way to both keep the secret and share it, all without any of this ever reaching the conscious mind.'

'But what *was* the secret? Lydia's mother was a married woman, and Lydia and Tanis were adopted children. What experience of incest could she have been alluding to? Do you think it was something from the mother's own childhood?'

'It might have been that,' he said. 'But time and changes in life tend to soothe and relieve ancient pains if they are consciously expressed, as Lydia's mother appeared to have been doing. It seems to me more likely that she was describing something which was causing her great pain at the time she spoke of it.'

I thought over all that I had heard of Joseph Krieger and his family, and remembered the words of Prosper Sainton.

'There was a daughter who died . . .'

'A daughter? Whose daughter?'

'A daughter of Joseph Krieger and his wife, who died before Lydia and Tanis were adopted.'

'Died? How did she die?'

'I don't know. I don't even know exactly when she died. But wait – there is something.' I tried to recall exactly what I had read in the old diaries of the French violin professor. I cast my mind back . . . I could see myself sitting in Professor Wessely's office . . . I could almost see the notebook in my hands. 'Her name was Xanthe. A friend of the Kriegers wrote about her in the winter of 1848. He had met Mrs Krieger somewhere, and she had mentioned this girl who had died, who had been sent to the country for her health, and who had died there. And then later I found out that Mrs Krieger refused to be buried at Highgate, where her husband had purchased a family tomb. She asked to be buried with her daughter instead.'

'In the country. The girl was sent to the country for her health,' the doctor repeated attentively. 'It is a phrase which so often indicates pregnancy. Does it not?'

'Well,' I said. 'I suppose it sometimes does. But I was imagining that Xanthe was a child. Prosper Sainton wrote . . . well, I guess he wrote nothing indicating whether she had died recently, or many years before they spoke, or how old she was when she died. But Mrs Krieger cried, and said she wished she had children to take care of, and Sainton wrote that she was too old to have any more.'

'So, she may have been in her late forties or even fifty or more at that time. This would indicate that the girl who died may not have been so very little.'

'Yes.'

'She might have been fourteen, fifteen, sixteen, and still been referred to as a child who died.'

I digested this idea.

'So you think that Xanthe Krieger might have died in childbirth?'

'Childbirth itself, perhaps, or else the consequences of giving birth at too young an age. Twice. Is it not possible?'

'Oh, my God. Yes, it is. And the little girls—'

'The little adopted girls—'

'From the countryside—'

'Were Xanthe's children. Fathered by her father.'

'Oh, my God.'

'Years of incest. Under the mother's eyes.'

'Perhaps she did not understand at first.'

'But she must have realised when the first child came. She must have tried desperately to put a stop to it.'

'Maybe she believed that she had.'

'But then, a second child came.'

'When Xanthe died, the mother must have seen her husband as a murderer.'

'Yet at the same time, the horror of it all would finally cease . . .'

'And she would have insisted on adopting the babies.'

'And he could not refuse.'

'And then he died himself, and the whole thing was buried in a grave of total silence.'

'How did he die?'

Until this point, my remarks and the doctor's had fused together as if produced by a single mind. But this last question of his started me.

'I don't know. Why do you ask?'

'Don't you see?'

'No! What do you mean? Can you believe—'

'Yes. He would not have been able to stop. The *pulsion* of paedophilia and incest is a disease.'

'You think – he turned his attention to Lydia?'

'I think it is certain that he did, or began to.'

'Horrible, for his wife!'

'And then he suddenly died.'

'He suddenly died,' I repeated as his meaning sank in. 'I see what you mean. She couldn't bear it any more.'

'What would you have done?'

'I think – I think I would have taken the children and gone off somewhere, far away.'

'But she was not the same type of woman as you are. She was probably a dependent, submissive character, who had been made more so by the domination of such a husband. It would be easier for such a person to take control within her domestic sphere than to flee. And then, she was motivated by something more than merely saving the remaining children. There may have been a desire for revenge.'

'Revenge?'

'For the sacrifice of the daughter by the father.'

We spoke simultaneously.

'Agamemnon.'

'Clytemnestra.'

CHAPTER TWENTY-TWO

Is the capacity to murder a character trait? Or are we all potential murderers within?

No – some faced with the choice of life or death will choose life at all costs, others will choose death. Not all can kill.

Like the capacity to go on a stage and enthrall a crowd, the capacity for murder belongs to only some.

Can it be inherited?

I must ask Carl.

Joseph Krieger died suddenly. Perhaps he was ill. Perhaps he committed suicide. But perhaps not.

He created havoc beyond compare in the heart of his family; he had caused horror and the death of his daughter, and suddenly he stood before a fresh temptation, another child, a little one, a fragile one, the very fruit of his horrendous sin, whose life was in his hand to crush and destroy.

If he were capable of feeling remorse or shame, such a temptation itself could be a motive for suicide. It could, indeed. Yet nothing in the picture of him that had put itself together in my mind from all the pieces I had collected from different sources indicated any sign of a capacity for those emotions.

If Mrs Krieger had put an end to her husband's life, and abandoned him in death to his lonely tomb, I could not but feel that it was a deserved judgement for his crimes. But that was not the only question. I also had to ask myself whether Tanis Cavendish had played a similar role in the death of her adopted son.

It was not the first time that this thought had assailed me. I had thought of her once before, on perceiving as a possible motive the necessity of preventing it being brought to Lord Warburton's attention that she had a mad sister interned at Holloway. But my theory had collapsed completely when I discovered that the person who paid the monthly fees for Lydia's hospitalisation was no other than Lord Warburton himself. The whole cycle of realisation, suspicion and disproval had occurred within a space of less than two hours; I had simply felt like a fool, and not spent any further time on the hypothesis.

Now, unable to find rest even in the rhythmic rumble and chug of the sleeping-car that was carrying me back across France, I could think of nothing else. My theory was alive again, for even if Lord Warburton knew about Lydia, it was clearly out of the question that he could ever be allowed to learn of the events the doctor and I had just realised – the dreadful truth of the parentage of his prospective wife.

Sebastian had understood it all; of that I felt certain. For nearly half a century, Lydia had kept her secret from everyone, including herself. But he had understood what even she had not. He had been imbued with the family atmosphere; he had carried inside himself all the family inheritance of ideas and attitudes; he had been familiar with all the expressions, the tensions, the nuances of mood and the subjects of reserve of the woman who had raised him. Seeing her reactions over the years to the natural questions of a child concerning births, parents, his own origins and hers, he must have gleaned, if not exactly an inkling of the truth, at least something of the sensitive atmosphere surrounding all the words that we had discovered in Lydia's writings. Perhaps for him, conditioned by living with her as he was, those same words had leapt off the page as they could not have done for anyone else.

Anyone else but Tanis. A mere baby at the time of the facts, she could not even have conserved the unconscious memories that her sister had retained. Yet she had grown up with Lydia, and with Mrs Krieger, the woman who loved her but was not really her mother, who had lost her only child to the evil of the man that she called her husband, and who never planted any other than yellow flowers on his grave; *yellow – Xanthe*, the meaning of the dead child's name in Greek – as an eternal reminder of his crime. Mrs Krieger, who had brought up the children of that crime by herself, who had visited the grave with them each year, and who had let them see where her grief truly lay – and where it did not. Impossible to guess what

Tanis actually, consciously knew. But whatever it was, something of it had been silently transmitted to the boy she had brought up.

He must have had a thousand bits of fragmented knowledge that could have come together as he spoke with Lydia and read what she wrote, forming a sudden, coherent and terrible whole. Now, finally, the mystery of his possessing his grandfather's famed genius found its natural, if dreadful, explanation. Now he could finally comprehend the meaning of the reticence and seeming indifference of the father who had raised him, but who was, in fact, not his true father; a reticence that extended even beyond death to his very legacy. It must have all made sense to Sebastian on that day.

Why had Lydia been sent to Holloway, to be shut away there forever? She was sweet and gentle; she could easily have lived outside. To be sure, she would not have been the only case in our severe times of a woman sent off to a madhouse on account of an illegitimate birth, but these poor creatures do not generally remain there, forgotten and unvisited, for twenty-five years! There are charitable institutions that concentrate upon the rehabilitation of such unfortunate creatures, and insist upon their release, even seeking gainful employment for them once it is deemed that they have been brought back to a sense of moral responsibility. No, this was something else; this was to be an eternity of enforced silence. Tanis knew something, and she knew that Lydia knew something. But Tanis could control herself and Lydia could not; her writings poured forth unrestrainedly, filled with revelations that, if visible to Tanis, could become visible to anyone sufficiently probing;

anyone, for example, who might fall in love with Lydia, and learn to understand her.

No wonder Tanis Cavendish wanted her sister to disappear forever. Between the trances and the pregnancy, she probably had no difficulty convincing her husband that Lydia was quite mad and better shut away. The rigid mentality of society under our dear Queen, in regard to all moral questions, would have made this normal, even seemly, twenty-five years ago, although now we may hope that times are slowly beginning to change widespread attitudes towards such things. But Sebastian must have had understood all this.

And what had happened then?

He had seen Lydia, he had read what she wrote, he had understood more than he had ever expected to, and he had returned home on that fateful 31st of December. So much was certain. No one knew the exact time of his arrival at the flat. Mrs Cavendish claimed that she had already left for the centennial ball; Lord Warburton had confirmed her punctual appearance there, and neither the police nor anyone else had seen any reason to doubt her words. Finding the house empty, then, Sebastian had decided to swallow poison, write to Claire and retire to bed to die alone?

Ludicrous! Absurd! Quite out of the question.

And if Mrs Cavendish had not yet left the house when Sebastian had arrived straight from the train from Virginia Water? If she had been waiting for him, in order to go to the ball together as planned? Then there would have been a violent confrontation; of this I could not have the slightest doubt, for the two would have been at terrible cross-purposes. Sebastian would have bitterly reproached her for her lies and her deeds, and demanded, perhaps even with threats of immediate revelation, the instant release of the woman he had just discovered to be his true mother.

Mrs Cavendish would have remained cool. A long explanation, perhaps, filled with gentle reminders of the necessity of keeping up appearances. A promise to discuss everything in detail, to make amends. And a nice cup of coffee laced with arsenic for an emotionally ravaged boy who would fling himself on his bed in rage and confusion, unable to face the idea of going to a party.

Sebastian was no longer her son; he had never been her son, in truth, but now that both mother and son were aware of that fact all pretence was abolished. Mrs Cavendish would have put on her hat and left the house, promising no doubt to talk everything over in the morning, but actually concerned above all to prevent Sebastian's knowledge from ever reaching Lord Warburton's ears. And what would Sebastian have done, alone at home, before the poison drove him into the agony of death?

He would have written to his beloved; to the one person in the world with whom he shared everything. He would have told her that he felt sullied within by the knowledge of his terrifying heritage of lies, cruelty, incest and murder. He feared, perhaps, that such an inheritance lay at the root of the wild forces he sometimes felt within himself – 'the devil within', as Rose had described it. He would have cried out in despair that such a person could not marry, could not engender yet more children to carry on the curse! Rose had told me that he was extroverted and generous. He would never have meant Claire to suffer for the rest of her life without understanding why he was doing what he was doing, and what it all meant.

Darling Claire,

How can I say this to you? I've found out something about myself – I can't go on with it any more. I'm sorry. I'm so sorry. Cursed inheritance – it's too dangerous to take such risks. Please try to understand.

This was not a suicide note, but a confession; an outpouring into another, gentle heart of the horror and disgust that now filled his own; an attempt to purify himself by releasing her from the loathsome attachment.

What would have happened had he lived? She loved him; she would not have accepted release, and perhaps he would have married her anyway. And then what? Perhaps her quiet normality would have tamed him with time, or perhaps he would have ended a slave to his own inherited power, dominating and subjugating the world around him as his grandfather had, carrying on the family burden of evil, and transmitting it onwards to yet another generation.

In any case, that curse was ended now.

CHAPTER TWENTY-THREE

'So this is also London,' said Carl, looking about him. 'Another London. Nothing like the one I have visited with such pleasure so many times. Here is another world altogether.'

We were sitting together in a hansom cab, looking for all the world like a couple, and the ambiguity of the situation worked strangely upon my nerves. Hansom cabs will accommodate two, but only in conditions of the most suggestive intimacy, especially when it is very cold, so that even withdrawn deeply under the sheltering hood and with the wooden slats firmly closed over one's legs, the warmth of the other occupant forms an irresistible attraction. Carl Correns had been paying the most assiduous attention to me since our first meeting, and the fascinating information he had given to me about the true nature of inheritance, combined with his ardent interest in my detective activities, had led me little by little during the course of a dozen or more pleasant rambles, teas and visits to confide all the difficulties of the case to him, and to discuss, analyse and theorise over them with him at length and in great detail. It was a pleasant change to have so supportive an ear and an arm, without the reserve and even the hint of unspoken disapproval that discouraged me from discussing these things with my husband, however much I knew that I could count on him one hundred per cent in the final pinch. The fact was that although Arthur would always stand by me and had done so significantly more than once, I knew that in his heart of hearts he was repelled by the signs of human cruelty and tragedy that invariably emerged during my investigations, and that he preferred insofar as possible to know nothing about them, taking refuge instead in an abstract world of numbers and equations.

But Carl was a professor of biology, not of mathematics, and the vagaries of the life force had an entirely different meaning for him. Just as the use of a mathematical law to explain the unfathomable mystery of inheritance had fascinated him so that he devoted years of his life to resurrecting and reproving Mendel's forgotten theory, so was he fascinated by the application of logic and reasoning to the mystery of human behaviour. Each time I saw him, he asked for news of my progress and my discoveries. His youthful face behind the generous blonde beard was radiant with fervour and excitement as we talked, and although we both kept up a polite pretence that this enthusiasm was purely inspired by the stimulation of detection, it eventually became clear to me that it was my presence quite as much as my work which caused his blue eyes to shine with such intensity.

Absorbed by all that I was discovering, I had pushed this observation to the back of my mind for weeks, cheerfully taking things at their face value, letting myself be warmed by Carl's ardent interest, so different from Arthur's quietness, and avoiding asking myself questions. But now something had changed, for I needed more than a willing ear; suddenly, now, I found myself in a situation where I was in need of actual masculine assistance in the plan I had outlined in my mind. A plan whose goal was to surprise the revelation of a truth that I feared might otherwise be entirely and definitively unprovable.

There was Arthur, and there was Carl, and I stood between the alternatives thus presented and contemplated them both. Arthur, stable and loving and dependable, but hating it all; Carl, an unknown quantity, exciting and eager and more than willing.

I chose to ask Carl, not knowing exactly what I was choosing when I did so, not knowing exactly where it was all going to lead. I asked him to help me discover the truth, and within myself I was aware that I was referring not only to the truth about Sebastian's death, but to another truth as well, which desperately called for clarification from within the depths of ambiguity: a truth about the state of my own heart.

Thus it was that I sat in a hansom cab for the first time in my life with a man who was not my husband, pressed together in a proximity so intimate, in spite of the heavy winter coats and wraps, that I found myself quivering with a mixture of nameless feelings, not least of which was acute embarrassment. Carl reminded me of a medieval knight; they chose and served their fair ladies with strong arms and absolute devotion, quite regardless of whether or not the ladies in question were married. It did not appear to have been a question of any importance in the Middle Ages, and, as far as Carl's mentality was concerned, it did not seem to have increased in relevance since then. But I myself felt torn a hundred ways, between inclination, desire, interest, and the beginnings of what might be a new love, compared to a deeply established and tender one.

There was no use troubling myself over this knotty problem at present. I put my feelings to one side, and decided to concentrate on my plan, or, to be precise, on its first part, which consisted of a visit to Mrs Munn. Thus we drove through the miserable streets of Bermondsey, a splendid steak-and-ale pie of the most generous dimensions reposing in a large box that Carl held upon his knee. The hour was close to supper time, darkness was falling rapidly, and the poverty and misery of the streets through which we drove seemed diminished by the crystal purity of the frosty air, and by the near-absence of ragged passers-by, all but the most courageous of whom had been driven indoors by the cold.

Mrs Munn and her husband lived in the little curve of Jacob Street, separated from the Thames by the Bermondsey Wall, but quite near enough to suffer from all of the unhealthy vapours emitted by that river, what with the filth from sewage and the waste from the leather tanning factories in the area. Having been there on his bag-returning mission, Ephraim had been able to describe the place to me very precisely. I was rather ashamed of that incident, it must be admitted, and determined, perhaps a tad immorally, to make no mention of it whatsoever (let alone provide a much-deserved apology), but I really preferred Mrs Munn to continue perceiving me as a benevolent and beneficial presence in her life. We came out of the cab, Carl paid the driver, and I led him – sniffing the air and looking about him in all directions as though to absorb to the full this new experience of an unknown London – straight to Mrs Munn's door, and knocked firmly.

She opened it, as I had been certain that she would. A woman like Mrs Munn, with an invalid husband at home, is not likely to be gadding about at suppertime on a dark winter evening. She was amazed to see me, and even more so Carl who, with his Teutonic elegance and beautiful hat, looked quite incredibly out of place in the dirty street, but she invited us quickly inside, probably as much in order to close the door as soon as possible and keep out the freezing draught as from some rusty and little-used sense of hospitality. Still, though, she did not seem displeased to see me, and it was almost with a smile that she called out to her husband that good gracious me, here was company, here was a visit, she didn't know why.

The fire burned low and the single room was chilly; only a few lumps of coal remained in the scuttle next to the hearth. The only other light was given by a lamp that stood on the table, shedding a small pool of clarity outside which everything else was in semi-darkness. Half the room was taken up by a tumbled bed in which sat a dishevelled man, peering at us with a mixture of curiosity and hopelessness. The only other pieces of furniture were a few wooden chairs, one of them of a particularly solid construction, with a square backrest and a footrest also.

The sight of the pie, which I took from Carl and presented to Mrs Munn at once, caused a stir of excitement. Placing it in a large dish, she set it to heat in front of the fire while I rather awkwardly introduced Carl, not knowing at all exactly how to describe him or explain what he was doing there with me. But Mrs Munn did not seem unhappy to have a strong, able man in the house, and immediately requested the guest to help her install her husband in his special chair. This job, which must have been quite an effort for Mrs Munn to accomplish by herself, was the work of a moment between the two of them together, her expertise aided by Carl's strength, and Mr Munn was settled at the table with pillows behind him, a rug around him, and the light upon him. There were more introductions and explanations, and the poor man's manifest pleasure in the unexpected change to his evening routine warmed the atmosphere.

'Pleased to meet you,' he said, shaking hands all around. 'Betty told me all about the talk she had with you,' he added to me.

'I told Bill everything you said,' she put in, setting some plates and glasses upon the table.

'It seems you want to know more about why the young man took poison, over there where Betty works,' went on Bill, speaking alternately with his wife in the kind of seamless duo which denotes endless years of closeness, and smiling up at her as she dished up the four rather tired potatoes and the drop of gravy that she had been preparing for their dinner. She now provided each of us with one of these, handed a knife to her husband, and set the pie in front of him to be cut.

'I have much more to tell you,' I said. 'I have come on purpose to tell you everything I know, and to ask for your help with a plan that I have, if you agree with me.' And as we ate, I embarked on a complete explanation of the entire story, including all my hypotheses and suppositions, and the details of the tangled and cruel past of the Krieger family.

'That poor young girl, with such a father, and dying like that,' said Mrs Munn, when I had completed the tale. Her tone held all the simplicity of a background which recognises suffering as an intrinsic part of human life, and does not turn its face away and utter sanctimonious nothings from behind its fan when it encounters it face-to-face, as so many of the ladies I frequent would feel the need to do; not necessarily from a feeling of superiority, although it often appears that way, but from a sense of shame at the very existence of certain phenomena that will not allow them to look them directly in the eye.

'Yes, the first and worst victim of the whole story was the eldest daughter, Xanthe,' I said. 'I do not see how there can be any forgiveness in this world or the next for that kind of sin. I should like to discover her grave, and visit it someday.'

'One girl died, one girl locked away, and now a young man dead,' said Mr Munn thoughtfully. 'It doesn't stop, does it?'

'No,' I said. 'It doesn't stop. It cannot be a question of chance. It is all related; it must be.'

'He was a handsome, lively lad, Master Cavendish,' said Mrs Munn. 'Not one to poison himself. That's what I thought.'

'But you think he didn't poison himself at all, don't you?' said Mr Munn, looking at me astutely. 'You think he was poisoned because he found all this out and someone didn't want it known. Isn't that it?'

'I don't know what I actually believe,' I quickly qualified my thoughts. 'Let me say that I suspect it. I think that it might be the case, and I am determined to find out. If Sebastian's death was murder, I do not want it to remain hidden and secret forever as the other crimes did.'

'But who would have done such a terrible thing?' said Mrs Munn, looking as though she knew exactly what I was about to say.

'The obvious candidate is Mrs Cavendish,' I replied firmly. 'She is the one who had most to lose from the facts becoming known to her future husband or to society in general, and she may very well have still been in the house when Sebastian returned home. If he left Holloway after the end of visiting hours there, he might have arrived home as early as six or seven o'clock. She says that she had already left for Lord Warburton's, and she certainly did arrive there, but their paths still could have crossed, perhaps even for just a few minutes.'

'But her own son!' cried Mrs Munn.

'He wasn't really, you know. Her sister was really his mother, and on that day they both knew it.'

'Still, though, it was she who raised him.'

'But you told me yourself that their relations with each other were pleasant but never close.'

'It's not so much whether it's likely she did it,' intervened Mr Munn, 'but whether it's more likely that she did it or that he did it. Someone did it. The poison was given. That's certain. And there doesn't seem to have been any reason for him to do it himself. You were surprised enough about it when it happened, Betty, weren't you? So if it's between him and her, then why not her?'

'Or someone else, a third person who came to the flat that evening,' I said. 'The fact is, we don't know, and it will be virtually impossible to prove anything at all unless we take some kind of radical step.'

The firelight flickered over the miserable room with its bed in the corner in which the invalid spent his days, the shaky wardrobe and the table that now looked rather dismal with the plates containing nothing but a few crumbs. But the two faces before me, wrinkled, gnarled with the thousand strains and stresses of a life of illness, hard work and poverty, were nevertheless alight with human feeling and the effort of imagination. Carl hovered over us all without speaking, but listening intently to every word.

'Go on,' said Mr Munn, 'tell us what you think happened. And what you want to do.'

'This is my idea,' I said. 'I believe that Sebastian returned from Holloway very angry, found that his mother was still in the flat, and confronted her with what he had discovered. He couldn't blame her for the dreadfulness of all that had happened in the past, of course, nor even for having kept it all from him. But I think he could not bear to discover that his real mother had been imprisoned in a madhouse all these years; especially not now that he had seen her, and knew that she was really not mad at all. Holloway is a luxurious and superior place, but it is nevertheless an asylum for insane people, and for the patients it is not much more than a prison. Sebastian must have seen in Lydia what anyone would see: a beautiful, gentle, sweet person, a victim who might arouse anyone's chivalrous sympathy – and on top of that he found a mother, and realised that twenty-five years of life had been stolen from her, and twenty-five years of a true mother's love from him. Anyone can understand that he must have been livid.'

'Yes, that's right. He'd have been furious,' agreed Mrs Munn. 'When he was angry, he was very angry; hot anger, not cold anger like his mum. Anything could have happened if she was still at home when he came back. But you'll never get her to admit it even if she was. She had already left, so she says and so she'll always say. There was no one to see or hear.'

'Well,' I said quietly, 'but perhaps there was someone. Perhaps *you* were there, Mrs Munn. Perhaps you came back for something you had forgotten, and when you reached the door, you heard the two of them quarrelling, and listened for a while, not wishing to walk into the middle of a scene.'

She looked at me with surprise and a shadow of fear reflected in her face. 'I wasn't, though,' she said tensely. 'Worse luck.'

'Hush!' said Mr Munn. 'The lady's saying something – I think I see.'

'This idea is a little risky,' I said, 'but here it is, for what it's worth. I think that if you were to write a letter to Mrs Cavendish saying that you knew she was at home when her son returned, that you came back the way I said, and you heard what they were saying, she could not but react. What I am suggesting is that you do something to provoke her to react very quickly and strongly. If we once see exactly how she responds to such a letter, then, I think, we will know the truth.'

'Why, she'd just deny it all,' said Mrs Munn.

'We mustn't leave her that possibility, if what I suspect is indeed true. I suggest that you write her a letter in which you say you heard her and her son together and you know that she lied to the police. Tell her that you stayed and listened, and that you heard all they said – but don't say what you heard. Tell her that she must bring you some money by tomorrow night. Give her the letter tomorrow evening when you leave the house, and suggest that she meet you at midnight in some lonely place near here.'

'That's too dangerous. I won't have that,' said Mr Munn. 'That's blackmail; it's illegal for one thing, and too risky for another. Why, someone who kills once may kill again! What could poor Betty do in some lonely place if Mrs Cavendish decides to murder her?'

'I will be the one to go and meet Mrs Cavendish, not Mrs Munn,' I said. 'I do not think my plan is really dangerous for either of you. If she is innocent, she will know that Mrs Munn must be lying, and she will say so. Think of it from her point of view. If she never saw Sebastian that night, then she will know that there was nothing to hear, and so she will know that Mrs Munn cannot really know any secrets.'

'But the law is severe against blackmailers,' objected Mr Munn. 'If she really didn't do it, we might find ourselves hauled up before the magistrate.'

'Not to mention out of a job,' added Mrs Munn. 'Couldn't you write her the letter yourself?'

'It wouldn't be believable coming from me,' I said. 'I

am a complete stranger. I was acquainted with neither Sebastian nor her on the day he died; why would I have been coming to their door? She would take me for a professional blackmailer horning in on a case from the newspapers, call my bluff and deny everything. I might succeed in blackmailing her by threatening to tell her secrets to Lord Warburton, but I would never have any chance of obtaining a confession. Your situation is different. For you to have returned there for something you forgot after having left the house would be quite believable, and you would be a witness to a lie concerning the actual murder.'

'But I didn't even go to the flat on that day,' she objected. 'It was a Sunday.'

'Oh, so it was. Oh dear. Couldn't you say you left something there on the Saturday, and had to come back for it?'

'When I was going back in to work the very next morning?' she said.

'You could say it was to take some food, knowing that she and her son would both be out,' intervened her husband suddenly. 'The Lord knows it wouldn't have been a crime, and we need it sorely. If it wasn't for the food that used to come from the house there, we'd have starved years ago. Since the boy died it's been terrible. Betty's whole salary practically goes just for the rent, and she's got to have a coat and skirt to go to work in.'

'So you think I should do it?' said Mrs Munn, turning to her husband. 'If she's done nothing, I'll lose my job without a reference. I'd have had to find another place anyway, when she gets married, but that's to be in another six months, and she'd have given me a good letter at least.'

'I will help you find another job,' I said, 'and write you a reference myself. Would you not be happier working in a larger family? I have a lot of friends. I am sure we can find something. If you were going to be looking for a job anyway, then we might as well start right now, don't you think?'

She looked at me gratefully, and I determined to help her find work by every means in my power, not hesitating to resort to a lie or two if necessary. With all my London acquaintances, I felt reasonably certain of success.

'There's still the problem of her taking Betty to the police over the blackmail,' said Mr Munn.

'She would never do that,' said Mrs Munn. 'She wouldn't want the publicity. She'd call my bluff and put a stop to it.'

'I believe you are right,' I said. 'Still, if that happens, I am quite prepared to declare that I wrote your letter myself, and that you had nothing to do with it. I do have a certain talent for forgery,' I added modestly, 'and I am not too much afraid of the police; I have several friends at Scotland Yard. What matters to me above all is what she says when she confronts me, expecting to see you. You must lend me a bonnet, so that from a distance she is not aware of the change. I am counting on being able to tell from her reaction whether she is innocent or not. As I said, if she is, she will not hesitate to deny everything, knowing that she is in the right, and that it is quite impossible that either you or I can know anything really significant. If she said that to my face, in that situation, I would believe her. But on the other hand, if she really did see Sebastian that night, then we must write your letter so that she thinks that you know it for a fact, and denial would be useless.

The letter will be a little delicate to write, but we can do it together. Shall we begin now?'

I had prepared writing-paper and pen in my handbag, just in case, but she had some at home already, of an inferior but very authentic-looking quality. In an inversion of the natural procedure, we used mine to write a rough draft, with much discussion over each line and phrase, arriving finally at the following result.

Dear Mrs Cavendish,

I am very much in need of money and I am sure you would be willing to help me out if you could. The fact is that last December 31st I came to your flat in the early evening. I thought that you and Master Cavendish would have left for the ball already and that I would be able to get something to eat from your larder. I know this is a dishonest thing to do but it was the night when everyone was celebrating the New Century and we did not even have a sausage with our mash. Master Cavendish was in the habit of giving me a gift of money each New Year, and flowers also, but he had been away and had not had the chance. Anything I took, I would have put back.

Anyway, I was in front of your door and before I could go in I heard that you and he were both inside the flat and you were talking very clearly. I could overhear most of what you were saying, especially the young master who spoke up very loud when he was vexed. I know you told police that you had already gone away from the flat when he came home.

I am telling you this because I am in need of

money very badly for my husband who is an invalid and can't work. I don't wish to cause any trouble to anyone. It's best to keep this secret but I am in very much of a hurry, so I am asking you to come to meet me at the south tower of Tower Bridge tonight at midnight and bring one hundred pounds and a written reference for me to look for another job.

Yours sincerely,

Elizabeth Munn

I then dictated it to Mrs Munn for her to write it out on her own paper in her own writing. I preferred this method to her copying it, for I wished to preserve any particularities of spelling that might help the letter appear absolutely convincing.

'You must give her this, or leave it at the house tomorrow after work,' I told her again. 'Just in case of any worry at all, I think it would be best if you spent the evening somewhere else, with some neighbours or friends near here.'

'If I really thought he had taken the poison himself, I wouldn't be doing this,' said Mrs Munn, folding the letter and sealing it. 'I think it would be an evil thing to do. But after all you've told us, I don't believe that any more: I believe you. Your explanation makes more sense. It's as simple as that. I think she must have given him the poison, and I don't want to work for a murderess any more. I shall go there tomorrow, but it will feel strange. I wish I didn't have to.'

'Let us not judge before we know the facts,' I said. 'When you leave work tomorrow, Carl and I will be waiting for you outside, and we will accompany you home to make sure you arrive here safely, and help bring you and Mr Munn to some other place. The rest is up to us.'

'You will come and see us, and tell us what happened?'

'Of course we will, as soon as we possibly can. Leave everything to me. Thank you for trusting me,' I added, shaking Mr Munn's hand and that of his wife, and taking the rusty bonnet she offered for my disguise.

'I do trust you,' said Mrs Munn. 'It's important to right a wrong.'

CHAPTER TWENTY-FOUR

Through the darkness of the winter night we walked, and I was not leaning on Carl's arm so heavily uniquely for the pleasure; the pavement was slushy and slippery and both of us stumbled from time to time in the darkness. I felt the tension in his arm and his body, but also the strength, and it lent me confidence and courage.

Well before the appointed time, we were walking up the road leading onto the splendid Tower Bridge, one of the most recent engineering marvels of London. There was no discontinuity between road and bridge, and we found ourselves looking down over the thick wrought metal parapet into the chill black water below, under the stars in the black sky above, whose expanse was crossed above our heads by the giant double band of the bridge's upper level.

When we came to the south tower, Carl entered and

concealed himself by the stairs inside. I, feeling strangely unlike myself in Mrs Munn's bonnet but filled with a sense of alertness and clarity that dominated my fear, stood under the archway in the icy chill of the winter air, holding my dim little lantern, and waited. As the minutes ticked past, I reflected on what I was doing, and recalled all the evidence that had led me to my final conclusions. A hundred times I asked myself if Mrs Cavendish might be perfectly innocent of the death of the young man that she had raised as her own child. In a sense, it was easier, and more desirable, to believe so. If she did not come, or came but denied everything in the letter, I knew that my conviction of her guilt would seriously waver.

If, on the other hand, my guesses corresponded to reality, she would not, she simply could not doubt that what the letter claimed was the plain truth. She would not deny it because she *could* not deny it. It would not just be a question of her word against Mrs Munn's in front of police, or even in the public arena. If Mrs Munn also knew the secrets of the past, she could reveal them, and they could be verified, and Mrs Munn's word would be proven to be the true one. In that case, she would have to react swiftly: in fact now.

There was nothing to do but wait in the cold and silence. Invisible within the tower, Carl was an abstract; I knew he was there, yet could not feel his presence in my heart. I knew that his ardent feelings were straining towards me like fingers of desire, but they could not touch me in that bitter darkness. No one passed at all, the bridge was silent and empty, and I stood shivering in the night air, waiting, waiting, waiting. I heard Big Ben strike a quarter to midnight, and then, after what seemed like an hour, midnight. The chimes were so deep and strong that they shivered the air, and other chimes answered them from bell-towers near and far across all London. So loud and manifold were the echoes that I nearly missed the smaller, nearer sound of quiet footsteps approaching, yes, undoubtedly approaching along the bridge.

It was Mrs Cavendish. Tall and handsome, her upright bearing did not betray for a moment the slightest hint of disquiet, nor for that matter of anger, fear, or any other visible emotion. She had seen my bonnet glimmering in the ray of light from my lantern before I had noticed her, and was walking directly towards me with all the quiet authority of her character. I braced myself.

'Oh!'

Even one so versed in self-mastery as Mrs Cavendish could not restrain the surprise and confusion of seeing an unfamiliar face in the place of the well-known one she had expected. The surprise had the effect I had wanted; she hesitated for a moment, her own strategy, whatever it might have been, momentarily thrown off course. Perhaps she thought, for a moment, that I was there by chance and had nothing to do with the letter she had received. I held up my lantern, she looked at me straight in the face, and her expression changed.

'I recognise you,' she said. 'I saw you backstage after Sebastian's memorial concert, with the musicians. And you were at the little boy's scholarship ceremony as well. Have you been following me? Who are you? What are you doing here?'

'I am here,' I said with as much quiet poise as I could

muster, but wishing that she was not quite so much taller, 'because of the letter you received from Mrs Munn.'

'What do you know about that letter?' she said sharply.

'Everything,' I replied calmly, 'since Mrs Munn wrote it together with me. I know that you lied to the police when you said that you had already left for Lord Warburton's party when Sebastian came home on the night that he died. You were still there when he arrived, and he confronted you with everything that he had discovered that day: the identity of his true mother, where she was, who put her there and why, and the truth about your own mother who was also your sister; all the infamy from the past and all the lies from the present. I know everything about it.'

She stared straight at me, her eyes unnaturally large. I stared back, knowing that if she now said that my words were false, *must* be false, for she had never seen Sebastian on that day, I would believe her. I looked straight back at her, giving her the chance. But instead, she said,

'What business is it of yours?'

'Murder is everyone's business,' I replied.

'Murder!' she snarled with sudden antipathy. 'What do you know about murder? That was no murder – it was suicide!'

I hesitated, startled, then pulled myself together. She had been there, or at least she was not denying it. She had been there with him.

'It was not suicide – you killed him!' I burst out. 'When the police know that you lied about not being there that night, they will realise that as well as I do. And when they know the reasons for your quarrel – when Lord Warburton knows – when everyone knows – do you think they will not ask you who made the cup of coffee that Sebastian drank that night?'

My words were hard, yet once again they contained a challenge as well as an accusation. If she had not done it, let her defend herself! Her eyes were locked into mine and mine gave her another chance, and yet another. *Say it – say that he took the poison after you left, and I will believe you. Tell me that he was destroyed by your words, by your acts, but not by your hand; that you destroyed him unintentionally; that your heart is filled with regret and despair, and I will believe you.*

But it did not happen that way. Instead, my words freed Tanis Cavendish of the need to lie, for her lie had served only the single purpose of silence, and mine indicated that that precious silence was to be necessarily and inexorably shattered and lost for ever.

'It was suicide,' she said passionately. 'I tell you that it was, for Sebastian could very well have chosen to live! I gave him the chance, and he took it and flung it to the winds. I told him what I would do to satisfy his miserable romantic fantasies about his victimised long-lost mother. I would have had her taken from Holloway if the place shocked the poor dear boy so badly. I would have set her up in some house somewhere where she would have been well looked after. What did I care, as long as she was kept where she couldn't cause any more harm than she had already done! That selfish vixen, set from a child on destroying everything I was trying to make of my life, hell-bent on pouring out on paper things that should be hidden from every decent God-fearing person until they are erased from human memory! She wouldn't stop! She

341

wouldn't stop! She wouldn't let them cure her – she liked playing with them, toying, showing her sick little secret, and enjoying the feeling that they still couldn't guess what it was. "Oh, what have I written?" she would say in that mincing voice of hers. Was she really too stupid to read her own words, or was she just pretending? I knew what she was writing – knew it from the very beginning. Who did she think she was fooling with all those half-hidden mixed-up fathers and children and abominations? I saw my father reaching for her, touching her; I may have been only two years old but the memory is burnt into my brain, how he reached for her and pulled her onto him and she screamed and struggled and my mother screamed and struggled and my father railed and hit and swore and then my mother put the white powder into his drink and he died. I saw it all but I could grow up and never speak a word, not to Lydia or to anyone else, not a single word in my entire life, because that was the only way to make it go away and everything become right! Oh, how I hated Lydia, that blabbermouth Lydia, trying to wreck everything with her sick little games, filth leaking from her pen while she went singing about the house like an angel. Oh, how I hated music, and talent – that damned, hateful talent that would not shut its devil's mouth but must yowl, yowl my secret out in music from generation to generation!'

She paused for breath, and I reached out my hand and grasped hers, for however horrible her deed, the pain in her words and the horror she described was beyond any that my life had given me to witness before. But she ripped it out of mine with enmity.

'For the first few years of my marriage, I thought I

342

had won,' she said, her jaw strained with the effort of controlling her white-hot anger sufficiently to speak. 'The doctor couldn't cure Lydia, but he was such a dunce that he seemed to have no idea what she was ranting about either, and anyway, she was far away. After four years I hadn't conceived a child and the doctors said I never would, and I knew it was for the best: no more fruit from the rotten tree. Then I thought I'd mended the cracks once and for all and locked away the wrong and could go on living in the sunshine of the right and the good. It was the only time I ever knew happiness. All could have been well, all was well. And then what had to happen? Lydia, the angel Lydia, comes home from Basel pregnant – like a common whore, a mad whore, back she comes to London and it all starts again; the shame and the disgust and the loathsomeness and the filth of it all, everything I thought I had finally escaped. Thank God that Edward agreed with me about what was best to be done with her. He didn't understand, of course; he saw nothing of her perverse tricks, he simply thought she was loose and quite mad, and I was glad that he did, and grateful to him because even though I was her sister, he never thought that I might also be mad. I rue the day that we decided to adopt her brat. I wish he had died at birth, and his mother with him! I should have known that nothing good could come of our stock. I fell for those blue eyes, that open little face of his that looked so good and so healthy, and I let myself be dragged into giving our family's rotten blood one more chance – more fool me! Nature had stopped the trail of horror with me. Why did I force it back into existence again? Idiot that I was – twenty-five years of seeing him grow up into *her* – hearing him play the violin like *him* – the devil's fingerprints all over the boy no matter what I tried to do!

'Through all the years I kept on working to make everything right and decent and true and straight. I never gave up, not for one moment. My dear husband died and I was going to marry again – a man of honour, a man of standing, a man who knew about my sister's state and accepted the situation with tolerance and generosity and compassion. Everything was under control – and then it all has to start again, like a nightmare, with that idiot Sebastian digging up these things that he was never meant to know, and trying to smash all my life to pieces again! I always knew he would do it sooner or later, child of sin and monstrosity that he was, even if I was the only person to know it! He came back that night and demanded that his dear sweet mother come to live with us; yes, with us, nothing less than that, knowing that everything was certain to come out in the end if that madwoman started her writing tricks in public, with all the craze there is these days about automatic writing and trances and such rubbish. I spit on it all, and all the filth it pretends to hide, and the people rushing to peek at the filth just as they rush to the public dissections of the naked corpses in the hospitals, pretending it's all for the sake of scientific knowledge – the prurient liars!

'I tried to reason with him, but he wouldn't listen to reason; oh no, he wouldn't listen to reason. He was going to talk to Lord Warburton. Everything was my fault; his mother was sweet Rapunzel and I was the evil witch that had locked her away in a tower and stolen her child away from her! Little could he understand that evil is what I've struggled to fight off all my life while it's dogged my steps and stood whispering over my shoulder that I'd never be rid of it as long as a drop of my father's blood still ran on the face of the earth! Fool, idiot, imbecile that he was, thinking that I'd let him run about with his heart on his sleeve, gasping out my secrets to the world at large! Oh, I was right to do what I did; it's no use your standing there with your narrow little morals thinking how good you are and how bad I am. I know that he'd have let everything out. Why, when I came home that night, I found the letter he'd written to that silly fool of a Claire, telling her he couldn't marry her because he'd discovered incest in his background – *incest*. Yes, he wrote down the very word that I spent fifty years refusing ever to hear, think or speak; and madness, too; madness and incest, all so terrible, and dear, darling Claire would understand, of course, that he couldn't marry her now because he felt tainted, the poor dear, and one never knew what dreadful things one might pass on to one's children and he couldn't take the risk. Such a load of rubbish it all was, nothing to do with whether they should go on with their silly marriage or not – all he really wanted was to *tell, tell, tell* – all anyone has ever wanted to do is *tell, tell, tell* – no one knows how to keep a secret, not even the ones you'd think would most want it kept! Filth! Corruption and filth and defilement! Pursuing me everywhere while I struggle to keep clean from it, and you come here accusing me with your nasty little mind and probably thinking how wonderful and how righteous you are, when you understand nothing about it, nothing at all! How dare you!'

Her hands shot out with a speed that took me by surprise

and with tremendous strength she dragged me towards the wrought iron railing at the edge of the bridge. I felt her trying to lift me and push me over. The barrier was very thick and hard to grasp and not particularly high. I clung to the railings with my arms, not finding a purchase for my fingers, afraid to let go of it to struggle with her, and screamed for Carl. If he had not been there, I could have screamed myself blue without being heard by a soul on that miserable night, but, thank God, he had been watching everything from the shadows of the tower, and the moment I cried out, he leapt forward and, seizing me by the arm, pulled me strongly towards him and enfolded me tightly. He might have done better to snatch at Mrs Cavendish instead of me, for seeing that her victim was lost to her grasp, she disappeared with such suddenness that at first we could not comprehend where she had gone. But a moment later, when the beating of our own hearts slowed down, we heard the faint echo of her feet running upwards – yes, undoubtedly, she was running up the tower stairs and the sound of her steps echoed down to us through the night.

Carl let go of me and ran into the tower. I followed him, up one flight, two, three, four – the staircase went round and round in a crazy square that seemed never to end, and my chest was burning; Carl was ahead of me, but Mrs Cavendish was already at the top and out onto the narrow walkway, high above the water, under the stars. We heard a jagged scream, muffled by the thick stone walls, and I did not hear, but imagined I heard, the faint sound of a splash far below. Panic overwhelmed me. I clamped my hands over my ears, but I heard my own voice from within myself, crying in uncontrollable horror. Carl came down and wrapped me in his arms, then opened his coat and wrapped it around me as well, pressing me to his chest. We remained so for long minutes. Then I looked up at him.

Carl had offered me love and admiration and his help and protection at this critical moment. But life makes our decisions for us, for his arms as he held me did not have the power to still the shuddering inside me, and I longed for something else: for another pair – for someone who alone could help me reason away the dreadfulness of it all, by showing me that every other alternative to what had just happened would have been worse. Carl was at my side, but I knew now that he meant nothing to me. I looked up at him and saw the face of a kind stranger.

'I need Arthur,' I heard myself say.

His blue eyes were filled with understanding and resignation.

'Of course,' he said. 'Come. I think we must first go to the police. There are things that must be done.' He laid my head against his chest and patted Mrs Munn's bonnet gently. 'Do not worry. I will not leave your side until you are safe at home in Cambridge where you belong.'

HISTORICAL FACTS AND
PERSONAGES

The fame of geneticist Gregor Mendel (1822–1884), reclusive monk and scientific genius, is so widespread today that it is difficult to imagine that the importance of his work was entirely unrecognised, and the work itself ignored and forgotten for several years after his death.

Like Darwin and other scientists, Mendel compared the effects of cross and self-fertilisation on plants whose characteristics were simple and easily identified and compared. But the difference is that Mendel was able to explain his observations via the theory of alleles and the theory of probability. His seminal paper dates from 1865; Darwin certainly knew nothing of it, since he made no mention of it in *The Effects of Cross and Self-Fertilisation in the Vegetable Kingdom*, published in 1876, in which he gives detailed results of very similar experiments to Mendel's, without, however, deducing the theoretical model explaining them.

Carl Franz Joseph Erich Correns (1864–1933) learnt of Mendel's work through a botanist friend of his parents who had been acquainted with them. The ideas contained there fascinated him enough to set him to try to reproduce them, as soon as he found himself with a university position that offered him the freedom to organise his own experiments. It took him eight years of work to confirm Mendel's results, and he published his findings in 1900, championing their originator and giving the name of *Mendel's laws* to the probability theory governing heredity. Strangely enough two other scientists, Hugo de Vries and Erich von Tschermak-Seysenegg, published similar rediscoveries of Mendel's work in that very same year (de Vries without citing Mendel's work, causing something of a conflict between him and Carl Correns). It seems that at the turn of the century, the time was finally ripe for Mendel's discoveries to emerge and be generally understood. Coming as it did contemporaneously with Freud's discoveries in psychology, this was the beginning of the application of Mendel's theory to explain the inheritance of human traits, both physical and mental (insofar as many mental traits are also of physical origin), culminating in the work of the Human Genome Project.

As for the story of the medium Hélène Smith, it is entirely historical down to the last syllable of her Martian language. Quite famous at the end of the nineteenth century, when automatic speech and writing were highly fashionable, Mlle Smith's visions gave rise to a number of written analyses.

The most important of these was the book *Des Indes à la Planète Mars (From India to the Planet Mars)* by the Swiss professor Theodore Flournoy, which was the main source of information on this subject.

In what concerns the musical aspect of the book, it should be noted that the professors of the Royal Academy who appear there, Prosper Sainton, Alexander MacKenzie, Alessandro Pezze and Hans Wessely, were all real people, as was the young student Wolfe Wolfinsohn, who (although in reality he was about a decade younger than in the story) indeed went on as predicted to become an extraordinary chamber musician, first violin of the legendary Stradivarius quartet. The description of the difficulties facing women cellists at the time is also historically accurate; there was, however, a small number of enterprising young women who did manage to overcome all obstacles to reach the pinnacle of international success. One of the first of these, if not the very first, was May Mukle, a student of Alessandro Pezze. The Wolfe Wolfinsohn String Quartet Prize and the May Mukle Prize for cello students are both still awarded yearly at the Royal Academy of Music.

RAMAGE'S DEVIL

Lord Nicholas Ramage, eldest son of the Tenth
Earl of Blazey, Admiral of the White, was born
in 1775 at Blazey Hall, St Kew, Cornwall. He
entered the Royal Navy as a midshipman in
1788, at the age of thirteen. He has served with
distinction in the Mediterranean, the
Caribbean, and home waters during the war
against France, participating in several major
sea battles and numerous minor engagements.
Despite political difficulties, his rise through the
ranks has been rapid.

In *Ramage's Devil*, Captain
Ramage, in his thirteenth
recorded adventure, is in conflict
with Napoleon again. During the
uneasy peace after the signing of
the Treaty of Amiens Nicholas
Ramage marries and while on
honeymoon at a friend's château
in France, war breaks out. In
hiding from Bonaparte's secret
police, Ramage hears that a
mutinous British brig has sailed
into Brest. Taking charge
of it could offer a means of
escape . . .

Dudley Pope, who comes from an old Cornish family and whose great-great-grandfather was a Plymouth shipowner in Nelson's time, is well known both as the creator of Lord Ramage and as a distinguished and entertaining naval historian, the author of ten scholarly works.

Actively encouraged by the late C. S. Forester, he has now written sixteen 'Ramage' novels about life at sea in Nelson's day. They are based on his own wartime experiences in the navy and peacetime exploits as a yachtsman as well as immense research into the naval history of the eighteenth century.

Available in Fontana by the same author

1. Ramage
2. Ramage and the Drum Beat
3. Ramage and the Freebooters
4. Governor Ramage R.N.
5. Ramage's Prize
6. Ramage and the Guillotine
7. Ramage's Diamond
8. Ramage's Mutiny
9. Ramage and the Rebels
10. The Ramage Touch
11. Ramage's Signal
12. Ramage and the Renegades
14. Ramage's Trial
15. Ramage's Challenge
16. Ramage at Traflagar

DUDLEY POPE

Ramage's Devil

FONTANA/Collins

First published by
The Alison Press/Martin Secker & Warburg Ltd 1982
First issued in Fontana Paperbacks 1983
Fourth impression September 1987

Made and printed in Great Britain by
William Collins Sons & Co. Ltd, Glasgow

For the late Frank Casper,
sailor, navigator and friend

FINISTÈRRE

Pointe de Corsen

St Pierre

Fort de Délec

The Lion Battery

Fort Mengam

Portzic

Fort du Toulbroch

The Gullet

Le Conquet

Abbey St Mathieu

Anse de Bertheaume

Les Fillettes

Pointe des Espagnols

CHÉNAL DU FOUR

Pointe St Mathieu

Cornouaille

Baie de

Pierres Noires (Black Rocks)

Anse de Camaret

IROISE RIVER

Camaret

Camaret Peninsula

Anse de Dinan

Cap de la Chèvre

ENGLAND

Dover

Plymouth

Portsmouth

Calais

Boulogne

ENGLISH CHANNEL

Amiens

Channel Islands

Cherbourg

Rouen

R. Seine

Golfe de St Malo

Caen

Falaise

PARIS

Ushant

St Malo

Landerneau

Brest

Finistèrre

Rennes

FRANCE

Île de Sein

Douarnenez

L'Orient

Orléans

Angers

Tours

R. Loire

Miles

0   50

Nantes

Poitiers

La Rochelle

BREST

Penfeld River

Kerhuon

St Louis
Church

Port of
Brest

Chateau

Laninon

Presqu'île de Plougastel

RADE

DE

- *Baie de
Daoulas* -

BREST

Roscanvel

*Anse du
Fret*

- *Anse du
Poulmic* -

FINISTÈRE

Crozon

N

W   E

S

BAIE DE DOUARNENEZ

Miles

0   1   2   3   4   5

Douarnenez

DJC

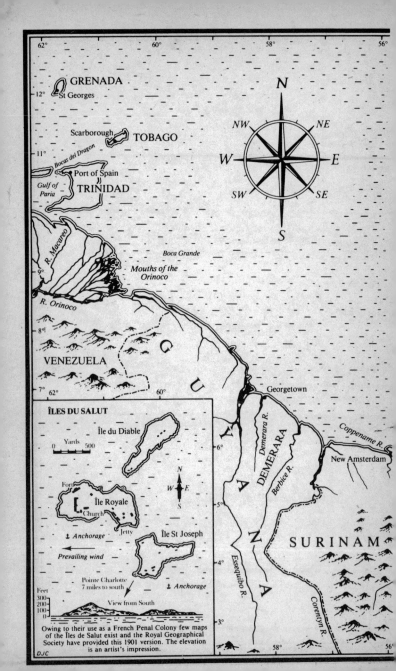

GRENADA
12° St Georges

N
NW   NE
W   E
SW   SE
S

Scarborough   TOBAGO

11°   Bocas del Dragon
Port of Spain
Gulf of Paria   TRINIDAD

R. Macareo

9°

Boca Grande

Mouths of the Orinoco

R. Orinoco

8°

G

VENEZUELA   U

7° 62°   60°

Georgetown

6°

Demerara R.

DEMERARA

Berbice R.

Coppename R.

New Amsterdam

ÎLES DU SALUT

Île du Diable

0   Yards   500

N
W ✦ E
S

Fort
Île Royale
Church

⚓ Anchorage   Jetty

Île St Joseph

Prevailing wind

Pointe Charlotte
7 miles to south   ⚓ Anchorage

Feet
300
200
100
0   View from South

Owing to their use as a French Penal Colony few maps
of the Îles de Salut exist and the Royal Geographical
Society have provided this 1901 version. The elevation
is an artist's impression.

DJC

SURINAM

5°

Essequibo R.

4°

Corentyn R.

3°

58°   56

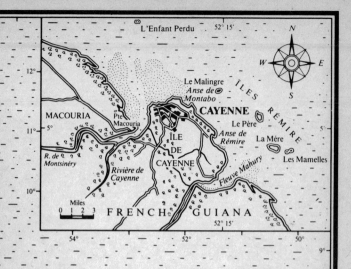

L'Enfant Perdu 52° 15'

N
W · E
S

12°

Le Malingre
Anse de
Montabo

ÎLES RÉMIRE

MACOURIA

Pte
Macouria

CAYENNE

Le Père

5°

Anse de
Rémire

La Mère

Les Mamelles

11°

R. de
Montsinéry

ÎLE DE
CAYENNE

Rivière de
Cayenne

Fleuve Mahury

10°

Miles
0 1 2 3

FRENCH   GUIANA

52° 15'

54°   52°   50°

9°

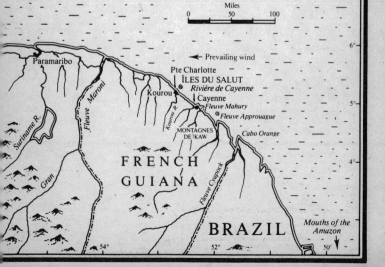

ATLANTIC   OCEAN

8°

7°

Miles
0   50   100

6°

← Prevailing wind

Paramaribo

Pte Charlotte
ÎLES DU SALUT
Rivière de Cayenne

Kourou

Cayenne

Suriname R.

Fleuve Maroni

Kourou R.

Fleuve Mahury

Fleuve Approuague

5°

Gran

MONTAGNES
DE KAW

Cabo Orange

FRENCH

GUIANA

4°

Fleuve Oyapock

BRAZIL

Mouths of the
Amazon

54°   52°   50°

CHAPTER ONE

They were both lying, propped up by an elbow, on the bristling carpet of short, coarse grass which was fighting for its life on top of the cliff, the roots clinging desperately to the thin layer of earth and finding cracks in the rock beneath. The browning leaves struggled against a wind which, although this afternoon little more than a brisk breeze, still whipped up a fine, salty spindrift from the swell surging on to the rocks below and sent it high like invisible smoke across the top of Pointe St Mathieu.

The Atlantic swell, from this height looking like slowly rippling wrinkles, swept in lazily from the west to hit first the barrier of tiny islands and rocky shoals stretching a dozen miles from Ushant, over on their right, down to the Black Rocks, which were in front of them and five or six miles to seaward. After surrounding each rock and islet with a fussy white collar of foam the swells rolled on inshore to smash against the front of the cliffs sixty feet below with a strangely remote booming that they felt rather than heard, like the tiny tremors of a distant earthquake.

Above them the sky was strewn with white cottonball clouds which seemed to be looking down on the rollers and the cliffs, pleased at finally making a landfall after a long but boring Atlantic crossing. But to the two pairs of eyes long accustomed to the brilliant, almost gaudy sharpness of tropical colours, the sea and sky background seemed washed out, faded and without energy.

Gulls hovered like kites on the wind currents coming up the cliff face and sometimes wheeled over them, as though curious and wanting to see why this dark-haired man and young, tawny-haired woman should be there alone and just looking seaward, not tending cattle or sheep, their horses tethered by the reins to pieces of rock jutting like teeth. Close by, two brown and white cows cropped the grass with indifference, as though they were supposed to graze a particular area by nightfall, and knew that they were comfortably ahead of their schedule, moving so slowly that the bells round their necks only occasionally gave muffled clangs, apparently reluctant to interrupt the whine of the wind and the distant thunder of the waves.

The occasional contented sigh, the sudden indrawn breath, the gentle touch of a finger, the woman's occasional toss of the head to move strands of tawny hair that blew across her face and tickled, revealed an erotic atmosphere (though neither of them thought of the word) not entirely due to the splendid isolation of Pointe St Mathieu which, with one exception, seemed to be saying that up here, on a sunny afternoon, nature was pausing briefly at the second phase of the cycle of birth, love and death, and smiling.

The exception stood behind them, grey, stark, shadowed in the sun yet not menacing. The ruin of the old Abbey St Mathieu was still solid, the walls forming geometrically precise angles with the flying buttresses. It looked as though it had been lived in until some unpredictable giant or unexpected storm had lifted off the roof and hurled it away.

A couple of artillery batteries, one to the left and the other to the right, with their guns still in position, were the only other signs that humans had ever passed this way.

'Les Pierres Noires,' Ramage commented, gesturing down at the handful of black shapes scattered in the sea below them like sheep crouching against the wind on a distant moor. 'Known to the Royal Navy as the Black Rocks. It seems strange to be looking down at them from up here, from France. Having the French view ... If these were normal times – wartime, anyway, because that's all I can remember – the French lookouts up here would be watching Ushant over there' – he pointed to the rocky island just in sight, the last in a series of smaller ones leading to it like enormous stepping stones – 'making sure no English ships sneaked along the Chenal du Four inside that great shoal, or round the southern end to get into the Iroise river.

'How different it looks from a British frigate!' he added, the dreaminess leaving his voice. 'There'd be the Black Rocks sticking up like ancient teeth and beyond you'd see this line of cliffs with the ruins of the abbey on top. And of course Le Conquet' – he pointed to the right – 'and the other villages to the north, although from the deck of a frigate the cliffs mean you can only see church towers and steeples. Le Conquet's tall open steeple: I remember that well, a cone-shaped skeleton.

'And French and English alike are here just to watch the Gullet. That's the mouth of the river down there' – he pointed over the edge of the cliff to their left – 'round the corner, as it were, and running up to Brest itself.'

She nodded across to the other side of the Gullet. 'What's that headland over there?'

'The Camaret Peninsula, forming the south side of the Gullet, with plenty of guns to keep out *rosbif* trespassers. The little town of Camaret is well inland. I remember seeing Camaret Mill once, but we had gone very close in and had a scare when the wind dropped on a flood tide.'

Sarah said: 'All this must remind you of Cornwall.'

He paused, lost for a moment in memories. 'Yes, because apart from the cliffs and hills the village names would be hard to distinguish, Delabole, Perranzabuloe, Scorrier, Lanner, Lansallos, Trelill, Lanivet, Lelant, St Levan – all good Breton names: could be within twenty-five miles of here!'

She nodded, and he added: 'And in Cornwall – Portsall, Lesneven, Lanion, Lannilis, Crozon, Plabennec, Kerlouan . . .'

'It's extraordinary,' she commented. 'Still, I think one can distinguish the Cornish ones.'

'Can you?' he smiled, eyebrows raised.

She nodded. 'Oh yes, even though I'm not Cornish.'

He laughed and leaned over to kiss her. 'Don't be cross with your new husband because he's teasing you. The first names are Cornish – the ones you thought were Breton. All the second are here in Brittany!'

'But . . .'

'Just listen to these: St Levan and Lesneven, Lanivet and Lannilis, Perranzabuloe and Plabennec . . . the first of each pair are Cornish, the second Breton. I can forgive you for mistaking them! And Botusfleming, Lansallos, Lesnewth, Lezant, Trelill – they hardly sound very Cornish, but they are.'

Sarah smoothed the olive green material of her dress, not bothering that the wind ruffled her hair. 'Brest . . . the blockade of Brest . . . I've heard you and your father talk about it,' she said thoughtfully. Her voice was deep; he reflected that he seemed to hear it with his loins, a caress rather than a sound. She was watching a bee circling a buttercup, thwarted as the breeze bent over the golden bell. 'We can't see the port from here, can we?'

He shook his head. 'Bonaparte's main naval base on the Atlantic coast is well up the Gullet. One has to sail in close under the cliffs (with these and other batteries pelting you if you're

British in wartime) and usually there's a soldier's wind to let you run in. All the way up to Brest the Gullet narrows like a funnel and there are three forts on your larboard hand – if memory serves they're Toulbroch, Mengam and de Delec; we'll be able to see them on the way back – and one on the other side. Plus various batteries.'

He half turned, resting on an elbow and looking across at the hills beyond Brest and at the ruined abbey in the foreground. It was built many centuries ago and obviously had been abandoned for at least a hundred years, but he tried to think what men had quarried the rock and hammered and chiselled the blocks to shape to build a monastery on what is one of the bleakest spots in Europe. Here during winter gales it must seem the Atlantic was trying to tear away the whole continent. Were those monks of the Middle Ages (or earlier?) scourging themselves by establishing their home on one of the windiest and most storm-ridden places they could find? Did they think the harshness made them nearer to God? Were they seeking absolution from nameless guilts?

'This must be the nearest point in France to Canada and America,' Sarah said.

He shook his head. 'Almost, but Pointe de Corsen is the most westerly.' He pointed northward along the coast. 'Look, it's over there, about five miles, beyond Le Conquet. Hundreds, indeed thousands of English seamen know it because it's a good mark when you're working your way through the Chenal du Four, keeping inside of Ushant and all those shoals...'

He fell silent, looking westward, until finally Sarah touched his cheek. 'Where are you now?'

He gave a sheepish laugh. 'Running the *Calypso* into Brest with a southwest wind. Earlier I was beating in against a northeaster, with all the forts firing at me. I was scared stiff of getting in irons and drifting ashore.'

'Southwick wouldn't let you do that,' she said teasing.

Like Ramage, she remembered the *Calypso*'s white-haired old master with affection. She said: 'I wonder what he's doing now?'

He shook his head as if trying to drive away the thought. 'By now he and the *Calypso*'s officers and men will probably have the ship ready to be paid off at Chatham.'

'What does "paid off" really mean? I thought it was the ship, but it sounds like the men.'

It was hard for him to avoid giving a bitter answer. 'Officially it means removing all the *Calypso*'s guns, sails, provisions, cordage and shot (the powder will have been taken off and put in barges on the Thames before she went into the Medway), and then the ship, empty except for a boatkeeper or two, will be left at anchor, or on a mooring. They may take the copper sheathing off the hull.'

'Why "may"?' she asked, curious.

'Well, you know the underwater part of the hull of a ship is covered with copper sheathing to keep out the teredo worm, which bores into the wood. Now some peculiar action goes on between the metals so that the ironwork of things like the rudder gets eaten away. Not only that, but after a year or so the copper starts to dissolve as well, particularly at the bow: it just gets thinner. So when a ship is laid up she is usually first dry-docked and the sheathing is taken off.'

'You still haven't explained "may" – and there's a strange look on your face!'

He sighed and turned back to look at her. 'Well, you know my views on this peace treaty we've signed with Bonaparte, and that neither my father nor I – nor most of our friends – believe Bonaparte truly wants peace. As a result of the Treaty, he's already had more than a year to restock his arsenals and from the Baltic get supplies of mast timber and cordage which we had cut off for years by blockading places like Brest. So now he's busy refitting his fleet: new sails, masts, yards. New ships, too. Now – or very soon – he'll be ready to start the war again.'

'Yet all the French we've met in the past weeks seem happy with the peace,' Sarah protested.

'We've only talked to two types – innkeepers, who smile readily enough as they take our money, and the monarchists who've returned to France from exile and have been trying to get back some of their possessions. They have to believe that Bonaparte really wants a permanent peace; otherwise they're admitting to themselves that they'll soon be exiles in England once again – only this time probably for the rest of their lives.'

'You keep on saying Bonaparte will start the war again, my darling, but what proof is there? After all, the ministers in London aren't fools!'

'Aren't they? Have you met Addington or any of his Cabinet? And Lord Whitworth, the British minister in Paris, can't have

15

looked out of the Embassy window – or else they're ignoring his dispatches in London.'

'The British government might be stupid and the French innkeepers greedy, but that hardly proves Bonaparte is going to war again!'

'Perhaps not, but we'll know for sure when we ride back through the port of Brest. Will the sight of men o' war being refitted in large numbers convince you?'

'Nicholas, why did you propose Brittany for the last part of our honeymoon?' she asked suspiciously.

'Don't you like it?' He was suddenly anxious, the picture of a nervous bridegroom anxious for his bride's comfort. 'The weather is fine. Not much choice of food, I admit, but the inns are not full of our countrymen – they go directly to Paris!'

'You haven't answered my question!'

Her eyes, green flecked with gold, were not angry; they did not warn that she felt cheated or duped. It was obvious she would accept it if he gave the real reason. Only evasions or half-truths would upset her, although good food was rarely spoiled by being served on fine china. He leaned over and kissed her. 'I have another wife,' he confessed solemnly. 'I married you bigamously.'

She undid the top two buttons of her dress, recently collected from a French dressmaker using materials Sarah had brought with her from England. 'The sun has some warmth in it, if you wait long enough, but not enough to tan. Yes,' she said matter of factly, 'I knew about that when you first proposed. Anyway, your mother warned me. In fact she used almost the same words. She said what a shock it had been for her as a new bride when she realized that *her* husband had another wife. She was very relieved that I already knew about you and your first bride, the Navy.'

'Well, we met under unusual circumstances.'

She blushed as he reached over and undid the next two buttons of her dress, pulling back the soft material so that he could see her breasts.

'Bonaparte has done one thing for us – the French fashions help lovers,' he said, and kissed a nipple, touching it with his tongue so it stiffened.

It was strange, she reflected, that you held your husband naked in bed; you even walked round the bedroom naked in front of him, and it all seemed quite natural. Yet out here in the sunshine, lying on the grass with bare breasts, she felt shy, as though this was the first time that Nicholas had unfastened a button. But how right he was about French fashions! Unlike in London, bare arms in the drawing rooms were commonplace here and very few French women of fashion bothered with corsets, although those sensitive of their plumpness wore narrow stays. And the flimsy materials! Often they were almost transparent, and most respectable women wore petticoats, but she had seen several women who passed for respectable wearing dresses that revealed their whole body when they stood against the light, and it was quite extraordinary how often they found themselves in front of a window. Still, anything was welcome that freed women from the constriction of corsets: why should women have to live as though squeezed in a wine press for the sake of fashion? Nevertheless, she pictured some women she knew and imagined them freed of corsets: it would be like slitting the side of a sack of corn!

She felt her breasts hardening as he pretended to inspect her nipples for the first time, commenting on their colour and size. Did he really like large nipples?

'Very well,' she said, concentrating with great effort, 'so the Navy is your first wife and you are honeymooning in Brittany with your second on secret business. *What* business?'

'It's no secret,' he protested. 'Our *passeports* are in order: the French authorities admitted us – welcomed, almost – to the country, enchanted that we are on our honeymoon, so if I happen to be able to count up the number and type of ships being fitted out in Brest, and perhaps La Rochelle and L'Orient . . . well, that would be only the natural curiosity of a couple interested in ships and the sea. After all, you have only just completed a voyage to India and back, and you love looking at ships – don't you?'

'Of course, dearest,' she said with a smile. 'And having closely inspected my breasts, taken my virginity, counted the ships and returned to London at the end of your honeymoon, what do you report to whom – and why? Surely the Admiralty must know what is going on in the French ports?'

'If not what happens on nearby clifftops. No, the Admiralty as such is not the problem. The man who seems to be completely hoodwinked by Bonaparte is the First Lord of the Admiralty, Lord St Vincent. He's laying up ships of the line and frigates. That in itself doesn't matter so much because they could be commissioned again in a few weeks, but he's letting go all the prime seamen: they are being turned loose and are just disappearing like chaff in the wind, looking for work. You can commission all the ships again in a month and get them to sea – *providing* you have the seamen.'

'But, dearest, surely an admiral like Lord St Vincent realizes all that?'

'Of course he realizes he needs trained seamen to commission ships and get them to sea. His mistake is he doesn't believe we need the ships. He doesn't think we'll be at war again with Bonaparte for another five years.'

'Five years? Why not seven, or nine – or three?'

'He's attempting a complete overhaul of all the dockyards – to get rid of the theft, corruption and inefficiency which ranges from commissioners at the top to workmen at the bottom. It will take at least five years.'

'So, my dear, do you think your honeymoon in Brittany will result in Lord St Vincent changing his mind and not paying off any more ships?'

The whimsical note in her voice took the sting out of the question, and he frowned as he answered. It was a fair question and hard to answer satisfactorily. 'It's almost too late to stop him paying off ships: most are already laid up. No sooner had we arrived home in the *Calypso* than (as you well know) I had orders to go on round to Chatham and lay her up. That means all those men I've been collecting together for years, from the time of my first command, the *Kathleen* in the Mediterranean, will be turned out of the Navy the moment the *Calypso* is laid up.'

'And the commission and warrant officers – Southwick, Aitken and the others, yes and young Paolo – what happens to them?'

'Well, they'll join another ship if they can find a berth, but hundreds of lieutenants and masters will be after a few dozen jobs. Paolo should find another ship because my father has enough influence to arrange a midshipman's berth. There's virtually no limit on the number a ship can carry: it depends on the captain.'

She sat upright to avoid the sun dazzling her and wondered if it could possibly tan her bosom a little. Her nipples were so large and brown. Did Nicholas prefer small pink ones, she wondered again. He seemed more than satisfied with them as they were, although she realized new husbands were unlikely to be critical.

18

'So you lose everyone once the ship is laid up again,' she commented. 'Supposing a month later – a month after you are back in London – the Admiralty commissions the *Calypso* again and gives you command?'

'I can ask for the officers, and for Southwick, and if they're not employed I'd probably get them. But the men – not one, unless they heard about it and volunteered, because they'd be scattered across the country, or perhaps serving in merchant ships.'

'And if the war started again?'

'I still wouldn't get them back. They'd volunteer or be pressed and be sent to whichever ship needed men most urgently. I'd have to start all over again. My name is well enough known that volunteers would join, hoping for prize money. But – well, you saw that I knew just about everything concerning every man in the *Calypso*.'

'Yes, you seemed to be father confessor to men twice your age. Anyway, at least we're not at war,' she said and touched his arm. 'At least you're not away at sea and I'm not sick with worry in case you have been wounded. Killed even.'

'That's a cheerful thought for a summer's afternoon!' he protested.

'Every time I hold you in bed, I feel a scar,' she retorted. 'Like knots in a log. You've been lucky so far, the shot or sword cuts have not damaged anything vital. Why, you've done more than enough already to be able to resign your commission and just run the St Kew estate.'

'My mother has been talking to you!'

'Not really. She would like you to, and so would your father.'

'He has no faith in the Admiralty or politicians.'

'That's hardly surprising, considering what they did to him. If they hadn't made him the scapegoat so many years ago, he would probably have been First Lord now, not St Vincent.'

Ramage shrugged his shoulders. 'Perhaps – but I wouldn't have done so well.'

'Why on earth not?'

'He would have been so determined that no one should accuse him of favouring his son that I'd probably still be a lieutenant commanding a cutter, probably on the fishery patrol off Newfoundland.'

'So although you might complain about Lord St Vincent's

policies, you've done well enough, thanks to him.' Sarah was unsure why she was sticking up for St Vincent, who had always seemed taciturn, almost boorish, when she had met him.

'Thanks to his predecessor, Lord Spencer. He gave me my first chances in the early days – the chance to win my spurs, as it were.'

'So you have a honeymoon task – to get enough information to persuade the First Lord and the Cabinet to change the country's policy towards Bonaparte!'

'Not quite,' he said wryly. 'Just to convince the First Lord to keep enough ships in commission. I – we, rather – don't *want* war; we just want to be ready because we think it is coming.'

She buttoned up her dress. 'Come on, let's get on our way. War *may* be coming, but it's certain we have only a few weeks of our honeymoon left and Jean-Jacques expects us for an early supper.'

Sarah riding side-saddle brought a stop to the daily life in each village: women stood at the doors of their houses or shops, or came down the paths to the gates in response to cries from their children.

'We're probably the first foreigners they've seen since before the Revolution,' Ramage commented, keeping a tight rein on his horse, which was nervous at the shrill cries and cheers of the darting children.

'They wonder what nationality we are,' Sarah said. 'There'd be fewer smiles if they knew we were English.'

'Yes, they won't like the *rosbifs* here. Still, we could be Spanish, or even French: here in Brittany anyone from another province is a foreigner!'

'But we are obviously *aristos*,' Sarah said quietly. 'They probably think we escaped the guillotine at the Revolution and with the peace have returned from exile . . .'

Ramage shrugged his shoulders. 'I am not very worried about that! It's more significant that Fort du Toulbroch, Fort de Mengam and the Lion Battery are still fully manned, as though the war was still on and a British squadron might sail up the Gullet any moment.'

'I can see another fort ahead of us. There, just to the right of that church.'

'Yes, the church is at St Pierre and the fort is de Delec, less than a mile short of Brest. This side of it, anyway.'

'How many sides are there?'

He laughed and explained: 'The port is built on both sides of the entrance of the Penfeld river, just where it runs out into the Gullet. From what I remember of the charts and from what Jean-Jacques said last night, the arsenal is this side, by the entrance to the river. Then as you go upstream there's the repair jetty, and a couple of dry docks and another arsenal. Then on the other side, to the east, there's the Château with high walls: an enormous fortress complete with gate and towers. There are barracks further inland. The commander-in-chief's house is in the centre of town, the Hôtel du Commandant de la Marine, in the Rue de Siam, although why I should remember that I don't know! There's a naval college nearby. All along this side of the river are more quays, for another arsenal which is probably used for storing guns and carriages. On the road to Paris at the main gate, the Porte de Landerneau on the north side of the town, there's the hospital. I remember the map of the town in the Hydrographic Office at the Admiralty, drawn ten or fifteen years ago, noted that the pile of garbage from the hospital was polluting the water. And the cartographer was called St Nicolin. Strange how one's memory dredges up these odd items!'

'Look,' Sarah said, 'I can see masts. Like trees that have lost their leaves.'

'Yes, there's just one more village, Laninon, before we reach the port. Ah, over to the right you can now see the ships at anchor in the Roads in front of the port. Yards crossed, sails bent on – why, it really does look as if Bonaparte is preparing a fleet. To send to India, the West Indies, the Cape . . . ? Eight . . . nine . . . eleven ships of the line. Thirteen . . . fifteen . . . sixteen frigates. Four transports. And various others – corvettes, frigates *en flûte* –'

'What are they?' she interrupted.

'Frigates with most of the guns removed and fitted out as transports. And,' he continued, listing what he saw, 'they're anchored out in the Roads, ready to sail. I wonder what we will see along the quays once we get into the port . . .'

She shivered. 'I don't like this, Nicholas. Supposing they stop us in the port and want to see your documents? You captured and sank enough French ships for them to know your name only too well. They could accuse you of being a spy.'

'Hardly a spy,' he protested. 'My papers give my full name. There's nothing secret about our visit – we're on our honeymoon. I'm not writing down lists of ships ... And remember, there's nothing to prevent a French naval officer visiting Portsmouth, or Plymouth – nor anywhere he wants in England. He could probably set up an easel in front of Southsea Castle and paint all the ships he saw riding at anchor at Spithead, and with half a dozen small boys and a sergeant of fusiliers watching him admiringly.'

'Yes, but remember what Jean-Jacques said,' Sarah reminded him.

'Dearest, poor Jean-Jacques is a stranger in his own country. He's lived in England as an exile since 1793. Nine years. A long time.'

'He realizes that. Imagine leaving a château empty, except for vandals, for nine years ... Still, I must say he's done everything to make us comfortable. Thank goodness he brought linen, crockery and cutlery with him from England. The place might be short of furniture but it's still more comfortable than the back of this horse!'

As they jogged along the lane skirting the coast and passing through the village of Laninon before reaching the Penfeld river, Ramage noted the state of the road. Apart from its width it was little more than a deserted track pocked every couple of yards with large potholes. Yet it was obviously the most important road for the defence of Brest because it was the only link (without going miles inland and swinging out again) with the three forts and the Lion Battery. The defences of Brest were between the port and Pointe St Mathieu, but quite apart from rushing out field artillery or cavalry, it was unlikely a company of soldiers could hurry along here on a dark night without a quarter of them spraining ankles in potholes. Yet summer was the time to fill potholes so that cartwheels and horses' hooves packed down the earth.

By the time they returned to the château, to be greeted by Jean-Jacques, they were weary, feeling almost stunned by the monotonous trotting of the horses. Jean-Jacques' valet, Gilbert, busied himself with buckets of water, filling the only bath in the house. This, a large circular basin about twelve inches deep, had been found outside – the Revolutionaries had used it for watering their horses. Now, with it sitting on a thick bath mat on the dressing room floor Gilbert walked back and forth from the kitchen stove with buckets and jugs of hot water. Finally, with

22

six inches of hot water in the bath and some jugs of cold left beside it, he reported all was ready and left.

Those buttons! Being constantly in the company of a woman with a beautiful body (with a body, he told himself proudly, which delighted a French dressmaker who took pride in cutting and stitching her material to emphasize or take advantage of every nuance of breast and thigh), buttons took on a new meaning for him. Previously they were devices for holding together pieces of cloth; now they could be a gateway to ecstasies.

Slowly she undid the buttons of her dress, starting at the bottom so that finally with a quick shrug of her arms the whole dress slid to the floor, and as he started up from the armchair she said: 'No, dearest: poor Gilbert has spent the whole afternoon boiling this water – let's use it while it is hot.' More buttons, more shrugs, and she stood naked, pleased at his obvious pleasure in watching her. Yes, her breasts were firm; yes, her hips were generous without being plump. Yes, her buttocks had that pleasing fullness: so many Frenchwomen, she noticed, had the flatness of young boys.

She turned slowly, and then picked up the towel. 'You bring the soap,' she said, and he stood up and began to undress, thankful that while in France he found it easier to forget breeches, which the French seemed to associate entirely with the aristocracy, and wore the trousers which the *sans-culottes* had adopted as a garment and a slogan.

By the time they had bathed and dressed, Sarah wearing a pale yellow dress which was low cut in the latest fashion, Ramage was sure he would doze off at the dinner table. However, in the high-ceilinged dining room, sparsely furnished with a table and five chairs, they found Jean-Jacques in high spirits. He had, he told them, just been able to trace some more of the furniture left behind and stolen by looters when he fled the Revolution.

Stocky, with crinkly black hair, a nose so hooked that in some lights he looked like a contented puffin, and dressed as though Louis XVI was still on the throne, instead of long ago executed by a revolutionary mob, Jean-Jacques wiped his mouth with a napkin. 'Landerneau, out on the Paris road, that's where I found them,' he said. 'A dining table, twelve chairs, the sideboard and wine cooler.'

'Who had them?'

'The mayor. He was using the table and four chairs; the rest

23

were stored in his stable. Luckily his wife was proud of the table and kept it well polished.'

'What happens now?' Sarah asked.

'Tomorrow I am sending my bailiff and a couple of carts to collect everything. With plenty of straw to protect the wood.'

'The mayor doesn't claim they're his?' Ramage asked.

'Oh yes, although of course he doesn't deny they were once mine. He claims the Revolution put an end to all private property.'

'You had an answer ready for that!' Ramage could imagine the conversation.

'Oh yes. He had half a dozen silver tankards on the sideboard with someone's crest on them, so I said in that case I'd take three since he had no claim to them. His wife nearly had hysterics!'

'But you haven't made a friend – a mayor can be a dangerous enemy,' Sarah said.

'The Count of Rennes has few friends in Brittany after the Revolution,' Jean-Jacques said grimly. 'My real enemy is Bonaparte, so I need hardly care about the mayor of little more than a hamlet. And since Héloïse – well, stayed behind – when I went to England I have no sons to inherit the title or this château. Rennes,' he said quietly, as though talking to himself while he stared back through the centuries, 'the ancient capital of Brittany. Two hundred years ago we were one of the half dozen most powerful families in the country. Now the last survivor is reduced to retrieving sticks of his furniture from the local thieves. Where are all my paintings, my silver, my gorgeous carpets, the Gobelins tapestry which ran the length of that wall?' – he gestured to one side of the long dining room – 'the Venetian glassware which has been handed down from father to son for generations? Being used by oafs.

'I don't begrudge oafs their possessions, but they are just as content swilling rough wine from pottery mugs. They get no pleasure from looking at and using a Venetian goblet; indeed, it just means they get short measure. To them, a Gobelins is a piece of cloth that keeps out a draught, or makes a good tarpaulin to prevent hay blowing off a rick. I could accept the local people stripping this château when the Revolution began if I thought they'd *appreciate* the treasures they stole. But . . .'

Ramage wanted to change the subject to cheer up the Count, whose grandfather had begun the family friendship with the

Blazeys, but there was a difficult question to ask, and now was obviously the time to get the answer.

'Héloïse – have you seen her?'

'The Countess of Rennes, in the eyes of my Church still my wife, though no doubt divorced by some new law of the Revolution? No, I last saw her here nearly ten years ago, when she refused to escape with me.'

Sarah knew only that the Count had spent his exile in England alone while his wife stayed in France, and could not resist asking: 'Why did the Countess stay?' A moment later she could have bitten her tongue.

The skin of Jean-Jacques' face suddenly seemed too tight for the bone structure, but he struggled to present an unconcerned smile. 'She agreed with the aims of the Revolution, or at least she said she did. She was very young then. It goes back a long time: she hated her father, who was of course one of the King's favourites, and she imagined the King once snubbed her at Versailles. Hardly the stuff of revolution, one might think, but she brooded so that when the mob from Brest and Nantes and Angers came yelling through the gate, crying death to the King (and the Count of Rennes) she met them in old clothes and invited them in and served them my best wine. Meanwhile I escaped with my valet and my life. She was very beautiful. Still is, I expect. She is the mistress of one of Bonaparte's generals, I believe: a former corporal, who is not too proud to bed a citizeness who has an old title in her own right and another by marriage.'

He signalled to one of the servants, indicating that the glasses were empty. 'The candles are getting low, too,' he said, and apologized to his guests. 'Before long we'll be reduced to using rush dips.'

Sarah said: 'You know, all that riding has made me so tired . . . Perhaps Nicholas will give you your game of backgammon.'

The Count stood at once, apologetic. 'Of course, both of you must be worn out: how thoughtless of me to keep you up talking of sad yesterdays. Yesteryears, rather. But tomorrow perhaps we shall dine at a more suitable table – I must be the first Count of Rennes to entertain in his own dining room with his guests seated round a scrubbed kitchen table.'

Ramage laughed and turned to Sarah. 'In Jean-Jacques' defence, I should explain that the house he bought in England was furnished with the finest English furniture he could find!'

'Ah, the house in Ruckinge. You know Kent, my dear? Not Ruckinge? I was fortunate enough to be able to carry jewellery with me when I left here for England and by selling some I could buy a house in Kent. Although I love that house, my heart is really here, even though the château is almost empty. I spent my childhood here. My father's father's father – so many forebears – grew up here and died of old age. The vaults in the chapel are nearly full. There'll be just enough room for me. Perhaps the original builder saw into the future and knew how many of us he would need to accommodate!'

'You seem to be full of gloomy thoughts tonight,' Ramage said as he helped Sarah from her chair.

'Yes, and as your host I am appalled that I have to put you in a suite over in the east wing furnished only with a bed, two chairs, commode and a single armoire. And no curtains at the windows.'

'You should see the great cabin of a frigate,' Ramage said dryly.

The Count led them to the door and once out of earshot of the two servants said: 'I met an old friend today. He lives at La Rochelle but travelled to Rennes by way of L'Orient to arrange some business. He was an officer in the old Navy and like me escaped to England. He says that five ships of the line and six frigates are being prepared at La Rochelle, and seven and eleven of each in L'Orient. How does that compare with Brest?'

'Eleven and sixteen,' Ramage said grimly. 'So twenty-three ships of the line and thirty-three frigates are being commissioned along the Atlantic coast. I wonder what's going on at Toulon?'

'I must admit that's a large fleet for peacetime,' Jean-Jacques said, and then added, as if to reassure himself that there was a future: 'But I am sure Bonaparte wants peace now. At least, he wants to – how do you say, you "consolidate". You've seen how he has sent most of his soldiers home to reap the harvest. There are many hundreds of miles of roads still to be repaired – thousands in fact. Today France is a whole country where reaping, ploughing and sowing will take every available man this year if the people are not to starve. Already he is gambling on a good harvest – a bad one would topple him. People will go short in time of war, but with peace they want full bellies.'

Ramage shook his head. 'Ten bad harvests won't topple a man who controls the biggest army and the most powerful police force the world has ever seen.'

'Still,' the Count persisted, hope overcoming reason, 'Bonaparte has concluded a peace with the Russians, and Britain is isolated. The world is at peace. I have no need to remind you that by the Peace of Amiens England has surrendered most of her colonial conquests – and in return Bonaparte has given up the deserts of Egypt. He has all he wants. You don't suppose he needs Spain, Portugal, the Low Countries, Scandinavia . . . ?'

'I do, but I'm probably in a minority,' Ramage said. 'Bonaparte has kept control of the Italian states and Switzerland.'

'But he knows he can't beat the British at sea. Think of the Battle of Aboukir Bay – what a disaster for France! He is a soldier; he has created a great army. But he can't use it to attack England because the Channel is in the way. He realizes this. And that is why he sends his soldiers home.'

'But why does he prepare his Navy – the Navy you say he knows cannot defeat the Royal Navy?'

Jean-Jacques held out his hands, palms uppermost. 'Perhaps to make sure they are in good condition before he stores them away – or whatever you sailors call it.'

'Perhaps,' Sarah said, taking Ramage's arm. 'You must excuse the bride for dragging her groom off to bed, but she is going to sleep standing on her feet!'

CHAPTER TWO

She was lying on her side with her back to him, and for a moment he marvelled that the female body had been so shaped that in this position it fitted the male so perfectly. But sleeping alone in a swinging cot at sea – for him that would from now on be an almost unbearable loneliness. Quite why horses should now be galloping with harness jingling he did not know, and he opened his eyes to find the first hint of dawn had turned the room a faint grey.

Horses? Harness? Now, as he shook the sleep cobwebbing his head, he heard shouted commands coming from the centre of the château; from the wide steps leading up to the front door.

He slid out of bed and walked to the window, cursing the coldness of the marble floor although too impatient to find slippers.

A dozen men on horseback, blurred figures in the first light. Perhaps more. Now he could just distinguish that they were dismounting. Some were hurrying up the steps, sword scabbards clinking on the stone, while a single man held all the reins.

One man was making violent gestures at the great double door – presumably pounding on it with his fist. Then he heard more horses and another five or six men cantered past the window towards the others. Soldiers. Even in the faint light it was possible to distinguish them – and only cavalry would have so many horses.

She was standing behind him now; he could feel her breasts pressing into his shoulder blades. 'What is it?' she whispered. 'It's so cold. Why aren't you wearing a robe? You'll get a chill.'

'French cavalry,' he said briefly. 'Quickly, dress in riding clothes. Don't try and light a lamp.'

He hurried across the room and pushed their two trunks so that, from the door, they were hidden by the armoire and commode. He then bundled up the clothes they had been wearing the previous evening and which they had been too tired to do more than drape over the chairs, and pushed them under the bed.

'What are you doing?'

'Hurry, darling. Something's happened and these soldiers aren't here on a search for Army deserters. They look more like an escort for Jean-Jacques or me. The second group was leading a riderless horse.'

'You don't think . . . ?'

'The mayor of Landerneau may be trying to keep his furniture by telling the *préfet* some tale. Don't forget Jean-Jacques is very vulnerable – he's only recently returned from exile.'

She shivered as she sorted out underwear. 'And he has the notorious Captain Lord Ramage staying in his house.'

'That can't be a crime,' Ramage said as he pulled up his trousers, but his voice was doubtful, so that what was intended as a statement sounded like a question. 'Anyway, whatever they're up to I can't think the soldiers know anything about us. One spare horse . . . that's for Jean-Jacques.'

'The officer in charge can easily leave two of his troopers behind, or have two of Jean-Jacques' horses saddled up for us. Or make us walk.'

'Let's rely on them not knowing we're here!'

'The servants,' Sarah said, ignoring her husband's attempts to reassure her, 'can they be trusted? Will they tell the soldiers we are here?'

'If you hurry up, we won't be here, darling,' Ramage said, reaching for his jacket. 'We'll be hiding in another room, so if the French soldiers search our suite they won't find us.'

'Dearest,' she whispered, 'do up my buttons.' She turned her back to him so that he could secure her coat. By now, he noticed, it was getting appreciably lighter. He had been thinking that the first cavalry had passed only a couple of minutes ago, but he realized it was now nearer five.

'There – now, my lady, hurry up or –'

He stopped and listened to the gentle but persistent tapping at the door. Tap, tap, tap – and then a hissed 'Milord ... milord...'

He recognized the voice: Jean-Jacques' valet Gilbert, a tiny, almost wizened Breton who had gone to England to share his master's exile and then returned after the Treaty of Amiens.

Ramage hurried to the door and the moment he had opened it the valet slipped through and shut it again.

'Ah, milord – and milady, of course – you are dressed.' Gilbert glanced round the room, noted the trunks and the lack of clothing and toilet articles lying about. 'You are prepared, then: this suite looks deserted – they will say the English have flown, if indeed they know you are supposed to be here. Quickly, please follow – I take you to a small room where you must hide.'

'But what –'

'I explain in a few minutes, milord: first, to safety!'

The valet shut the window ('No Frenchman would have a window open,' he explained) and they followed him out of the room, along the corridor away from the main part of the château, down a staircase where it was so dark they had to grip the rail and feel for the next step before moving, until finally the valet opened a door.

'An old storeroom, milord,' he explained. 'No one would seek you here, and there's a side door leading into one of the gardens.'

He extended a hand to Sarah. 'There is a small step up, milady. I am afraid there are simply these old packing cases, but we hope you will only have to wait an hour or two before returning to your suite.'

Ramage felt like a piece of flotsam swirling round rocks at the mercy of random waves, but before he had time to ask, the valet said: 'I have a message from the Count, milord, and some information I – er, well, I happened to hear. I took the liberty of listening beyond the door.

'The message from the Count is that he thinks France is again at war with Britain and you must escape. That was all he could say before the cavalry officer and his men came in to arrest him.'

'But you heard more?'

'Yes, sir, it is indeed war. The most important thing the cavalry officer said as he arrested the Count – on direct orders from Paris – was that Lord Whitworth, your ambassador in Paris, had left the capital on the twelfth of this month. He said this was close to a declaration of war. Then on the seventeenth the British authorities had detained all French and Dutch ships in their ports and issued commissions to privateers.'

He paused a moment, pulling at his nose as though that would stimulate his memory. 'Yes, then on the next day, the eighteenth, the British declared war on France and on the nineteenth ships of the Royal Navy captured some French coasting vessels off Audierne – almost in sight of Brest and, of course, in French waters.

'Then, according to the cavalry officer, on the twenty-third Bonaparte issued an order to detain British men between the ages of eighteen and sixty who are liable to serve in the British Army or Navy.'

Ramage glanced at Sarah. It was now the twenty-fifth of May. Britain and France had been at war for exactly a week. Yet yesterday when the two of them spent much of the day out on Pointe St Mathieu there had been no sign of police guarding the roads, no sign of a blockade; not a frigate on the horizon.

The valet seemed to have more to say, but whatever it was, he was not enjoying the prospect.

'Well, Gilbert, is that all?'

'No, milord, I regret it is not. You appreciate that my purpose in listening at the door was to obtain information to pass to you . . .'

'I am sure you were doing exactly what the Count would wish you to do, Gilbert, and we are grateful.'

'Well, milord, the cavalry officer stressed that the Count was being arrested on the orders of Bonaparte but as the result of information laid by the Countess – the former Countess, I mean.

And she had told the authorities that he was likely to have English guests staying with him. That was why I wanted you to leave your suite quickly.'

'But they'll look in the trunks . . .'

Gilbert shook his head. 'I doubt it, sir: the suite looked unoccupied when I came to you. Not only that, it is hardly where you would *expect* to find guests . . .' There was no mistaking Gilbert's horror at the choice of rooms forced on the Count by the Revolution. 'The Count's own suite has even less furniture. Anyway, the soldiers will start their search in the kitchen –'

'The *kitchen*?'

'Oh yes, milord, straight to the kitchen – to look for wine. I sent Edouard there at once to make sure there was plenty readily available. Once the officer has taken the Count away and the soldiers start searching, they will be half drunk. I do not think it will be a careful search.'

'They were taking the Count away at once?' Sarah asked.

'The officer gave him ten minutes to dress and pack a small bag, milady.'

Ramage was conscious that what he did from now on would govern whether or not he was marched off to a French prison as a *détenu*, but he was much more frightened of Sarah's possible fate. A selfish thought slid in before he had time to parry it: being married did indeed mean you had given a hostage to fortune. Now he could understand Lord St Vincent's dictum, that an officer who married was lost to the Service. Quite apart from Sarah's own safety in a case like this (which was admittedly unusual), would a happily married officer risk his own life in battle with the same recklessness as a bachelor, knowing that he now had something very special to lose? And if he had children . . .

He looked up at Gilbert. 'What will they do to the Count? Guillotine him?'

'It is possible, milord, but – if I may speak freely – I think the Countess, the former Countess rather, will probably make sure his life is saved. I thought they were happily married – until the Revolution, when she became caught up in the fever. Transportation is likely – I believe many Royalists who were not executed were sent to Cayenne, which I'm sure you know is a tiny island in the Tropics off the coast of French Guinea, in South America. Priests, masons, monarchists, indeed anyone out of favour with the Republic, are sent to Cayenne.'

'What do you suggest we do now? Obviously we want to get back to England.'

Gilbert nodded cautiously. 'The first priority is to avoid you falling into the Republic's hands. The second is to get you back to England. If you will excuse me, I will go to see what news Edouard has. The soldiers will have been talking freely to him, I am sure; a good revolutionary always assumes a servant is downtrodden and sympathizes with him.'

With that Gilbert seemed to vanish through the door, but Ramage realized the man was so deft and light-footed he could open a door, go through and close it again, with less fuss than most people reach for the knob.

Once they were alone, Sarah smiled affectionately and took his hand. 'We should have been married a month or so earlier, then we would have been back home by now,' she said. 'Or had a shorter honeymoon. Anyway, now you don't have to worry about convincing Lord St Vincent not to pay off any more ships.'

'No, it looks as though the Cabinet at last became suspicious of Bonaparte. Withdrawing our ambassador from Paris must have startled Bonaparte, who will have been full of his own cleverness in getting us to sign that absurd treaty last year. Now we've suddenly slapped his hand. No more than that, though, considering the size of his Army.'

'You'll have to fight him at sea, then!' Sarah said cheerfully, and then could have bitten her tongue for the second time in less than twelve hours.

'I'm hiding here,' Ramage said bitterly, 'and someone else is commissioning the *Calypso* in Chatham. He's the luckiest captain in the Navy if the men haven't been paid off yet, because he gets the finest ship's company.'

Suddenly she had an inspiration. 'That means you are lucky. He will keep the men together, all ready for you to resume command when you escape.'

'Providing I escape and providing the Admiralty are prepared to turn out a captain for me,' he protested. 'Neither seems very likely at the moment.'

'If you are captured – I'm sure we won't be – they'll release you on parole. Then you can make for the coast and steal a boat, or something.'

He laughed sourly. 'My love, you have a simple approach to it all but the Admiralty don't share it. Parole, for instance.'

'What is difficult about that?'

'Well, giving your parole means giving your word of honour not to escape, and you are freed to live outside the prison. You pay for your board and lodging, of course.'

'There's bound to be a "but", though,' she said gloomily.

'There certainly is. If you break your parole and escape to England, the Admiralty don't welcome you. In fact they might send you back. They certainly won't employ you.'

'Why ever not?'

'Because you gave the French your word of honour and you broke it.'

'But there is a war on! The French killed their king. They guillotined thousands of innocent people.'

'True, and probably will go on executing more, but the Admiralty's view is that you don't have to give your parole. If you do, then you must keep your word.'

'So what on earth can a captured officer do?'

'Refuse parole. That means he stays in prison, but it also means that if he *can* escape and get to England, he really is free and can expect to be employed again.'

'Do the Admiralty actually check?'

'I presume so. There's a French commissioner in London, you know.'

'Not when we're at war, though.'

'Oh yes. He's a fellow called M. Otto, Commissioner for the Exchange of Prisoners. Every now and again we exchange Frenchmen we've captured for an equal number of Britons that the French have taken.'

'Let's not talk about prisoners,' Sarah said. 'We'll get out of this somehow. Gilbert – we can trust Gilbert. I fear for Jean-Jacques, though.'

He shook his head. 'No, I think Gilbert is right: that damned wife, or whatever she is, won't want him executed: it wouldn't do her reputation any good. The widow of a traitor. Transportation – yes, he could be sent to Cayenne, and that's one of the unhealthiest places in the world. But death there is not certain. Not as certain as being strapped down to the guillotine here.'

'And what about us? I don't want to sound selfish but we are foreigners in the middle of the enemy camp!' Her smile was wry; he was pleased to see that his new wife neither showed fear nor attempted to blame him for the fact they were caught in a trap.

'When Gilbert comes back we'll hear if the French authorities know we're here and if they're looking for us. I don't think Jean-Jacques registered us anywhere or reported to the authorities that we were staying with him. I think he should have done – at the *préfet*'s office, perhaps – but he wouldn't bother because he thought it was not the *préfet*'s business whom he chose to entertain.'

'That attitude is all right in England, but I can't see Bonaparte and his merry men agreeing.'

'No, but although the French know the names of every foreigner who has entered the country, unless they have their present addresses, it doesn't help. Remember,' he said bitterly, 'if the French are arresting all the visitors, it means they are breaking their word.'

'In what way?'

'Well, everyone visiting France has to get a *passeport* from the French. That's a guarantee, a document permitting the foreigner to pass through the ports of France and travel about the country. Now, having granted these *passeports*, it seems Bonaparte is breaking his word.'

Sarah nodded but said with casual sincerity: 'Yes, that's true, but anyone – and that includes us – who trusts a man like Bonaparte or the government of France cannot complain if he is cheated. "Honour" is a word that the French deleted from their vocabulary when they executed the king. Any nation that cheerfully executes a whole class of its people for just being born into that class is wicked and mentally sick. A Frenchman could be born an aristocrat but be poorer than the local gravedigger, yet the aristocrat was dragged off to the guillotine, and the gravedigger went along to cheer the executioner.'

'We shouldn't have come here on our honeymoon,' Ramage said wryly.

'Where else? Prussia isn't very appealing. The Netherlands and Italy – Bonaparte will be arresting all foreigners there. Spain – who knows. Anyway, we are really learning something about the French.'

She sat down on one of the packing cases. 'What happens if the French soldiers find our trunks in the suite?'

'Well, they won't find us. Don't forget they came at dawn, so they'll assume we've escaped.'

'That seems too good to be true,' she warned.

'No, it's obvious when you think about it.'

'Where do we go now? This storeroom is rather bare!'

'Back to our suite eventually, because it'll probably be the safest hiding place in France.'

'Our suite? But . . .'

'"It's been searched by the cavalry, so the *rosbif* and his wife *can't* be there",' he said, imitating the precise speech of an officer reporting to a senior. 'They'll be searching everywhere else for miles around.'

There was a faint tapping at the door and Ramage opened it. Gilbert slid in, a reassuring smile on his face. He bowed to Sarah.

'You must find that box uncomfortable, milady.' As soon as Sarah reassured him, he turned to Ramage and took a deep breath.

'Edouard used his ears and eyes carefully, milord, and he acted as a simpleton so that he could ask silly questions – and sprinkled some shrewd questions among them.

'Anyway, it means this. As far as the Count is concerned, because France is now at war with England again and the Count spent all those years in England, he is regarded as an enemy of the state. He was denounced and the authorities in Paris sent orders to the *chef d'administration* in Rennes to arrest him.'

'Where is he being confined?'

'Ah, that's my next piece of information. He will be confined in the Château in Brest, the naval headquarters. He and many others not yet brought in.'

'What others?'

'Landowners like the Count who returned from exile, people who in the past year or so have fallen out of favour with Bonaparte or the local *préfet* or even a local chief of police. Priests who have spoken out too boldly. People to whom some of those in authority owe money . . .'

'Why the Château at Brest – to be near a convenient ship?'

Gilbert nodded. 'They will be transported to Cayenne as soon as a ship (a frigate, the cavalry captain said) can be prepared.'

'So the Count had how long – a year? – back in is home . . .'

'Eleven months, sir. Now, concerning you. The officer knew you had been staying here but Edouard was naturally a great supporter of the Republic and told the officer that you had received a warning yesterday evening and fled, leaving your trunks behind. This was confirmed by the Count, who was still in the room.

'The Count pretended anger – he said you were under the

protection of *passeports* issued by Bonaparte. The cavalry officer just laughed and produced a handful of papers and read them to the Count – I think because he had some idea that the authorities could blame him for your escape.

'Anyway, the first was a letter from the *préfet* at Rennes addressed to you by name, milord, telling you of a decree dated a few days ago. It enclosed a copy of the decree that made you a prisoner of war, from the second *Prairial* in the eleventh year of the Republic, which is a few days ago. The decree was signed by the First Consul, and with Bonaparte's signature was that of M. Marot, the Secretary of State.'

'And her ladyship?'

'No mention of wives, milord. Edouard had the impression that the letter was simply a copy of one being sent to all foreign males. He thought that women and children were not affected.'

Ramage looked squarely at the little man. 'What it means now, Gilbert, is that you and Edouard and the rest of the staff are harbouring enemies of the Republic. You could be guillotined. We must go.'

'I assure you Edouard and I are true patriots, milord; we are not harbouring enemies of the state because this house has already been searched carefully by a company of cavalry which had ridden specially from Rennes.'

Ramage held the man's shoulders. 'Gilbert, thank you. But there is too much risk for you.'

'Sir, please stay. The Count would wish it. England gave me a home, as well as the Count, when we were refugees. And there is no risk now for you or us: the house has been searched. And we are already making inquiries about their intentions for the Count and to see if it is possible to hire a fishing boat to get you to England, or even the Channel Islands.'

'Who is making inquiries?' Ramage asked.

'The second cook and her husband, Louis, a gardener, always take a *cabriolet,* how do you call it –?'

'A gig.'

'– ah yes, a gig. Well, they go into Brest each week to buy fish and other things. The *gendarmes* at the Landerneau Gate – that's where everyone has to show papers when entering or leaving Brest –'

Ramage was curious and interrupted: 'Is it possible to get into Brest without papers? No one asked us.'

'But of course, milord. You rode across the fields without knowing. Otherwise you simply leave the road half a mile before the town gates and go round them through the fields. There are gates on the road but no wall round the town. The risk now the war has begun is being stopped later somewhere in the town by a patrol of *gendarmes*.'

Ramage nodded and glanced at Sarah, a glance noticed by Gilbert. 'Ah yes, when it comes to getting you to the fishing boat, you dress as a French married couple going to market – or travelling to visit relatives or looking for work. You will have documents –'

'What documents?' Ramage asked.

'Genuine documents, I assure you, milord. You will have French names of course, and your French accent, of Paris, will need modifying. Thickening, to that of the Roussillon or Languedoc, for instance: you know both areas. We need to choose somewhere specific, a long distance from here – where if the *préfet* in Brest wants to check, he knows it would take three or four weeks, so he is unlikely to bother. But if it was Paris' – he shrugged his shoulders expressively – 'a courier leaves for there daily.'

'You have been giving it all careful thought!'

'When we returned from England,' the valet admitted, 'I did not share the Count's optimism for the future in France. The Count thought we would have many years of peace. For myself, I thought the Treaty was like two prize fighters having a rest during a bout. I advised the Count not to leave England, but alas, the nostalgia for this château overcame the love he had developed for the house in Kent. Now I fear the Count will travel the road to Cayenne . . .'

'And you – what will happen to you?' Sarah asked anxiously.

'I took the precaution of supplying myself with papers – and of course, like Edouard and Louis and the rest of the Count's staff, it is well known how deeply we hate the *aristos*! We work for them in order to eat!'

'And your stay in England – how will you explain that?'

'Oh yes, the Count threatened me so I had to go with him. The *gendarmes* are always most sympathetic with those who have suffered at the hands of the *aristos* . . . They even congratulated me on persuading the Count to return to France at the peace . . .

I think even then the *préfet* knew the Count (with many scores of other exiles) was walking into Bonaparte's trap.'

Gilbert then struck the palms of his hands together like a pastry-cook dusting off flour. 'We must cheer ourselves. I think it is safe for you to return to your suite and I will serve you breakfast. It will be safer if you eat there – not all my plans have worked.'

Intrigued, Ramage asked: 'What went wrong?'

'The cavalry suddenly arriving. I had paid out a good deal of money to make sure we had enough warning to allow the Count to escape.'

'I should think the *préfet* received the orders about the Count from Paris during the night,' Ramage said. 'As soon as he read them he sent out the cavalry and at the same time hoped to pick us up.'

Gilbert nodded slowly, considering the idea and finally agreed. 'That would account for it. I do not like to think that I was cheated – or betrayed.'

CHAPTER THREE

The meals, Sarah commented, were superbly cooked, and although the choice was limited, the food was plentiful; their suite was large and airy, even though the furniture was sparse. The view from the windows was spectacular, if you liked the Breton landscape, harsh to English eyes accustomed to rich greens and unused to the great jagged boulders scattered here and there like distorted hay ricks. Her only complaint was that they had not been able to leave the rooms for three days.

Ramage pointed out that their plight hardly compared with that of Jean-Jacques: he would be in a cell at the Château in Brest, a huge citadel both had agreed was cold and grim even when they saw it on a sunny afternoon only a few days ago (although it seemed a lifetime). Whereas Jean-Jacques at best could look forward to confinement for years in one of the unhealthiest places in the Tropics, the worst that could happen to them would be for Nicholas to be taken off to Valenciennes, where prisoners of war were held, while Sarah had to live with a French family for the rest of the war.

Sarah had declared that she would stay as near as possible to wherever her husband was incarcerated – they had all agreed that he would not give his parole. The unspoken agreement was that if they were discovered and captured, Nicholas would try to escape to England while Sarah would, if necessary, be left behind. She refused to consider that the French might punish her as a reprisal for her husband's escape.

The knock on the door was gentle but at the wrong time: Gilbert had taken away the dirty dishes only half an hour ago, and was not due to bring the first course of the next meal – Ramage took out his watch – for another four hours.

Gilbert slipped in and gave a dismissive wave with his hand as he shut the door and saw the look of alarm on their faces.

'The cook and gardener are back, milord. You would not have heard the horse's hooves because of course they came to the servants' entrance.'

Sarah sat down again, realizing that the sudden tension made her feel faint and that Gilbert would be quick to notice if she went white.

Ramage raised his eyebrows, not wanting to betray impatience by asking a question, but he noticed a curious tension in the Frenchman.

'You understand the word "brig", milord?'

'In English? Yes, it is a type of warship.'

'Ah, so they did get it right,' he said. 'Now, the news of the Count is bad, but no worse than we expected: he has been sentenced to transportation to Cayenne: he and fifty-three other *déportés* are being held in the Château and will sail in a frigate which is being prepared. The ship sails in about a week, the gardener believes: some of her guns, powder and shot are being unloaded to make room for prisoners.'

'What is the name of the frigate?' Ramage asked.

'*L'Espoir,* so the gardener understands. She was pointed out to him. Boats are taking out provisions, and it was said that carpenters are building special cells. Not to imprison the *déportés* all the time; only when they are punished.'

Ramage noticed that 'when': Gilbert knew enough of the Republican way to know that no monarchist would reach Cayenne without being punished for something, however minor; an important part of being a staunch Republican was to show that one was a staunch anti-Royalist, and the most effective methods were to betray someone (an easy way of settling monetary debts in the early days of the Revolution was to accuse your creditor of being a secret Royalist: the guillotine quickly closed that account) and to cheer lustily every time the guillotine blade crashed down. A woman had become famous in Paris because she sat quietly knitting beside the guillotine day after day – in three minutes it could dispatch a victim from him standing to his head rolling into a basket.

'We ought to find out exactly when *L'Espoir* intends to sail,' Ramage said.

'You hope we can make an attempt to rescue the Count?' Gilbert asked hopefully.

Ramage shook his head. 'You, Edouard, the gardener and me to capture a frigate? Four against at least a hundred, and the garrison of the Château as well if you tried it in Brest?'

Gilbert nodded. 'I grasp at straws, milord.'

'It's all we have to grasp,' Ramage said. 'I had in mind only that if we can escape to England before *L'Espoir* sails, perhaps I might be able to warn the Admiralty so that a watch is kept for her. But Gilbert, you mentioned a brig. What brig?'

'Ah yes, that was just some gossip the gardener's wife heard. Not the gardener,' Gilbert said tactfully, as though not wanting to cast any doubt on the intelligence of womanhood in Sarah's hearing, 'he was at the meat market, and she heard about this at the fish market.'

Gilbert was a splendid fellow, Ramage told himself, and his only fault is that for him the shortest distance between two points is a well embroidered story. His listeners needed patience, and it was a defect in Ramage's own character, he admitted, that he had been born with little or none.

'Yes, the gardener's wife – her name is Estelle, by the way – overheard two fishmongers discussing a brig which had arrived in *Le Goulet* the evening before, escorted by a French corvette.'

'Why "escorted"?' Ramage asked.

'Oh, because the brig is English, milord, and with the war now resumed one would expect an escort, no?'

Ramage nodded and managed to avoid looking across at Sarah: he knew she would be hard put to avoid laughing as she saw him struggling not to snap at Gilbert, swiftly drawing the story from him like a fishmonger filleting fish.

'Anyway, this brig has a name like *Murex*. It seems a strange name, but Estelle was sure because one fishmonger spelled it to the other.'

'Yes, it would be *Murex*,' Ramage said, and remembered another 10-gun brig of the same class, the *Triton*, also named after a seashell (not the sea god, as many thought). She had been his second command, and she had stayed afloat during a hurricane in the West Indies but, dismasted, then drifted on to the island of Culebra. By now there would be very little of her skeleton left: the teredo worm would have devoured her timbers and coral would be growing on any ironwork while gaudy tropical fish swam through whatever was left of the skeleton.

'Were many killed and wounded when the *Murex* was captured?' Sarah asked.

'Killed and wounded, milady?' a puzzled Gilbert asked. 'I don't think anyone was hurt. The captain and the officers, perhaps, but I doubt it.'

Ramage had a curious feeling that he was dreaming the whole conversation: that he was dreaming about a fairy tale entitled 'The Two Fishmongers'. The time had come to be firm with Gilbert.

'Start at the beginning and tell us what Estelle overheard in the fish market. Now, she is in the fish market and she hears two fishmongers talking.'

'Well, she was to buy salt cod. There was plenty of that. Then she wanted some halibut – but she could find none. What, she asked herself, could replace the missing halibut? Bear in mind she would be cooking it: the first cook, Mirabelle, refuses to cook fish: she says that a woman with her delicate pastry should not be asked to meddle with scaly reptiles – that's what Mirabelle calls them, milord, "reptiles".'

'The fishmongers,' Ramage said patiently.

'Ah yes, Estelle was discussing with them what to buy in place of the halibut. She had the sauce in mind, you understand. Well, the second fishmonger joined the discussion, and while Estelle was thinking, asked the first fishmonger if he had heard about the English brig arriving.

'The first fishmonger had not, and the second – his name is Henri, a Gascon, and he has trouble making people believe his stories: not for nothing do we have the word "gasconade".'

'And then . . .' Ramage prompted.

'Henri then told how this brig had been sighted in the Chenal du Four by the lookouts now stationed on Pointe St Mathieu. Then they noticed the strange business about her flag.'

Once more Gilbert came to a stop, like a murex (or a winkle,

Ramage thought sourly) retreating into its shell after every few inches of progress. Dutifully Ramage encouraged him out again.

'What about the flag, Gilbert?'

'She was flying a white flag above the English colours. Had she been captured? the sentries asked themselves. But why a *white* flag – one would have expected a *Tricolore* over the English.

'Anyway, they passed a message round to the Château and a corvette which was anchored close by was sent out to investigate. She returned with the English brig following, only now the white flag had been replaced by the *Tricolore*.

'If you want my opinion, milord' – he paused politely until Ramage nodded – 'the brig had already surrendered, but the corvette met her before she started coming into *Le Goulet* and put men on board and claimed to have captured her. That way they get a reward.'

They must be optimists, Ramage thought. The British Admiralty courts were notoriously fussy and the agents corrupt when awarding prize money, and he doubted if Bonaparte's Navy even bothered with prize courts. The corvette had been sent out to check up on a vessel already flying a white flag which traditionally meant surrender or truce. He raised his eyebrows in another variation of prodding Gilbert to continue.

'This English brig now flying the *Tricolore* over the English colours, and with her guns still – how do you say, withdrawn, not in place for firing...'

'Not run out.'

'Ah, yes. This brig is anchored in front of the Château and many important men – including the *préfet maritime* and Admiral Bruix, the *commandant de l'Armée navale* – are rowed out to the ship. They stay about an hour, and then after they return the crew of the *Murex* – her name can be read from the shore you understand – are brought on shore and given accommodation in the Château, while French sailors are taken out to guard the rest.'

'The rest of what?'

'Well, the officers, and a few seamen,' Gilbert said, clearly surprised at Ramage's question.

'But why are the officers and a few seamen being left on board? Who were the men brought on shore and lodged in the Château?'

'Why, they are the mutineers, of course!' Gilbert said. 'The officers and the seamen who did not mutiny are kept on board as prisoners of war. That,' he amended cautiously, 'is how Estelle understood it from Henri.'

The ship's company of the *Murex* brig mutinying within a few days – almost hours – of the resumption of war and carrying the ship into Brest to hand her over to the French? Ramage looked at Sarah, as if appealing to her to assure him that he had misheard. She stared at the floor, obviously stunned.

Who commanded the brig? He could be a lieutenant – almost certainly would be. The *Murex* would probably have left Plymouth or Portsmouth before war began. Most likely she was based on the Channel Islands.

But what caused a mutiny? The mutinies at the Nore and Spithead had brought better conditions for the Navy and he had never heard any murmurs of discontent since then. There was occasional loose talk of malcontents among Irish seamen; a few captains also complained of the activities of the London Corresponding Society, which some had blamed for the Nore and Spithead affairs, but the subsequent inquiry had produced no proof.

A mutiny in a single ship, Ramage felt instinctively, was the captain's fault. Either he was too harsh (like the late and unlamented Hugh Pigot, commanding the *Hermione*) or he was too slack, failing to notice troublemakers at work among the ship's company. The troublemakers did not have to be revolutionaries: far from it. There were always men who genuinely enjoyed stirring up trouble without a cause and without a purpose, and they usually became seamen or Members of Parliament, depending on their background. Either way, they talked shrilly without any sense of responsibility, like truculent whores at a window.

The *Murex*. Ideas drifted through his mind like snowflakes across a window – and, he admitted sourly, they had about as much weight. He looked up at Gilbert and smiled. 'Don't look so sad: now's the time to plot and scheme, not despair!'

The Frenchman shook his head sadly. 'We need a company of *chasseurs* or an English ship of the line, milord,' he said. 'Three or four of us against Bonaparte . . .'

'Don't forget Bonaparte was alone when he sent the Directory packing! From being a young Corsican cadet at the artillery school he rose to be the ruler of most of Europe . . . Don't despair, Gilbert; come back in half an hour and we'll talk again. First, though, tell me who we can count on among the staff.'

'All are loyal, sir. I mean that none will betray us. For active help: well, Edouard, Estelle and her husband Louis – who was a fisherman before becoming a gardener when the authorities confiscated his boat – will actively help. The others may not care to risk their lives.'

'But those two men and the woman would?'

'Yes, because they all hate the new régime. Not that it's very new now, but they have all suffered. Estelle and Louis lost their fishing boat and then had to sell their little cottage in Douarnenez: Edouard's father should be buried in the cemetery at Landerneau, on the Paris road, but instead the body is in a mass grave near the guillotine they set up in Brest.'

'What did the father do?'

'A terrible crime,' Gilbert almost whispered. 'He was the Count's butler. He decided to stay here in France when the Count escaped to England because he could not see any danger from his own people for a butler. But he was denounced to the Committee of Public Safety as a Royalist.'

'On what evidence? That he worked for the Count?'

'Milord, you do not understand. If you are denounced, you are not brought before the kind of court you are accustomed to in England. You are first locked up, and next day, next week, next month – even next year – you are brought before a tribunal, the denunciation is read out, and you are sentenced. You might be asked for your explanation, but no one will be listening to it. The sentence is the same, whatever you say – the guillotine.'

'Does Edouard know who denounced his father?'

'No, but he knows the names of the three members of the tribunal.'

'What does he intend to do?'

'We Bretons are like your Cornishmen, milord: we have long memories and much patience. Edouard is prepared to wait for his revenge. Nor is he alone: there have been many unexplained accidents in the last year or two, so I hear: farms catch fire, the wheel comes off a *cabriolet* and the driver is killed or badly hurt ... it seems that a band of assassins occasionally prowl the countryside. It was only six months ago that members of tribunals stopped having armed guards at their houses. But now, milord, I will leave you for half an hour.'

When the door had shut, Sarah patted the bed beside her.

'Come and sit with me – I suddenly feel very lonely.' She leaned over and kissed him. 'If I said what I felt about that, you'd blush.'

'I'd like to blush. For the last few hours I've felt pale and wan.'

'If you'd told Gilbert to come back in two hours, I'd lure you to other things.'

'I had thought of that, but Gilbert will be expecting to hear of a plan worthy of Captain the Lord Ramage – one that frees Jean-Jacques and gets us all safely back to England.'

She looked at him carefully, as though inspecting a thorough-bred horse at a sale. 'A slight turning up at the corners of the mouth . . . a brightness in at least one eye . . . a jauntiness about the ears . . . Or am I mistaken?'

'You're in love,' he said solemnly. 'I can produce plans as a cow gives milk, but they curdle as soon as you look at them.'

'What are the chances of rescuing Jean-Jacques?'

'You know the answer to that question.'

'Yes, I suppose I do. What are the chances of us escaping?'

He paused a minute or two. 'Better than they were, I think. It depends on how the French authorities regard the mutineers from the *Murex*. Yes, and what they intend to do with the officers and the seamen who did not join the mutiny and are still on board as prisoners of war.'

'Why is all that important?'

He shrugged his shoulders. 'I don't know. That's the worst of plans. Most of the time they're just ideas. Occasionally, if you're lucky, you can throw an idea at a problem and it solves it. That's how swallows make those nests of mud in odd places.'

'And was doing that what made Captain Ramage famous in the Navy for his skill and daring?'

'Captain Ramage is famous at the Admiralty for disobeying orders!'

'They do say,' Sarah said, 'that being too modest is another way of bragging.'

'Well, skill and daring have landed Captain Ramage with a wife in a château a few miles from Brest while his ship is at Chatham, which is only a war away.'

'You make it sound as though you're sorry you married me.'

He took her in his arms. 'No, my dear, I'm blaming myself for not having married you sooner: then I'd be taking the *Calypso* out of the Medway and you'd be safe in London or St Kew, starting to write a passionate letter to me saying how you miss me.'

Sarah sat up and patted her hair as there was a gentle knock at the door. Ramage realized with a guilty feeling that he had nothing to say to Gilbert. Well, maybe he could think aloud, but that seemed like cheating a man who trusted you.

CHAPTER FOUR

Sarah put the triangular red scarf round her head and knotted the ends under her chin. Then coquettishly she spun round a couple of times so that her heavy black skirt swirled out and up, revealing knee-length and lace-edged white cotton drawers.

Ramage frowned and then said judiciously: 'Yes, there's a certain rustic charm, despite the revolutionary scarf. Your complexion is just right: you have the tan of a country wench who helps with the harvesting.'

'You are a beast! You know very well this is the remnants of a tropical tan!'

'I do, yes,' Ramage teased, 'but I was thinking of the *gendarmes* you might have to charm.'

'You don't think my accent is adequate?'

'Oh yes – thanks to Gilbert's coaching you are a true Norman from Falaise. Just remember, in case they question you, that William the Conqueror was born in the castle there, his wife was Matilda, and the Bayeux tapestry is very long!'

She walked round him. 'You don't look right, Nicholas. That hooked nose looks far too aristocratic for you to have survived the guillotine, although I admit your hair looks untidy enough for a gardener. Those trousers! I'm so used to seeing you in breeches. Isn't it curious how the revolutionaries associated breeches with the monarchists? Personally I should have thought trousers are much more comfortable than *culottes*. If I was a man I think my sympathies would be with the *sans-culottes*. I'd cry "*vive les pantalons!* To the bonfires with the *culottes*!"'

She inspected his hands. 'You have worked enough earth into the skin, my dear, but they still don't look as if they've done a good day's hoeing or digging in their entire existence. And there's something missing ... Ah, I have it! Slouch, don't stand so upright! When you stand up stiffly peering out from under those fierce eyebrows, you look just like a naval officer dressed for a rustic fête. Ah, that's better.'

'Now surely I must look like the henpecked husband of a Norman shrew.'

'Yes,' she agreed, 'why don't you bear that in mind. Think of me as *la mégère*. With this red scarf round my head, I must say I feel the part!'

Gilbert slipped into the room after his usual discreet knock on the door. He excused himself and inspected Sarah closely. Finally he said: 'The shoes, milady ... they are most important.'

Sarah gestured to the pair of wooden clogs. 'And they are most uncomfortable!'

'Yes, milady, but you must wear them so that they seem natural. We are extremely lucky that Estelle had a pair which fitted you, even if those that Louis found for ...'

'Even if Louis has enormous feet and I feel as though I'm wearing a couple of boats,' Ramage grumbled.

'Yes, sir, but the socks?'

'The extra socks do help,' he admitted. 'I had to put on three pairs, though.'

'But the coat and *pantalons* – perfect. You have adopted to perfection the, how do you say, the *stance,* of a man of the fields.'

Ramage glared at Sarah, defying her to make a facetious comment.

Gilbert himself was dressed in black. The material of the trousers was rough, a type of serge; the coat had the rusty sheen denoting age and too much attention from a smoothing iron. He looked perfect for the role he was to play, the employer of a young couple who was taking them to market.

He was carrying a flat canvas wallet, which he unbuttoned as he walked over to the table. 'Will you check through the documents with me, sir? From what Louis reports, we might have to show them half a dozen times before we get back here.'

With that he took out three sets of paper and put one down on the table as though dealing playing cards for a game of patience.

'The *passeports,*' he explained. 'Foreigners need one type, and every Frenchman visiting another town needs a different sort: he has to get it from the local Committee of Public Safety,

47

and it is valid only for the journeys there and back. Now, milady, will you examine yours.'

Sarah picked it up. The paper was coarse and greyish, and at the top was printed the arms of the Republic. The rest comprised a printed form, the blank spaces filled in with a pen. She was now Janine Ribère, born Thénaud in Falaise, wife of Charles, no children, hair blonde, complexion *jaunâtre*. (*Jaunâtre?* She thought for a few moments, combing her French vocabulary. Ah, yes, sallow. Well, certainly Gilbert was not trying to flatter her!) Purpose of journey: multiple visits to Brest to make purchases of food from the market. She nodded and put the page down again.

Gilbert gave her another which had a seal on it and a flourish of ink which was an unreadable signature. It was smaller, had a coat of arms she did not recognize, but bore the name of the department beneath it.

'This, madame, is a certificate issued in Falaise, and saying, as you can see, that you were born there, with the date. And beneath the *préfet*'s signature is a note that you removed to the province of Brittany on your marriage. And beneath that the signature of the *préfet* of Brittany.'

'All these signatures!' Sarah exclaimed. 'Supposing someone compares them with originals?'

Gilbert smiled and took the sheet of paper. 'If he does he will find they are genuine. *Préfets* sign these papers by the dozen and leave them to underlings to fill in the details.'

'But how did you get them?'

'That's none of our business,' Ramage said. 'Where did *we* get them from officially?'

'Madame had this issued to her by the *mairie* in Falaise and it was signed in Caen (the *préfet* gives the name). Then she had the addition made at the *préfecture* here. The *passeport*, too, comes from the *préfecture* in Brest. I shall point it out to you.'

He took a second set of papers. 'These are yours, milord. The same kind of documents but you see there is one extra – your discharge from the Navy of France. Dated, you will notice, one month before your wedding. The ship named here was damaged in a storm at Havre de Grâce and is still there. You were discharged and were making your way home when you met a young lady in Caen and you both fell in love . . .'

Gilbert tapped the paper which had the anchor symbol and the heading 'Ministry of the Marine and Colonies' and, like the others, was a printed form with the blanks filled in. 'You are of military age, so you will have to show this everywhere.'

'And you? Have you the correct documents?' Ramage asked. 'You aren't taking any extra risks by coming with us?'

Gilbert shook his head. 'No, because I have all the necessary papers to go shopping in Brest. I am well known at the *barrières*. You have told madame about the difference between foreigners and French people passing the *barrières*?'

'No. We've been busy making these clothes fit and I would prefer you to explain. My experience in Republican France is now several years old: I'm sure much has changed.'

Gilbert sighed. 'To leave the *ancien régime* and go to England ... *then* to return to Republican France. Now it is the guillotine, the tree of liberty, *gendarmes* every few miles, documents signed and countersigned ... no man can walk or ride to the next town to have a glass of wine with his brother without a *passeport* ... few men dare quarrel with a neighbour for fear of being denounced out of spite, for here the courts listen to the charge, not the defence –'

'The *barrières*,' Ramage reminded him.

'Ah yes, sir. Well, first there is the curfew from sunset to sunrise: everyone must be in his own home during the hours of darkness. To travel – well, one has the documents you have seen. You need plenty of change – at every *barrière* there's a toll. The amount varies, depending on the distance from the last *barrière*, because they are not at regular intervals.'

'A large toll?' Ramage asked.

'No, usually between two and twenty *sous*. It wouldn't matter if the money was spent on the repair of the roads – which is what it is supposed to be for – but no one empties even a bucket of earth into a pothole. But luckily we have our own gig because travelling by postchaise is very expensive. Before the Revolution a postchaise from here to Paris was about 250 *livres*; now it is 500. No highwaymen, though; that's one triumph of the Revolution!'

'Highwaymen!' Sarah exclaimed. 'You mean that France now has none?'

'Very few, ma'am, and the reason is not particularly to our advantage. We now have many more mounted *gendarmes* stopping honest travellers, and instead of money and jewellery they demand documents. Truly "money or your life" has now become "documents or your life". So as well as the *gendarmes* at the regular *barrières*, there are ones who appear unexpectedly on horseback, so no one dares move without papers. But,' he added, tapping the side of his nose, 'there are so many different documents and so many signatures that forgery is not difficult and false papers unlikely to be discovered.'

'How many *barrières* are there between here and Brest?' Ramage asked.

'Three on the road, and then one at the Porte de Landerneau, the city gate on the Paris road. We could avoid it by going in along the side roads, but it is risky: if we were caught we would be arrested at once.'

'Whereas our documents are good enough to pass the Porte without trouble?'

'Exactly, sir. Now, if I may be allowed to remind you of a few things. As you know, the common form of address is "Citizen", or "Citizeness" . Everyone is equal – at least in their lack of manners. "Please" and "thank you" are now relics of the *ancien régime*. Rudeness is usually a man's (or woman's) way of showing he or she is your equal – although they really mean your superior. Many *gendarmes* cannot read – they know certain signatures and have them written on pieces of paper for comparison. But don't be impatient if a *gendarme* holds a paper upside-down and "reads" it for five minutes – as if it has enormous importance. They are *gendarmes* because they have influence with someone in authority. Neither the Committees of Public Safety nor the *préfets* want illiterates, but often giving a job to such a man is repaying a political debt from the time of the Revolution.'

Gilbert paused and then apologized. 'I am afraid I am talking too much . . .'

'No, no,' Ramage said quickly. 'And you must get into the habit of giving orders to "Charles" and "Janine". Lose your temper with me occasionally – I am a slow-thinking fellow. Poor Charles Ribère, he can read slowly and write after a fashion, but . . . even his wife loses her patience with him!'

A smiling Gilbert nodded. He found it impossible to toss aside the natural politeness by which he had led his life. Since he had been back in France, some Frenchmen had called it servility: why are you so servile, they had sneered: man is born free and equal. Yes, all that was true, but man also had to eat, which meant he had to work (or be a thief, or go into politics). Working for the Count was very equable: he lived in comfortable

50

quarters, ate the same food as the Count and his guests, but in
his own quarters without the need (as the Count often had) to let
the food get cold as he listened to vapid gossip. But for these
revolutionary fools he could have expected a comfortable old
age with a good pension from the Count, and probably a cottage
on the estate, here or in England.

'Servility' – yes, that was what these Republican fools called
it. Elsewhere, particularly in England, it was called good
manners. Please, thank you, good morning, good evening –
according to the Republicans these were 'servile phrases'. A true
Republican never said please or thank you. But he had never
listened to the Count, either: the Count *always* said please and
thank you and the suitable greeting every time he spoke to one
of his staff. In fact, a blind man would only know who was
servant and who was master because the Count had an educated
voice: his grammar, too, betrayed his background of Latin and
Greek, and English and Italian. Gilbert had once heard him
joking in Latin with a bishop who laughed so much he became
nearly hysterical. No Committee of Public Safety would ever
understand that normal good manners were like grease on axles
– they helped things move more smoothly.

'I think Edouard will have the gig ready for us by now,' Gilbert
said, making a conscious effort to avoid any 'sir' or 'milord'. 'We
are going to buy fruit – our apples have been stolen – and
vegetables: the potatoes have rotted in the barn. And indeed they
have. We need a bag of flour, a bag of rice if we can buy some,
and any vegetables that catch your fancy. I am tired of cabbage
and parsnip, which is all we seem to grow here. A lot of salt in
the air from the sea makes the land barren, so Louis says, but
I think it is laziness in the air from the Count's good nature.'

Gilbert gestured towards two wicker baskets as they reached
the back door. 'We take these to carry our purchases – you put
them on your laps. I have all the documents here and will drive
the gig, because your hands are occupied.' He winked and then
looked startled at his temerity in winking at a milord and a
milady. Ramage winked back and Sarah grinned: the grin,
Ramage thought in a sudden surge of affection, of a lively and
flirtatious serving wench being impertinent, Impudent. Ador-
able. And what a honeymoon – here they were setting off (in a
gig!) at the beginning of an adventure which could end up with
them all being strapped down on the guillotine. So far, the
Committee of Public Safety (though perhaps the Ministry of

51

Marine would step in, but more likely Bonaparte's secret police under that man Fouché would take over) could accuse Captain Ramage of disobeying the order to report to the local *préfet* as an *otage*, because to call them detainees and not hostages was polite nonsense. Then of course he was carrying false papers and dressed as a gardener – proof that he was a spy. And he was lurking around France's greatest naval base on the Atlantic coast … Yes, a tribunal would have only to hear the charges to return a verdict. And Sarah? A spy too – did she not carry false papers? Was she not assisting her husband? Was she not also an *aristo* by birth, as well as marriage? *Alors*, she can travel in the same tumbril, and that valet, too, who was a traitor as well as a spy.

As he helped Sarah up into the gig and heard a disapproving grunt from Gilbert (husbands might give wives a perfunctory push up, but they did not help them), he thought bitterly that their luck had been unbelievably bad. First, that the war had begun again while they were on their honeymoon – after all, the peace had held for a year and a half. Then that they should be staying with Jean-Jacques. Admittedly they would have been arrested if they had been staying at an inn, but the point was that they were now involved with *L'Espoir* and trying to think of a way of rescuing the Count of Rennes. *Noblesse oblige*. He was becoming tired of that phrase – his first love, the Marchesa di Volterra, was back in Italy because of it, and possibly already one of Bonaparte's *otages*, too. An *otage* if she had not yet been assassinated.

So, heavily involved with keeping himself and Sarah out of the hands of the local Committee of Public Safety, trying to rescue Jean-Jacques, and getting all of them (including the faithful and enterprising Gilbert) back to England, it was not just bad luck, it was damnable luck which brought the *Murex* through the Chenal du Four and into Brest with a mutinous crew on board.

Or, he allowed himself the thought and at once felt almost dizzy with guilt, why did the mutineers not put the officers and loyal seamen in a boat and let them sail back to England? Why keep them on board and bring them into Brest, where the French had anchored the ship, landed the mutineers and left the officers and loyal men on board the brig with an apparently small French guard? Now every *gendarme* in the port would be on the alert in case one of the loyal men escaped from the *Murex*; every fishing boat would be guarded – perhaps by soldiers – so that the chance of stealing one and getting back to England would probably be nil. Damn and blast the mutineers – and her captain, for not preventing the mutiny! He was not being fair and he found he had no *wish* to be fair: he wanted only to find someone to blame for this mess.

Lord St Vincent! The name slid into his thoughts as Gilbert flipped the reins so that they slapped across the horse's flanks and started it moving. Yes, if Lord St Vincent had not given him, as his first peacetime orders, the task of finding a tiny island off the Brazilian coast and surveying it, he would never have met Sarah. If they had never met they would never have fallen in love and from that it followed they would never have married or be here on a prolonged honeymoon through France. Which, he admitted, was as disgraceful a thought as any man should have so near breakfast.

The country round the château was bleak. Or, rather, it was wild: it had the harsh wildness of parts of Cornwall, the thin layer of soil sprinkled on rock, rugged boulders jutting up as though scattered by an untidy giant. The small houses built of tightly-locked grey stone, some long ago whitewashed, roofed by slates, a small shelter for a horse or donkey, a low wall containing the midden. Life here was a struggle against nature: crops grew not with the wild profusion and vigour of the Tropics – to which he had become accustomed over the past few years – but because men and women hoed and dug and ploughed and weeded from dawn to dusk.

Gilbert became impatient with the horse, a chestnut which looked as though it was not exercised enough and heartily resented being between shafts. Perhaps, Ramage thought sourly, it was a Republican and resented having to work (if jogging along this lane rated the description 'work') for Monarchists.

'Pretend to be asleep – or sleepy, anyway,' Gilbert said as they approached the first village. Ramage inspected it through half-closed eyes, and for a moment was startled how different it was from all the villages he had seen up to now. A few moments later he realized that the village was the same but his attitude had just changed. He had been a free visitor when he had seen all the other villages on the roads from Calais to Paris, south across Orléans and the Bourbonnais, among the hills of Auvergne, and to the northwest up towards Finisterre through Poitou and Anjou ... Towns and villages, Limoges with its superb porcelain and enamels, the fourth-century baptistry of the church near Poitiers which is France's earliest Christian building ... Clermont-Ferrand, where Pope Urban (the second?) sent off the first Crusade in 1095 (why did he remember that date?), the châteaux and palaces along the Loire Valley ... Angers with the château of seventeen towers belonging formerly to the Dukes of Anjou, and no one now willing to discuss the whereabouts of the tapestries, particularly the fourteenth-century one which was more than 430 feet long. And Chinon, on the banks of the Vienne, where Joan of Arc prodded the Dauphin into war. No, all these towns had been impressive and the villages on the long roads between them for the most part interesting (or different, anyway), but they had been at peace – with England, at least.

With England: that, he suddenly realized, was significant, and he wished he could discuss it with Sarah but it had to be talked about in English, not French, and it was too risky talking in English when they could be overheard by a hidden hedger and ditcher.

The French had been at peace with England but not yet with themselves. He had been surprised to see that the enemy for the people of all the villages, towns and cities of France was now their own people: the members of the Committees of Public Safety at the top of a pyramid which spread out to *gendarmes* enforcing the curfew and standing at the *barrières* demanding *passeports,* the old enemies denouncing each other in secret, the banging on doors in the darkness, when no neighbour dared to look to see who the *gendarmes* were bundling away.

Liberté, Egalité, Fraternité – fine words. They had stretched France's frontiers many miles to the north, east and south, but what had they done for the French people? Now every able-bodied young man would have to serve again in the Army or Navy, and there was no harm in that if they were needed to defend France. But France would be attacking other countries: earlier France was everywhere the aggressor, even across the sands of Egypt.

That was looking at the phrase in its broadest sense, yet the picture those three words summoned up for him was simple and one that fitted every *place* in every city, town and large village in France.

The picture was stark and simple: two weathered baulks of timber arranged as a vertical and parallel frame, and a heavy and angled metal blade, sharpened on the underside, sliding down two grooves. A bench on which the victim was placed so that his or her neck was squarely under the blade, a wicker basket beyond to catch the severed head. Weeping relatives and wildly cheering onlookers – that dreadful melange of blood and hysteria. Of the three words, the guillotine must stand for *fraternité* and *égalité* because *liberté* was represented by the other part of the picture. This was the rusted metal representation of the Tree of Liberty. Usually it was little more than an example of the work of a hasty blacksmith and always it was rusty. And sometimes on the top was placed a red cap of liberty, faded and rotting, rarely recognizable as a copy of the old Phrygian cap.

And the gig had stopped and Gilbert was getting out and saying something in a surly voice, using a tone Ramage had never heard before. Yes, they had arrived at the *barrière*. It was in fact simply three chairs and a table in the shade of a plane tree on one side of the road. Three *gendarmes* sat in the chairs and one had called to Gilbert to bring over the documents. Gilbert was carrying not just the canvas wallet but a bottle of wine.

Pretending to be asleep, hat tilted over his face, Ramage watched. Gilbert took out the papers – leaving the bottle on his side of the table, as though putting it there to leave his hands free – and handed them to the *gendarme*, who still sat back in his chair and gestured crossly when Gilbert first placed the papers on the table. To pick them up the *gendarme* would have to lean forward, and this he was reluctant to do. Gilbert put the documents in the man's hand, and the *gendarme* glanced through them, obviously counting. He then looked across at the gig and handed the papers back, holding his hand out for the bottle.

Gilbert walked back to the gig, resumed his seat, slapped the reins across the horse's rump and the gig continued its slow journey towards Brest. The other two *gendarmes*, Ramage noticed, had never opened their eyes.

Beyond the village, Gilbert turned. 'You saw all that – obviously they are not looking for any escapers. That is the routine, though: two sleep while the other reaches out a hand.'

'So our papers are not –'

The thud of horses' hooves behind them brought the sudden command from Gilbert: 'Don't look round – mounted *gendarmes*. Pretend to be asleep!'

A moment later two horsemen cut in from the left side, then two more passed on the right and reined their horses to a stop, blocking the narrow road.

'Papers!' one of the men demanded, holding out his hand.

'Papers, papers, papers,' Gilbert grumbled. 'We have only just showed them back there, now the four horsemen of the Apocalypse want to look at them again . . .'

One of the *gendarmes* grinned and winked at Sarah. 'We like to check up on pretty girls on a sunny morning – where are you going, *mademoiselle*?'

'Madame,' Sarah said sleepily. 'To Brest with my husband.'

Her accent and the tone of voice was perfect, Ramage realized. The *gendarme* was flirting; she was the virtuous wife.

The *gendarme* looked through the papers. 'Ah, Citizeness Ribère, born twenty-two years ago in Falaise. You look younger – marriage must suit you.' He looked at Ramage. 'Citizen Ribère? Off to Brest to buy your wife some pretty ribbons, eh?'

'Potatoes and cabbages, and rice if there is any,' Ramage said with glum seriousness. 'No ribbons.'

The *gendarme* laughed, looked at Gilbert's *passeport* and handed the papers back to him. '*You* buy her a ribbon, then,' he said, and spurred his horse forward, the other three following him.

'Was that normal?' Ramage asked.

'Yes – but for, er Janine, I doubt if they would have bothered to stop us.'

They passed the next couple of *barrières* without incident, although at the second two of the *gendarmes* were more concerned with their colleague who was already incoherently drunk but unwilling to sleep it off out of sight under the hedge. He had spotted the bottle that an unsuspecting Gilbert had been clutching as he alighted from the gig and probably saw a dozen. Finally, while Gilbert waited patiently at the table, the other two dragged the man away, returning five minutes later without apology or explanation to inspect the papers.

As they jogged along the Paris road into Brest, Ramage spotted the masts of ships in the port. Some were obviously ships of the line and most, he commented to Sarah, had their yards crossed with sails bent on. The French seamen had been busy since the two of them had spent the afternoon at Pointe St Mathieu.

Five *gendarmes* lounged at the Porte de Landerneau, the gate to the port, but they were too concerned with baiting a gaunt priest perched on an ancient donkey to pay much attention to three respectable citizens in a gig, obviously bound for the market.

The road ahead was straight but the buildings on each side were neglected. No door or window had seen a paintbrush for years; the few buildings that years ago had been whitewashed now seemed to be suffering from a curious leprosy.

'This leads straight down to the Place de la Liberté and the town hall,' Gilbert had explained in French. 'Just beyond that is the Hôtel du Commandant de la Marine. Then we carry on past it along the Rue de Siam to the river. While we jog along the Boulevard de la Marine you'll have a good view of the river as it meets *Le Goulet,* with the arsenal opposite. Then to the Esplanade du Château. There we'll stop for a glass of wine under the trees and you can inspect the Château.'

He laughed to himself and then added: 'From the Esplanade it is only two minutes' walk to the Rue du Bois d'Amour ... in the evenings the young folk dawdle under the trees there and look down *Le Goulet* at the ships and perhaps dream of visiting the mysterious East.'

'But now, the young men have to be careful the press gangs don't take them off to the men o' war,' Ramage said dryly.

'Yes, I keep forgetting the war. Look,' he said absently, 'we are just passing the cemetery. The largest I've ever seen.'

'I'll keep it in mind,' Ramage said in a mock serious voice. 'For the moment I have no plans to visit it.'

Gilbert finally turned the gig into the open market place, a paved square, and told Ramage and Sarah to alight. Sarah looked at the stalls while Gilbert secured the horse and groaned. 'Potatoes ... a few cabbages ... more potatoes ... a few dozen parsnips ... Louis may be right about the soil at Finisterre!'

There were about twenty stalls, wooden shacks with tables in front of which the sellers spread their wares and gossiped.

Gilbert said: 'We'll walk to the end stall; I have a friend there.'

Despite the lack of variety, the sellers were cheerful, shouting to each other and haggling noisily with the dozen or so buyers walking along the line of tables. The man at the end stall proved to be one Ramage would normally have avoided without a moment's thought. His face was thin and a wide scar led across his left cheek, a white slash against suntanned skin. His hair was unfashionably long and tied behind in a queue. He wore a fisherman's smock which seemed almost rigid from frequent

57

coatings of red ochre, which certainly made it waterproof and, Ramage thought ironically, probably bulletproof too.

He shook hands with Gilbert, who said: 'I am not introducing you to my friends because – to onlookers – we all know each other well.'

The Frenchman immediately shook Ramage's hand in the casual form of greeting taking place all over the market as friends met each other for the first time in the day, and he gave a perfunctory bow to Sarah, saying softly: 'The Revolution does not allow me to kiss your hand, which is sad.'

'Now,' Gilbert said, 'I shall inspect your potatoes, which are small and old and shrivelled and no one but a fool would buy, and ask you what is happening in the Roads.'

'Ah, very busy. The potatoes I have here on display are small and old because I have already sold twenty sacks to the men from the Hôtel du Commandant de la Marine, who were here early. Paying cash, they are. They tried buying against *notes de crédit* on the Navy, but suddenly no one in the market had any potatoes, except what were on these tables.'

'Why the Navy's sudden need for potatoes?'

'You've heard about the English mutineers? Yes, well, you know the English exist on potatoes. All the mutineers are now billeted in the Château and demanding potatoes. On board their brig there are still prisoners and their guards, demanding potatoes – it seems the ones they have are mildewed. And that frigate over there, *L'Espoir,* is leaving for Cayenne with *déportés,* and they want more potatoes . . .'

'Who had your sacks?' Ramage asked.

'Nobody yet. They paid extra to have them delivered – it seems that with so many ships being prepared for sea, with the war starting, they're short of boats. So I pay a friend of mine a few *livres* to use his boat and the Navy pays me many *livres*!'

Ramage thought a moment. 'Are you going to carry all the sacks on your own?'

'I was hoping my nephew would help me when he's finished milking.'

Ramage glanced at Gilbert then at the man. 'Two of us could help you now.'

The Frenchman pulled at his nose. 'How much?'

Ramage smiled as he said: 'Our services would be free.' He looked at Gilbert, seeking his approval. 'We could carry the potatoes down to the jetty in the gig.'

Gilbert nodded enthusiastically. 'Then Janine can look after it while we go out to the *Murex*.'

'The loyal men who are prisoners of war in the English ship do not speak French,' the man said pointedly.

'If I needed to speak to them, it would be in whispers.'

The man nodded. 'It would have to be,' he said. 'Much discretion is needed.'

Gilbert walked away from the tiller and took a rope thrown down from the *Murex*'s deck. As he turned it up on a kevil he shouted forward at Ramage in well simulated anger: 'Hurry up! Not so tight – you'll jam our bow into the Englishman. We want to lie alongside her, not butt her like a goat!'

'Yes, citizen,' Ramage called aft in a remorse-laden voice. 'These ships, I am used to a cart with wheels...'

Several French seamen lining the *Murex*'s bulwarks roared with laughter and in a glance Ramage counted them. Seven, and the fellow at the end, probably the bosun, had been giving orders. Was that all the French guard, seven men? It seemed likely, though he would soon know.

'Here,' a voice called down in French and the tail of another rope curled down. 'Secure that somewhere there as a spring.'

He saw that Gilbert was already making up another rope as a spring, so that the fishing boat was held securely against the brig. A glance aloft then showed that some British seamen, prisoners, were working slowly and obviously resentfully under the shouts and gesticulations of a French bosun, who was becoming more and more exasperated that he could not make himself understood as he tried to get them to rig a staytackle to hoist the sacks of potatoes on board.

Again Ramage counted. More than a dozen prisoners, though some of the men reeving the rope through the blocks were officers. Obviously the French guards were practising *égalité.*

Another shout from the *Murex*'s deck brought a stream of curses from Gilbert and the vegetable seller (Ramage had established his name was Auguste), and something landed with a thump on the deck beside him. It was a heavy rope net.

'Spread it out flat on the deck, then put two sacks in the middle,' the bosun shouted. 'Hurry up, or this ship will never sail!'

Ramage hurried with the net and found it easy to make the job last twice as long as necessary while appearing to work with ferocious energy. While he was untangling the thick mesh he slowly inspected the *Murex*.

She had been out of the dockyard for only a few weeks: that much had been obvious as the fishing boat had approached because the brig was rolling at anchor enough to show that her copper sheathing was new, each overlapping edge of a sheet helping make a mosaic still bright and still puckered where the hammers driving home the flat-headed sheathing nails had dented the metal.

Her hull, a dark grey with a white strake, showed that her captain was a wealthy man: he had been prepared to pay for the paint himself, because the dockyard's meagre ration was black. Some captains who wanted a particularly smart ship paid for the gold leaf to line out the name on the transom, and pick up decorations on the capstan head. The captain of the *Murex* was one of them.

With the net spread out on the only flat part of the fishing boat's deck, the tiny fo'c'sle, Ramage climbed down into the little fish hold and hauled a couple of sacks up to the coaming. The stench was appalling: whoever had to eat these potatoes would think they had been grown in Billingsgate fish market.

Auguste's lopsided face appeared over the edge of the coaming. 'You are doing well,' he muttered. 'A clumsier oaf straight from the farm never set foot in a fishing boat.'

'How many guards, do you reckon?'

'Seven, but we'll know for sure when we get on board.'

'Can we manage that?' Ramage asked.

'The knot I shall use to secure the net for the staytackle hook is almost impossible to undo – and I am an impatient man! Here, sling up that sack!'

Gilbert arrived to help haul the first two sacks to the net, and the two Frenchmen gathered up the four corners. Auguste produced a short length of rope to secure them together while Ramage played the simpleton with the dangling end of the staytackle, using it to swing on until one of the French guards quickly slacked it so that Ramage suddenly dropped to the deck with a yell of alarm. That established his position as far as the French guards were concerned: he was the buffoon, the man who fell down hatches and on to whose head sacks of potatoes dropped.

Auguste knotted the corners of the net, took the staytackle and hooked it on, and shouted up to the *Murex*'s deck to start hauling. There was a delay: the French guards were not going to haul sacks of potatoes aloft, but Ramage saw equally clearly that their British prisoners, tailing on to the tackle, would have the French bosun demented by the time the last sack was on board.

'Don't stand under the net,' he warned Auguste and Gilbert, and a moment later the net and two sacks came crashing down on the deck again, making the little fishing boat shudder as it caught the forestay a glancing blow and set the mast shuddering.

Auguste sent up a stream of curses and warned the French bosun that he, the commandant of the port, the Navy, and the Minister of Marine himself would all be responsible for any damage done to the boat. A moment later the bosun was swearing in French at the British seamen, who were swearing back in the accents of London, the West Country and Scotland. One man, they were protesting, had tripped and brought the rest of them down, but the French bosun, not understanding a word, was threatening them with the lash, the noose, the guillotine and prison, and as he ran out of ideas, Auguste restated his warning, adding that it was not worth losing a fishing boat for the profit on a few sacks of potatoes.

Finally, amid more shouting than Ramage had thought possible from so few men, the net and its sacks were slowly rehoisted and hauled on board the *Murex*. A run-amok choir, Ramage thought, well primed with rum, could not do better.

Auguste gestured to Ramage and the two men scrambled up the brig's side, followed by Gilbert. The bosun and two French seamen were crouched over the net, struggling to undo Auguste's knot. Ramage and Gilbert were by chance within four or five feet of the British seamen who had been hauling on the tackle.

As all the French guards hurried to help the almost apoplectic bosun undo the knot, Ramage hissed at the nearest man, who from his creased and torn uniform must be one of the brig's lieutenants: 'Quickly – don't show surprise and keep your voice down: I am Captain Ramage. How many loyal men are there on board?'

The lieutenant paused and then knelt as if adjusting the buckle of his shoe. 'Captain, two lieutenants, master, eleven seamen.'

'And French guards?'

'Seven. They keep half of us in the bilboes while half are free.'

'Who commands?'

'Lieutenant Rumsie.'

'Where do the French keep you?'

'At night all of us are kept in irons in the manger.'

'The guards?'

'Two sit with muskets, the rest sleep in our cabins and use the gunroom.'

Gilbert suddenly called to Auguste, asking if he needed help with the knot, and Ramage realized that a French seaman with a musket was walking along the deck towards them, not suspicious but simply patrolling where the prisoners were working.

Ramage decided there was time for one last question.

'Are the mutineers coming back on board?'

'No, and the French are asking Paris what to do with us prisoners and keeping us on board until they hear.'

With that the net opened, the two sacks were hauled clear, and the perspiring bosun signalled to the Britons to hoist again.

Auguste scrambled back on board the fishing boat, followed by Gilbert and Ramage, who once again climbed down into the fish hold as the two Frenchmen unhooked the net and spread it on the deck again.

As they came to the coaming to lift out the sacks, Auguste muttered: 'Did you find out anything?'

'From the English, yes.'

'What do you want to know from the bosun?'

'Are they taking the job of guarding very seriously?'

'I can tell you that without asking. It is a holiday – they have jars of rum in the gunroom and one of them was boasting to me that most of them stay drunk all day and sleep it off at night. The bosun is so drunk at the moment he sees two nets, four knots and eight sacks each time we hoist.'

'Good, then just find out how long they expect – here, you'd better hoist up this sack while I get the other ready.'

When Auguste's head appeared at the coaming again Ramage finished the question: '– expect to be guarding these men and what the French Navy intend doing with the *Murex*.'

'Very well. The bosun will probably invite us all below for a drink anyway, when we've finished loading.'

It was clear no one was really in a hurry: Auguste tied the net with his special knot and then as soon as the sacks were swayed on board he climbed up to help untie it.

Gilbert and Ramage went on board each time, casually sitting on the breech of a gun close to the prisoners so that Ramage could continue talking to the lieutenant, who had recovered from his surprise sufficiently to have questions of his own.

'Why are you here, sir?'

'Caught in France when the war began again. Trying to avoid capture. Are the rest of your men loyal?'

'They don't want to be prisoners of the French,' the lieutenant said carefully.

'Where's the captain?'

'He's under guard in the master's cabin. Sick, I believe.'

'What's his trouble?'

'Rheumatic pains. He can hardly move.'

The net was being hoisted over the side and the three of them climbed down into the fishing boat once again.

Auguste leaped over the coaming to grasp a sack and said: 'Trouble with the English captain.'

'So I've heard.'

'Rheumatic pains. Makes him bad-tempered. Bullied the men and most mutinied.'

'How long do the prisoners stay on board?'

'Who knows? They won't be short of potatoes, anyway,' Auguste said.

As soon as the last sacks were pulled off the net, the French bosun mopped his forehead with a dirty piece of cloth and mumbled drunkenly: 'English rum – we all deserve some. Follow me.' He stumbled aft and went cautiously down the companionway to the gunroom.

Ramage felt he was walking back in time: the *Murex* was almost identical with his second command, the *Triton* brig. There was more fancy work covering handrails, all of it well scrubbed until a few days ago, and the captain must have an obsession for turk's heads: the knots were neat but there was one on every spoke of the wheel, whereas usually there was only one on the spoke which was uppermost with the rudder amidships.

The brasswork was dulling now because it had not been polished with brick dust for several days, presumably since the mutiny. The deck was reasonably clean but unscrubbed, stained here and there by the French seamen who chewed tobacco.

He followed the others down the companionway. The gunroom was stuffy because the French did not believe in keeping skylights open. Why did they not use the captain's cabin? Probably not enough chairs: brigs were sparsely furnished and the gunroom made a better centre for meals and card playing. It was a rectangular open space formed by a row of cabins on each side. The cabins were little more than boxes made of canvas stretched across light wooden frames, and the only substantial parts were the doors. Over the top of each door was painted the rank of its normal occupant – the lieutenants, marine officer, master and surgeon.

The table filling the centre of the gunroom was filthy now, spattered with dried soup, crumbs and crusts of bread and dark stains of red wine. The racks above several of the doors had once held the occupants' telescopes and swords, but were now empty – the first Frenchmen to board the mutinous ship must have done well, probably relieving the mutineers of their loot before they were taken on shore.

The bosun gestured to everyone to sit on the two forms beside the table, on which stood a large wicker-covered rum jar whose fumes filled the gunroom.

The bosun and three guards. Four in all, and he had counted seven, a figure confirmed by the lieutenant. So now three Frenchmen were guarding the prisoners. There was a muffled groan from one of the cabins and Auguste, Gilbert and Ramage all looked inquiringly at the bosun, who grinned.

'The English captain. His rheumatism is bad. Saves us guarding him because he can't move.'

Gilbert reached for a battered metal mug and the bosun took the hint, lifting the rum jar and beginning to pour into a sorry collection of mugs. A French seaman said: 'One of the mutineers spoke some French, and before he was taken to the Château he told me the captain had been in his cot since the day after they sailed.'

'Why did they mutiny?'

'The rheumatism made the captain bad-tempered, so this *rosbif* said. He used to order many floggings. Hurting other people seemed to ease his own pain. He should have tried this,' the seaman said, lifting his mug of rum. 'But they said he did not drink. Prayed a lot, though it didn't seem to ease his problems.' The man gave a dry laugh. 'In fact praying seems to have brought him many troubles!'

'The mutineers – they are Frenchmen now, eh?' Gilbert asked as he raised his mug in a toast to the bosun.

'Frenchmen?' The bosun was shocked. He considered the matter, taking hearty sips of his rum. 'No, not Frenchmen. After all, if they mutinied against their own officers, they could mutiny against us. They have no loyalty to anyone, those buffoons.'

Ramage was startled to hear the man talk such reasonable sense. So, the mutineers were not welcome in Brest.

'But you are glad to have the ship!' he said.

The bosun shrugged. 'For me, it is of no importance: we have enough ships now – you can see the fleet we are preparing. This brig I do not like. It goes to windward slowly.'

'But surely the mutineers will be rewarded?' Ramage persisted.

'Oh yes, they'll be given a few *livres* each at the Château, and thanked. Who knows, if the English Navy hear that they get a good reception at Brest, perhaps they'll bring in some frigates, or maybe even ships of the line!

'We'll thank them for their ships,' the bosun continued, topping up his mug from the rum jar, 'but I expect we'll make sure the men leave the country after signing up in neutral ships. The Americans will be glad of them – they speak the same language. And the Dutch and the Danes are always glad to get prime seamen.'

'So these men that refused to join the mutiny,' Ramage persisted, managing to introduce a complaining whine into his voice, 'they won't be punished? Not executed or flogged?'

'Of course not,' the bosun said impatiently. 'They'll be taken off to the prison at Valenciennes or Verdun or wherever it is that they keep them. The first prisoners of the new war,' he added. 'Come on now, let's drink to thousands more!'

CHAPTER FIVE

The Café des Pêcheurs, halfway along the Quai de la Douane and overlooking the entire anchorage, was aptly named: at least twenty fishermen, most of them in smocks as liberally coated with red ochre as Auguste's, were playing cards, rolling dice or sipping wine at the tables outside. And arguing. Ramage listened to some of them and was amused by the vehemence that the most innocent of subjects could provoke among these bearded and rough-tongued men.

They eyed Sarah curiously: few women other than whores ever came to such a café, but because she was with Auguste she was accepted and spared any teasing or coarse remarks.

For the moment the three men and Sarah were sitting silently, looking across at the *Murex* over on their right hand and *L'Espoir* to their left. Boats were going out to the frigate, unloading casks, and returning empty to the Quai de Recouvrance, on the other side of the Penfeld river. It was from there, Auguste told them, that ships were supplied with fresh water and salt meat and fish.

The fishermen's café was a good place to talk. The few people who did not want to play cards or roll dice naturally went to the tables along the edge of the quay, and Ramage had already noted that no one could get within a dozen feet of their table without being seen, so it was impossible to overhear their conversation. And that, Ramage thought to himself, is just as well . . .

'*Alors*, Charles,' Gilbert was saying, hesitating over the name because he was really addressing a formal question to Captain Lord Ramage of the Royal Navy. 'What do you think about Auguste's proposal?'

While Ramage had sat in the gig telling Sarah what he had learned from his visit to the *Murex*, Auguste and Gilbert had walked down the road and the fisherman had taken the opportunity to tell Gilbert that he wanted to escape to England: that he and his brother Albert were completely disillusioned by the Revolution and had heard enough from Gilbert to know that England was preferable. But, he had asked, knowing nothing of their plans, hopes and fears, how was he to get there?

Ramage knew that for the moment it boiled down to one single question: did he or did he not trust Auguste, whom he had met only two or three hours earlier?

Obviously Gilbert did – he had known the man from boyhood, long before the Revolution. But Gilbert had been in England for several years. Did he know what Auguste and his brother had been doing here in Brest during those bloody years following the Revolution?

'Tell me, Auguste, were you a fisherman during the Revolution?'

Auguste told him what he and his brother had done: they had smuggled out Royalists, taking them half a dozen at a time, concealed in their fishing boat, southwards to Portugal and safety. They had continued to do that until a few months before Bonaparte signed the Treaty with England – then they had had a running fight with a cutter of the French Navy, finally escaping. 'That was when I collected this,' Auguste said, pointing to the scar on his face.

'Our fishing boat was so badly damaged by gunfire that we guessed we would be betrayed the moment we put into a French port, so we landed our refugees safely on the coast and then we sank our fishing boat and rowed ashore with our little skiff. We came back to Brest a few weeks later, and no one asked questions. But we could not fish any more; instead we grew vegetables on the piece of land our father left us.'

Ramage nodded. The story seemed both likely and straightforward. Sarah suddenly asked: 'What makes you approach my husband because you and your brother want to go to England? Bonaparte's men are hunting us, while you all have proper documents as French citizens. Surely you can steal a fishing boat more easily than we can.'

Auguste looked first at Ramage, unused to having a woman enter a conversation in this way, and noting the nod said: 'Obviously I know you are English and if you, m'sieu, are caught you will be made a prisoner of war. But you do not seem to me – nor you, madame – the sort of person to let yourselves be taken prisoner. I think you are planning to get back to England. Gilbert has said nothing – and his silence,' he added with a grin, 'bears out what I think.'

The man *looked* a scoundrel: a once handsome rogue. The type of person you did not trust without a lot of checking. Auguste had trusted him and Gilbert and taken them with him out to the *Murex,* and while they were drinking with the French bosun, Auguste had spotted the trend of Ramage's and Gilbert's questions, and asked some of his own.

If a man trusts you without question, then you can trust him.

Ramage found himself thinking that with the same clarity as if he was reading a printed text. Auguste had got them out to the *Murex* and back safely: obviously he was a man of ingenuity. At this moment Ramage knew only too well he needed the help of a man of ingenuity who knew his way around Brest.

It was too risky telling Auguste and his brother to come out to Jean-Jacques' château: *gendarmes* might be suspicious, and later might remember them passing the *barrières*. Anyway, this café was a good safe spot for what could be only a preliminary chat.

'I have no plans at the moment,' Ramage admitted. 'I have come into Brest now simply to look, and hope to get some – well, inspiration.'

'You can speak freely; I shall not betray you,' Auguste said calmly.

Ramage smiled. 'I would speak freely if I had anything to say. You could betray us in a few seconds by waving to those two *gendarmes* standing under the trees over there.'

'True, true,' Auguste said. 'Well, let's start by you saying what you *want* to do. How to do it can come later.'

'That is simple. First I would like to rescue the Count, then I would like to take him and Gilbert back to England.'

Auguste rubbed his nose as he looked carefully at Ramage. 'I am sure you would. But with a force comprising yourself, your wife, Gilbert, Louis and now myself and my brother Albert, you are outnumbered by about three hundred men.'

'Only about two hundred and fifty,' Ramage said dryly. 'But I was simply answering your question.'

'Yes, and I was teasing. But to be serious, your loyalty to the Count is admirable and what I would expect from an English *aristo* and from Gilbert. However, there is not a chance. The Count and fifty others (all of whom probably realize they are lucky to have escaped the guillotine and regard transportation to Cayenne as an acceptable alternative) are heavily guarded on board *L'Espoir*. This I can assure you. In fact, at the risk of distressing you, I can tell you that all of them are in irons and will remain so until *L'Espoir* sails in a few days' time. In fact, you may have guessed that the French government is being particularly cautious about this first voyage to Cayenne in the new war.'

'Is that why boats are taking out water and provisions? I should have thought it would be quicker and easier to bring *L'Espoir* alongside at the Quai de Recouvrance so that they can load directly from carts,' Ramage said.

'The commandant of the port has orders from Paris to take no risks with these exiles, so he is keeping the frigate at anchor, with other frigates round her. I think he dreams of all the *déportés* leaping over the side and swimming to the shore, or a British fleet sailing up *Le Goulet* to rescue them.'

68

Ramage looked at Gilbert. 'I think you realized there was no way,' he said gently. 'Even with fifty men.'

The Frenchman nodded. 'Yes, but one hopes for miracles. From what I know of you, citizen,' he said, a slight emphasis on the word to indicate he was really using Ramage's title, 'if any man could have done it, you could.'

'Who have we here?' Auguste asked Gilbert, who looked questioningly at Ramage and, when he nodded, leaned across and whispered the name.

The Frenchman turned and looked at Ramage, his eyes bright and his lean face creased into a grin. 'Captain, you are famous in Brest. If only Bonaparte knew ... he'd give me the province as a reward for betraying you.'

'You flatter me,' Ramage said.

'The thought does not seem to alarm you,' Auguste commented.

'You have only to shout to the *gendarmes*,' Ramage said. 'Mind you your brother would get the land, not you.'

Auguste raised his eyebrows. 'My brother?'

'Yes, because I presume he is your heir. You could shout – but you'd never draw the breath to replace the one that you used. I have a heavy kitchen knife hidden in my right boot.'

Auguste gave a sudden bellow of laughter and slapped his knee. 'Done!' he said, as though he had just concluded a business deal, and Ramage saw the performance was for the benefit of any curious onlooker, but 'Done' meant he had given his word; he was part of whatever Ramage might plan.

'Your interest in the – er, the potato ship. Were you looking for ideas, and did you find any?'

'I was looking. Nothing very certain has come yet. Something is hovering over my head, like a sparrowhawk in the distance.'

'Fifteen prisoners on board her, if you include that rheumatic wreck of a captain. Seven French guards. Five of us, unless you include madame.'

'Include madame and exclude that captain,' Ramage said. 'Five does not sound a very lucky number.'

The *Murex,* like the *Triton* and the other 10-gun brigs, was a handsome little ship, although too small to have a graceful sheer like the frigates. Anyway, the French always designed beautiful ships, so it was unfair to compare the *Murex* with the other vessels anchored in the Roads. He thought of the *Calypso,* a French frigate which he had captured and, by a stroke of luck, been given to command. In any anchorage she was always one of the handsomest ships.

Did Bonaparte ever wonder at the contradiction that the French built the best ships but could not fight 'em? And how irritating it must be for the little Corsican that usually the British kept the original French names once they captured ships and put them into service! One of the biggest ships in the Royal Navy today was called the *Ville de Paris*! One could not imagine the French calling one of their flagships the *City of London*. And some of the best ships at present in service had been captured from the French and often the names kept – the frigates *Perle*, *Aréthuse*, *Aurore*, *Lutine*, *Melpomène*, *Minerve*, for instance. And the 80-gun *Tonnant* and the *Franklin* (which had been renamed *Canopus*), as well as the 74s *Spartiate*, *Conquérant* and *Aquilon* (now called the *Aboukir*, in honour of the battle in which Rear-admiral Nelson had captured them). Then *Le Hoche*, 80 guns, had been a little too much for their Lordships at the Admiralty, who had renamed her *Donegal*, but *Le Bellone*, 36 guns, had been changed to *Proserphine* only to avoid confusion with the 74-gun *Bellona*. *La Pallas*, 40 guns, had been renamed *La Pique*, which showed their Lordships had no prejudice against French names! There were dozens more. And of course there were the Spanish and the Dutch ...

He suddenly realized that the two men and Sarah were watching him. Obviously they thought his silence was because he was thinking of daring plans to get them all to England, whereas in fact he had been daydreaming over ships' names.

'Yes,' he said lamely, 'let's say fourteen prisoners on board the *Murex* and half of them in irons during the day. All of them are put in irons for the night, so the guards can safely sleep.'

Sarah coughed as if asking permission to join in the planning, but she did not wait for anyone to nod encouragement. 'M'sieu Auguste cannot get a fishing boat – one large enough for us to sail to England?'

'No, madame, I regret I cannot. If I could, we would sail tonight. But now the commandant of the port has given fresh orders. All fishing boats with a deck – even a small foredeck – (all except open boats, in other words) must have two armed soldiers guarding them if they are in port for the night. Apparently the order comes from Paris and is the result of the renewal of war.'

'Yes,' Gilbert said, 'Bonaparte realizes that there are hundreds like the Count, and Charles here, who will be trying to escape if they are not already locked up.'

Ramage said: 'But you could get a rowing boat?'

'Yes,' Auguste said cautiously, 'but I do not wish to row to England in one!'

'No, but that means we can always go fishing in *Le Goulet*. I enjoy fishing and I am sure Gilbert does, too.'

'The port commandant disapproves, though,' Auguste said. 'He hasn't forbidden it yet, but the sentries on the men of war occasionally fire a musket if they think a fisherman is too close, just as a warning.'

'Any casualties?'

'Not yet.'

Ramage nodded. 'At night a moving boat is a difficult target, and if the fishermen keep a respectable distance . . .'

'Yes, the sentries are really only warning. And I hear that many captains of ships dislike having their sleep disturbed by random musket shots!'

Ramage nodded again. Firing muskets at anchor would certainly disturb a captain's rest, and half an hour would pass before he received an explanation and dozed off again.

'Gilbert, if you would pay for our wine, I think we had better buy some fruit and vegetables to satisfy the curiosity of the *gendarmes* at the *barrières* and bid our friend here *au revoir*.'

At the château, Louis met them with the news that a friendly neighbour of his wife's parents had told them that *L'Espoir* would be sailing in three or four days for Cayenne. The *Chef d'administration de la Marine* at Brest, Citizen Moreau, was rushing everything apparently, because the British declaration of war had taken Paris unawares and the First Consul was anxious to get this group of Royalists and priests on their way to Cayenne before the Royal Navy re-established the blockade of Brest. There was also talk of *L'Espoir*'s decision to beat out directly to the southwestward after leaving Brest, hoping to hide herself in the wastes of the Atlantic once she was out of sight of Pointe St Mathieu.

Ramage thanked Louis for the information. Since they could do nothing about *L'Espoir* and her sad human cargo, he could only note that the frigate's captain was intending to do what he would have done in the same situation. In fact, *L'Espoir* stood little risk of being intercepted because Cayenne was so far to the south round the bulge of South America that British ships of war and privateers bound for the West Indian islands would be crossing the Atlantic well to the north of her course. By staying far to the south, *L'Espoir* might risk getting beyond the belt of Trade winds and run into strong ocean currents, but she was embarking extra provisions and water, probably as an insurance against a long passage. From memory, the Île du Diable, better known to the English as Devil's Island and referred to by the French as 'Cayenne', the name of the nearest town on the mainland, sat precisely on the fifth parallel of latitude, only 300 miles from the Equator, a hot and humid hell on earth.

Louis added, almost as an afterthought, that two *gendarmes* had called to ask if there had been any sign of the Englishman, but they had been told the agreed story: he had stayed a few days before the Count had been arrested and left, as far as anyone knew, to visit friends somewhere in Provence. Why had the Count not reported that he had strangers staying in the house, as required by State Ordinance number 532, dated 1st *Vendémiaire* year VI? Louis had shaken his head sadly and told the men that the Count, although a very law-abiding man, had not been living in France at the time of the Ordinance and probably knew nothing about it. But Louis had almost been trapped by his own inventiveness: had the Count had other visitors – not necessarily foreigners, but people 'not normally inhabiting the place of habitation' – staying and whom he had not reported to the *préfecture*? Louis said he did not know what the Count reported. The *gendarmes* themselves had said he had not reported the Englishman but for all Louis knew the Count *had* reported them and the *gendarmes* had lost the record. At this, Louis related gleefully, the police had been so embarrassed that it was clear that losing papers was not unknown.

Gilbert's comment had been brief and acute: clearly the authorities were not too concerned about the Englishman and accepted that he had moved on. Much more important, they did not realize that he was the Captain Ramage who had played such havoc with their ships in the previous war; if they thought he had been a guest of the Count, then strict precautions would be taken at Brest. This had not been the case, he said with a grin, at the *barrières*.

Ramage had been momentarily startled by Gilbert's use of the word 'previous', but of course he was right: that war had begun in February 1793 and ended officially with the signing of the

72

Treaty in April last year, 1801. After eighteen months' peace Britain had now declared war, obviously alarmed by French preparations, but it was another war. What would it be called? The last one had gone on long enough, but with Bonaparte in possession of a huge army – it was said that he could mobilize a million men – how the devil could Britain alone (she had fought most of the last war alone) defeat him? The Royal Navy could only fight where there was water enough to float ships.

He cursed his daydreaming; once again Gilbert, Louis and Sarah were watching him and waiting, as though expecting brilliant ideas to spout from his mouth like water from a firehose the moment men started working the pump handles. He shook his head in a meaningless gesture and, taking Sarah's hand, led the way to their rooms. As soon as he had shut the door she poured water from the big jug into the porcelain basin on the washstand.

'I feel dirty from the top of my head to the tips of my toes,' she said, hanging her coat on a hook and beginning to unbutton her dress.

Ramage sank back on the bed, wishing there was an armchair. 'I am weary too. So I shall sit here and watch you undress and then watch you wash yourself from the top of your head to the tip of your toes. It is one of the greatest joys of being your husband. I'm sorry I'm too weary to undress you.'

She slid the dress down and stepped out of it as once again Ramage marvelled at how natural and beautiful she looked in the coarse underwear lent her by Louis' wife. Next she undid the white ribbon – carefully-sewn strips of linen, in fact – of the shift, which was like a long apron, and unwound it.

She smiled at him and watched his eyes as she unbuttoned the bodice and slowly took it off, revealing her breasts in a movement which stopped Ramage's breath for several moments. The breasts seemed to have a life of their own; the nipples, high and large, were dark, like seductive eyes.

Still looking at him, she slid down the frilled knickers and stood naked without embarrassment. Standing naked before your husband for his inspection, she seemed to be saying, was the natural end to a day's journey into the enemy's camp.

'You approve?'

She knew he did but wanted reassuring.

'The left breast . . . is it not a fraction lower than the right?'

A look of alarm spread across her face as she hurried to the dressing table. The large looking glass originally fitting into the frame was missing and the only one available was the small handheld glass from her travelling bag.

She held it at arm's length, twisting and turning, peering first at one breast and then the other. Then she held the glass to the side, trying to line up the nipples. Finally she put the mirror down in exasperation.

'I can't see them properly!'

Hard put to keep a straight face, Ramage said: 'As you walked, it seemed to me it is actually the right one that's lower. Come over here and let me take a look.'

Then she realized he was teasing. 'Are you too tired to undress yourself?' she whispered.

Ramage nodded. 'I shall have to rely on my wife.'

Gilbert went into Brest the next day to make arrangements with Auguste and returned to say that both the fisherman and his brother would be ready and had begun collecting weapons. So far they had six pistols and shot, two blunderbusses, three heavy daggers, a cavalry sabre and two cutlasses. When Ramage marvelled at such a collection, Gilbert had grinned. The authorities in Paris lacked popularity in Brittany, he said, so that when a drunken soldier flopped asleep into a ditch or a cavalryman riding alone was thrown from his horse and found unconscious, they were usually returned to their barracks alive but always unarmed. Occasional raids on armouries, sudden and unexpected affairs, meant that many of those not entirely in favour of the First Consul's régime had weapons hidden among the beams of old barns or concealed in sacks of grain.

On the second day, while Ramage and Sarah roamed through the great house admiring the architecture and feeling guilty at envying Jean-Jacques because of his present situation, Louis went into Brest. There was no need to take unnecessary risks and arouse suspicions, Ramage had decided, and Louis and his wife passing through the *barrières* once a week would seem normal enough while Gilbert passing along the road alone in the gig once a day might start a *gendarme* asking questions.

Many of the rooms of the château were completely bare, stripped by looters of furniture, carpets, hangings, curtains, and occasionally complete doors. Damaged ceilings showed where chandeliers had been torn down; some staircases lacked banisters.

Yet the house, although almost empty, maintained its dignity. It had none of the delicacy and fine tracery, carefully balanced winds and imposing approaches of many of the châteaux of the Loire and Dordogne. It was four-square, and not concealing its origins – a defended home of the counts of Rennes. The battlements of thick stone were crenellated so that men with crossbows and later muskets could hide behind them and fire down on attackers; the enormous (and original) front door, studded with iron bolts that would blunt and deflect an attacker's axe, was so massive that a much smaller door had been built more recently to one side.

Ramage was staring out of a window, one of scores and now grimy, with paint lifting from the frame in a discreet warning that rot was at work beneath, when Sarah took his arm and said quietly: 'Where are you now?'

He gave a start, and then smiled without turning. 'I was thinking that it's the top of the springs tonight.'

She sighed and shook her head. 'Springs and neaps – I know they're something to do with the moon and the tide, but . . .'

'A sailor's wife and you don't understand the tides!'

'A sailor's wife who admits she doesn't understand, and expects her all-wise and adoring husband to explain.'

'The sun and the moon both pull the sea. When they are in line, both on one side of the earth or on opposite sides, they pull most and that's when we get the highest high tides, and the lowest low. They are called spring tides. They coincide with the new moon (the moon on the same side of the earth as the sun) and the full (when on the opposite side). When the sun or moon are at right-angles to each other in relation to the earth their pull is weakest and we get the smaller tides which are weaker and called neaps. So the springs are the highest and strongest around new and full moon, and the neaps are the smallest and weakest at first and third quarters.'

'Nothing to do with the seasons then – spring, summer and so on?'

'Nothing at all. It is a full moon tonight so there are spring tides. The highest in terms of sea level but also the strongest in terms of current. When the tide starts to ebb, it will flow out very strongly through the Gullet.'

'And that is important?'

'It would be if you were fishing from a small boat. Why, if you lost an oar you could drift to America!'

'Make sure you take plenty of bait,' she said. 'Am I such a stupid woman that I can't be told what you are planning?'

'I'd tell you if I knew. I'd talk it over if I thought you could help me get an idea. The fact is that *L'Espoir* sails for Cayenne with Jean-Jacques today or tomorrow and here I am, walking through his empty house, helpless and hopeless.'

'My dear, how can you expect to rescue one man from a frigate?'

Ramage shrugged. 'My men in the *Kathleen,* the *Triton* and the *Calypso* in the past did what people reckoned impossible, and we did it *only* because to others it *was* impossible.'

'But your men – the splendid Southwick, and Aitken, Jackson and Stafford: dozens of them – are all in Chatham on board the *Calypso.* You are' – she gave a wry smile – 'in France on your honeymoon, hunted by the French.'

'Not all the French; only Bonaparte's men.'

'About one in ten thousand are not Bonaparte's men. You won't collect a very big army in Brittany to overthrow him.'

'No,' he admitted. 'But I need very few. I agree we can't save Jean-Jacques, so we have to save ourselves: you and me, Gilbert and Louis (and his wife if she wants to come) and now Auguste and his brother. Five men and one, perhaps two women.'

'We are a long way from England. There always seems to be bad weather in the entrance to the Channel. Why don't we travel overland towards Calais? We'd have only twenty miles or so to row or sail to England, compared with – what, a hundred and fifty to Plymouth?'

Ramage turned and pulled her towards him, and kissed her gently. 'My dear, you are right in one respect: it is a much shorter sea crossing from Calais. But that's what makes it dangerous. The French *expect* escapers to try to cross there. Every rowing boat is chained up at night. There are big rewards offered – big enough to overcome most scruples. Brest is so far away from England that the French are more casual in the way they guard boats.'

'But they are putting soldiers on board the fishing boats here at night!' she protested.

'Yes, but they are the large ones with fish holds, those large enough to make the voyage to England safely in almost any weather.'

'Are you proposing we all go in a rowing boat?' She was not frightened at the idea but obviously surprised and dismayed.

'No. I'm not proposing anything at the moment, beyond a couple of hours' fishing at night in the Gullet. Auguste is providing a boat for us.'

'Why fishing? You hate fish and fishing. Why the sudden interest?' she asked suspiciously.

'A romantic row in the moonlight so that you can see all the pretty ships at anchor.'

'Most romantic,' she said with a rueful smile. 'We'll have four men as chaperones. Can we hire an orchestra, and perhaps a troupe of wandering minstrels?'

CHAPTER SIX

Auguste sighed in the darkness and admitted: 'The price is good at the moment, but in truth I hate the smell of potatoes.' He pulled fretfully at a couple of sacks, trying to find himself a more comfortable position in the little hut. 'And madame, you must be very uncomfortable?'

'I had not realized potatoes could be so hard,' Sarah admitted, 'but if my husband is to be believed, we'll soon be sitting on the hard wooden seats of a boat and probably thinking of potatoes with nostalgia . . .'

And how long would Nicholas be? He had talked for half an hour with Gilbert, Louis, Auguste and his brother Albert, and now he had gone for a walk along the quay. She saw now that he had been very clever. Although he had told her back at the château that he had no plans for their escape, in fact he had an idea. Certainly as he had explained it to the men, speaking softly in the darkness of Auguste's hut in the fruit and vegetable market, he had sounded diffident. Not nervous, but almost shy, so much so that first Auguste and then Gilbert had tried to reassure him. Then, as he explained his idea piece by piece, like stripping an artichoke, they had discussed it among themselves, exclaiming from time to time at its soundness, like antiquarians examining old china or an early edition of a book and agreeing on its authenticity.

The more they had exclaimed, the more diffident Nicholas had become, putting up reasons why his idea would never work and declaring he did not want anyone to risk his life in such a stupid venture. 'Stupid venture', a phrase which translated well into

French, was the one that definitely turned the tide, though whether a neap or a spring, she did not care. At that point, the four Frenchmen rallied together to persuade Nicholas that the plan – by now it had graduated from an idea – was not only possible but certain of success and Sarah sensed that in their own minds it had become *their* plan: one of which Captain Ramage had now to be convinced.

Then she realized that as far as Nicholas was concerned it had been a plan all the time but was such a gamble that its only chance of success was to have it carried out by men who were convinced it would succeed. What was that phrase Nicholas had once used? 'Better one volunteer than three pressed men.' So with four volunteers he had the equivalent of a dozen. And, of course, his wife! Louis seemed to be bearing up bravely, she thought, to the fact that his wife had decided not to come. Louis said she would go to her parents as soon as she was sure he had escaped. Between them they had prepared a likely story of Louis throwing her out of the house – of the servants' quarters of Jean-Jacques' house, rather.

Sarah sensed that both Louis and his wife had reached the stage where they bored each other. In another year it would be followed by dislike and that would turn to hatred. The wife missed life on the farm where she had been brought up, obviously preferring feeding the pigs and mucking out the cattle to feeding humans and making beds, and as she was the only child, she would inherit the farm on the death of her parents. Clearly, Sarah realized, each thought the parting had come amicably and at the right time. And, not surprisingly, the other servants had decided to stay behind.

Where *was* Nicholas? This was worse than being a young girl waiting to grow up, or a pregnant woman waiting for her hour to come. Or, she thought bitterly, a sailor's wife waiting for her man to return . . .

Ramage looked in the darkness across the Brest Roads. 'Roads' – a strange name but one usually given to the anchorage in front of the port. Well, even though it was dark but cloudless, giving the stars a chance to prove themselves before the moon rose, there was plenty of traffic in the Roads; it seemed as busy as Piccadilly after the Newmarket Races, when winners wanted to celebrate and losers wanted to drown their sorrows, and the

Duchess of Manston always gave a ball at which it was forbidden to talk about racehorses.

Spanish Point over there, forming the south side of *Le Goulet*: the Château black and menacing, its walls now sharp-edged shadows. Somewhere over there in the Roads, *L'Espoir* was at anchor, and by now Jean-Jacques would be on board, a prisoner, probably awake and thinking of his home or his future in the tropical heat and sickness of the Île du Diable. Boats were going out to the frigates and ships of the line, many more than would normally be taking officers to and fro. There was no doubt that the ships were being prepared for sea in great haste.

He paused against the trunk of a huge plane tree, hidden from the sharp eyes of any patrolling *gendarmes*. The masts of the distant ships were like leafless shrubs lining twisting paths. The ships of the line were easy to distinguish, while one, two, three frigates and more were over to the right, towards Pointe des Espagnols. Further round to the left, partly hidden by the cliffs rising up at Presqu'île de Plougastel, were more frigates. Where was *L'Espoir*?

Ah, there was the *Murex* brig, much easier to spot because she had only two masts and was much closer. And it was near the top of the tide; almost slack now, and the ebb would start in half an hour or so.

Anchored ships were something like weathervanes on church steeples. If the wind was strong and the current weak they indicated wind direction, but if the current was strong (as it would be at spring tides) and the wind weak they showed the direction from which the current was coming.

On a calm night at slack water, when the current stopped flooding in and paused before ebbing like a bewildered man on a ballroom floor, ships headed in various directions, and those carelessly anchored and usually lying to single anchors would drift and foul neighbours.

He cursed softly because at night distances were always hard to estimate, although by some good fortune the *Murex* brig had been anchored more than half a mile from the nearest ship, a frigate. And she was near enough to where he stood to see that only a single boat floated astern of her on its painter. Either the rest of her boats had been hoisted back on board or they were being kept in the dockyard. In other words, it was unlikely that the French guards had been reinforced and, more important, if they were not expecting visitors in the shape of senior officers, they would be keeping the rum jar tilted, with all the prisoners in irons.

He shivered, but was not sure if the goosepimples came from the chill of the night or the knowledge that he could no longer delay going back to the hut to start everyone moving. Sarah was the problem: she was his hostage unto fortune, although she must never realize it. When the *Calypso* went into action he had worried about Paolo, who was Gianna's heir and nephew; now it was Sarah. Would he ever go into action having given no hostages, with nothing to bother him but the fight itself? There was always something to stop him concentrating all his thoughts on the action. He shrugged and then smiled at the stupidity of such a movement alone in the darkness.

Probably most captains of the King's ships were often in this same predicament – especially, he told himself, if they were married. Yet if you had a wife, and perhaps children, you thought of them whether they were in a house in the quiet countryside or if the wife was waiting nearby in a rowing boat: in one instance you were worrying about her being widowed and the children made fatherless; in the other you were worrying about her safety. Either way, you were worrying; either way you were preoccupied. So perhaps Earl St Vincent was right when he said that if an officer married, he was lost to the Service . . .

Sarah and the four men waiting in the hut clearly expected to start off at once. He took out his watch. Yes, by now the French guards would have soaked up enough rum to ensure they were befuddled, if not in a stupefied sleep.

He gestured towards the lantern and told Gilbert: 'Bring it with you, otherwise all of us stumbling along in the dark will arouse suspicion. Now, have we the fishing lines? Ah,' he nodded as Auguste and his brother held up coils of thin line. 'And bait?' Sarah rattled the bucket she was carrying.

Two *gendarmes* passed them on their way to the jetty and one said cheerfully: 'Good fishing. It's a calm night!'

'Too calm,' Auguste answered dourly. 'The fish prefer some wind to ruffle the water.'

Once the *gendarmes* had passed, Auguste explained: 'Fishermen always grumble. I don't think the fish care about the waves; they have enough sense to stay below them.'

'Unless they bite a hook,' Louis said.

'Ah, no, they're biting the bait, not the hook.'

'They cannot have so much sense: a meal hanging from a line is obviously bait.'

'Yes,' Auguste agreed sarcastically, 'sensible fish eat only from a plate.'

Ramage led them to the avenue of plane trees lining the quay but told Auguste to lead them on to the boat: a sentry might become suspicious of the leader of a group of fishermen who seemed uncertain which was his boat.

He dropped back to walk with Sarah who, careful to act the role of the obedient fisherman's wife, even though it was late at night, had followed the menfolk.

'Feeling nervous?'

'No, not nervous. At the moment I'm thankful not to be smelling potatoes but not sure' – she rattled the bucket – 'if sliced fish is a welcome change. Do you enjoy fishing?'

'This is my first experience,' Ramage admitted. 'I let the men tow a hook when they want, because fish makes a welcome change from salt horse. But towing a line from a rowing boat, or casting with a rod along a river bank – no.'

'You've no patience, that's why,' she said.

He was saved from admitting that by Auguste stopping above a boat moored stern to the quay. 'Well, my friends,' he said loudly, 'I hope your muscles are all working smoothly. Now, someone haul in the sternfast so that I can jump in and slack the anchor rope: then we can get her alongside and put our gear on board.'

The boat's stern was four or five feet from the dock and Louis went down the narrow stone steps to untie the sternfast from a ring that slid up and down a metal rod let into the vertical face of the quay, allowing for the rise and fall of the tide. He cursed as he nearly slipped on the green weed.

'Farmers,' Auguste's brother commented unexpectedly. 'That's what we are, farmers going out for a night's fishing.'

No one answered as he went down to help Louis, then called up to Auguste: 'All is ready for the real fishermen to step on board.'

It took five minutes of hauling, pushing and banter for the four Frenchmen to get on board and hold the boat alongside the steps for Sarah and Ramage to climb in. The lantern set down on one of the thwarts revealed the inside of a hull which seemed to have been painted with dried fish scales and decorated with the sun-dried heads, tails and fins of past catches. The worst of the smell was for the moment masked by the sewage running into the Penfeld river from a large pipe a few feet upstream from the steps.

With Sarah seated on a thwart, the wooden bucket of bait on her knees, Ramage and Auguste counted up the oars. Four, held down by a chain wound round them and secured by a padlock. 'I have the key, here,' Auguste said in answer to an unspoken question. 'Now, I want you two, Louis and Albert, to stand in front of the lantern: cast a shadow over the bow.'

Ramage saw a pile of fishing lines and a coil of rope, and as soon as the lantern light was shadowed he saw Auguste pulling them aside and for a moment a flash of steel reflected a bright star.

'They're here,' Auguste muttered. 'Six cutlasses ... two, three large daggers ... five pistols – no, six ... a bag of shot ... flask of powder, and another of priming powder ... You said no muskets.'

It was a remark which sounded like a reproach.

'Believe me,' Ramage said, 'muskets are too clumsy for boarding a ship. If they're loaded, there's always the danger of the lock catching on clothing so the musket fires just when you're trying to be quiet. A pistol tucked in the top of the trousers – that is enough. Anyway, cutlasses or knives tonight: no shots except in an emergency.'

'But we can carry pistols?' Auguste asked anxiously.

'Yes, of course,' Ramage assured him. 'Now, let's get away from here and start fishing nearer the *Murex*. Bottle fishing – none of you ever heard of that, eh?'

Both Auguste and Gilbert repeated the phrase, which certainly lost something in translation. 'No, never "bottle fishing",' Auguste finally admitted. 'For what kind of fish?'

Ramage laughed and explained. 'In the West Indies, smuggling is even more common than in the Channel, only out there it is called "bottle fishing" when it involves liquor.'

'What is it when it is silk for ladies?' Auguste asked slyly.

'No need to smuggle silk out there: no customs or excise on that,' Ramage said.

Auguste unlocked the padlock and unwound the chain securing the oars. 'We are ready,' he said. 'The fish are waiting for us.'

The men took up their places on the rowing thwarts, leaving

Sarah to sit at the aftermost one. They would use a tiller to avoid having to give orders to the oarsmen.

Auguste boated his oar and then scrambled forward to the bow to begin hauling in the weed-covered rope and the anchor while his brother cast off the sternfast, leaving it dangling from its ring on the quay wall. Would the boat ever return to use it again? Ramage thought not.

Gilbert tentatively pulled at his oar and nearly fell backwards off the thwart as the blade scooped air instead of digging into water.

'Don't let go of the oar,' Auguste snapped. 'Dip the blade deeply and just try and keep time with the rest of us.'

'I know how to do it.' Gilbert's voice had a determined ring. 'I'm out of practice.'

'And the palms of your hands will soon be sore,' Auguste added unsympathetically.

'I can see the *Murex*,' Sarah murmured. 'She's in line with the western end of the Château.'

'Ah, a woman who knows the points of a compass,' Albert said.

The oars creaked, the thwarts creaked from the men's weight and their exertions, and as Ramage crouched he was sure his spine was beginning to creak too. The smell of last week's fish was now almost overwhelming and seemed to be soaking into his clothes. Then he could just see the western edge of the Château, stark and black against the lower stars. The only lights over there were from a high window and a few gun loops, vertical slots that, because of the thickness of the wall and the changing bearing, soon cut off the light from the lanterns inside.

Sarah put her bucket down beside the lantern as Ramage said: 'We are at the meeting point of the Penfeld and *Le Goulet*.'

'Stop rowing, men,' Auguste said, and then announced formally: 'Your fishing captain now hands over to your fighting captain.'

Ramage laughed with the rest of them and looked forward at the *Murex* brig. She was a good half mile away and it was still slack water, with the ships heading in different directions. A frog's view of models on a pond. For a few moments the familiar shape of the brig once again brought back memories of the *Triton*. He remembered her best at anchor in some West Indian bay during a tropical night when her masts and yards cut sharp lines in a star-littered sky. Up here in northern latitudes fewer stars were visible, for reasons he could never understand, and they were not nearly so bright, as though the atmosphere was always more hazy.

To fish or not to fish? He looked slowly round the horizon. No other boats were following them out of the Penfeld; the nearest ships to the *Murex* were half a dozen frigates and ships of the line at least half a mile beyond. Various boats moved under oars (and he could see one under sail making poor progress because of the light wind) taking officers and men out to the ships. None had that purposeful, marching sentry movement of a guard boat: the war, he guessed, was too new for the French to have started regular patrols in the Roads, and anyway lookouts along the coast (at Pointe St Mathieu, for instance) would most likely have reported that the English had not yet resumed the blockade; that no English ships were on the coast.

He coughed to attract their attention and as a way of accepting the transition announced by Auguste. 'I think madame can throw that bait over the side; she must be tired of the smell of fish.'

A clatter showed Sarah had not waited to hear if anyone disagreed.

'Good, now let's get our oars on board, before someone lets go and we lose a quarter of our speed. Auguste, can you issue the weapons you have hidden up there?'

The Frenchman scrambled forward, fumbled for a minute or two, and then stood up again, clutching several objects.

'Cutlasses,' he said. 'Here, Gilbert, take a couple before they slip from my arms. Ah, and one for you, captain, and one for me. I shall put mine under my thwart. Careful with your feet when you sit down again, Gilbert.'

With that he bent down and burrowed under the coils of lines again. 'Four knives . . .' his voice was muffled as he dropped them behind him, ' . . and the pistols.'

'You have six, I believe,' Ramage said. 'We'll have one for madame.'

'Of course!' Auguste said. 'I remember Gilbert telling me she is a fine shot. I shall load it for her myself. Now . . .' he pulled the coil of lines to one side, '. . . ah, the flask of powder . . . and the priming powder . . . and the box of balls and wads. Here, Gilbert, pass things aft, starting with the knives.'

For the next five minutes the men were busy checking the flints, flipping them to make sure they gave a good spark, but hiding them under a piece of cloth to conceal their unmistakable flashing. Then they loaded the pistols, putting them on half-cock.

Louis and the two brothers were wearing high fishermen's boots and slid their knives down into them. Ramage and Gilbert wore shoes and so had to tuck the knives into the waistband of their trousers. Ramage was thankful the cutlasses had come with belts, but decided against slipping his over his right shoulder and instead pushed it under the thwart.

'You were right about muskets being too bulky, captain,' Auguste commented. 'With knife, pistol and cutlass, I have all the weapons I can handle.'

'Yes – but everyone remember: use the pistol only to save your life: shots might arouse the sentries in another ship, or alarm a passing boat.'

'Is madame content with her pistol?' Auguste inquired.

Sarah said: 'Yes, it is much like the English Sea Service pistol: clumsy and heavy!'

'Yes, but remember how roughly the sailors treat them,' Auguste said, beating Ramage to it, 'and when you've fired, you can always throw it at the next target.'

By now, Ramage was having second thoughts about his original plan. If a sentry challenged, they could probably gain several important seconds by innocently protesting that they were fishermen; seconds which could be converted into yards, and a closer approach.

'Auguste, what would you be using out here – a seine or long lines?'

Auguste thought for a few moments. 'Long lines, I think.'

He guessed what Ramage had in mind and added: 'One could use either, and I doubt if a sentry would know anyway! And it won't matter that we have no bait!'

Although they were not rowing, and there was very little wind, the Château was slowly drawing astern and the western bank where the Penfeld ran into *Le Goulet* was now closer, showing the direction the boat was drifting.

'The ebb has started,' Ramage said. 'The rest of us can start rowing again while Auguste puts over some lines.' He moved into the fisherman's seat.

Sarah took the tiller and gave occasional directions to the four oarsmen as Auguste struggled with the lines. 'Hold up the lantern, madame,' he said finally, 'otherwise I shall be the only fish these lines catch.'

'You need only two or three,' Ramage said. 'No one will notice.'

'That's true,' Auguste said and put over one and then another, feeding out the lines expertly. 'Shall I sit aft and pretend to watch?'

'As long as you have your cutlass and knife ready under the thwart,' Ramage said. 'In fact you can take over as coxswain from madame, and start by giving me a distance.'

Sarah quickly pointed out the *Murex* to the Frenchman, who exclaimed: 'Why, we are close! Much closer than I thought!'

'That's the ebb taking us down.' Ramage then glanced over his shoulder and was also startled to find the brig now only about five hundred yards away: already her masts and yards were standing stark against the stars like winter trees with geometrically precise branches. 'Auguste, we'll row past at about a pistol shot and then, if nothing happens, turn under her bow and even closer under her stern and then if we still see no one, board this side.'

Sarah suddenly murmured in English: 'Nicholas, I am frightened. The *Murex* looks more like a house full of ghosts.'

'I'd prefer ghosts to French *matelots*,' he said lightly, while Gilbert, who had understood, gave a reassuring laugh.

'How are you going to get on board?' she asked reverting to French. She undid the knot of scarf round her head, took it off and shook her hair free.

'I don't know at the moment,' Ramage said, his sentences punctuated as he leaned forward and then stretched back with each oar stroke. 'There might be a ladder hanging over the side, or a rope. Otherwise, it'll probably be a scramble up the side.'

Sarah was silent for a moment and then said quietly in English: 'There's a light on deck. A lantern, I think. It gets hidden as rigging and things get in the way.'

'Speak in French,' Ramage said, trying to hide his disappointment. 'We don't want our friends to think we have any secrets.' He turned away towards them and repeated Sarah's report.

'A warm night, so they're drinking on deck,' Auguste commented. 'It would be natural. That cabin we saw – the "gunroom" I think you called it, captain – was very small. It would get very hot down there.'

Ramage saw his ideas being thrown aside like men caught on deck by a blast of grapeshot. Five Frenchmen up on the *Murex*'s deck drinking with weapons to hand, and two more guarding the prisoners below, would be more than a match for the five of them down in the rowing boat: the *matelots* would have the advantage of height, as well as numbers. But despair, fear, alarm – all were contagious, so Ramage laughed. 'It'll soon be hot on deck for them too!'

They continued rowing in the darkness at the speed set by Auguste, with an occasional 'left' and 'right'. Auguste said he was not using the seamen's terms because not all of them understood them and anyway, facing aft, they would only get muddled.

'We are two ship's lengths from her,' Auguste muttered. 'How close before we begin our turn to pass?'

'One,' Ramage said. That would be thirty yards, or so. Close enough for Ramage to see what was happening on deck; close enough for any French seaman to see a fishing boat passing. Or perhaps to show whether or not rum fumes would allow French *matelots* to see that far.

'No lights showing at the stern – what does that mean?' asked Auguste.

'They're not using the captain's cabin.'

Sarah said: 'There are several men on deck sitting round the lantern – do you see them, Auguste?'

The Frenchman grunted and then counted aloud as an explanation why he had said nothing. '. . . three, four . . . five. Two missing. Are they guarding the prisoners?'

'They could be fetching more rum or lying drunk on the deck,' Louis said. 'Perhaps we should row round for another hour and keep counting. As soon as seven have fallen down drunk, we can board!'

Ramage only just managed to stop himself making the usual joke about one Englishman being equal to three Frenchmen. These men, apart from not being trained seamen, were good: they had the right spirit and they hated the régime. Do not, he told himself, underestimate hate: it drives men to show the kind of bravery they never thought themselves capable of, yet it can just as easily warp their judgement.

'She's close on our bow – we're just beginning our run down her starboard side,' Auguste reported to Ramage, his voice punctuated by the creaking of the four oars, the slap of the oar blades in the water, and hiss of the stem as the boat drove on.

'Ho! *Ohé,* that boat!' The hail from the *Murex*'s deck was

87

definite: the voice was sober. 'Answer!' Ramage told Auguste, whose voice carried better and had a local accent.

'Ho yourself!' Auguste shouted back. 'I don't like *rosbifs* shouting at me.' His voice sounded genuinely offended.

'We're not *rosbifs*!' the voice answered indignantly. 'We are honest Frenchmen *guarding* the *rosbifs*.'

'You speak French like a *rosbif*,' Auguste said sourly.

'Watch your tongue: I come from Besançon. Now, why do you fish so close to us?'

'Ha!' Auguste called back contemptuously. 'So you think you own the whole sea, eh? Why, you are even standing on the deck of a *rosbif* ship, not a good French ship.'

'Answer: why do you fish so close?' This time it was another, harsher voice: Ramage thought he recognized it as belonging to the bosun.

'To catch fish!' exclaimed Auguste. 'You're no seaman if you can't see that!'

'What do you mean? I'm the bosun; I command this ship!'

'For the time being,' Auguste said contemptuously. 'But you've not yet learned that fish always gather round a ship at anchor. They feed off all the weed and things growing on the bottom. They like the shade on a sunny day –'

'And from the light of the moon too, I suppose. Afraid it will drive them mad, eh?'

'And they like to eat the scraps you all throw over the side. Salt beef and salt pork may not seem very tasty to you, but to a fish it is a banquet.'

By now the boat was within a few yards of the *Murex*'s side.

'To save all this rowing, with my back giving me trouble again,' Ramage said in a lugubrious voice, 'can't we fish from your decks? Then our hooks go down where the fish are thickest.'

The bosun answered quickly. 'Yes – but you have to give us a quarter of your catch!'

'You're a hard man,' Ramage complained. 'Five wives and eleven children depend on what we catch.'

'You should have thought of that before you got married,' the bosun sneered. 'A quarter of your catch and I'll let you on board.'

'Oh very well,' Ramage said grudgingly, and Auguste, in an

88

appropriately officious voice, gave the orders to the men at the oars which brought the boat alongside.

Ramage murmured: 'Pistols if you can hide them; otherwise just knives.'

'The bait bucket,' Sarah whispered. 'Put the pistols in the bait bucket and I'll carry it with my scarf on top.'

Louis called up to the bosun: 'I'm coming on board with the painter while they coil our fishing lines.' He touched Ramage to get his approval.

Ramage turned to Sarah. 'You go after Louis and flirt with the bosun. I'll bring the bucket and give it to you to hold as soon as I can.'

He glanced up and saw that none of the French guards were looking over the rail. Swiftly he pushed a knife and its sheath down the inside of his trousers and made sure the belt was tight enough to hold it. It was a pity that the cutlasses would have to be left under the thwarts, but Gilbert and Albert were putting the loaded pistols into the bucket with the deftness of fishwives packing sprats. Sprat – improbably, he remembered, it was the same word in both English and French.

'Your scarf, madame,' Gilbert whispered, and Ramage said loudly, 'Now are we ready? Gilbert – supposing you go up, and then you and Louis can help the lady at the top.'

As soon as Gilbert started climbing the battens fitted like thin steps up the *Murex*'s side, Sarah began cursing, using words which would be familiar to a fisherman's wife but which Ramage was startled to find that she not only knew but used as though they were commonplace.

'Such steps – why no rope ladder? In this skirt? Do the *rosbifs* never have women on board? It's fortunate I wear no corset. Look the other way, you lechers; I am tucking my skirt in my belt.'

She grabbed the hem of her skirt and Ramage glimpsed long slim legs as she tucked in the cloth. 'This will occupy their thoughts!' she murmured to Ramage, and before he had time to reply she had grabbed the highest batten she could reach and started climbing.

'Forgive me, captain,' Auguste murmured to Ramage, and then called in a raucous voice to Louis and Gilbert on the *Murex*'s deck: 'Why you went aloft too soon! From here one sees *la citoyenne* quite differently!'

'Keep your eyes down, you old dog,' Ramage said hotly in

what he hoped was the correct tone for an aggrieved husband, but he found himself continuing to watch Sarah's progress. A young woman's legs in the moonlight: certainly they did not help concentration. And since the sight made his own throat tighten he could guess the effect on Auguste.

A jab in the ribs from the bucket and a casual, 'Your turn, and tell Louis and Gilbert to stand by to take the lines,' came from Auguste.

The lines! He had forgotten all about the fishing lines. The prospect of fishermen arriving without them was only slightly less absurd than the idea of a Royal Navy post-captain on his honeymoon climbing up the side of a surrendered brig holding a bait bucket filled with loaded pistols concealed by his wife's headscarf.

He slung the greasy rope handle of the wooden pail over his left arm and began the climb. Usually sideboys held out sideropes for the captain, and the first lieutenant waited on deck ready to give a smart salute. This time there would be a surly French bosun . . .

The bucket slid down his arm and hit the ship's side with a thud. Ramage's heart seemed to stop beating for a moment, but the pistols did not make a metallic clunk and anyway, he thought sheepishly, there's no one up there watching me. But as he slid the handle back to the crook of his elbow he saw that now there was: not the bosun but the man who presumably was the sentry.

Ramage's head came level with the deck, and in the moonlight he saw Sarah a few feet away, talking to the bosun. Amidships and sitting on forms round the grating, on which stood a lantern and a wicker-covered demijohn of rum, several seamen were watching idly.

As soon as the bosun saw Ramage he left Sarah and came over. 'You came with the potatoes,' he said, his voice only slightly slurred by the rum. He had not shaved for several days or washed – it seemed to Ramage for even longer. His jersey and trousers had the greasy and rumpled look that showed he usually slept 'all standing', the British seaman's phrase for sleeping fully clothed.

'A quarter of your catch, eh? That is agreed?'

'Yes, of course,' Ramage said, continuing to walk towards Sarah so that the bosun had to follow. 'Let's hope we get a good catch. My dear,' he said to Sarah, 'here is the bait bucket: look after it while we sort out the lines.'

He held the bucket low so that as she took it she would not reveal its weight by letting it drop a few inches, and at the same moment Ramage turned to the bosun to divert his attention and said querulously: 'Never get a good catch with a full or new moon, you know. Moonlight seems to frighten the fish, or put them off food.'

'A quarter, though,' the bosun muttered as Sarah took the bucket and turned aft, saying in the voice of a dutiful wife that she would help bait the hooks as soon as they brought the lines.

By now Albert was on board and hauling up fishing lines from a cursing Auguste, who was putting on a noisy and effective act of being afraid of being caught on the hooks.

Louis and Gilbert came up to help and Ramage, seizing the opportunity of gathering all his men close to the bucket so they could collect their pistols, called: 'Hoist up all the lines – we have more room to untangle them on this ship's deck. Look, there's plenty of space aft there.'

Ramage walked along the gangway and, noting that the only lantern on deck was on the grating, giving the drinkers enough light to see when their glasses were nearly empty, shouted down to Auguste: '*Merde!* Hurry up or it'll be dawn!'

The bosun watched. 'You'll catch yourself on those hooks,' he sneered.

'Then you won't get a quarter,' Gilbert said.

'We'll see,' the bosun said, and Ramage tried to decide whether or not he imagined a curious inflexion in the voice. Finally he decided that it was just the man's local accent combined with a normal sneering and bullying manner.

As soon as the lines were all on board, the four Frenchmen, led by Ramage, carried them aft to where Sarah waited. The light was poor and confusing, a muddling blend of faint moonlight and a weak yellow glow – an artist would call it a wash – from the lantern on the grating.

The bosun, Ramage noted thankfully, had remained at the gangway, and the sentry had gone back to rejoin his three fellow seamen sitting and sprawling on the forms. So the sentry had a musket – he had left it propped against the edge of the coaming – and Ramage saw there were two more within reach of the other sailors.

As Ramage busied himself with the fishing lines close to the taffrail, he managed to indicate to the men that he wanted them working with their backs to the bosun so that Sarah could give them their pistols. As the men moved casually into position Ramage suddenly thought of the fourteen Britons being held as prisoners somewhere below and the captain imprisoned by rheumatism. Eleven seamen, the master and two lieutenants – they would be in irons, probably somewhere forward on the lowerdeck.

Tonight the *Murex* brig, he thought grimly, certainly holds an odd collection of people, ranging from the daughter of a marquis to seven French sailors loyal to the Revolution, a post-captain in the Royal Navy, and a rheumatic lieutenant, and four Frenchmen who, although perhaps not entirely Royalist, were certainly against the First Consul.

When the ingredients were mixed together, he mused as he saw Sarah dip into the bucket and give Auguste a pistol, it would be like mixing charcoal, sulphur and saltpetre, each in themselves harmless but in the right proportion forming gunpowder and needing only a spark –

'Step back from those fishing lines!'

The bosun's sudden bellow paralysed the five men.

'Woman! Come over here!'

Rape, Ramage thought: the bosun and his men intend to rape Sarah. And only Auguste has a pistol: the bosun shouted before Sarah had time to give out the others.

'Oh, lieutenant!' Sarah said, her voice apparently trembling with fear. 'What do you want me for?'

'Ah, no, not for that yet,' the bosun boomed, although the regret at any delay was obvious in his voice. 'You'll make a good hostage against the behaviour of your husband and his friends.'

Ramage saw that the bosun was aiming a musket at them. The other men were now laughing but still sprawled on the forms, two of them holding mugs in their hands.

Ramage said: 'What are we supposed to do? We are poor fishermen. You gave us permission to fish.'

'Ah yes, but you do not keep yourself informed, citizen. From midnight, patrols are searching all the streets and houses of Brest to find more seamen. A thousand more. The First Consul needs many more men for all these ships,' he said, waving a hand towards the main anchorage. 'We received orders during the day

to see if any of the British prisoners in this ship want to volunteer
– and then tonight the five of you row past . . .'

'Oh my poor husband!' Sarah moaned, but Ramage noticed
she still clutched the bucket to her, like a mother clasping her
child.

Ramage took two steps towards her but the bosun snarled:
'Halt – another step and I shoot you dead.' He glanced over his
shoulder at his men. 'To arms, citizens! Cover them with your
muskets.'

There was a clatter as one of the forms tipped over, and
Ramage saw the men pick up their muckets and cock them. Five
muskets . . . He had not seen the others lying on the deck beyond
the coaming.

Now the bosun was getting excited by the nearness of Sarah.
'Ah yes, the fisherman's wife! Well, take a good look at him, my
dear, because you'll not see him again for a long time. A very
long time. Ever again, perhaps, if the English fight like they did
before.'

Ramage took another step forward but the bosun swung the
barrel of the musket. 'Stand still. We'll be taking you below in
a minute.'

With that he turned to Sarah. 'Yes, look well at your man.'
Then, with a sudden movement of one hand he ripped away the
front of Sarah's dress and as her breasts shone in the moonlight
he screamed at Ramage: 'Look! Look, you fish pedlar – you
won't see her again for a very long time. But' – he paused, staring
wide-eyed and slack-mouthed at Sarah as she tried to clutch her
dress closed with one hand, the other still holding the bucket –
'I'll look after her for you, won't I, my dear?'

He reached across and pulled Sarah's hand away so that the
torn dress again gaped open. 'Look after these wretches,' the
bosun ordered his men. 'Now,' he said to Sarah, almost
slobbering the words, 'you come down to my cabin!'

'No,' she said, calmly and clearly, 'and you put the musket
down on the deck and order your men to come over one at a time
and put their muskets beside it!'

The bosun stood, jaw dropped in surprise and then gave a
harsh, ugly laugh.

'Be careful,' Sarah warned. 'Your life is in danger.' Her voice
was cold but the bosun was too excited to notice.

'Oh, she has spirit, this one!' he exclaimed.

'No,' Sarah said, taking a step forward, 'a pistol.'

A moment later the bosun pulled in his bulging stomach as the muzzle of Sarah's pistol jabbed it.

'You would never dare! Ho!' he half turned to his men and called over his shoulder: 'Watch me pull this hen off her nest!' He reached out and grabbed Sarah's dress again.

Ramage saw the men beginning to move, uncertain what was happening because Sarah's hand holding the pistol was hidden from them by the bosun's bulky body. Suddenly there was a bright flash and bang and a scream from the bosun, who staggered back three steps and then collapsed on the deck.

'Seize her, seize her!' one of the *matelots* screamed and then, as Sarah made a sudden movement and said something to the quartet that Ramage did not hear, the man shouted urgently: 'No! Don't move! The cow has another pistol! Don't shoot, *citoyenne* – it was all in jest!'

By now Ramage was running towards the bucket, a hand groping for a pistol and cocking it as he kept an eye on the four *matelots*. In one almost continuous movement he was moving towards them with the pistol aimed. Behind him he could hear the thudding feet and then the clicking of locks as the pistols were cocked.

'My wife has dealt with the bosun. Unless you all put your muskets down I shall shoot you – the man nearest the mainmast. My friends – ah, here they are – will shoot the rest of you.'

He said to Auguste conversationally: 'I have the man on the right in my sights. The next is for you. Then Gilbert and then Louis.'

The four *matelots* seemed frozen by the speed of events. 'Muskets down on the deck,' Ramage reminded them.

Sarah said with the same calm: 'Shoot one of them, to encourage the others!'

The *matelots* heard her and hastily put the guns down on the deck. 'Collect them up, Gilbert and Albert. Now you,' he gestured to the nearest man, 'come here.'

As the *matelot* reluctantly walked the few feet, outlined against the brighter light thrown by the lantern and clearly expecting to be shot, Ramage wrenched his knife from its sheath and held it in his left hand.

'Closer,' he ordered. 'Come on, stand close to me, my friend!'

The *matelot* was a plump, pleasant-looking man with a chubby face, but now his brow was soaked in perspiration as though water was dribbling from his hair; his eyes jerked from pistol to knife and his tongue ran round his lips as though chasing an elusive word.

'Closer,' Ramage said as the man stopped a couple of paces away. Then, as he shuffled forward a step, Ramage's knife curving towards him flashed briefly in the lantern light and several people gasped and Sarah dropped the now empty bucket with a crash and tried to muffle a scream.

The *matelot* swayed, a puzzled vacant expression on his face, waiting for the pain to start, and everyone expected blood to spurt because clearly Ramage's knife had just eviscerated the man.

Instead his trousers fell down in a heap round his ankles.

'Next time it won't be your trousers,' Ramage said. 'Now, where are the keys to free the prisoners?'

The sailor stood, speechless and paralysed by fear.

Ramage prodded him with the pistol, forcing him to take a step back. The man had enough presence of mind to step out of his trousers and Sarah picked them up, checked if they had a pocket, and finding they had not, walked to the ship's side and threw them into the sea.

'It doesn't make up for my torn dress,' she said to no one in particular, 'but it is very satisfying!'

Auguste had taken command of his brother, Louis and Gilbert, and had them lined up with the muskets covering the other *matelots*. Auguste picked up the lantern and then, as an afterthought, put it down again, took the big bottle of rum and tossed it over the bulwark. 'Madame has the right idea,' he said, 'no one gets fighting drunk without spirits to drink and,' he added slyly, 'no man is a hero without his trousers.'

With that he took out his knife and cut the belts of the other three *matelots*, leaving them standing with their trousers round their ankles. 'Forgive me, madame,' he said to Sarah, 'but I am following your husband's example.'

'I am a married woman,' she said demurely.

'What a wife,' one of the *matelots* muttered. 'She uses a pistol like a filleting knife.'

'I need another lantern,' Ramage said to Gilbert. 'Will you get ours up from the boat? Take Louis with you and bring the cutlasses too. This fellow,' he tapped the sailor on the head with the flat of the knife, 'will suffer if his friends misbehave while you are gone.'

As soon as Gilbert and Louis returned with the lantern and cutlasses, Ramage commented: 'Time is short: that shot may bring over inquisitive people.' To the trouserless seaman, who seemed to be the senior of the survivors, he said: 'Now we free the British prisoners. If you want to live to an old age, you will help.'

The *matelot* haltingly explained that the irons had only four bars running through them, secured by four padlocks, and the four keys were on a hook in the cabin the bosun had been using. Suddenly Ramage remembered the other two guards. Where were they?

Ramage sent Gilbert with his lantern down the companionway into the gunroom ahead of the *matelot* and himself. The lantern lit the steps and showed the *matelot*'s movements clearly. Since the stroke that had cut his belt and lost him his trousers, it was clear that the man feared the blade more than the pistol, which surprised Ramage. Perhaps the wretched *matelot*'s imagination conjured up a more horrifying picture of what a knife could do to a man walking about clad only in a thick woollen jersey and a pair of felt shoes obviously cobbled up by a clumsy sailmaker.

The sailor pointed to the second lieutenant's cabin and followed Gilbert into it. The two men took up all the space and Ramage stood at the doorway, with the point of the knife just resting on the base of the *matelot*'s spine, so that he moved slowly and very obviously kept clear of Gilbert and the lantern.

Finally he reached round very slowly, offering four large keys to Ramage, like an acolyte at communion. 'These are the ones, sir.'

'You carry them. Call to the other two guards and warn them to put their weapons down, or you'll die. Now we go and undo those padlocks.'

The next cabin was empty. 'The captain was here,' the *matelot* said hastily, 'but he was so ill they took him to the hospital yesterday.'

Ramage felt a surge of relief. He had not looked forward to interviewing a captain who drove his crew to mutiny, whatever his state of health.

The two guards were collapsed in a drunken stupor and the prisoners were lying at the fore end of the lowerdeck. Iron rings protruded from the deck so that metal rods through leg irons

96

needed only a padlock at one end – the other was too bulbous to pass through the eye – to secure each of the four rows of men. They all looked up, and although blinking and squinting in the lantern light, all were wide awake, obviously roused by the pistol shot.

Ramage decided it would be easier to ensure their attention if he left them prone on the deck for a few more minutes so he waved the *matelot* to one side, telling him to be ready.

'Gentlemen,' Ramage said loudly. 'I am Captain Ramage, of the King's Service. I spoke to one of your lieutenants while delivering potatoes – ah,' he pointed, 'it was you. Very well, in a few minutes you will all be free. I have this fellow here and three other French seamen on deck as prisoners and the bosun is dead – you heard the shot. But listen carefully: in addition to this man' – he gestured towards Gilbert – 'there are three other Frenchmen up there, dressed in fishermen's clothes. Two of them do not speak English but all three are responsible for your rescue. So be very careful.

'I shall put the six French guards in the open boat we came out in, and cast them adrift so that they can row into Brest Harbour with one oar and report what's happened. That will save us guarding prisoners, and there's been enough killing for tonight.'

There was some murmuring from three men who Ramage guessed were the lieutenants and the master. Very well, he would deal with them in a moment.

'The guards will report that the *Murex* has been recaptured by the English and sailed. Anyway that will be obvious to anyone standing on the beach. So, within ten minutes at the most of those irons being unlocked, I want this ship tacking down the Gullet under topsails. We'll let the anchor cable run to save time.

'Two more things. My wife is on deck.' He then let a hard note come into his voice. 'Any orders I give will not be questioned. I have taken command of this ship. I do not have my commission but it is dated September 1797. Nor do I have orders from the Admiralty, but anyone doubting my authority can go off in the boat with the French guards and become a prisoner of war.'

CHAPTER SEVEN

The description of him dressed in a French fisherman's smock and trousers, and standing on the quarterdeck of one of the King's ships with his wife beside him wearing a badly torn dress cobbled up with sailmaker's thread, would soon, Ramage mused, be another story added to the fund of bizarre yarns which already seemed to surround him.

At least a westerly gale was not screaming over the ebb tide and kicking up the hideous sea for which Brest Roads were notorious; at least the stars were out and the moon had risen. And if there had been no war, he would regard this as the start of a pleasant voyage. But now in an instant it could all turn out very difficult. If one of those anchored French ships opened fire and the three forts lining the cliffs along the Gullet followed suit, then in this light wind the *Murex* would be battered . . .

He picked up the speaking trumpet and the coppery smell seemed to complete the series of memories taking him back to the *Calypso,* to the *Triton* and then to the *Kathleen.*

'Let that cable run, Mr Phillips . . . Foretopmen there: let fall the foretopsail . . . Stand by, maintopmen!'

Strange orders, but ones carefully phrased because he had so few seamen. That delivery of potatoes had saved him – knowing how many men he would have available to handle the ship had allowed him to work out a rough general quarter, watch and station bill for two lieutenants, master and eleven seamen.

And what a bill! Seven sail handlers: four seamen for letting fall the foretopsail, three for loosing the maintopsail. Then the foretopmen had to slide down swiftly from aloft to haul on the halyards, and as soon as the yard was up, they had to hoist the jibs and staysails. The maintopmen in turn had to race down to tend their own halyard and then help the four remaining seamen who were to haul on sheets and braces to trim the yards and sails.

Of those four, two would have been helping the second lieutenant, Bridges, to let the anchor cable run . . . The master, Phillips, would be on the fo'c'sle, making sure that the cable ran out through the hawse without snagging, and the headsails and their sheets did not wrap round things in that tenacious embrace so beloved of moving ropes. And he wondered if Swan, the young first lieutenant who was now waiting at the wheel, could remember how to box the compass in quarterpoints! It was something he would have known when he took his examination for lieutenant and, having passed, would have forgotten it . . .

Damnation, this wind was light . . . Better not too strong with such a tiny crew, but he needed enough breeze to get those topsails drawing and give him steerage way over the ebbing tide – by the time the *Murex* was drawing level with Pointe St Mathieu he would have dodged enough rocks and reefs to sink a fleet. The first of them was just abreast Fort de Delec, the dark walls of which he could already see perched up on the cliff on his starboard hand.

Ah! At last the foretopsail tumbled down as the men slashed the gaskets. He had made sure they had knives (it meant raiding the galley) to save valuable time: untying knotted gaskets (it was sure to be the last one that jammed) could cost three or four minutes.

Two men were coming down hand over hand along the forestay! The other two were coming down the usual way, using the shrouds. A puff of wind caught the sail so that it flapped like a woman shaking a damp sheet. To Ramage's ears, by now abnormally sensitive to noise, it seemed every ship in the anchorage must hear the *Murex*'s foretopsail sounding like a ragged broadside.

Now the maintopsail flopped down with the elegant casualness of canvas in light airs.

A rapid thumping, as though a great snake was escaping from a box, ended with a splash and a cheerful hail from Phillips: 'Cable away, sir!'

'Very well, Mr Phillips,' Ramage called through the trumpet and warned Swan at the wheel, 'Be ready to meet her – the bow will pay off to starboard but for the moment the ebb has got her!'

The brig, with her bow now heading north as though she wanted to sail up the Penfeld river and into Brest, was in fact being swept sideways by the ebb down the Gullet towards the wide entrance, a dozen miles away and stretching five miles or so between Pointe St Mathieu on the starboard side and the Camaret peninsula to larboard.

The seamen were like ants at the base of each mast. Up, up, up! The heavy foretopsail yard inched its way upwards on the halyard and then a bellowed order saw it settle and the sheets tautening, giving shape to the sail.

The wind was still west; the feathers on the string of corks forming the telltale on the larboard side reassured him about that as they bobbed in the moonlight.

'I can feel some weight on the wheel now, sir,' Swan reported, as Ramage saw the maintopsail yard begin its slow rise up the mast. Damnation take the foretopmen, they had to make haste with those headsails: brigs were the devil to tack without jibs and staysail drawing, and already the *Murex* was gathering way as though she wanted to run up on the rocks in front of the Château.

Ramage lifted the speaking trumpet. He had to make them get a move on without frightening them into making silly mistakes.

'Foretopsail sheet men – aft those sheets! Brace men – brace sharp up!' Strangely-worded orders, but he had no afterguard.

Now he could see the sail outlined against the stars and it was setting perfectly, and Swan was cautiously turning the wheel a few more spokes.

'Maintopsail sheet men, are you ready? Take the strain – now, run it aft! Another six feet! Heave now, heave. Right, belay that! Now, you men at the braces, sharp up!'

The flying jib, jib and staysail were crawling up their stays – with this light breeze and their canvas blanketed by the foretopsail, three of the four seamen were hauling a halyard each...

'Amidships there! Hands to the headsail sheets ... Take the strain ...' He watched as the sails slowed down and then stopped their climb up the stays. 'Right, aft those headsail sheets ... Foretopmen, pass them the word because I can't see a stitch of the canvas from here!'

Cheerful shouts from forward and the moonlight showing the topsails taking up gentle curves indicated that his unorthodox method of getting under way and passing sail orders to a handful of seamen, all of whom would normally be doing just one of those jobs, was working.

'Don't pinch her, Mr Swan,' Ramage warned the first lieutenant. 'Just keep her moving fast, and then we'll have control. We'll have to put in a few dozen tacks before you put the helm down for Plymouth.'

Ramage paused and wiped the mouthpiece of the speaking trumpet, which was green with verdigris.

'You nearly ran down the *matelots* in the fishing boat as you were setting the maintopsail,' Sarah said. 'They hadn't made much progress.'

'I didn't hear you reporting,' Ramage teased.

'No, you didn't,' she said shortly. 'I didn't start the Revolution or the war.'

'Remind me to tell you how much I am enjoying our honeymoon, but first we must tack.'

And, he thought to himself, if the *Murex* hangs in irons we'll drift on to the rocks on the headland in front of the arsenal and opposite the Château: the current sets strongly across them on the ebb.

A quick word to Swan had the wheel turning, and he could hear the creak of rudder pintles working on the gudgeons, an indication of a quiet night.

Then he gave a series of shouted commands to the men at sheets and braces and slowly (too slowly it seemed at first, convincing him he had left it too late) the *Murex*'s bow began to swing to larboard, into the wind ...

'Not too much helm, Mr Swan, you're supposed to be turning her, not stopping her ...' A first lieutenant should know that. Now the jibs and staysail were flapping across.

'Headsail sheets, there!'

The men knew what to do; that much was obvious in the way the sails had been set. So now he need give only brief orders which took care of the trimming.

'Braces! Altogether now, haul! Now the sheets!'

A glance ahead showed the brig now steady on the other tack.

'Mr Swan,' Ramage said quietly, walking over to the wheel, 'I think you can get another point or two to windward ...'

He watched the luff of the mainsail and then the leech.

'And another couple of spokes?'

Swan turned the wheel two more spokes but his movements lacked certainty: he was clearly nervous.

'Come now, Mr Swan,' Ramage said, a sharper note in his voice. 'I don't expect to have to give the first lieutenant compass courses to steer to windward. Now look'ee, you can lay the Pointe des Espagnols – that's the headland on your larboard bow.'

With that he turned away and said to Sarah, 'Can you see

L'Espoir over there at anchor? I think she's gone: sailed while we were having our trouble with the bosun.'

She turned and looked over the larboard quarter at all the ships moonlit against the black line of low cliffs with the town of Plougastel in the distance. Unused to allowing for a change in bearings she took two or three minutes before finally reporting: 'No, she's not there. But she can only be...'

'Yes,' Ramage said, 'half an hour or so,' and noted it was time to tack again: the brig was moving along well and the ebb was helping hurry them seaward. He went over to Swan and gave him the new heading for when they had gone about.

'Follow the cliff along from Brest. You see the village of Portzic? Now, just beyond that next headland – you see the building? That's Fort de Delec. You should be able to lay it, but if a messenger has reached them they'll open fire. And just beyond, on top of the cliff, is the Lion Battery. If the fort and battery begin firing at us, we'll tack over to the other side.'

There was no need to tell Swan that on the other tack they would be heading for the Cornouaille Battery on the Camaret peninsula, and if the fire from that became hot enough to force them to tack northwestward again back to the Pointe St Mathieu side, they would be steering for the next fort, at Mengam, with three isolated and large rocks also waiting in the fairway for them...

The *Murex* went about perfectly: the headsails slapped across as the bow came round and were swiftly sheeted in; both topsails were braced sharp up on the larboard tack; Swan moved the wheel back and forth three or four spokes and then reported: 'I can lay a bit to windward of the Lion Battery, sir.'

Already the Château was dropping astern fast and Ramage watched the irregular shape of Fort de Delec. Distance was always hard to estimate in the darkness, but a mile? At night an object usually seemed closer – so to the French gunners the *Murex* would seem to be just within range. Just? Well within range, and Sarah murmured: 'I imagine Frenchmen staring along the barrels of guns...'

It seemed to be tempting fate to make a reassuring comment, and anyway she was not frightened. 'If they're going to open fire, it'll be in the next two or three minutes,' he said.

She held his arm in an unexpected gesture, and he was startled to find she was trembling. 'Will it look bad if I go below if they start shooting?'

He gripped her hand. 'Of course not. But it will be more frightening.'

'*More* frightening? I don't understand.'

'Dearest, if you stay on deck and see where the shot fall, you'll see there's no danger. If you go below you'll be waiting for the next shot to come through the deck and knock your head off!'

'I feel cold and shaky all of a sudden,' she said. 'Not frightened exactly. Apprehensive, perhaps.'

'When you shoot a man with a pistol you usually feel shaky afterwards,' Ramage said dryly, and added: 'I feel cold and shaky every time after I've been in action. I think everyone does.'

He looked up at Fort de Delec again. He felt he could see down the muzzles of the guns. Yes, there was the straight line of the walls; there were the embrasures. The moon had risen high enough now that he knew he would see the antlike movement of people if the guns were being loaded and trained round. It was a confounded nuisance commanding a ship which had no nightglass and no telescopes. No log or muster book for that matter – the telescopes had presumably been looted, and all the ship's papers would have been taken away by the French authorities. And charts – well, the only relevant one he had glanced at by lantern light just before getting under way, 'A Draught of the Road and Harbour of Brest with the adjacent Coast', must have been copied from a captured French one, but even then gave only one line of soundings from the town of Brest right along the Gullet, stopping as it reached the first of the three rocks, Mengam, and the man at the lead could be calling out twenty fathoms amidships as the bow hit the rock.

Another couple of minutes and they would tack again and then he wanted plenty of lookouts. With luck he would be able to leave Mengam safely to one side so that on the next tack to the northwest he could pass close to the last of the three rocks, which was in fact a small reef appropriately named Les Fillettes.

The Cornouaille Battery was silent, but that was to be expected: a boat would have to be sent over to the Camaret peninsula to raise the alarm, although they would pick it up from the other forts. This next tack would bring them within range of Fort de Mengam. Was the fort named after its silent ally in the middle of the Gullet, or the other way about?

He lifted the speaking trumpet as Sarah murmured: 'Anyone

raising the alarm at these forts and batteries would use the same road we rode along that afternoon from Pointe St Mathieu.'

'Now my dear, you can understand my interest in the number of guns each of them mounted.'

'You didn't explain,' she said.

'I'm always interested in French forts. I hardly expected we'd be sailing out in these circumstances!'

She shivered and turned to look back at the town and harbour. 'No, you were hoping eventually to sail your own ship in, on some wild escapade.'

'Yes,' he admitted, 'one never ignores a chance to learn about an enemy, but I prefer having my wife beside me!'

'You are being more polite than a new husband needs to be: I am a nuisance!'

He began shouting orders through the speaking trumpet and once again the *Murex*'s bow swung across the eye of the wind to the southwest: once again straining men hauled at the sheets and braces to trim the topsails. If only he could set the courses as well; then with more than double the amount of canvas drawing the brig would be out of the Gullet and into the Atlantic, passing the Pointe St Mathieu to starboard and the shoals to larboard off the Camaret peninsula, like a stoat after a rabbit.

He walked up to the mainmast, partly to leave Swan on his own and help him gain a confidence which had probably been badly battered by the mutiny, and partly to place extra lookouts. He called for Auguste, Albert and Louis.

'You know the Mengam?' he asked.

'Yes, captain, I was just coming to warn you: it is very near.'

'And the one beyond, and then Les Fillettes?'

'Yes, I know them all; I have fished around them dozens of times. In fact the Mengam is fine on the bow. You – yes, you can see it. Look . . .'

He stood beside Ramage, who saw they would pass clear and instructed the three Frenchmen to watch for other rocks. He walked aft to point it out to Swan, who seemed to have benefited from being left alone at the wheel. He had more life in him; he said, in the first time he had spoken except in answer to a question: 'I thought it'd be the batteries we'd be dodging, sir, not the rocks.'

Ramage then remembered that the *Murex* had been brought in

while it was still daylight. 'You were able to watch the scenery as you came in?'

'No choice, sir: we – those who had not mutinied – were all penned up on the fo'c'sle.'

'What about the mutineers?'

Swan laughed at the memory. 'Well, the French who came on board drove them all below. You see, sir, I was the only person in the ship who spoke any French, so when the French boarded us and asked why we were flying a white flag, I said some of the men had "misbehaved".'

'So they thought we – the officers and the loyal ship's company – were bringing the ship in and handing her over, and the mutineers had been trying to stop us. So for a couple of hours or so the mutineers were knocked around – until we anchored off Brest and English-speaking Frenchmen came out!'

Ramage calculated that they would be clear of the Gullet on the next tack, and Sarah joined him as he walked forward to pick up the speaking trumpet. As he gave the first orders for the tack which would turn the *Murex* to the northwest, Auguste came up and pointed ahead.

'Sir, Les Fillettes are ahead. You will pass clear when you tack.'

'Thank you, Auguste. Ah yes, I see them.'

There was no reason to point them out to Swan, who was now giving the appearance of enjoying himself. The moonlight was strong enough to give a clear picture of the deck, and as they tacked the men were quicker at freeing a rope or making it fast on cleat, kevil or belaying pin.

Now Swan was steadying the ship on the new tack as sheets and braces were trimmed, and as Ramage put the speaking trumpet down beside one of the guns and gave a contented sigh, Sarah said: 'We're almost out of this beastly river. Is that –?'

'Pointe St Mathieu? Yes. It seems a long while ago . . .'

'In some ways. Certainly, as we sat up there in the sun and looked out across here and up towards Ushant, I never expected to be sailing out of the Iroise in the dead of night. Yet' – she paused, and he was not sure if she was choosing her words carefully or deciding whether or not to say it – 'yet the way you looked out at the Black Rocks, and Ushant, and across this estuary to the Camaret peninsula – you were recording it, not looking at it like a visitor. You were noting it down in the pilot book in your head, ready for use when the war started again. Our

105

ride back to Jean-Jacques' – you were more interested in the forts and batteries than anything else!'

'No,' he protested mildly, 'I saw as much beauty as you did. I just made a note of the things that might be trying to kill me one day, like the guns in the batteries and forts.'

'But has all that *really* helped you now – as we sail out?'

'Oh yes, although I was gambling that the commandant of the port, or the commander of the artillery, or the commander of the garrisons, would all disagree about whose responsibility it was to warn the forts.'

'Do you have to gamble when you're on your honeymoon?'

He squeezed her arm. 'It's better for the family fortunes to gamble with roundshot rather than dice!'

Sarah laughed and nodded. 'Yes, I suppose so: if a roundshot knocks her husband's head off, at least his widow has the estate. But if he gambles at backgammon tables she has a husband with a head, but no bed to sleep in!'

Ramage stood at the taffrail of the *Murex* in the darkness and mentally drew a cross on an imaginary chart to represent the brig's position. She was now clearing the gulf of the Iroise, which stretched from the high cliffs and ruined abbey of Pointe St Mathieu over there to starboard across to the Camaret peninsula to larboard.

Ahead was the Atlantic, and the English Channel was to the north, round Ushant, which stood like a sentry off the northwestern tip of France. The Bay of Biscay, with Spain and Portugal beyond, was to the south. Astern, to everyone's relief, was Brest, and about 300 miles due east of it was Paris.

So that was it: from here, a tack out to the northwestward for the rest of the night and then dawn would reveal Ushant to the northeast, so that he could then bear away. He then had a choice: either he could run with a soldier's wind to the Channel Islands to get more men (having the advantage of a short voyage with such a small ship's company), or he could stretch north (perhaps nor'nor'east, he had not looked at the chart yet) for Falmouth or Plymouth.

The advantage of either port was that once he reported and handed over the *Murex,* he and Sarah could post to London or go over to the family home at St Kew, not far from either port. On second thoughts London would be better: their Lordships would certainly need written reports, and it would do no harm to be available when Lord St Vincent read them, concerning both his escape and the size and readiness of the French fleet in Brest, and the *Murex* episode.

Anyway, the *Murex* was now making a good six or seven knots; the courses had been set once they were safely out in the estuary and drawing well. A couple of seamen at the wheel were keeping the ship sailing fast, with Swan occasionally peering down at one or the other of the dimly lit compasses in the binnacle, his confidence restored.

Sarah was asleep down in the captain's cabin; Ramage himself was weary but warm at last, thanks to Sarah finding a heavy cloak in the captain's cabin and bringing it up to him. Dawn was not far off and the sky was clear with the moon still bright, although there was now a chill greyness that seemed to be trying to edge aside the black of night. The *Murex* was not just butting wind waves with her weather bow and scattering them in spray that drifted across like a scotch mist, salting the lips and making the eyes sore: now she was lifting over Atlantic swells that were born somewhere out in the deep ocean.

Very well, he told himself, the time had come to make the decision so that the moment daylight revealed Ushant on the horizon, he could give Swan the new course, for Falmouth, Plymouth or the Channel Islands.

Or southwestward, to start a 4,000-mile voyage to Cayenne, without orders, without much chance of success, to try to rescue Jean-Jacques and the other fifty or so people declared enemies of the French Republic?

He walked back and forth beside the taffrail and then stood looking astern at the *Murex*'s curling wake. There was one thing in the brig's favour. One thing in *his* favour, he corrected himself (there was no point in trying to shift the responsibility on to the poor *Murex*). Yes, the one thing in his favour was that he knew he was only a few hours behind *L'Espoir*. As a frigate she was much bigger, but more important she had fifty extra people on board, all of whom had to be kept under guard. So the frigate would be carrying extra men, seamen or soldiers, to make up the guard. Twenty-five? Extra in the sense that they were in addition to the normal ship's company. Whoa, not so fast; she was armed *en flûte,* so she would have only the guns on the upperdeck, say half a dozen 12-pounders. And that – being armed *en flûte* – meant she needed only sufficient men to fight six or eight guns, not the thirty or so which had been removed to make room for the prisoners. Against that, the French in Brest were very short of seamen: that had been the last piece of information given out by that wretched bosun before Sarah shot him. The *Commandant de l'Armée navale de Brest* would certainly favour fighting ships at the expense of transports like *L'Espoir*.

Yet the French were in a hurry to get these prisoners on their way to Cayenne before the British re-established their standing blockade of Brest, which would otherwise have made the capture of *L'Espoir* a distinct possibility. In turn that could also mean that these fifty prisoners were of considerable importance: people that Bonaparte wanted out of France at any cost and incarcerated in Devil's Island.

So apart from the importance of Jean-Jacques – which from the Royalist point of view was considerable – what about the others? What value would the British government put on them? In other words, if Captain Ramage acting without orders attempted with a brig and a dozen or so men a task for which a fully-manned frigate would not be too much, and succeeded, what then? Pats on the head, a page in the *London Gazette,* a column or so in the next issue of the *Naval Chronicle,* the grudging but heavily-qualified approval of the First Lord.

But if Captain Ramage failed in this self-appointed role of rescuer riding a (borrowed) white horse, what then? Well, the resulting court-martial would make the trial establishing his father as a scapegoat for the government look like a hunt cancelled because of heavily frozen ground. At best, Captain Ramage would spend the rest of his life on half-pay. At worst? Well, at least being cashiered with the disgrace of being 'rendered incapable of further service in his Majesty's Naval Service'.

Yet it really boiled down to ignoring the Admiralty. By chance he had been able to recapture a British brig from the enemy, and without his activity the *Murex* would have been added to the French Navy. That was where the chance ended. Did he owe it to Jean-Jacques to try to rescue him? A debt of honour? That was using a rather high-flown phrase, but supposing Ramage had been seized and taken off to some improbable prison, and Jean-Jacques had escaped and knew where he was? Jean-Jacques would attempt a rescue. That was all there was to it, really, although the Admiralty would certainly not agree.

To make an enormous dog-leg course to call at Plymouth to get provisions, men and water would wreck everything because it would probably mean that a couple of frigates would be sent in his place, and a vital week lost – at least a week; more if there was bad weather. It would take a couple of days to convince the port admiral at Plymouth of the importance of such a rescue and pass a message to the Admiralty (though with the new telegraph, Plymouth could send a signal to London and get a reply in a few hours), then watering and provisioning the frigates would take another day or so ... By the time they were clear of the Chops of the Channel (and perhaps driven back by a westerly storm or gale) *L'Espoir* would be a third of the way to Cayenne; a third of the way to the Île du Diable. At this moment, though, the *Murex* brig was only a matter of hours behind her. Yet without enough men to do any good and perhaps short of provisions and water. But no more than fifty miles ... If *L'Espoir* had careless or apathetic officers of the deck, poorly set sails and inattentive men at the wheel, plus the feeling that once clear of Brest they were safe from the Royal Navy, the smaller *Murex*, sailed hard, would be able to make up the gap.

'I'm going below for half an hour,' he told Swan. 'Report when you can see Ushant.'

Sarah was awake, unused to the swinging cot, which was little more than a large hammock with a shallow, open-topped frame fitted in it, like a box in a net bag.

'I preferred going to and from India,' she said teasingly. 'A proper bed is more comfortable.'

'You wait until there's rough weather. Going to windward in a blow and that cot will swing comfortably, while a fixed bed tosses you out.'

'How do I get out of it, anyway?'

'You don't; you're marooned!'

'Do you want to get some sleep?' she offered, sitting up with her tawny hair tousled, naked because she had only the clothes she had worn in the fishing boat. The lantern light seemed to gild her and he turned away quickly, reassuring her and telling her to stay in the cot. Stay in the cot, he thought to himself, or the captain will not concentrate on his charts ...

He put the lantern on the hook in the beam just forward of the desk. The charts were rolled and stowed vertically in a rack fitted on one side of the desk. Checking what charts were there meant removing each one and partly unrolling it. He sat at the desk and made a start. English Channel, western section, including the Scilly Islands; English Channel, eastern section, including the mouth of the Thames and the Medway. North Sea ... in four sections. Ireland, the southern half. The Channel Islands. St Malo to Ouessant (the French spelling and the detail showed it was probably copied from a captured one). Ushant to Brest and south to Douarnenez ... Those were probably the charts for her last patrol ... Half a dozen more left. North Atlantic, southern section ...

Ramage unrolled it. It covered from the southwestern corner of Spain to the eastern side of the West Indian islands, and down to the Equator, yet giving very little detail of the South American coast. There was Trinidad – which anyway could be identified by its shape. No reference to Cayenne, though; it must be about there, just a kink in the ink line of the coast, north of Brazil.

He looked at the remaining charts. A French one of the islands of St Barthélemy, St Martin (with the southern half owned by the Dutch and given its Dutch name, St Maarten), Anguilla and well to the north, just a speck, Sombrero. Then another two of the group just to the southward, Nevis and St Christopher. And two more, St Eustatius and Saba. A detailed chart of Plymouth ... and Falmouth ... and, finally, the Texel, showing the northwestern corner of the Netherlands.

All in all, Ramage thought wryly, he was no better off than he would be with a blank sheet of paper and his memory; in fact he was going to have to draw up a chart or two for himself. For the moment, though, he had to try to put himself in the French captain's place.

When sailing from Europe to the West Indies or the northern part of South America, the trick was to pick up the Trade winds as soon as possible without getting becalmed in the Doldrums. Which meant sailing where you could be reasonably sure of finding steady winds. Every captain and every master had his own invisible signpost in the Atlantic; a sign which said 'Turn southwest here; this is where the northeast Trade winds begin.'

For Ramage it was 25° North latitude, 25° West longitude. And – he took a pencil from the desk drawer and a crumpled sheet of paper which he smoothed out enough to make it usable.

According to the copied French chart, St Louis church in the centre of Brest, just north of the Château, was 48° 23′ 22″ North, 4° 29′ 27″ West. That, within a mile, was where L'Espoir had sailed from, and she was bound first to the magic spot, 25° North,

25° West. Which ... was ... about ... yes, roughly seventeen hundred miles to the south-southwest.

Then, from the magic point it was to Cayenne ... about ... another 2,000 miles, steering southwest by west. Say 4,000 miles altogether, and let no one think that steering southwest by west from the magic point would bring him or his ship to Cayenne: he would probably start running out of the Trades by the time he reached 12° North; from then on he would be trying to fight his way south against a foul current which ran northwest along the coast of Brazil. Caught in the right place, it helped; but if the wind played about, whiffling round the compass (which it could do in those latitudes) then the current would sweep the helpless ship up towards the islands – towards Barbados, for example, where the British commander-in-chief was probably lying at anchor in Carlisle Bay.

Ramage looked at his brief calculations again and then screwed them up.

Sarah asked: 'When do you think we shall be in Plymouth if this weather holds, dearest?'

'In about three months.'

'No, seriously. Our families will be worrying.'

'I expect the Rockleys will be worrying about you, but mine will make a wrong guess and give a sigh of relief that I am safely locked up in a French prison while they will expect you to be lodging with a respectable French family.'

'Is that how it would have been, normally?'

He shrugged his shoulders. 'I should think so. Anyway, my parents will not be worrying, and I'm sure as soon as they get the word they will be calling on your people.'

'But we'll be back in London before then, won't we?'

He was sure she suspected the idea that was popping in and out of his mind like an importunate beggar.

She said, in a flat voice: 'It would be madness to go after *L'Espoir*. You'll lose the *Murex* and everyone on board. A scout's job is to raise the alarm, dearest. Losing everything won't help Jean-Jacques, but getting help will ...'

He nodded and was startled when she said: 'You took so long to make up your mind.'

She was making it easier for him, and he took the opportunity as gracefully as possible. 'I needed to give it a lot of thought.'

She sat up in the cot, swung her legs out on to the deck and holding one end firmly stood up. She walked over to him and,

111

standing to one side, gently held his head against her naked body. 'You had two choices, dearest, Cayenne or Plymouth. Two choices. But you know as well as I do there was really only one that you could take.'

'Yes, but ...'

'But in the same circumstances another captain would have had only one choice: he would have gone to Plymouth!'

He nuzzled against her, his unshaven face rasping slightly on her warm skin, his chin pressing gently against her breasts. 'I suppose most other captains wouldn't have to choose because they do not usually meet people like Jean-Jacques.'

CHAPTER EIGHT

Ramage had just gone on deck after Swan called that they could now sight Ushant, and the deck lookouts had been sent aloft when both men heard the hail.

'Deck here!'

'Foremost lookout, sir: sail ho! Two sail!'

'Where away?'

'Two points on the starboard bow, sir, frigates I reckon.'

'Very well, keep a sharp lookout.'

Swan turned to Ramage, saw that he was already looking over the bow, and heard him cursing. 'Those blasted mutineers – I wish they'd left us the bring-'em-near. Even a nightglass!'

'They must have spotted us ten minutes ago, probably more. They'll recognize the rig...'

'And guess we're the *Murex* – perhaps sailing under the French flag?'

Ramage shook his head. News did not travel that fast. 'I doubt if the Admiralty yet know anything about the mutiny. In a day or two they'll read about it in the *Moniteur*: half a page of French bombast about oppressed English seamen fighting for their *liberté, fraternité* and *égalité*.'

'Yes,' Swan said bitterly, 'at the price of treason and making sure that fifteen of their shipmates go into a French prison.'

'That's what is meant by *fraternité*,' Ramage said laconically.

'That westernmost frigate has tacked,' commented Phillips, who had come on deck when he heard the hail.

'And the other one is bearing away a point or so,' Ramage noted. 'They're taking no chances. If we try to make a bolt for it, one can catch us to windward ánd the other to leeward.'

'But they recognize our rig,' Swan protested. 'The French don't have any brigs like this one!'

'They had one briefly, until last night,' Ramage said. 'Remember, in wartime all sails are hostile until they prove themselves otherwise. I presume we still have a set of signal flags.'

'Yes, sir,' Swan said and took the hint. 'I'll have our pendant numbers bent on ready.'

'Deck there!' Once again the lookout was shouting from the masthead, the pitch of his voice rising with excitement.

'Deck here,' Swan called back.

'More sail, sir, just beyond those frigates. Must be a couple of dozen, I reckon, and some of them seventy-fours and bigger.'

'Count 'em, blast it!' Swan shouted. 'Divide 'em up and count 'em.'

Ramage counted the days since the declaration of war. Yes, it might be. Indeed, if there were ships of the line it had to be, so there would be an admiral. Which meant so much explaining to be done; so much persuading to be done.

'Deck there, foremasthead here . . . I'm counting as we lift up on the swell waves, sir . . . Looks like at least six o' the line – one of 'em bigger'n a seventy-four – and seven frigates, including the first two.'

'Very well,' Swan said. 'Report if you sight more.' He turned to Ramage. 'Well, sir, can't be French and I don't think they're Spanish.'

'No, it'll be the Channel Fleet coming out to blockade Brest again . . . Well, they've had eighteen months' rest, but winter will soon be here.'

Phillips gave a dry laugh. 'The equinoctial gales will be along . . . then they'll dream of being "Close up with the Black Rocks with an easterly wind"!'

Both Ramage and Swan laughed, but both were thankful they were not serving in the blockading fleet. The Black Rocks . . . The description really stood for the twenty-five or thirty miles from the island of Ushant in the north to the Île de Sein in the south and, covering the entrance to Brest rather than the Rocks themselves, must make up the most iron-bound coast in the world: for almost every day of the year it was a lee shore wide open to the full fury of the Atlantic.

Yet by a quirk of nature the ships of the Royal Navy, forced to blockade Brest, were fortunate. The French fleet could leave Brest only with an easterly wind. A strong wind with much west in it left them unable to beat out of the Gullet and meant that they were also blockaded by nature.

The blockading British fleet's line-of-battle ships could stay twenty, thirty or even forty miles out to sea, so that they had plenty of room when the westerly Atlantic gales turned into storms lasting a week ... A captain with his ship under storm canvas could pull down his newly-tarred sou'wester and curse that he had ever chosen the Navy, but apart from keeping station on the admiral if possible (it never was in a full storm) it was more miserable than dangerous.

As a precaution a line of frigates, each within sight of the other, linked the fleet with the French coast. But with west in the wind the admiral could be sure that nature was his ally, keeping the French penned in. France was in fact unlucky because the perfidious English had along their Channel coast large and sheltered harbours which they could enter whatever the weather – Plymouth, Dartmouth, Falmouth, Portsmouth and the area inside the Isle of Wight, Dover and the Thames estuary.

The French were plagued with much higher tides and all their main Channel harbours – Calais, Havre de Grâce, Cherbourg and Boulogne – were artificial. The first of any size which was natural was Brest – which, as the Admiralty stated it – was 'outside Channel limits'.

So a west wind kept the French penned in; but the situation changed immediately the windvane on the church of St Louis de Brest swung round: an east wind tried to blow the blockading Royal Navy out to sea and gave the French a fair wind for slipping out of the Gullet while the blockaders beat back again to close the door.

Indeed, as Ramage knew from experience, that is why the blockading fleet had the frigates – as soon as the wind turned east the British frigates moved close up to the Black Rocks: close in with the Black Rocks, a couple of miles seaward of Pointe St Mathieu. They were, he reflected, a suitable name for rocks when you were commanding a frigate on a dark night in an easterly gale and peering with salt-sore and weary eyes for a sight of the white collars of breaking seas that would enable you to give hasty helm and sail orders to save the ship.

'Close up with the Black Rocks with an easterly wind' – words written on most midshipmen's hearts, and worthy of being carved on many a captain's tombstone, Ramage thought wryly. Still, it was worse for the admirals – they might have to spend a couple of years out here, shifting their flag from ship to ship while captains and seamen had a brief rest when they returned to Plymouth for water, provisions or repairs. The wear and tear on masts, spars and cordage keeping a close blockade off somewhere like Brest was beyond belief.

With her courses furled, the *Murex* was lying hove-to, her backed foretopsail trying to push her bow one way and maintopsail to turn it the other and the pair of them leaving the brig in a state of equilibrium, rising and falling on the swell waves like a resting seagull.

'The cutter is ready to be hoisted out, sir,' Swan reported. 'Two of the Frenchmen, seeing how short-handed we are, volunteered as boat's crew. Six men should be enough in this wind and sea.'

Ramage nodded. 'Someone is standing by to help Bridges with the flags?'

'Yes, sir.'

'And you can guess what the first signal will be.'

'I think so, sir,' Swan said with a grin.

The two frigates, one approaching from the north and the other from the northeast, were a fine sight: both had all plain sail set to the royals and Ramage guessed the one to the northeast was commanded by the senior of the two captains – the other was deliberately letting her reach the brig first.

Sarah, standing beside him and wearing her hastily repaired dress, said quietly as she watched the frigates: 'Should I go below, out of sight?'

'Most certainly not!' Ramage said. 'I'm anxious to show off my new bride! No,' he added, 'we have no signal book and very few men, so we want these fellows to guess at once that something's wrong. We don't want them to rush past hoisting a string of flag signals giving silly orders we can't read.'

'Can they give you orders?'

'Yes, if they are senior. If they were made post before me, in other words.'

'If their names are above yours in the *List of the Navy*? How will you know that, without looking them up in Mr Swan's copy as soon as you are introduced?'

Ramage grinned complacently. 'I know the names of the thirty or so lieutenants who were above me in my year, and all those in the two preceding years, so it's not too difficult!'

'What do you think will happen now? I was just beginning to look forward to the idea of getting back to London.'

'I don't know. It might be difficult to persuade the Admiral that fifty French Royalists being transported have any importance.'

'Who will the admiral be?'

'I don't know. Lord St Vincent commanded the Channel Fleet until the change of government saw him made First Lord. Now the war has started again, who knows . . .'

'Perhaps Lord Nelson. You know him, so it shouldn't be too difficult . . .'

'Perhaps, but I doubt it. After Copenhagen, I don't think the public – which means the politicians – would want to see him doing blockade duty. You don't have to be a brilliant tactician to blockade Brest.'

'No, but you need to be a brilliant tactician if the French fleet sails from Brest and you have to stop it!'

She was sharp-witted and wide awake. Ramage had to admit that, and said: 'You're right, and from what we saw in Brest, that admiral over there' – he nodded towards the British ships of the line beating up towards Ushant – 'will have to stay awake.'

The French coast was beginning to drop below the horizon: the coast of gaunt, high cliffs was now little more than a thick pencil line on the eastern horizon.

Sarah gestured towards it: 'I think our honeymoon is officially at an end now. Have you enjoyed it, dearest?'

'If honeymoons are always as exciting as this, I think I will get married more often!'

She wrinkled her nose at him. 'I didn't care much for the company, but I enjoyed seeing France.'

'Ah, yes, the French way of life. One of the most complex of life's puzzles: how can such selfish people create such an interesting atmosphere? It must be a quirk of the weather,' he added teasingly. 'Take away the wine and the cheese and what do you have left?'

'Lots of *gendarmes* at the *barrières*!'

Swan coughed as he approached. 'The easternmost frigate, sir: she's hoisted the Union at the mizen topmasthead and our pendant.'

'Very well, acknowledge and hoist out the cutter.'

'Aye, aye, sir.' Swan paused a moment, looking embarrassed.

'Well?' Ramage said, eyebrows raised. 'Say it!'

'I was wondering, sir, if you'd sooner wear breeches – I have a spare pair left which would fit.'

'No – they'll have to put up with a *sans-culotte*. They're good French fisherman's trousers, and this smock – why it smells more of potatoes than fish!'

A slatting of canvas made Ramage glance up to see the frigate tacking to the northwest. He guessed she would stand on for a mile or so, tack again until she was half a mile to windward of the *Murex*, and then heave-to.

'They've not heard about the mutiny,' Ramage said loudly and both Swan and Sarah swung round.

'They haven't, sir? How can you be sure?'

'Guns,' Ramage said laconically. 'Neither ship has her guns run out. Not the way you'd approach a mutinous ship.'

And probably all her captain wants to know, so he can make a signal to the admiral and show that he is awake, is what ships we have sighted recently in the area, because we look as though we are on a regular patrol.

The *Murex*'s cutter was hoisted out, Ramage was on board and the men bending their backs to the oars by the time the frigate had hove-to. At the last moment Swan had shouted down that she was the *Blanche*; that the lookout had been able to read her name on her transom and one of the seamen had recognized her.

Fifteen minutes later the cutter was alongside; the *Blanche*'s seamen caught the painter the first time it was thrown (by Auguste, Ramage noted) but missed the sternfast, but even before the officer of the deck began shouting Ramage had jumped for the battens and was scrambling up the side.

At the top, the moment he stepped on deck, a lieutenant stood in front of him.

'Stand aside, blast you: your captain is the first up!'

The senior officer was always the last in and the first out of a boat, and instead of the expected young lieutenant falling over his sword and with his hat awry, here was a man dressed more like a fisherman!

'I am the captain,' Ramage said quietly. 'Before you –'

'Master-at-arms!' roared the lieutenant, 'get this man out of my way!'

'– before you make a fool of yourself, lieutenant,' Ramage repeated without changing the tone of his voice, 'I suggest you listen because I shan't tell you twice.'

The lieutenant, tall and plump but with a weak mouth and chin hinting at self-indulgence, paused a moment and for the first time looked at Ramage's face. The deep-set eyes, the slightly hooked nose, the thick eyebrows . . .

'Who the hell are *you*?' he demanded.

Ramage realized that this must be the frigate's first lieutenant, and the captain would be down in his cabin.

'Most of the ship's company of that brig mutinied last week and ran her into Brest. I and a few others recaptured her and sailed her out last night. Now, either fetch your captain or take me to him.'

'And who the devil do you think *you* are, to give *me* orders.'

'My name is Ramage.'

'Well, you can dam' well – Ramage? Lord Ramage?'

The man in fisherman's clothes just nodded his head.

'Oh my God, sir, I had no way –'

'I know that. Your captain . . . ?'

'Of course, sir, at once.'

'Who is he?'

'Captain Wells, sir. Captain John Wells.'

The man then ran the few steps to the companionway, watched open-mouthed by the *Blanche*'s master and a lieutenant of Marines, who stood too far away to hear the conversation but had seen their first lieutenant move like a recoiling gun.

Wells . . . John Wells. No, that name was not in the last list of post-captains that Ramage had seen, so he must have been made post after Ramage and therefore was junior to him. That was one hurdle cleared; there was nothing like a little seniority . . . And it probably meant that he was senior to the other frigate captain, too. It should not be too difficult to get a dozen men to help sail the *Murex*.

'If you'll come this way, sir . . .'

The lieutenant combined nervousness, doubt, uncertainty and embarrassment into an interesting melange which manifested itself in him taking off his hat, turning it round completely, and putting it on again.

'You did say "Lord Ramage", didn't you, sir?'

'You said "Lord": I merely said "Ramage". I don't use my title in the Service.'

'No, quite, sir: I remember in the *Gazette*... It is simply that we did not expect...'

Ramage turned aft towards the companionway, feeling smug at his self-control: the temptation of pointing at the unmanned guns and closed ports had been almost irresistible.

Captain Wells had been given post rank late in life: Ramage guessed he was well past fifty, and like his first lieutenant he was plump, and what would have otherwise been a pleasant face with sandy eyebrows was spoiled by eyes too close together.

Now he stood at the bottom of the companionway staring up at the apparent fisherman coming down the steps with all the assurance of a Gascon. Not, Ramage thought to himself, that Captain Wells would know the meaning of 'Gasconade' or its derivation. Nor did Wells know how he was going to get any proof of the extraordinary story that the first lieutenant had just gabbled out.

Wells gave himself time by saying: 'Won't you come in?'

Ramage remembered that his own cabin, couch and sleeping place in the *Calypso* frigate were larger: the French allowed their captains more room.

Wells gestured towards the single armchair and while Ramage sat down, seated himself at the desk and began taking the cap from an ink bottle.

'Ah ... well now, perhaps you had better report to me in your own words and if you'll speak slowly, I'll write –'

'No reports, written or otherwise, to anyone except the commander-in-chief,' Ramage said flatly. 'My name is Ramage, and I do not have my commission but you can confirm the date from your copy of Steel's List, which I see you have on your desk. I was in France on my honeymoon – you have no doubt seen my wife on the *Murex*'s quarterdeck – when the war started again. We escaped arrest, saw the *Murex* being brought in with a French escort and discovered that most of her ship's company had mutinied. The officers and a dozen or so loyal seamen were left on board and my wife and I' – Ramage decided Gilbert and the others would forgive the exaggeration – 'with the help of four

119

Frenchmen overpowered the guards, freed our men, and sailed the ship out of Brest. Then you came along.'

'But look here, I've no proof –'

'You don't need any, Wells,' Ramage snapped. 'Send a dozen of your men over to help those poor souls sail the *Murex,* and make a signal to the admiral. You'll have fun with the Signal Book. I don't recall anything which quite covers this situation.'

'But Ramage, I can't –'

'Tell the admiral why you can't, Wells, but I'll tell you just one more thing, after which I want a dozen topmen sending down to my cutter and I'll be off to join the fleet. Time, Wells, hours and minutes rather than days: I am desperate to save time.' With that Ramage was out through the door and halfway up the companionway before Wells had time to draw a breath.

He was calling to the first lieutenant to have his boat ready when Wells came up the companionway, took one more look (a despairing look, it seemed to Ramage) and seeing his first lieutenant busy, called to the master to send a dozen topmen down into the boat without waiting for them to collect their gear.

'You *will* let me have them back?' he called after Ramage, as anxious as any captain to keep prime seamen.

'Yes – as soon as we're hove-to near the flagship. You can escort us down there!'

CHAPTER NINE

Reginald Edward Clinton, knight, vice-admiral of the blue, was a bachelor and, Ramage decided at first sight, every child's idea of what Father Christmas should look like. He was plump and round-faced, the red complexion contrasting with a pair of startlingly blue eyes, which rarely moved. The admiral had a habit of swivelling his whole head when he wanted to shift his gaze. The effect, Ramage decided, was like aiming a gun.

But Admiral Clinton was decisive. He listened to Ramage's story without interruption and then asked a series of questions, starting with those referring to the beginning of Ramage's visit to France and ending with a request for the numbers and rates of the French ships anchored in Brest. After writing down the figures and the state of readiness of each of them, he put the cap back on the inkwell, wiped the tip of his quill pen with a piece of cloth and said casually: 'You captured and then commanded the *Calypso*, didn't you?'

'Yes, sir. I still do – or did. She was being paid off and laid up at Chatham when I went on leave.'

'Hmm. Well, she wasn't actually paid off – the war was started again. In fact I have her with me. Commanded by a fellow called Bullivant.'

'Edward Bullivant, sir, son of the Navy Board contractor?'

'The same one,' the admiral said, his voice flat. 'What sort of officers did you have?'

'Not one I would change – indeed, sir, not one I would ever want to exchange.'

'Master?'

'A man called Southwick. He'd been with me from the time I was given my first command.'

'And the surgeon?' Clinton asked casually.

'A brilliant man. Used to have a practice in Wimpole Street.'

'Oh? Then why is he now simply a surgeon in a frigate?'

'Drink, sir. Lost all his patients. Came to sea.'

'That explains it all,' Clinton said, obviously relieved.

Ramage quickly decided to risk a snub. 'May I ask what it explains, sir?'

'Well, had a dam' strange signal from her at daybreak. Number 215 over her own pendant.'

Ramage thought for several moments. There were more than four hundred numbered signals in the book and 215 was not one he had ever seen hoisted or heard anyone refer to.

Clinton said: 'Number 215 means: *The physician of the Fleet is to come to the Admiral.* But hoisted over the *Calypso*'s pendant numbers I assume she is trying to reverse it – asking for the physician of the fleet to go to the *Calypso*.'

Physician. Ramage realized the significance of the word. Most frigates and all ships of the line had surgeons, but physicians were different. There were between two and three hundred surgeons in the Navy but only three physicians – Dr Harness (who had given his name to a special sort of cask), Dr Trotter (who was a friend of Lord St Vincent) and Dr Travis One of them would be on board this flagship.

121

'Why would she be wanting the *physician*?' Clinton asked, although it was obvious the question was rhetorical.

'The Signal Book, sir,' Ramage said. 'I don't think there is any signal for requesting medical assistance.'

'But why should she need it? Perhaps the surgeon has drunk himself stupid.'

Ramage realized that he had not completed his reference to Bowen. 'I think not, sir: his first ship was the *Triton* brig, which I commanded, and he stopped drinking.'

Clinton smiled benevolently: he was making allowances for the pride of a young captain.

'Not Bowen, sir – that's the surgeon. He was cured.'

'Who achieved *that* miracle?' Clinton demanded.

'Well, sir, the master and I saw him through the worst of it. As I said, he's a very intelligent man. A wonderful chess player.'

'Hmm – I hope he isn't trying to make pawns of us. She has the same officers and ship's company; only Bullivant is new. What do you think is going on?'

Had Bowen started drinking again? Or been injured himself? In that case, Bullivant would have asked one of the other frigates to send over her surgeon.

'Where is the *Calypso*, sir? I did not see her.'

'Some distance up to the northwest, in company with the *Blackthorne* frigate.'

'So she would be close enough to ask the *Blackthorne* to send over her surgeon?'

'Yes. The *Blackthorne* is nearer to us and relayed this strange signal. Who the devil would have thought up 215 over a pendant – it's clever, if they really need the physician of the fleet.'

'Or the physician's authority,' Ramage said and then realized that he had inadvertently spoken aloud what was only a random thought.

'What's that you say?' the admiral demanded. 'Authority? Medicine is what they want, I'd have thought.'

In for a penny, in for a pound, Ramage thought, and time was passing and he still had to persuade the admiral about *L'Espoir*. 'I was trying to see it from the *Calypso*'s point of view, sir. Sickness, fractures – all these can be dealt with by a surgeon. I was trying to see what the physician of the fleet had that a surgeon would not have, and medically – with respect – there'd be nothing of consequence. But the physician of the fleet would have *authority*. He would be reporting direct to you, and he could act on your authority...'

'But what the devil does the *Calypso* want to bother me about?' Clinton growled. 'I don't care if the second lieutenant has just ruptured himself: that's why she has a surgeon. Can't be scurvy or anything like that – we left Plymouth only a couple of days ago.'

Southwick, Aitken, Bowen, young Paolo, Jackson, Stafford – Ramage felt a great nostalgia. The Admiralty (having no choice) had appointed a new captain to the *Calypso*, but she would always be his ship: he had captured her from the French, refitted her in the West Indies, chosen her new name, taken her into action ... He knew every man on board and had promoted most of the officers. Every seaman had been in action with him several times and people like Jackson, Stafford and Rossi had saved his life – and he theirs, for that matter.

'Sir, whatever it is, I'm sure it's serious and unusual. I know Bullivant only by report, but I do know my officers. The first lieutenant, Aitken, thought of the signal: I'm sure of that. He's a very responsible young officer.' He remembered Clinton's slight accent and added: '– and comes from an old Scots family with naval connections.'

Clinton scratched his head, doubtful about something, although Ramage could not guess what. 'Let me think about it. Now, are we finished with this *Murex* mutiny business? I want a list of names of the mutineers, of course, and all the loyal seamen, and the warrant and commission officers, who can give evidence against them. The brig's first lieutenant can deal with that. The Navy Board will have the last Muster Book, so they can print up some posters naming these mutinous rascals. They'll have to serve in French and neutral ships, or starve, you'll see, and we'll catch 'em and stab 'em with a Bridport dagger, just like we did those villains from the *Hermione*.'

Admirals rarely used slang – at least, Ramage had not heard them – but 'Bridport dagger' was very appropriate. Some of the Navy's best rope, particularly hemp, came from the Dorset town of Bridport, and hemp was always used for the hangman's noose. The seamen, with their liking for the bizarre euphemism, had soon tied the town, the hemp, the noose and death into one tidy phrase.

'I'll have the list for you, sir, and that rounds off the *Murex* affair, but there is one factor: you remember I mentioned earlier that the Count of Rennes and about fifty other Royalists were being transported by Bonaparte to Devil's Island?'

Admiral Clinton nodded. 'Rennes? Isn't he the refugee fellow that has a place in England? Down at Ruckinge, I seem to remember. My place is at Great Chart, and my wife and I met him several times. A friend of the Prince Regent, I think.'

'The same person, sir. He came back to France at the peace. My wife and I were staying with him when he was arrested, as I was telling you, and his valet hid us. I have the valet on board the *Murex* – he's one of the four Frenchmen who helped me retake the ship.'

'The others – are they people like the Count?'

'I don't know who they are, sir, but *L'Espoir* was fitted out in great haste the moment Bonaparte heard that our ambassador was leaving Paris.'

'So we are too late to stop her escaping. *L'Espoir* is on her way to Devil's Island now.'

'She's only a few hours ahead, sir. She left Brest about half an hour ahead of the *Murex*.'

By now Admiral Clinton was lost in his own thoughts and talking to himself. 'Takes a frigate to catch a frigate – *en flûte*, you say, so she'll have fewer men and few guns . . . more guards because of the prisoners . . . Yes, I'd better spare a frigate: it'd be dashed difficult if the Prince heard that nothing had been done . . . but if I could take the Count of Rennes back with me . . . the frigate'd be a prize too, and there'd be my eighth . . .' He gave a startled jerk, as if surprised to find he was not alone in the cabin.

'Ah, Ramage. Yes, well, just had an idea about that dashed signal from the *Calypso*. You've got those extra men from Wells' frigate, so the *Murex* isn't short-handed now. Supposing you take her and go on board the *Calypso* and see what the devil it's all about. You know the ship so well.'

Ramage nodded and added the part that the admiral had omitted: 'It will save you detaching any of your frigates, too, sir.'

'Quite, quite,' Clinton said, as though the thought had never occurred to him. 'Give me time to think about the Count of Rennes and *L'Espoir*, so if I have any more questions later you can answer them when you get back from the *Calypso*.'

'If there is any urgency, sir, a situation which I think calls for the physician of the fleet, should I repeat 215 and the *Calypso*'s pendant?'

Clinton thought for a moment. 'That would also mean that this flagship had to come up to the *Calypso*?'

'Yes, sir. I was thinking only of saving time in a dire emergency.'

'Very well. But look 'ee Ramage, you're a sensible fellow. I've read all your *Gazettes*. Bit inclined to go your own way – that wouldn't do if you were serving under me, mind you – but you succeed. So my orders to you – I'll have them put in writing: it'll only take a couple of minutes – are to go on board the *Calypso*, and sort out whatever is the problem. I must hurry to get into position off Brest – from what you say, Bonaparte has several ships he'd like to get out before I arrive to shut the door. Now, wait on deck while I get my dam' fool secretary to write up your orders. Get the *Calypso*'s position from Captain Bennett, and anything else you need. Looks as if you'll need to visit your tailor as soon as possible.'

Ramage grinned. 'There's a lot to be said for trousers when you're climbing up a ship's side, sir; breeches are tight.'

Clinton said: 'Very well. Unless you find it absolutely necessary to hoist 215, you will come up and report to me personally. Use your discretion. I have an odd feeling about this *Calypso* affair ... Bullivant must have just been made post ... Influence of the father, I suppose ...' Again the admiral seemed to drift away in a reverie, and Ramage quietly left the cabin.

Captain Bennett took Ramage into his cabin and unrolled a chart. 'The fleet will be here' – he indicated a line thirty miles to the west of Ushant – 'and there'll be the usual frigates here, here, here and (providing this odd signal does not mean the *Calypso* has to go back to Plymouth) here. The admiral likes a couple of frigates with him, to investigate strange sail.

'Do you want to note down any latitudes and longitudes?' he asked.

Shaking his head, Ramage said: 'I should be reporting back in a few hours. How far do you estimate the *Calypso* is to the north?'

'Well, the *Blackthorne* is in sight of us and the *Calypso* can see her. Say twenty miles. This is a five-knot wind for a brig like the *Murex* – she must have a clean bottom.'

'She's clean,' Ramage said, 'but with only a dozen hands I haven't been pressing her!'

'A dozen, eh?'

'And four landmen, only one of whom speaks English!'

At that moment a bespectacled young man came into the cabin after the Marine sentry announced him.

He handed a slim volume and a sheet of paper to Ramage. 'A copy of the Signal Book and the admiral's orders, sir: he particularly wants you to read them before you leave the ship.'

Murmuring 'If you'll excuse me,' to Bennett, he read the copperplate handwriting and stylized wording. The phrases were dignified, those used by their Lordships and admirals for scores of years. They added up to the fact that whatever happened the man giving the orders took no responsibility for the results, while the man receiving them had no choice . . . However, in this case Admiral Clinton had obviously consulted Steel's List and found that Ramage was senior to Bullivant, and the orders, which of necessity were phrased with no knowledge of what was the matter, gave Ramage authority 'to rectify, make good, issue orders and otherwise do what is required for the benefit of the King's Service in relation to the vessel herein described'.

Ramage folded the orders and tucked the paper down the front of his shirt. 'If you'll excuse me,' he said to Captain Bennett and used his pen to sign the receipt for the orders and for the Signal Book which the young secretary had been holding out.

As he climbed down into the cutter he felt himself being pulled in two directions. Up to the north, something strange was happening to the *Calypso,* a ship he had come to love and a ship's company he regarded as his own family. Out to the west, *L'Espoir* was carrying Jean-Jacques and fifty other victims of Bonaparte to Devil's Island, which meant harsh imprisonment probably ended eventually by a quick death from the black vomit.

Ramage watched as the small cutter was hoisted on board and heard Swan preparing to get the *Murex* under way again. The extra dozen seamen would mean the *Murex* could stretch to the northward under courses as well as topsails.

As soon as Swan came aft, Ramage handed him the new copy of the Signal Book. 'Have someone sew up a canvas bag and find a weight to put in it. That Signal Book must be kept in the bag and the whole thing thrown over the side if . . .'

'Yes, sir,' Swan said. 'Anyway, now the ship isn't deaf and dumb any longer!'

'We might regret that,' Ramage said. 'The admiral will be changing all the signal numbers now the French probably have *Murex*'s original book.'

'Oh no, sir, I forgot to tell you. I was on deck when the mutiny started and the Signal Book and private signals were on the binnacle box. I managed to throw both over the side before the mutineers got control of the ship. I'll take an oath on that, sir.'

Ramage sighed with relief but said: 'I wish you'd told me that earlier. The admiral is already choosing the number to add to all those in the Signal Book, and drawing up new private signals.'

'Well, I know the penalties for signals, so . . .' Swan said, and both men knew the phrase usually added to them when they were issued. The new private signals handed over by the admiral's secretary, Ramage noted, had two paragraphs of warning: 'The captains and other officers to whom these signals are delivered are strictly commanded to keep them in their own possession, with a sufficient weight affixed to them to insure their being sunk if it should be found necessary to throw them overboard . . . As a consequence of the most dangerous nature . . . may result from the enemy's getting possession of these signals, if any officer . . . fail in observing these directions, he will certainly be made to answer for his disobedience at a Court Martial . . .'

Which was why Swan wanted to make it clear that he had disposed of the signals. But he would certainly be tried – a court-martial could clear a man of any suspicion just as well as it could find him guilty.

'You have witnesses?' Ramage said. 'You may need them.'

Swan said: 'Yes, I understand, sir. Phillips saw me, and the two men at the wheel, who did not mutiny.'

'Good, they'll be sufficient. Now, let's start carrying out our present orders. First, steer north-northwest, and warn the lookouts to watch for two frigates, one French-built. Both of them are well to the north of the fleet. We have to visit the northernmost one, the French-built.'

'Like your last ship, the *Calypso*,' Swan said, smiling at the thought.

'She is the *Calypso*,' Ramage said, and gestured towards the taffrail. As the two men walked up and down the windward side, out of earshot of the men at the wheel and the quartermaster, Swan pausing from time to time to shout orders through the speaking trumpet to get the brig under way, Ramage described what had happened, and why the *Murex* was being sent to the *Calypso*.

'Captain Bullivant,' Swan said. 'Just made post, obviously. We served together as lieutenants in the *Culloden*.'

'A pleasant fellow, eh?' Ramage said, realizing that Swan would be careful not to criticize one captain to another but hoping the man would realize that he needed to know as much as possible.

'He had his friends,' Swan said carefully. 'His father is one of the biggest contractors to the Navy Board.'

'I heard about that,' Ramage said. 'Salt meat, isn't it?'

'Yes, sir,' Swan said, unable to keep a bitter note out of his voice. 'You know, a cask of salt beef, and stencilled on the outside it says "Contains fifty-two pieces" . . .'

'And when the master counts them, there are only forty-seven,' Ramage finished the sentence. 'And although every ship in the Navy notes it down in the log – the contractor's number on the cask and the number of the pieces short – and although the log goes to the Admiralty and the Navy Board can trace the contractor in each case from the number, nothing is ever done about it.'

'But the Bullivants of this world and the people they bribe at the Navy Board get richer,' Swan said, thankful that the new temporary captain of the *Murex* needed only a pointing finger, not a detailed chart.

The two men walked over to the binnacle, and after a look at the compass card and a glance up at the luffs of the sails, Ramage nodded to the quartermaster.

He was, Ramage noted, one of the original men of the *Murex*, but Swan had already said that he was only an ordinary seaman. He wondered why the *Murex*'s captain had not rated the man 'able'. Perhaps he had a bad record, a good seaman but a heavy drinker. All too many men disobeyed the regulations and 'hoarded their tot' – instead of drinking their daily issue they kept it until the end of the week so they could get very drunk. They knew before they put aside the very first tot that if they got drunk they would probably be flogged, but all too many seasoned topers reckoned a dozen with the cat-o'-nine-tails a fair exchange for ending Saturday night in an alcoholic stupor.

With the wind almost on the beam, the brig was sailing fast. Already the line-of-battle ships making up the fleet were on the *Murex*'s starboard beam, and in half an hour they would be well aft on the quarter, their hulls beginning to sink below the horizon, hidden by the curvature of the earth.

There was little for him to do until the *Blackthorne* and the *Calypso* were sighted, so he went below to talk to Sarah. As soon as he saw her sitting on the settee, he remembered the family's London home in Palace Street. There Mrs Hanson, the butler's wife, was also the housekeeper, and Ramage had once heard her describe a disgruntled person as 'on the turn, like yesterday's milk in a thunderstorm'.

Sarah's expression showed that she was far from happy; Mrs Hanson would regard it as definitely curdled. No wonder the *Admiralty Instructions* forbade officers to take their wives to sea in wartime!

'So you're back,' she said bleakly. 'Are we bound for Plymouth now?'

'No, not yet,' he said. 'One of the frigates with the fleet is the *Calypso* and –'

'But she's yours!' Sarah exclaimed, suddenly coming to life.

He shook his head. 'With war breaking out so quickly and the First Lord having to send out a Channel Fleet, he would have taken every ship that could get to sea. Obviously the *Calypso* had not been paid off, so as I wasn't there a new captain was sent down and he took her round to Plymouth to join Admiral Clinton.'

'Clinton? The Scots family?'

'I think so: he speaks with a Scots accent. Why?'

'He was out in the East Indies once and I met him when he called on father. I think he's quite well regarded.'

'Yes, we're lucky he's commanding the Fleet.'

'It hardly matters, surely, if we are going to Plymouth.'

'Dearest, I have no idea whether we'll be sailing for Plymouth or Jamaica or the Cape of Good Hope. All I know is that Admiral Clinton has given me orders which I am carrying out. They should take only a few hours, but' – he softened his voice – 'they concern a ship, men and the sea, so nothing is certain.'

She gave a ghost of a smile, as if to start making up for her earlier tartness. A start, but by no means an acceptance of the fact she was now (for the first time in their brief marriage) very definitely the moon in her husband's life; the Navy was the sun. This was, of course, precisely what the Countess of Blazey had warned her about before the wedding. Sarah admitted to herself that she had thought Nicholas's mother was being too protective (of both of them) when she warned that Navy wives always came second. Well, that had not prevented the Countess's own marriage being a most successful one – the Earl of Blazey, apart from being one of the Navy's finest admirals until falling victim to politics, clearly loved and was loved by his wife.

'Am I allowed to know what Admiral Clinton's orders are?'

'Of course!' he said, snatching at the tiny olive branch which was being inspected rather than proffered. Quickly he explained how the *Calypso* had hoisted what seemed a bewildering signal. It took longer to explain that there were only three physicians in the entire Navy, while surgeons were numbered in hundreds, but she was intrigued.

'What do you expect to find?'

'I have absolutely no idea; nor has the admiral, which is why he is sending me.'

'But this new captain, Bullivant, what . . . ?'

'I'm sure he is not going to be very pleased to see me!'

'Why not? I should have thought that –'

He cut her short. 'Just imagine it. The *Calypso* is not famous but people know about her. I captured her, was put in command, and took her into action several times. All the officers and many of the ship's company would be regarded by a new captain as "my" men because normally he selects his own officers when commissioning the ship – certainly his first lieutenant and midshipmen, and probably the master.

'This wretched fellow Bullivant – I feel sorry for him. He knows that whatever he does, from how he wears his hat to the way he gives orders, everyone on board is comparing him with the previous captain. It can't give him much confidence. He must hate the thought of me – I know I should!'

'You wouldn't, you know: you'd just make sure you did everything better – and quicker, too. You are one of the lucky people who have confidence in themselves.'

Ramage's laugh was bitter. She could never guess the hours before going into action when he had completely lost confidence in himself and his plans, and would have changed them completely but for there being no time or no obvious alternative. Even as late as two nights ago, when he led the four Frenchmen and Sarah to capture the *Murex* – did she think he had no doubts and fears? Well, perhaps it was better if she (along with everyone who had served with him in the *Calypso*) thought he had not.

He heard shouting from aloft, and then Swan's question to the masthead lookout. 'Where away? . . . You are sure? . . . French built from the sheer? Very well, keep a sharp lookout!'

Then the shout from the top of the companionway, 'Captain, sir,' but by then Ramage had given Sarah a hasty kiss and his foot was already on the first step.

Swan repeated the bearing. 'Dead ahead, sir, and the lookout says he sees her well as we lift on the swell waves. Thought I glimpsed her sails for a moment.'

'Strange how helpless one feels without a bring-'em-near,' Ramage commented. 'I should have borrowed one from the flagship.'

'I can't see anyone giving up his glass, even for Captain Ramage,' Swan said jocularly.

'There!' called the master, 'I glimpsed a sail then. That's her, dead ahead!'

CHAPTER TEN

An hour later the brig and the frigate crossed tacks, the *Murex* passing half a mile ahead.

'No signals flying,' Swan commented.

'So I see. But now we are to windward of her, so hoist her pendant and make number 84.'

Swan snapped out an order to two seamen, who began hoisting the three flags forming the *Calypso*'s pendant numbers, and told two more to hoist eight and four.

'*Pass within hail,* isn't it, sir?' Swan asked. 'You have the book,' he said apologetically, 'but I'm presuming it hasn't been changed.'

'Yes, but whether or not Captain Bullivant chooses to obey is another question. He might assume a brig is still commanded only by a lieutenant.'

'I think if I was him and a brig tacked across my bow and gave a peremptory order, I'd assume she had a senior officer on board!'

'We'll see,' Ramage said. 'In the meantime, have 173 bent on and ready for hoisting, and have number one gun on the larboard side loaded with a blank charge. There's no need to send the men to quarters: have Bridges and a couple of men do it. Here's the key to the magazine. It was still in the desk drawer.'

Swan was enjoying himself hoisting flag signals with orders for Bullivant, that much was obvious, and his enjoyment revealed more about Bullivant than his earlier comments. Ramage handed him the Signal Book, knowing that the first lieutenant could not remember the meaning of 173.

He quickly leafed through the pages, which were cut at the side with the signal numbers printed in tens.

'Ah,' Swan said, 'a gun and that should produce results!'

'Yes, we'll tack again; they're ignoring 84.'

Ramage saw Bridges and two men running to the forward gun on the larboard side, where seamen in answer to Bridges' earlier shouted order were already casting off lashings.

Out came the tompion; a man held the flintlock in position and hurriedly tightened up the wing nut to clamp it down. The gun was quickly run in and a cartridge slid down the bore and rammed home. The gun was run out again, a quill tube pushed down the vent and priming powder shaken into the pan.

Bridges held up his hand in a signal to Ramage, who was watching the *Calypso* as she sailed on, approaching their starboard bow.

'Mr Swan, we'll pass very close across the *Calypso*'s bow . . .' Ramage gestured to the two seamen who had bent on the three flags representing the signal 173, *Furl sails*.

Ramage watched the *Calypso* out of the corner of his eye and said to the seamen: 'Leave up the pendant numbers but lower 84.'

By now Swan was bellowing orders and the brig's bow was turning to starboard, canvas slatting, the ropes of sheets and braces flogging, spray flying across like fine rain as the bow sliced the tops off waves. Then, with Swan giving the word to haul, the yards were braced round and sheets trimmed so the sails resumed their opulent curves. The *Murex* began to leap through the water again – right across the *Calypso*'s bow.

'Oh, nicely, nicely!' Swan exclaimed. 'Less than half a cable – we'll be able to throw a biscuit on to her fo'c'sle as we pass across her bow!'

'Stand by,' Ramage shouted, and saw the gun captain kneel with his left leg thrust out to one side, the triggerline taut in his right hand.

The *Calypso* was a fine sight, bow-on and just forward of the *Murex*'s beam. Men were peering over the bulwarks; Ramage thought he saw the lookout at the foremasthead gesturing down to the deck.

'Hoist 173!' Ramage said to the seamen and watched the three flags soaring upwards. He turned forward. 'Mr Bridges, fire!'

The gun spurted flame and smoke, and a moment later came the flat 'blam' of an unshotted gun firing, the standard signal drawing particular attention to a hoist of flags.

Ramage watched the *Calypso* for the first sign that she was altering course or clewing up sails. There was only one more signal that he could make (108, *Close nearer to the Admiral*) but if Bullivant ignored that too, what next?

Were the luffs of the courses fluttering slightly? As the *Murex* passed across the *Calypso*'s bows the frigate's masts had for a few moments been in line, but now the brig was hauling out on the *Calypso*'s beam and it was hard to distinguish an alteration of course. But ... yes ...

Swan exclaimed: 'She's bracing her courses sharp up, sir! Yes, I can see men going up the ratlines. There, she's starting to clew up!'

Ramage judged distances and times. Better than Bullivant he knew how long it would take to clew up the big forecourse and the maincourse, the lowest and largest sails in the frigate; then, as the *Calypso* slowed down the foretopsail would be backed, the yard braced sharp up so that the wind blew on the forward side. With well trained crew and Aitken and Southwick, she could be hove-to a good deal faster than the smaller but undermanned *Murex*.

'She's heaving-to,' Ramage told Swan. 'Cross her bow again and then as soon as we're to windward, heave-to.' Was there any point in sending the *Murex*'s men to general quarters? Ten guns, five each side, and only a dozen or so of the men had ever fired them. No one would know his position in a gun's crew. No, there would be chaos, and ten guns against the *Calypso*, with her well trained, experienced crew, would do about as much harm as the shrill cursing of bumboat women.

'As soon as we've hove-to, I want the cutter hoisting out to take me across to the *Calypso*.'

Swan looked anxious, his eyes flickering from Ramage to the frigate. 'Sir, Bridges and Phillips are quite competent to handle this ship. May I come with you to the *Calypso*? Not because I'm being nosy,' he added hastily, 'but I'd be happier if you had an escort.'

Ramage had been thinking not of an escort but of something that might prove more necessary. 'Yes – but you'll be coming as a witness. Keep your eyes and ears open. Try and remember exact phrases. I can't tell you more than that because I don't know what the devil we're going to find.'

As the cutter surged down and rounded up alongside the *Calypso*, Ramage recognized several of the faces watching from over the top of the bulwark, but no one was waving a greeting and no one was standing at the entryport.

Aitken? Southwick? Young Paolo? They must be on board, and although they could never expect to find their old captain arriving alongside in a brig's cutter, surely some of them would have recognized him by now, since he had deliberately stood up in the sternsheets of the cutter for the last hundred yards. Surely *someone* would be watching through a telescope. The whole episode of a brig making peremptory signals to a frigate was unusual enough to make the cutter's arrival a matter of considerable importance.

It seemed only a moment later that the cutter was alongside and Ramage leapt for the battens just as the cutter rose on a crest. He sensed that Swan was right behind him. A rope snaked down from the *Calypso* to serve as a painter.

No sideropes, so the *Calypso* was not extending the usual courtesy to the commanding officer of another ship o' war, but perhaps there had not been time to rig them. There had, of course, and Ramage knew it, but he also knew that when Aitken and Southwick proposed it, Bullivant might have refused.

Up, up, up . . . cling to the battens with your fingers, keep your feet flat against the side of the ship to prevent the soles of your shoes from slipping . . . Yes, that gouge in the wood there was so familiar and that scarph in the plank there . . . He could remember the actions in which the hull had been damaged.

Suddenly his head came level with the deck and a moment later he was through the entryport, standing on the deck itself and staring into the muzzle of a pistol held by a man he had never seen before but who was wearing the uniform of a post-captain. He had a single epaulet, showing he had less than three years' seniority, Ramage noticed inconsequentially.

'Stop!' the man bellowed. He was young, stocky, with a round face mottled with – was it anger? The pistol in his right hand was beautifully made, the barrel damascened, the silver and gold tracery of inlaid patterns catching the sun. The silver tankard in his left hand also had an intricate design worked all round it. And the man, who seemed too excited to string together a coherent sentence, took a pace forward as Swan stepped on deck.

'Stop, both of you!' He gestured with both hands as though shooing a hen back into her coop, and an amber liquid spilled from the tankard.

'You see, pirates! Look at him, a *sans-culotte*! A Republican pirate. And the other one . . .' he paused, catching his breath and then unexpectedly took a long drink from the tankard. '. . . He's wearing the . . . the *King*'s uniform . . .'

Ramage saw that the speech was becoming more slurred and the man's eyes were glazing. The man – Ramage guessed it must be Bullivant – turned and pointed. Ramage recognized the lieutenant in Marine's uniform as Renwick, now white-faced, fear showing in the way the lips were drawn back. Ramage had seen Renwick facing broadsides, muskets fired at close range, pistols from a few feet, dodging the slash of cutlasses, but the Marine officer always grinned because he loved battle. Fear? A moment later he realized why.

'Shoot these men!' Bullivant screamed. 'Come on, you have your file of Marines ready! The devil's work . . . that's what these French swine are doing . . .' His speech was slowing and Ramage glanced round.

There they all were, in a circle of men with fear on their faces: Aitken, the Scots first lieutenant, Wagstaffe, the red-haired and freckle-faced Kenton, his face red and peeling from the effect of wind and sun, young Martin, the fourth lieutenant, and old Southwick, his white mop of hair as usual trying to escape his hat and suddenly reminding Ramage of straw sticking out from under a nesting hen. And Paolo, his normally sallow face now white, his hooked nose bloodless, as though he was some young Italian model for a Botticelli painting.

Then Ramage saw that every one of the men on deck, seamen and Marines, was watching him, horrified by Bullivant's words. Renwick was making no move. The sergeant of Marines stood firm. Yes, they must be thinking, their old captain has by some magic come back, dressed as a French fisherman, and their new captain has just given orders to shoot him.

Now the signal for the physician of the fleet made sense: Bullivant had been driven mad by drink and presumably Aitken had hoisted that signal at a time when Bullivant could not see it – when he was below.

Where was the surgeon, Bowen? Even as Ramage glanced round once again, he saw the surgeon coming up the companion-way, carrying a big flask. Now everyone was watching Bowen, and Bullivant was smiling: it was the vapid smile of an idiot, ingratiating and welcoming.

'Ah, Mr Bowen ... Welcome, you bring me sustenance ... you see the demons I face.' He waved both pistol and tankard towards Ramage and Swan. 'Here, you are just in time.' He held out the tankard and Bowen poured liquid from the flask. Bullivant took a sip, swallowed and then gulped like a calf at a cow's udders.

Swan, pressing with his elbow, caused Ramage to look down. The *Murex*'s first lieutenant had a Sea Service pistol tucked in the waistband of his breeches and was trying to draw Ramage's attention to it while Bullivant, head back and tankard to his lips, had his eyes closed.

This situation was what every officer dreaded. Relieving a captain of his command was juggling with the risk of being charged with treason. What was madness on the high seas could appear to be perfectly sane behaviour when the captain soberly described it to a row of hard-faced officers forming a court-martial in the peace and quiet of a guardship's cabin in Plymouth or Portsmouth. The whole edifice of discipline was built on the authority of a senior officer – a seaman obeyed a bosun's mate who obeyed the bosun who obeyed a lieutenant who obeyed the captain who obeyed a captain senior to him or an admiral who obeyed the Admiralty: it was all in the Articles of War ... Many covered every aspect for maintaining command – numbers XIX, XXII (carrying the death penalty for anyone even lifting a weapon against a superior), and XXXIV ... and of course, XXXVI, the so-called captain's cloak, covering 'all other crimes' not covered by the Act. None provided the means of depriving a man of command ...

Bullivant was not just senior to all the officers and men of the *Calypso*; his commission appointing him to command the *Calypso*, signed by the Lords Commissioners of the Admiralty, and which he would have read out aloud to the ship's company when he first came on board ('reading himself in'), would have enjoined everyone to obey him, and given warning that they failed to do so 'at their peril'.

Only one thing could save them all from a crazed captain, and that was a more senior officer. There was no signal in the book that Aitken (as the second-in-command) could make to warn the admiral; he could only, Ramage realized, ask for the physician of the fleet and rely on him to declare the captain unfit to command.

That was the only thing unless a senior officer came on board ... and that was why Admiral Clinton had made sure Ramage was higher up the Captains' List than Bullivant. Ramage was senior. A higher link in the chain of command ...

Ramage pulled the pistol clear and held it out of sight behind him. All this might be of significance at a court-martial charging that Bullivant was first threatening an unarmed senior officer with a pistol. To this, Ramage realized, Bullivant at the moment had the perfect defence: he did not know Ramage, who was not in uniform, and genuinely mistook him for a Frenchman.

The hell with courts-martial and niggling points of law; this was the *Calypso* and Renwick had just been told by his captain to order his Marines to shoot Ramage. Now was the time to act, while everyone was paralysed by the outrageousness of the order.

Ramage waited until Bullivant lowered the tankard and then stepped forward.

'Captain Bullivant, I believe?'

'Yes, I am. Listen, Bowen, this dam' fellow speaks passable English!'

'I am Captain Ramage, and I have been ordered by Admiral Clinton to board your ship and satisfy myself on certain matters.'

'Captain Ramage? Absurd. Ramage is on the Continent. Prisoner of Bonaparte. With his new wife. Ramage's, not Bonaparte's. Spy, that's what you are. Rich, Ramage is dam' rich; he wouldn't wear fisherman's clothes. That brig – I ask you, where has she come from, eh? Shoot you and sink her, doing my duty. Says he is Captain Ramage, Bowen, what do you think of that, eh?'

'He is Captain Ramage, sir,' Bowen said loudly and clearly. 'I have served with him for several years, and so have all the ship's officers, and they recognize him too.'

'Well, I don't. I command this ship. Admiralty orders. Have m'commission. I read it out loud when I first came on board. Death, that's what happens if you disobey me –'

Ramage said crisply: 'I have identified myself to you and been recognized by all your officers. Now, I relieve you of your command, Captain Bullivant. You are a sick man. You will go to your cabin and place yourself in the surgeon's care while I take this ship to the admiral.'

Bullivant flung the tankard at Ramage. It spun through the air, spilling a tail of liquor, and crashed against the bulwark. He then lifted the pistol and, his face creasing with the effort of concentration, said carefully: 'You are the Devil dressed . . . as a French fisherman . . . You want me . . . to surrender this ship, Satan . . . but I shall shoot first . . .'

He tried to pull back the hammer with his thumb to cock the pistol but, glassy-eyed, it was obvious that he could probably see at least two, perhaps more, flints. And Ramage, although holding a pistol behind his back, was helpless: he could not shoot a besotted man.

It might work, Ramage thought. Suddenly he realized it was exactly the hint that Bowen was trying to give. He cursed himself for being so slow and turned and said casually to a seaman: 'Jackson, pick up that tankard and give it back to Captain Bullivant.'

Yes, Bowen had the idea; Bowen, of all people, the man who regularly drank himself senseless until Ramage and Southwick cured him by using a ruthlessness neither had thought the other capable of: Bowen would know. Bowen knew – or could guess – what was going on in Bullivant's befuddled mind, and Bowen had already removed the cap of the flask . . .

Jackson, holding out the tankard, approached Bullivant, whose face was streaming with perspiration, and said as though unaware that the man was wrestling with a pistol: 'Your tankard, sir.'

'Wha'? Wha's that? Oh, tankard, eh? I've got a set like that. No good empty.'

But Bullivant's attention was now on the tankard; he had lowered the pistol but being right-handed was obviously wondering how he could take the tankard. By then Bowen was beside him, holding up the flask.

'I'll fill it for you, sir. Now, Jackson, hold it steady.'

Ramage heard the suck and gurgle of the liquid as it ran from the flask and Bullivant watched with the fascination of a rabbit cornered by a stoat.

'There we are, sir, almost full. I'll have to refill this flask, though. Now, if I take the pistol you'll have a hand free for the tankard, sir . . .'

In a moment Bullivant was sucking greedily at the tankard while Bowen tucked the pistol inside his coat. He motioned to Ramage and Jackson to keep still.

It was then Ramage realized that every man in the ship seemed to be staring at Bullivant and holding his breath: it was as though there had been complete silence for an hour. Instead, Ramage knew he had been on board only a very few minutes and a frigate lying hove-to made a good deal of noise: canvas slatted, the waves slopped against the hull, the backed foretopsail yard creaked its protest at being pressed hard against the mast. It seemed that all these noises started again when Bullivant began drinking.

But what was Bowen waiting for? There was nothing to stop Ramage ordering Renwick to detail a file of Marines to take Captain Bullivant down to his cabin: he had the authority by virtue of his seniority and, much more important, the confidence of knowing that at the court-martial that was bound to follow, each one of these officers would give evidence of precisely what happened: none would back and fill to save his own skin from possible reprisals from Bullivant's cronies or people over whom Bullivant's father had influence. Aitken, Wagstaffe, Kenton, Southwick, Renwick, Martin, every seaman – they would be only too anxious to tell a court on oath exactly what had happened in these few minutes – and what had happened in the preceding few days. He had led these men in and out of action, he had been wounded several times alongside them, he had saved Jackson's life more than once and Jackson had saved his twice as many times.

Yet why were they all standing there? It was a curious scene, unreal, yet he thought he would never forget it. Bullivant, cocked hat now awry, breeches and white silk stockings stained – from urine rather than brandy, it seemed – and face streaming with perspiration. The eyes closed now, even when he lowered the tankard and took a few breaths . . . Bowen quite calm, looking as if he was just waiting for a patient to don an overcoat, Jackson with his sandy and thinning hair tidy as usual, shaven yesterday if not today, and wearing a blue jersey and white duck trousers, Southwick like a jovial bishop unable to avoid listening to a stream of blasphemy, Aitken with colour back in his face and watching Ramage like a hawk, waiting for orders, Paolo the same – in fact Ramage realized the boy was holding a long and narrow dagger which he must have drawn while Bullivant was fumbling with the pistol: Paolo's complexion was once again sallow, and although the boy was still balanced on the balls of his feet ready to move quickly, it was clear from his expression he knew he would not now be using the dagger and Ramage knew him well enough to gauge the boy's disappointment. Wagstaffe, Kenton, Martin ... and the seamen, Stafford and Rossi, who were closer than he realized, and he guessed that somehow they had closed in stealthily once they recognized their old captain.

Then nearly two hundred men groaned. No, not a groan, it was a sigh, everyone breathing out after holding their breath, and a startled Ramage looked back at Bullivant in time to see him sitting on the deck and then slowly bending backwards, like a carpet unrolling, until he was sprawled flat, his cocked hat lying to one side, the tankard still clasped in one hand and the remains of the brandy spreading a slow stain across the planks of the deck.

Bowen gestured to the Marines, but before he could say anything Ramage had stepped forward. It would matter at a trial who gave the next orders, and although Ramage knew he did not give a damn for himself, the future of the officers could be damaged unless he was careful.

'Bowen, Captain Bullivant seems to have lost consciousness...'

The surgeon knelt beside the man, rolled back an eyelid, loosened the badly-tied stock and stood up again. 'He is unconscious, sir,' he said formally, 'and in my opinion –'

'In your opinion,' Ramage interrupted, 'is he capable of carrying out his duties as captain of this ship?'

'No, sir, under no circumstances. Nor will he be for several –'

'Days?'

'– for several days, sir.'

'Have him taken below to his cabin for treatment,' Ramage said.

Now the formalities were over and, while Bowen called over some Marines, Ramage turned first to Southwick. As a warrant officer, the master was junior to the lieutenants, but he was old enough to be the father, even the grandfather, of any of them, and the bond between him and Ramage could not be measured by normal standards.

As Ramage reached out to shake the old man's hand he was startled to see tears running down the weathered cheeks, although the kindly mouth was smiling. 'Sir . . . sir . . . when your head came up the ladder I thought I was dreaming . . . where were –'

'We'll exchange news later; now we have work to do!' He shook hands with the lieutenants, Paolo and several of the seamen who rushed up, still hard put to believe their own eyes and anxious to touch him, as though that would make everything a reality. Then he beckoned to Swan, and together they walked aft.

'What a five minutes, sir!' Swan exclaimed. 'You look down the muzzle of a pistol like a man looking in a window. My blood ran cold even though he wasn't aiming at me!'

'He saw five or six of me and wasn't sure which one to shoot at.'

'Even so,' Swan said, 'five to one are not good odds!'

'Well, it's over now. If I hand over the *Murex* to you and give you orders to rejoin the flagship, can you manage? No one will ever know if you don't feel up to it, so don't be afraid to say.'

'No, sir, thanks but I'll be all right. If you'll just give me the latitude and longitude of the rendezvous.'

'You can sail in company with us. I have to take this ship to the admiral. Do you want some more men?'

Swan shook his head. 'No, sir, so I'll get back to the *Murex*. What about her Ladyship? Shall I send the cutter back with her?'

'No, we can't spare the time, but as long as you make sure no one else overhears, you can tell her what you saw.'

'Any other message for her Ladyship, sir?'

'Tell her that Southwick, Stafford, Jackson and Aitken – no, just tell her that all the officers and ship's company of the *Calypso* send her their regards.'

Swan looked puzzled. Ramage could see that the lieutenant was wondering how on earth a captain's new wife could know all the men in his previous ship. 'They saved her life once, Swan. If you have time and if she's agreeable, get her to tell you about it: it'll help you pass the time as we beat back to the Fleet.'

*

Ramage stood on the fore side of the quarterdeck with Aitken as they watched the *Murex* brace up the foretopsail yard and then bear away to the rendezvous, the clewed-up courses soon set and drawing.

'Handsome little ships, those brigs,' Aitken said. 'Any nostalgia, sir?' he asked, knowing Ramage had commanded the *Triton*.

'Yes and no. "Yes" because they are handy – we tacked that one out of the Gullet with only a dozen men, and looking back on it we could probably have made do with eight. "No" because I found it strange being in that particular one, where most of the men had mutinied and handed over the ship (and their loyal shipmates) to the enemy. It's as though treachery rubs off like soot, marking everything and leaving a distinctive smell.'

'Aye, evil has a distinct smell, and all of us can recognize it. In our case it's the smell of brandy.'

'It has been bad, eh?'

'Almost beyond belief, sir. We could see no end to it. There's nothing in the Articles of War or the *Regulations and Instructions* about it. Bowen reckoned medical reasons were the only safe way, but for the first day or so, when the drink wasn't in him, he was bright enough. Cunning and fawning, but shrewd. It seemed to me, sir, that if we took away his command and then he was cunning enough to keep off the liquor for a few weeks before the court-martial, at the trial he could make it all look very different...'

'Yes, that's the danger. When you look at something from different directions, you get different views.'

'And Bowen knew all about the effects of drink. That's how we came –'

Ramage held up a hand to stop him. 'I'm sure the ship's officers didn't conspire against the captain, Aitken, because that's forbidden. As you know, Article XX specifies death as the only punishment for anyone "concealing any traitorous or mutinous practice or design". So don't mention anything resembling conspiracy – the listener immediately becomes guilty as well.'

Aitken grinned. 'I understand that, sir. Well, it's wonderful to have you on board again.'

Ramage nodded and looked across at the *Murex,* now a couple of miles away. 'I think we can get under way now and rejoin the admiral with the brig. Admiral Clinton is a very puzzled man.'

They walked forward again and Aitken picked up the speaking trumpet. Ramage realized that since he last stood here a couple of months or so ago, as they tacked up the Medway to Chatham, he had married, been to France, escaped capture when the war broke out again, recaptured the *Murex* brig, and relieved the new captain of the *Calypso* of his command. What he had not done was try to rescue Jean-Jacques.

'I'm going below to see Bowen and his patient,' he told Aitken. He gave him a folded piece of paper. 'Here is the rendezvous, and you'll sight the fleet before nightfall. Ignore the *Blackthorne* if she starts making signals – there's no signal in the book to describe what we're doing.'

Below in the great cabin he found Bowen sitting in the chair at the desk while in the sleeping cabin Bullivant, undressed and now in his nightshirt, was breathing heavily in a drunken stupor, his lips flapping like wet laundry each time he exhaled.

Bowen hurriedly stood up as the Marine sentry announced Ramage, who gestured to him to remain seated.

'I'll take the armchair. It's good to see you, Bowen. I wish it was under happier circumstances ...'

'Oh, I hope everything will turn out all right, sir,' Bowen said vaguely. 'For the moment we have about an hour before Captain Bullivant recovers consciousness and descends into the hell of *delirium tremens.*'

'Hell seems the right word: he seems obsessed with it. He recognized me as the Devil when I came on board.'

'Oh yes, Satan is very real to him. For the past five or six days this ship has reeked of brimstone. The captain had all the lieutenants sprinkling the quarterdeck with holy water laced with brandy in an attempt to exorcize it, but without success.'

'This conversation never took place,' Ramage remarked, 'so tell me the story from the beginning.'

'Well, you know a good deal of the circumstances if you remember how I came to serve with you in the *Triton* brig,' Bowen said with disconcerting frankness.

'There are two kinds of heavy drinkers: those who drink secretly until they are stupefied, and those who don't give a damn and get drunk openly. Captain Bullivant is a secret drinker, so no one – except perhaps his family and his wife if he is married – knows. But from my own experience I can tell you he has been drinking hard for years. Four or five years, anyway: look at the

143

veins under the skin of his face, at his nose, at his eyes when they are open. And he looks ten or twenty years older than he is.'

'But when he joined the ship,' Ramage prompted.

'Ah, yes. We had fallen behind in paying off the ship because of difficulties with the dockyard, and just as well. We (that is, Mr Aitken, because of course you were on leave) suddenly received orders to commission the ship at once, and the dockyard commissioner warned us war was likely again any moment. He also said that if you did not return from France in time, the First Lord would appoint a new captain.

'We had the ship ready in what must be record time and Captain Bullivant appeared and read himself in as the new commanding officer. Very brisk, he was, and delighted with everything Aitken and Southwick had done. He made a very good impression on every person who saw him, except one man.'

'And that was you.' It was a comment, not a question.

'Yes, I knew the symptoms which no one else ever recognizes. The constant sweating, the tiny tremor of the fingers when the hands are extended, the slightly glazed appearance of the eyes and the feeling they are never quite in focus, the smell of cashews on the breath . . . the apparent temperance and lack of interest in wine and spirits. When his luggage was brought on board, I had a word with Jackson and he made sure each trunk was checked. One clinked – full of bottles, carefully packed and only two loose ones.'

'And after he had read himself in?'

'All went well the next day: orders arrived from the Admiralty to proceed to Plymouth and put ourselves under Admiral Clinton's command. We were off the Nore that night and we suddenly found ourselves in the middle of the Harwich fishing fleet. Aitken sent for the captain, who came up on deck so stupefied he could not stand without holding on to something. That was the first time we heard him see the Devil.'

'What did he look like?' Ramage asked.

'Well, we didn't see him since he only existed in the fumes affecting Captain Bullivant's brain, but we certainly heard *where* he was: about fifty yards on one bow and then on the other, preparing to rake us.'

'With empty bottles, I suppose.'

Bowen grinned as he shook his head. 'No, he was on the fo'c'sle of a three-decker which was "painted in orange stripes like a glorious sunset" – Captain Bullivant's exact words, though he didn't explain how he distinguished colour in the dark. All this took the lieutenants and Southwick by surprise, sir: I had kept my earlier observations to myself – I had not realized he had reached the stage of recurrent *delirium tremens*. I was mistaken: I should have warned Aitken.'

'But the *Calypso* did not sink any of the fishing vessels?'

'No, mercifully. Anyway, eventually I quieted down the captain and got him back to bed. Next morning he was – to the layman's eyes – perfectly normal, but in the secrecy of this cabin he drank himself into a stupor every night until we arrived in Plymouth . . . There Aitken talked to me about reporting it all to Admiral Clinton.'

'What was your advice?'

'Well, sir, I thought of my own cunning when you and Southwick were trying to cure me and decided Captain Bullivant was a clever man, well aware of his weakness and with enough influence at the Navy Board through his contractor father to make useless anything we could do. Admiral Clinton was busy getting his fleet to sea, so if Aitken had appeared in the flagship with a story of Satan stalking the *Calypso,* I suspect we would have been sent a new first lieutenant, not a new captain.'

'So the Fleet sailed. Then what happened?'

'Well, that was all Captain Bullivant was waiting for: he left the entire running of the ship to Aitken. He gave orders that he was "not to be bothered with signals", and that Aitken was to execute all orders from the flagship "without troubling" him. From this we expected he would stay drinking down here in his cabin, but every now and again he would emerge raving about the Devil. He would chase him out of his cabin and up the companionway to the quarterdeck, and would then sight him behind the binnacle, behind a carronade, trying to climb the ratlines . . .'

'Was there anything you could do?'

'Frankly none of us had the courage. If we had bundled him below and he had later remembered it, any of us – Marine, seaman or officer – could be tried for striking a superior officer, or mutiny. So we all looked for Satan, exorcized the quarter-deck . . .'

'That signal for the physician?'

'That was when his delirium was reaching the crisis. Yesterday he had the ship's company mustered aft and inspected them.'

'Well, there's nothing unusual about that,' Ramage commented, feeling he ought to say something, however mild, in Bullivant's defence.

'No, sir, unless you are looking for the Devil himself – and find him hiding in the bodies of three men!'

'Which three?' asked a flabbergasted Ramage.

'The seaman Rossi, the Marchesa's young nephew Paolo Orsini – and Southwick!'

'I can understand Rossi and Orsini – they have sallow complexions and black hair. But Southwick – I always think he looks like a bishop.'

'That's exactly what Captain Bullivant said! He denounced Southwick because he said it was impossible for a bishop to be serving as the master in one of the King's ships, therefore he must be the Devil in disguise.'

'But how did this cause a crisis?'

'He swore he would hang a Devil a day until the ship was free of them. Southwick was the first and due to be executed at sunset today.'

'But the men would never haul on the rope!' Ramage said. The whole thing was unthinkable.

'Sir,' Bowen said very seriously, 'the minute he gives anyone an order and is disobeyed, that's a breach of enough Articles of War for a death sentence at a court-martial . . .'

'So . . . ?'

'So, I told Aitken that the only way out was to use "medical grounds" to get the admiral involved. I had a plan in case that failed (the signal for the physician of the fleet, I mean) but I couldn't then be sure it would work. Luckily it did when I used it . . .'

'The tankard of brandy and the flask?'

'Yes, sir. It's the timing that is difficult. To judge how much is needed to tip the man over the edge into oblivion – well, that depends on how much he has drunk in the previous few hours, and whether he has eaten.'

'You timed it perfectly.'

'I thought all was lost when he threw the tankard at your head. Thank goodness you realized what I had in mind.'

'I was very slow. I was surprised to see you offering him more drink. Then, quite honestly, I remembered what used to happen when Southwick and I were curing you.'

'"Completing my medical education" would be a more tactful word, sir, than "curing"!'

'As you wish. Anyway, thank you. On my behalf and the three Devils'!'

'Yes, well, Aitken and young Orsini thought of that signal. I told Aitken we should stake everything on medical grounds, and between them they thought of that signal. Aitken could only keep it hoisted for ten or fifteen minutes at a time.'

'That was long enough. The *Blackthorne* repeated it and it reached the admiral.'

'And he sent you at once?'

Ramage laughed dryly. 'No, if the majority of the *Murex* brig's men had not mutinied and carried the ship into Brest . . . And had I not been near Brest on my honeymoon . . . And had not my wife and I had the help of four Frenchmen so we could retake the *Murex* . . . And had we not managed to sail out and accidentally meet Admiral Clinton and the Fleet . . . And had the *Calypso* not been my old ship . . . No, but for all those circumstances, Mr Sawbones, I don't think your signal would have attracted the attention it deserved. Still, all's well . . .'

'But will all this end well?' Bowen asked anxiously. 'We still have him' – he gestured to the door of the sleeping cabin – 'in there. Supposing the admiral doesn't . . .'

'Oh, he'll do something about him, I am sure. Who you'll get in his place I do not know. Probably the first lieutenant of the flagship – that's usually the person who gets the first vacant frigate command.'

'But the *Calypso*'s still inside Channel limits.'

'She won't be when the admiral makes the appointment: Brest is outside the limits. He wasn't born yesterday!'

'And you, sir?'

Ramage hesitated, thinking of *L'Espoir,* which, even while the *Calypso* and the brig rejoined the Fleet, was ploughing her way towards Cayenne, towards Devil's Island. Everything depended on Admiral Clinton. Would the Prince of Wales's friendship with a French refugee have any effect? Probably not. Almost certainly not. And even if it did, Clinton must have his own favourite frigate captains, and one of them would get orders which could bring him glory or, if he failed, square his yards for ever!

'I expect I'll be taking the brig back to Plymouth and reporting what I know of the mutiny to the Admiralty.'

'And your wife, sir? Is her Ladyship still in France? You mentioned her when you talked of retaking the brig.'

'Yes, we escaped together and she is on board the *Murex*. She wanted to come with me to board the *Calypso*, but I was rather worried about what I might find.'

'I hope her Ladyship submitted with good grace.'

'Well, you know her Ladyship, Bowen. I doubt if anyone would call her submissive,' Ramage said.

Bowen laughed and his memories of Lady Sarah Rockley, as she was before her marriage, were of a lively and high-spirited woman of grace and beauty who would captivate all the men in a drawing room and leave the women seeming as flat as ale drawn last week.

CHAPTER ELEVEN

Admiral Clinton sat at his desk with the alert wariness of a stag lurking in a stand of low trees at the far end of a glen. He was trying to decide whether the five men in front of him were innocent visitors or a quintet likely to board him in a cloud of smoke.

'Well now,' he said finally, his Scots accent broadening, and Ramage remembered Sarah's reference to the family, 'so here ye all are. Let me see . . .

'Yes, Dr Travis, the physician of my fleet, I know *you* well enough, and so I should since I see you every day. Are ye comfortable in that old armchair?'

Travis, tall and gaunt, everyone's idea of a dour man of medicine, had obviously qualified in Edinburgh, and his brief 'Aye' was all he would allow himself for the moment.

'And m'flag captain – are you comfortable, Bennett? I know ye prefer standing but with this headroom and you so tall, it worries me!'

Except for Travis, the others laughed dutifully: Captain Bennett was only an inch or so over five feet; even his hair, wiry and sitting on his head like a bob major wig, did not come within five inches of the beams.

'Then there's Captain Ramage. Lord Ramage, by rights, but

he saves us any possible embarrassment by not using his title. You're a jealous man, otherwise you'd have brought that beautiful wife with you.'

Ramage smiled, not at all certain whether or not the admiral was making a polite joke. 'She has only a fishwife's torn smock to wear, sir, so she decided to wait for a more appropriate occasion.'

Clinton gestured at Ramage's trousers and shirt. 'You'd have made a good pair. I've been a sailor too long to judge a ship by the patches in her sails.'

He looked round at the settee. 'Well, Mr Ramage, perhaps you'd introduce these gentlemen . . .'

'Sir, Lieutenant Aitken, the *Calypso*'s first lieutenant. He has served with me in the Mediterranean and the West Indies.'

'Aye,' Clinton told Aitken, 'he's been telling me all about you. What he doesn't know – nor do you – is that I knew all about you long ago.'

He gave a laugh at the look of dismay on the young lieutenant's face. 'Man, you look as though the parson's just accused you of deflowering all the young women in the village. Y'father was another Aitken, master, was he not, and he served with me in the *Ramillies*, *Britannia* and this ship, the *Culloden*, before I hoisted my flag. I owed a lot to y'father and I've kept an eye on you from the day y'went to sea, but you've made your own way without needing a dram of help so I've held m'peace.'

Aitken was obviously startled at this news and stammered his thanks, to be cut short by Clinton. 'Ye've served Mr Ramage very well, and it looks to me as if Mr Ramage feels towards the Aitken family as I do. Still, we all have the rest of our lives to live and,' he added, his voice taking on a friendly warning note, 'a great deal of both good and bad can happen before we go to our graves.'

A sombre silence had fallen over the great cabin and in Ramage's imagination the mahogany of the desk, wine cooler and table seemed to grow darker, but Clinton seemed not to realize the effect he had unwittingly made.

'And you must be the *Calypso*'s surgeon – Bowen, isn't it? You and Mr Aitken have had a worrying time, I imagine. Now, who starts? Perhaps we'd be better starting at the end, then Dr Travis can be about his business.'

Which was another way of saying, Ramage reflected, that

Travis would not have to listen to things that he could be questioned about later at a court-martial.

'How did you find the patient?'

'Mr Aitken was justified in signalling for the physician of the fleet, sir. This is no reflection on the medical capacity of Mr Bowen, who I truly believe understands a great deal more about this type of illness than I do.'

'Don't stop man, you've only just started!' the admiral exclaimed impatiently.

'Acting on your orders, I boarded the *Calypso* frigate as soon as she hove-to near the flagship,' Travis said in a monotonous voice, obviously nettled by the admiral's remarks, 'and I asked Captain Ramage why the ship had made the signal requesting the fleet's physician. He said that the captain of the frigate, a certain Captain William Bullivant, was confined to his cot unconscious and not in a fit condition to exercise command of the ship.'

'Oh, go on, man!'

'Captain Ramage commented to me,' Travis said heavily, 'that the nature of Captain Bullivant's illness was such that not only could he not exercise command, but it led him for long periods to act in a manner prejudicial to the King's business.'

Everyone in the cabin realized that Travis had spoken slowly and with great care a sentence which was carefully phrased, intended not just for the ears of the commander-in-chief but the five or more captains and flag officers who might be forming a court-martial or court of inquiry.

'Did you examine the patient?'

'I was introduced to the ship's first lieutenant and her surgeon, but before discussing the case any further I went below and examined the patient. I have my notes here,' he said, pulling a sheaf of papers from a leather case. The admiral watched for a moment as Travis began sorting them out, and then groaned.

'No, no, Travis, don't start pouring Latin words all over me. I'm just a simple Highlander, not one of your brilliant Edinburgh scholars.'

Travis glared at the admiral, sat up straight in the armchair and put the papers back in his case. 'In words of one syllable, sir, Captain Bullivant was in a drunken stupor. He has been having attacks of – if you'll permit me that Latin – *delirium tremens*, and he was proposing to have the master, a midshipman and a seaman hanged at sunset.'

Clinton's face paled. It took him only a moment to connect the

Bullivant family and the Navy Board, the besotted captain of a frigate and the dangers for junior officers, and another moment to realize that the whole problem had landed in his lap like a haggis sliding away from the carver's knife.

'You can testify about the man's medical condition; you don't know about the hangings.'

'I do, sir,' Travis contradicted, and he said with some precision: 'I confirmed the captain's intentions with each of the three men and my witnesses were Captain Ramage and Lieutenant Swan, the first lieutenant of the brig.'

'Very well, doctor, and thank 'ee. I'm sure you have plenty of work waiting for you.'

'I have that,' Travis said. 'You'll be wanting a written report?'

'I'll talk to you about that later.'

As soon as Travis had left the cabin, Clinton looked at Ramage. 'It was as bad as that?'

'Worse, sir. Bullivant was going to shoot me when I came on board: he reckoned I was Satan, too.'

Clinton permitted himself a wintry smile. 'A pardonable error of identification, some might say.'

Ramage gave an equally wintry smile. 'With a loaded pistol at less than five paces, sir.'

'Too close, too close,' Clinton agreed, and turned to Bowen. 'When do you think the drinking started?'

'Years ago, sir. Secret drinking. As the months pass it takes a glass or two more to produce oblivion. Finally the brain is deranged, although at first not all the time. For a long time the patient probably manages to control his drinking so that he stays this side of *delirium*, but suddenly he is put under a strain – given the command of a ship, for example. He feels himself inadequate so he has an extra glass or two, or three or four. And he passes over the line into *delirium*. A few hours later he recovers from that particular attack, craves more drink . . . and so it goes on. Fifty glasses are not enough; one is too many.'

'How long will it take to cure this man?'

'That is a question better answered by Dr Travis, sir.'

'I am asking you,' persisted the admiral.

'You won't like my answer, sir.'

'When you reach my age and rank you rarely like *anyone*'s answers about *anything,* so that's not relevant. You were cured of the same thing.'

'Yes, sir, but the cause – what drove me to drink – was not the same.'

Ramage was pleasantly surprised at the way Bowen was carefully making his points: the admiral was leaning forward, like the close relative listening anxiously for the diagnosis.

'What's the difference? A drink is a drink. One man's body is like another. It's the liver isn't it. Gets damaged?'

'It's really the mind, sir,' Bowen corrected gently. 'It's the mind that starts a man drinking, although the liver eventually kills him. The patient we are concerned with started drinking – in my opinion, of course – because it helped him forget his feelings of inadequacy.'

'Inadequacy? Inadequacy?' Clinton turned the word over like a dog with a bone. 'What did he feel inadequate about?'

'Commanding a frigate, sir. He was also unlucky enough to be given the *Calypso*.'

'Bowen, you are talking rubbish.'

Ramage, too, was startled to hear the surgeon declaring it was Bullivant's bad luck to be given the *Calypso*, although he thought he understood the rest of the point Bowen was making.

'You asked for my medical opinion, sir, and if you'll allow me, I had one of the best practices in Wimpole Street until I ruined it all with drink. So, drink, drinking, its cause and consequences – that is a subject I know a great deal about. If I was as expert in naval strategy and tactics, I would be the admiral of the red.'

Clinton nodded because for the past few years, as he had begun climbing up the ladder of flag rank, he had been surrounded by sycophants: he found that many captains brave enough in action were too quick with the fawning 'Yes, sir, no sir' in this cabin: he found he still enjoyed seeing an officer's features tauten and hear him say 'If you'll allow me sir' as a preliminary to flatly contradicting a commander-in-chief who could destroy his career with the wave of a hand.

'I appoint you temporarily an admiral of the red wine,' Clinton said dryly. 'So explain his "inadequacy" and why he was "unlucky".'

'As Lieutenant Bullivant on board a ship of the line or a frigate, the patient simply obeyed orders. Sighting land, changes in wind strength or direction, tacking or wearing – every captain's standing orders set down that he is to be called, so the patient never had to decide whether that was a particular headland, whether he had to reef or furl, tack or wear. His whole life at sea was to ask a senior when he was in doubt; to report and obey.'

'Yes, yes, I understand that much,' Clinton said.

'Suddenly – perhaps as a result of patronage, perhaps because he had proved to be a good lieutenant –'

'Perhaps a combination of both,' Clinton interrupted sarcastically.

'Yes,' Bowen agreed, 'perhaps. Anyway, he was suddenly made post and given a frigate in emergency conditions with no previous experience of command: with the war about to start again he was ordered to take over the frigate in Chatham, get her ready for sea immediately – remember, she was in the process of paying off – and join your fleet for blockade duty off Brest, notoriously the worst job the Navy has.'

Clinton nodded encouragingly. 'So far we are only stating in a medical voice what we all know.'

'Agreed, sir; I could have said that in a naval voice. However, I will now proceed, if I may, in my Wimpole Street voice.'

Clinton grinned: he was beginning to like this whimsical sawbones. He had heard enough about young Ramage to know that by now he must be a shrewd judge of men, and had been impressed at Ramage's earlier references to Bowen and his lieutenants and the master. Bowen must have sewn him up a few times too, come to think of it, because Ramage had been wounded often enough.

'You can talk in a Wimpole Street voice, but don't send me a Wimpole Street bill because you're still a ship's surgeon!'

'And I wouldn't exchange any of it.'

'Easy to talk,' Clinton commented.

Ramage said quietly: 'With the late peace, sir, Mr Bowen came with me in the *Calypso* on a long cruise beyond the Equator.'

Clinton pushed his chair back to the full extent of the chain which secured it to the deck against the ship's roll.

'Hmmp . . . that only tells me you are loyal if not wise, Bowen, but go on. Your patient' – Ramage noted that Clinton was still keeping the episode at arm's length – 'has just been given a frigate and orders to join my fleet.'

'Well, sir, he's now on his own. When the officer of the deck reports a landfall, a change in wind direction or strength, the decision to reef or furl, tack or wear, the decision what to do is now entirely the patient's: he's alone in his cabin or on the windward side of the quarterdeck. Oh yes, up to a point he can accept the suggestions of the master or the first lieutenant on points of seamanship and navigation, but there are very many decisions which only the captain can make.'

'Yes, yes,' Clinton said impatiently.

'The problem is that our patient,' Bowen said in a flat voice, 'can't bring himself to make those decisions. He suddenly realizes that despite years of training and all the family money and patronage and the fact he has now been given a ship, he's not competent to command it.'

'Who says so?' Clinton demanded.

'I do, sir,' Bowen said promptly. 'I am not competent to judge his seamanship but I can judge him as a leader – or his attempts at leadership.'

'Unlucky,' Clinton interrupted. 'You said he was unlucky to get command of the Calypso. Why? Is she a difficult ship to handle? Crank, tender, slow to windward? Truculent ship's company? Leaking decks? Why unlucky, eh?'

'Had he been given command of a frigate which had been commanded by an average captain, a ship and captain which never featured in the London Gazette, a frigate a man served in and forgot the name a year after, I'm sure everything might have been made to serve. He would have been able to hide his sense of inadequacy. But what happened? Well, I don't wish to embarrass Captain Ramage, who wears his fame lightly, but the Calypso and her captain are perhaps the best known in the King's Service. Our patient knows that in everything he does on board, every decision he makes and every order he gives, he will be compared to Captain Ramage. He thinks it's a comparison made daily by the officers and men and that it's a comparison bound to be made at the Admiralty or by a commander-in-chief. "He's not a patch on young Ramage" . . . You may not have said it yet, sir, and you may never have said it at all, but the patient can imagine you saying it.'

'Very well, you've explained "unlucky". Now explain the delirium tremens,' Clinton said grimly.

'You may not know the patient by appearance, sir. No? Well, he is handsome but with a weak face. By that I mean if you judge a man's character to a certain extent by his face, you would not expect this man to have a strong will. As a lieutenant he delighted in strong drink. By inclination, perhaps, because he liked the taste. However, I think it more likely he needed a dram or two

154

to bring him abreast of the rest of the officers in whichever ship he served. So the liking for drink was already there. He may have discovered – in fact from my own experience I am sure he did – that a few drinks made him quite as good in his own estimation as the next man, perhaps even better.

'What happens if you put a weak man prone to drink into a position where he feels inadequate (and thus *is* inadequate)? Well, sir, I suggest that at first the man does what he did before – looks to the tankard or the glass to make his decisions and blunt his cares. But soon he feels he needs more proof, and the cares increase. So does the drinking in proportion.

'It has to be drunk in secret, of course, so the patient increasingly feels guilty because he thinks he would be finished if anyone (even his personal servant) knew he was drinking to make himself fit to do his job.'

Clinton growled: 'We still haven't got him in a *delirium*.'

'It doesn't take long. Some months for a newcomer to drink; some weeks for someone who has been an average drinker; but only a few days if the man has been a secret and heavy drinker for a long time.'

'You can't say what the patient was doing before he joined the *Calypso*,' Clinton objected.

'I can, sir, if you'll pardon me for contradicting you. I recognized him as a heavy drinker the moment he joined the ship.'

'Am *I* a heavy drinker?' Clinton suddenly asked.

Bowen looked round the cabin. 'A very large wine cooler. A rack of cut-glass decanters which a duke might envy. And racks of wine and spirits glasses. They could belong to a heavy drinker; or let us say a connoisseur of wine and spirits. A *bon vivant*, in fact. However, you asked if I thought you were a heavy drinker, so I look at you and not the glassware. In fact, sir, I had by chance made up my mind – made a diagnosis, if you would prefer it – when I first came into the cabin, before I looked round.'

'Well?' Clinton demanded. 'A heavy drinker or a light one?'

'I would say,' Bowen said slowly, 'giving it due consideration, and allowing for the responsibility resting on your shoulders, and the fact that you come from Scotland, where more whisky is distilled than rainwater collected ... I would say you probably have a glass of wine with your dinner, and perhaps a glass of port afterwards. No more.'

The admiral's face fell: he reminded Ramage of a Father Christmas recognized by the children as the butler dressed up.

'I've given up the port,' he admitted, 'because I was afraid of the gout. Well, Mr Sawbones, after that display, I admit I'm now more prepared to listen to you. So let us suppose your patients drinks himself into a stupor (from time to time, I'm thinking, when the pressures get heavy) because –'

'No, sir,' Bowen interrupted, 'he's past the "from time to time": he needs liquor to get out of his cot of a morning; he needs liquor to get him past the noon sight. He needs liquor because he's afraid of the devils with glaring eyes and demons with sharp tongues and all the clammy, crawling beasts that are waiting to attack him: all those horrible things that come with *delirium tremens*. And don't think they're imaginary, sir. They are to the onlooker; to the victim they are terrifyingly real.'

'So what do we do about your patient?'

'Are you asking from the medical point of view or are you concerned with the *King's Regulations and Admiralty Instructions* and the Articles of War, sir?'

'Damned if I know,' Clinton admitted. 'It's an entirely new situation as far as I am concerned.'

'Medically, a captain, master and Marine guards have nursed a man through *delirium tremens* in a few days – that I know because the patient was me – but it is hard work. Yet the following days are almost more important – getting the patient interested in life again and giving him the confidence to face it without using a bottle of liquor as a pair of crutches. I like chess, and Mr Southwick, the master, played endless games with me. Captain Ramage even learned to play to help out. I was very lucky.

'Discipline is out of my field, of course, but you may want a medical opinion on the disciplinary aspect, sir. In my opinion, which I will give you in writing, the patient is completely incapable of commanding a ship: indeed, he is both unfit and incapable of leaving his cabin.'

Clinton stood up and sighed. 'My orders are to start and maintain a close blockade of Brest with this fleet. Provisioning and watering the ships and trying to outguess the Atlantic weather, Bonaparte and every ship's propensity for wearing out, is normally agreed to be enough to keep an admiral occupied. Your damned patient, Bowen, is going to cause more problems than the rest put together.'

The phrase 'your patient' was finally too much for Bowen, who stood up, white-faced and almost rigid with anger, and said stiffly: 'Sir, that he is my patient is a very unfortunate coincidence. Had I any say in the matter, he would never have been employed as a lieutenant; whoever then made him post did something akin to treason.'

And that, Ramage thought, is how Bowen was court-martialled under at least two of the Articles of War, but he was wrong: the admiral turned to the surgeon and smiled.

'Some flag officers suffer from spasmodic deafness.' He waved a dismissal to Bowen and Aitken. 'Well, gentlemen, thank you. Mr Ramage, will you stay a few minutes with Captain Bennett?'

Sitting at the end of the highly polished rosewood table with Bennett halfway down one side on his right and Ramage to his left, Admiral Clinton no longer looked like an amiable Santa Claus: the grey-blue eyes which could twinkle were now glinting like the sharp blades of two freshly honed épées.

'This conference never took place, which is why my nincompoop of a secretary is not present taking notes. But I want privately to hear your personal opinions of this fellow Bullivant. Bennett?'

The admiral's flag captain was only five feet tall but had achieved some fame (and the unexpected cheers of his men) when his ship's company mutinied at the Nore some years earlier. Some wretched man had made an insolent remark to Bennett about a matter unconnected with the mutiny, and in front of several hundred mutinous seamen, Bennett had taken him by the ear to the entryport, pushed him over the side, and then coolly told the leader of the mutineers to fish him out because he probably could not swim.

Bennett's first words showed he had not lost his directness. 'That surgeon fellow was right: Bullivant should never have been made post,' he said emphatically.

'Salt beef and salt pork supplied by the father: that's what mattered. Thousands of casks, and plenty of cumshaw scattered among the right people in the Navy Board, and your eldest son doesn't need much ability. It's unfortunate for the seamen, officers and admirals who suffer the consequences ... In my opinion, sir, there's only one thing to do: send him back to

Plymouth in the *Murex* brig with signed reports by Bowen and Dr Travis about his "sickness".'

'It's a serious matter, relieving him of his command.'

Ramage realized that the admiral was wavering, and he thought of the *Calypso* and her officers and ship's company. 'Sir, the consequences of not doing so will be worse.'

'How so? Relieving a captain of his command is serious enough!'

'You are relieving him only on medical grounds, sir,' Ramage reminded Clinton. 'You are not saying he is incompetent. But the consequences of leaving him in command – well, yesterday, there could have been three murders by him or a mutiny by the ship's company. There's bound to be mutiny if you leave him in command.'

'*Bound* to be mutiny? You don't have much confidence in the men you've spent so long training,' Clinton said sarcastically.

'On the contrary, sir: I have *complete* confidence in them: that's why I know they'd mutiny.'

Bennett was watching him shrewdly. He knows, Ramage realized, but the admiral has been too remote from the day-to-day handling of a ship's company for too long.

'Do you *really* mean you're confident they'd mutiny?' Clinton demanded angrily.

Ramage nodded. 'Yesterday, sir, Captain Bullivant said he would hang three men, Midshipman the Count Orsini, who happens to be the nephew of the ruler of Volterra and one of our allies; the master of the ship, who is certainly the most competent seaman and one of the bravest men I know; and an Italian seaman called Rossi, a man to whom I've entrusted my life on several occasions.

'Bullivant was going to have them hanged at sunset because after inspecting the entire ship's company he identified them as Satans. I trust, sir, that any seaman would mutiny rather than obey such an order to put nooses round their necks and haul them up to the yardarm.'

Ramage knew he was white-faced, and he kept his fists pressed down on the table to hide the trembling: he could feel perspiration soaking through his shirt but mercifully it did not appear on his face, which felt cold and clammy, as though he was about to faint.

'Quite,' Clinton said calmly. 'However, it seems to me the

only one now left with his neck in a noose is the commander-in-chief.'

'That's what he's there for, sir,' Bennett said cheerfully. 'I agree with Ramage completely. I know what the Articles of War say and don't say, but I'd sooner the seamen mutinied than obeyed the "lawful" orders of a brandy-besotted madman. That's something the Articles don't allow for, and they should. Loyalty is what matters. Men who'd mutiny because of their loyalty to their officers and shipmates are the men I want round me when I go into battle.'

'We aren't in battle, we're blockading Brest, and judging from the last war the only action we're going to see is dealing with a drunken maniac,' Clinton grumbled.

'At least you're outside "Channel limits", sir,' Bennett said. 'That gives you more freedom.'

'Leaves me short of a post-captain for the *Calypso*.'

Bennett glanced across the table at Ramage. 'A post-captain commanding a brig is a bit overweight.'

Clinton waved dismissively: 'Ramage has to go to England with the brig: they'll need him at the inquiry into the mutiny and recapture, and for the Bullivant affair. Commanding a *prize* brig, don't forget.' The idea raised another train of thought for the admiral. 'Hmm, that's an interesting point. There's no question that Ramage *captured* the damned ship: he didn't "retake" her because he wasn't part of the original ship's company. He, his wife and four Frenchmen. He's the only one entitled to prize money.'

'His wife will help him spend it!' Bennett said jocularly.

'So you'll be back in Plymouth in a couple of days. Lucky fellow,' Clinton said, and then added: 'Why so gloomy? Sailing home after your honeymoon and with a sack full of prize money!' Then a sudden thought struck him. 'What about that young Scots first lieutenant? We ought to do something for him. Make him post into the *Calypso*?'

Ramage remembered an attempt a year or more ago when Aitken was offered command of a frigate and the post rank that went with it; he had said he preferred to continue sailing with Captain Ramage. But now was not the time to mention that to a Scots admiral. Aitken could make the point later, if necessary.

Bennett rubbed his ample chins and looked down at the table. 'If I was Ramage, sir, I'd be eating my heart out over the

159

Calypso. And weren't you telling me earlier that he was concerned over this French count who is being transported to Cayenne – a friend of the Prince of Wales, didn't you say, sir?'

Ramage decided that Bennett was a man to whom he already owed a debt of gratitude worth more than a brig.

'Bennett,' Clinton said, his voice rasping, 'you have an unhappy knack of mentioning things I'm trying to forget.'

'Sir, I shouldn't forget that the Prince of Wales is unlikely to forget a commander-in-chief who forgot his friend being carried off to a certain death in Cayenne . . .'

And now, Ramage thought, the repetition of 'forget' and 'forgot' means the ace of trumps has gone down on the table. Or it's the bait dangling in front of the fish. Or the snare carefully placed outside the rabbit hole.

'Blast it, Bennett. I've been tossing up between the Prince of Wales and Lord St Vincent ever since Ramage mentioned the Count of Rennes. And it's probably not only the Count: if there are fifty of them, half are bound to be Royalists who went back to France after exile in England and know Prinny. At least half, probably more.'

'You are caught between the devil (*pace* Bullivant) of the Admiralty and the deep blue sea of the Prince, seems to me, sir.'

'It's all right for you to joke about it,' the admiral complained. 'I'm the one who has to choose.'

'Oh, I chose when you first told me about it yesterday, sir,' Bennett said blithely.

'You did, eh?' the admiral exclaimed, his voice now truculent, the accent becoming more pronounced. 'Surprising how easy it is to choose when you don't have the responsibility.'

Ramage expected Bennett to react strongly, but instead the little man picked up the quill pen lying on the table and waved it back and forth as though fanning himself.

'I'm like that surgeon fellow, Brown, or whatever his name was. I'll put it in writing if you wish, sir. As your flag captain I'm expected to give you professional advice when you ask for it.'

He paused and then tapped the table with the feather of the quill. 'My views are simple. Question number one, what do we do with the drunken Bullivant? Wrap him up, in a canvas straitjacket if necessary, and send him home in the *Murex* brig with reports by Bowen and Travis tucked in his pocket.'

He tapped the table twice. 'Question number two, who is to command the *Calypso*? There's only one possible man, and that's Ramage here. He's not needed for the *Murex* because her first lieutenant is a capable fellow, saw the mutiny and can write reports and give evidence. Also he deserves his chance of getting command of her from the Admiralty. I'm assuming Ramage here is resigned to his new wife returning to England without him.'

He tapped three times. 'Now, the third question, what to do about the ship of exiles. She's a frigate now armed *en flûte*. She must look very much like the *Calypso*. She'll sail like her – except, since she's French carrying exiles, she'll be short of men and will most likely shorten sail at night. And she left the Gullet about thirty-six hours ago.

'What you are to do, sir, brings us back to the devil and the deep blue sea. Well, consider the devil in the shape of the First Lord of the Admiralty and the rest of the Board: they're political appointments. Lord St Vincent was appointed by Addington and will probably be replaced (along with the rest of the Board) by Addington's successor. So that devil can come and go. But now let us look across the deep blue sea ... One day the Prince will be King. He will probably have a long life – they're a long-lived family – and no doubt he inherits the long memory, too.'

He grinned at Admiral Clinton. 'I'll give you my recommendations in writing, sir, but you'll have to take my word for the reasoning behind them.'

'Oh, you're a droll enough fellow,' Clinton said, mellowing slightly. 'Watch out that one day I don't drop *you* over the side. Ramage, call that nincompoop of a secretary for me: I seem to have a number of orders to write, and I want them all carefully copied into my order book. Especially those intended for you.'

CHAPTER TWELVE

The abominable Bullivant had changed nothing in the great cabin: the desk was polished, the keys were still in the locks of the drawers. The settee was the same as usual, its dark-blue cover not torn or stained. The armchair was unmarked (except by the passing years flattening the springs). The man's possessions had been stowed in his trunks and sent across to the *Murex*. Yet although he had been on board for only a few days he had left an invisible atmosphere: now Ramage knew how the owner of a house felt standing in a room which had been rifled by a burglar.

He sat down at the desk, jerking open one drawer after another. Nothing had been removed, nothing added. Letter book – that was still here, and he flipped open a few pages. Bullivant had not written any official letters or, more likely, the clerk had not copied them into the letter book. Order book – yes, the Board order giving Bullivant command of the *Calypso*, followed by the Admiralty order to him to join Admiral Clinton's fleet were here, and so was Clinton's order to Bullivant telling him to place himself under the admiral's command. Nothing else.

The 'Captain's Journal' was here, started the day Bullivant joined the ship, and Ramage put it in another drawer without reading it. Yes, here was the muster book, and an entry indicated the date that Bullivant had joined the ship 'as per commission'. No one had noted that he was replacing Captain Ramage, who was on leave. Now there was a nice point – in noting that Bullivant had gone to the *Murex* 'by order of the commander-in-chief', did Ramage now note that Captain Ramage had taken (resumed?) command 'as per commission', thus having taken command twice without ever having (officially) left the ship? Or did he ignore Bullivant's brief command?

Some tedious quillpusher at the Navy Board could worry about that bureaucratic problem, and no doubt the correspondence ensuing would continue for another ten years. He noted that no seaman had been discharged and no new men had joined the ship.

He put the muster book and letter book back in the drawer, and took Admiral Clinton's order from his smock. Soon he would be back in uniform. Several officers in the flagship had offered spare uniform frocks and breeches, stockings, shirts and stocks, but Ramage guessed that his own clothes would still be in the *Calypso,* and indeed almost the first thing his steward Silkin had reported was that his trunks had been brought up from the hold and all the clothing was being washed or cleaned or ironed with a sprinkling of vinegar to get rid of the musty smell.

He opened Admiral Clinton's two sets of orders and read the

second one again. The admiral and Captain Bennett had drawn them up in a hurry, which ensured brevity.

'Whereas I have received information,' Admiral Clinton's orders began, 'that the French national frigate *L'Espoir* sailed from Brest very recently carrying as prisoners a large group of men and women accused by the French government of disloyalty and sentenced to transportation and exile in Cayenne, you are hereby required and directed to proceed with all possible dispatch in His Majesty's ship *Calypso* under your command and make the best of your way towards Cayenne and intercept the said French national frigate *L'Espoir* and free the prisoners and carry them safely to a port in England, reporting at once to my Lords Commissioners of the Admiralty the success of your mission . . .'

He slid the letter between two blank pages in the order book and put the volume back in the drawer, locking it. It was lucky that Bullivant never bothered to put a key in his pocket – every drawer in this particular desk had a different lock.

The shouting, stamping and scuffling on the deck overhead had finally stopped and Ramage listened for feet clattering down the companionway, to be halted at his door by the Marine sentry, who would then call out the person's identity.

He sat back and sighed with sheer pleasure. It was exciting to be back – he had spent so long in this cabin it seemed like home. Indeed, it was his home. Certainly sitting at this desk dressed as a French fisherman was unusual, but there was no time to wait for Silkin's smoothing iron to finish its work.

Since boarding the ship he had used the first fifteen minutes to listen to Silkin (who regarded his sartorial report as the most important the captain would want to hear) and then come down to the great cabin and read his orders once again. He had done this while Aitken prepared the ship for the next step.

And now there were the footsteps clattering down the companionway, and the clank of a sword hilt held high but not high enough to prevent it catching one of the steps.

The thump of feet and clatter of a musket indicated the Marine sentry coming to attention. Two voices, a question (from the sentry, one he would have had to ask even if the visitor had been his own mother), and a reply.

Then a tap on the door and the sentry's voice: 'Captain, sir – the first lieutenant!'

'Send him in.'

And in came a smiling Aitken, crouching slightly because of the low headroom, his sword held clear with one hand, his cocked hat under his arm.

'Ship's company mustered aft, sir.'

'Aitken' – Ramage stood up and walked towards the young Scot, his hand extended. As they shook hands, Ramage added: 'I'm glad to be back and I'm glad I have the same officers.'

'Thank you, sir. We held our breaths when we heard the British ambassador – Lord Whitworth, I think it is – had left Paris, but when you didn't come back from your honeymoon we guessed that the French had captured you and her Ladyship.'

Ramage gestured down at his smock and trousers. 'You didn't expect to meet me off Ushant in this rig! Well, you should see her Ladyship – she's dressed as a fishwife.'

He led the way up the ladder and out on deck. The Marines were lined up in two ranks against the taffrail; Southwick, the lieutenants and Orsini were at the starboard end of the front file, and the seamen formed the other three sides of the square so that the quarterdeck was a box of men.

Ramage had mustered all the men not through any overweening conceit but, because of that confidence always existing among men who have fought beside each other many times, he knew that they wanted to see him and be reassured.

The drunkard who had briefly taken his place had been hoisted out lashed on to a stretcher shouting and screaming that the seamen at the staytackle were doing the Devil's work. Now Bullivant was on his way to Plymouth in the *Murex* and he could only feel sorry for Sarah. She will, he thought grimly, see and hear what we went through with Bowen. Still, it is a bare 120 miles from Ushant to Plymouth and the *Murex* should stretch over to the northeast at a good six knots, so that Sarah will have to put up with it for only twenty-four hours. Then she would post to London and very soon the thought of the recent excitement would be like a half-remembered dream.

On top of the main capstan: the ship was not rolling enough to make it difficult for him to balance, and he could look round and see everyone, except for two or three Marines hidden by the mizenmast. But it was a dam' cold wind: the downdraught from the mainsail seemed to go straight through his smock. The advantage of full uniform in a northern climate was its warmth, although it was too hot for the Tropics – the cocked hat, for instance, seemed to gain a pound in weight for every ten degrees of latitude it moved south, so that near the Equator it was about as comfortable as a knight's helmet.

Now the Marines were standing stiffly to attention, the lieutenants frozen to the deck, and the seamen looking up at him, some grinning, some straight-faced, but none sucking teeth. Few captains seemed to realize that the presence or absence of the sucking of teeth revealed more about the men's attitude, happiness or discontent, than anything else.

He spoke a few words of greeting as he pulled the first of Admiral Clinton's orders from the front of his smock and the Marines and lieutenants unfroze. The seamen knew only too well what was coming next and made sure they were standing comfortably.

Ramage unfolded the paper and began the ritual of 'reading himself in'. Until that was completed he could not officially give any orders and expect them to be obeyed; he had purposely made 'stand at ease' a gruff comment rather than an order, and the helm order to Southwick was to save time. Then he began reading.

'By virtue of the power and authority to me given as commander-in-chief of His Majesty's ships and vessels comprising the Channel Fleet, and being off Brest and outside the Channel limits, I Reginald Edward Clinton, Vice-Admiral of the Red, do hereby constitute and appoint you captain of His Majesty's ship the *Calypso* frigate, willing and requiring you forthwith to go on board and take upon you the charge and command of captain in her accordingly ...'

Ramage paused for breath, cursing the man who had originally (probably a hundred years ago) drawn up the wording, never considering the poor captain who had to recite them loud enough so that over the sound of the wind and the sea every man in a ship's company could hear them. Well, almost all the seamen were grinning now, and he continued.

'... Strictly charging and commanding all the officers and company of the said *Calypso* frigate to behave themselves jointly and severally in their respective employments ... and you likewise to observe the General Printed Instructions ... Hereof nor you nor any of you may fail as you will answer to the contrary at your peril; and for so doing this shall be your warrant ...'

That last sentence meant just what it said: lieutenants, post-captains and admirals had been court-martialled and broken for failure. The commission of course covered any orders given by superiors, and the admiral's actual orders had a vagueness about them explained partly by the lack of much knowledge about *L'Espoir*, her prisoners and her route, but also so worded that whatever happened (in case of failure) the admiral could not be blamed. Admiral Clinton had been careful to note that he and Ramage were 'outside the Channel limits', because within Channel limits only the Board of Admiralty could appoint captains.

Ramage folded the orders and tucked them back inside his jersey: he had 'read himself in', he was (once again) commanding the *Calypso*. As soon as he had 'read himself in', Ramage reflected, a captain usually made a speech to the ship's company (threatening, inspiring, flatulent, boring – different styles). But all these men, all the names attached to the sea of faces surrounding him, knew him well: they had gone into action with him, boarded enemies beside him, pistol, cutlass or boarding pike in hand. Some had been blown up with him, most had seen him brought back unconscious from wounds. There were no words to say to such men.

He just looked round slowly at all the men, raised his right hand in a salute that suddenly reminded him absurdly of a Roman emperor's gesture, and jumped down from the main capstan amid a swelling roar of cheers: 'Three cheers and a tiger,' and apparently led by Southwick.

Well, he was back. Where was *L'Espoir*?

The sea now had the is-it-mauve-or-is-it-purple? of the deep ocean, with white horses stippling the tops of a few wind waves while swell waves slid beneath them. The *Calypso* was pitching slightly and rolling heavily, the masts and their yards creaking and the bulging sails frequently flattening and slatting as a particularly quick roll suddenly spilled the wind for a minute or two.

Astern the sun had lifted over the line of distant black cloud lying low and flat on the eastern horizon like a shadowy baulk of timber floating on the sea, and quickly the last of the stars were dazzled away and the sky overhead turned pale blue and cloudless.

In a few hours they would be crossing that invisible line of latitude 23 degrees 27 minutes North, marking the Tropic of Cancer, and, Ramage reflected thankfully, at last they seemed to have picked up the Trade winds.

For the previous few days it had been a damp and dreary ritual. During the night the wind dropped, leaving the *Calypso* wallowing in a confused sea which bounced her up and down like a doormat being shaken and made everything movable creak, rattle or bang. In Ramage's cabin even the wine glasses clinked in their rack as though toasting each other. Two drawers full of clothes which had not been shut properly skidded across the painted canvas that served as a carpet on the cabin sole, spilling silk and lisle stockings, handkerchiefs, stocks and shirts as though a dog was making a nest in a draper's storeroom.

Dawn each day had revealed thunderstorms building up all round them, the lower clouds foaming upwards towards a higher layer which soon cut off the sun. From time to time Ramage had stood at the quarterdeck rail, picturing *L'Espoir* scores of miles ahead and sailing in different weather, the Trade winds sweeping her south and west to Cayenne, sails bulging, the French captain cheerful as he marked his chart and filled in his journal to record a fast passage from Brest.

In the *Calypso,* Ramage, almost stifling with frustration, had looked up at the sails hanging down like heavy curtains, chafing against rigging, the foot of each one wearing against the mast since the sails of the King's ships were cut with a straight foot, not the deep curve favoured by merchant ships deliberately to avoid the chafe but reducing the area of the sail, something a ship of war could not afford.

Clew up to save some of the chafe or furl and avoid any at all? Or leave them so that he would not lose a minute once the first gust of wind arrived? But when it came (this week or next) would the wind be just a nice gust or would it be a roaring blast from one of those great thunderstorms that would send topmen hurrying to furl as courses were hastily clewed up and Aitken doubled the number of men at the wheel so that four stood a chance of preventing the overpressed frigate broaching as she raced to leeward, barely under control?

Should he risk losing a mile or so of progress, should he risk that heart-stopping bang of sail torn in half by the brute strength of the wind and then the thudding and thumping of the pieces slatting, or should he furl everything and wait for the wind to set in properly?

Eventually while he argued back and forth with himself and Southwick paced up and down, a lonely figure on the lee side of the quarterdeck, or Ramage stopped and barked at the quartermaster or chatted with the officer of the deck, in this case Martin, whiffles of wind had been spotted by the lookout at the foremasthead (a man having to hold on for dear life, and Ramage would have forgiven him if he had been too dizzy to spot anything). But the dancing shadows on the water were coming from the south. Anyway, anything was better than having the ship slat and bang herself to pieces, so they had braced up the yards and trimmed the sheets and found that, with the swell from the east and the lightness of the wind, the best they could lay and keep the sails asleep was west by north. They could pinch her to west by south but she slowed like a carriage miring itself in mud.

For the rest of each of those days they had jogged along at four and five knots, with the wind falling away at night and dawn bringing more thunderstorms. And the glass had fallen a little.

Except for this morning: while it was still dark the wind had again set in light from the south but he noticed that the glass had stopped falling and went on deck to find the sky was full of stars, already a good deal brighter than usual in northern skies. As dawn had begun to push away the dark of night the wind backed slightly – the coxswain had reported it as fluking around southeast by south, and the *Calypso* would just lay southwest by west. An hour later it was a steady east-southeast with the *Calypso* almost laying the course.

By noon it had backed another few points so that Southwick marked the slate in the binnacle box drawer and recorded the wind as northeast by east, with the ship making seven knots with all sails set to the royals and laying the course. More important, the ship's company were getting the stunsails up on deck ready for hoisting. The Trades had really set in? They could only hope. The noon sight – with Southwick, Aitken and Ramage himself on deck with quadrants and sextants measuring the sun's altitude – gave the latitude as 24 degrees 06 minutes North. Orsini had also taken a sight, which involved only turning the adjusting screw of the sextant to get the highest angle the sun made and did not depend on the accuracy of the chronometer. The young midshipman had achieved all that without difficulty but had stumbled over the simple calculations which involved the sextant angle and the sun's declination. The latitude which he finally admitted to Southwick had to be wrong, as the master pointed out with mild irony, since it placed the *Calypso* on the same latitude as Edinburgh.

Ramage was allowing a knot of southeast going current but previous experience showed this was too much. However, like Southwick who was a cautious navigator, he preferred that any error put the reckoning ahead of the ship: if the ship was ahead of the reckoning she could (and many did!) run on to unseen rocks and reefs guarding the destination.

As he was taking the noon sight, Ramage felt sure the Trades were setting in with their usual abruptness. At the moment only a few of the typical Trade wind clouds – small, flat-bottomed with rounded tops and reminding him of mushrooms – were moving in neat lines apparently converging on a point beyond the western horizon.

Trade wind clouds were a never-failing entertainment in the Tropics. In fact, he reflected, weather in the Trades could also be alarming for a Johnny Newcome, whether a seaman or officer fresh to the Tropics. In crossing the Atlantic, often one would find at dawn a band of low, thick cloud to the east (to windward and therefore, one would think, approaching) which would become black and menacing as the sun rose behind it: obviously, one would think, the herald of a strange tropical storm or gale, or at least a devastating squall.

The beginning of the day in the ship usually meant that for an hour or two every man was fully occupied, and then the Newcomes would suddenly remember (with more than a stab of fear) and look astern for that low, black cloud. But a quick glance to the eastward would show a clear horizon and an innocent sun rising with all the grace and smoothness of a duchess composing herself for a portrait artist.

So by nine o'clock the sky would be clear from horizon to horizon and the sun just beginning to hint that soon it would have some warmth in it. Then the parade of the mushrooms would begin.

He called them mushrooms but they really started in the distance as rows of white pinheads on a pale blue velvet pincushion. They would gradually move to the westward, keeping in neat lines but each pinhead beginning to expand like a fluffy ball of cotton growing on its bush. On and on to the westward they would move, and the sun warming the air would make the clouds blossom larger, but they would still stay in orderly and evenly-spaced lines, like columns of well drilled soldiers advancing across a plain. Sometimes the shapes would change: while the bottom stayed flat, the top would take up a grotesque shape, like a bun determined to alarm the baker's wife.

For Ramage the actual growth of the lines of cloud was the least of it. The fun came in looking at each of them. With flat bottom and bulging top, many were like recumbent effigies on the tops of tombs; with others the white vapour curved and twisted into the shape of faces staring up into the sky. In the course of fifteen minutes, ten chubby, long-faced, pug-nosed or long-nosed politicians familiar from cartoonists' broadsides, a dozen friends, and a dozen more bizarre but identifiable shapes would sail past on their way westward.

Occasionally, often in the late afternoon towards sunset, the western sky would slowly turn into the most horrifying scarlets and oranges, livid purples and ominous mauves, as though a child was being introduced to watercolour washes, and it seemed that within hours a most devastating hurricane must roar up against the wind and bring enormous seas to set them all fighting for their lives. But by nightfall the sky was usually clear again and sparkling with its full complement of stars and no hint of where the gaudy clouds had gone or why they had appeared.

The first flying fish always excited the ship's company: as soon as the ship slipped into the warmer southern seas most men would glance over the side as frequently as possible, hoping to be the first to glimpse the tiny silver dart skimming a foot or two high in a ridge and furrow flight over the waves to vanish as quickly as it appeared. What seemed the upper quadrant of a slowly turning and very thick wheel was the curving back of a dolphin, and always good for a yell, and sometimes a dozen or so of them would play games with the ship, racing to cut across the bow from side to side and so close that it seemed the cutwater must hit them.

For Ramage, though, there was a particular assignation in the Tropics, and he always felt cheated if he was not the first to sight it. It was the unusual rather than beautiful white bird which could be mistaken for a great tern, but for the fact that its tail, three times as long as its body, comprised a couple of long thin feathers trailing in a narrow V. The beak of the Tropic bird was red or yellow and the wings were narrow and pointed like those of the tern with the fast beat of a pigeon. Strangely enough it seemed to be a bird of the islands and headlands, one that was used to jinking and diving, and which would not stray far from land. And what was the purpose of that tail?

The birds in fact lived in colonies – he knew of several at St Eustatius and Nevis, in the Leeward Islands (each island, coincidentally, was easily identified because of the huge topless cone at one end revealing an old volcano). A passage between St Martin and St Barthélemy on one side and Saba, St Eustatius and St Kitts and Nevis on the other usually produced a dozen or more Tropic birds flying across the channel.

Yet Ramage had seen them here in the middle of the Atlantic, fifteen hundred miles and more from the nearest land, flying with just the same quick, almost nervous wing beats, as though due back at the nest in twenty minutes. It seemed to make little difference whether its destination was fifteen or fifty miles away. Nor fifteen hundred: that was simply the middle of the Atlantic between the Canary Islands and Barbados. To reach one from the other (or any land) the bird had to fly nearly three thousand miles. Did it just fly day and night without stopping? He had never seen one resting on the water like a seagull. And another strange thing was that all those he had seen out in the Atlantic were always flying directly east or west, never to the north or south. On the last voyage, he remembered looking up at eight o'clock in the forenoon to see his first Tropic bird of the passage flying due east, directly over the ship. Then, at four o'clock in the afternoon, he had seen one flying due west, again passing right over the ship. The same bird? His ship's destination, Barbados, had been two thousand miles to the westward. Yet, he remembered, every Tropic bird he had ever seen out in the Atlantic had passed directly over the ship: he had never seen one flying past in the distance. Nor did the bird ever dip down towards the ship, as though looking for a resting place or a tasty scrap of food.

Other species of birds often came on board, though of course they were usually much nearer land. Still, an old Barbados planter he had once spoken to said Tropic birds lived on flying fish and squid, diving down for them. The planter called it the boatswain bird, and the French had several names, different in each island – *paille-en-queue, paille-en-cul,* and *flèche-en-cul.* Straw tail, arrow tail – there were a dozen ways of translating it, but the Spanish *contramaestre* was the nearest to the English boatswain bird.

He waved to Aitken to cross the quarterdeck and join him.

'Horizon looks very empty, sir,' the young Scotsman commented. 'Seems you only realize how big the Western Ocean is when you're looking for someone.'

'We could have overtaken her. Or she could be to the north or south. Or ahead of us.'

'Aye, it'll be only a matter of chance if we sight her. Ten different captains have ten different routes for making this crossing.'

'So you're not very hopeful?'

'No, sir, not with the difference in time.'

Ramage nodded. 'Once she was a complete night ahead of us – ten hours of darkness – there was always the chance of us accidentally overtaking her. And with two or three hundred miles' difference in position, there's the weather, too. She could be stretching along comfortably with a northerly breeze while we are beating against a southerly. She could have a soldier's wind with stunsails set and we could be becalmed.'

'At least we're catching up now!' Aitken gestured to the stunsails, long narrow strips of sail each hanging down from its own tiny boom and hoisted by a halyard out to the end of a normal yard so each stunsail formed an extension of the sail, like an extra leaf at the end of a table.

'Catching up or outstripping?' Ramage mused. 'I can't see Frenchmen hurrying with a ship full of prisoners: they could be treating it all as a comfortable cruise and be in no rush to get back to France – it'll be winter by then, too. They've no idea they're being chased.'

The two men walked aft from the quarterdeck rail, past the companionway leading down to the captain's cabin, then abreast the great barrel of the main capstan, with the slots for the capstan bars now filled with small wedge-shaped drawers containing bandages and tourniquets, ready at hand if they should go into action. Past one black-painted gun on its carriage, and now a second. Then came the binnacle box, like an old chest of drawers with a window on each side, a pane of stone-ground glass revealing a compass which was far enough away not to affect the one on the other side but so placed that the man on either side of the wheel had a good view.

Now the double wheel. Normally the man to windward did most of the work, pulling down on the spokes, but with the ship running before the wind as she was now doing, yards almost square and stunsails drawing, each helmsman paid attention and the quartermaster's eyes never stopped a circuit which covered the luffs of the sails, the telltales streaming out from the top of the hammock nettings, and the compass.

The telltales – Ramage was thankful to see them bobbing so vigorously. Four or five corks threaded at ten-inch intervals on a length of line, with half a dozen feathers embedded in each cork, and the whole thing tied to a rod and stuck up in the hammock nettings, one each side, might not be everyone's idea of beauty, but after those days of calm and light headwinds, they were a wonderful sight.

Now they were passing the captain's skylight – built over the forward side of the great cabin it was a mixed blessing: it provided air and light, and he could hear what was going on, but sometimes the quarterdeck was a noisy place: at night there could be the thunderous flap of sails followed at once by the officer of the deck cursing the quartermaster, and the quartermaster cursing the helmsmen for their inattention . . . The officer of the deck at night would regularly call to the lookouts (six of them, two on the fo'c'sle, two amidships, and one on each quarter) to make sure they were awake and alert . . . Then, Ramage thought sourly, there would be one of those 'Is-it-isn't-it' conversations, probably between the sharp-eyed young Orsini and the officer of the deck. One would think he glimpsed a sail, or land, or breakers in the darkness. The other would be equally sure there was nothing. The muttered but heated debate would be enough to make sure that a drowsy Ramage wakened completely, and often, although he knew there was no land for a hundred miles, he would pull on a cloak and go on deck – there was always a chance . . .

Finally the last gun on the starboard side and a few more paces brought them up to the taffrail and time to turn back, both men turning inwards, a habit which ensured no interruption if they had been talking.

'This Count of Rennes, sir?' Aitken said cautiously. 'You've met him?'

'He has been a friend of my family since long before the war began.'

'Ah, so you feel all this personally, too, sir?'

'Yes – but he escaped to England at the Revolution and lived in England until the recent treaty. He still has an estate in Kent. But we're chasing *L'Espoir* because he's one of the most important French Royalists alive today.'

'And he won't be alive for long if they get him to Cayenne. That Devil's Island is well named, so I've heard.'

'There are two or three islands. I think the French call them the Îles du Salut. One is for convicts and another for political prisoners.'

'I have some notes on Cayenne and the islands,' Aitken commented. 'Taken from some old sailing directions from the Seventies. They probably haven't changed much!'

'You have them on board?'

'In my cabin, sir. I checked as soon as you mentioned where L'Espoir was bound.'

'We'll go over them soon, just in case.'

'That's where you'll catch the rabbit, sir,' Aitken commented. 'A poacher doesn't set a snare in the middle of the field; no, he puts it just outside the burrow. Then you catch the rabbit when it runs for home!'

Ramage stopped for a few moments. Yes, Aitken's simile made sense: why comb the Atlantic? Three thousand miles was the distance, and assuming the Calypso's lookouts could see ten miles on each beam in daylight, they were searching a swathe three thousand miles long and twenty miles wide – sixty thousand square miles. Which, to continue Aitken's simile, must be like walking across a county unable to see over the top of the grass. Cayenne was the burrow: that's where he had to set the noose.

Yet ... yet ... He resumed walking with Aitken.

'It doesn't leave us room or time to make any mistakes,' he said. 'If we're off the coast of Cayenne and L'Espoir heaves in sight, she only has to cover five miles or so and she's safe.'

'But if we're patrolling that stretch of the coast with all our guns run out, sir,' Aitken protested.

'You might just as well leave them unloaded with the tompions in,' Ramage said grimly. 'I can hardly fire into a ship where a quarter of those on board are likely to be those I'm ordered to rescue ...'

'Then how are we ... ?' Aitken broke off and came to a stop facing Ramage. He shook his head. 'I've spent many hours trying to decide the route L'Espoir would take, so that we could intercept her, but I didn't think of ... Yet it's so obvious!'

'Not that obvious,' Ramage assured him. 'Neither the admiral nor his flag captain considered it in drawing up my orders!'

'We're going to have to bluff 'em,' Aitken said dourly.

'Bluff won't help much: the French will see Devil's Island close to leeward and all they have to do is make a bolt for it.'

'Would they risk damage to their spars with land so close to leeward?'

'Of course. From what I've read, it's a mud-and-mangroves-and-sand coast and it's theirs, so even if we sent all their masts by the board, the ship would drift on to a friendly lee shore and the French would march their prisoners off at low water. Not quite that, because there's ten feet or so of tide, but you know what I mean.'

'But L'Espoir's people would know they'd then be marooned there for months, until the next batch of prisoners are sent out. Worse than that, until the next ship arrives that manages to break our blockade of Brest.'

Ramage thought of the problem often facing captains: how to train their officers fully to consider all the enemy's advantages without getting too overwhelmed or depressed to think of ways of overcoming them. An overwhelmed or depressed officer was almost as dangerous as an overconfident one. Well, perhaps Aitken would get there by himself.

'The French captain may have guessed that a British frigate is after him,' Ramage said, without adding the corollary that he would have had a long time to think of his advantages and disadvantages.

'I don't see why, sir,' Aitken said politely but firmly. 'In fact, if you'll pardon me, I think it'll be just the opposite. He'll be treating it like an unexpected cruise.'

'But he can't be sure he won't be intercepted somewhere by a patrolling British frigate.'

Ramage almost grinned at the effort Aitken, usually a very patient man, was making not to show his complete disagreement with this sort of reasoning. In other words, Ramage thought, it's working: Aitken really is considering!

'Sir, no ship that he meets, not one, whether French or British, Spanish or Dutch, will know that the war has started again: the news can't possibly have reached them yet. Cayenne and Devil's Island won't know of the new war until L'Espoir arrives, and her captain knows that as long as he smiles and waves if he sights a British frigate, he's in no danger because the British frigate will think the world is at peace.

'The *Calypso*, sir,' Aitken continued emphatically, 'is the most westerly British ship that knows the war has started again.

If we've overtaken *L'Espoir,* then we are the westernmost ship in existence.'

Ramage nodded agreement. 'We can be thankful Bonaparte didn't send out a dozen frigates from Brest the moment our ambassador left Paris: in areas off Madeira and the Canaries they could have captured dozens of John Company and other ships all bound to and from England. But he didn't because he's a soldier and not a sailor, and anyway they're very short of seamen in Brest.'

'Aye,' Aitken agreed. 'That Bonaparte seems to be a bonny soldier and we can be thankful he didn't take to the sea. Anyway, *L'Espoir* will have no reason to think the *Calypso* knows there's a war.'

'Wouldn't she be suspicious at seeing a British frigate so far south on this coast? About eight hundred miles south of the nearest British naval headquarters, Barbados?' Ramage continued testing Aitken.

'Sir, the *Calypso*'s French-built, and apart from the fact that she's a little smarter than the usual French national ship, there's no way she'd know we're British unless we're flying our own colours.'

Now Aitken was straying from the point Ramage wanted him to discover and consider.

'Yes, I agree with all that but – and it's a big "but" – Bonaparte never forgives anyone who makes a mistake. In France there's a very complicated secret police system under which everyone is supposed to report on everyone else. One effect is that anyone failing to carry out his orders is likely to be accused of treason. Failure is frequently labelled treachery to the Revolution. And that usually means the guillotine – few brought before the courts in France are ever found not guilty.'

'So you think that the captain of *L'Espoir* will have considered that among the possible risks and dangers, sir? That he won't regard this voyage as a cruise, even though he is certain to be sailing ahead of the news of war?'

'Look at it another way, Aitken: forget the naval aspect. The captain of *L'Espoir* is carrying out the orders of the admiral at Brest, but he is a realist: *he* knows that the orders really come from the Ministry of Police, from that man Fouché, in fact. His written orders may have said that he was to carry fifty *déportés* from Brest to Devil's Island and hand them over to the *préfet,* but he knows very well that those fifty men (and their women)

176

are regarded by Bonaparte at the moment as being the fifty greatest traitors who can be transported instead of guillotined. Now do you follow?'

Aitken shook his head. 'I don't think so, sir. It seems quite straightforward to me, but from the tone of your voice obviously it isn't!'

'Well, if somehow the captain does not deliver those fifty prisoners to the *préfet* in Cayenne, but instead they escape or are rescued by a British ship, so that Bonaparte and his police can't get at them, then –'

'Ah, I see!' Aitken exclaimed, his voice a mixture of triumph and disbelief. 'He would be accused of treachery – of deliberately allowing those fifty to escape.'

'Exactly. Ministers in power and Bonaparte himself always need scapegoats. The captain of *L'Espoir* knows that. No one commands a French national ship of war today solely because of his seamanship. Remember, in the first six months of the Revolution France destroyed many of her best officers, so today most of her captains are former boatswains; men who've survived all those earlier régimes. The captain of *L'Espoir* has survived – for nine years. He knows how to do it; he's an expert. So you can be sure he hasn't ruled out the chance of interception.'

'How does that affect us, sir? He must still be sure he is sailing ahead of the news of war.'

'Come now, forget that aspect. He has fifty valuable prisoners on board – valuable particularly because they could lead him to the guillotine. Surely he must have at least one overwhelming advantage . . .'

'Well – oh yes!' Aitken exclaimed. 'Fifty hostages! No one attempting a rescue would dare risk harming them! Yes, he knows no one dare fire a broadside into him. By God, he's as immune from harm as a pirate holding a nun in front of him.'

'Exactly, immune from broadsides, and he doesn't have to give a damn about arriving disabled on a lee shore. If he hands over the prisoners to the *préfet* safely at the cost of losing his ship the Minister of Marine might be lenient as long as he gets a favourable report from the *préfet*. Mind you, the captain and ship's company will be marooned in Cayenne and half might die from the black vomit and the survivors be captured on their way back to France in another ship . . .'

Aitken said suddenly: 'What do we do if we sight *L'Espoir* this afternoon, sir?'

'I've no idea,' Ramage admitted. 'We might send their masts by the board or tear their sails to shreds with langrage, but we'd still have to carry the ship by boarding and if the captain uses the prisoners as hostages and threatens their lives, we're still no nearer rescuing anyone.'

'It's a worry, sir,' Aitken commented, and Ramage was irritated by the Scotsman's tone: he spoke in the 'Yes, well, the captain's bound to think of something' voice. However, as Aitken now knew well, this time there was no way.

Admiral Clinton was lucky, Ramage thought sourly as he turned yet again at the taffrail: if the Count of Rennes and his fellow prisoners were not rescued, or were killed, the commander-in-chief would certainly incur the disfavour of the Prince of Wales, but that was all, because his orders (as far as they went) were quite correct. But Captain Ramage, whatever the verdict of a court-martial, could be sure that at best he would spend the rest of his life on the beach, drawing half-pay. No one would say anything out loud, but at the Green Room in Portsmouth, at Brooks's, White's and such places, there had been too many of his *Gazettes* published by the Admiralty for there not to be jealousy of 'that fellow Ramage'.

Nor would half-pay now be so boring and frustrating; in fact, with Sarah beside him it could be very lively. They would live at St Kew and running the estate would keep them busy. Yet he knew that while the war against France lasted and there were ships of the Royal Navy at sea, only half his heart would be in Cornwall. That, Sarah would know, might prove the most difficult thing to deal with.

He shook his head to dispel the thoughts: what on earth was he getting so depressed about, putting himself on half-pay when they had not even sighted *L'Espoir*?

Five minutes later, as Aitken wrote on the slate and Ramage continued pacing the windward side of the quarterdeck, there was a hail from aloft.

'Deck there – foretopmast lookout here!'

CHAPTER THIRTEEN

Mess number eight was the rather grandiose official description of one of the well-scrubbed tables and two forms flanking it on the *Calypso*'s lowerdeck. It was on the larboard side abreast the forehatch, which ensured a bitterly cold draught in winter in northern latitudes, but as the *Calypso* under Captain Ramage's command had spent most of her time in the Tropics or the Mediterranean, the members of the mess were content.

The outboard end of the narrow side of the table fitted into the ship's side and the other was suspended from the deckhead by two ropes. Each of the forms on the long sides of the table seated four men, so that each mess in the ship comprised no more than eight men.

The mess had its own equipment. There was the bread barge, a wooden container in which the bread for the mess was kept. The bread was ship's biscuit, made in the great naval bakeries, and at the moment it was fresh, a word used to describe a square of hard baked dough which was still hard, not soft and crumbling, the happy home of the black-headed and white-bodied weevils which felt cold to the tongue but had no taste.

The bread barge was in some ways a symbol of the mess. The number eight was carefully painted on the tub-shaped receptacle and beside it was the mess kid, a tiny barrel open at one end with what looked like two wooden ears through which was threaded a rope handle. Also marked with the mess number, it was used to carry hot food from the copper boilers in the galley to the table.

The carefully scrubbed net bag folded neatly on the bread barge and with a metal tally stamped '8' fixed to it was the 'kettle mess', the improbably named object in which all hot food was cooked, because boiling in the galley's copper kettles was the only way it could be done. The *Calypso*'s cook, like those in each of the King's ships, was the man responsible for the galley in general, the cleanliness of the copper kettles and the fire that heated the water in them, but that was the limit of his cooking.

Each mess had its own cook, a man who had the job for a week. Number eight mess's cook this week was Alberto Rossi, a cheerful man who was nicknamed 'Rosey' and usually corrected anyone who called him Italian by pointing out that he came from Genoa, which in Italian was spelled Genova, so that he was a Genovese. If number eight mess decided in its collective wisdom that it would use its ration of flour, suet and raisins (or currants) to make a duff, Rossi's culinary skill would extend itself to mixing the ingredients with enough water to hold them together, put them in the kettle mess and make sure (with tally safely affixed) that it was delivered to the ship's cook by 4 a.m. and collected at 11.30 a.m., in time for the noon meal.

For this week when he was the mess cook, Rossi was also responsible for washing the bowls, plates, knives, forks and spoons of the other members of the mess, and stowing them safely. And, because bread, even if not appetizing, eased hunger, he had to make sure the bread barge was full – any emptying being ascribed to the south wind. Stafford, noting it was barely half-full, might comment: 'There's a southerly wind in the bread barge.'

Nor were the points of the compass limited to the compass and the bread barge: tots of rum were also graded. Raw spirit was due north, while water was due west, so a mug of nor'wester was half rum and half water, while three quarters rum would become a nor'nor'wester and a quarter of rum would be west-nor'west and find itself nobody's friend.

The seven men now sitting at mess number eight's table piled up their plates and basins. Three used old pewter plates, but four, the latest to join the mess, used bowls and looked forward to the *Calypso* taking her next prize, Rossi having explained carefully that a French prize years ago had yielded the three pewter plates in defiance of the eighth Article of War, which forbade taking 'money, plate or goods' from a captured ship before a court judged it a lawful prize. There was an exception which the three men interpreted in their own way – unless the object was 'for the necessary use and service of any of His Majesty's ships and vessels of war'. Admittedly such objects were supposed to be declared later in the 'full and entire account of the whole', but as Stafford said at the time with righteous certainty in his Cockney voice: 'S'welp us, we clean forgot.'

'Feels nice to be warm again,' Stafford remarked, wiping his mouth on the back of his hand. 'England's never very warm but the Medway's enough ter perish yer. The wind blowin' acrorst those saltings . . . why, even the beaks of the curlews curl up with the cold.'

'Curlew? Is the bird? Is true, this curling?' Rossi asked, wide-eyed.

Jackson, the captain's coxswain, who owned a genuine American Protection issued to him several years earlier, shook his head. 'Another of Staff's stories. All curlews have long curved beaks whether it's a hot day or cold.'

'Anyway, I'm glad we're back in the Tropics,' Stafford said cheerfully. 'Don't cross the Equator, do we?'

Jackson shook his head. 'Not even if we go all the way to Cayenne. What's its latitude, Gilbert?'

The Frenchman shook his head in turn. 'I am ashamed,' he said, 'but I do not know it.'

When another of the French asked a question in rapid French, Gilbert translated Jackson's question, and the Frenchman, Auguste, said succinctly: '*Cinq.*'

'Auguste says five degrees North,' Gilbert said.

'Five, eh? When we're in the West Indies, up and down the islands, we're usually betwixt twelve and twenty,' Stafford announced, and turned to Jackson. 'There, you didn't know I knowed that, didja!'

'Knew,' Jackson corrected automatically, and Stafford sighed.

'Oh, all right. You didn't knew I knowed that, then.'

'*Mama mia,*' Rossi groaned, 'even I know that's wrong. Say slowly, Staff: "You didn't know I knew that." How are these *Francesi* going to learn to speak proper?'

'Don't sound right to me,' Stafford maintained. 'And I come from London. You're an American, Jacko – Charlestown, ain't it? And you're from Genoa, Rosey. So I'm more likely to be right.'

Jackson ran his hand through his thinning sandy hair and turned to Gilbert. 'You'd better warn Auguste, Albert and Louis that if they are going to speak decent English, they'd better not listen to this picklock!'

'Picklock? I do not know this word,' Gilbert said.

'Just as well, 'cos I ain't one,' Stafford said amiably. 'Locksmith, I was, set up in a nice way of business in Bridewell Lane. Wasn't my business if the owners of the locks wasn't always at 'ome; the lock's gotta be opened.'

Gilbert nodded and smiled. 'I understand.'

'Yer know, the four of you are all right for Frenchies. Tell yer mates wot I said.'

Gilbert translated and considered himself lucky. Just over a year ago he was living in Kent, serving the Count while they were all refugees in England. Then, with the peace, the Count had decided to return to France (and Gilbert admitted he wished now he had taken it upon himself to mention to the Count the doubts he had felt from the first). Then everything had happened at once – the Count had been taken away to Brest under arrest, Lord and Lady Ramage had managed to escape, they had all recaptured the mutinous English brig and now the four of them were serving in the Royal Navy!

His Lordship had been very apologetic, although there was no need for it. Apparently he had intended (this was when he expected to sail the *Murex* back to England) to keep them on the ship's books as 'prisoners at large', and recommend their release as refugees as soon as they reached Plymouth, so they would be free to do what they wanted.

Gilbert could see his Lordship's motives, but he was forgetting that three of them – Auguste, Louis and Albert – did not speak a word of English and would never have been able to make a living. Serving in the Royal Navy, at least they would be paid and fed while they learned English, and life at sea, judging from their experience so far, was less hard than life in a wartime Brest, and no secret police watched . . .

Anyway, his Lordship had explained this odd business of 'prize money'. Apparently it was a sort of reward the King paid to men of the Royal Navy for capturing an enemy ship, and as the *Murex* had been taken by the French after the mutiny, she became an enemy ship, so recapturing her meant she was then a prize.

Apparently, though, after they had recaptured the *Murex* and sailed her out of Brest, it seemed that only his Lordship would get any prize money because he was the only one of them actually serving in the Royal Navy. That seemed unfair because her Ladyship had behaved so bravely. Certainly neither he nor Auguste, Albert nor Louis had expected any reward, but his Lordship had thought otherwise and he had talked to the Admiral, who had agreed to his proposal. The result was that if the four of them volunteered for the Royal Navy, their names would be entered in the muster book of the *Calypso* and (by a certain free interpretation of dates) they would get their share.

So here they were, members of mess number eight, and Auguste and Albert were put down on the *Calypso*'s muster book as ordinary seamen while he and Louis were still landmen, because they did not yet have the skill of the other two.

And this mess number eight: although no one said anything aloud, Gilbert had the impression that while Jackson, Rossi and Stafford were not the captain's favourites – he was not the sort of man to play the game of favourites – they had all served together so long that they had a particular place. It seemed that each had saved the other's life enough times for there to be special bonds, and Gilbert had been fascinated by things Jackson had explained. Gilbert had noticed his Lordship's many scars – and now Jackson put an action and a place to each of them. The two scars on the right brow, another on the left arm, a small patch of white hair growing on his head . . . It was extraordinary that the man was still alive.

However, one thing had disappointed Gilbert: no one, least of all Jackson, Stafford and Rossi, seemed to think they had much of a chance of finding *L'Espoir*. Apparently once she left Brest she could choose one of a hundred different routes. Oh dear, if only the Count had stayed in Kent. The estate he bought at Ruckinge was pleasant; even the Prince of Wales and his less pleasant friends had been frequent guests, and the Count never complained of boredom. But undoubtedly he had a *grande nostalgie* for the château and, although expecting it, had been heartbroken when he returned to find everything had been stolen. He had –

The heart-stopping shrill of a bosun's call came down the forehatch followed by the bellow 'General quarters! All hands to general quarters – come on there, look alive . . .' Again the call screamed – Jackson said the bosun's mates were called 'Spithead Nightingales' because of the noise their calls made – and again the bellow.

Gilbert followed the others as he remembered 'General quarters' was another name for a man's position when the ship went into battle. He felt a fear he had not experienced in the *Murex* affair. The *Calypso* was so big; all the men round him knew exactly what to do; they ran to their quarters as if they were hunters following well-worn tracks in a forest.

Ramage snatched up the speaking trumpet while Aitken completed an entry and returned the slate to the drawer.

'Foremast, deck here.'

'Sail ho, two points on the larboard bow, sir: I see her just as we lift on the top of the swell waves.'

'Very well, keep a sharp lookout and watch the bearing closely.'

Ramage felt his heart thudding. Was she *L'Espoir*? Keep calm, he told himself: it could be any one of a dozen British, Dutch, Spanish, French or American ships bound for the West Indies and staying well south looking for the Trades. Or even a ship from India or the Cape or South America, bound north and, having found a wind, holding it until forced to bear away to pick up the westerlies.

If the bearing stayed the same and the sail drew closer the *Calypso* must be overhauling the strange vessel, and it was unlikely that the *Calypso* was being outdistanced. If the sail passed to starboard, then whoever she was must be bound north; passing to larboard would show she was going south.

Southwick had heard the lookout's hail and came on deck, his round face grinning, his white hair flowing like a new mop.

'Think it's our friend, sir?'

'I doubt it; we couldn't be that lucky. She's probably a Post Office packet bound for Barbados with the mail.'

Southwick shook his head, reminding Ramage of a seaman twirling a dry mop before plunging it into a bucket of water. 'We'd never catch up with a packet. Those Post Office brigs are slippery.'

'Could be one of our own frigates sent out by the Admiralty with dispatches for the governors of the British islands, telling them war has been declared.' Ramage thought a moment and then said: 'Yes, she could be. She'd have sailed from Portsmouth before the Channel Fleet, of course, and run into head winds or been becalmed.'

He looked round and realized that it had been a long time since he had given this particular order: 'Send the men to quarters, Mr Aitken. I want Jackson aloft with the bring-'em-near – he's still the man with the sharpest eyes. I must go below and look up the private signals.'

He went down to his cabin, sat at the desk and unlocked a drawer, removing the large canvas wallet which was heavy from the bar of lead sewn along the bottom and patterned with brass grommets protecting holes that would allow water to pour in and sink it quickly the moment it was thrown over the side.

He unlaced the wallet and removed five sheets of paper. They were held together by stitching down the left-hand side, so that they made a small booklet, a thin strip of lead wrapped round the edge hammered flat and forming a narrow binding.

The first page was headed 'Private Signals' with the note 'Channel Fleet' and the date. The first two paragraphs, signed by Admiral Clinton, showed their importance: they were, with the Signal Book, the most closely guarded papers on board any ship of war.

Ramage noted that the wording of the warning was similar if not identical to that in the document he had studied with Lieutenant Swan on board the *Murex*.

Any ship of war passing through the area cruised by the Channel Fleet would have a copy of this set of flag tables for challenging and distinguishing friend from enemy. The system was simple: depending on the day of the month (the actual month itself did not matter), there was a special challenge with its own answer.

There were four main vertical columns divided into ten horizontal sections. The first section of the first column contained the numbers 1, 11, 21, 31, and referred to those dates. The section immediately below had 2, 12, 22, with 3, 13, 23 below and then 4, 14, 24, until the tenth section ended up with 10, 20, 30, so that every day in a month was covered.

The next column had the same two phrases in each of its ten sections: '*The first signal made is* –', and '*Answered by a* –', and referred to the next two columns. The third was headed by 'Maintopmasthead', and gave the appropriate signals to be hoisted there, while the fourth and last column headed 'Foretopmasthead' gave the signals to go up there.

Ramage noted that today was the eleventh of the month, and the date '11' was the second in the first column. The 'first signal' made would be a white flag with a blue cross (the figure two in the numeral code of flags) hoisted at the maintopmasthead and a blue flag with a yellow cross (numeral seven) at the foretopmasthead. One ship or the other (it did not matter which) would challenge first with those two, and be answered by a blue, white and red flag (numeral nine) at the maintopmasthead and a pendant over blue pierced with white (numeral zero) at the foretopmasthead. Numeral flags hoisted singly by a senior officer had a different meaning, but these were given in the Signal Book and there could be no confusion.

The last page of the booklet gave the private signals to be used at night – combinations of lights hoisted in different positions, and hails. Ramage noted that whoever thought up the hails must have an interest in geography: the month was divided into thirds, with the various challenges and replies being 'Russia – Sweden', 'Bengal – China', and 'Denmark – Switzerland'.

To complicate the whole system, the day began at midnight for the flag signals (corresponding to the civil day), while it began at noon for the night signals, and thus corresponded with the noon-to-noon nautical day used in the logs and journals.

Ramage repeated the numbers to himself – two and seven are the challenge, nine and zero the reply. He put the signals back in the wallet, knotted the drawstrings, and returned it to the drawer, which he locked.

How long before Jackson would be reporting?

The cabin was hot: he longed for the loose and comfortable fisherman's trousers, but they had been taken away with the smock by a disapproving Silkin, whose face was less lugubrious now he had the captain regularly and properly dressed in stockings, breeches, coat, shirt, stock and cocked hat. That the breeches were tight at the knees and the stock became soaked with perspiration and chafed the skin of the neck (and rasped as soon as the whiskers began sprouting again three or four hours after shaving) was no concern to Silkin: to him those discomforts were the sartorial price a gentleman had to pay, and Silkin regarded any article of clothing as 'soiled' if it was only creased.

Ramage knew that by now the men would be at general quarters: indeed, the Marine sentry had already reported that the men who would be serving the two 12-pounders in the great cabin and the single ones in the coach and bed place were waiting to be allowed in to cast off the lashings and prepare the guns, hinge up the bulkheads and strike the few sticks of furniture below the gundeck. Ramage picked up his hat and left the cabin, nodding to the guns' crews as he went up on deck and pulling the front of his hat down to shield his eyes from the sun, which glared down from the sky and reflected up from the waves.

He told Aitken the flag numbers for the challenge and reply, said he did not want the guns run out for the time being, and then joined Southwick standing at the quarterdeck rail, looking forward the length of the ship. Men were hurrying about but none ran: each had that sense of purposefulness that came from constant training and which led to them using the minimum of effort needed to do a task. The decks had already been wetted and sand sprinkled, so that if the ship did go into action the damp planks would stop any spilt powder being ignited by friction and the sand would prevent it blowing about as well as stop feet slipping.

The flintlocks had been fitted to the guns. Powder boys holding cartridge boxes sat along the centreline, one behind each pair of guns, while each gun captain had fitted the firing lanyard to the lock, the lanyard being long enough for him to kneel behind the gun and fire it well clear of the recoil. A small tub of water stood between each pair of guns with lengths of slowmatch fitted into notches round the top edge and burning so that any glowing piece fell into the water. They would be used only if a flintlock misfired. The cook had just doused the galley fire at the order for general quarters, and the slowmatch were the only things burning in the ship.

Below, 'fearnought' screens, thick material like heavy blankets, would have been unrolled and now hung down to make the entrance to the magazine almost a maze. Where men had now to jink about to get in, it was sure no flash from an accidental explosion would penetrate. The gunner was down inside the magazine, wearing felt shoes so that there could be no sparks inside the tiny cabin which was lined first with lathes and then plaster thickened with horsehair, and that covered with copper sheeting. The only tools allowed inside were bronze measurers, like drinking mugs on wooden handles, and bronze mallets for knocking the copper hoops from barrels of powder.

Close to each gun, stuck in spaces in the ship's side where they could be quickly snatched up, were cutlasses, pistols and tomahawks – each man knew which he was to have, because against his name in the General Quarter, Watch and Station Bill would be a single letter, C, P or T.

In less than a minute, Ramage knew, just the time it would take to load and run out the guns, cock the locks and fire, nearly two hundred pounds of roundshot could be hurling themselves invisibly at an enemy, each shot the size of a large orange and able to penetrate two feet of solid oak. Yet to a casual onlooker the *Calypso* was at this very moment simply a frigate ploughing her way majestically across the Western Ocean, stunsails set and all canvas to the royals rap full with a brisk Trade wind, the only men visible a couple of men at the wheel, three officers at the quarterdeck rail, and a couple of lookouts aloft.

Yet all this was routine: in the Chops of the Channel a frigate might be sending her ship's company to quarters every hour or so, as an unidentified and possibly hostile vessel came in sight. In wartime every strange sail could be an enemy. Admittedly, one saw a great many more ships in the approaches to the Channel and few would prove to be enemy, although so-called neutral ships trying to run the blockade were numerous. For a surprising number of people, Ramage noted, profit knew no loyalty – or perhaps it would be truer to say that whichever nation provided the profit had the trader's loyalty as a bonus.

'Deck there – mainmasthead!'

That was Jackson, and Ramage let Aitken reply. The American's report was brief.

'Reckon she's a frigate steering north, sir. Too far off to identify but you'll see her in a few minutes, two points on our larboard bow.'

Aitken acknowledged and turned to Ramage, who nodded and said: 'Take in the stunsails, Mr Aitken.'

As soon as Aitken gave the order, there seemed to be chaos as men ran from the guns, some going to ropes round the mast, to the ship's side where stubby booms held out the foot of the sails, and others went up the ratlines.

Bosun's mates' pipes shrilled and they repeated the order: 'Watch, take in starboard studding sails!'

After that it was a bellowed litany, making as much sense as a Catholic service in Latin to a Protestant but curiously orderly and impressive.

Main and foretopmen were standing by waiting for the order to go aloft, along with men named boomtricers in the station bill for this manoeuvre. Then the orders came in a stream – 'Away aloft . . . Settle the halyards . . . Haul out the downhauls . . . Haul taut . . . Lower away . . . Haul down . . .' As the tall and narrow rectangles of sail came down and were quickly stifled on deck before the wind took control, more orders followed to deal with the booms, still protruding from the ends of the yards and the ship's side like thin fingers.

'Stand by to rig in the booms . . . Rig in! . . . Aft lower boom . . . Top up . . . Ease away fore guy, haul aft . . .'

Then, to the men stifling the sails on deck: 'Watch, make up stunsails.' Aitken raised the speaking trumpet: 'Stand by aloft . . .'

The quartermaster was already giving orders to the men at the wheel: with the starboard stunsails down and no longer helping to drive the ship along, the larboard stunsails, yet to be taken in, were trying to slew her round to starboard and needed a turn on the wheel to counteract them.

Then came the same ritual for the larboard stunsails, until with the canvas rolled, the booms taken in and the topmen and tricers down from aloft, Aitken gave the final order: 'Watch carry on at general quarters.'

At last Ramage let his brain function again. He had tried to shut it off when the sail ahead was first sighted: he wanted to store the sound of that first hail until, perhaps half an hour later, Jackson would report that the vessel was a French frigate similar in appearance to the *Calypso* and steering the same course: evidence enough that they had finally caught *L'Espoir* – although quite what he did then, he did not know.

Now, however, his lack of ideas did not matter: the ship was unlikely to be *L'Espoir* because she was going in a different direction. A frigate, yes, but following the sea roads imposed by the wind directions, probably bound for Europe but first having to go north nearly to Newfoundland before turning eastward, unless she wanted to try the slower Azores route.

Probably Royal Navy, possibly returning from the Far East or South America, but more likely the Cape of Good Hope. Anyway, she would not know the war had started again, and if she was British he was obliged to give her captain the news. Nor could he begrudge the time because *L'Espoir* could be ahead or astern, to the north or the south, so any delay or diversion could lead to her discovery. Patience, Ramage thought, as he glanced aloft at the tiny figure of Jackson perched in the maintop. It was the one thing needed by the captain of a ship of war, it was one of the virtues he had always lacked.

'Look,' Stafford said, pointing at the shiny metal rectangle of the flintlock, 'you see the flint there, just like wiv a pistol or musket.'

He waited for Gilbert to translate to Auguste, Albert and Louis and then continued: 'Only you don't have no trigger like a hand-gun. Instead the lanyard – well, translate that.'

He paused because he really meant that the flintlock of a great gun did not have the kind of trigger that you put your finger round, and he was rapidly realizing that a good instructor was a man who could explain complicated mechanisms and thoughts

189

in a simple way. Jackson was good at it. The captain was fantastic.

'Yers, well, this lower bit is the trigger: when yer put a steady strain on the lanyard (yer *don't* jerk it),' he emphasized, 'it pulls the trigger part up towards the ring the lanyard threads through down from – translate that!' he exclaimed, having lost both the lanyard and the thread of his explanation,

Gilbert looked up politely and said gently: 'Stafford, we can see very well how it works. Your very clear explanation – it is not really necessary.'

'Ah, good,' sighed a mollified Stafford, with a triumphant glance at Rossi, who had earlier been jeering at the Cockney's attempts to explain the loading and firing of the *Calypso*'s 12-pounders. 'Now, here is the pricker.' He held up a foot-long thin rod, pointed at one end and with a round eye at the other, and for which he as second captain of this particular gun was responsible.

He passed the pricker, which was like a large skewer, to Gilbert to inspect and waited while the others looked. 'Ze prickair,' Auguste repeated. '*Alors.*'

'No, just "pricker",' Stafford corrected amiably. 'Now, you saw the flannel what the cartridge is made of and what 'olds the powder. Well, now, forget that for a minute and we'll go back to the lock. That's got to make a spark what fires the gun ...'

He waited for Gilbert's translation and noted to himself that the French seem to make things sound so difficult.

'Well, you see this 'ole 'ere leading down into the barrel – same as in a pistol, the touch'ole. Well, instead of just sprinklin' powder in the pan and lettin' it fill up the touch'ole, so that when the flint sparks off the powder and sends a flash of flame down the touch'ole to set off the charge ... No, well, in a ship the roll or the wind could ... well, we put a special tube in the touch'ole and sprinkle powder in the pan and cover the end ...'

Gilbert translated a shortened version.

'Now, just remember that. But the flash down the touch'ole won't go through the flannel of the cartridge. Ho no, nothing like. That's why we use the pricker. Before we put in the tube, we jab the pricker down the touch'ole and wriggle it about so we're certain sure it's made an 'ole in the cartridge right under the touch'ole, and that means if you looked down the touch'ole you'd see the powder of the cartridge – if the light was right, o'course.'

Gilbert translated but the other three men, who had already worked it all out, having seen the little tubes in their special box, were beginning to suck their teeth.

'*Now,* in goes the tube and we pour some powder into the pan and cover the end of the tube, just to make sure the spark of the flint really makes it take fire ... The tube explodes (well, not really, it makes a flash, which goes down the touch'ole of course) and that explodes the powder in the flannel cartridge –'

'And forces the shot up the barrel and out of the muzzle,' Gilbert said quickly.

'That's right! Good, I'm explaining it clearly enough, then,' Stafford said smugly. 'Next, now we know 'ow to fire the gun –'

'We must learn how to load it,' Rossi said triumphantly. 'You forgot that!'

'I was goin' to explain the dispart sight,' Stafford said sulkily.

'Only the gun captain uses that,' Rossi said. 'Leave it to Jackson to explain.'

'Oh well,' Stafford said in the most offhand manner he could contrive, but which did not reveal his relief as he realized that in fact he did not really understand how a dispart sight worked, 'we'll do loading now.'

Gilbert coughed. 'We watched when you had gunnery practice the day before yesterday,' he said. 'It is the same as for a pistol except you "swab out" the barrel. "Swab out" – that is correct, no? And you "worm" it every few rounds with that long handle affair which has a metal snake on the end. To pull out any burning bits of flannel cartridge which might be left inside –'

'Yes, very well, I'm glad you've understood that,' Stafford said, tapping the breech of the gun with the pricker and preening himself in the certainty that the Frenchmen's understanding was due to his explanation. 'The rest is obvious: you saw how we use these handspikes' – he pointed to the two long metal-shod bars, like great axe handles – 'to lift and traverse the gun. "Traversing" is when you aim it from side to side, and you say "left" or "right", not "forward" or "aft". Now, to elevate the gun, you –'

'Lift up the breech using a handspike as a lever,' Gilbert said.

'That's right,' Stafford said encouragingly. It was not as hard to explain difficult things as he had expected, even when your pupils are Frenchmen who do not speak a word of English.

'Then,' Gilbert continued, reminding Stafford of his role as translator, 'you pull out or push in – depending on whether you are raising or lowering the elevation – this wooden wedge under the breech. What you call the "quoin", no?'

'Well, we pronounce it "coin", but you are understanding.'

Rossi chuckled and said: 'Tell the Frogs about "point-blank".'

Gilbert grinned at the Italian. 'We have a *rosbif* explaining to a *frog* with a *Genovese* watching. What is a *Genovese* called?'

'I don't know,' Rossi said expansively. 'Tuscans call us the Scottish of the Mediterranean, but who are Tuscans to cast stones?'

'Why Scottish?' Stafford asked. 'You don't wear kilts or play a haggis or anything.'

'You eat haggis,' Rossi said. 'It is some kind of pudding. They make it from pigs, I think. No, Scottish because the *Genovesi* are said to be – well, "careful" I think is the word. We don't rattle our money in our purses.'

'Ah, "mean" is the word, not "careful",' Stafford declared.

Rossi shrugged. 'I am not interested in the word. Is not true, not for the *Genovesi* or the *Scozzesi*.'

'Point-blank,' Stafford said, 'is the place where a roundshot would hit the sea if the gun barrel was absolutely 'orizontal when the shot fired. About two hundred yards, usually. The shot doesn't go straight when it leaves the gun but curves up and then comes down: like throwing a ball. There!' he said to Rossi. 'Yer thought I didn't know!'

Shouts from aloft cut short Rossi's mocking laugh and Gilbert began translating for the other three.

CHAPTER FOURTEEN

'She's hove-to on the starboard tack, sir,' Jackson shouted down from the mainmasthead. 'Waiting for us to come down to her.'

'What is she?'

'Frigate, looks as though she could be French-built, sir, but she's too far off to distinguish her colours.'

Ramage turned aft and began to walk, hands clasped behind his back, oblivious of the glances of the guns' crews on each side of the quarterdeck.

A French frigate: 32 guns or so, a hundred and fifty men or less in peacetime, and her captain with no idea the war had started again. Unless she had sighted *L'Espoir*. In which case she would know not only about the war but where *L'Espoir* was perhaps only a few hours ago. In the meantime, the fact that she had hove-to, waiting for the *Calypso* to run down towards her (like an affectionate dog rolling over on its back in anticipation of a tickled belly) meant that she had recognized the *Calypso* as French-designed and built: her distinctive and graceful sheer would be seen particularly clearly as she approached, taking in her stunsails.

Ramage walked between two guns and then looked out through a port. The Trades were kicking up their usual swell waves with wind waves sliding across the top of them. Not the sort of seas for ships to manoeuvre at close quarters; seas in which a cutter with strong men at the oars would have to take care. An accidental broach in those curling and breaking crests – which seemed sparkling white horses from the deck of a frigate but were a mass of airy froth which would not support a man's body or a boat any more than thick snow carried carriage wheels or horses' hooves – was something that kept a coxswain alert.

He turned forward again at the taffrail, cursing softly to himself. Devil take it; he wanted to concentrate all his thoughts and all his efforts on catching *L'Espoir* and rescuing her prisoners, without being bothered by another frigate, least of all French. An enemy which had to be attacked.

Yet ... yet ... He reached the quarterdeck rail and turned aft again, unseeing, walking instinctively, almost afraid to move or yet stand still because out there just beyond his full comprehension, like the dark hurrying shadows on a calm sea made by tiny whiffles of a breeze that came and went without direction or purpose, refusing to strengthen or go away, intent only on teasing, like a beautiful and wilful woman at a masked ball, there was a hint of an idea.

Well, at least he could see the wind shadows of an idea, and they hinted where this frigate could fit in. Taffrail, turn forward ... So let us consider the arguments against this vague, floating idea, or anyway what little he could grasp of it. Damage to the *Calypso*'s spars ... But they were still far enough north to make Barbados under a jury rig ... Seamen needed as prize crew and Marines as guards ... Now those dark whiffling shadows were becoming a little sharper, the edges more distinctly outlined . . . Quarterdeck rail and turn . . .

No more hails from Jackson but, he suddenly realized, both Southwick and Aitken had been standing where he turned, waiting to say something but unwilling to interrupt his thoughts. He swung back to them.

'Sir,' Aitken said, 'the ship ahead is now in sight from here on deck. We can't make out her colours but from the cut of her sails and her sheer, she looks French all right. Shall we hoist our colours? Do you want the guns loaded now and run out?'

Ah, how one decision depended on another, but the sequence had to have a beginning. In this case the beginning was positively identifying the ship ahead as French. French-built with French-cut sails almost certainly made her one of Bonaparte's ships, because the last year and a half of peace ruled out her being recently captured by the Royal Navy.

Very well, she is French. 'Don't hoist our colours,' Ramage said. 'She probably wouldn't be able to see them anyway because we're dead to windward. Have the guns loaded. Canister, not roundshot, and grape in the carronades. We want to tear her rigging and sails, not splinter her hull. Don't run them out, though.'

He thought a moment. 'Have a dozen men rig up a line of clothes on the fo'c'sle. Laundry always looks so peaceful.' He grinned. 'Tell them that anything lost will be replaced by the purser.'

'Pusser's slops' were never popular with any seaman proud of his appearance. 'Slops', the name given to the shirts, trousers, material and other items which could be bought from the purser, who combined the role of haberdasher, tobacconist, and general supplier whose profit came from the commission he charged, were usually of poor quality. The shirts all too often came, so the men grumbled, in two sizes – too large and too small. Likewise the trousers were too long or too short. All were too expensive, as far as the men were concerned. The 'pusser' was rarely a popular man, and in most ships the victim of scurrilous stories. He was, the seamen of the Navy claimed, the only person who could make dead men chew tobacco. The miracle was performed when a seaman died or was killed and an unscrupulous purser put down in his books that the man had drawn a few pounds of tobacco, the price of which would be taken from the wages owing to relatives while the tobacco remained in the purser's store to be sold again. Careless pursers had even charged men who never touched tobacco.

Daydreaming ... Again Ramage cursed his habit of letting his mind go wandering up byways when his thoughts should stay on the highway.

He waited until Aitken had finished passing the orders and watched Martin, Kenton and Wagstaffe down on the maindeck supervising their divisions of guns. He looked around for Orsini and found the young midshipman waiting beside the binnacle. His role when the ship was at general quarters was to be near the captain, ready to run messages. He had once heard the boy complain to Martin that being the captain's *aide de camp* sounded a fine job in action, but Mr Ramage never wanted any messages taken anywhere ...

Well, Paolo could hardly complain with any justification: since Gianna had first asked Ramage to take her nephew to sea as a midshipman and teach him to be an officer in the Royal Navy, the lad had been in action half a dozen times or more; he had even been given command of a prize while in the Mediterranean.

Gianna. No matter how hard he tried to shut her out, and no matter how he and Paolo had tactfully not talked about her when he had rejoined the *Calypso,* she came back. Not because of a broken love affair, because it was not really like that, and since Gianna had left England he had met Sarah and they had fallen deeply in love and married. Still, that did not mean he was not very worried over Gianna's safety or did not have affectionate memories of her.

It had been a relationship which now had a strange air of unreality about it: could it have happened to him, had she really existed? Well, she had and did because that handsome youngster over there, one of the most popular people in the ship as far as the men were concerned, was her nephew. Yes, she was the ruler of Volterra, a small state in Tuscany; yes, she had fled before Bonaparte's Army of Italy, and been rescued by Lieutenant Ramage, who had carried her to safety ... Yes, they had both fallen in love and she had gone to England as a refugee and lived with his family, and yes it was obvious now that with such differences in religion the Catholic ruler of Volterra could never marry the Protestant heir to one of the oldest earldoms in the kingdom.

It had taken Bonaparte to end it all, though, just as he had, some years ago, then simply the General commanding the Army of Italy, unknowingly started it. Then, when Britain and France had signed that peace now called the Treaty of Amiens, Gianna had decided it was safe to return to Tuscany: that it was her duty to return to her people . . . Ramage, his father, many people, had warned her not to trust Bonaparte, that the peace would be brief, that she risked arrest by Bonaparte's police at best, assassination at worse, but she had gone. She had travelled to Paris with the Herveys while he had sailed on a long voyage with the *Calypso*, lucky to remain employed and in command in peacetime, and by bizarre circumstances he had met Sarah, returned to England and married her – and found there was no news of Gianna. No one knew if she had arrived in Volterra or not. The Herveys confirmed that she had left Paris safely, but that accounted for only the first steps on a long journey. Then, while he and Sarah had honeymooned in France, the war had started again, and with it went the last chance of knowing about Gianna.

Daydreaming again, and now the French ship was hull-up on the horizon. He looked with his glass. Yes, backed foretopsail and lying there like a gull on the water, rising and falling as the crests and troughs of the swell waves slid beneath her and carried on westward. Sails in good condition. French national colours hoisted. Guns not run out. A hoist of flags at the foretopmast-head, probably her pendant numbers identifying her.

It might work. Surprise, that great ally, could quadruple one's apparent size (or quarter them if you're the one surprised). But he would have to do it himself: it was unfortunate that Aitken did not speak good French.

He beckoned Aitken and Southwick closer and explained his plan. He then told Southwick to call Jackson down from aloft – he was not needed as a lookout any more. Southwick gestured down to the maindeck. 'Stafford and Rossi, sir? And one or two of those Frenchmen?'

They were all serving at the same gun, and the *Calypso* was not short of men. Auguste and his brother could be useful. Gilbert and Louis would be too clumsy. Ramage told the master the names and ordered him to be ready to hoist out a boat.

Formality: oddly enough, that would eventually save time. It might trip him up, too, but a boat cloak too would be normal and hide much. 'Orsini,' he said, 'fetch my sword and boat cloak from the great cabin. Get your own boat cloak too. I see you have your dirk!'

Paolo grinned and nodded as he turned to the companionway. The dirk, a short sword two feet two inches long and, as he readily admitted, little more than a broad-bladed dagger, was one of his proudest possessions, but despite that he was a realist and usually carried a seaman's cutlass as well, using the dirk as a *main gauche*. Ramage guessed he dreamed of the day when he exchanged the midshipman's dirk for a lieutenant's sword, with its elaborate hilt.

The main and forecourses were being clewed up. Seamen hurried to hook the staytackle on to the cutter, ready to hoist it out. Jackson waited until the last tie was undone and the canvas cover pulled clear before, as the captain's coxswain, climbing into the boat to check over the oars, rudder and tiller, pull the bung from the small water breaker lashed beneath one of the thwarts and confirm that it was full of fresh water, and finally put the large bung in the boat itself: it was normally left out to drain rainwater.

Stafford and Rossi were already up on the gangway with Auguste and Albert, cutlass belts over their shoulders and pistols stuck in their belts, but Ramage guessed from their stance that the two Frenchmen were puzzled and bewildered because Gilbert's translation of the instruction to arm themselves and go to the gangway with Rossi and Stafford would have been the only orders they received.

At that moment Paolo appeared, a sword in one hand and two boat cloaks slung over the other arm. 'Put them down there, beside the capstan. Now, listen a moment,' Ramage said.

Quickly he outlined what had happened so far – which Paolo had seen anyway as the *Calypso* rapidly approached the unknown frigate – and added his intentions. 'Now, go and tell those two Frenchmen what they need to know. It's time you polished your French.'

After that everything happened with the speed of an impatient child shaking the coloured chips in a kaleidoscope. The ship once ahead was now fine on the starboard bow and men had left the guns to stand by at the sheets and braces controlling the foretopsail and yard. Jackson had the cutter's crew mustered on the starboard gangway. The boat would be hoisted out on the weather side, so everyone would have to work fast, but the lee side would be open to too many prying French eyes.

He lifted the glass and looked at the ship and was startled to see that she was close enough for him to notice the uniforms (or lack of them) on the quarterdeck. He glanced at Aitken, who already had the speaking trumpet to his mouth while Southwick stood by the quartermaster close to the wheel.

The wheel began to spin and the *Calypso*'s bow started to swing slowly to starboard to put her on a curving course bringing her close to windward of the French frigate. Sails began slatting while Ramage put the telescope in the binnacle drawer, picked up his sword and clipped it on to the belt, and slung the cloak over one shoulder. He thought a moment and then flattened his hat and put it under his left arm. Paolo followed his example and, with the sails thundering aloft as the ship swung and the great foretopsail was backed, the two of them went down the steps to the gangway.

The ship slowly came to a stop, the wind now blowing on the foreside of the foretopsail, and the cutter swung out and over the side. Wagstaffe gave a brief order here and there but mostly used hand signals. In a few moments the boat was in the water, the bow held by the painter while the sternfast kept the boat close in to the rope ladder which had been unrolled over the ship's side.

Jackson was first down the ladder, the wind catching his sandy hair, and before Rossi, who had followed him, had jumped into the boat, the American was shipping the rudder and the tiller. The rest of the men scrambled down, the last one followed by Orsini.

'Here!' Ramage shouted, throwing down to Jackson his rolled-up boat cloak, with the hat inside. The coxswain waited until Ramage was on board and sitting in the sternsheets and then pulled the boat cloak round him to hide his uniform. Ramage pushed his sword to one side to make the wooden grating a more comfortable seat, and then watched the enormous bulk of the *Calypso* seeming to move sideways as the men at the oars rowed the cutter clear.

Jackson eventually put the tiller over so that the cutter passed under the French frigate's stern to come along her lee side. '*La Robuste*, sir,' he commented. The name meant nothing to Ramage. He counted up the gunports. Sixteen this side, so she was a 32-gun frigate. About the same size as the *Calypso* but not built from the same plans: her sheer was flatter, her fo'c'sle was longer, and he had the impression her transom raked more sharply.

Ramage saw several faces looking down at him over the

taffrail and gave a cheery wave, which the men answered enthusiastically. He glanced at Paolo sitting opposite him. The lad had a wide grin on his face: no sign of any doubts or fears.

Suddenly every damned thing seemed to be happening at once, Ramage thought, and then realized it was his own fault because he would let his concentration wander. The cutter's bowman had hooked on with his boathook and while men pulled and hauled to secure painter and sternfast, Ramage stood up to find that the French had also unrolled a rope ladder, so he did not have the nail-breaking and finger-twisting climb up the battens. He pushed his sword round under his boat cloak and clutched his hat, guessing that no one on *La Robuste*'s deck would recognize it for what it was.

He leapt for the ladder and immediately started climbing, glad that Paolo was only a couple of rungs below him because his weight stopped each wooden slat trying to swing inwards. More jerks followed as the rest of the men followed and this was the moment of danger: would any of the French officers look down past Ramage and Orsini and notice that the seamen were carrying cutlasses? Ramage let his boat cloak flow out.

Up, up, up – now his eyes at deck level; four more steps and he was on the deck itself with four men standing in a half circle to greet him – presumably the captain and three lieutenants.

Ramage paused, punched his cocked hat into shape, jammed it on his head and, undoing the buckle of his boat cloak, swirled it off and tossed it to Jackson, who was now standing beside Paolo at the entryport.

'Captain Ramage, of His Britannic Majesty's frigate *Calypso* at your service,' he said in French to the heavily-jowled and sallow-faced man with iron-grey hair who seemed to be the captain.

'*Britannic?*' the man muttered disbelievingly. He was a stocky man who had seemed taller than Ramage, but as he turned to look at the *Calypso* hove-to close by he protested: 'She is flying no –' he stopped and then, arms extended and palms uppermost, he said angrily: 'When she first hove-to she had no colours. She is French-built. Naturally, I think she is French.'

Ramage shrugged his shoulders and smiled. 'You are free to think whatever you like.'

The Frenchman's shrug made Ramage's look like a feeble twitch. 'Of course, of course.' He introduced himself. 'Citizen

Robilliard, commanding the French national frigate *La Robuste*, at your service. May I –'

As he turned to introduce his officers, Ramage interrupted him calmly. 'Citizen Robilliard, a moment please. You are now the former captain of the former French frigate *La Robuste*, which is now a prize to His Britannic Majesty's frigate *Calypso*...'

'But ... *mon Dieu*, citizen,' Robilliard protested, 'the war is over. It is all finished. We are friends. Where have you been that you do not know?' He slapped his thigh and started to roar with laughter. 'Ah, it is the English humour! You make a joke because –' he saw Ramage's face and his voice tailed off. He took a deep breath. 'No, you don't make a joke, Captain Ramage. You come from Europe. We have just come from the Batavian Republic. You have news ...'

Suddenly Ramage felt sorry for this amiable man, whose accent showed he had grown up not far from Honfleur.

'Yes, hostilities have begun again. Brest is blockaded – my ship is part of that fleet.'

'And you are bound ...'

'... for the West Indies,' Ramage said. 'Now, m'sieu, you and your ship's company must consider yourselves my prisoners.'

'But this is absurd,' Robilliard protested, and then looked in the direction of Ramage's pointing finger. The *Calypso*'s guns were run out while the French guns were still secured, well lashed down and ready for bad weather.

Ramage said to Paolo in Italian: 'Collect papers, charts and signal books from his cabin. Take a couple of men with you.'

Robilliard scratched his head, still unwilling to accept what he had heard. 'I can't believe this. You have documents? A newspaper – *Le Moniteur*, perhaps? There must be a written declaration – you just come on board and tell me that you have taken my ship prize! Why no!' he exclaimed, as though suddenly losing his temper. 'You are just pirates!'

'You are familiar with Brest?'

Robilliard nodded his head cautiously. 'I was blockaded in there for three years.'

'When did you sail?'

'As soon as the peace was signed. In fact we carried the dispatches informing the governor of the Batavian Republic.'

Ramage beckoned to Auguste and Albert. 'These two men can tell you the names of all the important ships in Brest three weeks ago, as well as the names of the Navy and Army *commandants*, and answer any questions you care to ask. They are French. I was in Brest until after the war began; I can give you a certain amount of information.'

Auguste said: 'It's all true, citizen. The English ambassador left Paris, war began and Bonaparte arrested all the English in France, whether officers on leave or women. Bonaparte now makes war on women.'

Robilliard flushed and then said angrily to Ramage: 'This is ridiculous. Why, I could seize you, and then your ship would never dare open fire for fear of killing you!'

A series of metallic clicks made him look round and he was startled to find that three seamen, Jackson, Stafford and Rossi, were standing close with broad grins on their faces and pistols aimed at Robilliard, and each man swung a cutlass as a parson might use his walking stick to knock the head off a dandelion.

'Captain,' Ramage said, 'we are wasting time, my ship would certainly open fire if necessary, my second-in-command has strict orders about that. But you would not be alive to hear the first broadside that might kill me. You have been tricked by the perfidious English, captain, just as I was tricked by the perfidious French less than a month ago. There is no dishonour: no need for you to fire a broadside "for the honour of the flag".'

Robilliard still shook his head disbelievingly. 'I have only seventy-six men because we were short when we left Brest and have had much sickness in Batavia and at sea, but how can you keep us all prisoner . . . ?'

'That is no problem,' Ramage said and signalled to Jackson. 'Give me your pistol,' he said in English, and then switched back to French to say to Robilliard: 'We are agreed, are we not, that you and your ship are my prize?'

Robilliard shrugged his shoulders and looked round at his three lieutenants. They were all young men, their faces frozen with the shock of finding an English frigate poised to rake their ship and her captain on board *La Robuste*.

'What do you say, *mes braves*?'

'We have no choice,' the oldest of them said without much conviction.

'You must remember you said that when a committee of public safety accuses me of treachery,' Robilliard said bitterly. 'We have no choice, certainly, but I don't want any of you claiming to be heroes if we are exchanged and get back to France.'

'Don't worry,' Ramage said and waving to Jackson to go aft. 'My dispatch will make it clear you had no knowledge of the war.'

'A lot of good your dispatch would do me in France!'

'I expect it will be published in the *London Gazette,* which is as good as *Le Moniteur.* Certainly, I'm sure that Bonaparte has it translated and read to him.'

Robilliard was watching Ramage closely. 'Yes, I believe you.' He spelled out his name. 'And make sure you put in the "Pierre", because there is my cousin, too, and although he does not command a ship he is a scoundrel – no, I didn't mean that –'

'I understand,' Ramage assured him.

'But so many prisoners,' Robilliard said as he watched the Tricolour flutter down as Jackson hauled on one end of the halyard. 'How will you ... ?'

'Leave that problem to me,' Ramage said. 'You are not short of provisions?'

'Water, but not provisions. With so many dead from sickness, I could have doubled the rations of the living.'

CHAPTER FIFTEEN

Ramage and Aitken sat at the desk, Ramage in his normal chair and the first lieutenant opposite, trying to make himself comfortable on a chair that normally served at the dining table in the coach. Aitken was hurriedly writing notes, quill squeaking, as Ramage translated from various pages of the small pile of documents in front of them.

'Ah, here we are,' Ramage said happily, 'some of the answers about Cayenne. This is' – he glanced at the title page – 'a sort of pilot book published three years ago, so it is reasonably up to date. Take notes as I read it aloud.'

He turned over a couple of pages. 'It begins with a word about the currents to expect off the coast of French Guiana. There are two – well, we knew that. The first starts close off the African coast, near to the Cape Verde Islands, and is caused by the Trade winds blowing across the Atlantic. Yes, well, we know all about that, too. It reaches to within ...' he paused, making the conversion, 'to within thirty-five miles of the coast, or a depth of eight fathoms, where a second current, produced by the tides, meets it. And there is the water pouring out of the Amazon and the Orinoco. Well, it's the heights not the rates that interest me.

'Hmm, numerous other rivers between the Amazon and the Orinoco carry down vast quantities of mud, tree trunks and branches ... these accumulating along the shores have built up a border of low ground.' The pilot was written in stilted French and translation was difficult. 'Mangroves generally cover it between high and low water. At low water this border seems impassable: at high water there are sometimes channels accessible to vessels ... Ah, here we are: "The only ports are at mouths of rivers ... there are usually bars at the entrances and shoals in the channels ... Larger ships can anchor to wait for high water without risk because no violent tempests ever occur in this region ..."

'That's comforting; I dislike "violent tempests". The mariner "can wait for a local pilot or send boats ahead to make soundings".'

Aitken reached out for the inkwell. 'Except for the mangroves and the lack of "violent tempests", it sounds rather like the east coast of England!'

'Yes. Now for the general information: the French have owned Cayenne – Guiana, rather – since 1677 ... It stretches about two hundred and fifty miles along the coast and goes more than a hundred miles inland ... The land is low along the coast which runs roughly north and south with a mountain chain running east and west ... Produces and exports pepper, cinnamon, cloves and nutmegs. Nothing,' Ramage noted, 'that isn't used for seasoning food!'

He read several more pages without bothering to translate but finally hunched himself in his chair and squared up the book. 'Here we are ... During the summer the current runs strongly to the northwest off this coast ... Heavy breakers generally ease at slack water ... Tide rise just over eight feet at springs, four or five at neaps ...

'Now, we're interested in twenty-seven miles of coast between the River Approuague to the south and the River Mahuri to the north. The land is so flat you can see it at only seven or eight miles from seaward ... behind it, though, are the Kaw mountains, a level ridge not very high. Now, the Mahuri river –'

He broke off, cursed and shut the book with an angry gesture and stood up. With his head bent to one side to avoid bumping it on the beams overhead he strode round the cabin, watched by a startled Aitken, who then picked up a piece of cloth and busied himself wiping the sharpened point of his quill. He knew better than to ask what was the matter. Was the vital page missing? The Scot did not trust anything French. The good luck of finding a French pilot book would obviously, he considered glumly, be cancelled by there being pages missing . . .

Ramage sat down, face flushed, and opened the pilot book again. 'Cayenne . . . Cayenne . . .' he said crossly. 'Wouldn't anyone in their right mind assume that any wretched Frenchman deported "to Cayenne" was being sent to a penal colony on the island of Cayenne, which is in the middle of the entrance to the Cayenne river?'

Aitken thought for a moment but could see no danger in agreeing. 'Yes, sir, that seems a reasonable assumption; indeed, a very logical conclusion.'

'Yes, but any ship laden with prisoners and anchoring off the Îles de Cayenne in the Rivière de Cayenne would find herself some twenty-five miles too far south!

'Having no charts or pilots, I'd assumed the three Île du Salut, which include Devil's Island, were in the Cayenne river.' He tapped the book. 'Now I find they are three almost barren little lumps of rock seven miles offshore and twenty-five miles north of Cayenne, river or island. So, tear up what you've written and let's start again . . .'

'A good job we found *La Robuste*,' Aitken said, 'Otherwise . . .'

'Otherwise we'd have looked very stupid,' Ramage completed. 'Right, we start at Pointe Charlotte. The coast is low and sandy, plenty of mangroves up to the high-water-mark, occasional clumps of trees behind, and isolated rocks sitting in the mud to seaward.

'By a stroke of luck, or just the kindness of nature, there is a high, cone-shaped hill nine miles inland: on a clear day you can see it for twenty miles, so you don't have to rely on the mangroves for a landfall.

'Right, now we get to it. The coast is trending west-northwest when you reach Pointe Charlotte, which is three miles northwest of the Kourou river, which is marked by three small mountains "all remarkable objects at a long distance, and good guides for the entrance to the river".

'To distinguish Pointe Charlotte from a thousand other points, it has some rocks at its base,'Ramage said ironically. 'Of more interest to us, though: if you stand on Pointe Charlotte and stare out across the Atlantic, hoping perhaps to see Africa, you'll see instead "a group of three small rocky islets", and they *are* small, occupying a space of about half a mile.

'As far as I can understand from this pilot, the island farthest out in the Atlantic is the northernmost, Île du Diable, 131 feet high; the one on your left is the largest and highest, Île Royale, 216 feet; and to the right is the nearest, the southernmost, and the smallest, Île St Joseph.'

'Which is the one we're particularly interested in?' Aitken asked.

'I think Île du Diable, or Devil's Island, and the blasted pilot simply says it is forbidden to land on any of the islands without the written permission of the *préfet* at Cayenne because St Joseph and Royale are "convict settlements" while Diable is a settlement for "*détenus*", which I'm sure means "prisoners" but not people who have actually been convicted, although I'll check it with Gilbert because he knows better than I the finer shades of meaning in Revolutionary France.'

'What about anchorages?' Aitken asked. Captains concerned themselves with tactics, first lieutenants worried about anchorages.

'The pilot makes a great song and dance that the lee of the islands provides the only sheltered anchorage along the coast – otherwise you have to go up one of the big rivers. Yes, here we are – five cables southwest of the western end of Royale, soft mud, five fathoms, well sheltered from easterly winds. Ah, Royale seems to be the headquarters – it has a fort guarding it to seaward, a church on the hill, and a jetty on the south side. Diable – well, that has only "a fortified enclosure" for the *détenus*. St Joseph: a poor anchorage a cable to the south in hard mud – that is all it has to offer the world . . .'

'Are there any rocks and shoals?'

'Plenty,' Ramage said, 'and too many to mention. The positions this pilot gives are too vague to be of much use. Hmm . . . "generally, a vessel coming in sight of the fort on Île Royale will result one hour later in a canoe with a local pilot waiting close under the northwest corner of Île du Diable . . ." He'll guide you to the recommended anchorage I've just mentioned southwest of Île Royale.'

Ramage closed the book. 'That's all it says about the Îles du Salut. More important, though, is that *L'Espoir* will presumably have a copy . . .'

'. . . and so will wait for a pilot and anchor there?'

'I hope so,' Ramage said, 'but I hope it doesn't mean we have to try to capture three rocky islands.'

Wagstaffe walked the starboard side of *La Robuste*'s quarterdeck and reflected that commanding a ship was a satisfying experience, even if the ship was a prize frigate and all he had to do for the next few hundred miles was stay in the wake of the *Calypso*. This was easy enough in daylight but at night it was difficult to follow the triangle of three poop lanterns. In fact, in the last couple of nights he had gone to his cot and fallen asleep to waken almost at once, certain that the three lights had gone out of sight, and the officer of the deck (Kenton the first time and Martin the second) had been startled to find the commanding officer suddenly flapping round the deck in a boat cloak, staring forward, grunting and going below again, all without a word of explanation.

Well, Wagstaffe told himself, how on earth did one explain all that to junior lieutenants? Now he thought about it, both Kenton and Martin were sensible enough to report the moment they lost sight of the lights – indeed, there'd be enough yelling in the darkness, with the officer of the deck shouting questions at the lookouts and making a noise which would come down the skylight like a butt full of cold water.

It is easy enough to be brave and confident when the sun shines bright, he thought defensively, but hard on a dull cloudy day when it is raining. Harder still at nightfall, and dam' nearly impossible at three o'clock in the morning. Three o'clock courage, that's what he lacked. It's what distinguished Captain Ramage from most other men:he had it in abundance. It was also, Wagstaffe admitted, what kept Captain Ramage's officers poised on the balls of their feet all the time. Not because he yelled and screamed when things went wrong: perhaps it would be easier if he did. No, it was that chilly, quizzical and questioning look from those dark eyes set under thick eyebrows that was far more reproachful than words. They seemed to say: 'I trained you and trusted you: now look what you've done . . .'

Wagstaffe lifted his 'distance staff' and held it up. He was proud of it because it was so easy to make and to use. He had been told to keep one cable astern of the *Calypso* and in her wake. One cable was 200 yards precisely, not 150 or 250. It was a distance which anyone in the *Calypso* could check with a quadrant or sextant in a few moments because of the two simple facts: if you knew the height of an object (in this case a mainmast) and the angle it made from you, it was easy enough to work out how far away it was: the mast made the vertical side of a right-angled triangle and the angle was opposite, between the base and hypotenuse. And of course the base was the distance, in this case two hundred yards.

However, to avoid having to get a quadrant or sextant out of its box to measure the angle, it was easy enough to cut two notches in a short stick at appropriate distances apart so that when you held the stick vertically at arm's length, the lower notch was level with the *Calypso*'s after waterline, and her mainmasthead touched the upper notch. If the mast appeared shorter than the distance between the notches, *La Robuste* was more than 200 yards astern: if taller, they were too close.

In fact it was not too difficult to keep station because both frigates were almost the same size and of course French-designed and built, with the sails cut by French sailmakers. Providing *La Robuste* set the same sails, and providing the men at the wheel, the quartermaster and the officers of the deck stayed alert in this sun (which was really getting some heat in it as the latitude decreased) it was easy.

What had Captain Ramage in mind? The series of rendezvous he had given to Wagstaffe, a latitude and longitude for each day, in case they lost each other during the night and were not in sight at dawn, ended up at five degrees North and fifty-two West, which was the South American coast at Cayenne . . . The French kit of charts on board *La Robuste* did not include French Guiana, except as a half-inch square on the chart of the south part of the North Atlantic. Cayenne, Devil's Island . . . Wagstaffe shivered. It was probably no healthier than it sounded. Devil's Island was said to be the place Bonaparte sent his enemies. Well, it must be a big island because the Frenchman had a lot of enemies. And friends, too, judging from England's lack of allies.

Sergeant Ferris, the second-in-command of the Marines on board the *Calypso*, undid his pipeclayed crossbelts and unbuttoned his tunic. Sitting on the breech of one of the guns was not exactly resting in an armchair but the breech was in the shade and the breeze blowing the length of the maindeck was cool, even if *La Robuste*'s bilges stank so that the last foot that the pump would not suck out swirled back and forth with the frigate's pitch and roll and occasionally made the maindeck smell like a Paris sewer.

Jackson walked up and sat on the truck on the after side of the gun and leaned back against the breech. 'Coolest spot in the ship,' he said.

'Aye,' Ferris said, 'count yourself lucky you're not a Marine and wearing this damned uniform.'

'Trouble with the French prisoners?'

'No, not yet. A couple of them started quarrelling with each other and some of my lads had to stop them, so we've put them all in irons, each man one leg, so they're sitting in rows facing each other and staring at the sole of the other fellow's foot. Still, forty-six prisoners is not too bad since I've got half the *Calypso*'s Marines, and we've got that 12-pounder trained on 'em.'

'Yes, but that's just a bluff,' Jackson said. 'If we have to fire it down the hatch the recoil will turn the gun upside-down!'

'The Frogs don't know that,' Ferris said philosophically, 'and if only half the canister catches them it won't leave many alive.'

'More likely put a hole in the hull,' Jackson said.

'Don't worry. Just go down in the hold and sit down with one ankle held by the irons, and I can tell you that inside ten minutes the muzzle of that 12-pounder will seem to measure two feet in diameter and be winking at you like death himself.'

Jackson's laugh was mirthless. He had fought the French for too long to have much sympathy for them. 'What about Gilbert?'

Ferris puffed out his lips and then opened his mouth as if blowing out a plum stone. 'Don't make a mistake about that fellow! He may be small and he may be a Frog – it's easy to forget that because he speaks such good English – but you should see him when he gets worked up!

'Before we took half the prisoners over to the *Calypso* he talked to all of them below decks (this was while you was ferrying across our seamen) and gave 'em a warning. All French to me, of course, but I understood everything he said just by watching the faces of the prisoners! I think a lot of it was religion – Diable, that means the Devil, doesn't it? Well he went on a lot about him, and they shuffled about a lot, as though they were scared of the Devil. There was another chap they were scared of, too, someone called More. What with him threatening 'em with the Devil and More, and us Marines, too, we had them French twittering like frightened starlings.'

'Until the two started fighting.'

'Yus, but I think they are so scared that they very easily get on each other's nerves. Anyway, a day or two in irons won't hurt 'em. Given half a chance, Gilbert and his chaps would have beaten the two of them. Yet they're French too – why do they hate the fellows in this ship so much, Jacko?'

'It's not just this ship: they hate all Frenchmen who support Bonaparte. I don't know much about it myself but of course Gilbert and Louis worked for the Count of Rennes, who Bonaparte is shipping to Cayenne in the frigate we're trying to catch.'

'Cayenne? That's a sort of pepper, isn't it?'

'Yes, it comes from French Guiana, which is near Brazil. It's a deadly sort of place – makes islands of the West Indies like Antigua seem as healthy as Bath. Die like flies there, according to the captain.'

Ferris nodded and flapped the front of his tunic back and forth like a fan. 'I can believe it. But what does the captain want with this frigate, *La Robuste*? Halves our strength in men, even if it doubles the number of ships. But doubling the number of guns and halving the number of men to fire them,' his voice assumed the monotonous drone of a drill sergeant, 'is militarily unsound, Jacko.'

'Tell the captain,' the American said. 'He may not have considered that. Or,' he added sarcastically, 'he might be considering it only from a naval point of view, not a military one.'

Sergeant Ferris patted his stomach. 'Yes, that could be so,' he agreed judicially, completely missing the tone of Jackson's voice. 'Yes, I agree, he might have some particular naval plan in mind.'

Wagstaffe looked at his makeshift journal. There was something very satisfying about the book, which had been made up by young Orsini stitching together the left-hand side of a dozen sheets of paper. How satisfying to write boldly across the top (normally it was only a matter of fitting names in the blank spaces

209

of a printed form) 'Journal of the Proceedings of –', he paused a moment: this was an unusual situation. He then continued, '– the former French national frigate *La Robuste*, presently prize to one of his Majesty's ships, Lieutenant Wagstaffe, commander.' He had added the date and then carefully ruled in nine columns, and today, as he glanced down them, the ship's progress was becoming more obvious.

The date occupied the first two columns, the third recorded the winds (which had stayed between southeast and northeast the whole time), then came the courses (which were unchanged) and the miles covered from noon to noon, which were usually around 175. The latitude and longitude occupied the next two columns and showed to a navigator's eye the progress they were making to the southwest.

The next column, bearing and distances at noon, had been left blank, and there was only one entry under 'Remarkable Observations and Accidents', which recorded putting all the prisoners in irons for twenty-four hours after two of them had started fighting.

Across in the *Calypso*, Ramage had just worked out the noon sight and compared his position with those of Aitken and Southwick. They tallied within three or four miles, and with the ship rolling and pitching with following wind and sea, so that taking a sight was like trying to shoot a hare from the back of a runaway horse, that was close enough.

He opened his journal and under the 'Latitude' column wrote 6 degrees, 45 minutes North; next to it was recorded the longitude, 52 degrees, 14 minutes West. The Îles du Salut, according to the French pilot book, were 5 degrees, 17 minutes North and 52 degrees, 36 minutes West, so . . . they were . . . yes, ninety miles on a course of south by west a quarter west. Which meant no change in the course, but because they were making eight knots and he wanted to bring the mountains in sight soon after dawn, both the *Calypso* and *La Robuste* were going to have to reduce canvas: a little under five knots would bring the mountains in sight at daybreak so that the ships' companies would be breakfasted by the time the three islands were sighted. Providing of course the visibility was reasonable. Often there was a haze along a lee shore, presumably caused by the sea air meeting the land air, and the mistiness thrown up by the waves breaking on rocks and sandy beaches.

He wiped the pen, put the top on the ink bottle, and replaced everything in the drawer. He found Southwick and Aitken on deck.

'If the chronometer is not playing games, and if there's not a radical change in the speed of the current as we close the coast . . .' Ramage said.

'Ninety miles, I make it,' Southwick said.

'Which means we might run up on the beach in the night,' Ramage commented. 'Mr Aitken, we'll try her under topsails, and then a cast of the log, if you please. Five knots will be quite enough, so we can furl the courses and get in the t'gallants and royals.'

Aitken picked up the speaking trumpet while Ramage went aft to the taffrail and looked astern at the *Calypso*'s wake. Despite the speed she was making and the wild rolling, the wake was no more than the first wrinkles on a beautiful woman's face: the French designer had produced a fast and sea-kindly hull which slipped through the water without fuss.

La Robuste was a fine sight. He could imagine how often over the past days Wagstaffe, Kenton and Martin had been measuring the angle to the *Calypso*'s mainmasthead, to maintain that magic distance of a cable. He smiled to himself because although Wagstaffe might not realize it, the next few minutes were something of a test. Wagstaffe was a fine seaman and steady, a good navigator and popular with the men. He had shown himself, in other words, to be an excellent lieutenant. He could and did carry out orders with precision. And, as Bowen had pointed out to Admiral Clinton, this is what Bullivant could do. Bullivant had only failed when he made the enormous jump from taking orders as a lieutenant to making decisions and giving orders as a captain.

How about Wagstaffe?

The *Calypso*'s bosun's mates finished the shrill notes of their calls and bellowed orders: now came the thud of bare feet as the men ran to their stations. Sails would not be furled as fast as usual, since half the *Calypso*'s men were now over in *La Robuste*, but – he took out his watch – with similar ships and similar sails set it would be interesting to compare times.

The squeal of ropes rendering through blocks, the shouts of bosun's mates, the grunts of men straining as they heaved on ropes . . . And the great rectangle of the maincourse, which for days had been billowing in a graceful curve, suddenly crumpled

211

and distorted as the wind spilled when the lower corner of each side began to be pulled diagonally towards the middle.

And damnation, *La Robuste* was beginning to clew up her maincourse, too! Wagstaffe had plotted his noon position against the latitude and longitude of the Îles du Salut: he must have realized that the two ships would have to slow down to avoid arriving in the night, and he had his men waiting out of sight, waiting for the first wrinkles to appear in the *Calypso*'s maincourse . . . Yes, Wagstaffe passed the test . . .

Looking forward again and upward Ramage could see the men on the *Calypso*'s mainyard furling the sail neatly and securing it with gaskets, the long strips of canvas keeping it in place. He glanced at his watch and then looked at *La Robuste* and waited for the last gasket to be passed. The *Calypso* won by under half a minute, and that victory could no doubt be explained by defects in *La Robuste*'s running rigging and the poor state of her gaskets – he had seen two tear in half, weakened by the heat and damp of a year in Far Eastern waters.

Forecourses were clewed up and then furled and *La Robuste*'s time was better, allowing for the fact that Wagstaffe had to wait for the *Calypso* to make the first move because his orders were to conform with the *Calypso*. In topgallants . . . the same. Obviously the Calypsos in *La Robuste* were enjoying themselves.

It was going to be a busy afternoon – preparations for making a landfall were, in this case, the same as for entering harbour, and as soon as the last sail was furled and the last topman down on deck again, Ramage nodded to Southwick, who was responsible for the fo'c'sle and all that went on there. The heavy anchor cable would have to be roused out while the blind bucklers closing the two hawsepipes would have to be taken off. That was always a difficult job under way with a following sea, since the bucklers were fixed securely to prevent seas coming in through the hawseholes.

One end of the first cable would then be led out through the starboard hawse and back on board again and secured to the ring of one of the two anchors on the starboard side. Then the end of a second cable would be led out of the larboard hawse and back to the ring of one of the two larboard anchors. People were often surprised that a ship the size of a frigate in fact carried six anchors and eight cables (seven of them each eighteen and a half inches in circumference and 720 feet long). But such people had never seen a ship at anchor in a high and a heavy sea.

The covers needed taking off the boats and a couple of quarterdeck guns should be loaded with blank charges in case it was necessary to make an urgent signal to *La Robuste*. And ... well, Ramage admitted, that was about all. All that was needed next morning was the sight of the three mountains close to the mouth of the River Kourou, Pointe Charlotte and the Îles du Salut. Still, he'd be quite satisfied if they sighted the 'very remarkable conical hill' called Mont Diable in the pilot book but presumably Montagne du Diable, and which should warn in good time that he was a little too far south. Diable, diable ... it had started off with Bullivant in his delirium seeing Satan; now English devils in the imagination were going to be replaced by French *diables* in fact.

CHAPTER SIXTEEN

There they were, three flat-topped islands still grey in the distance and overlapping so that there appeared to be only two. That would be Île du Diable just coming clear on the left while Île Royale and Île St Joseph merged to the south. As his body swayed with the rolling of the *Calypso,* making it difficult to hold the telescope steady, they moved from side to side in the circular lens as though being viewed through the bottom of a drinking glass.

He turned aft to train the glass on *La Robuste*'s quarterdeck. Yes, they too had sighted the islands; there was Wagstaffe hunched with the telescope to his eye and Kenton, Martin and Orsini standing in a row beside him at the quarterdeck rail like inquisitive starlings.

It had been disappointing at dawn when the first light seemed to spread outward from the ship and nothing had been in sight. The traditional cry of 'See a grey goose at a mile' had brought in the six lookouts stationed on deck round the ship and sent two aloft, and they had reported a clear horizon.

Then suddenly, as though a bank of fog had drifted away to reveal them (though the fog familiar in higher latitudes was of course unknown in the Tropics), they were ahead. Obviously

213

there had been a haze hiding the coast until the sun lifted over the horizon and burned it up.

Ramage sighed, a natural reaction but one which led Southwick to ask: 'You expect trouble, sir?'

Trouble? They were too far off for him to be sure. If a frigate's masts showed up behind Île Royale, revealing that *L'Espoir* had arrived (and had time to send her prisoners over to Île du Diable), then yes, they had trouble. The idea, plan, gamble – he was not sure what to call it – that had come to him several days ago like a wind shadow, and the outline of which had since sharpened, as though someone had used a quill to run an inked line round it, would have been a waste of thought if *L'Espoir* had beaten them in.

More important, Southwick's question merely emphasized that the idea was just a gamble. You could put other fancy names to it, he told himself sourly, but it was still a gamble: he was like some pallid player putting a small fortune on the turn of a dice in the final desperate throw that could lose or save a home which had been in the family for generations and was a son's rightful inheritance. So if there were masts, he had lost; if there were no masts, he had won.

Won? That was nonsense. If there were no masts, then he had not yet lost, which was a far cry from winning. No, what Southwick's innocent and well-meant question emphasized, Ramage admitted to himself with bitterness, was that by pinning everything on beating *L'Espoir* to the Îles du Salut, he had not fully considered the consequences of losing the race.

If *L'Espoir* had not arrived, then the prisoners were still on board the frigate, and frigates were not invulnerable. But if *L'Espoir* had arrived, then the prisoners by now would be imprisoned on the Île du Diable in what the French pilot book called a 'fortified enclosure', and the whole purpose of these fortifications was to keep people (rescuers, in this case) out.

Southwick was still awaiting an answer.

'If *L'Espoir* is here, yes,' Ramage said.

'Because she'll have put her prisoners on shore?'

'Yes. There must be hundreds of prisoners on the island – perhaps more than one island. We can't be sure they still keep all the criminals on one island and the political prisoners on another.'

'I wonder if Bonaparte sees any difference in the two sorts,'

Southwick commented. 'He's just as likely to put 'em all together.'

'That would mean our fifty would be among perhaps five thousand others; and five thousand prisoners means how many guards?'

Southwick gave one of his famous sniffs. They came of a standard strength, but he could give each one a particular meaning. This one indicated that the whole thing was absurd and not for the serious consideration of grown men.

'Even at one guard for every twenty prisoners, plus all the camp followers and cooks and administration people, we'd never stand a chance,' the master said. 'To find out if *L'Espoir*'s there we've got to get in sight of that fort on Île Royale, so they'll sight us and we lose surprise.'

'Yes,' Ramage said, and changed the subject, which was thoroughly depressing him. 'Now, we'd better start working out the positions of those reefs and shoals.'

'Aye, I have 'em noted from the pilot book,' Southwick said. 'The main bank is over there, between one and two miles nor'nor'west of Royale.' He pointed over the starboard bow.

At that moment Ramage saw Renwick down on the maindeck and called him up to the quarterdeck. The Marine captain's face was as usual burned a bright red from the sun and the skin of his nose was peeling, but he gave a smart salute.

'How are the prisoners?' Ramage asked.

'Very subdued, sir. They haven't forgotten that man Gilbert. I don't know what he said before they were brought over here, but it frightened them!'

Ramage nodded. 'Keep them subdued.'

Supposing there were no masts. Oh yes, he had this wonderful idea, but what about the pilot? The garrisons on the islands? He shook his head and left a puzzled Renwick standing on the quarterdeck as he clattered down the companionway to the great cabin, nodding to the sentry.

He sat down at his desk and looked at the sketch he had made of the three islands based on the information in the pilot book. Why was he looking at it? He knew the outlines and positions by heart. He pushed the sketch aside and took out the French pilot book and began reading the reference to the Îles du Salut. The words blurred into meaninglessness: he knew them by heart, so why was he reading it yet again? He put the book back in the drawer and stood up impatiently. What the devil was wrong with

215

him? Impatience, he told himself, that's what's wrong. It needs patience to wait until we are closer to the islands so that we can be sure about the masts.

Islands! Even at this distance that was obviously an absurd word for three long lumps of rock lying like broken grindstones half a dozen miles off a flat coastline fringed with mangroves, marshy land and almost stagnant water and buzzing and whining with biting insects.

At least the islands do not suffer from a shortage of water: the rainfall must be so heavy that perpetual dampness and mildew, not drought, is the problem.

Up on the quarterdeck he said to Southwick: 'Hail the lookouts. No, better still, send a man aloft with a glass.'

'Yes, sir,' Southwick said, but added: 'You did say that Royale was 216 feet high, and Diable 131, didn't you, sir?'

Ramage glared at him. 'Yes, and the truck of a frigate's mainmast won't show clear from behind 'em.'

'Yes, sir, so I was thinking . . .'

'Nevertheless send a man aloft with a glass.'

'Aye aye, sir.' Southwick knew the strain of waiting. They had left the Channel Fleet how long ago? Nearly three weeks. For twenty days they had looked for *L'Espoir* and the captain had shown no sign of strain. Now all the tensions and anticipations of three weeks, when everyone had wondered if they would catch *L'Espoir* or beat her to Cayenne, were being compressed into an hour.

The new lookout soon hailed the quarterdeck. With the bring-'em-near he could make out some buildings on the largest island. They were low down on the seaward side, he added.

Ramage nodded: that would be the fort on Royale, and by now the French lookouts would be reporting the approach of two frigates. Was there one *préfet* in command of the three islands? Or was he a soldier, a garrison commander? It did not matter a damn, really; Ramage knew he was just trying to keep his mind occupied. He turned and began to walk back and forth along the few feet of deck between the quarterdeck rail and the taffrail, occasionally looking astern at *La Robuste* and allowing himself a glance at the islands only once every hundred times he completed the stretch.

Eventually Southwick said: 'We should close the coast a little more to the north, sir. Then we know we'll be clear of that bank of rocks and can stretch down to the anchorage. Unless you want to wait for a pilot.'

'Yes, we'll heave-to and wait for the pilot, if he's not there waiting for us.'

'But ... well, sir, won't the pilot realize that ...?'

Southwick did not bother to complete the question.

'If we don't pick him up, he'll come over to us after we've anchored.'

'Yes, I see, sir,' Southwick said and did not understand at all. To him, the prospect of anchoring the two frigates close in under three French islands which were probably bristling with batteries was something that did not bear thinking about.

The *Calypso* hove-to just long enough for the frigate's cutter to be hoisted out and rowed to *La Robuste* to collect Paolo, Jackson and the four Frenchmen, and bring them on board. Gilbert and his men had been puzzled and nervous from the moment that Wagstaffe, after reading the instructions delivered by the boat's coxswain, had ordered them away.

They were brought up to Ramage on the quarterdeck and he smiled the moment he saw their long, nervous faces. He led them aft to the taffrail and, speaking quickly in French, gave them their instructions. They talked among themselves, embarrassed, for a couple of minutes and then Auguste nodded reluctantly.

'Me, sir. They've chosen me.'

'Very well,' Ramage said. 'I'm sure you'll do it well. Go down to the great cabin. Silkin is there. Gilbert, you go with him, as translator.'

With the cutter now towing astern – the shallower water brought calmer seas so there was no need to hoist it in again – the *Calypso* steered for the western end of Île Royale, followed by *La Robuste*. Seen from this angle, against the flat land of the shore, the island seemed like the end of a lozenge, crowding Île St Joseph, which was much smaller and only ninety feet high. The resulting channel was wide but the water brown, obviously shallow. Here and there short branches of wood floated on the sea but did not drift, merely moving up and down. Southwick pointed out several to Ramage, who tapped the old man on the shoulder. 'You're lucky to have your navigation confirmed like that – the local fishermen have put their pots down round the bank, and those bits of bough are their buoys. The only trouble is you don't know if the pots are for lobsters and therefore close to rocks, or fish, in which case they'll be further away.'

'All the same to me, sir,' Southwick declared cheerfully. 'I don't want to take us within a mile of that bank! And these islands – I wouldn't want to stay here a week, let alone a year. If I was a Frenchman I'd take care I didn't fall foul of Bonaparte and get sent out here.'

'If you were a Frenchman you might not have the choice. The Count of Rennes just wanted to be left in peace.'

Southwick sniffed in agreement, recognizing that in two sentences the captain had summed it all up.

'At least we beat *L'Espoir*,' he said, gesturing at the empty anchorage. 'Tell me, sir, did you expect to?'

'Hopes were fighting fears. When it was dark I didn't expect to, but if it was a nice sunny day with a fresh wind – well, I hoped.'

'And now, sir?'

Ramage purposely misunderstood the question. 'We heave-to and wait for the pilot off the western end of the island, then we'll anchor a cable further seaward than he says. Four fathoms, soft mud, single anchor. I told Wagstaffe in the orders I sent across to anchor as far inshore of us as he dared, so the gap between the two ships is at least a cable, preferably two.'

Southwick was puzzled. 'I hope young Wagstaffe doesn't run on the mud. Soft mud and a lee shore. Think of the suction on that hull . . .'

Laughing at the thought, Ramage said casually: 'We can always use the boats to lay out an anchor or two for him; then all hands to man the capstan. With the fiddler standing on top to set them trotting, we'd soon have him off!'

Southwick looked like a bishop to whom the suffragan's wife had just made a very improper suggestion, but Ramage saw no point in explaining everything in detail because there was a good chance he would have to abandon the plan. Which plan? There were two now and he was muddling himself. Well, he meant the one he had just explained to Gilbert and his men, the one which had occurred to him only a couple of hours ago. Call that the first plan, even though it was the last to arrive in his head. The second plan, which followed only if the first was successful, was the original idea, the one that had come like a wind shadow, and it was surrounded with ifs as thick as a blackthorn hedge intended to keep boys out of an apple orchard. The second plan did not even begin until *L'Espoir* hove in sight. Providing the first worked, and providing *L'Espoir* hove in sight, then there would be plenty of time to tell Southwick all about the second.

'Deck there, mainmasthead here!'

'Deck here,' Aitken bellowed up, not bothering with the speaking trumpet.

'There's a strange little craft ahead of us, sir: through the glass it looks like a canoe with a sail on a sprit. Four men in it.'

'Very well, keep reporting it,' Aitken said and turned back to Ramage. 'That'll be your pilot, sir,' he said with a first lieutenant's usual lofty disdain for local pilots.

'Heave-to to leeward of them so they can drop down to us. Now, our colours are stowed. Mr Southwick, tell the men no one is to speak English while the pilot boat is near. Nor is any bosun's mate to use his call. There's no need for the pilot to mistake us for an English frigate . . .'

'Mistake us?' Southwick repeated the phrase and then took his hat off, scratched his head, and ran his hand through his hair before jamming his hat back on. He took up the speaking trumpet and bellowed the length of the ship. Without much apparent effort his voice carried Ramage's order to every man.

'Now stand by to back the foretopsail, Mr Aitken,' Ramage said and could have bitten his tongue. Aitken knew what to do, and giving him unnecessary orders must be irritating.

Now he could see the pilot boat with the naked eye. Yes, it was a large dugout canoe, with a stubby mast and, like a canted boom, a sprit stuck out diagonally, holding out the square sail. And it was an old sail obviously sewn up from odd pieces of cloth. But for all that the canoe was skimming along, and through the glass he could now see there were three blacks actually handling the boat while a white man tried to sit in a dignified manner. But, judging from the urgency with which one of the others scooped water over the side using a calabash shell as a bailer, he must be sitting in a few inches of water.

The movement of the pilot canoe so intrigued him that Ramage did not notice that the *Calypso* was turning head to wind to heave-to until her bow swung and the canoe and Île Royale suddenly shifted from the larboard bow to amidships on the starboard side.

Ramage walked over to the skylight above his cabin and called down in French. He listened to the reply, laughed and looked round for Louis and Albert, who were still waiting by the taffrail.

'Wait for Gilbert and Auguste at the top of the gangway,' he told them in French. 'You really understand what I want you to do?'

'Indeed we do, sir,' Louis said. 'We are proud to be able to do it!'

Ramage nodded and grinned. One Englishman was usually reckoned to be equal to three Frenchmen, but not these Frenchmen. What had changed them? Gilbert and his three friends probably held their own political views as strongly as a Revolutionary sailor in Bonaparte's Navy. Was it leadership? He shrugged because he had no idea: it was so, and for the moment that was all that mattered.

The pilot canoe was only a hundred yards off, and he walked back to the skylight and warned Gilbert and Auguste, but there was no reply and a moment later he saw them joining Louis and Albert at the gangway.

Ramage took off his coat and untied his stock, bundling both up with his hat and stuffing them under one of the guns.

'Mr Aitken ... Mr Southwick ...' he pointed at what he was doing, and each man hurriedly removed his hat, coat and stock.

Now the master, his white hair caught by the wind, could pass for – well, a rural dean, an amiable grocer, a tenant farmer who was now leaving the heavy work to his sons ...

'You still don't look like a Republican, sir,' Southwick said doubtfully. 'Perhaps the hair? Too tidy?'

Ramage ran his fingers through it. 'You have the advantage of me, I must admit,' he said wryly.

'The breeches and silk stockings, sir?' Southwick said, his voice still doubtful. 'Don't forget those whatever they're called, the *sans cullars*.'

'*Sans-culottes*. No, don't worry, we don't need to dance on top of the hammock nettings!'

With that Ramage left Aitken and Southwick on the quarter-deck and went down to the entryport where Auguste stood watching the canoe, which was now beginning to round up to come alongside, one of the men casting off the sheet and stifling the sail by standing up and clasping it to him as he reached for the mast. The other two blacks picked up paddles and began

220

paddling the canoe the last few feet in the calm water provided by the *Calypso*'s bulk.

Ramage gestured to Auguste, who took the telescope Ramage held out to him. Tucking it under one arm and straightening his shoulders, the Frenchman said with a grin: 'I shall find it hard to be an ordinary seaman again, sir.'

Ramage stood to one side beside a gun while Auguste went back to the entryport and Gilbert, Louis and Albert stood close to him.

There was a faint hail and Albert hurried forward with the coil of rope he was holding. From the top of the hammock nettings he threw an end down to the canoe and one of the blacks seized it. The canoe was almost level with the entryport when the pilot began to stand up.

Auguste leaned over slightly to shout down at him. 'M'sieu, listen carefully. This frigate and the one astern have come from Brest, and a third is due any day – we lost company with her.'

'Very well, captain,' the pilot answered. 'There is plenty of room in the anchorage. You bring us many prisoners, eh?'

'We bring you possible sickness and death,' Auguste said sadly. 'Brest has *la peste*. We lost five men from it the day after sailing. The other frigate' – he gestured astern – 'lost nine. I dare not think what has happened with the third frigate: I suspect we lost sight of her because she had so much sickness . . .'

'The plague? Brest a plague port? Nine – no, fourteen – dead? Quarantine! You must stay at anchor! No one to come on shore. Six weeks from the last case. Here, cast off!' he snapped at the seaman, who let go of the rope as though it was a poisonous snake.

As the canoe drifted away the pilot stood up and shouted: 'I will report to the governor, but six weeks you stay –'

Auguste and Gilbert screamed back at him: it was an injustice, it was mocking their misery, it would leave them short of medical supplies and provisions . . .

Louis and Albert joined in. There was no wine and very little water left. Now they would get the black vomit, as well as having the plague, and anyway what authority had the pilot to give such orders?

'I'll show you!' the white-faced pilot screeched back as the canoe drifted away. 'No one is to come near the shore: you stay on board. Tell the second frigate and the third when she comes in because I am not coming out again for six weeks. I know the governor will order sentries to shoot at anyone approaching the shore. That's an order; I have the authority!'

'Assassin, cuckold, pederast, Royalist traitor!' Auguste bawled and stood aside to give the others a chance while he thought up more insults.

'You wait until the Minister of Marine hears of it!' Gilbert bellowed. 'Then you'll be a prisoner here, not the pilot!'

The pilot knew he was far enough away to be at a disadvantage shouting against the wind, but he took a deep breath. 'Perhaps – if you live long enough to get a message to Brest. But you'll all leave your bones on the beach over there ...'

'Your mother was a careless whore!' Auguste yelled and then shook his head. 'It's a waste,' he grumbled, 'he's too far away.' He handed the telescope back to Ramage. 'Was that satisfactory, sir?'

A grinning Ramage patted him on the back. 'Perfect. As I watched you all it was obvious the *Calypso* had at least four captains!'

'Sir,' Aitken called anxiously, 'we're running out of sea room!'

'Bear away and anchor when you're ready!' Ramage shouted and hurried back to the quarterdeck, passing Southwick on his way to the fo'c'sle. By now the pilot was a quarter of the way to a jetty which was just coming into view on the south side of Île Royale.

As he climbed the steps Ramage was thankful his idea had effectively ensured that no one would be coming out to the anchored ships, but he wished the pilot had not taken fright so quickly: Auguste had not been able to ask the pilot to remain in his canoe but lead the way to the anchorage.

Aitken shouted to a seaman standing in the chains, ready with the lead: 'Give me a cast!' Then he gave orders to brace up the yard and trim the foretopsail sheets so that the *Calypso* turned for the last few hundred yards to the anchorage.

The leadsman reported. 'Six fathoms, soft mud.'

Ramage had already explained to Aitken the importance of the *Calypso* anchoring in the right place, so that *La Robuste* could position herself, and he kept both topsails shivering so that the *Calypso* had little more than steerage way.

Ramage watched the luffs of the sails and kept an eye on the quartermaster, who would signal the moment the *Calypso* was going too slowly for the rudder to bite. He glanced astern and noted that Wagstaffe was handling his ship perfectly.

'Five fathoms ... five fathoms ...' the leadsman's chant was monotonous but clear. He heaved the lead forward so that it dropped into the water and hit the bottom just as the mainchains passed over it. A quick up-and-down tug on the line confirmed that the lead was actually on the bottom, and by the feel of the piece of leather or cloth in his hand, marking the depths, he sang out the fathoms and feet.

The *Calypso* was now moving crabwise to the unmarked spot where Ramage intended to anchor, and Southwick's upraised arm showed that all was ready on the fo'c'sle. The anchor, stowed high up and parallel with the deck when on passage, had been lowered almost to the water. Ramage's eyes swept the luffs, saw the men at the wheel, and said: 'Down with the helm!'

Had he left it too late? Was the *Calypso* now going too slowly for the rudder to work effectively, or had the quartermaster (very sensibly) given the warning a few seconds early? In fact they could lower the anchor and, as soon as it held, the cable would swing the frigate round head to wind. Effective, but not very seamanlike, and the cable going under the hull was likely to wrench off copper sheathing.

But the *Calypso*'s bow was coming round ... one point, two, three ... speeding up now ... six, seven, eight ... fourteen, fifteen, sixteen ... And with the wheel amidships and the foretopsail once again aback, because the yard had not been hauled round to compensate for the turn, the *Calypso* slowed.

Ramage walked to a gunport and looked over the side. The water was muddy and several pieces of palm fronds and odd branches were floating. But they stayed in the same place: the *Calypso* was stopped. Then they began moving towards the bow ... the frigate was beginning to move astern.

Ramage signalled to Southwick and heard first the splash of the anchor and then the thunder of the cable running through the hawse. And yes, the usual smell of burning as the cable, finally dry after being stowed for weeks in the cable tier, scorched itself and the wood of the hawsehole as it raced out.

A quick order to the topmen had the main and mizentopsails furled, but he waited for the signal from Southwick which would indicate that the foretopsail now thrusting the *Calypso* astern had dug in the anchor.

He returned to watching the rubbish. Finally the palm fronds and broken branches slowed down and then stayed alongside. He watched a rock on Île Royale which was lined up with a headland on Île du Diable. The two remained lined up. If the rock had moved out of line that would have been proof that the anchor was dragging and the palm fronds were drifting in a current moving at the same speed as the frigate.

Ramage then jumped up on to the breech of a gun to watch *La Robuste* anchoring. She ended up positioned perfectly, and as her anchor hit the water, Ramage saw that the pilot's canoe had just arrived at the jetty.

'They're in a hurry,' Aitken commented.

'I'm not surprised: the pilot has never had such a startling report to make the governor,' Ramage said.

'Now what do we do?'

'We hoist out all the boats and wait,' Ramage said. 'Wait and practise.'

CHAPTER SEVENTEEN

Sergeant Ferris was, usually, a patient man. He had a rule that he would explain something three times to a Marine or seaman he regarded as intelligent and four times to a fool. But no one valuing his pride, sanity or eardrums would dare cause a fifth. If he had any sense he would do what Marine Hart was doing.

Hart made up in bulk and loudness of voice what he lacked in intelligence, and this resulted in him being, at six feet two inches tall and sixteen stone, the largest of the *Calypso*'s Marines with a bellow that sounded like a bull with spring fever.

Ferris, now commanding the Marine detachment in *La Robuste*, was thankful that Hart was an amiable man. This was due less to his nature than the fact that it was almost impossible to insult him. When he accidentally trod on someone's foot and was promptly called a 'bloody great big oaf', Hart would grin and say proudly: 'Ah, I am big, ain't I?' Hart had been a Marine for more than a year before he discovered to his surprise that an oaf was neither a special sort of promise nor a swear word.

'Let's have one more go, men,' Ferris said, although he knew the twenty Marines in his party understood that he was using 'men' instead of 'Hart' because the man was liable to sulk if he thought he was being singled out. Hart, who was also left-handed, was not difficult or dangerous when he sulked but it was, as Mr Renwick once remarked, like having a stunned elephant lying at the foot of the stairs.

'The idea is this. We have one hundred and sixty Marines and seamen, an' that's dragging in every man that can wield a cutlass or fire a pistol.'

To Sergeant Ferris a cutlass was always a cutlash, no matter how many times he heard Mr Renwick and the *Calypso*'s officers pronounce it correctly. On one occasion Renwick had taken him to one side and explained that it might be bad for discipline if privates heard such an ordinary word mispronounced. Ferris, a great believer in pipeclay and discipline, agreed wholeheartedly. 'So,' Renwick said, promptly sweeping into the linguistic breach, 'it's pronounced "cutlass".'

'S'right, sir,' Ferris agreed, 'cutlash, like I always say.'

Ferris looked round at his twenty men, careful not to glare at Hart. 'Now the captain reckons that eighty men (that's half the total: half one side and half the other) is too many to h'act h'as a disciplined force.'

Anyone except Hart who had served under Ferris knew that under stress (except of course in action), the sergeant sprinkled his sentences with both too many and too few aitches. He was not particular where they fell: a word with a vowel at its threshold was always a convenient spot.

'So h'it h'as been decided to divide the entire force, one hundred and sixty Marines and seamen, h'into eight parties each of twenty men. 'Ow h'about that, 'art, do you understand?'

'Yus, sergeant,' Hart said, nodding his head like a bear trying to disperse buzzing flies.

'Right. Now h'each party will 'ave its h'own h'objective.'

Hart was not alone in trying to sort out the sergeant's aspiration.

'Ours will be the starboard gangway. We clear h'it. I do not want' – he spaced the words and emphasized them – 'h'any of the h'enemy left alive on the starboard gangway.'

'Wot about the fo'c'sle, sergeant?' Hart asked lugubriously.

'None of your affair, my man: you just confine your h'activities to the starboard gangway.'

Hart digested this and then asked: 'Wot about the quarter-deck, sergeant?'

Ferris took a deep breath. They were a good crowd, he had

ιo admit that. They did not quarrel among themselves or try to dodge sentry duty in the more cramped parts of the ship, and they all agreed that Hart when possible should be the sentry at the water butt on deck, when it was in use, rather than, say, sentry at the captain's cabin, where the headroom was five feet four inches, leaving Hart with a surplus of ten inches. But why Hart? What had Ferris ever done, he asked himself, to have a Hart?

'None of your affair, my man,' he repeated firmly, 'you just confine your h'activities to the starboard gangway.'

'But sergeant, what happens when we've done 'em all in on the starboard gangway? Don't seem fair that the fo'c'sle and the quarterdeck men and the rest of 'em get a bigger share than us. After all, we are Marines.'

Ware, Ferris suddenly remembered. In Hertfordshire. That was where Hart came from. 'Where?' 'Ware.' Yes, Ferris could remember that puzzling conversation with Marine Hart years ago.

But for once Hart was asking a good question. Once they'd cleared the gangway, were they expected just to stand there? Toss bodies over the side? Or what? Anyway, it gave him a chance to encourage Hart.

'That is a very pertinent question, my good man, and I'll raise it with Mr Wagstaffe.'

'Oh sergeant,' Hart said hastily, 'I wasn't trying to be pertinent: it just seemed we was being discrimbulated against.'

Not being pertinent? Ferris's brow wrinkled. He had never seen Hart so apologetic. What was wrong with 'pertinent'? It was a sergeant's word, like 'my man' was a sergeant's phrase. Suddenly he added two letters and saw the reason for Hart's apology.

'H'oh no, "pertinent" and "impertinent" are two h'utterly different words. "Pertinent" means – well, it's a good question. "Impertinent" is being rude to someone of a higher station, like a sergeant, or a lieutenant.'

That left 'discrimbulated'. Who would dare discrimbulate against Sergeant Ferris's party of men? That would risk a flogging. At least, it sounded as if it would. But ... well, that word had a sort of left-handed sound about it. Then Ferris sighed.

'Hart, my good man, you mean "discriminate". Believe me, no one's trying to discriminate against us. Mr Renwick was there

226

when Mr Ramage drew a diagram of the ship's deck h'on a sheet of paper, and he divided it h'up into fo'c'sle, maindeck, starboard gangway, and larboard, quarterdeck and lowerdeck. Obviously most people are going to be on the maindeck, so four parties go there, one to the fo'c'sle, one to the quarterdeck, and one to each gangway: eight parties, one hundred and sixty men, plus a few under Midshipman Orsini to rescue the Royalists.'

'If you say so, sergeant,' Hart said. He did not understand, he was not convinced, nor, Ferris firmly believed, did the big ox *want* to be convinced. Like a bull giving an occasional bellow for no reason, and not because of any bad temper, Hart had these mild attacks from time to time.

On board the *Calypso,* Ramage filled in the last couple of lines of the day's entry in his journal. He had a strange 'someone-else-is-writing-this' sensation when he noted the *Calypso*'s position, under the 'Bearings and distance at noon' column as 'Western extremity of Île Royale bearing north by east $^3/_4$ east five cables'. Nor was it often one could be so exact, but here in the lee of the islands the sea was calm and the wind steady, and as the French pilot book gave the heights of the three islands Paolo had been set to work with sextant and tables working out the distance. His first two attempts put Île Royale eleven and then seven miles away, but by the fifth sextant reading and set of calculations his answer coincided with Southwick's.

Ramage usually left the 'Remarkable Observations and Accidents' column empty, and the events of today, the first complete day after they had arrived and anchored, were so far unimportant, but if there was a court-martial the record might be important. He made an abbreviated entry:

'French pilot's canoe came within hail mid-afternoon inquiring number of *déportés* on board both frigates and intended for island. Told sixty-two and more due in third frigate. Told that Governor's orders are for both frigates and third when she arrives to remain at anchor in quarantine for six weeks after death or complete recovery of last case of cholera. Lieutenants Martin and Kenton returned on board until *L'Espoir* arrives. Ships' companies employed A.T.S.R.'

He hated the initials for 'As the Service required' but at this rate he would soon run out of space. There was no need to describe it as meaning scrubbing decks, setting up or replacing rigging and whippings, mending sails, and all the thousand and one jobs a sailor in a ship of war (or any ship for that matter) was heir to. And the sudden torrential rains that seemed to arrive out of a reasonably clear sky at three-hourly intervals meant that the quarterdeck awning was stretched with one corner dropped to catch water. If they could fill butts at the present rate each man would have something like a gallon of fresh water a day – something he had never experienced before. He could drink as much as he wanted; more important, he could rinse his clothes properly. Using the urine collected in the tubs in the head gave enough ammonia to bleach clothing, but rinsing in salt water always meant that everything dried only to get damp on a humid day.

It would soon be necessary to send a boat to the mainland one night: the purser was complaining that he had only nineteen wreaths of twigs left for the cook to light the galley fire, and there was precious little wood left. So a wooding party would have to be sent out. And green wood needed more twigs to get it burning . . . Curious how planning the rescue of the Count of Rennes was built on the foundations of wreaths of twigs. 'Wreaths' was an absurd name, yet in the Navy Board's list of 'Tonnage with respect to stowage', forty wreaths of twigs were noted as weighing a ton. Out of curiosity he searched through a drawer and found the list – yes, six jars of oil, forty bushels of oatmeal, 252 gallons of wine, 1,800 pounds of cheese in casks, 450 pieces of beef, 900 pieces of pork, 200 empty sacks, wooden hoops for 420 hogshead or 600 kilderkins, 240 gallons of vinegar, forty wreaths of twigs . . . each item weighed a ton. Wreaths – did the gypsies call them that when they went from door to door in towns selling kindling?

He looked at his watch. By now the *Calypso*'s parties of men should be waiting on the lowerdeck. Wagstaffe had just arrived on board from *La Robuste* and Aitken, Kenton, Martin and Renwick would be ready. Very well, *aux armes, citoyens*.

It was hot down on the lowerdeck but eighty seamen and Marines stood to attention as Aitken barked an order when Ramage came down the ladder, once again wearing his French trousers and a white shirt – with a powerful glass it was possible for anyone on the hill of Île Royale to inspect the ship's deck, so neither Marines nor officers could wear anything but what would be usual on board a French ship of war. Ramage was delighted that his stockings, breeches and coat were back in the trunks, and Silkin was now busy stitching up white duck bought

228

from the purser into shirts and trousers. It was not seemly, Silkin had complained, that the captain should be wearing trousers cobbled up from 'pusser's duck'.

Ramage looked round at all the faces and found most of them were grinning. He had never before had such a large group muster on the lowerdeck, and the presence of the lieutenants and the ship's present position accounted for the air of excitement which was as heady as the smell of hops to leeward of a brewery.

'Fall out the officers,' Ramage said, 'and all of you make yourselves comfortable.' Unaware of Sergeant Ferris's problem he added: 'I am going through all this once. Then if there's anything someone doesn't understand, ask questions.'

He looked round at the men again and said in level tones: 'What is the difference between an axe and a hammer? Let's say the head of each is a chunk of metal weighing eight pounds. If you hit a plank with the hammer, you get a dent. But if you hit a plank with an axe, you get a deep cut the length of the blade.

'Why a dent with one and a deep cut with the other? Well, you've already guessed that the hammer's eight pounds when it hits the plank is spread over an area of the head likely to be twice the size of a guinea. But the eight pounds of the axe is concentrated on the blade – say four inches long by less than the thickness of a sheet of very thin paper. That's why you use an axe to fell a tree, not a hammer. Obviously you wouldn't use an axe blade to drive in a nail, either; you want the energy spread out over the flat head.'

He looked round at the sailors. Yes, they understood the similes, even though they were puzzled why the captain was suddenly sermonizing like one of Mr Wesley's men.

'Now supposing you want to smash a plank of wood into kindling. You can have an eight-pound hammer or you can have an eight-pound axe – you have the choice. Or you can have eight one-pound axes or hammers.

'Supposing you were in a hurry: instead of an hour you had only five minutes to smash that plank into kindling. Wouldn't you be better off using your eight pounds of weight by chopping with eight one-pound axes rather than one axe weighing eight pounds?'

Several men immediately said yes, and the rest of them quickly muttered their agreement.

Ramage looked round and spotted Stafford. He pointed at the

Cockney. 'Why would we be better with eight smaller axes, Stafford?'

'Well, sir, stands ter reason, dunnit: eight blades choppin' away at eight different places is better than one big blade – that's if you want the plank as kindlin'.'

'Exactly. For chopping down a tree . . .'

'Oh well, sir, the one big blade, o'course.'

'Good. You all notice I am talking of a plank and not the tree: if it was a tree we'd be using the big axe to chop *in the same place*; because it's a plank for kindling we use eight small axes chopping *in several places*.'

Most of the men were nodding, reminding Ramage of a flock of pigeons. This business of speaking to them in parables was, in this instance anyway, a good one. And anything that helped maintain some sort of discipline in the heat of battle was all to the good. He found it difficult to control himself in the roar, smoke, flame and shouting of battle afloat, so he could not blame the seamen for regarding action on board an enemy ship as a concentrated group of men fighting a series of hand-to-hand actions, cutlass against cutlass, boarding pike against pistol, tomahawk against musket. This was the hammer method, and usually it worked: the owner of any unfamiliar face was killed or taken prisoner.

'Very well, the "plank" we might be attacking using the several small axes method is, I hope, the French frigate *L'Espoir* when she arrives.'

From the satisfied 'Ahs' and the way that the men wriggled to make themselves more comfortable, as though settling in for a long session, Ramage knew that only a handful of men had thought that far ahead.

'Now, capturing *L'Espoir* – providing she arrives here and providing we are still here to meet her – is going to be the most difficult job we've ever undertaken. Not the most dangerous, just the most difficult. You saw how the "plague" trick worked, and you'll remember that Mr Orsini did a similar thing once in the Mediterranean. You were all with me when we dealt with the renegades at the Ilha Trinidade. But this time each of us will be fighting with one hand tied behind his back.

'There are fifty prisoners on board *L'Espoir* that we are under orders to rescue. We won't know where those prisoners are being kept in *L'Espoir*; we don't even know if the captain will be desperate enough to threaten to kill them unless we let him go free. Of course we can't use our great guns for fear of killing the prisoners. Now, listen carefully.'

Quickly he outlined the plan, explaining how each group of twenty men would be under a particular leader and would have its own task. 'So you see,' he concluded, 'the frigate is a plank of wood, and the eight groups are the eight small axes. Has anyone any questions?'

Jackson stood up. 'Yes, sir. When do we expect *L'Espoir*?'

The *Calypso*'s gunroom, occupying the after part of the lowerdeck, was just far enough forward to clear the end of the tiller as it moved from side to side in a great arc, responding to the lines led down to it from the barrel of the wheel, but not far enough to be out of range of the harsh squeaking of the pintles of the rudder blade grinding on the gudgeons which supported them. When the *Calypso* was under way the rudder moved constantly, but the noise was almost lost in the symphony composed of water rushing past the hull and the creaking of the whole ship working as she flexed like a tree in a strong wind to ride across the troughs and crests of the waves.

The gunroom was an open space between four large boxes on one side and three on the other. The boxes were in fact cabins formed by three walls, or bulkheads, made of painted canvas stretched tightly over battens, with the ship's side forming the fourth. Each had its door, and each door had a stone-ground glass window in the upper half. Over each door was a sign bearing a carefully painted rank – surgeon, first lieutenant, and second lieutenant on the starboard side, Marine officer, third lieutenant, master and fourth lieutenant on the larboard side.

A table and forms fitted most of the remaining space, though the object like a thick tree trunk at the after end was the mizzenmast, while the hatch on the larboard side, between the table and the master's cabin, and on which everyone stubbed a foot at least once a week, was the scuttle to the magazine, a reminder if any was needed that the ship's officers lived just above several tons of gunpowder.

Forward of the gunroom were two smaller cabins on the starboard side (for the gunner and the carpenter) and two to larboard, occupied by the purser and the bosun. A large cabin forward of the bosun's box was the midshipmen's berth, built to be the home of up to a dozen who could range in age from fourteen or fifteen to fifty, but at present the sole inhabitant was

Midshipman Paolo Orsini, who thus had more space than anyone else in the ship except the captain.

Forward of these cabins the Marines had their tables and forms, and at night slung their hammocks, and forward of them was what was usually called the 'messdeck', because the seamen forming the rest of the ship's company lived there, six or eight men to a table or 'mess' and slinging their hammocks at night.

Right in the bow, most of the time with a leg in irons, were the *Calypso*'s half of *La Robuste*'s prisoners, guarded by a couple of Marines with muskets. For a couple of hours in the morning the French prisoners were freed for exercise but, as Ramage had told Renwick, it was unlikely they would be kept on board for more than a few days; not enough to worry about them being in irons.

In the gunroom, with the day's work in the ship completed and only the anchor watch, lookouts and prisoners' guard to keep men from their hammocks and cots, the ship's lieutenants sat in their cabins or at the table.

The cabins were tiny and airless – there was room only for the cot, a canvas or metal bowl for washing, a trunk usually up-ended, a leprous mirror stuck in the best place to catch what little light squeezed through the skylight under the half deck, and a rickety canvas chair which usually collapsed when the ship rolled violently, forcing the occupant to retreat to the forms, which were bolted to the deck.

Kenton, the red-haired and freckle-faced third lieutenant, was the smallest of the ship's officers but his chair had recently broken completely and it was only the suddenness of the collapse that saved him trapping any fingers. Now, as he waited for a carpenter's mate to make him a new chair, he had to sit on a form, munching the last piece of fruit cake he had brought with him from home, and which was edible only after he had scraped off a thick layer of mildew.

William Martin, the fourth lieutenant and son of the master shipwright at Chatham, was in his cabin behind Kenton and softly played his flute. Kenton did not particularly like the tune that 'Blower' was playing and called to Aitken, who was sitting in his cabin filling in reports on provisions which should have been handed to the captain's clerk last week.

'When does the captain reckon *L'Espoir* will arrive?'

He rubbed his nose while waiting for a reply. Kenton, like Renwick, never tanned and the tropical sun meant his face was always scarlet and usually peeling. He had tried rubbing the skin with butter, goose grease (which was awful: his clothes reeked of it for days) and soap, but nothing helped.

'The captain doesn't "reckon". He can only guess, like you or me. He's hoping, obviously, but he's trying not to be influenced by the fact that one of the prisoners is a close friend.'

'Yes, what's that all about?' Kenton asked.

'I thought you knew.' Aitken was always careful to separate information that the officers should know from gossip. Sometimes the dividing line was thin.

'No, I've only heard what Southwick's said.'

'Well, the captain and Lady Sarah were on their honeymoon in France and staying with this friend, the Count of Rennes, when the British ambassador left Paris. Bonaparte's police arrested many Royalists before they knew the war had started again.'

'Why didn't they arrest the captain and Lady Sarah at the same time?'

'Oh, that's how we came to have those four Frenchmen on board: Gilbert managed to hide the captain and his wife; then with the other three retook the *Murex*.'

'Yes, I heard some of the seamen saying that her Ladyship shot dead a Frenchman.'

'She did. Saved all their lives, I gather.'

Kenton sighed, a deep sigh that seemed to go on as a descant to Martin's flute. 'What a lovely lady she is. The captain certainly finds 'em. I used to think the Marchesa was the loveliest woman I ever saw until Lady Sarah came along. I'm glad I didn't have to choose between them!'

'Keep your voice down; there's no need for Orsini to hear you going on about his aunt.'

'She went back to Italy, didn't she? Hey!' Kenton sat up suddenly. 'Do you suppose the French arrested *her* as well?'

'Arrested or assassinated?' Aitken said sourly. 'No one knows yet. She reached Paris and left for Volterra, but there's no proof she ever reached Italy.'

'I don't like this making war on women.'

'At least some of the women make war on the French,' Aitken commented. 'Think of Lady Sarah!'

'Yes. I'm sorry we missed that. That's the first time the captain's been in a scrap without us for a long time.'

'Ha, a long time!' Southwick rumbled from his cabin, where

he was stretched out on his cot. 'You're a new boy! I've been with him since he was given his first command!'

'Yes,' Kenton said. 'That was the *Kathleen* cutter, wasn't it? Tell us about the first time he came aboard and what you thought of him.'

'Corsica, that's where it was,' Southwick said, a nostalgic note in his voice. 'Bastia. Nice harbour with all those fortifications. Commodore Nelson – well, he was only a commodore then – gave orders that –'

A hammering on the deckhead had all the officers grabbing their swords and pistols from the racks over their doors and hurrying for the companionway, Kenton muttering: 'I thought I heard a hail!'

CHAPTER EIGHTEEN

The sun was setting, and within half an hour it would plunge below the mangrove swamps and distant hills lining the mainland. Already Île Royale and Île St Joseph seemed to have changed shape as the shadows lengthened and moved round, the sun lighting the crest of fresh hills and darkening valleys.

The captain was on deck: they all knew that because when he wanted to spend some time alone pacing up and down, he had told Martin, who was officer of the deck, that he could go below for an hour.

They looked questioningly at the captain as they reached the quarterdeck, and he simply gestured seaward.

There, like a grey swan gliding on the far side of a lake, a frigate had just come in sight round the end of Île Royale.

'She looks French-built,' he said, and told Orsini: 'Go aloft with a bring-'em-near and see what you make of her. You, Kenton and Martin, had better get over to *La Robuste*.'

Ramage then looked again at the approaching ship, at the Île Royale which was a grey, black-streaked monster crouching close by, and at *La Robuste*, anchored abeam. From pacing the quarterdeck he knew the wind was steady from the southeast at ten to fifteen knots.

Speeds and distances. Although the approaching frigate had at first been hidden behind the Île Royale, now she had drawn clear he could see she had only three miles to reach the point where she would expect the pilot canoe to be waiting.

I command L'Espoir and am at the end of the long and potentially dangerous voyage across the Atlantic, he told himself. My pilot book tells me where to anchor (there, where two frigates are already anchored) and that I should find the pilot just off the western end of Île Royale.

However, there is no pilot. I curse because, apart from anything else, the sun is too low to penetrate the water enough to show reefs and rocks, and the sea is too smooth in this lee to break. And soon it will be dark. What do I do?

Obviously I assume the two anchored frigates have seen me approaching. The pilot book tells me where the bank of dangerous rocks is, and the two frigates indicate the anchorage. One or both of the frigate captains will notice that the pilot does not meet me and if I try to get to the anchorage they will have warning guns ready. So I shall creep in under topsails, and if I get too near the bank a frigate's guns will warn me, and if it gets too shallow my own leadsman will warn me.

Yes, Ramage told himself, that is what he would be thinking and doing himself, and he was damn'd sure that is what the French captain was thinking and doing. The Frenchman would be concentrating his thoughts first on the outlying rocks and reefs and then on the shallow banks with soft muddy bottoms. And at the back of his mind there would be the prospect of a good supper at the governor's house with fresh meat instead of salt tack, and fresh fruit and fresh vegetables.

Aitken was inspecting La Robuste with a telescope. 'I can see Wagstaffe watching. There are a few men on deck and they look very French.' He closed the telescope and looked aloft and forward to check the Calypso. 'We do, too, sir.' He sniffed in a fair imitation of Southwick. 'And I can't wait to have the men back at work with the brick dust putting a shine on our brasswork. It's so green that the ship begins to look like those copper roofs in Copenhagen.'

'I didn't know you'd ever been there.'

'Copenhagen, Elsinore, Christiania, Malmö, Stockholm ... Yes, I know the Cattegat and Skagerrak, sir. In fact every time I see some weathered copper or brass I think of Copenhagen. Those spires and towers make it a lovely city. You know it?'

Ramage nodded, and both men were aware that they were using this inane conversation to pass the time. As they watched,

L'Espoir seemed to slow down, but they knew that it was their own reactions quickening.

Opening his telescope again and carefully lining up the focusing ring he had filed in the eyepiece tube, Ramage looked carefully at the peak at the western end of Île Royale. The church stood shadowed and the big western door closed. The flagstaff was bare and there was no movement round the building.

Obviously the garrison commander or *préfet* had listened to the pilot's story that Brest had *la peste* and that although the two frigates already arrived had lost only a few men, a third frigate still on her way was believed to have lost many more. The garrison commander would assume that this frigate was the third and that she, even more than the other two, must be prevented from bringing *la peste* to the three islands which were already crowded with convicts and *déportés*. Only one hospital, the pilot book said, and Ramage could picture it: built of stone, small windows, one or perhaps two small wards, four beds in each, and nearby a cemetery situated in a place where there was a reasonable thickness of earth on the rock. And both hospital and cemetery within a short distance of the church: one did not walk far in the sun in a latitude of five degrees North, and funerals were always held within twenty-four hours of death.

Funerals! His mind had a macabre twist at times. Ah, *L'Espoir* was furling her courses. Quite unconsciously he began counting the seconds, which merged into minutes, and he began extending his fingers so he could keep a better tally. Finally both courses were furled and he turned to find Aitken grinning at him.

'Short of topmen, short of petty officers, or just aren't in a hurry, sir? I saw you timing them.'

'Just French,' Ramage said. 'Latins measure time by different watches and clocks than us!'

Now *L'Espoir* was abreast the western end of the Île Royale and began turning in a graceful arc until she was head to wind and, in a few moments, hove-to just where the pilot canoe had been waiting when the *Calypso* and *La Robuste* arrived. Now only a few sodden logs marked fishpots . . .

Ramage glanced at his watch and then turned to look at the sun, which was a perfect red orb with the lower edge exactly its own diameter above the horizon. The French captain had about fifteen minutes to decide that the pilot was not coming out tonight and make for the anchorage . . .

Exactly five minutes later *L'Espoir*'s foretopsail was braced up and she bore away towards the *Calypso* and *La Robuste*.

'Send the parties to their stations, Mr Aitken,' Ramage said quietly, and went down to his cabin to collect his pistols and sling a cutlass belt over his right shoulder.

Back on deck, Ramage steadied the glass against the rigging and studied *L'Espoir,* a graceful but weather-worn ship, in the circular frame of the telescope's lenses. Certainly he had no doubt that she was *L'Espoir*: he had seen in Brest that she was, very unusually, painted a dull russet red: a red very similar to the colour of rust. And, as the last of the sun caught her side squarely, he could see why that colour had been chosen: rust weeps from dozens of bolts streaked her hull as though the tails of dull red cows had been nailed to her side. The paint almost disguised the weeps but they were as obvious to a seaman's eye as the sobs after a weeping woman dried her eyes.

Ramage walked to the taffrail and looked over the stern. Three of the *Calypso*'s boats were streamed astern on their painters and the fourth was just securing to the end of the boat boom, after taking Kenton and Martin to *La Robuste.* A rope ladder hanging down from the outer end allowed men to climb up on to the boom; a line running parallel with the boom to the ship's side acted as a handrail.

Ramage had been amused at the sight of many of the men sitting round on the maindeck with 'prayerbooks' (the small blocks of Portland stone used as holystones to clean the deck), sharpening cutlasses and squaring up the three-sided tips of boarding pikes. He had forbidden them to hoist up the big grindstone on deck because it made a harsh noise and while no man, however sharp his cutlass, could resist 'having a whet' on the stone, the unmistakable noise would carry to Île Royale and Île St Joseph, and make some people wonder.

Or would it? Was he being too cautious? Could anyone on the three islands ever believe that the two frigates anchored close by were British? Fortunately the Tricolour was never run up at the flagstaff by the fortress on the seaward side. He had long ago noticed that while in Revolutionary France waving the Tricolour and yelling revolutionary slogans was very popular, it was only in Royalist Britain and on board her ships that colours were hoisted and lowered at set times.

Had the *Calypso* and *L'Espoir* been arriving at a British island with its own governor they would have fired a salute, and the fort would have replied. Had Bonaparte decreed special days on which his Army and Navy were to fire salutes? The Royal Navy, with its very long history, had only six, three of them for the King (birthday, accession and coronation), and the others on the Queen's birthday, the anniversary of the Restoration of Charles II, and what was called 'the Gunpowder-Treason' on 5th November. Anyway, L'Espoir was not firing any salutes, so obviously salutes were regarded as a waste of Revolutionary gunpowder.

Yes, the captain of L'Espoir had chosen where he was going to anchor and the frigate was coming round in a broad sweep which would save her having to tack. And Ramage looked forward at Southwick and Aitken, who were watching from the forward end of the quarterdeck. He nodded and smiled.

The dull red hull of L'Espoir now seemed black as the sun finally dipped below the horizon, and Ramage was thankful that twilight in the Tropics was brief. He walked forward to the quarterdeck rail and Aitken, in trousers and a loose smock, his narrow and intense face giving him the look of a Revolutionary, commented: 'He timed his arrival perfectly!'

'To suit us, yes! An hour earlier would have given him time to be rowed to Île Royale to report to the governor, and the French sentries opening fire might have led to him discovering the deception. Half an hour later and he would have anchored for the night at the pilot station and waited until tomorrow. Then he certainly would have gone over to the island.'

'As it is, he might come over here expecting to be invited to supper,' Southwick said.

'Oh, I'm sure he'll have supper on board here tonight. What do you propose offering him? The last of the hens had its head chopped off a few days ago.'

'Gunpowder soup, a cut off a roundshot, grapeshot stuffed with canister ... Does that sound appetizing, sir?'

At that moment a slatting of sails made them look towards L'Espoir, which was rounding up, foretopsail aback, halfway between the Calypso and La Robuste. The new frigate's quarterdeck was perhaps a hundred yards away, and Ramage saw a man, obviously her captain, lift his hat and wave it in a greeting.

Ramage waved back, followed by Southwick and Aitken, and L'Espoir came to a stop and then gathered sternway as the wind pushed against the forward side of the foretopsail. An anchor splashed into the water as Ramage again put the telescope to his eye.

Enough men on the fo'c'sle to deal with the anchor; enough topmen waiting at the foot of the shrouds to go aloft and furl the sails. Enough, but fewer than *L'Espoir* would have had if she was not armed *en flûte*.

L'Espoir's anchor cable was making less and less of an angle with the water as she moved astern and more cable was paid out; finally she stopped, the curve in the cable disappearing as it was straightened by the weight on it, and at last her captain was satisfied the anchor was well dug in. Both topsails were furled, and while the topmen were busy aloft the rest of the ship's company crowded the side, staring at the other two frigates, the islands and the distant low shore.

'Their first sight of the Tropics,' Southwick commented. 'A line of mangroves and three big lumps o' rock with pretentious names.'

'Not pretentious to those prisoners,' Ramage reminded him. 'When they sensed the ship was in calmer waters, and then heard the anchor go down ... They know it could only be the Île du Diable. No doubt quite a few of them expect to leave their bones here.'

The light was going fast now; already a dozen of the brighter stars and planets were showing through as if shy of anyone knowing they had been there all the time but outshone by the sun.

'I'll go and get meself ready, sir.' Southwick excused himself and went down to his cabin in the gunroom.

'That sword of his, sir,' Aitken said. 'Is it a family heirloom or something? I've never seen anyone using a two-handed sword!'

'Two-handed and double-bladed,' Ramage said. 'He doesn't jab or chop with it; he whirls round like a dancer spinning with a scythe. With his white hair flying and him bellowing like a livid bull, nothing clears an enemy's ship's deck faster!'

He looked at his watch, having to hold it up to catch the last of the light. 'Just seven. Let's hope Wagstaffe has his people ready.'

'Your orders were clear enough, sir. An hour after sunset, if she came in during the evening.'

Ramage went to the larboard side and looked through the port.

Île Royale, just forward of the beam, was beginning to blur at the edges, the darkening sky making a smoothing background to the otherwise stark outline. Already *La Robuste* was difficult to see against the distant mangroves, and the russet-coloured *L'Espoir* seemed to have gone to sleep, as though the flurry of activity with anchoring and furling sails had exhausted her.

On board the *Calypso* men were placing lanterns in the normal positions, as though she was greeting the night in the normal way at anchor. A sharp-eyed observer might have wondered why there was no lantern at the entryport – but then, he might think, who was likely to come on board?

'We can start, Mr Aitken,' Ramage said eventually. 'Start by getting those boats still astern hauled round to the boom.'

Nearly every man in the *Calypso*'s ship's company was now on the maindeck and gathered in groups of twenty around the officers. There was one small group by the mainmast, one which Ramage thought of as 'Paolo's Party'.

Paolo stood in front of the four Frenchmen and inspected them. It was now dark and the men were almost invisible: like Paolo and everyone else in the ship, their faces, necks, hands and bare feet were smeared with lampblack, and each man had a wide strip of white duck tied round his head, covering his forehead and knotted behind, the ends left to hang down.

'Now, keep your hands from those headbands,' Paolo instructed in French. 'They're the only thing that will distinguish you from the French crew: remember, our people in *La Robuste*, and all the men here, have orders to kill or capture anyone without headbands – except the *déportés*, of course.'

'We understand, m'sieu,' Auguste said. 'We follow you.'

Ramage stood at the inboard end of the boom. 'Mr Renwick, your men should board.'

Renwick, indistinguishable from a cook's mate who had spent the last hour cleaning out the galley coppers, led the way past Ramage followed by his twenty men, and Ramage was surprised how far it was possible to distinguish the white headbands. Renwick was at the end of the boom and beginning to scramble down the ladder, yet his bobbing head was clear.

'Now Mr Southwick ... mind that meat cleaver of yours!'

Ramage felt rather than saw the master grip his hand and shake it. 'Thanks for letting me go, sir,' the old man said. 'M'sword was getting rusty!' he murmured.

He could just see Renwick's boat drifting clear, the men lifting the oars from their stowed positions along the thwarts. Binding all those damned oars with old cloths, bits of worn sail canvas and finally new duck had caused more trouble than anything else. The duck for the headbands and the oars – ah, Ramage felt angry at the thought of it. That blasted purser, asking to whom he should charge it! Well, admittedly the purser would have to pay unless he received a written authorization from the captain to issue it, but that was hardly the moment to burden everyone with bureaucracy. Probably the wretched fellow wanted the signature on the paper before the captain left the ship in case the captain did not come back alive! Anyway, Southwick saved the wretched man's bacon by declaring there was a grave risk that many yards of duck and sail cloth, some messdeck forms and tables, a couple of dozen worn pistols and twice as many muskets, along with fifty cutlasses whose blades were now so pitted they'd serve better as saws, were going to be written off as 'damaged or lost in battle'.

Eighteen, nineteen, twenty ... That was Southwick's party. 'Mr Aitken ...' The first lieutenant looking, Ramage thought, as 'lean and hungry' as any yon Cassius with blackened face, led his men out on to the boom just as Southwick's boat drifted clear and close to Renwick's.

Again Ramage counted. Yes, that was Aitken's party.

'Orsini ...' The midshipman led his four men along the boom.

'Jackson ...' the coxswain appeared out of the darkness, 'Lead on.' Yes, he recognized the outline of Stafford. A muttered *'Buona fortuna, commandante,'* came from Rossi. Nine ... eleven ... fifteen ... twenty.

Then Ramage was standing there alone except for a shadowy figure. 'Well, bosun, it's the first time you've had command of a frigate! Look after her until I get back!'

'Good luck, sir,' the bosun said. 'I'd prefer to be coming with you.'

'I know, but tonight you have to look after the *Calypso*.'

As Ramage walked out along the boom, hearing the wavelets slapping below, he cursed his own softheartedness. The man who should have been left in command was the gunner, a wretchedly weak-willed man whom Ramage had been intending to replace for a year or more, but the prospect of a long battle with the Board of Ordnance and the Navy Board had made him keep the fellow. It was said that Southwick had not spoken a word to the man for more than a year ...

He hitched his cutlass round to the centre of his back and pushed on the two pistols in his belt, and then went down the ladder. He stepped over feet and reached the sternsheets, to find himself with Paolo and the four Frenchmen, the rest of his own group being further forward. Jackson called softly to the man at the bow, who pulled the painter through the block and the boat drifted clear of the ship. The large black mass blotting out the stars on one side was the *Calypso*: the three shapes close by were the other boats. Over there was Île Royale which, like the *Calypso*, was only identifiable because of its outline against the stars.

CHAPTER NINETEEN

Ramage was never really sure whether it was a hiss or a purr, but the sound of a boat's cutwater slicing through a calm sea was very restful, like going to sleep on board the ship with wavelets faintly tickling the hull. The men were breathing easily because they were rowing at a comfortable pace and the oars were groaning softly in the rowlocks instead of squeaking and clicking: the cloth lashings and the greasy slush from the cook's coppers wiped into the open-topped square rowlocks were effective.

The boat came clear of the *Calypso*'s stern and Ramage had his first glimpse of *L'Espoir* from sea level. She seemed huge, black and menacing. No, perhaps not menacing – there were several lanterns casting yellowish cones of light on deck and reaching up to the under side of the yards which poised over the ship like eagles waiting to plunge.

Beyond he could just distinguish *La Robuste* in the distance: specks of dim light showed her position. At this very moment Wagstaffe should be leading four boats towards *L'Espoir*. Ramage was not too concerned that the two groups of boats arrived simultaneously because if one attacked before the other the French would concentrate on trying to beat it off and the second would take them by surprise. Hopes and fears: at this time they ran through one's thoughts like a pair of playful kittens.

In England it would be about half past eleven o'clock at night. Sarah would be in bed. Asleep? Probably, but perhaps lying awake thinking about him. If she was awake, he knew she was thinking about him. That was not conceit. It would have been if he had thought it before their honeymoon, but since then he had discovered that she needed him as much as he needed her, and that he occupied most of her life just as she occupied what was left of his after the Navy's demands were satisfied. Loneliness, he had realized, was something no bachelor really understood. Loneliness was a happily married man (or woman) sleeping alone, the absence of a loved one. Gianna . . . In Volterra it must be about half past one o'clock in the morning. Tomorrow morning, as far as they were concerned here. What was she doing? How was she? Where was she? *Was* she? He tried to drive the thought away. Was Paolo, sitting next to him in the sternsheets, thinking about his aunt? Was he wondering if Bonaparte's secret police had murdered her, or had her securely locked up, something which for a woman like her would be a kind of death –

'*Qui va là?*'

The challenge from the deck of *L'Espoir* was casual: there was no alarm in the sentry's voice. Nor, Ramage realized as his body unfroze from the first shock of the hail which had brought him back from Volterra, London, warm nights with Sarah at Jean-Jacques' château near Brest, anything but friendly expectancy.

And casually, a comforting and confident casualness, came Auguste's amiable reply, his Breton accent deliberately more pronounced than usual.

'Our captain is visiting your captain, citizen. Did you have a good voyage from Brest?'

Some night birds fussed in the distance and he recognized the squawk of a night heron. And another. They must be flying from Île Royale to the mangroves on the shore. And that squeakier note – and again. Oystercatchers? Perhaps. What about that damned sentry? Twenty yards to go. Would he be watching just this one boat he had first sighted? Or would he look beyond and see three more that, however stupid he was, would give the lie to Auguste's reply?

'One gale and five days of calm. What ship?'

'We are *L'Intrépide*, and that's *La Robuste* over there.'

'Your captain's name, citizen?'

243

Ramage hissed: 'Keep rowing: lay us alongside, whatever happens.'

'Citizen Camus, and who is he visiting?'

'Who is he visiting?' asked the puzzled sentry. 'Why our captain you said, citizen.'

'And what's your captain's name, you mule?' Auguste asked crossly.

'Magon,' said a deeper voice. 'I am the captain of *L'Espoir*. But rest on your oars . . .' the voice sounded harsh yet uncertain. '*L'Intrépide*, you say? That wasn't *L'Intrépide* that I saw. And Camus – I don't know that name.'

Would Auguste pull it off, delay for a couple of minutes? 'Pretend you're the captain!' he hissed at Gilbert. 'Interrupt in a moment!'

'I don't expect you do; we're bound for Brest from Batavia,' Auguste said, repeating the story Ramage had given him earlier.

'But even so,' the doubting voice said from *L'Espoir*'s deck, 'I don't even remember "Camus" as a lieutenant.'

'*Merde!*' exclaimed Gilbert angrily, as though he was the Camus in question and whose patience was now exhausted. 'I haven't heard of "Magon" either, and *L'Espoir* hasn't exactly distinguished herself, has she; you probably spent all the last war safely blockaded in Brest. Took a peace treaty to get you out again, eh? Now you're at sea' – Gilbert paused a moment and Ramage thought he too had heard a shout from the other side of the ship – 'you've forgotten your manners. Good night, citizen. I'm not sitting here in my boat listening to that sort of welcome when I come to pay a visit!'

'No, no, you misunderstand me, citizen,' Magon said hastily, 'it's –'

He broke off as two pistol shots snapped across the frigate's deck and in the distance Ramage heard the night herons squawk in alarm. 'Alongside!' he shouted. 'Stand by to board, men!'

It seemed only a moment later that men were tossing oars and the cutter slammed against the frigate's hull and suddenly he could smell the humid, almost sickly smell of the weed that had grown along her waterline, and there was the reek of garlic, even down here.

Ramage leapt for the battens and both ahead and astern heard shouting in English and the thud, thud, thud of the spiked heads of tomahawks being driven into the hull planking to make steps for the men to board.

Bellowing and shouting he climbed, fingers gripping the edges of the battens, feet pressing sideways for footholds and his legs heaving and thrusting him up. Suddenly he was standing on *L'Espoir*'s deck and a man he guessed to be Captain Magon was wresting a musket from the sentry, who was clearly paralysed by the shouts and shots suddenly disturbing the tropical night.

Ramage dragged a pistol from his waistband and cocked it as he aimed at Magon, but the man pitched forward as another pistol firing beside him left Ramage's ears ringing. Ramage just had time to see in the light of the lantern hanging in the shrouds that Magon was bearded, then he turned towards the quarter-deck, shouting to his men.

There was a lantern on the binnacle: as he ran up the steps towards it, cutlass in his right hand, pistol in his left, he saw the one man on the quarterdeck, probably the officer keeping an anchor watch, running towards him, the blade of a cutlass he held over his head glinting in the dim light. The man was shouting almost hysterically and from three feet away he slashed downwards.

Ramage held up his own cutlass horizontally, the parry of quinte, and the man screamed and stepped back to slash again. He must have been a butcher before going to sea, Ramage thought, noting that the man had bared his right side. A quick lunge, a gurgle, and he was leaning over the collapsed man desperately tugging his cutlass free. How many times had he shouted at men under instruction that a cutlass was a slashing weapon: using the point was a quick way of getting cut down as you tried to withdraw from a body which invariably wrapped itself round your blade.

Jackson, Rossi, Stafford and more than a dozen other men now stood round him but, except for the body at Ramage's feet, the quarterdeck was now empty. 'The gunroom!' Ramage shouted and led the way down the companionway, which would bring them out first by the door to the captain's cabin and beside the second companionway to the gunroom.

Aitken and Renwick's boats had come alongside just ahead of Ramage's cutter, and the first lieutenant, uttering wild Scottish battle cries, scrambled down from the gangway on to the maindeck where French seamen, hurrying up from the lowerdeck where they had been having supper, found themselves running straight into bitter fighting.

Renwick's men were dropping down on to the maindeck from further forward just as Aitken, realizing the value of lanterns, seized one and held it aloft and began the desperate game of hide-and-seek among the guns.

Paolo and his four Frenchmen, who had run along the larboard gangway to the forward end, dropped down and hid behind a couple of guns as dozens of yelling Frenchmen came rushing up the forehatch ladder, some of them – Paolo guessed them to be petty officers – pausing to open up arms chests and throw cutlasses on the deck for the men to grab.

The captain had been most emphatic, so Paolo did not mind hiding behind the gun with Auguste, while Gilbert, Albert and Louis crouched under the barrel of the next one forward. 'Orsini,' the captain had said, and Paolo could hear the words even now, 'you are not to get involved in the fighting: I have enough fighters; I want talkers!' But it was hard just crouching here and watching those men giving out cutlasses. The five of them could – but no, the captain had been emphatic.

He heard a dreadful screaming from right aft amid the shouting and cursing of a dozen men yelling in both French and English. Pistol shots, the clang of cutlass blades – *accidente*, the worst noise was coming from the gunroom: all the ship's officers and warrant officers must have been trapped there – and, Paolo knew only too well, they would have swords and pistols in racks outside their cabin doors. But with all these wretches rushing up from below and snatching up cutlasses it was not a question of cutting off the snake's head . . .

Southwick had scrambled up over the starboard bow, helped by a couple of seamen and thankful that the anchor cable was thick because it was a struggle to get up on to the fo'c'sle. A French seaman emerged from the head, protesting loudly at being interrupted, but within moments he had been cut down and his body thrown over the side.

The master was just about to lead his men in a sweep across the fo'c'sle to clear out the group of men where the gangway met the fo'c'sle when the reflection from a lantern showed a white band.

'Calypso!' Southwick roared and heard a querulous Sergeant Ferris say: 'Can't find any more bloody Frenchies, sir! We've cleared the starboard gangway.'

'Calypso!' came a shout from the group on the other side and Southwick discovered Lieutenant Martin complaining that the larboard gangway was clear and he thought Mr Ramage and the rest of them were either aft on the maindeck or down on the lowerdeck.

'Calypsos!' Southwick bellowed, a sudden fear catching him: the fear that there was a good fight going on and he was missing it. 'Follow me!' He led the rush aft along the starboard gangway, pausing a moment to look at the maindeck and find a rope ladder to scramble down, but he was beaten to it by Martin and Ferris, who jumped.

There were many writhing men but little light on the maindeck: Southwick saw a couple of lanterns hooked up on the beams, and then, his eye caught by a dancing light aft, he saw a shouting and a grinning Aitken holding a lantern high with one hand, his cutlass slashing with the other.

Southwick stepped forward, both hands grasping his great sword. He paused a moment to look at the head of the nearest man, saw it had no white band, and swung. The shock of blade on bone jarred and he took a couple of steps forward to the next man.

Wagstaffe shouted to his men to get to the main hatchway but the noise drowned his voice. Wagstaffe realized too late that he and Kenton had made a mistake: the moment they had seen the starboard gangway cleared they should have secured the fore, main and afterhatches and cut down *L'Espoir*'s ship's company as they scrambled unarmed up to the maindeck. Now dozens, scores of Frenchmen, were on the maindeck, snatching up cutlasses from the arms chests. Wagstaffe led his men across to the other side of the ship.

God, that noise in the gunroom!

The fighting was now almost entirely on the maindeck, with Southwick, Ferris and Martin slashing their way aft along the starboard side to meet Aitken and his men working forward, and Wagstaffe, Kenton and Renwick slashing and jabbing their way forward along the larboard side. Right aft, one deck lower, Ramage and his men fought through the gunroom with little room to swing a cutlass and all their pistols empty. Ramage eyed the swinging lantern: the remaining Frenchmen could have saved themselves if they had cut that down, but it seemed they dreaded the darkness.

Paolo watched the forehatch. No one had come up it for two, perhaps three minutes. *'Andiamo!'* he said to the four Frenchmen, and then realized that with his excitement he had lapsed into Italian. 'Come on!' he corrected himself, added a very English 'Damnation!' and then said: *'Allons, messieurs!'*

The lowerdeck was well lit: candles flickered at the tables and it took him a moment to realize that the curiously stark shadows on the deck were overturned forms. There was a great deal of shouting and cutlass clanging right aft, round the gunroom, but in his imagination Paolo could recall the captain's voice giving him orders.

He turned forward, picking up a lantern, and followed by the four Frenchmen passed the last of the tables.

'Déportés!' he called, and Gilbert, his voice agitated and cracking with emotion, started to shout but it ended as almost a scream: *'M'sieu le Comte!* Here is Gilbert! Please, are you there!'

Paolo held the lantern higher. They were there all right, row upon row, men next to women, each held flat on the deck by a leg iron round the ankle, and waving near the back was a man who Paolo could see was too overcome with emotion to speak.

Paolo seized Gilbert's arm and pointed and gave him the lantern, and with a gasp of relief the Frenchman stumbled forward, trying to avoid the other prisoners but lurching as his feet caught ankles, eyebolts and the rods linking the leg irons. Now every one of the prisoners seemed to be shouting at once, every one of them and at the top of his voice or her voice. It was absurd; of that Paolo was sure. It was unseamanlike. Ungentlemanly and unladylike, too.

'Silence!' he shouted. *'Silence! Silence!'*

He paused for breath. Yes, now he had silence down here except for the blood pounding in his ears, but right aft and on the deck above there was more shouting, screaming and clanging of cutlasses than he had ever heard before.

'Ladies and gentlemen!' he said, to consolidate the silence he had brought to this part of the ship. Then he could think of nothing to say. Fifty or more white faces stared up at him; a hundred or so eyes glinted in the candlelight as Auguste brought up another lantern. *Mama mia,* what would the captain say to these people if he was standing here!

'Ladies and gentlemen, I must apologize for the noise.' A woman started laughing, a laugh which rose higher up the scale and ended suddenly as someone reached across and slapped her to stop the hysteria.

248

'I am from the *Calypso*, one of His Britannic Majesty's frigates and commanded by Captain Ramage, and –'

'Count Orsini, I think!' The voice came from the back.

'At your service,' Paolo said carefully, an Italian count suspecting he was addressing a French one but determined not to give too much ground. 'You have me at a disadvantage, m'sieu.'

'I am Rennes, and Captain Ramage told me about you.'

Then Paolo remembered the rest of his orders. 'Forgive me for a moment. Now, ladies and gentlemen, we shall try to release you, once we have found the keys, but please stay here until Captain Ramage comes and tells you to move: unless you are wearing one of these white headbands, you might be killed!'

At the other end of the lowerdeck Ramage was cursing fluently in Italian, with Jackson and Stafford providing a descant of obscene English. There was a small doorway at the after side of the gunroom and the five Frenchmen (Ramage was unsure if they were officers or seamen who had been trying to escape from the messdeck) had managed to get through it, slashing and parrying with swords, and vanished into the darkness beyond. It was the tiller flat, a space the width of the ship across which the great wooden arm of the tiller moved in response to the wheel turning above. And now anyone going through that black hole was asking to be cut down by the men who could remain hidden behind the bulkhead.

Five men: of no consequence. With the captain dead they would soon surrender.

'You men' – he pointed to five of his group – 'stay here and stop those fellows coming out. More important' – he pointed down at the thick wooden hatchcover – 'that's the magazine scuttle, so guard it!'

With that he was running up the companionway to the maindeck and was just in time to see twenty or so Frenchmen retreating before Southwick, Ferris and Martin, but fighting back-to-back with twenty more who were slowly driving Aitken and fewer than a dozen men aft, trapping them against the capstan.

Aitken was still slashing with his cutlass and turned away shouting incomprehensible encouragement to his men when Ramage saw one of the Frenchmen break from the group and run towards Aitken, holding his cutlass like a pike.

There was no time to shout a warning – Aitken would never hear it – and Ramage hurled his cutlass, leaping after the spinning blade. The hilt caught the side of the Frenchman's head, he staggered, and a moment later Ramage had an arm round the man's neck and they both swayed, a shouting Aitken flicking away the cutlass of another attacker but still unaware that he had nearly been cut down.

The Frenchman was burly, two or three inches taller than Ramage, and he wore no shirt. His body was slippery from perspiration, but now, no longer stunned, he wrenched away from Ramage's grasp after punching him in the face, took a step back, and lifted his cutlass for the slash that Ramage knew would split his head in two, and for the moment he was too dizzy to do anything but stand there.

The Frenchman's blade swung up, only the sharp edge shiny; Ramage registered dully that the blade must be rusty and only the cutting edge clean. Up, up the blade went and the Frenchman's eyes held his: the head was the target and the Frenchman was not going to be distracted.

The Frenchman's face contracted slightly, the body flexed and the right shoulder twisted an inch or two as the muscles drew at the arm. Ramage sensed rather than saw that not one of his own men was within ten feet and no one had noticed this lonely and one-sided duel.

The Frenchman was grinning: two teeth missing in front at the bottom. Unshaven. The arm coming down now. Sarah. Jean-Jacques. Such a waste, but no pain –

But the arm was still upraised and the Frenchman was looking up and tugging. In an instant Ramage realized that the man had held the cutlass too vertically as he raised it for the final blow and the point had caught in the deckhead above. As he struggled to free it, Ramage moved two paces closer, kicked the man in the groin and then picked up his own cutlass. That made seven.

He turned to join Aitken and found that in the few moments of the strange duel, which had seemed at the time to be lasting ages, his own party had combined with the first lieutenant's and driven the Frenchmen forward again, squeezing them against Southwick's party.

Ramage jumped up on to the capstan head and crouched to avoid the deckbeams. It was easier to look across the maindeck from here. Two, four, eight ... twelve ... thirteen ... sixteen ... All the rest wore white bands round their heads. And here were Southwick, Ferris and Martin coming along the starboard side, grinning.

'Just going to give Aitken a hand!' Southwick said and led his men in a scramble over the cranked pump handle.

So apart from a few unwounded but surrendering Frenchmen, the maindeck was suddenly secure. But the *déportés*? For a moment he had a clear picture of fifty people in irons at the fore end of the lowerdeck, their throats cut by some rabid Revolutionary.

Jackson was beside him now, with Stafford and Rossi. 'Lost you for a moment, sir,' the American said.

'It was a long moment,' Ramage said, 'but come on!'

He jumped off the capstan and snatched up a lantern lying on its side, flipped open the door and straightened the wick. Fortunately it could only just have been knocked over because the wax had not run. He shut the door and clattered down the companionway to find himself outside the gunroom again. What the devil had made him go up on the maindeck after leaving those five men on guard? The whole reason for the voyage and this attack was waiting at the forward end of the lowerdeck, and he remembered with sick fear that Paolo had not reported, nor Gilbert, nor Auguste.

He was past the afterhatch; there, like a vast tree trunk, was the mainmast. Now the mainhatch and past these forms lying over the deck, an indication of the way the Frenchmen had been surprised.

Candles alight on the tables. There was a lantern, two lanterns, moving about right up forward, and now he could see a mass of bodies lying on the deck. And two or three men moving among them – murderous Republicans cutting the throats of the *déportés*?

He was concentrating so carefully on not tripping in the half-darkness that he was almost among the slaughtered *déportés* before he realized it, and he looked up with his cutlass raised to find that the nearest rabid Republican killer with the lantern was in fact Paolo.

'Your friend is in the last row, sir,' Paolo said calmly, not realizing how close to death he had been. 'I understand that the key to unlock these irons is in the captain's possession. A Captain Magon, I believe.'

Ramage stepped over the prone people to where Gilbert was kneeling. There, his ankle held by a leg iron, was Jean-Jacques, who looked up and grinned and said: 'I hardly expected to see you here. Is Sarah with you?'

CHAPTER TWENTY

Ramage stepped out on to the jetty where the group of Frenchmen stood with a white flag on a staff, and the wind tugged at the similar white flag being held up in the cutter's bow. Gilbert and Paolo followed and as Jackson stood a French officer held up a hand and said in French: 'Only one man, the captain.'

Ramage stopped. 'Where is the island governor?'

'At the fortress, waiting for you.'

'My letter suggesting a truce said we meet and negotiate on this jetty.'

The French officer shrugged his shoulders. 'It is not my concern. My orders are to escort you to the fort.'

Ramage turned to his men. 'We go back to the ship.' He then said to the French officer: 'I shall return in half an hour. If the governor is not here, *L'Espoir* will then be blown up.'

'But her crew!'

Ramage raised his eyebrows in what he hoped was a cold and callous glare. '*What* about them?'

'They will all be killed!'

'The survivors, yes. Many were killed last night. The rest . . . well, that depends on the governor. Half an hour then. If he is not here, we shall sail at once, and *L'Espoir* will vanish a few minutes later.' He looked across the anchorage and laughed. 'Perhaps not vanish: you will see plenty of smoke and an abundance of wreckage!'

'A moment,' the French officer said hurriedly, 'we can reach an accommodation.'

'I assure you that we cannot,' Ramage said stiffly. 'I talk only to the governor. No one on Île Royale, the Île du Diable or the Île St Joseph – or for that matter down in Cayenne – is performing a favour for me. I am offering him the lives of sixty-four French seamen from *L'Espoir*. They treated the *déportés* so shamefully they will never be exchanged from England. The wounded certainly will not survive the voyage . . .' he paused and composed himself for another cold-blooded laugh. It came out quite satisfactorily judging from the look on Jackson's face. '. . . And I have grave doubts about the unwounded. My men have no sympathy . . .' He gave an expressive shrug and waved a hand towards the broad Atlantic on the other side of the island, a gesture which he saw achieved its purpose in conjuring up a picture of shark fins cutting through the water.

The Frenchman pointed towards the seaward end of the jetty. 'm'sieu, you speak French like a Frenchman. Walk a few steps with me –'

'Tell your party to stay by the boat,' Ramage snapped as he saw a couple of lieutenants begin to follow.

The officer snapped out an order which froze the men. Lot's wife, Ramage thought, and looked curiously at the officer. He did not recognize the man's uniform, which was well cut in green cloth. It had black buttons with a design or initials on them. If his rank was a captain or major, one would have expected . . . His thoughts were interrupted as the man tried to smile, indicating that they should walk the few paces which would take them to the end of the jetty and out of earshot of everyone else.

When they stopped, Ramage turned to the man and guessed the answer before he said: 'Well?'

'There is no need to go to the fort; we can negotiate here.'

'You command the garrison?'

'I command all three islands.'

'And you are?'

'General Beaupré.'

'Prove it.'

He was a solidly built man with a flowing black moustache and brown eyes that were friendly. Not at all what one expected of a jailer, Ramage decided.

'Lieutenant Miot!' Beaupré called.

'*Oui, mon général?*'

Ramage nodded. 'All right – you are a general. We negotiate. I have three French frigates, not two – the two farthest from us I captured recently, one last night and the other last week. The nearest I captured a couple of years ago and she is now commissioned into the Royal Navy.'

'You want to exchange something for the two frigates?' General Beaupré was incredulous.

'No, I was simply introducing you to the situation. *L'Espoir*, the frigate that arrived last night, was bringing you more than fifty *déportés*.'

'Yes, I guessed that. They would be kept on the other island.' He pointed. 'The Île du Diable is for *déportés*, who are of course

253

political prisoners. The criminals are kept on Île St Joseph and here, on Île Royale.'

'I am not interested in the criminals,' Ramage said. 'I will exchange my prisoners, the men from *L'Espoir* and *La Robuste*, for all the *déportés* you have on the Île du Diable.'

The general's face fell. 'But I don't have any *déportés*!'

'Where are they?' Ramage demanded.

'With the treaty that ended the war, they were all sent back to France. Why should we detain them in peacetime? I have only criminals now. And what people they are. Every one of them, men and women, think nothing of murder! But *déportés* now, why that is absurd.'

'Because we are all at peace, eh?'

'Yes, of course,' the general said. 'When you mentioned *déportés* in *L'Espoir* – that was a slip of the tongue, was it not? You meant "convicts".'

Ramage shook his head slowly, angry with himself for not realizing. His note sent on shore earlier had merely said that the ships did not have *la peste* on board, that the shooting and shouting of the previous night had been caused by the capture of *L'Espoir* by men of the Royal Navy. Ramage had suggested a truce to discuss the disposal of French wounded and prisoners; he had forgotten the most important item of news.

'No, *déportés*. The war has started again.'

The general paled. 'War,' he muttered. 'I thought it was piracy. War ... I suppose *L'Espoir* also brought dispatches giving me the news.'

'I expect so,' Ramage said. 'We have not gone through all the papers yet. However, what about the exchange?'

The general faced Ramage squarely. 'I have no *déportés*. If you wish, we will visit the three islands and you can question any one you like. Convicts – yes, scores, and you are welcome to them. The *déportés* in *L'Espoir* would have been the first for a year, and the buildings for them on the Île du Diable are falling down – termites, white ants, the rain ... Nothing lasts, be it buildings or men. Termites or the black vomit,' he said hopelessly. 'We're all exiles here ... the convicts are locked up at night. But are their jailers free?'

He suddenly shook his head, apparently startled that he should have been confiding in not only a foreigner but now, apparently, an enemy.

He said: 'Shall we inspect this island first and then go to Diable and St Joseph? Once the sun gets up ...'

Once the sun gets up these islands must be among the hottest, most unpleasant and unhealthy in the world, but that was not the reason Ramage shook his head. The general had obviously been speaking the truth about the *déportés,* and when the man rambled off on that brief soliloquy it was because he knew that a new war only prolonged his stay on the islands, where the sun, sea, the fevers and the swamps ensured that the jailer was as much a prisoner as the jailed.

'I accept your word,' Ramage said. 'Our boats will start landing the French wounded as soon as I return on board and give the order. Then we will land the French seamen we hold as prisoners, first from *La Robuste* and then from *L'Espoir.* All this under a flag of truce, eh?'

'A flag of truce,' the general echoed. 'You are being generous,' he admitted, 'since I have nothing to give you in return.'

Ramage was not about to tell him that prisoners were a confounded nuisance in a ship of war. 'Very well, then we are agreed.'

'Your name,' the general said. 'I read it on the letter. Of course you know it is a French word, too. But I know you by reputation. I can only hope you go back to *La Manche:* my countrymen would not welcome your arrival to Martinique or Guadeloupe . . .'

Ramage stood up from behind his desk and smiled at Aitken and Wagstaffe. 'Very well, then, each frigate is to keep a couple of cables apart by day, and one cable by night, and the rendezvous is Carlisle Bay, Barbados.'

'Thank you, sir,' Aitken said. 'Being *L'Espoir*'s temporary first lieutenant is going to be good experience for Kenton.'

Southwick, who was staying in the *Calypso* with Ramage, laughed and commented to Wagstaffe: 'And young Orsini will learn a lot being your second and third lieutenant!'

Ramage said to Wagstaffe: 'Are you happy with just Martin and Orsini? Until we get up to Trinidad the wind can chop about.'

'We'll be all right, sir. Do you think the admiral there will buy 'em in?'

'Two frigates in good condition with no damage – except for a few nicks from pistol balls in one of them? I should think he'll be only too glad. You'll all be rich men!'

'They haven't done too badly up to now,' Southwick said. 'Enough in the Funds to retire as knights of the shire!'

'And you!' Wagstaffe exclaimed. 'Since you began serving with Mr Ramage, you've made enough money to buy ten taverns and ten breweries to supply them!'

'I'm not complaining,' Southwick said, and turning to Wagstaffe said seriously: 'You could let young Orsini think we shall be depending on his positions.'

Wagstaffe nodded. 'I'll let him *think* that, but I expect he'll come along with some workings that put us in the middle of the sugar cane in Demerara!'

As the two lieutenants left the cabin with Southwick, Ramage walked through to the coach, where a Frenchman was busy writing. 'Jean-Jacques, we sail in half an hour. Judging by the way that quill is bobbing, you've now recovered enough to tell me what happened when they arrested you in Brest.'

'Yes, yes,' the Frenchman agreed. 'But first you must tell me the – how do you say, "the butcher's bill"?'

'Yes, and it makes a sad story. *L'Espoir* had 127 officers and men on board when she anchored here last night, and fifty-four *déportés*. The captain and two of the three lieutenants were killed in our attack, and twenty-seven petty officers and seamen. Thirty-three more were wounded.'

'More than half of them killed or wounded,' Jean-Jacques said. 'They fought hard.'

Ramage was silent. The French had fought hard, but they knew they were fighting to survive. Most men tried to stay alive. The bravery came when you risked your life just to save others or obey orders. Jean-Jacques looked up at Ramage.

'Because we *déportés* were the cause, I hardly dare ask your casualties: it is like asking a man how many of his family have just been killed.'

'Eight killed and nineteen wounded. Three of the wounded won't see another sunset but the others will be standing a watch before we land you all at Portsmouth.'

'Sarah. You said last night that she was safe and well. I prayed that she would have come to no harm under my roof.'

'Gilbert and Louis . . .'

'Yes, they obeyed my orders. These other two, Auguste and Albert, tell me about them. I was too excited and too exhausted to understand about a ship called the *Murex*. A British brig, Gilbert said, and Sarah shot the man in command? Tell me,' he said anxiously, 'was that not . . . well, rather drastic?'